Beauty's Beasts

By Alex Hanson

Beauty's Beasts

First paperback edition October 2023

Cover Design: Atra Luna Design
Illustrations: Hugor and Hugorky Rodriguez from Ink the Tea
ISBN 979-8-9853751-4-5
Published by Alex Hanson

Author's Note

This story is not a dark romance, but it does include some dark topics and scenes that some readers might find disturbing. Below is a full content list for *Beauty's Beasts*, but please be warned, there may be spoilers. This list includes the good, the bad, and the ugly and is ordered randomly.

Beauty's Beasts contains content that includes but is not limited to: asexuality rep, non-binary rep, genderfluid rep, mutism rep, amputee rep, misogyny, transphobia, homophobia, deadnaming, animal death (stillborn), assault, kidnapping, human sacrifice, religious trauma, strong religious themes, chasing, gore, violence, amputation (off page but described in detail), monster genitalia, biting, mating, grand mal seizure (on page and described in detail), dirty talk, exhibitionism, begging, oral sex, rimming, breeding kink (no pregnancies), cream pie, cum play, body horror and disfigurement, death of a sibling, bondage, ass spanking, clit spanking, hair pulling, edging, primal play, spanking with a switch, throat holding and squeezing, anal sex, rejected mates, double penetration, PTSD, depression, self-degradation, spanking with a belt, purity culture, gun violence, death of a parent, body mutilation, grief, voyeurism, chronic social anxiety, throat fucking with breath play, group sex, self-sacrifice, live animal birth, resurrection, & character death.

Beauty's Beasts contains scenes of graphic nightmares and night terrors that depict gruesome violence, death, suicide, and torture. These scenes can easily be skipped if they become too intense, and you won't lose any important story aspects.

Beauty's Beasts includes two blood relatives who share a lover, but the two related characters don't engage in sexual activities together or engage with their love interest sexually in the same scenes.

Beauty's Beasts includes a character who is a sex-averse asexual, meaning he does not experience sexual attraction toward others and has no desire to engage in most sexual activities. Please note that just because someone is asexual, that doesn't automatically mean they are sex-averse. This character happens to be sex-averse, but many asexuals can and do engage in and enjoy sex. If someone tells you they are ace, please don't assume they don't ever enjoy or engage in sexual activities.

Alright, I'm done now. On with the spicy goodness!

For the gays and the theys.

You are not broken.
You are not damned.
Remember who the real beasts are.

Playlist

Listed in no particular order

YouTube and Spotify links available at mxalexwrites.com

Love Myself – Hailee Steinfeld
The Village – Wrabel
Labour – Paris Paloma
Weak – Seether
i hope ur miserable until ur dead – Nessa Barrett
Family Tree – Ethel Cain
Heaven Was Full (I'm Headed Straight to Hell) – TX2
Limits – Bad Omens
The Vengeful One – Disturbed
You're Mine – Disturbed
The Sound of Silence – Disturbed
The Siren – Nadiiife
Freaking Me Out – Ava Max
Salt – Ava Max
Finally // beautiful stranger – Halsey
You should be sad – Halsey
Afterlife – Avenged Sevenfold
Bat Country – Avenged Sevenfold
Kill The Noise – Papa Roach
Way Down We Go – KALEO
Save Yourself – KALEO
The Steeple – Halestorm
The Fruits – Paris Paloma
Graveyard – Nicole Rayy
She Keeps Me Up – Nickelback
Burn It to the Ground – Nickelback
Again – Noah Cyrus ft. XXXTENTACION
Frozen – Madonna & Sickick
Savin' Me – Nickelback
Mansion (feat. Fleurie) – NF
Hate Me – Eurielle
Nameless – Stevie Howie
Hard Times – Ethel Cain

Just Pretend – Bad Omens
THE DEATH OF PEACE OF MIND – Bad Omens
Aimed to Kill – Jade LeMac
Judgment Day – Five Finger Death Punch
The Humbling River – Puscifer
The Valley – Nadiiife
Angels Fall – Breaking Benjamin
When I'm Gone – 3 Doors Down
Feel Something – ILLENIUM, Excision, & I Prevail
I'll Wait – Kygo & Sasha Alex Sloan
Sleepsong – Secret Garden

Evangeline

For thou hast possessed my reins:
thou hast covered me in my mother's womb.
I will praise thee;
for I am fearfully and wonderfully made:
marvelous are thy works;
and that my soul knoweth right well.

-Psalm 139:13-14 KJV

Chapter 1

I am not a woman.

I repeat those words to myself again and again as I walk the cobbled street toward the general store, and I get nothing but stares and glares from those I pass along the way. A group of ladies walking the opposite way down the lane spot me, and they move over as I get closer, their dresses whispering across the stone path and their parasols bumping together as they try to give me as wide a berth as possible. One of them huffs in disgust, her eyes sliding up and down my outfit as her lip curls.

I'm wearing a pair of my father's old riding boots and pants as well as a shirt and vest set I made myself since my father's are never big enough in the chest for me. When I left the house not an hour ago, my mother had a fit when she realized I was headed into the village.

"Evangeline," she hissed between gritted teeth. "Go change that outfit this instant!"

"I'm far beyond the age where you can tell me what to wear, Mother," I replied. "And my name is Evan today."

She huffed. "Keep it up, girl. There are already far too many whispers in the village about your behavior as of late. What will you do if they decide you're a witch or some other evil spirit sent by the devil to torment us all? Do you want to end up sent with The Offering?"

"They don't send women with The Offering," I said with a roll of my eyes.

"Aren't you the one claiming you're anything *but* a woman? You can't have it both ways."

She had a point.

I meet the eyes of the lady who huffed at me and give her a smile.

"Mornin'," I say in the deepest voice I can manage.

I've been practicing masculine mannerisms in the mirror for days like today, days when it makes my skin itch to wear any of my dresses or to fuss over my hair. My long, dark brown locks are currently twisted up under a cap I stole from my best friend last summer. I tip it at the ladies as I stroll past.

The huffy one looks like she was just asked to swallow a frog, and I can't get the smile off my face for the rest of my walk to the store.

A bell tinkles as I walk in, and the shop owner's son—my best friend, Will—looks up from a book he's reading behind the counter and grins.

"Good morning," he greets. He quickly assesses my outfit, his eyes moving up and down my body in much the same way the lady's did out on the street. His face is much warmer than hers, though, as he asks, "It's Evan today then?"

I smile and nod.

Will has been my closest friend since we started school, and we've been practically inseparable since, much to the dismay of both our families. 'It's not right for a boy and a girl to spend so much time together', they always argued. 'Girls shouldn't be climbing trees and playing in muck, and boys shouldn't be attending tea parties and playing with dolls.' And yet, despite their protests, they never outright barred us from seeing each other, probably because they knew we'd simply sneak around and do it anyway. By allowing it, at least they knew what we were up to… most of the time, anyway.

Will was the first person I told when I realized I was not a girl. He'd listened and asked questions then immediately started calling me by my chosen names: Evan on my masculine days, Eve on my feminine ones, and Evangeline on the days when that still fit me best. He was the one who came up with referring to me as they/them instead of she/her or he/him. I loved the idea and loved him even more for the respect and understanding he showed me when I needed it most. Even now, two years later, no one else is as considerate of my feelings as Will, except maybe my father, who's my only other source of support.

"I came to pick up my mother's order," I say.

"I figured as much. It's perfect timing." Will leans closer and lowers his voice even though we're the only two in the store. "Those items you ordered came in yesterday."

My heart skips a beat. "Really?"

Will winks and disappears into the back room, coming back with two parcels wrapped in brown paper and my mother's basket filled with her monthly order. The packages are larger than I expected. I'll have to make two trips to get everything to my cart on the other side of the village.

"You know your mother will have a thing or two to say about these," Will says as he pushes the parcels toward me across the counter.

"My mother always has something to say," I reply. "I may as well give her something new to complain about."

Will chuckles. "Want some help carrying these?"

"Can you leave the store right now?"

"My father is due back any minute. Can you wait?"

"For you? Eh, I suppose." I slide my arms across the counter and gaze up at him. "Give me a sweet for my trouble?"

Will rolls his eyes and reaches to the shelf behind him where they keep the hard candies. He fishes a peppermint sweet from a jar and hands it to me.

I pop it in my mouth. "You're the best."

"Hurry up and get it gone by the time my father gets back, would you? He'll make me pay for it if he sees me slipping you sweets."

I smile at him with the candy stuck between my teeth.

Will shakes his head and replaces the jar.

The front door dings again as someone else comes into the shop.

Will looks past me and stiffens. "Good morning, Pastor."

I quickly turn toward the shelves to the left of the counter and stare at the displays of watercolors and paintbrushes to hide my face.

Pastor Elias IV has been the head of our local church for three decades now. His son, Elias V, is slated to take his father's place when he retires. Ever since I came out as… not a girl, both of them have been absolute thorns in my backside, and I don't feel like dealing with that today. Not that I ever do.

"Good morning, young man," Pastor Elias greets Will. "Don't tell me your father has you stuck in here all day."

"No, Pastor. Just for this morning while he runs a few errands."

"That's good. It's too fine a day for someone so young to be cooped up out of the sun."

I roll my eyes at the tins of pastels. Pastor Elias treats anyone who's unmarried as if they're still teenagers. Will is twenty, like me, but until he takes a wife, Pastor Elias will talk to him as if he's barely more than a child.

"I'll be running along to help my brother mend fences as soon as my father gets back," Will replies.

I almost laugh. Will doesn't plan to do any such thing. As the youngest of four brothers, he gets away with just about anything, and avoiding any form of physical labor is Will's number one priority. That's why he's here taking care of the store this morning, I bet. He likely volunteered, knowing he'd be free to go about his day after his father returned while his brothers are stuck working on fences.

"You be sure to do that," the pastor says sternly. "In the meantime, be a good lad and fetch my wife some sugar, coffee, and two candles."

"Coming right up."

Pastor Elias holds out a small basket, and Will takes it as he steps around the counter. I have to move to give him room to squeeze past me, and that's enough to make the pastor notice me.

"Beautiful day, isn't it?" he asks.

I squeeze my eyes shut. "Sure is," I answer, praying my voice is deep enough he won't recognize it.

Will side-eyes me as he reaches for the candles on the next set of shelves. "How's your wife, Pastor?"

Thank you, I mouth as the pastor focuses again on Will instead of me.

"Oh, she's fine. Just fine. She's been teaching our youngest to sew." He chuckles. "Poor girl is struggling something fierce, but her mother won't let her give up. 'You'll need to know how to mend your husband's clothes someday, girl', she says. 'Every decent wife does'."

The two men chat back and forth until Will sets the basket of goods on the counter and gives the pastor the total. When the pastor pays and picks up the basket, I think I might've gotten away with avoiding him, but my hope shatters when he turns his attention back to me.

"I don't believe we've met," he says. "Are you new around here, young man?"

I slam my teeth together, say a prayer, and turn around.

Pastor Elias sucks in a breath. "Evangeline," he utters in horror.

I force myself not to grimace at the name.

"What on earth are you wearing?" he demands to know, but then he shakes his head as if no answer I give him could ever excuse such behavior. "It's no wonder your mother worries you'll never find a husband."

I raise my chin and straighten my back. "It's a good thing I don't want one of those then, isn't it?"

I expect another horrified gasp or perhaps for him to go red in the face in anger, but he surprises me instead by raising a single brow. The smile he gives me makes me take an uncertain step back.

"We'll see," he says simply, then he turns and leaves the store without another word.

"What do you think he meant by that?" I ask.

"I have no idea," Will replies. "But knowing him…"

"It can't be good."

Will's father walks in while we're still staring at the door. When he sees me, he pauses, his brows furrowing even more than usual. Will's father has had a permanent scowl on his face since Will's mother died years ago, but whenever I'm around, that scowl turns downright deadly.

"Evangeline," Will's father greets me cautiously.

"Good morning, sir," I say cheerfully. I'm always as pleasant as possible with Will's family. I want to keep our friendship and don't want to give them any more reasons to forbid him from seeing me.

Will gathers my parcels from the counter. "I was going to help them carry these things to their cart. You don't need me anymore, right?"

Will's father flicks his eyes between us a couple of times. "I'd like you to help me reorganize the storage room, Will."

Will shrugs. "I'll just carry these to the cart and come right back then."

Defeat settles in Will's father's eyes. Coming up with some other reason why Will can't walk with me would make it obvious he's lying to keep us apart, and he knows it. He grunts and walks past us.

I gather my mother's basket.

Behind the counter, Will's father falls into a coughing fit. It's a wet, hacking sound that makes me pause.

"Are you alright?" I ask.

He waves away my concern. "Fine," he wheezes. "Just fine. A lingering cold, nothing more."

Will doesn't seem worried, so I bid his father good day and follow him outside.

We walk up the street together, and where I was met with silent judgment on my way to the store, Will is greeted with happy hellos and waves on the way back to my cart. He jerks his chin, calling to various people and asking after others, his face never losing its bright smile. His hair is short, straight, and dark brown. He keeps it brushed back out of his face and swept to the side, but every now and again, a clump will fall forward over his left eye. He looks the most handsome that way, so handsome that many often wonder why he isn't already married.

I'm the only one who knows why.

No one greets me as we walk or even looks my way. That's one of the best things about being around Will. I'm a tiny shadow walking beside a beacon of light so bright no one ever sees me. And, in private, I return the favor by being the only one Will can trust with his darkness.

We make it back to my horse and cart where I left them tied to old man Oren's fence without incident. Will plops my packages into the cart and takes the heavy basket from my arm to lower it in over the side for me as well.

"Thanks," I say.

Will leans against the cart. "This month's Offering list was sent out yesterday."

I cock a brow at the troubled look on his face. "And?"

He avoids my eyes. "And I don't know if it's wise for you to be strutting around in men's clothes right now."

I cross my arms. "Not you too."

"Don't give me that look. You know I'm not like them." He jerks his chin back toward main street. "I get it. I mean, I don't *get* it, but I believe you feel what you say you feel, and I don't care what clothes you wear or what name you ask me to call you. But you know *they* don't understand. And what they don't understand, they fear." He leans toward me. "I don't want to see you dragged out of the village at the next full moon."

The fact that this is the second time today someone has cautioned me about this unnerves me a little, but I swallow it down. "You're beginning to sound like my mother."

"Maybe she knows what she's talking about this time."

I huff.

Will sighs. "Look, I'm not telling you what to do. God knows you're going to do what you want anyway. I'm just asking you to be careful until The Offering is over."

"And then what?" I snap. "There will be another Offering next month, and the month after that, and the next one as well. Am I to hide my true self each time? Is that what you'd ask of me?"

Will is silent, but his eyes remain worried.

I force myself to dull the sharpness of my tongue. "I know you're only saying these things to try and protect me," I say more calmly. "And I know you're not like the others. But hiding won't change who I am. I won't live a lie anymore. I just want to be me. These people will either accept me exactly as I am, or they'll do what they feel they must."

"You don't mean that," Will says in a panic, taking a step toward me. "You don't mean that you'd rather be sent to The Deadwood than—"

"It was killing me, Will. Living as a woman was killing me from the inside. I can't go back to that. I won't. If it comes down to it, I'd rather die a quick death at the hands of the devil than a slow wasting one trying to earn these people's approval."

Will hangs his head.

"I'm sorry. That wasn't a commentary on *your* life choices."

"I'm not upset at you, Evan. I envy you."

I blink in surprise. "Envy me? Why?"

"I wish I was brave enough to live my truth."

I take both his hands in mine, my heart aching for my friend. "Choosing a life of peace over one of constant conflict and ridicule isn't cowardly. I don't blame you for it. People are cruel. We both deserve better."

Will nods and squeezes my hands. "Yes, we do."

The clearing of a throat nearby makes us both jump. Old man Oren is standing by his back gate, staring at us with a crooked, toothless grin.

"Don't make me send word to your parents that you two need a chaperone in each other's company," he says sternly.

I drop Will's hands as if they've suddenly become hot coals.

Will merely laughs. "You'd never tattle on me, Oren," he says with confidence. "You like the extra chewing tobacco I slip into your deliveries far too much."

Oren gives Will a pointed look, spits a stream of said tobacco on the grass, winks, and walks away.

I shake my head with a snort.

"He's become a bit of a gossip since his son moved away, so maybe you should go," Will says.

I nod and climb up into my cart.

Will smiles as I take up the reins. "My hat looks better on you than it ever did on me."

I make a show of tugging the hat down more securely on my head. "Good, 'cause I have no plans to give it back anytime soon."

Will laughs as he steps back from the cart, and I click my tongue at my horse as we head off down the road back toward home.

Chapter 2

I set my mother's basket on the kitchen table and immediately head for my room.

"Evangeline," my mother hollers after me. "I'd like your help with dinner, so don't go running off and getting filthy."

I roll my eyes and don't reply.

Just about every day for the past two weeks she's dragged me into the kitchen to "help with dinner" while she shows me how to properly bake bread, make preserves, and cook her various recipes. I know what she's doing. She's hoping some time doing good old "women's work" will make me suddenly want to be a wife and mother myself. Whenever I can get away with it, I duck out of the house and spend the afternoon in the barn with my father, riding in the lower pastures, or fishing in the river at the southern edge of our property instead. Mother never complains about the fish I bring back for her to cook, but she always fusses over the worm guts and scales on my clothes.

Up in my room, I shut the door and wrap a piece of twine around the knob and a bent nail I've pounded into the wall. It's the only way to keep my mother from barging in no matter how many times I've asked her to respect my privacy.

My room is the one place that's completely me. No matter how much my mother complains, I refuse to let her dictate a single piece of furniture or décor in here. The walls are a muddy brown, something I did myself last summer when I got tired of staring at the pastel pink that hadn't changed since I was an infant. My mother was livid when she saw it, but my father was impressed I managed not to get a single drop of paint on the floor. I've helped him paint barns, sheds, and fences enough over the years to know what I was doing.

There's a set of shelves across from my bed that used to be filled with books when I was little, but now they hold feathers, bones, interesting-looking rocks, and a stick I found in the woods with a twisted knot on the side that looks like a tiny face. There's a stack of letters from Will that he wrote to me during a summer he spent with his aunt in the city. I'd wanted to go with him, but my mother threw a fit and said it wasn't proper for an unmarried woman to travel so far alone with an unmarried man. Will felt terrible leaving me behind. He wrote me just about every day while he was away, and he has a similar stack of letters from me in the drawer of his nightstand, though it's much smaller than mine. It turns out I'm not very good at putting my feelings down on paper.

There are still a few books on the shelves as well, though they're much different from the fairytales my father used to read to me. Books on math, science, economics, and engineering now line my shelves. My mother hated them the moment she first discovered them.

"Young ladies shouldn't be reading such things," she lectured.

"What were you even doing in my room anyway?" I asked.

She ignored the question and rounded on my father. "Don't you have anything to say about this?"

"So what if the girl wants to learn a thing a two?" my father asked. "She's not harming anyone."

"It's not *proper*," my mother replied, her voice going all squeaky on the last word. "What man will want to marry a girl who spends more time with her nose in a book than learning how to cook and sew?"

"The right one?" my father said with a shrug.

Mother didn't talk to either of us for a week.

It was one of the calmest weeks we'd had in years.

In a way, I feel bad for my mother. She wanted a little girl long before she even got married; she's told me so many times throughout my life. But then it took so long for her to get pregnant after marrying Papa she was afraid she couldn't have children at all. My arrival was the answer to my mother's countless, tearful prayers, but my birth didn't go according to plan. Papa told me once that there was a moment he was afraid neither I nor my mother would make it through the night, but made it we both did. In the morning, though, as the doctor was packing up, he took Papa aside and explained just how close the situation came to Papa's fears. He said having more children was a significant risk for both my mother and any of her future children. After he left, Papa told my mother the truth, and they decided together, right then, that I would be an only child.

I am all my mother will ever get, and I haven't turned out at all like she wanted.

My mother wanted a daughter to dress up, to teach how to bake and how to clean, then, one day, to marry off in a beautiful ceremony attended by the whole village. She's already made my wedding dress, even though I've told her at least a dozen times I don't plan to ever get married. I know I should be grateful, but I'm frustrated.

All of that is wiped from my mind, however, as I throw my parcels onto my bed and start untying the strings and unwrapping the paper with shaking hands.

Over the past six months or so, there have been more than a few occasions when I've woken up Sunday morning to discover it's an Evan day. This always depresses me since Sunday is church day and I'm expected to dress my best. Sitting in the pew in my Sunday dress and slippers with that ridiculous bonnet my mother insists I wear makes me feel like a prisoner in my own skin, but I never had anything masculine to wear that was church appropriate.

Until now.

I finger the dress pants and crisp white dress shirt that falls out of the first package. The advertisement in the magazine promised they could make them to fit any body type as long as I provided the proper measurements. I spent an hour measuring every inch of my body to be doubly sure every number was correct before mailing in the form. I would have to make my own jacket to wear during the colder seasons, but I have months before I have to worry about that.

I quickly unwrap the second package and set my new pair of black dress shoes next to the clothes on my bed. Will helped me figure out my men's shoe size. He had me try on some of his old shoes his mother packed away in their attic before she died. We eventually found a pair that fit me perfectly, though I had to order these in a boys' size. They look just like adult shoes, so I doubt anyone will notice the difference.

I go to my dresser and fish out a cravat I saved from being donated to the church last winter. It was old and threadbare in places when it came to me, but by the time I was done fixing it up with a needle and thread, it looked almost brand new. I set it on top of the shirt and pants. My heart is thumping like crazy in my ears, and I know this excitement will see to it this Sunday is an Evan day so I can try it all on. I'm tempted to do so now but tell myself it will be worth it to wait. I hold the pants to my body and squeal with delight when I see they are indeed the perfect length. They do look a bit big in the waist though, and I wonder if Will has a belt I can borrow for—

"Evangeline!" my mother calls up the stairs. "Come down here, please."

I groan then quickly tuck my new treasures away around my room in places I know my mother won't find them. The shoes are the only thing I struggle to hide, but I eventually find an old blanket in my closet and wrap them in that before tucking them into a back corner, out of sight.

I hear voices as I start down the stairs.

"Can I offer you some tea, Pastor?" my mother asks.

I stop halfway down the staircase. What's the pastor doing here? Is this about earlier at the store?

"No thank you," the pastor replies.

"Elias?"

"Oh, no thank you, ma'am."

The pastor's son, Elias V, is here as well. I take one step backward up the stairs, debating whether or not I should hop out my bedroom window and disappear down to the river until sundown. My plan is thwarted, however, when my father rounds the corner of the sitting room and spots me. He gives me an apologetic smile.

"You may as well come down," he says quietly. "They're here to see you."

I grimace.

My father snorts and beckons me down the stairs.

"Has the mare had her baby yet?" I ask as I descend.

My father's favorite mare is due to foal any day. The fact that he's in here and not in the barn where he's been practically every minute for the past few days tells me that whatever I'm about to walk into must be serious.

"Not yet. Let's get this over with. We no doubt both have better places to be."

I nod, and we head into the sitting room together.

Pastor Elias and his son are sitting side-by-side on our long couch. My mother sits across from them with her back straight, her legs delicately crossed at the ankle, and a teacup balanced on her knee. When I walk in, all three of them look over at me, and I feel instantly uncomfortable as they fall silent. Elias V's eyes widen, and he looks at his father, who bobs his brows as if to say, "I told you so."

I frown at them both.

"Evangeline," my mother calls sweetly. "Come and sit down. You have guests."

I'd rather eat a whole bowl of boiled beets, but I force my feet into motion and take a seat in the chair beside my mother's. My father remains standing on my mother's other side.

"The pastor and his son came to speak with you," she goes on. "Well, to speak to all of us, really."

"Oh?" I say, pretending to be interested as I look over at the men in question. "What about?"

The pastor clears his throat and claps his hands once. "As you all know, my son will one day take my place as the head of our church. As the future shepherd of our flock, it's important that he stand as a pillar of society and a prime example of the type of person we should all strive to be. For a man of God, that's a husband and a father to as many children as the Lord blesses him with. I'm not getting any younger." The pastor laughs but quickly stops again when no one else joins in. "Elias and I have talked and decided it's well past time he marry and start his own family. At the age of thirty-five, he's strong, handsome, and has his own little homestead right next to ours with ample land to expand as his family grows. All he needs now is a wife."

The pastor turns his eyes on me.

My stomach rolls so hard I fear I may be sick. "You… you want… you're asking me to…?"

"I think you and my boy would make a fantastic match," the pastor says with a smile. "Your parents agree."

I look at my mother and father. Mother looks delighted. She's practically bouncing in her chair. Papa looks highly uncomfortable, but he doesn't deny the pastor's statement.

"We were thinking a fall wedding would be beautiful, Evangeline dear," my mother says, her voice all soft and dreamy. "Oh, it's going to be perfect."

My mouth falls open. "I haven't even said yes yet!"

"Well, of course you'll say yes," my mother says with a huff. She gives our guests a nervous smile. "Our pastor is asking you to marry his son, darling, the man who will lead us all to God's holy land. There isn't a higher honor you could ask for."

I scoff in disgust and look at Elias, who hasn't said a single word.

"Why do you want to marry me?" I ask him.

His father opens his mouth to answer, but Elias holds up his hand. The way the pastor immediately falls silent unnerves me almost as much as the way Elias' eyes bore into mine with an intensity that makes me squirm.

"The men in my family have always led our community on the path of righteousness," he says. His voice is much deeper than his father's. "It's our job to lead those who stray back to the proper path. It's no secret that you've wandered, Evangeline. You've cast yourself away from the path. I'm honored to be the one to lead you back to it again."

Instant rage makes my entire body hot, and I glare at him. "You want to marry me because you think it's your job to *fix* me? Is that it?"

My mother sucks in a breath, but the pastor waves his hand, much like his son did a moment ago, and she stays silent.

Elias grins at me. "Just look at yourself, Evangeline. Look at what you're wearing. Have you had a single suitor these past few years? You're twenty years old and still living at home with no hopes to marry. How much longer until you're a burden to your family?"

"I am not a burden," I say heatedly. "I help my father with everything around the farm and—"

"She does men's work?" Pastor Elias asks angrily.

"Evangeline does as she pleases," my father says, though it lacks bravado. "And she's as much help as the hands I hire each year."

"God help us," the pastor says. "It's worse than I thought."

"You are an unmarried woman," says Elias V, still staring me down. "And that means the decision isn't yours to make." He looks at my father. "I'm asking for your daughter's hand in marriage, sir. Do you accept?"

My eyes snap to my father, who holds my gaze for a long moment. I nearly hold my breath.

"I won't force Evangeline to marry a man she doesn't want," he finally says. "If you want my daughter's hand, Elias, you'll have to earn her affection first."

My mother spits my father's name like a curse while I sigh in relief.

The pastor shakes his head.

Elias looks at me again. "I'm not one to back down from a challenge."

I roll my eyes and get up from my chair. "My answer is no, Elias. Now, if you'll excuse me, I have chores to tend to."

I walk out of the room without waiting for a reply.

As I'm pulling my boots on by the back door, I hear Elias say, "Don't worry. I'll bring her around."

"Don't count on it," I mutter under my breath as I grab the egg basket and flee outside.

I don't make it halfway to the chicken coop before I hear heavy footsteps behind me.

"Evangeline," Elias calls.

I don't stop, but I have just enough time to say a quick prayer for patience before he catches up to me anyway.

"Can I speak to you privately?" he asks.

"Is that not what you're doing right now?" I ask bitterly.

"I know it seems like this proposal comes from nothing but the desire to change you—"

"That's exactly what this is, by your own admission!"

He speeds his steps and comes around me to block my path. I refuse to let him and keep walking, forcing him to walk backward.

"While it's true your family is worried about you and my father fears you may lead our little congregation off the righteous path, those things are not why I didn't hesitate to say yes when my father asked me if I would consider marrying you."

I stop walking. "Then why do you really want to marry me?"

Elias smiles. "For years, I've watched you come to church every Sunday in those flowy, delicate dresses you wear with your hair falling around your shoulders or spun around the top of your head like an angel's halo, and I always thought you were beautiful."

I wrinkle my nose. I haven't worn my hair like that in at least four years, and the thought that he was watching me even then makes me uncomfortable.

"Think of the life you could have with me," he continues. "If I was your husband, no one would dare speak ill of you or question your place on God's path ever again. You could live the life you choose, and no one would say a word."

"The life I choose? So, you'd let me dress however I like and use whatever names suit me?"

He takes his time, choosing his words carefully before he answers. "In private, you could wear and call yourself whatever you like. In public, I would ask that you dress appropriately and use your given name. Appearances are important, and your behavior would reflect directly on me as your partner in life."

I shake my head. "That's not enough."

He sighs. "Evangeline—"

"Stop calling me that," I say through gritted teeth. "My name is Evan today."

The bones of his jaw jut out as he clenches his teeth together, biting back the remark he obviously wants to make. "Why fight this?" he asks instead. "You and I both know your parents want this. Your mother will continue to plan our wedding; she may even announce it in the paper. My father will consider you his future daughter-in-law. And I'm not going anywhere."

He takes a step toward me, and I refuse to back away.

"Even if I have to come here every day to ask," he continues, "I promise you, you will one day accept my proposal." The way he says it makes it sound like a threat. "Whether by necessity or your own desires, you will take me as your husband. What will happen when your father can no longer run this farm? What happens when, God forbid, he passes and there's no male heir to take this land? What will you do then? Would you deny your aging parents the stability my name and money can give them as they grow old? You can't be that selfish."

His words sting, as he meant them to. Of course I don't want my family to suffer or become homeless. Despite the truth in what he's said, using my station as a woman and only child against me is a low blow.

I scowl at him. "You're a beast, Elias. If you think you can manipulate me into marrying you, you're sorely mistaken. I am not some damsel in need of rescuing."

"No, you're not. It's one of the things I admire most about you."

"And yet it's the one thing you're all trying so hard to change."

"Would it not be enough that I will gladly submit to your wishes in the privacy of our own home?"

I fix him with a pointed stare. "No."

I step around him and continue on to the chicken coop. He, thankfully, doesn't follow me this time.

Chapter 3

Sunday morning arrives, and I'm giddy with joy as I wash my face and brush and braid my hair. I pin the braid flatly to the top of my head then pluck the pieces of my outfit from their hidey-holes about my room with butterflies in my stomach. As excited as I am to wear these clothes today, I also know their reception may not be pleasant. I'm willing to take that risk, especially when I stand in front of my full-length mirror and inspect myself.

I look handsome.

The pants are indeed a bit too large at the waist, but I don't care. I put Will's hat on to complete the look and smile. Looking at me now, one could barely tell I was not born a man. It fills me with so much joy, I nearly cry.

The next thing I'll order is a men's scent—either a soap or an oil—something other than the flowery stuff my mother slathers on my clothes when she washes them.

"Evangeline," my mother calls. "We're going to be late!"

"Coming."

I adjust my cravat and tuck a stray strand of my hair up under my hat before heading downstairs.

I don't even make it to the door before my mother starts yelling.

"You march yourself right back upstairs and change into your Sunday dress this instant!" she demands with her hands on her hips.

"I thought you said we were going to be late," I say innocently.

"I've had just about enough of your lip, young lady. Go throw your dress on, and I'll take down your hair on the way."

I take a deep breath, and in a steady voice reply, "No."

My mother seems to swell before my eyes. "You'll do as I tell you."

"This is what I'm wearing to church today, Mother. Standing here arguing with me over it will only make us miss service because I'm not changing no matter what you say."

She rounds on my father. "Say something!"

My father studies me, his teeth chewing an anxious hole in his cheek as he does. "How much does this mean to you?" he asks me softly.

"Everything," I say with conviction.

He nods and turns to my mother. "Go and get in the wagon."

Her mouth falls open. "You're not seriously considering allowing her to—"

In a temper quite rare for him, my father cuts in, "What do you suggest I do? Drag her, kicking and screaming upstairs and dress her myself? Evangeline is not a child anymore. She will do as she sees fit to do. If you're so worried about wagging tongues, perhaps you should get moving and get in the wagon so we're not the last to arrive at service this morning."

My mother's bottom lip trembles for a moment before she turns with a huff and stomps outside.

My father and I both cringe as she slams the screen door shut.

"She'll likely ignore us longer than a week this time," he says.

"We can hope."

"Evange—Evan." He takes my shoulders in his hands and stares directly into my eyes. "I won't pretend to understand what's going on with you, but I know you're not a fool. You wouldn't be doing the things you do and facing such controversy if this wasn't what you truly felt was right. But I worry about you, as any father would. Are you certain you won't consider Elias' marriage proposal? His position in the village and his family's fortune would see to it you were cared for no matter what the rest of them think."

"If I marry Elias, he'll force me to be who I am not. I would be trading one hell for another."

"But at least you would be guaranteed a future."

"That's not a future I want, Papa." I take his hands from my shoulders and hold them in my own. "Please don't worry about me.

I've made my choice, and I'm prepared to deal with the consequences of it."

My father's eyes are tired and sad. He's been sad ever since his mare had her foal, a beautiful black colt.

He was stillborn.

It always breaks my father's heart to lose an animal, much less one he'd been looking forward to for so long. I don't want to cause him more pain, but this is important to me. After a long silence, he nods again. He unclasps his leather belt, yanks it through the loops of his pants, and holds it out to me.

"Those pants are too big for you," he says.

I snort as I take the belt and thread it through the loops of my own pants. "I ordered them through a catalog."

"They look nice." Once I've got the belt buckled, he says, "Now tuck in that shirt. That's right, all the way around. Perfect." He offers me his arm. "Well, let's go then."

I take his arm with a squeeze, and we walk out to the wagon to join my mother, who scowls at the floorboards and ignores us both as we climb aboard and head for the village.

*****

Father drives faster than usual to church so we arrive right on time. As we pull into the front yard, I notice the stares but keep my eyes fixed forward. Beside me, my mother slouches down in her seat as if that will make her disappear. We pull up to the fence, in line with the other wagons, and head for the church. Pastor Elias is standing out front to greet everyone as they come in, as usual. When he sees me, his eyes get so big they look ready to pop out of his head. I brace myself for a lecture, but he rips his eyes away from me and shakes my father's hand instead.

"Good morning," he says. "So good to see you." He tilts his head to shout in the door for his son before greeting my mother next, who manages the smallest smile. Their eyes meet, and it seems to me like an unspoken understanding passes between them. I wonder briefly what might've been discussed in the house after I left to tend the chickens the other day.

Elias V is quick to come at his father's call. As soon as he appears, he takes one look at me and his back snaps straight.

"Elias," says the pastor, "I thought perhaps you might like a moment with Evangeline before the start of service."

Elias smiles. "That's an excellent idea." He moves around his father and takes me by the elbow. His grip is hard, almost painfully so.

I try to take back my arm, but he refuses to let go. "Elias—"

"Come along," Elias orders.

"Stop!" I say loudly. "Let go!"

Elias doesn't stop, nor does anyone come to my rescue as he marches me around the corner of the building. Once we're out of sight of the others, he backs me against the wall of the church and finally releases me. I'm furious now, so I shove him away.

"What is the matter with you?" I snap. "What gives you the right to—"

Elias backhands me across the face.

I lean back against the wall in a daze and touch my burning cheek.

"Don't you ever lay your hands on me," he sneers. "And I don't want to see you in this outfit again, do you understand me? As your future husband, I forbid you from wearing anything other than proper lady's attire in the company of others from now on. Now, you will get on your horse, go home, and change into that nice Sunday dress you wore last week. Then, you will come straight back here and join me in the front row for service at my side as my betrothed."

My chest is heaving, and hot tears burn in my eyes. I drop my hand from my face and stand up straight. "No!" I shout. "I'm not your betrothed. I won't marry you, Elias. I wouldn't marry you if you were the last man on this miserable earth!"

He curls his lip back at me, and I brace myself for another strike.

"Hey!" Will runs over and forces himself between me and Elias. He shoves Elias, much like I did, only with enough force Elias is pushed several steps back. "Get away from them," Will sneers, and he shoves Elias again. "You like to be a bully? Fine. Bully someone your own size then." Another shove. "Come on, coward. Or do you only like to pick on those you perceive as women?"

Elias' face is red with fury as Will continues to taunt him, and the longer the exchange goes on, the more I worry for the safety of my friend. I take Will's hand and try to tug him back.

"Will, stop."

He yanks his hand out of mine.

"Will, please!"

Will finally stops shoving Elias but continues to glare at him as he says, "Don't ever touch them again."

Elias glares right back, first at Will, then at me. "You'll both regret this," he promises before stalking off.

As soon as Elias turns the corner and disappears, Will spins and puts his arms around me.

"Are you alright?" he asks.

"I think so."

He takes my chin in his hand and turns my head to inspect my face. He runs a finger across my abused cheek, and I wince as he brushes over a freshly-forming bruise.

"I'll kill him," Will hisses.

"You'll do nothing," I tell him sternly, and I yank my chin from his hand. "It would only bring you trouble as well as me."

"What are you going to do, Evan? He's determined to have you. Your mother was in the village yesterday telling everyone who'd listen how excited she is for your upcoming wedding."

I groan.

At the soft clearing of a throat, we both look over to find the baker's son, Jacob, standing awkwardly near the front corner of the church.

"Pastor Elias asked me to fetch you," he says, looking at Will. He then turns to me and says, "But he told me to tell you you're not welcome in church dressed as you are, Evangeline. I'm to escort you home."

"*I'll* be taking them home," Will declares sternly, but then he softens as he says, "Thank you, Jacob."

Jacob nods and disappears back around the corner.

Will continues to stare at the spot where Jacob was standing long after he's gone. When he finally turns back to me, I say, "We both deserve better."

Will leans his head down and touches his forehead to mine. "Let's run away," he says softly. "Both of us."

My heart skips a beat. "Where would we go?"

"My aunt's. It's plenty big enough for two guests until we can find other arrangements. We could both start over somewhere more accepting."

I consider it. I'd be leaving Papa to tend the farm alone with the hired help, but that'd be no different than if I were to go and marry Elias like they want me to. Leaving with Will and staying with his aunt sounds much more pleasant, all things considered.

"Do you think she'd take us in?" I ask, barely daring to hope.

"I know she'd gladly give *me* a room." He grins. "I'm her favorite. It shouldn't take much convincing to get her to agree to give you one too. She's an old spinster herself by choice. She'll understand."

"How soon can you get a letter to her?"

"I'll send one out tomorrow with the rest of the mail. I should hear back within a week or two. The Offering is tonight, then we'll have a whole month to plan our escape." He gives me a pointed look. "Can you be good until then?"

I smile mischievously. "I'll try my best."

He laughs. "Come along, heathen." He motions toward the front of the church. "I'll take you home."

Will unties his family's horse from the fence then gives me a hand up into their wagon.

As soon as he sits down beside me, I ask, "Can we take the south road home? I'd rather avoid the rest of the village if we can today."

"Good idea."

Chapter 4

The south road forks off from main street at the old windmill and swings south—as its name suggests—for about a mile before swinging north again and reconnecting with the main road just before my family's farm. It's the perfect route to take to avoid other travelers since it's only ever used once a month to deliver The Offering. The only downside is that it runs dangerously close to the edge of The Deadwood, a place anyone with good sense avoids at all costs.

Will and I often found much-needed solitude on the south road growing up. Though there are endless stories of horrible monsters breaking through the dense brambles to eat people alive who dare walk too close to The Deadwood's border, we've never seen a single beast nor known a single person who's been killed by one. We've occasionally heard strange sounds coming from within The Deadwood—long howls or the cries of animals we couldn't identify—but they were always far off in the distance and never close enough to make us anxious as we played in the long grass or picked wildflowers nearby.

There's a tree we used to climb with branches high enough we could see over the tops of The Deadwood's thick, arching branches and brush. We couldn't see very far, though. Since it's always winter inside The Deadwood, the blowing snow hides the notorious castle from view year-round. Will and I used to sit side-by-side on those high branches and speculate if it even exists at all.

We pass that tree on our way back to my farm, and we both glance past it to the large stone arch at the edge of The Deadwood that marks the halfway point of the south road. This is where the village makes the monthly Offering, but I've never understood how since the entire arch is grown over with tight, interwoven vines. And yet, somehow, they get a whole wagon load of food through it every month on the full moon.

As well as the occasional human.

It has only happened three times since I was born, but every once in a while, someone commits a crime heinous enough to be sent with The Offering into The Deadwood. I don't remember anything about the first two who were sent in my lifetime, but I remember the last one. Two years ago, the owner of the local feed mill killed his neighbor's only son while out hunting. He'd mistaken the youth for a deer in the early morning light, a tragic accident. The boy was only twelve. After his death, the sentencing was swift, though the mill owner had to be imprisoned in the church's cellar for two weeks while he waited for the next full moon. We could hear him calling out to his family throughout the two services we held while he was chained up down there, and I watched his loved ones cry as they sat listening to him beg to see them just one more time.

The whole thing gave me nightmares for months.

Not one of the people sent with The Offering has ever been seen again. It's our belief that they are dead, likely eaten by the ancient demons our legends say reside in those woods. This is our form of execution, reserved for men who've sinned far beyond the capacity of Pastor Elias to save their souls. Up until recently, I'd believed what my parents told me: that those sent with The Offering deserved their fates, that they were evil sinners no longer worthy of our pity or our mercy.

I'm not sure I believe that anymore.

*****

That night, I dream about The Great War.

Our legends tell of a war fought so long ago that no one in our village can trace their lineage back far enough to find a relative who lived through it. This war—waged between great winged beasts large enough they blocked out the sun for days at a time—ended with the creation of The Deadwood. What the war was fought over and where the beasts who waged it went afterward is a mystery even to our old stories, but The Deadwood and its magic winter is enough for us to believe in what little our stories have remembered about that time. Pastor Elias likes to preach about The Great War at least once a season, to praise God for ending it, and to remind us of our monthly sacrifice in the form of The Offering that keeps the demons still roaming in that forest of death satisfied enough they never leave it.

I see those great winged beasts circling high above me now, colliding and ripping at each other's wings as they fight their great war. Every so often, one of them drops dead out of the sky. It's raining beasts and blood, and I am afraid. Not of the creatures in the sky—not even for myself, I realize in surprise—but for my world, my home, and the ones I love. I reach my hand up toward those flying, snarling creatures as if asking to join them in battle, a battle for all that I hold dear.

I don't realize I'm crying until someone shakes me awake.

A man I don't recognize is standing in my room, and I scream.

"Shut up, you," he snarls as he rips me out of bed.

My legs get tangled in the bedding, and I fall to the floor. Another man comes in, and they both yank me to my feet by my arms and carry me between them out into the hall and down the stairs.

"Mother! Father!" I scream, but no help comes. "Let me go! Who are you? What do you want?"

I get no answers.

I'm marched out the front door of the house where I shield my eyes against the light from dozens of torches. The men at my arms march me down the front steps and across the yard toward a gathered crowd, then they throw me to the dirt.

I settle on my knees, shivering from cold, fright, and shame all at once. I'm in nothing but my thin nightgown. I tug it down over my legs to hide as much of myself as possible, both from the night chill and the dozens of eyes watching me. At the front of the crowd stands Elias, his father, and both my parents.

"What's happening?" I ask, even as I guess the answer.

"Evangeline," says Pastor Elias, "our congregation has decided your recent behavior must be the acts of a soul corrupted by the devil. You've shamed your family and refused their attempts to bring you back to the path of God. You've rejected the body God has given you, his gift of flesh, and you refuse to fill the role of a proper, God-fearing woman. This is your last chance at redemption."

Elias V takes a step forward and peers down at me. "Evangeline, you'll either agree to take me as your husband so that I may lead you back to God's righteousness and cast out the wickedness in your soul"—he takes another step forward—"or you'll go with The Offering tonight. You'll make your choice now in front of these witnesses. Marry me or be cast into The Deadwood to the mercy of the demons that dwell within."

I glare at the gathering in front of me, mostly men, though I notice Will is not among them, for which I am thankful. I look at my parents.

"You'd let them do this to me?" I ask.

"I spoke against it," my father says tearfully. "I'm so sorry, Evangeline, but I was outvoted."

"And right you should have been," my mother spouts. "It's your pampering that's put her in this position in the first place." She looks at me. "But she'll choose wisely now. Right, Evangeline? You'll listen like a good girl and stop this foolishness, won't you?"

I can tell by my mother's face that she truly believes that. She thinks this is all just some hard lesson for me to learn, a test to push me to do what she's wanted all along. What they all want.

I think of Will.

We both deserve better.

I look at Elias.

"I will not marry you," I announce.

"Evangeline!" my mother cries.

"I am *not* a woman!" I scream. "No marriage, no amount of faith, no number of *beatings*"—I spit that word right up at Elias with as much venom as I can muster—"will change who or what I am. I am neither a man nor a woman, and I will not be forced on any path."

My mother steps toward Elias. "She doesn't mean that," she says pleadingly. "Elias? You know she doesn't mean that, right?"

Elias and I lock eyes, and I hope he can see how deeply I hate him in mine.

He must because he grimly shakes his head.

"She's made her choice," he says. "Bring her."

"Elias, no!" my mother screams. "This is not what we discussed!"

Rough hands yank my arms forward as one of the men who kidnapped me from my bed ties my wrists together in front of me.

"I told you I would try," Elias tells my mother. "But it has to be her choice to come back to God's path. She's chosen the devil's instead."

A rope is looped under the tie at my wrists, and I'm tugged to my feet. The bindings dig into my skin as I'm pulled across the yard. The crowd parts to reveal The Offering cart, and the other end of my rope is tied to the back before they urge the horses into motion, and I'm dragged along behind the cart toward the south road. The crowd follows.

My mother is sobbing back where they left both her and my father in front of the house.

I still don't see Will.

I struggle to keep up with the cart. I'm barefoot and shivering with cold, but what concerns me more is the rain that begins to pour a few minutes later. I'm quickly drenched, and my nightgown clings to me, the wet fabric barely more than see-through now that it's wet. Several of the men snicker, and one trips me. I go down hard on the rocky road, scraping skin off my knees and arms. The cart doesn't stop, and I'm dragged several feet before I'm able to get my feet under me again. Another man throws a rock at me, which hits me in the mouth. They laugh when I cry out in pain.

It seems I've gotten what I wanted at last: they no longer see me as a woman.

They no longer see me as human at all.

No one deserves this fate.

I fall many more times before we arrive at the arch. The bottoms of my feet burn and throb. I'm freezing and covered in gashes from rocks, both ones I've fallen on and ones I've had thrown at me. At last, they pull the cart off the road and stop to unhook the horses. I sink to my knees in the tall grass, thankful for the break. It's short-lived.

Elias yanks me up by the hair, and I scream. The cart is now pulled by several of the largest men, and Elias marches me forward with it, still holding tight to my hair so that I have to walk on my toes. We stop again in front of the arch, and the vines shake then slowly slither away like snakes until the arch is clear. There is a narrow path beyond that leads off into the dark and snowy unknown. The men push the cart through the arch.

Elias finally releases me, but once the cart comes to a stop inside The Deadwood, the rope attaching me to it is long enough that I'm still standing outside of the arch. Elias grabs me again by the front of my nightgown and brings his face an inch from mine.

"I didn't want you as my wife anyway," he sneers. "I bet you'd be as cold as they come both in bed and out."

I spit blood in his face. "I hope you burn in hell!"

"Evangeline!"

My best friend comes running up, still dressed in his night clothes as well, the fabric every bit as soaked as mine. He must've run all the way from his bed. The men hold him back, but he pushes against their arms, desperate to reach me.

The sight breaks me, and the tears finally come. "Will!" I cry out.

Elias shakes me, drawing my attention back to him. "You'll burn first," he says with glee, then he shoves me back and kicks me hard in the middle, sending me stumbling through the arch.

I slam into the back of the cart, and it knocks the wind out of me.

"Evangeline!"

"Will," I utter between coughs. I slowly get to my aching feet and turn back toward the arch, but it's already half-covered with vines again. "Will!"

"I'll find you!" Will screams. "I'll find you, Evange—"

The last of the vines groan as they slide into place, and I'm left standing in the snowy lane, shivering and bleeding.

I am in The Deadwood.

In the distance, something large roars, and it no longer sounds so far away that I don't have to worry about it eating me.

Chapter 5

The precariousness of my situation hits me in full force when I start to shiver violently. The water in my hair and clothes is already going stiff in the frigid wind. My head is throbbing, and I can barely feel my feet. I quickly climb up into the cart to escape the snow on the ground and hug my legs to my chest. I pull up the slack from the rope, work it loose from between my wrists, and toss it away in disgust before working the binding off with my teeth. I tug my nightgown down over myself and huff hot air underneath, but the wind whips right through the fabric, stealing any heat I manage to produce. My white nightgown is splotched with blood and mud, and every inch of my body aches or burns, my knees worst of all, which are both skinned raw.

I want to cry, but that would only waste the few precious minutes I have left. I need a plan. I peer around at The Offering on the cart for anything I could wrap around myself to keep warm, but the food is all packed in wooden crates. There's not even a single burlap sack to be found.

I stiffen as the ground rumbles so hard the cart slides forward a few inches. Something heavy just hit the ground somewhere down the lane, and I peer cautiously over the top of the crates into the darkness. I don't see anything, but I hear the occasional snap of a twig and the crunch, crunch, crunch of heavy footsteps in the snow.

Someone's coming.

Or some*thing*.

I duck back down and assess my options. Whatever is coming is either here to collect The Offering or was drawn here by the noise of my arrival. Is it friendly? Is there such a thing as a friendly beast in this place?

The footsteps are close enough now that I should be able to see the creature if I look again, but I can't bring myself to. It might see me. Of course, it will anyway if it inspects the contents of the cart. I take that chance and sit completely still, huddled behind the crates. The footsteps stop, and there's a moment of terrifying silence before the cart begins moving again. It's being pulled by… whatever is out there. Perhaps that means the beast's attention is on the lane ahead and not the cart it's pulling. I dare another peek over the crates.

At first, all I see are a pair of large, leathery wings. They're so large they brush against the branches and vines on either side of the lane. A flow of long, stark white hair falls down the creature's back between the wings. A single arm the size of four of mine is stretched back, holding on to the hitch of the cart and pulling it down the lane as if it weighs nothing at all. I glance down and see two massive, muscled legs clothed in plain brown leather above wide feet tipped with talons instead of toes. Its skin is a deep, dark blue or perhaps purple, I can't tell in this light.

Demon, my mind screams.

As I crouch there, gawking, my foot slips in the water and snow in the wagon and bumps against one of the crates. I quickly duck back behind cover, but the damage is done.

The cart stops.

I cover my mouth with both hands to stifle the sound of my breathing as I begin to hyperventilate.

The footsteps start again, getting louder and closer with each step. I squeeze my eyes shut and wait until I hear them beside the cart to my right, then I bolt left. My limbs are slow from the cold and my fingers can't grip the wood of the cart hard enough. As I hop over the side, I slip and tumble down into the snow, but at least there is a whole cart between me and that thing now. I quickly peer around for which way to run, but there's only one way to go.

I take off down the lane.

I don't dare look back, but it doesn't matter, I can hear the demon's footsteps and feel the ground rumbling underneath me as its feet pound against the earth. It's running too and gaining on me quickly. I finally spot an opening in the dense overgrowth on the left side of the lane and dive for it. The hole is small, and thorns and sticks claw at me as I squeeze through, but I manage to tunnel my way, slowly but surely, into The Deadwood.

The creature begins snapping off branches and stomping down brambles, but I'm picking my way over and under them faster than it can tear through them. Eventually, I don't hear it at all anymore, and I hope that means it gave up and decided to leave me alone. I don't stop.

The snow hasn't managed to penetrate this deep into The Deadwood, so the ground is warmer, but the constant scraping of the wood and thorns against me makes my entire body burn. After what feels like an eternity swimming through hell, I finally emerge into a clearing. There's a mound of wind-swept snow blocking my way, and I climb over it to find this isn't a clearing, but a pond. I step out cautiously onto the ice, but it seems solid. My feet protest again at the cold, but I opt to give the rest of my battered body a break for a moment and cross this empty space then re-enter The Deadwood on the other side.

About halfway across the pond, I hear the flap of massive wings behind me and break into a run. I only make it a few steps before a large body smashes into the ice right in front of me. I scream and fall on my backside, scrambling away from the demon as it stands up and stares down at me through pure white eyes that seem to glow in the dark.

The demon is at least half again as tall as a human man and twice as wide in the shoulder. The wings, now fully extended, stretch twice its width out on either side. It wears no shirt, just simple leather pants. Its limbs are bulky and muscled, and its neck is thick. It has a large brow above those two glowing white eyes, a flat nose, and a wide mouth with two rows of vicious-looking teeth I can see as it pants. It has fangs. A forked tongue flicks out and licks its upper lip as it takes a step toward me.

"Stay away!" I scream. I can't get my feet underneath me as I slip and slide on the ice.

The creature surprises me by kneeling down on one knee.

I pause.

It raises an arm and sticks its hand out, palm facing me.

All at once, my fear drains away. I sag against the ice as a wave of calm flows over me, and I'm suddenly so tired I can barely keep my eyes open.

The creature comes closer, still staying down on one knee.

The fear threatens to return. I shouldn't let it reach me, and yet I can't move, both because of my fatigue and because of the calm that washes over me a second time.

Of course there's nothing to be afraid of. Why was I running? That's so silly.

As the adrenaline fades, the pain and the cold hit me hard, and I whimper.

The creature comes even closer and turns its hand, this time offering it to me as if to help me to my feet, my feet that are bleeding so badly they're staining the ice red.

I roll onto my knees.

It shuffles closer.

I reach out.

My hand slides into the demon's, and it's so warm that I instinctively reach for it with my other hand as well, craving that heat to thaw my frozen fingers. The massive hand closes around both of mine and tugs me closer.

I panic briefly when its arms wrap around me, but then that wave of calm washes over me again. Its arms are every bit as warm as its hands, and I can't get enough. I'm shivering so hard I can barely breathe through the spasms in my chest. Those two massive wings wrap in close, cocooning me inside them and blocking the icy wind as I huddle against the creature's chest, which is as warm as the rest of it. I look up through the small gap at the top of the wings into the demon's face.

"Whhhh… what… are you?" I stammer.

It doesn't speak, but a sudden flood of feeling washes over me, a feeling of safety, concern, and maybe a little awe.

Even without hearing the word, I understand.

Friend.

*****

I nod off in the demon's arms almost as soon as it begins walking. Where to? I have no idea, nor do I particularly care at this point. I am warm, and the sound of the creature's heartbeat beneath my head lulls me to sleep. I wake up a time or two as we walk, but it merely adjusts its arms around me each time, and I fall quickly back to sleep again.

I barely notice the sudden quiet when the wind disappears.

I pick my head up from the demon's chest, but I'm too weak and lay it right back down with a groan.

Everything hurts.

My head is still throbbing, every inch of my skin feels like it's been scraped off my body, my knees ache, and my feet pulse with bright pain with every beat of my heart. Even my teeth hurt, which is something I've never experienced before. I'm so stiff that when the arms that have held me for the past few hours—or maybe days, I don't really know—finally pull me away from that warm chest, every muscle in my body screams in protest.

I gasp and utter, "No."

I'm lowered onto something soft, but it brings me no comfort.

"What did they do to her?" asks a deep, rumbling voice.

"Walked her, half-naked, through the rain then tossed her into the snow would be my guess," answers another.

"Why would they send a woman here?"

"She must have really pissed someone off."

There's a moment of silence, then, "Don't start, Caliborne. This doesn't mean anything, so don't go getting all our hopes up. 'No man nor woman', remember?"

"This just means the zealots in the village have grown bolder, nothing more. Now we'll have to deal with *females* in the castle."

I open my eyes, though my lids feel as heavy as lead. I catch glimpses of a room made of dark stone, bright spots of burning fires I can't focus on, and a face, the same face I stared up at from those arms, except this one has coal-black eyes instead of white.

"I don't know if I can save this one." There's another stretch of silence, like someone is replying, only I can't hear them speaking. "It's in her lungs, Caliborne, I can feel it. If you think she looks sick now, just wait. This will get much worse before it gets better. I can keep her breathing and help fight infection, but I can't heal her, you know that. It might be kinder to—" More silence, then a sigh. "Alright. I'll try, but I make no promises."

Those black eyes come closer, and for a moment, I'm afraid again. But then the calm comes back, and I drift off to sleep despite my efforts to stay awake.

At least in sleep, I'm no longer in pain.

*****

I must be running a fever.

I try to talk, but by the time I get my mouth open, the words I was about to say escape me.

Where am I? Am I dead?

Is this hell?

My chest aches and there's so much pressure there, like a giant boulder has been placed between my breasts. It feels like it should be impossible to breathe, and yet air flows in and out of my lungs effortlessly, though each breath burns as if that air is made of flame.

"Fen, I think it's time to let this one go."

"No."

"You're exhausted, and she's not getting any better. Humans aren't like us. You've said yourself that sometimes it's kinder to end it. I know Caliborne is set on saving her, but if you told him—"

"I said no. Not this time."

"Why?"

"She's still fighting, and as long as she keeps fighting, I'll fight with her."

*****

The brief moments during which I am conscious are full of pain, nausea, and cold sweats. I'm shivering again, but only for a moment before those warm arms that carried me through the snow are back around me and that chest that kept me alive is pressed against me. I roll into it, warming my aching hands against leathery skin. Gentle fingers run up and down my back, comforting me.

I cry. I can't help it.

I ask for my father, but he never comes.

I ask for Will, but he doesn't come either.

I'm alone, but at least I'm warm.

Conquest

And I saw, and behold a white horse:
and he that sat on him had a bow;
and a crown was given unto him:
and he went forth conquering, and to conquer.

-Revelation 6:2 KJV

Chapter 6

I need a drink.

I also really need to pee.

It takes me several minutes to blink the sleep from my eyes and get them to focus. I'm in a bedroom, a large and rather beautiful one. The walls are rough-cut stone, but the room is furnished like any other. I'm currently lying in a giant four-poster bed and covered in deep purple down bedding. There's a dresser, an armoire, a vanity with a large oval mirror, and a window with thick purple curtains. It's daylight outside, but all I can see through the glass is blowing snow. I'm alone in the bed, though the blankets are pulled back beside me as if someone—or something—only just left it.

I try to sit up and gasp as pain lances through my middle and my legs when I do. I peel the blankets back and find myself dressed in a clean nightgown. All four of my limbs are heavily bandaged. The rest of me is covered in small gashes from my trek through The Deadwood and the rocks the men threw at me as I walked behind The Offering cart. There's a hideous bruise on my stomach where Elias kicked me, and my head still aches terribly, but at least the fever is gone.

I cover myself back up again. The room is chilly, and I don't think I'm in any position to get up anyway. I don't even know where I am.

Where is the demon?

It saved my life, but why?

I tense when I hear heavy footsteps outside my room. The knob turns, and the door opens as the creature lets itself in. It's holding a silver tray that looks like a toy in its massive hands. When it looks up and sees I'm awake, it pauses and slides the tray onto the nearby vanity without coming any further into the room.

"Who are you?" I ask, sliding back across the bed and preparing to jump off the other side if I have to, no matter how badly it may hurt.

It waves a hand dramatically down itself and shrugs.

It's such a human-like gesture that I almost laugh.

"I see you, but that doesn't tell me who, or what, you are."

Its face is expressionless and impossible to read. It picks up the tray again and takes a cautious step toward the bed.

I don't move.

The demon walks over and sets the tray on the bed beside me then backs away a few steps. There is a bowl of clear broth on the tray as well as a cup of what looks like hot tea. They're both steaming and smell mouth-watering. There's no silverware, so I pick up the bowl with both hands. It warms my chilly fingers as I tip it and take a sip.

It's very good.

I take another sip, humming as the hot liquid soothes my dry mouth and throat. I drink half of it before setting it down and trying the tea. It's good too but lacks any cream or sugar. I set it aside in favor of the broth again, quickly finishing it with a contented sigh before returning the empty bowl to the tray.

"Thank you," I say.

The creature bows its head at me and points to the tea.

"Oh… I don't like it black."

It nods in understanding and comes to take the tray.

"Do you have a name?" I ask.

The demon nods then takes a slip of paper from its pocket. It hands it to me before picking up the tray.

I unfold the little paper.

My name is Caliborne. You're safe here.

"Caliborne," I say softly.

The creature winks at me.

"Thank you for saving my life."

He bows his head again. At least I think it is a he. His bare chest has no breasts but still has two nipples like human men do.

"Are you… male?" I ask, my cheeks burning at the question.

He nods once.

"Are there others here like you?"

Another nod.

I wrinkle my brow. "Don't you talk? I heard voices before."

He shakes his head this time.

I study the little note again. "My name is… well, it's Evangeline, but I don't always go by that."

Caliborne studies me then raises his hand like he did that night on the pond, pointing his palm at me. My scalp tingles, like someone ran a finger up the back of my neck, then a flood of feelings I know aren't mine washes over me.

I feel wonder and trepidation laced with the tiniest hint of frustration.

"What was that?" I ask when the feeling subsides.

Caliborne points to his palm, then to his mouth, then to me.

"That's how you communicate?"

He nods.

"Do it again."

He complies, and again I feel the wonder, trepidation, and frustration swirl inside my mind, and this time I understand what he's trying to say: he's curious and a little bit uneasy.

"Are you afraid of me?" I ask, baffled.

He snorts and shakes his head.

"Then, I guess I'm confused."

"He's worried about you," says a deep voice, and another winged creature comes into the room. He's the same kind of creature as Caliborne, except he has vivid red hair and eyes instead of stark white. He's a full head shorter than Caliborne but bulkier, more muscled. He's also missing most of his left arm, and his wing on that side is slightly shredded at the bottom. What kind of creature is strong enough to do that to him? I probably don't want to know. "You almost died on us," he says. "Caliborne has been by your side since you got here."

"How long ago was that?" I ask.

"Four days."

"Who are you?"

"I'm Wexton." He takes a dramatic bow. "Nice to make your acquaintance."

"How come you can talk and Caliborne can't?" I ask.

Wexton straightens and looks at Caliborne. "I don't know. He's never told us." He smirks at me. "Get it?"

I smile a little, I can't help it.

"Anyway," he continues, "Caliborne here sat at your bedside and kept you warm these past four days while you slipped in and out of your fever dreams. He bandaged your wounds too." He slaps Caliborne on the shoulder. "Such a good little nurse, he is."

Caliborne merely looks at Wexton with that same expressionless face, but a moment later, Wexton laughs as some unspoken communication passes between them I'm not privy to.

"Where am I?" I ask.

"This place? It doesn't really have a name. Just 'home', I guess. Our home. Yours now too since your village sent you into The Deadwood. Once you enter The Deadwood, you can't ever leave again."

"Why?"

"That, little human, is quite a long story. Too long for me to get into right now. I'm on my way out to patrol."

"Patrol?"

Wexton smiles at me. "Who do you think keeps the beasts from breaking out of The Deadwood and ravaging your precious little village?"

"I thought you said no one can leave The Deadwood."

"Oh, she's sharp. I like her."

"I'm not a her."

Wexton blinks in surprise and looks at Caliborne.

Caliborne stares back.

"Alright then," Wexton says after a pause. "Maybe we've both got some stories to tell."

"I guess so," I say.

Wexton looks again at Caliborne. "I'll ask Fenmire to check if you need anything when he gets back, but you know how he is. Go drag him away from his books if you have to."

Caliborne nods.

Wexton leans closer to Caliborne. "Have you told Drixus yet?"

Caliborne shakes his head.

Wexton grunts. "Do you want me to?"

Another silent communication passes between them.

Wexton nods. "Alright, just don't wait too long."

"Are Fenmire and Drixus like you?" I ask.

"Ha! They wish. Isn't that right, Cal?" Wexton bumps his shoulder against Caliborne's.

Caliborne's face remains emotionless, but his eyes close as he shakes his head in obvious exasperation.

Their manner of speech and behavior is so odd and yet somehow endearing. They are massive, deadly-looking beasts, to be sure, and yet there's almost human-like brotherly affection between them. This isn't at all what I'd expected to find in The Deadwood.

"Do all the people sent with The Offering end up here?" I ask.

"Most do," Wexton says. He picks up my abandoned tea from the tray Caliborne is still holding and drinks it all in one swig. "There were a few we didn't get to in time, but that hasn't happened in a while."

I sink under my covers. "What happened to the ones who didn't make it?"

Wexton hesitates. "That's part of the long story I don't have time to get into right now." He sets the cup back on the tray. "By the way, what's your name?"

"That's also a long story."

Wexton tilts his head. "How can a name be a long story?"

"I guess you'll have to listen to it sometime and find out."

Wexton laughs. "Oh yes, I definitely like you. I'm glad you lived."

I smile. "Me too."

Wexton takes the tray from Caliborne. "See you around, little human," he calls as he leaves.

Alone again with Caliborne, I'm suddenly shy and don't know what to say, especially since he can't talk back to me anyway. I'm saved from saying anything at all, though, when he goes to a nearby cabinet and plucks out a large roll of bandages and a small, round tin. He brings them both to the side of the bed and sets them on the mattress.

He reaches for my arm, slowly, but I still flinch. He stops and holds his hand out, palm up and open. I slowly set my hand in his. It barely covers his palm. His fingers curl around my hand, and he gently tugs my arm out and untucks the end of the bandage wrapped around it. He unravels it, and I wince at the sight of my red and seeping skin. Once the arm is uncovered, Caliborne picks up the tin and twists off the lid to reveal a jelly-like substance inside. It's brown and smells awful.

"What's that?" I ask with a wrinkle of my nose.

He points to the jelly then to one of the worst gashes on my arm.

"A salve?"

He nods and dips his finger into the tin. The care he shows as he smears it across my wounds is touching, and I study his face as he works.

His eyes do indeed glow, it wasn't merely a trick of the light. It's as if a fire burns behind them. There are no whites and no pupils, just blazing white light. His lips are quite thick, and two long, curved fangs overlap the bottom one. Up close like this, I can see his ears through his hair. They're large and slightly pointed at the tops. I get a better look at his wings too. I can see bones between stretches of leather, and when I lean to the left, the torch on the wall shines through his right one, outlining the blood vessels under the skin.

"What *are* you?" I mutter, mostly to myself since I know he can't answer.

He's re-wrapping my arm now, but at my question, he pauses and studies me. He drops the bandage roll and raises his hand toward my face, stopping an inch from my cheek.

I wrinkle my brow and peer sideways at his hand before slowly leaning into his touch.

As soon as my cheek touches his palm, an image pops into my head… no, not an image, a moving picture. *I see Wexton standing with his hand on his hip. He looks irritated. Everything around him is fuzzy, but I can see him in perfect clarity as he says, "We need to get word to the other Gryxen somehow about—"* Then he's gone, and I'm once again staring at Caliborne's face.

"What was that?" I ask in awe.

Caliborne taps his finger against his temple.

"Was that a memory? Your memory?"

He nods and goes back to wrapping my arm.

"That word Wexton said, 'Gryxen', is that what you are? What your kind is called?"

Another nod.

"Can you all perform such tricks of the mind?"

He shakes his head no.

"Only you?"

A nod.

"Are you special then?"

No.

"So the others have powers too?"

Yes. He moves on to my other arm.

"Do my questions bother you?"

No.

Through carefully worded yes or no answer questions, I learn that the man who was locked in the church cellar is here somewhere, that I'm truly the only female human who's been sent with The Offering, and that the four names I've heard so far—Caliborne, Wexton, Fenmire, and Drixus—are the only ones of their kind within The Deadwood.

As I ask questions and Caliborne nods or shakes his head in answer to each, he tends to my arms and legs until they're each smothered in salve and wrapped in clean bandages. Once he's done, I'm tired again, and he must see it on my face because he flips the blankets up to my chin and all but tucks me in before cleaning up the soiled bandages and tugging the curtains closed over the window, plunging the room into near darkness.

"Wait," I say as I sit up. "I need… I need to relieve myself."

I'm embarrassed, but he only nods and slides a bedpan out from under the bed. He sets it next to me then turns around to give me privacy. I blush as I take it and do my business. It takes me a while since I'm still so stiff, and by the time I'm done, I'm completely exhausted, so much so that I don't even have the energy to feel bashful when Caliborne quietly takes the soiled pan and leaves the room with it.

I snuggle down under the covers, but despite how thick they are, they're not enough to cut through the chill in the room. The wind whistles through cracks in the walls and window, and I shiver. The cold isn't enough to keep me awake, though, and my eyes droop and drift shut as my body gives in to sleep.

I wake up again what feels like mere minutes later, but there's no light filtering in around the curtains anymore. I'm pressed against a familiar, warm body, and I huddle closer with a contented hum. I peek up through heavy eyelids to see two burning white orbs staring back at me.

"Why are you doing this, Caliborne?" I ask groggily. "Why work so hard to keep me alive?"

Caliborne, of course, doesn't answer me, at least not with words. He touches his palm to my cheek again, and I suddenly see myself cowering on a frozen pond, bruised, wet, and bleeding as I scramble backward across the ice.

As I watch Caliborne's first memory of me through his eyes, I feel pity for the wounded creature in front of me, anger at those who harmed it in this way, and impressed at its cunning in using The Deadwood against me. But most of all, I feel concern, concern for how pale this human's skin is, that its lips are turning blue, and that the clothing it's wearing isn't nearly enough to keep it alive in this weather.

It's only when I take a step closer and it shouts at me that I realize it's a female, and the revelation angers me more. They cast a helpless female out into the snow with no clothes and nothing to defend herself. She'll die if I don't get her home soon. I must make her trust me, and fast. I reach my hand out to her and calm her with my mind, telling her she is safe, that there is no reason to run. Once she's relaxed enough, I take her hand, and my body heat draws her in closer until I can put my arms around her.

Gods, she's freezing.

I block the wind with my wings. It means I can't fly home, but at least she's warm. I tuck her close to my chest and peer around, calculating the quickest path to the castle through The Deadwood. When I look down, she's staring up at me, and something inside my chest aches a little.

She's so small.

I hold her tighter, tuck my wings in closer, and begin the long trek home.

The wind and the snow disappear, and I'm once again staring at Caliborne's face, tucked in bed and curled up to his warm chest.

"You don't want to know what *I* thought when I first saw *you*," I say.

His chest shakes with silent laughter.

"Why don't you talk?"

He shrugs.

"Have you ever tried?"

No.

"Don't you want to?"

No again.

"Fair enough, I suppose."

I have so many questions, but they aren't ones I can frame for easy yes or no answers, and I'm too tired to dive into the deeper stuff right now anyway. I'm still in shock over everything that has happened since I was dragged from my bed by strangers. Now I'm lying in a much larger, grander bed, cuddling with the demon who saved my life after a whole village of humans—humans who've known me my entire life—cast me away for daring to be myself.

There's no doubt a lesson in that about what makes a true beast, but it slips through my fingers as I close my eyes and fall back to sleep in Caliborne's arms.

Chapter 7

I wake up to the sound of singing.

I don't understand any of the words, but it's definitely a song. I rub the sleep from my eyes and prop myself up on an elbow. Another Gryxen, this one with black hair and eyes, is sitting in a chair at the foot of my bed. He has his foot propped against the bedframe with his chair pushed back precariously on two legs. He's staring at the floor as he sings softly to himself. It's daylight again, though there's still nothing to see out the window but snow.

"Which one are you?" I ask sleepily.

He whips his head toward me and lowers his chair. "She wakes at last." His voice is not as deep as Wexton's, but it still rumbles a bit throughout the room.

"Where's Caliborne?"

"Fond of the big guy already?" His black eyes shimmer as he studies me. "Can't say I blame you. He has a soft heart."

"And you don't?"

He tilts his head. "I'm the rational one. I do whatever makes the most sense to me in the moment. I would've just let you keep running through The Deadwood and gone on my merry way."

"You would've left me to die?"

He considers this for a moment. "Maybe not. I can't say for certain. I wasn't there."

"You still haven't told me who you are."

He pushes his chair back onto two legs again. "I'm Fenmire. I'd ask for your name, but apparently, even something as easy as that is complicated with you."

"You can say that."

"Females," he scoffs. "You're all the same, no matter the species. This is the last thing we need."

"I didn't ask to be sent here," I say bitterly.

"And just why *were* you sent here?"

"I refused to marry the pastor's son."

"Why? Isn't marriage you humans' primary goal in life? That and offspring, of course."

"Not for me."

"Oh? A rebel, are we? I can respect that."

I narrow my eyes at him. "I'm not rebellious by choice. I simply refuse to pretend to be something I'm not."

"And what did the poor pastor's boy want you to pretend to be?"

"A woman."

Fenmire cocks a brow. "So then, do you call yourself a man?"

"I am neither a woman nor a man."

His chair comes down with a bang so loud it makes me jump. He leans forward. "Come again?"

The door opens and Caliborne walks in.

Fenmire looks up at him, gestures toward me, and asks, "Did you know about this? That our new *guest* claims to be neither man nor woman?" All sarcasm and jeering is gone from his voice now.

"I prefer to be referred to as 'they', not 'she'," I declare rather moodily.

Both Gryxen stare at me, one with no expression, the other, one of confused disbelief.

Fenmire says something to Caliborne in the same language he was singing in earlier.

Caliborne is silent, but whatever message he communicates back makes Fenmire huff and get to his feet.

"We need to discuss this," Fenmire says. "All of us. As soon as possible."

Caliborne growls with a pointed look at me.

"Fine," Fenmire barks. He marches over to Caliborne until there is barely a foot of distance between them. He's about the same height as Wexton, so he just reaches Caliborne's chin. "As soon as they're out of that bed, we're going to talk." He glances back at me, and the look on his face softens. His eyes are wide now with wonder, but there's also a worried crease in his brow.

Caliborne touches Fenmire's shoulder, but Fenmire brushes it off and stalks out of the room.

"He seems touchy," I remark once the door closes behind him.

Caliborne nods.

Now that the excitement is over, I assess myself from head to toe. I'm feeling much better today, more rested and less achy. My knees still burn horribly when I move them as well as the bottoms of my feet, but the rest of me moves with fewer protests. My headache is gone. I sit up against the headboard.

Caliborne hands me another slip of paper, a much bigger one this time. The handwriting is much different than the note he gave me yesterday. It's a list of simple meals, breakfast dishes.

"What's this?"

He points to me, pats his stomach, then points to the list.

"I'm to pick what I want to eat?"

Yes.

My stomach grumbles at the thought of food. "Can I have a 4-minute egg and a slice of ham? Some tea too but with cream and sugar this time?"

Caliborne takes back the list with a slight bow of his head and turns to leave.

"Was Fenmire upset because I said I'm not a man or a woman?" I ask.

Caliborne hesitates before shaking his head.

"What is my place here? Am… Am I a slave or…?"

He comes back to me and reaches for my face, stopping just before contact to let me decide. I lean my cheek against his palm.

I'm once again peering through Caliborne's eyes as he walks down a long stone hallway. A human man comes out of a room to my right, and I catch a glimpse of a neatly made bed inside before he shuts the door.

"Good morning, Caliborne," he greets cheerfully.

I wave at him as I walk by.

At the end of the hall, I walk into a kitchen. The sounds of pots and pans and sizzling meats are all around me. It smells mouth-watering in here. Three more humans bustle about making food. When they spot me, they all call out in greeting. One of them walks over, wiping his hands on a rag as he does. He's quite old and walks with a bit of a limp.

"What can I do for you, Caliborne?" he asks in a wheezy voice.

I hand him a paper.

"The newcomer is ready for a proper meal at last, eh?"

I nod.

He smiles at me. "Give me a moment, and I'll make you a list."

He shuffles off to the back of the room for paper and a pencil while I sneak bites of raw meat from a long counter where another man is chopping up ingredients for some human meal. He catches me popping a morsel of beef into my mouth.

"Caliborne," he chastises. "Stop that or there'll be none left for stew."

I raise my hand and point my palm at him. Without words, I joke that he could stand to eat a more meager stew for a meal or two. He laughs and pats his rounded belly.

"You're not wrong, friend," he says with a smile.

The older man comes back with his list. "Here you are," he says as he hands it to me. "I hope he feels better soon. We need a new face around here."

"Are you saying I'm ugly?" jokes the man at the counter.

"I'm saying it!" calls the third man who stands all the way at the other end of the kitchen, stirring a giant pot over a fire.

All three men laugh and return to their work. The atmosphere is light, the conversation cheerful, and the work done with pride.

This place is not a prison. It's a home.

Caliborne takes his hand back, and the memory fades.

"So, humans live here and help out willingly?" I ask.

Yes.

"Is there any other place to go in The Deadwood?"

No.

Knowing I'm the only female human here doesn't bother me, but the thought that there is nowhere else to go and I can't even go outside without freezing to death in a blizzard makes me sad. No more spring flowers, no more summer swims, no more long fall walks after harvest with Will.

No more Will.

I hug myself. The thought of never seeing him again makes my chest hurt.

He'd been there at The Offering. He'd run all the way from his family's farm in his pajamas and the rain to try and rescue me. He'd promised he'd find me somehow, but I don't see how that can ever happen. Unless…

"Is there a way into The Deadwood from the outside besides The Offering?" I ask.

No.

I turn away from Caliborne and bite my lip against the urge to cry. As badly as I wish Will were here with me, I don't wish The Offering on anyone, much less my best friend.

That strange tingle runs up the back of my scalp again, and a rush of anxious worry fills me. I look over at Caliborne, and he has his palm out, asking me, in his way, what's wrong.

"I miss a friend, that's all," I explain.

He nods in understanding then points at the list still in his hand and motions toward the door.

"Go ahead. I'm fine."

Caliborne leaves to get my breakfast, and I take the opportunity while he's gone to use my bed pan again. It's agony to stand. My knees and feet throb for the few seconds I'm up to get the pan, but I'm soon back in bed with an empty bladder, excited at the thought of a real meal, which arrives just moments later.

Caliborne comes back with the same silver tray as before, and he sets it on the bed beside me. At the smell of ham, I sit up and drag the tray into my lap. There's silverware this time, but before I can pick up my fork, he's asking to touch my face again. I let him, and this time I see myself lying in bed as I say, *"My name is… well, it's Evangeline, but I don't always go by that."* Along with the memory comes a deep sense of confusion and wonder.

"You want me to explain my name?" I ask once he takes his hand away.

Yes.

I consider it and eventually decide that, after saving my life and taking care of me like he has, I at least owe him this much. So, as I carefully crack open my egg and slice up my ham, I tell him my story.

"Like I told your friend, I consider myself neither a man nor a woman. I was named Evangeline by my parents when I was born. As a child, I started feeling like something was… off. Not wrong, necessarily, at least not all the time. There were days when I'd wake up and think, 'This is not the body I'm supposed to have'. On days like that, I hated the name I was given. But then, there were days when I woke feeling as if all was right in the world and that this body was perfect, but the name still didn't quite fit. And there were also days I felt indifferent, like I didn't care to think about my body or my name at all.

"As I got older, those feelings and the void between them grew. After a while, the days when I woke up feeling like I was born in the wrong body made me hate myself. When I told my parents about it, they were dismissive and assured me it would pass in time, but it only got worse. They didn't understand. No one understood. None of the girls at school felt this way; trust me, I asked. Then, on one of those depressing days when I couldn't stand my own skin, I was out on a walk with my best friend, Will, when it grew suddenly chilly, so he gave me his jacket to wear home.

"It was like something woke in me. The jacket was far too big for me, but the feeling I had while wearing a man's clothes was indescribable. The next time I felt like that, I went to my parent's room while they were out of the house and tried on my father's clothes. And I cried. I cried because it felt so good. Looking in the mirror that day, I knew the name Evangeline wasn't right anymore, not for this person who looked so handsome in their father's dress shirt.

"But there were still the days when putting on a dress and brushing out my long hair felt good, and I was deeply confused. Was I a man or was I a woman? I asked myself that over and over and begged my mind to decide, but it never did. And there were still days when neither dresses nor dress shirts made me happy. It was a confusing time until I accepted that I am neither a man nor a woman but something else, something that shifts like the weather or the seasons. To honor that, I gave myself two new names. On my masculine days, I like to be called Evan; on my feminine days, Eve; and on the ones where it makes little difference, Evangeline feels more fitting.

"So, my name is Evangeline, this is true, but it is also Evan and Eve. But, regardless of the name, I am not a he or a she but a they."

After my speech, I'm reluctant to look at his face, but Caliborne shows no emotion, as usual, so I have no idea what he thinks about all of this until he opens his palm and I feel contentment, acceptance, and joy.

He is happy and satisfied with my answer.

"Will you do something for me?" I ask.

He doesn't shake or nod his head but waits for me to make my request before he decides.

"Will you tell… or… show, I guess, the others what I've told you, so I don't have to repeat that story over and over?"

He nods.

"Thank you."

He points at my remaining breakfast—now cold but still delicious—and motions for me to continue eating. I smile as I pop a bite of ham in my mouth and sip my tea, which is perfectly sweetened.

"Fenmire says you have a soft heart," I say. "Does that mean you're the nicest?"

Caliborne rolls his eyes, and it's the most emotion I've seen on his face yet. It makes me laugh.

"Is this my new room, then?"

No. He points at himself, and I almost choke on my tea.

"This is *your* room?"

Yes.

"Oh." I almost apologize for intruding so long in his space, but then I remember I had no say in the matter. "Do I have my own room?"

Yes.

"When can I see it?"

He points toward my legs.

"Once I can walk?"

Yes.

"Fenmire mentioned a talk, some discussion that's to be had about me. Am I to be included in it?"

This time, Caliborne only shrugs.

"It's only fair. It's impolite to talk about others when they're not in the room."

Caliborne is silent as I finish my breakfast.

I set the empty tray aside and ask, "If it's always winter here, and you can't leave The Deadwood, is that why we must make The Offering each month? To bring you food?"

Yes.

"Do you truly let beasts into the village if we refuse The Offering?"

No.

"But our legends speak of great beasts coming out of The Deadwood to kill us all if we refuse to bring The Offering."

With his palm, Caliborne makes me feel great sorrow and crushing guilt mixed with self-loathing. Failure. That's what it is.

"You didn't mean to let the beasts loose?"

No.

"Where do the beasts come from?"

Caliborne walks over and taps his knuckle on the bedroom door.

"A door? And your job is to keep them from getting out of The Deadwood?"

Yes.

"Did you create The Deadwood?"

No.

"But you live in it, so you must know who did."

Yes.

"Perhaps they could let us humans out again. We never asked to be brought here, after all."

Caliborne shakes his head.

I sigh. "Wishful thinking, I know."

I hope they do include me in their talk because there are a hundred more questions I want to ask that will require much more than yes or no answers. For now, though, I am content as Caliborne moves my tray to the vanity and offers to help change my bandages again.

Chapter 8

I am flying over The Deadwood. Below me, some monster is tearing through the dense underbrush, but I can't see through the brambles and vines to find and kill it. I must find it and fast because, even in the blizzard, I know the edge of The Deadwood is not too far ahead.

I can't let it get out.

One of the taller trees nearby gives a violent shake, as if something large just ran into it, and I fly lower, scanning through the thick canopy for the beast below. I can't see it, and no more trees are moving here. I fly on, desperate now to find my enemy before it—

There is a mighty howl, but it's far ahead of me. Too far.

I fly faster, shooting blindly through the air as snow pelts my face and stings my eyes. With a mighty flap of my wings, I pull up short at the edge of The Deadwood and watch in horror as the beast crosses the human road and races across the field toward the village beyond.

I roar in defeat, angry and disgusted with myself for having failed.

A moment later, the screaming begins.

I wake up with a gasp.

A long, flat face framed with red hair and dotted with glowing red eyes is just a few inches away from my own. I jerk back with a small cry of shock.

Wexton doesn't pull away. He doesn't even seem sorry for startling me.

"You were dreaming," he says simply.

"Were you watching me sleep?"

"For a moment."

"Why?"

"You were mumbling and thrashing about. I thought you might be having a bad dream and was deciding if I should wake you or not."

"What time is it?"

"Nearly dawn."

I peer around the room. "Where's Caliborne?"

Wexton makes a show of fluffing one of the pillows before collapsing onto the bed beside me. I scoot far to the other side to create enough space for his massive wings.

"I don't know," he says with a smirk. "He didn't say."

"How often do you make that joke?"

"As often as I can."

"Can you influence emotions and show me memories too?"

"No, that's just Caliborne."

"Do you have some other powers?"

"Wouldn't you like to know." He gives me a brazen wink.

"You're back from patrol?"

"Sure am."

"Did any beasts get past you?"

"Me? Never."

"But you only have…" I clamp my mouth shut in shame.

Wexton doesn't look the least bit offended. "That just makes my victories twice as impressive."

"What happened to you?"

"That's a long story."

What a wiseass. I decide to beat him at his own game. "I guess that means it must be a boring one," I say sleepily. I even yawn to complete the ruse.

"Oh, it's anything but boring," he insists.

I roll over and put my back to him. "I don't believe you."

The bed creaks as he leans closer. "It'll give you nightmares."

"More likely it'll put me straight to sleep," I mumble.

The bed shakes and groans as he rolls over to face me.

I don't move.

He huffs. "Fine, I'll tell you, but don't say I didn't warn you."

I roll over to face him too. "I'm listening."

"Back when The Deadwood was first created—"

"How long ago was that, exactly?"

"About two thousand years, give or take a century or two. Anyway, back when it was first formed, we didn't know there would be great beasts coming through The Gate now and again to—"

"The Gate? Caliborne called it a door."

"Are you going to keep interrupting, or do you want to hear this story?" he grumbles.

I bite my lip to hide a smile. "Sorry."

"As I was saying, we didn't know to keep watch for beasts coming through The Gate, so when the first one came through, I was the only one out in The Deadwood. I was searching the perimeter for any way in or out besides the arch and—"

I sit up on one arm excitedly. "Did you find one?"

Wexton turns his head toward me, slowly, narrows his eyes to slits, and blows a gust of air into my face through his nose with an irritated snort.

I laugh and settle back on my pillow. I make a locking motion over my lips and stuff an imaginary key into his palm.

He nods once and makes a show of pocketing my key. "I'd almost completed a full pass and was about to head back to the castle when I heard a roar. The ground began to shake under massive footfalls, and when I found the source, the beast was already halfway to The Deadwood's border. It was headed straight toward your village, and I knew if I didn't stop it, it would break out and go on a killing spree. I headed it off, but it wasn't about to let me stop it.

"It was like something had possessed it. It was determined to break through the border, and so, when I landed in front of it, it never even slowed down. It barreled right into me—which hurt like a..." He clears his throat and continues. "It slammed into me, and I wrapped my arms around its massive neck and tried to throw it to the ground. It had horns, mind you, sharp ones, and a mouth full of razor-sharp teeth. I could hear them snapping in my ear as I clung to its neck. No wings that time, though, thankfully. It wasn't anything I'd seen before, so I had no idea how best to kill it, much less how to do so with my bare hands. As I stood there holding the beast back from breaking out of The Deadwood, I took too long deciding how best to handle it, and it managed to get its head around and clamp those teeth down on my side."

He waves a hand down his side from armpit to hip, and when I look closer, I can see the pattern of the beast's teeth in his leathery skin.

"You better believe that kicked my ass—sorry, my backside into motion. I punched it in the eye so hard it burst all over my hand." He lifts his stubbled arm as if to show me the hand that no longer exists. "I didn't move out of the way fast enough, though. It let go of my side and bit onto my arm instead. As I was flailing around there with my arm in its mouth, my wing ended up under the beast's paw. Its nails shredded it a bit, but I can still fly straight, so." He shrugs. "I was more upset about the arm because a moment later, it tossed its head back and forth and ripped it clean off."

I wince.

"Told you. Gruesome. Thankfully, the others heard the beast's roaring when it first came through The Gate and were quick to investigate the commotion. Thank Seerraf for that. I nearly bled to death as it was."

I can't help myself. I ask, "Who's Seerraf?"

"One of our gods, the oldest one."

"There is only one God."

He laughs a full belly, rumbling laugh. "Silly human. You have a lot to learn."

"Will you teach me?"

"About gods?"

"Gods, your kind, where you came from, The Great War, the creation of The Deadwood. All of it."

He studies me silently for a moment. "Perhaps, if you can learn to listen without interrupting."

"I make no promises."

"Then neither shall I."

"Caliborne tells me your kind is called Gryxen."

"That's the word in our language, sure. Your kind calls us demons."

I frown. "Demons are beings of hell sent to possess and torment our souls."

Wexton chuckles. "Hell has no interest in human souls."

"That's truly where you're from, then? Hell?"

"That's the name your people gave it long ago, but the image you've created of our world is not at all accurate to how it really is."

"What's it really like?"

"For one thing, we don't collect the souls of the wicked. We collect no souls at all. And our world is no pit of eternal fire. It's a lot like yours. It just so happens that The Gate opens to a desert on our end. The scorching heat and red sands have been mistaken for a burning pit by your kind."

"I still don't know what The Gate is."

"It's a doorway between your world and ours. The Gryxen—which translates from our language to yours as 'Gate Guardians'—are tasked with keeping the doorway closed to protect both our worlds from destruction."

"Gate Guardians," I mutter as I sit up. "So, that's not your race but your job?"

He considers this and nods. "That's one way to describe it, I suppose. But a job is something you can leave if you decide it's not the right fit for you. We are born as Gryxen. We can't ever not be Gryxen. Our 'race', as you call it, is Gruxa. Gryxen are a special kind of Gruxa born with wings specifically so we can fight in the air to protect The Gates since they reside in the sky in our world."

"What created The Gates?"

"Even we don't know that. The Gates have existed for as long as life has existed."

"How many Gates are there?"

"How many hairs do you have on your head?"

That is an impossible thing to calculate, so I shake my head.

Wexton nods. "Exactly."

"And they all connect my world to yours?"

"Heavens, no. There are several Gates in your world, and only one of them connects to my world."

"Where do the others lead?"

"You'd have to ask Fenmire. He's our historian."

I flop back down on my pillow. "It's all so unbelievable that I'd call you a liar if not for the fact that you just lying here beside me proves at least some of it is true."

"Oh, it's all true. And there's much more to it than what little I've told you. You'll learn it all very soon."

"You say that like it's inevitable."

Wexton falls silent, but I can see in his eyes that he's struggling not to say the words poised on his tongue. Eventually, he says, "We've waited for you for a long time."

I have no idea what that means, but when I open my mouth to ask him to clarify, the bedroom door opens and Caliborne returns with my breakfast tray.

Wexton smiles up at him. "Finally!" He bounds off the bed. "I don't know how you get any rest, Cal. This one just about chatted my ear off. I've gotten not a moment's peace since they woke."

"Me?" I bark in indignation. "You're the chatterbox."

"I didn't hear you complaining as you shot question after question at me."

I stick my tongue out at him.

Wexton marches over and slaps Caliborne on the shoulder before strolling out of the room without a backward glance.

"See you later, silly human," he calls from down the hall.

"Is he always like that?" I ask.

Caliborne nods with a soft huff.

I laugh as I prop myself up with pillows.

He brings me my food and sets the tray across my lap.

"I never see you eat," I say. "Aren't you hungry?"

No.

"Doesn't your kind need to eat?" I find it hard to believe otherwise.

Caliborne offers me his palm, and I set my cheek against it. I see a beast slain in the snow in The Deadwood, and I watch through his eyes as Caliborne begins butchering it much like my father does to the deer he hunts in our corn fields, except this creature's blood is black as ink.

"You eat the beasts you hunt?" I ask.

Yes.

"That makes sense, I suppose. There's no need to let that meat go to waste."

Caliborne nods in agreement then motions for me to eat while he gets ready to tend my arms and legs like he does every morning. It's sweet, really, the care he shows me day after day.

I think about how humans have labeled his kind as evil. Demons. The images Pastor Elias has painted over the years may look similar to Caliborne and his friends, but their mannerisms and behavior are nothing like what I imagined. Could it be true that we simply misunderstood? Even Pastor Elias admits our legends and scriptures aren't perfect accounts of our past. But how did we get it so wrong? Was it fear that warped the truth into the horrors we've come to believe? Or am I being lied to now? Perhaps these beings are after my soul after all, and this is all some elaborate trick to get me to trust them.

Caliborne gently shifts my leg out from under the blankets and unwraps the bandages. He's careful not to aggravate the worst of the wounds as he tends them with a soft touch. He looks up and catches me watching him, and he must read the worry on my face because he tilts his head curiously at me.

"Wexton told me about The Gate," I say. "I'm having a hard time believing such a tall tale. Hell is supposedly no different than Earth, demons are actually guardians, and my people have mistaken desert sands for fire and brimstone." I shake my head. "I was sent here to suffer," I say as tears burn in my eyes. "I was thrust through the arch as a wicked sinner in need of punishment, but all I've found is…" I wipe my eyes, but my emotions are overwhelming me. At the worst possible moment, I think of Will, and the tears spill over, trickling down my cheeks as I look up into Caliborne's blank face. "…is warmth and… acceptance." I blink up at him and whisper, "I'm so confused Caliborne."

He has salve all over his fingers, but he reaches out and wipes away first one tear then the other with one of his massive knuckles.

"I've been told for a long time that I am broken," I say. "But if they were wrong about all of this, perhaps they were wrong about me too."

Caliborne gives me an enthusiastic nod, lifts my chin, and taps me on the end of the nose before going back to work on my legs.

I watch quietly and eat my breakfast.

Chapter 9

Days pass during which I do nothing but eat and sleep and heal. It's rather boring, actually. Caliborne is with me during the day, but at night, he leaves after I fall asleep and doesn't come back until breakfast. I wake up to find someone else in my room each morning. It's usually Wexton, but once or twice it's Fenmire. The former usually climbs into the bed beside me to talk, though we don't discuss anything as deep as we did before. Perhaps Caliborne asked him not to talk about such things with me again, I don't know. Fenmire, on the other hand, seems reluctant to talk to me at all. He'll answer me if I ask him a direct question but refuses to initiate any sort of conversation himself. I try to respect that and leave him alone, but it makes for awkward silence while we wait for Caliborne to show up.

The fourth Gryxen, the one they call Drixus, never comes, and when I ask Wexton why I haven't met him yet, he gives me an ominous answer.

"Be glad Drixus doesn't come around," he says. "He's sour company these days."

Finally, a morning arrives when I wake up feeling the most well-rested I've been since I was dragged from my bed at my parents' farm. I refuse to call that place home anymore. I roll and stretch and peek over at the chair at the foot of my bed to see who's watching over me this time. It's Fenmire, but he's asleep with his head lolling down to his chest. I sit up, quietly, so as not to wake him, and study him as he sleeps. Without the permanent frown he wears all waking hours, he looks like Caliborne, except for the hair, of course. I decide not to wake him and bring back that scowl.

Instead, I slowly fold back the blankets on the bed and slide to the edge of the mattress. The bandages on my arms are gone as are most of the ones on my legs. Only my knees and feet are wrapped now, and even they pain me little as I stand up and stretch the stiffness from my muscles.

I've been in bed too long. My hair is limp and messy, and my body feels sticky all over. I need a bath, but I don't know where to go to get one.

I tiptoe past Fenmire and cross to the window where I shift the curtain aside to stare out at the blowing snow. The cold seeps in through the glass, cooling this side of the room so much it's nearly uncomfortable to stand here in nothing but my nightgown. I lean nearer the glass anyway, squinting my eyes to try and see through the blizzard. All I see is white. There is an icicle growing on the inside of the windowsill, and I wrap my fingers around it and pluck it off the stone. It's twice as long as my arm and makes me think of the times Will and I would pretend to sword fight with them in winters past.

I turn from the window and brandish the ice like I did back in those days, pointing it at the back of Fenmire's chair as if I'm about to run him through. The sheer weight of it breaks the icicle in half, and the end falls and shatters on the floor.

Fenmire jumps with a snort and rubs his face. He sees the empty bed and sits abruptly upright. When I don't materialize under the covers in front of him, he stands and glances around the room. His eyes land on me behind his chair and take in the whole scene, from my icicle sword—which I'm still holding out like a child's weapon—to the pieces of ice on the floor between us. He lifts a brow, and I swear I see the hint of a smile on his face before his scowl returns in full force.

"It's about time," he grumbles. "I thought we'd be stuck babysitting forever."

"I'm not a child," I grumble back, even though the icicle in my hand begs to differ.

Fenmire steps around the ice on the floor and takes the icicle from me. Again, a smile tugs at the corners of his mouth, but he hides it behind a mask of cold indifference. He looks down at my play sword in his hand, and I wait for the wisecrack I know is coming, but he surprises me by poking me in the stomach with the flat 'hilt' end instead.

"You like to play knight, do you?" he drawls. "You should try it with a real sword sometime."

"Is that what you fight the beasts in The Deadwood with?"

"Swords, arrows, maces… I beheaded one with my shield once."

"Will you teach me?"

He narrows his eyes. "Why?"

I shrug. "What else is there to do around here?"

"Work."

"Don't you ever have free time?"

"Yes, but that doesn't mean I want to spend it trying to train a human how to fight."

"You all seem to think I'm important. You've yet to tell me why, but don't you think it'd be wise to show me how to defend myself?"

"You'll never need to defend yourself." He says it with a bit of a growl as if the thought of someone or something coming near enough to hurt me makes him angry. I don't understand that since he's shown little more than contempt for me since I arrived. I stare up at him in confusion as he glares back down at me.

I reach out, wrap my fingers around the icicle, and tug.

He doesn't relinquish it.

I try again and end up pulling too hard and snapping it in half. We each now hold a short dagger of ice.

Tentatively, while watching his hostile eyes for his reaction, I tap my dagger playfully against his. When he doesn't move, I spin my weapon around his and tap it against the other side. Still nothing. I take a step forward and 'hit' his arm just above the wrist. He stands still as stone. I take another step—

Fenmire moves so fast, I don't have time to react before he's behind me with his dagger of ice to my throat. I yelp then laugh.

"You think it's funny, do you," he purrs near my ear. "You're my captive now. What will you give me in exchange for your freedom?"

I spin my ice dagger around and plunge it behind me toward him.

He snatches it out of my hand. "Nice try. So, what will it be? What price should I demand for my mercy?"

The ice of his blade is melting against my skin, and water begins dripping down my throat. It sends a chill through me, and I shudder. Fenmire tenses, and the ice pulls away from my throat. I want to explain to him that our game isn't what made me shake, that I'm not afraid of him, but before I can, the bedroom door opens.

Caliborne stands in the doorway with the same expressionless face he always wears, but his eyes narrow as they flick between me and Fenmire.

Fenmire immediately releases me.

I turn to Fenmire to show there are no hard feelings or regrets, but at the sight of my smile, his face falls into his usual mask of contempt, and he quickly turns away from me, tossing both our icy weapons toward the window.

"They're out of bed," he snaps at Caliborne. "It's time we all talked."

I turn to Caliborne too, who studies me, his eyes softening until he nods once.

"I'll tell the others," Fenmire says, then he stalks from the room, shutting the door a tad too hard on his way out.

"I'll make him like me if it's the last thing I do," I say stubbornly.

Caliborne snorts and sets my breakfast on the bed.

I pad around the room and gather the ice from the floor, tossing the pieces into my clean bedpan. "How does one take a bath around here?" I ask as I deposit the last of the shards. "And does this mean I get to see my own room now?"

Caliborne nods then points at my food.

I climb back into bed to eat. "I really do need a bath, though. I'm starting to smell."

As I uncover my plate of bacon and toast, he leans over and sniffs loudly at my hair.

I laugh and swat him away. "Take my word on it, will you?"

I hear the familiar rumble of laughter in his chest.

"Are there clothes for me to wear? I'm fine with wearing men's things most of the time, but it would be nice if I had some fabric to stitch a dress or two for the days when I'd prefer those instead. I'm good with a needle and thread."

Caliborne merely winks at me.

I have no idea what that means, so I shrug and dive into my breakfast.

Once I'm fed, Caliborne motions me back out of bed, and for the first time, we head out of his room. The hallway is drafty, but we don't walk far before he opens another door just down the hall from his own and ushers me into another bedroom.

This one is slightly smaller than Caliborne's, but the bed is just as massive. There's also a fireplace that's lit and crackling away across from the bed. I happily go to it, warming my hands near the grate as I peer around the rest of the room. There's a dresser and vanity here too, but no window, and I notice that the entire room is considerably warmer than Caliborne's. I'm thankful for that. There are also two armoires instead of one, which makes me tilt my head curiously and look at Caliborne for an explanation.

He strolls across the room and opens the first armoire. Inside is a mismatched collection of men's shirts and pants. I can tell most of them will need adjustments to fit me, but I can do that myself. The other armoire is empty, but Caliborne points to a pile of clothing on the floor beside it, neatly folded and stacked. He picks up a shirt and holds it out to me.

"Do you want me to put that on?" I ask.

He shakes his head and pinches the front of the shirt with his finger and thumb, rolling the cloth between them.

"Oh, cloth? I'm to use these things to stitch dresses?"

Yes.

I walk over and take stock of the items in the pile. Yes, these will do just fine. They won't be the prettiest dresses, but I can make several decent outfits with what I have here. I take the shirt from Caliborne with a smile.

"Thank you. This is perfect."

He takes my hand and shows me a sewing basket tucked beside the vanity. It contains a few decent needles but only one spool of thread. I'll have to make it count until I can find more. Caliborne takes a small leather satchel from atop the vanity and hands it to me. Inside is a bar of soap, a washrag, and a scrub brush.

"A bath?" I ask.

He nods and motions toward the armoires.

I take the hint and select the best shirt and pants I think will fit me for now as well as a thick pair of wool socks to wear on my feet since I don't see any shoes. With my arms loaded with clothes and my new wash bag, I follow Caliborne back out of the room and down the frigid hallway.

The hall is lit on both sides by golden sconces filled with fire. The ceiling is so high that two of the Gryxen could easily stand with one on the other's shoulders and still not reach it. There are also golden, flaming metal baskets hanging from the ceiling from long chains to try and brighten the space even further, but the natural dark shade of the stone, the long gaps between the sconces and baskets, and the lack of windows leave most of the hallway rather dark and gloomy with flickering shadows dancing across the walls cast by the flames.

Everything out here is made of the same stone as the bedrooms, but the texture is very odd, like it wasn't cut to build the castle but rather grew in this formation. There are no gaps or seams in the stone anywhere that indicates large sections of the walls and floor have been placed together, and there doesn't seem to be a division between the walls and floor but rather one clean ninety-degree angle in the stone. Surely this place was built somehow, the surfaces are far too perfect, and yet I can see no evidence of craftmanship at all.

We emerge from the hall into a foyer with a grand spiral staircase that leads both up and down. To the left of the staircase are the castle's large double doors, and I can hear the wind howling on the other side. We take to the stairs and head down, down, down. We walk down so many steps that, by the time we come to solid ground again, my world seems permanently tilted. I smell… I don't know what it is, but it isn't pleasant. It smells like rotten eggs or like some giant broke wind.

Caliborne leads me down another short hallway with no doors. Instead, it opens at the end to a wide-open space full of water, like a rock cave with a pond in the middle. The ceiling and walls here are jagged, not at all like the smooth interior of the castle above, which makes me think this is a far more natural structure. There's a small strip of stone, like a walkway, around the outer edge of the pond, which looks big enough to fit half the village in it comfortably. The air is filled with a steamy haze, and the temperature rises considerably when we cross the threshold.

"What is this place?" I ask in wonder. I've never seen anything like it.

Caliborne takes my clothes and wash bag then my hand and leads me to the water's edge. He kneels next to the pool, pulling me down with him, and dips my hand into the water.

It's warm, and I suddenly ache to go in, but at the thought of getting undressed, I hesitate.

Does Caliborne mean to watch? Does his kind care about nudity? I've never been naked around anyone but my own mother, and even that stopped several years ago. I'm suddenly nervous, unsure what I'm supposed to do.

Caliborne doesn't make me choose. He sets my clothes and bag next to the water and points back toward the hallway, then he leaves the pool room and sits with his back to the wall just outside, turned enough to give me privacy while I bathe but still close enough to hear if I call him.

I happily shuck my nightgown and leave it in a heap then sit at the edge of the pool. I unwrap my feet and dip them into the water. The heat feels amazing against my bruised and battered skin, and I quickly unwrap my knees too and shove off the edge into the water that comes up to my hips. I sink deeper with a moan I don't even try to stifle. For the first time since coming to The Deadwood, the last of the chill leaves my bones as I bob there in heated water up to my chin. I tip my head back and wet my hair as well.

The smell I noticed earlier is coming from the water, which makes me nervous to submerge my face, but I think Caliborne would've warned me if that was something I shouldn't do, so I risk it. I take a deep breath and sit down in the pool so that I'm completely under the water. I stay there until my lungs begin to burn and repeat the process three times before finally going back to the edge for my soap. I scrub my hair first then work down my entire body, switching the brush for the rag for my knees and feet where the cuts are still too sore. Once I'm finally clean, I lie back across the surface of the water and float there, letting the heat and the silence envelop me like a warm and calming blanket.

I could stay here forever, but I don't want to leave Caliborne waiting in the hallway for long, so I begrudgingly climb back out. Along the wall to my right is a shelf carved into the wall I didn't notice at first. There are rolled sheets, all mismatched, stuffed onto the shelf, and I grab one to dry off. It smells like the water, but I no longer mind.

Once I'm as dry as I can manage, I put on the blue shirt and brown pants I chose from my armoire. I roll the sleeves of the shirt clear up to the top and tuck the legs of the pants into the wool socks since they're all too long for me. I squeeze as much of the water from my hair as I can and soak up the rest with another sheet before braiding it. I rip a small piece of cloth from the bottom of one pant leg for a tie since I'll be trimming that part off eventually anyway. All I'm missing is Will's cap, but, surprisingly, my long hair doesn't bother me today.

It's an Evangeline day.

I throw the strap of my wash bag over my shoulder, gather up my dirty laundry, and approach Caliborne at the wall.

He glances over at me when I walk up, and his eyes slide up and down my frame. It reminds me so much of the looks I used to get in the village that I tense up.

"How do I look?" I ask nervously.

Caliborne gets to his feet and offers me his palm. When I set my cheek against it, I see myself the moment he first turned to look at me just seconds ago, and a feeling of wonder and awe passes over me.

They look like one of the warrior priestesses.

Another memory washes the other away, and my image is replaced by one of a female that looks like Caliborne, minus the wings. She's wearing similar leather pants, only black instead of brown, and a low-cut, billowing white shirt with a strange symbol on the front. Her dark brown hair is braided back out of her face and draped over her shoulder just like I'm currently wearing mine. There's a sword strapped to her hip. As Caliborne walks past her, she gives him a respectful nod.

"Gryxen," she greets.

Caliborne bows back, and a feeling of deep respect accompanies the gesture.

I smile as he takes back his hand.

"All I'm missing is the sword," I say, patting my hip where the weapon would be, then I laugh. "And about four feet in height."

Caliborne snorts and touches my chin affectionately.

He motions for us to return upstairs, but we take no more than a step before the entire castle begins to shake violently. Dust and bits of rock rain down around us, and I yelp.

"What's happening?" I ask in a panic.

Caliborne draws me closer by the arm and folds his wings protectively around us both as the tremors continue. From somewhere nearby, so near it brings the chill I only just washed away instantly back to my bones, comes the roar of some mighty beast. The shaking intensifies until I'm sure I'm about to be buried alive down here. I cling to Caliborne's arms as a full minute passes, then, just as suddenly as they began, the tremors stop.

As soon as the last bits of rock have settled, Caliborne draws back his wings and pats me, asking if I'm hurt.

"I'm alright," I say. "But what *was* that?"

He offers no answer. Instead, he sweeps me off my feet and into his arms and starts running up the stairs. We make it back up to the foyer in record time, and as soon as my feet touch the ground again, Wexton and Fenmire come running down the hall. Wexton carries a large golden sword in his hand. Fenmire has a mace under his arm, a shield in one hand, and a bow and quiver full of arrows in the other.

"Drixus only just went out," Wexton says in a rush. "He'll no doubt find the creature fast, but we need to move."

Fenmire throws first the quiver then the bow to Caliborne, who catches both effortlessly.

"Did something come through The Gate?" I ask.

"No time for armor," Fenmire says with a growl. "It's got too much of a head start thanks to that quake. Let's go."

Fenmire yanks open the front door, and a blast of icy wind sweeps across the foyer. He charges out into the storm, and Wexton is fast to follow him. Caliborne pats me on the shoulder and heads for the door himself.

"Caliborne?" I call after him in uncertainty.

He points his palm back at me, and I receive a short but powerful blast of confidence and pride before he slips out the door, shutting it behind him.

"Be careful," I whisper.

Chapter 10

I go back to my room since it's the only place I know to go and try to distract myself with sewing, but all that does is give me more time to think and worry as I stare absentmindedly into the fireplace, picking out the stitches in an old pair of pants.

A knock on my door sends me flying out of my seat, but it's only one of the kitchen staff bringing me lunch. I recognize him as the older of the three cooks from Caliborne's memory.

"Hello there," he says cheerfully.

"Hello," I say. "Are they back yet?"

"Not to my knowledge." He hands me my tray. "But don't you worry about them. They know how to handle themselves, and it takes them a bit to butcher the beasts and haul them back home."

I take the tray, eying the slices of meat on my plate as I ask, "We don't cook and eat these beasts, do we?"

"Oh, no. Only the Gryxen eat the beasts. Our bodies can't handle that meat, or so they say. They eat the creatures raw, and we humans eat what the village brings for The Offering each month."

"The Gryxen don't eat The Offering?"

"No, they stick to their beasts."

"Do we get our food from anywhere else?"

"No. The blizzard makes it impossible to grow or raise much of anything out here. The Offering is all we've got."

"The village doesn't even know they're the only thing keeping the humans here alive and that The Deadwood demons don't benefit from The Offering at all."

He nods. "It's a bit disconcerting having everything you thought you knew about the world turned on its head, isn't it? And there's so much to learn. After a while, I told them not to tell me anything more. My head is filled with enough wonders for one lifetime."

"What's your name?"

"Levi."

I recognize the name if not the man standing in front of me.

"You..." I choose my words carefully. "You were the last to come here, right? Before me, that is."

He hangs his head a bit. "I was. I made a grave mistake that I'll live with for the rest of my life here in exile." He looks at me again. "I remember you too. And your folks. You lived on the farm out by the south road, right?"

"I did."

"Your father used to buy grain from me every week. He brought you a time or two when you were little before your mother put a stop to that."

I nod. "I remember. Barely."

"I don't know why they sent you here, but I hope you find peace with it."

"Thank you. I hope the same for you."

He nods and heads back to the kitchen.

Lunch is hot chicken with rolls and roasted apples, but I barely taste it. I'm too busy listening for the sounds of the Gryxen returning from their hunt. I've finished my meal and have all the seams split in several of my fabric garments when there's another knock on my door. I half expect it to be Levi back for my empty tray but am pleasantly surprised to open the door and find Caliborne standing in the hall, slightly snowy but otherwise completely unharmed.

Without thought, I rush out the door and wrap my arms around him. "You're alright," I say, and the relief I feel nearly brings me to tears.

Caliborne is momentarily stunned at my show of affection. He puts a hand on my back, and when I pull away, he blinks down at me in confusion.

"I was quite worried there for a moment," I say, wiping my eyes.

He takes my chin in his hand, and his thumb strokes softly up my cheek.

I smile and pat the back of his hand. "I'm alright now."

He takes back his hand and bows his head before motioning off down the hall, not toward the staircase but toward the kitchen.

"Where are we going," I ask, but I step into the hallway anyway.

We walk together down the hall. The kitchen door is open at the end, and the same three men as before are bustling about inside. When Caliborne and I are spotted, they all call out separate hellos. I wave as we turn left at the end of the hall and continue down another corridor. Eventually, Caliborne shoves open a door to a room with a large table in the middle surrounded by the biggest stools I've ever seen. There's a fireplace in this room as well, and Fenmire stands beside it brushing snow off his wings. Wexton is sitting at the table drinking from a large goblet. They both look to be in perfect health as well.

"It's about time," Fenmire grumbles. He sits across the table from Wexton but glares at me then up at Caliborne. "Why are they here?"

I answer before Caliborne can. "If this is the talk you've all been planning for the day I can finally get out of bed, then I asked to be here."

"Do you think that's wise, Caliborne?" Wexton asks. He looks at me apologetically. "No offense, but you might not be ready to talk about some of the things we must discuss."

"Will you be discussing me?" I ask.

The Gryxen all shoot knowing looks at each other before Wexton answers, "Yes."

"Then I'd like to hear what you have to say."

Wexton glances at Caliborne, who nods once.

"Alright," Wexton says with a shrug, and he motions to the stool next to him.

I sit. Or, rather, I jump and then sit. The stool is twice the size of a human one.

Caliborne sits at the end of the table to my right.

"Try not to interrupt too much this time," Wexton tells me with a smirk.

I stick my tongue out at him.

"Like I told you before, about two thousand years ago—"

"Two thousand, one hundred, and forty-nine years," Fenmire barks.

Wexton rolls his eyes. "*Two thousand, one hundred, and forty-nine years ago,*" he says with such dramatic flourish that I giggle, "a sorceress named Reilanna plotted to come through The Gate and take over your world."

I stop laughing.

"It's the Gryxen's job not to let things like that happen," Wexton continues, "so of course, we stepped in. It was seven of us against her and a few lesser sorceresses, so we weren't worried. We'd seen her kind dozens of times. But, unlike those other times, we were betrayed by some of our own. Four of our brothers-in-arms turned traitor and sided with Reilanna, who promised them power, wealth, and lands in your world to oversee once she conquered your kind. The only ones who chose to stand against her are those of us in this room."

"But"—I glance around at each of them—"aren't there four of you trapped in The Deadwood?"

Fenmire turns on his stool to face the fire with his back to me as Wexton explains.

"Drixus sided with Reilanna along with his blood brother, Horthos. They were inseparable, so when Horthos joined Reilanna, it wasn't surprising that Drixus went with him. We fought Reilanna and our brethren for years, keeping her from coming through The Gate while holding back the magic the other Gryxen threw at us. We managed to keep them at bay, but we were losing. The Gate was slowly opening under their onslaught until, one day, Reilanna betrayed those who had sided with her."

"Why would she do that if they were winning?" I ask.

Wexton opens his mouth to answer but doesn't get the chance.

"Because she's an evil, impatient witch," Fenmire sneers. "The Gate likely wasn't opening fast enough for her liking, or perhaps she knew she was going to win and decided she didn't want to share your world with the others after all."

"Reilanna managed to torture Breklen, Jothrik, and Horthos into giving her their powers," Wexton continues, "but when she went after Drixus, she couldn't break him. No matter what she did to him, he refused to give up his power. Eventually, she gave up on him entirely and settled for the powers she'd already stolen. She threw him through The Gate for us to deal with, expecting us to kill him for her."

"But we didn't," Fenmire says. The tone of his voice is one of bitter regret, and I get the feeling he'd wanted to end Drixus all those years ago but was outvoted.

"No, we didn't," Wexton reiterates with a cautious glance at Fenmire's back. "With our help, Drixus healed enough that, when Reilanna made her push to come through The Gate, he aided us in holding her back, and we were able to banish her from this world for good. She did not take that lightly, as you can imagine. As a parting gift to us, just as The Gate closed and sealed her in our world forever, she cast a spell."

Fenmire takes one long, deep breath and recites said spell aloud:

"If you love your precious humans so much, have your fates tied to them then. Live amongst endless winter and death and forfeit your home until a human releases you. Not just any human, mind you, neither a man nor a woman, but a human all the same, one willing and eager to bind themself to all four of you. Only then will you be free. But that freedom, in the end, will come at a cost so dire it'll crush your soul to pay it. The Gate will claim payment when the time comes."

"The spell created The Deadwood," says Wexton. "It didn't used to be such a wasteland. The forest was once green and thriving. Jothrik grew it as a natural wall that kept the humans away from The Gate when it first appeared. Reilanna twisted it into what it is today and bound us to it. We can't venture past its borders. Now, she waits on the other side of The Gate, sending her beasts through it whenever it pleases her in hopes of killing us."

"Or driving us mad," Fenmire mutters.

"Or that," Wexton concurs.

"Did she create this castle too?" I ask.

"No, the castle was already here. Horthos built it before he and the others betrayed us, when they fought with us on this side of The Gate to keep Reilanna in check. When Reilanna killed them, she stole those abilities."

"What power did she steal from the third Gryxen? Breklen, was it?"

"The power to control the weather. Hence, the never-ending blizzard she summoned around us as part of her spell."

"'*Neither a man nor a woman*'," I say thoughtfully. "You think the human who can break the spell is… me?" I look at Fenmire, finally understanding his reaction the first time I said those words to him.

"We don't know," Wexton says. "That's what we're here to discuss."

"It's too much of a coincidence," says Fenmire as he spins again on his stool to face the table. "How many humans claim to be neither a man nor a woman, much less find themselves cast into The Deadwood?"

"'*The Gate will claim payment*'," I say. "That sounds ominous."

"Not really," Fenmire says. "The Gate is nothing but a magical doorway. There's nothing sinister about it. It's just more of her riddles."

"'*One willing and eager to bind themselves to all four of you*'. What does that mean?"

"We don't know," says Wexton. "We tried for years to find a way around the spell but eventually gave up. Of the humans your village sent to us, none ever came close to the one Reilanna described."

"Until now," Fenmire says sourly.

"We started to think maybe there wasn't a way to break the spell at all and this was just a way for her to torture us forever."

"How do we find out if I can break it?" I ask.

"I have a couple ideas," Fenmire says. "Take them to The Gate and see if it reacts."

"Absolutely not," Wexton barks at the same time a low growl rumbles to my right.

Fenmire raises his hands defensively. "It was just a suggestion."

"I'll go if it will prove anything," I offer.

"You'd be far too close to danger if Reilanna chose that moment to send a beast through The Gate," says Wexton. "It won't matter if you are the key to breaking her spell if you're killed in the process of finding out."

"Do you want to hear my other idea or not?" Fenmire grumbles.

"*I* do," I say.

He rolls his eyes over to me so hard I have to bite my lip to keep from laughing, knowing that would only irritate him further. Oddly enough, that makes me want to laugh even more.

"Let's take them to the edge of The Deadwood and see if they can leave," he says.

The rest of us exchange glances.

"Did you try to go back through the arch after The Offering?" Wexton asks.

"No. It didn't occur to me to try."

Wexton nods thoughtfully. "That's a good idea, Fenmire. It would make sense that they'd be able to defy the spell's rules if they are indeed the one to break it."

Fenmire snorts. "I know. That's why I suggested it."

"I'm willing to try whatever you all think is best," I say.

"Like you have much of a choice," Fenmire sneers.

Wexton snaps his head around, and for the first time, there's anger on his usually-laughing face. "They most certainly do have a choice. Nothing will be done against their will."

Caliborne lays his hand over mine on the table in clear agreement with him.

Fenmire looks temporarily taken aback. "That's not what I meant!"

"What *did* you mean then?" I ask.

"Only that you're imprisoned here just like we are. If you want to leave The Deadwood and go back to whatever life you led before coming here—your friends, your family—the only way to do that is to help us. I didn't mean to imply…"

"It's fine, Fenmire," Wexton says. "As long as it's understood that Evangeline's… Erm…" He leans over toward me. "Is that the correct name today?"

I smile. "Yes."

He nods and turns back to Fenmire. "Evangeline's willingness to help trumps any and all others' desires or ambitions. That is, after all, part of the spell: *'willing and eager'*, remember?"

Fenmire nods.

Caliborne squeezes my hand before letting me go.

"So, it's settled then?" I ask. "You'll take me to the edge of The Deadwood?"

Fenmire is staring at me, his eyes so intense I want to look away like a chastised child, but I don't. I hold his gaze until he looks away first. He looks at Caliborne, and an unspoken conversation passes between them during which Caliborne uses his palm to send whatever feelings he's conveying and Fenmire either nods or shakes his head in reply. Eventually, Fenmire snorts, stands up abruptly from his stool, and marches out of the room without a goodbye.

"Meeting adjourned, I guess," Wexton says, and he leans back on his stool as he chugs the last of his drink.

"Was Drixus not included in this meeting because he betrayed you?" I ask.

Wexton sets his empty cup on the table. "Yes."

The frankness of his answer surprises me. "The spell mentions all four of you. I'll have to meet him eventually."

Wexton laughs. "Good luck with that. Drixus doesn't see anyone. He spends his days in his room, avoiding us."

"Why?"

He looks at me, and there's a mischievous twinkle in his red eyes I've come to recognize. "That, my dearest Evangeline, is a long story."

I channel my inner Fenmire and roll my eyes at him.

Chapter 11

I'm walking down the hall toward the kitchen. I can smell the food and hear the cheerful chatter of Levi and his cooks. I'm hungry, so I'm looking forward to seeing what they've cooked up for us today. Halfway down the hall, I stop as a sudden gust of wind whips down the corridor, bringing with it a blast of icy snow.

I raise my arms to shield my face, but the wind doesn't stop. When I lower them again, I'm no longer in the castle but standing in the frozen lane in The Deadwood. I'm wearing my old nightgown, which is sodden once more and sticking to me. My feet and knees ache, my stomach hurts, and my face burns.

"Caliborne?" I call out in a panic. "Where are you?"

You. You. You.

The word echoes all around me, growing in intensity until it's a snarl in my ear and no longer my voice.

"You. The one who would free them."

I have never heard this voice before, and yet I know exactly who spoke.

"Reilanna," I whisper to myself.

She laughs, and it's a cruel, terrifying sound.

I hug myself. "Caliborne!"

"You can't save him. You can't save any of them. You couldn't even save yourself." She laughs again, mockingly this time.

"I will *free them!" I shout into the wind. "If it's the last thing I do, I'll free them from your spell!"*

"Oh, believe me…"

I gasp. She's standing right behind me. I can feel her presence and her warm breath on my ear.

"...I'll make sure it's the last thing you ever do."

I wake up with a scream, and I swear I see a shadow in the corner of my eye as I jerk upright. I scramble out of bed and away from where I know Reilanna was standing a heartbeat ago. I land with a thud on the floor beside my bed, but when I look back, there's nothing there.

"It was just a dream," I tell myself quietly. "You're alright. She's not here. Just a dream."

I force myself to climb back in bed but can't bring myself to settle back down under the blankets. I sit there for a while, willing my heart to quit racing, and it doesn't take long for me to realize sleep is far out of my reach for the moment. I slip from bed again—more gracefully this time—and tread on quiet feet out the door and down the hall. Caliborne's door is shut, as usual, and I knock lightly on it, whisper-calling his name by the knob.

"He's not in there."

I jump with a startled yelp and spin around.

Wexton is leaning in an open doorway down the hall.

"Where is he?" I ask.

"The same place he's been every night for days now."

"Which is where, Wexton?" I ask in exasperation.

He smirks. "The forge."

"There's a forge here?"

"There's a little of everything in this castle. Horthos made sure we had all we needed."

"So, where is this forge?"

Wexton crosses his arms. "You shouldn't bother him right now, Evangeline."

I'm disappointed, but I nod and head back toward my room.

"I heard a cry earlier," he says, and I pause. "Was it you?"

"It was."

"Bad dreams?"

"You could say that."

"I'm pretty sure I just did." His smirk widens.

"Wiseass."

He snickers. "Well, out with it. What was it about?"

I hesitate.

"Come now, the best way to break a nightmare's hold on you is to speak it aloud."

I turn back around. "I dreamt of her. The one who put the spell on you."

Wexton pushes off the doorframe. "Reilanna?"

"Yes."

He runs a finger down one of his fangs thoughtfully. "It's been some time since she's come to any of us in our sleep."

I cross the distance between us until I'm standing in front of him. "I swear I saw her when I woke. She was standing beside my bed, leaning over me." I shiver.

He nods. "She's not here, not really, so you don't have to worry about her harming you. It's just one of her many torments. Perhaps it's a good thing she's started playing her games with you. She must feel threatened."

"She called me 'the one who would free them'."

Wexton takes my shoulders in his hands. "This is good, Evangeline. This is very good."

"I'm glad one of us is happy about my bad dreams."

He lets go of my shoulders. "Sorry." It's the first time I've ever seen him look chagrined. "It's just that, as I said before, we've waited for someone like you for a long time. You have no idea what it would mean to us to finally be free of this spell. We haven't been home in thousands of years. We had lives and loved ones before all of this happened."

"Has no one from your side of The Gate tried to break you out?"

"We have no way of knowing if any have tried, but obviously none have succeeded if they did. All that has come through The Gate since we sealed it against Reilanna are her beasts."

"How do they get through if it's sealed?"

"The Gate is not like a physical door. It's a magic gateway, like a portal."

"What's a portal?"

He scratches his chin as he considers how best to explain it to me. "Say you take a piece of string and stretch it from one side of a room to the other. Both ends are connected together by the stretch in the middle. Usually, to get from one end to the other, you'd have to walk. A portal is a direct connection between both ends. Simply walk through it at one end of the string and instantly materialize at the other. Do you understand?"

"I think so."

"Good. So, The Gate is like a portal with one end of the string residing in your world, the other in ours. But it's not a physical door. It doesn't connect two rooms that otherwise abut each other. There are millions of miles between them. It's magic that allows the transfer from one place to the other. Still with me?"

I nod.

"Now, for The Gate to transport a being from one world to the other, it requires power, but some beings require more or less power than others. For The Gate, the size of the being doesn't matter, it's how powerful that being is. The more powerful the being, the more power it requires to transport them.

"We sealed The Gate, but somehow, Reilanna kept it from closing completely. It's likely a part of the spell holding us here, like a link between her and her magic. But The Gate is not open enough to let a being as powerful as her come through. She would require a great deal of power to transport here, especially after draining our brethren of their magic. The beasts she sends, however, have no magic. They are simple creatures that require very little power for The Gate to transport here. She could send a beast the size of a mountain—she has before—and it would pass through The Gate with little difficulty."

"Does all of your kind possess magic?"

"Yes. That's likely why none have come through after us. The Gate doesn't have the power to send them."

"What about a human? Could someone like me slip through to your world?"

He ponders this a moment. "Probably. Your kind are certainly more evolved than beasts, but you don't wield magic. The Gate likely wouldn't require any more power for that. I don't recommend it though. The Gate opens high in the sky in our world. Unless you had wings or someone waiting to catch you at the other end, you'd never survive the fall."

"The last time I checked, I did not, in fact, have wings."

He snorts. "Best skip that idea, then."

I yawn loudly.

"Am I boring you?" he teases.

"I like your stories," I say as I rub my watery eyes. "I'm just tired."

"Go on back to bed. Reilanna won't bother you again. None of us have ever dreamt of her twice in a single night."

"Good to know."

"Goodnight, Evangeline."

"Goodnight."

As Wexton predicted, my dreams are free of Reilanna and her laughter for the rest of the night, but I still find myself wishing Caliborne had been in his room when I'd gone calling. I would've liked a warm chest to curl up to and a strong pair of arms to wrap around me, and something tells me he wouldn't have said no.

*****

It's an Eve day when I wake up, which is a tad disappointing since I've not yet begun to stitch a single dress. I pick another outfit from the men's armoire but leave my hair down and loose to satisfy my feminine urges today. When I look in the mirror, I see a girl about to go out and help Papa with chores, and that makes me smile.

After breakfast, I find Caliborne waiting for me in the foyer like we planned. Today, he will take me to the edge of The Deadwood, and while I'm excited to get out of the castle for a bit, I'm not so excited about having to go out into the storm to do it. It seems Caliborne already thought of this though. When I walk up, he wraps a large blanket around me from head to toe, tucking me in tight before hoisting me up into his arms.

"Will we walk or fly?" I ask.

He merely winks at me before trudging out the double doors into the snow.

The wind slams into me, but thankfully, the blanket Caliborne chose is thick and warm. I worm an arm up through the fabric to pull a fold of it up over my head as a makeshift hood. Tucked in his arms yet again, I am perfectly warm and comfortable. Caliborne shakes out his wings, and a few seconds later, we shoot straight up into the sky.

I cry out in surprise then laugh as the wind picks up even more. I have no idea how fast we're going since I can't see any passing landscape through the snow. I wonder how Caliborne knows where to go in so much blinding white. He doesn't look the least bit bothered by the cold or the blowing snow. Not that his face would show it if he was.

A trip that took hours on foot when we first met takes minutes in the air, and we're soon landing in the middle of the icy lane in front of the arch. Caliborne sets me on my feet, and I shiver. Not from the cold but from the fact that we've landed at the very spot I dreamt of last night. I look up at Caliborne who nods for me to lead the way.

So I do.

I clutch my blanket tighter around me as I step up to the arch. The vines don't move, so I come closer. Nothing. I look again at Caliborne.

He shrugs.

I slither an arm free of my blanket and reach out toward the vines. There's no movement, so I expect to feel cold, dead wood as my fingers make contact. I feel nothing. My hand disappears into the vines as if they aren't there at all, like they're an illusion. I take back my hand and study it. It's whole and unharmed.

"Caliborne?"

He steps up beside me and touches the vines himself, but where my hand slid right through them, his stops and splays across the wood. He knocks a knuckle against one, and it thuds dully. I reach for the same spot, and my hand disappears again. With one last look at my companion, who raises no objections, I walk forward and effortlessly step through the arch.

I'm met with blazing sunlight I have to shield my eyes against at first. I also immediately begin to sweat as summer heat engulfs me. I shrug off my blanket and stand there in complete shock.

I am out of The Deadwood.

I breathe deep of the fresh air and close my eyes at the feel of warm sunshine on my face. When I open them again, I laugh.

They tried to banish me, but they failed.

I stand there, basking in this small victory until a familiar voice calls my name, and my breath locks in my chest.

"Evangeline!"

Will is running through the grass next to The Deadwood. He has a sack slung over his shoulder and an axe in his hand. He flings both away as he nears me, and I stifle a sob just before my best friend slams into me, yanking me into a hug so tight my ribs protest, but I don't care.

"Will!" I cry as I cling to him.

He lifts me clear off my feet and spins us in a circle as I laugh with glee. When he sets me back down, he takes my face in his hands.

"How?" he asks. "How are you here?"

"It's such a long story," I say, then I laugh because I sound like Wexton. "You'll never believe me if I told you, but, Will, everything we thought we knew about The Deadwood and the creatures that dwell there is all wrong. Our legends have twisted this place into something ugly, but the truth is a tragedy."

"What do you mean?"

"The demons they say live in The Deadwood, they're not demons at all. They're warriors cursed by an evil sorceress thousands of years ago. They're…"

I turn back toward the arch, remembering that one such warrior is standing on the other side, waiting for me.

"I can't stay," I tell Will sadly.

"What do you mean? Of course you can. I heard from my aunt. She's invited us both to come stay with her; indefinitely, if that's our wish. We can leave this place like we planned."

My heart aches, for I still do want the life with my friend we'd planned not so long ago. But everything has changed. I can't leave. There are others who've placed their faith and trust in me to help them, and I can't abandon them now. And the more I think about it, the more I realize that I don't want to leave regardless, that a part of me can't wait to pass back through that archway and climb into the arms of the demon waiting for me in the ice and blowing snow.

Part of me can't leave Caliborne. Or Wexton. Or even Fenmire and his moods.

I take a step back. "I'm sorry, but there are things much bigger than me that I have to see to first. Please, go to your aunt's if that's what you wish to do. Don't let me stop you. I'm well taken care of, so you don't have to worry about me. Get out of here while you still can, but me, I'm staying here. I'm staying in The Deadwood."

To say he looks shocked is an understatement. "You want to go back in there? Why?"

"I plan to destroy The Deadwood once and for all. I can do it too. That I'm standing here in front of you now proves that I can."

Will studies me then looks at the arch. "Then take me back with you."

"What? You don't want that, Will. If you followed me into The Deadwood, you wouldn't be able to leave again. I'm the only one who can."

"I won't go to my aunt's without you. I won't leave you behind. You plan to destroy The Deadwood, yes?"

I nod.

"Then I'll come with you for now and help however I can. We can go to my aunt's afterward. Together."

I bite my lip, torn between insisting he stay here in case I fail and gladly taking him with me so I can have my best friend back. "Are you sure?"

Will gathers his bag and axe from the ground. "I've never been more sure."

"What about Jacob?"

At the mention of the baker's son, Will goes tense. "Elias has been watching us both very closely since you left. I don't know how, but I think he knows. About us. It's made spending time together difficult and dangerous." He hangs his head. "I'll be keeping us both safe by going away for a while."

"I'm sorry."

"I'm trying to talk him into going to my aunt's with us, but he's scared. He's never been to the city and doesn't want to give up his life here. I don't blame him, but I also know he can never be truly happy here, just like we can't."

"Give him time. He'll figure it out."

Will shoulders his pack higher with a nod of determination. "So how do we get through?"

We both turn toward the arch.

"I'm not even sure I can take you with me," I say.

"If you're the only one who can come out, it makes sense that you'd be the only one who could take others in."

"In theory, I suppose."

Will picks up my discarded blanket and hands it to me. "I've been out here almost every day since you left trying to break into The Deadwood. I've tried digging under it, climbing over it, and even chopping through it"—he spins his axe in his hand—"but those vines stop me every time."

"Let's give this a shot then." I reach out and touch the vines covering the arch, and just like before, my hand slides right through them as if they're not even there.

"Whoa," Will utters. He reaches out and touches the vines too, but they stop his hand just like they did Caliborne's.

I pull my hand back and take his. "Let's try it this way." I try to push our joined hands through the vines, but they stop Will's hand anyway. I wrap my arms around him and try to lean into the arch, but while my shoulder slips through the space, his does not.

Will slams a fist against the vines. "Damn it!"

"It's alright," I say with sudden inspiration as an idea occurs to me. "We'll wait until The Offering!"

"That was my backup plan in case I couldn't get through on my own."

It means I won't see Will again for a couple of weeks, but after that, we'll be together again, and I can live with that. "Make sure you're here when they push the cart through and run in behind it. I'll be waiting on the other side."

He looks down at me sadly. "Do you truly have to go back?"

"I do. But don't worry, I'm going to put an end to this madness for good."

He nods in woeful understanding.

"Can I ask a favor of you before I go?"

"Name it."

"Can I borrow your boots?" I point down at his feet.

He laughs. "I bet it's a might chilly in there without a decent pair."

We sit in the grass as he kicks off his boots and I pull them on and work up all the laces. They're big on me, but with the thick wool socks I'm wearing and a few hard tugs on the laces, I can at least walk in them. And my feet will finally be warm.

Back on our feet once more, Will and I hug goodbye, but it's only temporary.

"I'll see you soon," I promise as I wrap my blanket around myself.

"See you soon."

I wave as I step through the arch back into the freezing snow, and I almost run into Caliborne. He's standing with his back to me, and another familiar voice is yelling from further down the lane.

"You should've listened to me, damn it!" Fenmire screams. "What did you think would happen? I warned you."

"Caliborne?" I say uncertainly.

He startles and spins around.

"What's going on?" I ask.

Caliborne tugs me closer and curls his wings around each side of us to block the wind as we turn to face Fenmire. Through the gap in Caliborne's wings, I see Fenmire's scowl, but it softens when his eyes land on me.

"Aren't you on patrol this morning, Fenmire?" I ask. "Has something happened?"

Caliborne's hand brushes my cheek, and I lean into his palm.

Through Caliborne's eyes, I see Fenmire land with a slam in the lane, his face furious.

"What have you done?" he barks.

He knows, so I don't reply.

"How long have they been gone?"

Too long, and Fenmire knows this too.

He growls. "I told you to take them somewhere else. But of course, you know better. You always do, don't you? Now they've run off and we've lost our one chance of ever going home! You should've listened to me, damn it! What did you think would happen? I warned you."

Caliborne cuts off the memory at the point where I call his name.

"You thought I wouldn't come back?" I ask Fenmire.

He turns his face away, but I can still see the sadness and shame on it. "You have no reason to trust us. I figured once you realized you could go home, you wouldn't want to come back. You have family in the village, after all, and we're nothing to you."

"That's not true," I say. "You're my friends."

Fenmire snorts in disbelief.

"I'm here, aren't I?"

He studies me then looks at Caliborne. He opens his mouth to say something, looks back at me, and slams his mouth shut. A second later, he launches into flight, and the ground shakes beneath the force of his takeoff. I look up and squint through the blowing snow, but he's already far out of my sight.

"Maybe I underestimated how hard it's going to be to make him like me," I say.

Caliborne snorts again.

I turn and look up at him. "Were *you* afraid I wouldn't come back?"

He shakes his head.

I smile. "Liar."

He brushes a clump of hair from my face.

I consider telling him about Will and our plan but decide to keep that to myself for now. I'm not sure how Caliborne will feel about a human willingly throwing themselves into The Deadwood, and I don't want anyone to try and convince me to talk Will out of it. Selfishly, I can't wait until the full moon when I can have my best friend back again. Having that to look forward to makes me happy.

I take Caliborne's hand. "Let's go home."

Chapter 12

Even though I just bathed yesterday, as soon as we're back to the castle, I excuse myself to go downstairs to that wonderfully warm pool and soak away the chill from being outside. Caliborne doesn't come with me this time, which means I can swim for as long as I please. With clean clothes tucked under my arm, I all but skip down the hallway and into the pool room.

"Well, well, well," says Wexton, who's sitting in the pool with his back against the side, his arms splayed across the stone, and his wings tucked in tight to his body. "Back already?"

"Sorry," I say bashfully. I take a step back toward the door. "I didn't know you were down here. I'll come back later."

"Whoa, whoa. No need to rush off. This pool is plenty big enough for both of us."

It's plenty big enough for all four Gryxen and I to swim in it together, but I can't help but notice Wexton's pants sitting by the wall. I want to float naked in the hot water, undisturbed. I can't do that with a naked Gryxen in here too.

Can I?

If he stays on his side and I stay on the other, neither of us would see anything we didn't want to. And the company might be nice.

"Alright," I say with far more bravery than I feel. "Turn away while I undress."

He dutifully spins his back to me, and I wait to the count of ten to see if he plans to peek before I start shuffling out of my clothes. I undress quickly so he can't get any funny ideas and hop down into the water, ducking so it comes clear up to my chin. I glide my way over to the side of the pool opposite him.

"Alright, you can turn around now."

He settles back against the wall where he was before. "Did it work?"

It takes my brain an extra few seconds to realize he's talking about me leaving The Deadwood. "It did."

He slaps the surface of the water. "Guess that means you're our ticket out of here. How does that make you feel?"

"Um… a little nervous? But mostly, I'm just glad to help."

"I meant what I said before. Nothing will happen against your will."

"I know. We still don't know what I need to do to 'bind' myself to you though."

"We'll figure it out. Let's celebrate this victory first."

I dip my head under the water, slick my hair back from my face, and lean against the wall too while being careful to keep my chest well below the water line. "We saw Fenmire at the arch."

"Caliborne took you there after all, did he? I bet Fenmire was fuming at that."

"You can say that. He thinks I'll abandon you all at the first opportunity."

"Don't take it personally. He has his reasons to feel that way, and they have little to do with you or your character."

"Care to elaborate?"

"No."

I gasp in feigned shock. "You, for once, have nothing to say, Wexton? Are you feeling alright?"

"Go on, laugh it up, short stuff." He splashes water at me. "That story's not mine to tell. You'll have to get Fenmire to tell it to you."

I snort. "I don't see that ever happening. He doesn't like me."

"I don't think that's true. I think he does like you, which will make it even harder for you to get close to him."

"That doesn't make any sense."

"He'll come around. The real problem is Drixus. I don't know how you'll make any sort of connection with him. He doesn't talk to us anymore, visit with us, eat with us, nothing. He spends every minute he's not on patrol up in his room."

"Does he know I'm here?"

"He's been told, but don't expect him to care. He lost a lot in the war. More than the rest of us put together. It changed him."

I don't know what that means, but I don't want to ask. "I'll have to meet him eventually if this is going to work."

Wexton grunts. "I know. We'll figure that out too."

We both soak for a time in silence, and I lean my head back against the stone with a sigh. I don't even mind the smell of the water anymore. The heat melts the tension from my muscles until I feel like I could easily close my eyes and drift off to sleep.

Wexton groans, and the water splashes a bit as he pushes off the wall and extends his wings. "Well, I've got to get moving. I'm supposed to take over for Fenmire soon." He stands up, and my heart kicks into overdrive when I see his fully nude form clear down to his calves.

He has two penises.

I know my eyes have got to be as big as saucers, and I'm staring far too intently at his privates, but he *did* just flash me without warning, so I feel I'm entitled to a good stare.

His genitals are nestled at the groin like a human male's with two testicles dangling underneath as expected, but where a human man has just one shaft, Wexton has two, one right above the other. The top shaft is smaller than the bottom one, but both are larger than anything I've seen on a human. Though, I've only seen a couple of penises in my lifetime, so I don't have much to compare them to.

It's only after I take all of this in that I realize he hasn't moved.

I finally look up at his face, and he's smirking at me. It's obvious he did this deliberately to get a reaction out of me, and as much as I want to deny him the satisfaction, I can't help but narrow my eyes and stick my tongue out at him.

He laughs as he finally climbs out of the pool and wraps himself in a sheet. "Enjoy your soak," he calls to me before picking up his pants and heading for the stairs.

I blow a long breath of embarrassment out between my lips as I sink under the water to hide my burning face.

*****

"Will!" I cry, and I throw myself into my best friend's arms in the bright morning sunlight.

"Ah," says a voice near my ear that makes me cringe. "So you already have someone who means a great deal to you." I let go of Will and turn around, but of course, Reilanna isn't there. Her voice surrounds me as if she were one with the air. "He looks like fun."

"You leave him alone!" I scream into the wind.

Reilanna's laughter makes me want to cover my ears. The light begins to dim, and I look up as great black clouds billow up in the sky, blocking out the sun.

"You don't need him anymore, princess," Reilanna says. "You've got four demons to concern yourself with. Surely you can share this one."

I take Will by the hand. "Run!" I yell, but when I try to, Will doesn't move.

He struggles to lift his feet, and I look down to see The Deadwood's vines wrapped around his ankles. I take both his hands in mine and pull with all my strength, but even with my added leverage, he can't get his feet free.

"Go, Evangeline!" he yells. "Get away from here!"

"Not without you!"

Reilanna's laughter grows louder before the ground starts to shake. Will looks at me with panic in his eyes a heartbeat before the earth beneath his feet splits and the vines suck him underground. The hole quickly closes behind him.

"No!" I scream as I hit my knees and desperately claw at the dirt with my hands, but the soil is packed solid as if no hole had ever been there at all. "Give him back," I demand.

Again, the laughter, then she says right next to my ear, "As you wish."

The ground beneath my hands opens again and begins spitting out bright white bones.

"Will!" I scream as I wake up with tears soaking my face and pillow. There's a shadow in the corner of my eye next to my bed, and I snatch my pillow out from under my head and throw it. It lands on the floor with a thud, hitting nothing on its way down. "Go to hell, you heinous witch!" I yell for good measure. "I swear on all that's holy, if you touch him—"

I jump as my bedroom door opens.

My bravado fades and is replaced by sad tears at the sight of the person standing in the doorway.

"Caliborne," I utter.

He comes immediately into the room, shutting the door behind him, and crosses to my bedside. I sit up on my knees and hug him, soothed almost instantly by his warmth and scent. Instead of simply holding me, he scoops me up into his arms and sits on my bed with me in his lap. I wrap my arms around his neck with a squeeze.

Caliborne's silent comfort calms the storm, and I'm able to banish the nightmare quickly, though I fear I won't be able to go back to sleep tonight. Once I've calmed down enough, I notice the feel of Caliborne's long hair under my hands and how soft it is. I start playing with it, running my fingers through it to feel the tinkling softness between them. I pull away but still sit twirling a clump of his hair in my hand.

"I'm sorry," I say bashfully. "I'm not usually a crier."

He taps me on the forehead.

"I had a nightmare. Wexton says it's Reilanna playing games."

Caliborne growls low in his chest.

"She… she hurt Will," I say quietly. "In my dream. Can she do that in real life?"

No.

"Are you sure?"

Yes.

I sigh with relief. "Good."

He wipes the last of the tears from my cheeks with his thumb.

I take a larger section of his hair in my hands, draping it over his shoulder as I marvel at the softness of the stark white strands. "Beautiful," I murmur.

Caliborne takes my chin in his hands and tilts my face up to look into my eyes. As he does, he traces a single finger across my forehead, down the side of my face, and softly across my lips. He sets his palm on my cheek, and I watch him do it all again through his own eyes.

Beautiful.

My eyes are teary again when he takes back his hand, and when he lowers his face toward mine, I don't pull away. The press of his lips against mine is so gentle it makes my heart feel funny in my chest. I kiss him back a little harder while being cautious of his fangs. His hand slides up into my hair as he holds me closer. I brace my hands on his shoulders and turn my head, deepening the kiss as my heart starts thumping loudly in my ears.

What am I doing? And why does it feel so right?

When we break apart, I'm breathless and flushed. Though his face remains emotionless, his eyes are wide as he watches me, as if he's afraid I might flee. I don't, and I don't wait long before leaning back in. As we kiss again, it's more of the same soft tenderness, and I can't get enough. His lips are as warm as the rest of him, and they're just as much of a comfort. I have to break away from them to breathe, but I don't go far.

As I sit catching my breath, he nuzzles my cheek with his nose and rubs his hands across my back, and I can't help but feel a little grateful to Reilanna for the nightmare; her harmless dream hell was a small price to pay for this moment of pure heaven in a demon's arms.

*****

I wake up alone in the morning, to my dismay. I vaguely remember Caliborne tucking me in after I nearly fell asleep in his arms. Then I remember the kisses that happened before that and touch my hands to my face as my cheeks burn all over again. As embarrassed as I am, I remind myself that Caliborne kissed me first. It wasn't like I threw myself at him, and yet I feel like such a vixen.

Young, unmarried women are not supposed to kiss men like that.

But, then again, Caliborne is not a man, and I am not a woman, so I'm not sure that counts.

I laugh and flop down on my pillow. How ridiculous I am. I'm in The Deadwood far away from those who preached to me my entire life of chastity and dignity. Who cares what they might think if they knew? They have no say over my life anymore, and nothing about what Caliborne and I did last night feels wrong even now. It was sweet and tender.

Loving.

I touch my lips, remembering the heat of his against them, the taste.

I wouldn't mind doing that again. Not at all.

I flip back my blankets and hop out of bed. Bolstered by my good mood, I feel confident and strong, definitely an Evan day. I stroll to my armoires, dress in the most masculine outfit I can find, and pull on Will's boots. I braid my hair and frown at it in the mirror as I try and fail to knot it up on my head somehow. I'll have to hunt down a hat. Someone in the castle has to have one they won't mind parting with. Perhaps I'll ask the cooks. I roll my shirtsleeves up to the elbows and tuck in the bottom of my shirt.

I don't look as good as I did in my church outfit, but it'll do.

I grab my breakfast from the kitchen with a quick hello to Levi and his crew then head to the room where I met with Wexton, Caliborne, and Fenmire. I've since learned this is where they take their meals, so I carry my plate down the hall to see if any of them are up and eating breakfast as well. To my delight, both Wexton and Caliborne are at the table when I walk in. They both look up and stare at me as I come into the room and set my plate on the table at a seat across from them.

"Good morning," I greet as I hop up onto the stool.

"Good morning," Wexton replies, but then he quickly follows it with, "The humans usually eat down the hall."

I pause with my fork stuck in a slice of ham. "Do you want me to leave?"

"No, no! I just meant, if it makes you more comfortable, you could eat there instead."

"Why would I be uncomfortable here?"

He waves down at the table in front of him, and I regard his meal for the first time.

His plate is at least three times the size of mine and made of gold. Sitting atop it is a large chunk of what looks like meat but it's completely black. Not burnt black, I realize as he slices a piece off and it oozes black blood. It's raw. He pops the bite in his mouth, and a drop of black blood drips down his chin. He wipes it away with the back of his hand.

"Is that one of the beasts that came through The Gate?" I ask.

"Sure is," Wexton says as he saws off another chunk. He's holding the fork between his cheek and shoulder as he works the knife since he only has one hand. "I'd ask if you want a taste, but it turns out the meat from our world doesn't sit well with humans. We can eat your world's meat, but ours makes your kind sick if you eat more than a bite or two, even if it's cooked."

Caliborne cuts off a much smaller bite from his own plate and chews it silently as he watches the conversation before him.

"Is all meat in your world that color?" I ask.

Wexton stuffs his mouth full. "For the most part," he mumbles around his food.

"Does your kind bleed black as well?"

Caliborne nods.

I eat a bite of my ham. The sight of the black meat and blood doesn't bother me, but the way Wexton devours it does. He belches between bites, and I cringe.

"Pardon," he says.

"You should work on your table manners," I tell him.

Caliborne snorts.

Wexton smirks at me, stabs the remaining meat with his fork, and tears a bite off with his teeth. Black blood dribbles down his face and onto his plate, some missing the gold dish entirely and splashing onto the table. At that moment, Levi walks in holding a teacup and saucer.

"Evan, you forgot your—" He stops to stare at Wexton. All three of us stare back at him. "Tea."

The meat slips off Wexton's fork and slams into his plate, right on the edge, sending the dish spinning up off the table. A wave of black liquid arcs off the plate and splashes across his front, soaking his face and chest, then the dish falls onto the floor with a deafening clatter, leaving Wexton sputtering and dripping.

There's a moment of stunned silence in the room before I lose it.

I laugh so hard I can't breathe.

A few seconds later, Levi joins me.

Then Wexton does too.

Even Caliborne is shaking his head and snorting at the ridiculousness.

Just when the laughter starts to die down, the hunk of meat—which landed on the table—slides off the wood into Wexton's lap, and it all starts over again.

Levi eventually walks over and sets my tea next to my plate. I thank him through my helpless chortling, and he leaves, still laughing himself silly.

I turn to Wexton. "I thought your job was to defeat beasts." I point to the hunk of meat in his lap. "That one bested you from the grave."

He licks the dripping blood from his upper lip. "Wanna help me clean up? You seemed to enjoy the show last time."

My mouth falls open, and I look quickly at Caliborne. He seems unfazed by Wexton's flirting as he slices another bite of his food. My reaction, however, doesn't go unnoticed. Wexton's eyes flick between me and Caliborne, and I can practically hear the gears spinning in his head. I go back to my breakfast to hide my burning cheeks.

"Well, well, well," Wexton says in a low voice.

I ignore him.

Caliborne looks up at me and winks.

I smile and keep right on eating.

Fenmire walks in next with a giant plate heaped with black meat of his own, but he takes one look at me, growls to himself, and immediately leaves again.

I sigh.

"We can't all be easy to woo," Wexton says with a shrug.

I throw a piece of scrambled egg at him. "Go take a bath."

He gets up from the table, blows me a kiss, and walks out, leaving his entire mess behind.

"Who gets to clean that up?" I ask.

Caliborne motions toward the door. I assume that means Wexton will have to come back and do it, but I'm not sure.

I pick up my plate and round the table, setting it beside Caliborne on the clean side. I hop up into the stool and give him a smile. "Hello."

He nods down at me.

I eat a few more bites of my breakfast as I summon the courage to say what's on my mind. "About last night. I was feeling a tad bit vulnerable, so I'm sorry if… if I came on a bit too strong or… or crossed a boundary."

Caliborne sets down his knife and fork and turns in his seat toward me.

I look nervously up at him.

He takes my chin in his hand, tilts my face up, and kisses me on the lips.

It's a quick but no less tender kiss, and when he pulls away, he strokes my cheek and goes right back to his breakfast.

I smile to myself as I do the same.

Chapter 13

I don't see Caliborne for the next two days.

I half wonder if he's avoiding me, but that doesn't make sense after our morning-after kiss. I question Wexton about it, but he merely says Caliborne is working on a special project in the forge.

"Why does no one want to tell me where that is?" I ask.

"When humans started showing up with The Offering," Wexton says, "we opened the castle to them. Why wouldn't we? We aren't monsters, after all. But that meant we had to adjust to sharing our space with your kind. As more of you showed up, the more we shared our space, but the forge, it's always been ours. We don't allow humans in there. That's where we go to craft and maintain our armor and weapons or simply be alone to think, free of little human distractions."

It's a bit too much of a coincidence for me that Caliborne is spending so much time in his "thinking space" immediately after things between us changed.

Wexton must read the worry on my face, and for once his tone is free of mocking humor as he says, "I'm sure he'll be done down there soon, don't worry."

I don't say anything, I just go back to my room and my sewing, which is the only thing I've found to do to pass the time.

Then, on the third day, there is a familiar rumble as the whole castle begins to shake. Dust and small rocks rain down from the ceiling, and another roar, even louder and more ferocious than the one I heard in the pool room, resonates in my chest.

Another beast has come through The Gate.

I run out into the hall in time to see Fenmire rush by my bedroom door, mace and shield in hand.

"Who's on patrol, Fenmire?" I call.

"Caliborne!" he calls back. "Stay in your room, Evan."

Caliborne is on patrol, so he will be the first to face whatever nightmare Reilanna has sent us. That thought swirls in my stomach, turning my lunch sour.

I go back to my room like I'm told. "He knows what he's doing," I mutter to myself. "He's kept himself alive the past two thousand years. He'll be fine."

I force myself to go back to my sewing, but I fret the entire time, listening for any noise in the hall as the hours tick by.

Dinner comes and goes, and Levi is all hopeful smiles again. This is obviously something he's used to. I hope it'll be that way for me someday, but I'm doubtful.

It starts to get late, but there's no way I'm going to bed without knowing. I change into my night clothes and sit staring into my fire as the temperature in the room plummets. Even though they gave me a room as far away from the castle walls as possible, Reilanna's storm seems to seep through the very stone into every room, particularly at night. My fire burns twenty-four hours a day, though, so my room is always the warmest.

It's still not as cozy as Caliborne's arms and chest.

I get up and pace for a bit, standing by the door every so many minutes, listening, listening. Nothing. Listening, listening. Nothing. Then, finally, there is a screech of old hinges and the whoosh of wind whipping down the hall as the front doors open for a moment then shut again. I rip my door open and step out into the hall.

Caliborne is striding toward me wearing a full suit of armor. I know the Gryxen wear armor out on patrol, but I haven't had the chance to see it until now. It's gold and covers him from his head, which is protected by a helmet with wings on the sides, to his toes, which are stuffed into boots that come clear up to his knees. There are pants, a thick chest plate, shoulder pieces, sleeves, and even gloves, all gold, and it takes my breath away. Dressed like that and with a bow in his hand and his wings slightly open behind him, shadowing him as he walks down the corridor, he looks every bit like one of the warriors from Wexton's stories.

Something's wrong though. He's holding one of his arms, which is streaked with dark liquid over the gold of his sleeve. When he sees me, he lets go of the limb and straightens to walk with more confidence.

I'm not fooled.

I rush down the hall and meet him. "What happened?"

He waves a hand toward his injured arm as if it's no big deal.

"Let me help you?" I ask.

He touches my chin then nods.

"Where?"

He points to his bedroom door, so that's where we go.

In his room, he props his bow and quiver against his dresser and rounds up a large bowl and a few clean rags. I fill the bowl with clean water from the pitcher on his dresser as he fishes not one but three rolls of bandages from his cabinet. With my help, he removes his helmet and shakes his sweat-streaked hair from his face. Next, we unbuckle the shoulder plates then the chest piece. The gloves come off, and then we tackle the sleeves. His uninjured side is no trouble, but he grunts in pain when I try to pull off the other one. It takes a few minutes of gentle tugging and twisting, but eventually, the arm comes free, and I suck in a breath.

"Caliborne…"

At the place where his sleeve met the shoulder plate on that side, there is a deep, oozing gash that stretches across the entire top of his arm and down it several inches. It's so deep the flesh is gaping open, and I feel a bit lightheaded at the sight. The top of his sleeve of armor is sliced open, and there's something stuck at the bottom of the groove. I pull it out. It's a claw almost the size of my hand.

Caliborne takes it from me and inspects it. He sniffs the end and even licks it with his tongue before handing it back to me.

"What am I supposed to do with it?" I ask, glaring at the offending thing that hurt him.

He shrugs then starts working the buckles and ties open on his boots. I set the claw aside and help him strip off the last of his armor until he's once again in nothing but those leather pants they all wear night and day. The rest of him is, thankfully, unharmed.

I wet a rag in the bowl and hold it out, making my intentions known, and when he nods, I start cleaning the blood from his arm. The room is lit by nothing but a few candles, but I can see enough to know when the water turns pitch black. I dump it, fill it again, and continue working. When it's time to clean the wound, I hesitate, but he takes my hand and presses it down across the cuts. Though he grunts again, he encourages me to wipe at the mess until there's nothing but drops of fresh blood seeping from an otherwise clean wound.

I grab a roll of bandages, but he shakes his head and goes back to the cabinet. This time, he sits back down holding the largest needle and thread I've ever seen. He offers them to me.

"You want *me* to stitch *that*?" I ask, pointing at his ravaged arm.

He nods.

I look from the needle to the wound and back again. "Are you sure?"

Yes.

I take the needle. I'm good at sewing. Fabric. This can't be that much different, can it? With one final nod of encouragement from Caliborne, I get to work. I'm careful with every stitch to be sure I'm pulling the skin together in a way that won't leave a thick scar, so it takes me much longer than if I were stitching this same length in fabric, but once I'm done, I'm proud of my work. Caliborne's nod as he inspects it says he approves too.

Now it's time for bandages, and it indeed takes all three rolls to completely wrap the area. When all is said and done, it's taken about an hour, but my demon is tended to, and I'm relieved he wasn't more grievously injured. I start to clean up.

Caliborne stands up from the bed and touches my shoulder just as I'm about to gather the dirty bowl and go wash it.

"What is it?" I ask as I turn back to him.

He takes the rag and dirty needle from my hands and places them on the vanity, then he hauls me up into his arms and sits on the bed with me in his lap so that we're right back where we were three nights ago.

I don't question it. I merely nestle into his chest and put an arm around his neck.

"Was it scary out there?" I ask.

He shrugs as if being mauled by some vicious beast is an everyday occurrence, which, after two thousand years of it, I suppose it must feel that way.

I brush his hair with my fingers, working out the small tangles from his helmet. It must feel good because he closes his eyes with a low, groaning growl. Once it's detangled, I run my hands through it from scalp to tip, brushing sections over his shoulders to pet as I do. I don't notice at first, but his face slowly drifts closer to mine until our noses almost touch. I stop playing with his hair, and when he opens his eyes, they rake across my face, stopping at my mouth.

A second later, we're kissing.

I turn in his lap to straddle him and bury my hands in his hair while he cups my face, pulling me closer. I can't get enough. A rush of desire sweeps through my entire body making me hot all over. My heart threatens to choke me as it lurches into my throat. I open my mouth in silent invitation, and Caliborne takes it.

His forked tongue sweeps across mine, tentatively at first, tasting me, then harder, more demanding. I match his eagerness. His arms tighten around me, crushing me to his chest, and I whisper his name against his lips.

He stands up from the bed, still holding me tight in one arm, and folds back the blankets with the other. He slides me in under them and quickly follows me into bed, dragging me right back to his chest once we're both horizontal. His kisses begin again, but they soften as he dusts them across my entire face, not just my mouth.

I know what I want, what my body wants, but I've never been intimate with anyone before, and the thought sends little anxious butterflies fluttering in my middle even before I remember what I saw the day Wexton stepped nude from the pool.

Two penises.

And I don't even know what to do with one.

I must tense up because Caliborne pauses and pulls away enough to study my face.

"I'm nervous," I tell him honestly. "I've never…"

He nods that he understands.

"I want to, but I don't know the first thing about it. Will you show me? Slowly?"

Caliborne never smiles, but I swear I see one in his eyes.

He nods and takes my hand, guiding it to his chest where he presses it, palm flat, against his dark blue, leathery skin. He plucks at the bottom of my night shirt, and his hand disappears beneath it. He places his hand on my chest at the same place mine rests on his. His thumb strokes across the top curve of my breast, and I mimic the move on him. When his thumb slides down over my hardened nipple, I suck in a breath as a jolt of pure sensation shoots straight to my toes. I do it to him too, and he closes his eyes with a groan.

This giant warrior of a being just groaned at my touch.

I feel like such a vixen.

I lean in and kiss him again, seeking his tongue as well as his touch, and he gives it to me. We kiss and roam each other's chests until I'm a writhing mess and Caliborne is panting softly against my lips. I'm wet between my legs, something I've only ever experienced by myself in bed with my hand up my nightgown. This though? This is different. This is an intense need, and I'm soon bucking my hips every time Caliborne touches me somewhere new.

His hand disappears, and for a second, I'm terrified he means to stop us here, but then it's back again and gliding across my belly. His fingers slide under the waistband of my pants, and my heart starts beating so hard my chest aches. I'm supposed to be mirroring him, but I can't get my hands to move as his trails down, down, down to that aching wetness between my thighs. He coaxes my legs apart, and when his finger first brushes against my sex, I jump with a gasp.

Everything is so sensitive, but Caliborne is gentle, as always. He moves slowly, allowing me time to absorb each new precious sensation as he touches me. When his finger first strokes my clit, a sound escapes me that's so carnal I clamp my mouth shut, horrified, until he touches me like that again, and the sound repeats itself against my will. Caliborne kisses my neck, not fazed a bit by the fact that I'm now mewling in his ear, and his finger dips lower to probe at my entrance.

I hold my breath as he presses against me, and when my body relents and lets him in, I whimper. His hands are at least twice as large as a human man's, so the stretch of his finger is a bit uncomfortable at first, but he goes so slow, entering me and pulling back over and over, giving me a fraction more with each stroke, and my discomfort vanishes almost instantly. His thumb finds my abandoned clit and softly circles it at the same time he finally pushes his finger completely inside me.

I instinctively tilt my hips to match the angle of his hand and melt against him. He withdraws, and the hot, slick feel of him sliding out of me only reminds me where he's been. I want him there again.

As if he's reading my thoughts, his finger thrusts inside me again and stays there. With a bend of his finger, he puts pressure on a place deep inside me that makes me squirm.

He snakes his other arm out from under me and sets his hand against my face, and a familiar tickle creeps up the back of my neck before a flood of affection and raw, unabated desire rushes over me.

"Caliborne!" I cry out as my orgasm makes my entire body arch off the bed. His hand between my legs makes it stretch on and on long after he stops flooding me with feeling through his palm. But then, as soon as the storm begins to calm, the tingle inches up the back of my neck a second time.

The second orgasm hits just as hard and fast as the first, aided by Caliborne's touch both on my face and more tender places. I'm shaking as I come down off the high, but he gives me little time to breathe before doing it again… and again… and again.

Oh, I'm in trouble. Sweet, delicious trouble I hope never ends, and yet, long after I've lost count of the times I've peaked, I finally have to cry out for him to stop or else I'm afraid I'll faint. When he takes his hand out from between my legs, I realize I'm soaked down there and covered in sweat everywhere else, but I don't let that stop me from curling as close to him as our bodies will allow.

He holds me. It's Caliborne, so of course he does. Never mind that I completely forgot I was supposed to be touching him too. Never mind the fact that I was screaming by the end as well. At least I think I was, judging by how raw my throat is. I don't remember. I don't remember much about the last twenty or so minutes except for how amazing it felt to lie here bathing in pure pleasure. None of that matters as Caliborne's forked tongue gently licks the salty sweat from under my ear. He kisses the same spot a moment later.

I nuzzle my nose up under his chin and fall fast asleep.

*****

I wake up without having a single nightmare as I slept. I feel rested, relaxed, and very warm. Air tickles the top of my head every now and then, and I realize it's Caliborne softly snoring into my hair. It makes me smile. His arm is draped over me, heavy but comforting, and the other is looped under my head. I've used it as a pillow throughout the night. I even drooled on it. I wipe it away, and the movement wakes him. He blinks down at me and yawns with a rumble in his chest that makes me laugh.

"Good morning," I say.

He kisses my forehead in reply.

"I'm sorry about last night."

His brow crinkles a bit.

"We were supposed to be pleasing each other, and I ended up being the one receiving all the pleasure."

Caliborne snorts and kisses my neck, clearly unbothered by this.

"Really, Caliborne, I want to learn how to please you too," I insist.

He rolls away enough to study me, and I don't say anything else, choosing to let my words hang between us as he considers. Surprisingly, he gives me a curt nod and rolls onto his back with one arm tucked under his head. With the other, he gives a wave of invitation.

And now I'm nervous all over again. I want this but don't have a clue where to start.

No, wait, that's not true. Where did we start last night?

I scoot closer and put a hand on his chest, palm flat like he showed me yesterday, but then I decide I'd like to start a little higher than that and slide it up to his neck instead to trace the underside of his strong jaw with my finger. He tips his head back to give me better access, and I become familiar with every bump of his throat. They move as he swallows, which fascinates me for a moment.

I move on to his wings, only one of which I can reach. The top bone is very thick and curves up, ending at a bend, like a giant knuckle, where the bone starts to curve down instead. The leather skin that makes up the majority of the wing is much thicker than that on the rest of his body and is covered with small, soft hairs. There are bones that run the length of the wing clear to the bottom in between each vast section of leather. They look like massive, webbed fingers. The wing attaches to Caliborne's back behind his shoulder, which I can't see at this angle, but I can feel the muscles there flex as I run my fingers across the top of his wing and shoulder. The movement sends a ripple through his wing which flutters enough to rustle my hair with a soft breeze.

Next, I feel the jutting ridge of his collar bones on both sides, comparing them to my thin ones. When I finally reach his chest, he has his eyes closed again, and he sighs when my thumb traces across the tops of his pectoral muscle on first one side then the other, each at least twice as large as my hand. I muster the courage to brush across a single nipple, and I get that same low groan as before, which makes me bold, so I do it again on the other side. I sit up on my knees to free my other hand and do it again on both sides at once.

Caliborne's lips part slightly.

Not wanting to focus on a single place too long, I move downward and trace the sharp line at the bottom of each pec. Below them starts the stacked peaks and valleys of his abs, which are well-defined and hard as stone under soft leather skin. I run my fingers down each of them clear to his belly, which lacks a belly button, oddly enough. There are deep, curving dips above each of his hips that disappear below the waist of his leather pants, inviting me lower still.

His pants are held closed by leather laces and nothing else, so it's easy enough for me to pluck at the bow keeping it all together as if unwrapping a gift on Christmas morning. I peek up at Caliborne's face for any indication that he wants me to stop, but his eyes are still closed, either to absorb the sensations or to give me privacy to explore his body without feeling shy, I don't know which. I loosen the ties, peel back the cloth, and gulp.

Caliborne does in fact have the same anatomy as Wexton with two shafts and large, drooping testicles. Just as I observed on the other Gryxen, the top shaft is somewhat smaller than the lower one, but *unlike* the day I caught a glimpse of Wexton's… gifts, this time, they are obviously hard and swollen with arousal, which makes them even more impressive to behold. I sit staring at them in awe until I remember that Caliborne is waiting and likely wondering why I've stopped. Sure enough, when I glance back up at his face, I find him watching me, his eyes hooded as he studies my reaction to his naked body.

I smile nervously and go back to my task of learning exactly how to please him, but then I freeze. Is the top one more sensitive to touch? The bottom? Should I pay attention to the dangly bits or leave them alone? I don't even know the answer to that for a human much less a Gryxen. Thankfully, Caliborne senses my distress and takes my hand, wrapping it around the top shaft and squeezing to show me the pressure he likes. He strokes himself once with my hand under his from base to tip then lets go and closes his eyes again.

I continue on my own, marveling at the feel of his leather-wrapped rod sliding through my hand. The end of this shaft isn't bulbous like a human penis but rather tapers just a bit before ending with no slit or hole at the tip. The bottom shaft, however, mimics human anatomy with a more veiny texture and a definite bulb with a slit at the end. That must be the one that… procreates, I realize. What's this one for then, I wonder? I watch Caliborne's face as I take that second shaft in my other hand and stroke it in time with the top one. There's a slight intake of breath and a twitch of his hips when I do.

I smile and speed my strokes. Within minutes, I know I've found exactly how to please him.

He's not talking, but the sounds he's making tell me plenty. Caliborne's mouth is open, and his breath is coming in ragged little pants mixed with the occasional growly groan. After a few minutes, he reaches down and pries my hand from his lower shaft, so I focus solely on the top one. His legs start moving, at first with just an occasional flip of a foot or bend of a knee, but soon his feet are shuffling across the sheets, the claws at the end of each toe stiff and threatening to tear the cloth to ribbons. Then he stiffens and draws one leg up to pump his hips with a snarl that ends with a breathless cry. Afterward, he lays still on the bed again, breathing heavily.

I have to assume that was an orgasm, but isn't such a thing supposed to produce… something? Biologically, that's the point of any living creature having an orgasm, right? Was that why he took my hand from his lower shaft? To stop such a thing from happening? Interesting. A touch on my shoulder pulls me out of my curious musings as Caliborne fingers my night shirt and tugs. I scoot back up to his chest, and he pulls me against him under one arm.

"Did I do well?" I ask with a hint of laughter in my voice. He's breathless and slightly sweaty, so I suspect I did.

He peeks down at me through one slit eye then hauls me up for a kiss, a long and tender one that stretches on and on until I'm breathless too.

"I'll take that as a yes," I murmur against his lips.

I tug a clump of his hair over his shoulder and fan it out against his collar, rolling the strands across the bone as his breathing returns to normal. His fingers brush lightly up and down my arm bringing goosebumps to my skin, and I sigh in contentment.

"I thought you were avoiding me," I say softly.

His fingers stop, and our eyes meet.

He cocks his head in confusion.

"I didn't see you for days, and I thought I was the cause. Wexton says you've been working in a forge somewhere."

Caliborne nods.

"Can I see it?"

He shakes his head.

I huff. "Wexton said the same thing."

Caliborne's chest bounces as he chuckles silently.

"Fine then, keep your secrets. Just pop in and say 'hello' every once in a while, alright? I missed you."

He nods and kisses my forehead.

My stomach rumbles.

Caliborne laughs again and sets me aside to climb out of bed. He ties his pants back up as I lounge on his bed and watch. He catches me staring and winks at me, and I shake my head with a sheepish smile.

Once he's all put back together, I get up and we head out into the hall and toward my bedroom so I can dress before breakfast. We're not halfway to my room when the front doors slam open with a gust of wind. A gust of snow bursts into the foyer at the end of the hall, ushering in a wind-swept Fenmire, who curses as he forces the doors shut again. He shakes the snow from his shoulders and starts down the hallway toward us, but as soon as he spots us, he stops.

His eyes roam over me where I stand in my pajamas with Caliborne's arm at my back. It's quite obvious where we've just come from and where we're headed, and Fenmire's eyes narrow as he glares at us.

"I'm so glad I could take over the last of Caliborne's patrol last night so that you two could have the evening together," he gripes. "I do hope you *enjoyed* yourselves."

Beside me, Caliborne growls.

"Why are you determined to be so angry all the time, Fenmire?" I ask, genuinely curious.

"We have a job to do," he barks. "And as I stated before, you are a distraction. We can afford no such thing."

"I also happen to be the key to getting you all out of this hellish wasteland, or have you forgotten?"

He snorts angrily. "It's impossible to forget with you underfoot day and night."

"Then why fight it? We could at least be friends."

He snorts again, incredulously this time. "Is that what you call what the two of you were up to last night? Becoming friends?"

I cross my arms. "If you're determined to be a sour puss, don't let me stop you. I won't let you ruin my good mood though." I turn to Caliborne. "See you at breakfast?"

He nods and squeezes my shoulder before I head into my bedroom alone, leaving Fenmire glaring daggers at Caliborne from down the hall.

After I close my door, Fenmire says, "You're playing a dangerous game, I hope you know. Reilanna will do whatever she can to stop them from breaking the spell. What happens if you get attached and Reilanna comes seeking that payment she mentioned? Have you stopped to consider this might be exactly what she wants? To see something that matters to us be ripped away again in one of her cruel tricks? Or is this simply how you plan to discover exactly what it takes to bind them to us?"

I've never wished harder that Caliborne could talk so that I could hear his reply to all of that. My gut tells me Caliborne would never use me that way, but now that Fenmire has planted that seed in my head, it'll fester there until I dismiss it, I know. As for the rest, the fact that I can leave The Deadwood coupled with the dreams Reilanna sends to disturb me at night makes me fairly certain I'm a lot more than some cruel trick sent to torment them, though the bit about the 'payment' she'd need in the end still bothers me.

There are so many unknowns, and for a moment I understand Fenmire's concern and hesitation to get close to me. This could end badly for all of us, but what else is there to do but move forward and hope for the best?

Chapter 14

A few more days slip by during which I see very little of Caliborne, though he makes a point to eat breakfast with me each morning. I'm so bored. Sewing and swimming can only entertain me so far, and with the blizzard raging outside, I can't even go out and enjoy any fun winter activities. To escape my room, I finally go to the kitchen and ask Levi if I can help them in there. At first, I'm met with surprised looks from all three men, but then they happily accept my invitation and put me right to work.

For the first time in my life, I enjoy cooking, mostly because of the company I keep. Though at first, they're quiet in my presence, it takes no more than a day for the cooks to relax and start cracking their jokes and telling their stories. They make me laugh even though some of their tales and quips make me blush. It's nice to be accepted by a group of men as one of their own, and though their candor takes some getting used to, I find I appreciate it, especially on Evan days.

The nights are less fun.

Reilanna comes to me each night, each time with new horrors, and I watch her hurt Will, my father, and even my mother as well as Caliborne, Wexton, and Fenmire. I wake up in fright but quickly pull myself together, not wanting to give her the satisfaction of seeing me quake or cry.

"I'll banish you forever, you evil witch," I mumble to her in the dark. "You just wait and see."

The morning after one such terror, I find Wexton in the hall outside my room, leaning casually against the wall. He stands up straight when I appear.

"Were you waiting for me?" I ask.

"I was. Levi says you've been spending a lot of time in the kitchen, and it occurred to me you haven't been given a proper tour of the castle. There are a few other places you might find enjoyable."

"Such as?"

"The study, the stables, the library—"

"There's a library?" I ask in surprise.

"Well, we call it such, yes, but it's small and isn't stocked with fun fairytales like human libraries. It's Fenmire's pet project, filled mostly with scholarly stuff he spends his free time pouring over."

"Those are the sorts of books I like."

"Very well. Go have your breakfast then meet me in the foyer."

Caliborne is in a bit of a rush this morning, so he has time for no more than a quick kiss as he passes me on his way out of the dining room. I eat my breakfast alone but quickly, excited to see what secrets about the castle Wexton will show me. He's waiting for me in the foyer as promised afterward, and I smile sheepishly as I stroll up. We haven't spent much time alone since my recovery, I realize, and I'm nervous.

"Ready?" he asks.

"Where to first?"

"Let's start at the top and work our way down, shall we?"

I nod and let him lead the way.

We climb up the spiral staircase but stop only one floor up even though the stairs go higher than that.

"What's up there?" I ask with a nod up the remaining steps.

"That's Drixus' floor. The rooms up there are vacant except for his."

"Does he truly never come down?"

"He must at some point for the necessities, but I never see him. He moves about the castle like a ghost."

"Why?"

"Shame? Guilt? Depression? Trauma? Take your pick."

Wexton ushers me down the first-floor corridor, which is identical to the ground-floor one except the doors here are all open. He shows me the study, which is full of oversized furniture obviously better suited for a Gryxen than a human. There is a comfy-looking oversized chair by the far window, though, that looks like the perfect place to get lost in a good book. There's an abandoned card game strewn across a side table between two chairs, and I pick up one of the cards. It's easily twice the size of any playing cards I've ever seen.

"Put that back," Wexton says. "Fenmire will accuse me of cheating if you mess up his hand."

"The two of you were playing this together?" I ask in surprise.

"As grumpy as he is, Fenmire can be decent company sometimes. You'll see."

I put the card back where I found it with a grunt of uncertainty.

Across the hall is another open door, and I peek into a room strewn with bins of water, buckets, and long grates made of wooden dowels. "What's all this for?"

"Fenmire's projects. I'm surprised this door is open. He usually bars anyone from going in his workshop." He ushers me past the door and down the hall to the room at the end, which sits directly above the kitchen. "The library," he says, as I step over the threshold.

No doubt heated by the fires in the kitchen below, this room is the warmest on this floor. There are shelves about the room as one would expect, but they're sparsely stocked. There are perhaps two hundred books in total along four different stacks. There's a desk against the right wall strewn with books, papers, and pencils. I turn and wander between the shelves, but none of the books has a single title along the spine.

"You say Fenmire spends his time here?" I ask as I pluck down a book at random. I flip through a few pages, but it's in a language I don't know, so I quickly put it back.

"He's always up here," Wexton replies rather boredly. "He's out on patrol right now, though, so we're safe from his brooding for the moment."

"I can't read any of these," I say when the next book I open is also in another language.

"Over here." He points me to the last shelf, the one that's the least stocked of all. "These are all in your tongue."

I take one down and discover it's a tome about the Earth's creation and the evolution of my kind. There are drawings in the margins, diagrams cramped with tiny labels for body parts, dates, and regions. The detail is exquisite, the writing very neat and organized.

"Wow," I utter as I flip through a few of the pages. I put it back to select another and am pleased when this one is all about mathematics. The pages are filled with complex arithmetic and equations I've never seen even in my own advanced books at home. "Who wrote these?"

"Fenmire," Wexton says. He plucks his own book down and props it open against my shoulder as he leafs through it, though it's obvious he reads none of it before snapping it shut again and sliding it back onto the shelf. "He's a scholar by nature. Once we were cut off from his precious libraries back home, he felt compelled to build one of his own here."

I look back at the other books, the ones I can't read. Knowing they've all been handwritten by one person makes the collection seem much more impressive than it did at first glance. I put the book back and go to the desk, Fenmire's space, I assume. The papers scattered across the tabletop are filled with the same cramped but neat writing. I slide a few around, not wanting to mess up his space but finding myself utterly fascinated by the mind that must sit up here, hour after hour, with nothing but the scraping of a pencil over parchment for company. I slide one last sheet aside, and a splash of color catches my eye. From underneath the notes, I tug out three drawings.

The three figures are Gryxen—I can tell by the wings—but they're not the three I've come to know. One has salt and pepper hair and one black eye, one white that both glare up at me from the paper. The second has bright green hair and eyes and is smiling whimsically as if he's privy to the secrets of the world and doesn't plan to share them. The third and last one has hair and eyes of a rich, watery blue. His face is a little sad but also cautious as he watches me with a shrewd stare. They're each drawn in such stunning detail it feels as if I'm peering into their very souls.

"Are these the other Gryxen?" I ask. "The ones who betrayed you?"

"Yes," Wexton confirms. He taps the drawing of the salt-and-pepper-haired one. "Horthos." He taps the green-haired one next. "Jothrik." Finally, he taps the blue-haired one. "Breklen."

"These are beautiful. Did Fenmire draw them?"

"He did." Wexton picks up the drawing of Jothrik. "These were our friends for thousands of years. I'll never understand what possessed them to turn on us like they did. What could they have wanted in the human world that was worth raising their swords against us?"

"Perhaps they didn't act of their own free will," I offer. "Could they have been persuaded by magic?"

"I've often asked myself that over the years. It would explain why Reilanna wasn't able to break Drixus."

"How does that explain it?"

Wexton drops the drawing back onto the desk and smiles down at me. "Let's just say there are things more powerful than magic in our world."

"Like what?"

He chuckles. "Not my story to tell, remember?"

I click my tongue at him. "Tease."

He takes a step closer to me, and in a low voice utters, "You have no idea."

I shiver and blush and take a step back.

He cocks a brow. "What's the matter?"

I shake my head and turn my burning face back to the drawings on the desk.

A finger to my chin turns it back to him again. "Why do you hide your face whenever I bring that lovely color to your cheeks?"

My heart is thumping in my ears. "I shouldn't be blushing at your flirts."

He frowns. "Why not?"

"Caliborne and I are involved, as I'm sure you know."

He smiles. "I know very well. I heard you the other night, screaming all manner of things as he brought you pleasure across the hall. It was all I could do to stay in my room and mind my own business."

My mouth falls open. "You *heard* us?"

"Oh, I heard, and I imagined what you must've looked like sprawled across Caliborne's bedding, all pink with your chest heaving like it is now."

I snap my mouth shut, but that doesn't stop the heavy breathing.

He chuckles. "Yes, that must've been quite a sight. I'd love to see it myself sometime."

"Yes, well, as I said, Caliborne and I are already involved, so…"

"Silly human," he says with another chuckle. "There's something you should know about our kind."

"By all means, Wexton, enlighten me."

He slides closer, his face one of wolfish delight as he leans down and whispers, "We don't mind sharing."

"What… what does that mean?"

"It means that our kind often take multiple lovers. In some cases, even family share lovers and sometimes even share mates."

"Mates? What's that?"

He ignores my question. "Your kind places great value on monogamy, but our people find such a thing far too restrictive. After all, what could be better than having one person love you unconditionally? Why, having two, of course. Or three. Or more."

"Are you trying to trick me?" The whole thing sounds utterly preposterous.

"Ask Caliborne if you don't believe me. But the question remains: if he tells you what I've said is true, would you still turn that beautiful, blushing face away from me when I flirt with you?"

I know what he's really asking, and the truth is that I don't know the answer. Since Caliborne and I have become… more than friends, I've slammed the door shut in my mind on the idea of feeling such things for any of the other Gryxen. Truth be told, I find Wexton charming if not a little infuriating at times. Could I feel more for him if given the chance? Something tells me I could, even though it feels like a betrayal to think it. I've been taught all my life that love can only be found between two people, and that loving anyone outside of that pairing is considered a sin, a betrayal. But if all parties involved are aware and give their blessing…

It makes my head spin to consider such a thing, but Wexton still stands in front of me, waiting patiently for an answer to his question.

"I don't know," I say truthfully. "I haven't thought about it."

He nods in understanding. "Speak to Caliborne. If you wish, that is." He smirks at me. "Should you decide to discover how the rest of us can make you cry out in the night, I'm at your disposal."

My cheeks burn again, but this time I roll my eyes and give him a shove. It's like pushing against a brick wall, but he backs away and gives me space anyway.

"You're an absolute heathen," I say.

He smiles wickedly. "Yes, I absolutely am." He waves toward the door. "Should we continue on?"

I glance down at the three drawings one last time and tuck them away again under Fenmire's other papers before following Wexton out of the library and back down the hall.

We go down the stairs back to the ground floor, but instead of heading down the main corridor, Wexton ushers me through a door off to the right of the stairs that leads to a smaller hallway. It leads us away from the heart of the castle, and the wind gets louder the longer we walk. The temperature begins to drop too, and I'm soon rubbing my arms against the chill.

"The stables are up ahead," Wexton says. "It's warmer in there."

"Are we outside?" I ask.

"Technically, yes. This is a sort of covered walkway."

I shiver.

Wexton sidesteps nearer to me. "Here." He puts his arm around me and curls his wing on that side around to create a warm little bubble with his body heat.

"Thank you." I grip his arm to thaw my freezing fingers. He's just as warm as Caliborne. "Do all Gryxen have such high body temperatures?"

"Not just Gryxen. All Gruxa are significantly warmer than humans."

"Is your world warmer or colder than mine?"

He shrugs. "It depends on the region. Where we're from, it's hotter and very dry most of the time."

"You said The Gate opens above a desert?"

"The Vorisca Desert, yes. The Gate resides not a mile outside of our capital city, Michastiforo, at the edge of the Vorisca. That's why there were seven of us protecting it. Michastiforo is a major trading hub and the home of one of our largest temples. When The Gate formed so close to such a beloved landmark, it created quite a panic at first."

"How long have you and the others guarded it?"

"Since its creation."

"How long ago was that?"

"A little over three thousand years ago."

"You're three thousand years old?"

He chuckles. "I'm much older than that."

"Does your kind live forever?"

"In a sense. We do age, but it takes many thousands of years. And even then, our bodies don't decay with time like yours do."

"But you believe in God… or gods, right?"

"We do."

"How does your kind get to go to heaven if you never die?"

"I didn't say we never die. We can be killed by injury or illness like any living beings. Those who are fortunate enough to survive such things to advanced ages often choose to pass on, usually when the last of their friends and loved ones are no longer around to make life worth living."

"How does one choose to pass on?"

"In a ceremony at one of the temples. You lie upon a table as the priestesses pray for Seerraf to usher you home. Then you simply close your eyes and… stop breathing. It's peaceful and void of pain. I can think of no better way to go."

"And your god just takes them? All they have to do is ask?"

"The priestesses interview those who come to the temple wishing to pass on. If they suspect the desire comes from dishonest intentions or circumstances in their life that might be improved, they deny the request, but of those they approve for the ceremony, yes, Seerraf accepts them without question."

This notion of a god so actively granting his people's wishes stuns me to silence as we continue down the walkway.

"I sense I've upset you," Wexton says quietly.

"I'm not upset, exactly, just conflicted."

"About what?"

"Your god answers your people's prayers so effortlessly. It makes me wonder why ours doesn't." How many times have I prayed to a god I believed was deaf to my call since none of my prayers were ever answered? Does my god exist at all? Pastor Elias likes to preach about the righteous path, but perhaps we've all been led astray somehow.

"Oh, that's simple," Wexton says with a small wave of his hand. "Your god is too young."

"Too young? Like a child?"

"Not in the sense that he lacks maturity. He's just not powerful enough to play such an active role in his people's lives yet."

"How does a god become more powerful?"

"Through his followers. The more who worship a god, the stronger that god becomes. But the worship has to be genuine, not the work of false prophets who only want power for themselves. Fenmire can tell you more about all of that. It's quite complex."

"My god does exist though?"

"Oh yes, he exists. If a god has worshippers, he exists, though in what capacity is the question."

"If worshippers are all it takes for a god to exist, does that mean the devil is a god? Pastor Elias says there are people who worship him as such."

This question makes Wexton hesitate, which is a rare sight and instantly puts me on edge.

"Yes, he exists," he says, then he glances uncertainly down at me as he adds, "That's the name your people gave our god, Seerraf."

I stop walking. "Your people worship the devil?" I cry.

"I've already explained your people mistaken my world for a place of fiery torture you call 'hell', so it makes sense the god of our world would be known in yours as the lord of the underworld."

"But he's not evil, is he?"

"That's subjective."

"Is it?"

Wexton sighs. "To our people, Seerraf is one of the kindest and most forgiving gods. From what little I know about your culture, our morals and values don't differ so far to say that your people, if they knew the truth, would think he was in any way evil."

I mull all of this over as Wexton urges me to keep moving and we come to the end of the walkway. Just like in the castle pool room, the corridor suddenly opens up into a cavernous space, only this one is filled with the smell of animals and not rotten eggs. Wexton and I walk out onto a hay-strewn stone floor, and I am immediately overwhelmed with the sheer size of the place and the number of animals everywhere I look.

There are stalls and pens as far as the eye can see, all neatly aligned in rows on either side of a long walkway that cuts the space in half. And the animals. When Wexton mentioned stables, I'd pictured pack animals, maybe a cow or two, but from where I stand, I can see rabbits, raccoons, foxes, deer, and even a few elk. There are long wooden boxes encased in wire that run the length of the walls, but I can't see clearly enough from this distance to tell what they house. Four men bustle up and down the center lane, carrying various tools and feed and calling to the animals and each other as they work to take care of the creatures. There are birds perched on top of enclosures, and in one case, even on the shoulder of one of the workers.

I am utterly awe-struck, and I don't realize I'm frozen at the entrance until Wexton clears his throat.

"Impressive, isn't it?" he asks.

"Where did they all come from?" I ask.

"The woods. Before it became The Deadwood, it was a thriving forest tended by Jothrik. He could create and control animal and plant life. When Reilanna twisted their home into what it is now and summoned the blizzard, creatures came here for shelter. We took in as many as we could and simply allowed them to use this area as a safe haven. When humans started showing up at the castle, they took it upon themselves to take greater care of the creatures and turned this space into what it is today. There's even a lower level for storage and treating the sick or injured animals."

I walk down the aisle in a daze. Everywhere I look, little noses twitch at me, ears perk my way, and beady eyes follow my every move. Squeaks, chirps, and titters surround me. An elk snorts and stomps at the end of the lane, and one of the men chastises it for its impatience in waiting for its dinner.

"Hello!" One of the men calls to me, the one with a bird on his shoulder. As he makes his way up the aisle, I realize it's an owl. "Is this the newcomer at last, Wexton?" He doesn't wait for Wexton to answer before he offers me his hand. "I'm Percival."

"Evan," I say as I shake his hand. He's the youngest person I've seen yet. He can't be over forty. "When did you come to the castle?"

"Almost eighteen years ago. I was about your age."

Percival's hair is short, black, and very curly. It wisps out from under his hat every which way. He's about Will's height, and his eyes are kind and understanding. In them, I see the hint of a kindred spirit. I don't ask, that wouldn't be polite, but I have a suspicion his exile was similar to my own.

"Who's your friend?" I ask with a nod to the creature on his shoulder.

"This is Moon." He reaches up and scratches the owl on the side of its feathered neck. "She's the boss around here."

I laugh. "Really?"

"Oh yes. She oversees all the work we do down here, don't ya, girl?"

As if in confirmation, Moon hoots at him, spinning her head nearly upside down as she stares intently at me as if deciding whether or not I'm welcome in her domain.

Percival laughs. "We hand-raised her about ten years ago, so she thinks she's our little queen." He continues petting the bird affectionately. "And she's spoiled rotten, so I suppose she's right, in a sense." He gives me a sad smile. "She's the last of her kind down here. Once she's gone, there won't be any more like her in The Deadwood, so we let her have whatever she wants."

"That's sad but also kind of beautiful," I say.

Percival nods. "As are many things in The Deadwood." He waves a hand around at the vast room. "Would you like a tour?"

I look up at Wexton, who bows his head to me, letting me decide.

"Yes, please," I say with a smile.

Chapter 15

Over the next several hours, Percival introduces me to every animal with a name, which is all of them, I soon realize. The stables are kept neatly organized to maximize the space and prevent overbreeding. There are some instances where males and females are allowed to roam together, but most of the time, the sexes are kept apart to keep the population manageable.

There are short enclosures for smaller creatures with no interest in climbing and enclosures with wired roofs far above my head for the ones who could easily scale or jump even the tallest wall. There are burrowers like rabbits and badgers who spend their time digging in their straw bedding, there are playful ones like foxes who endlessly chase each other around their pens, and there are majestic ones like deer who spend their time watching and waiting for handouts, which their human guardians give out at frequent intervals. Everything from the smallest mice—which are housed in the long, wired enclosures I noticed along the walls before—to the tallest elk—who snorts rudely into my hair as I walk by his enclosure—has a place and a home here and is obviously well looked after.

"Better than spending your day in the kitchen?" Wexton asks me quietly as I hold a baby squirrel in my palms.

Throughout every introduction, every pat and snuggle, Wexton has watched and tagged along and never once complained of boredom or otherwise indicated there was anywhere else he'd rather be. The animals don't run from him either. Having been born here, they have no reason to fear humans or Gryxen.

I smile up at him. "Much better. Thank you for bringing me down here."

He reaches out and softly strokes the little squirrel in my hands with one finger. "You're welcome. Thank you for agreeing to spend the day with me."

"It must be really boring being stuck here for so many years," I say as I put the baby back in his hutch and close the door.

"That's not why I asked to give you a tour, but, yes, it all gets a bit tedious at times."

"I'm sorry."

He shrugs. "We're Gryxen. We're built to weather the harshest storms. Pun intended," he says with a nod toward the far end of the stables where two massive wooden doors seal off the cavern from the raging blizzard outside. "We'll get through this too. Especially now that we have you."

An anxious lump forms in my throat. "We still have no idea how to break the spell." The last thing I want is for him and the others to place all their faith in me only for it all to go wrong somehow.

Wexton touches my shoulder. "Just be you. The rest will reveal itself in time."

I nod. "I can do that."

A whistle from across the stables makes us both look up. Caliborne is standing at the end of the covered walkway, waving at us. He has a small box under his arm.

"Finally," Wexton mutters.

"Finally, what?" I ask.

Wexton merely smirks at me as he ushers me across the stables. "Perfect timing," he says as we join Caliborne. "Their stomach has been growling for an hour."

"No, it hasn't," I argue, but the organ immediately growls, calling me a liar. "What time is it?"

"Almost dinnertime," Wexton says. "We skipped lunch since you were too busy giving cuddles and kisses."

I stick my tongue out at him.

He returns the gesture, and I laugh so hard at the sight of a demon with his tongue out that I nearly wet myself.

"Run along, you," Wexton says as he gives me a firm yet gentle push on my lower back. "Go tame that ravenous beast you call a stomach."

"You're not coming?" I ask suspiciously.

"Percival asked me many moons ago to help mend one of the elk enclosures. I might as well help him with that while I'm down here."

I don't buy it, but I also don't question him, especially not when Caliborne puts his arm around me to tuck me close to his warm body as we turn to head back up the walkway toward the castle. As charming as I find Wexton and as much as I enjoyed his company today, this place, under this arm, against this body, this feels as much like home now as my bedroom back at my parents' farm.

I put both my arms around Caliborne's waist as we walk. "I didn't expect to see you again so soon," I say in happy surprise. "I spent the day touring the castle."

His fingers softly brush my arm, and he peers down at me as we walk.

"What's that you've got under your arm?" I ask.

He bobs both brows, and his eyes gain the same mischievous twinkle Wexton's do before some witty joke.

"What are you up to?"

A wink is his only reply as we continue up the frigid walkway.

The air slowly thaws as we move back into the castle, but I don't move out from under Caliborne's arm. We make our way to the kitchen only to be told dinner won't be ready for another hour as it's still early in the evening.

"That's alright," I say. I look up at Caliborne. "Can we talk somewhere in the meantime?"

His brow creases a bit, but he nods and waves me down the corridor toward the dining room. To my surprise, he leads me past that room and on down the hall where I've yet to venture. We take a set of stairs down, and the air grows cool again, but not nearly as cold as the trek to the stables. This is bearable in my long sleeve shirt and pants. We step out into a dark and empty section of the castle, and it's not hard to see why it's been abandoned.

The ceiling here has either fallen in or been ripped completely off, and for the first time, I can see the outside of what the castle looks like. I peer up at massive pillars of jutting stone that seem to spring straight up out of the ground and rise far past where I can see through the blizzard. There's the occasional branch off in different directions, but for the most part, the walls are sheer, broken only by the windows that dot various rooms. This section of the castle is surrounded by stone that blocks the storm raging around us, and a slow and peaceful snow falls in the stillness between us and the whipping winds high above. It drifts down in swirling wisps until it settles on the floor where it melts against the only stone that's able to absorb the sun's heat in the daytime. At night, this place must turn into a pure sheet of ice.

Right now, though, it's a winter wonderland.

There's no rubble from the destruction, just a few walls left standing that used to separate the rooms here. It's like wandering an ancient ruin as I meander through open doorways and gaps in the walls, catching snowflakes on my tongue.

"Did this happen during The Great War?" I ask.

Caliborne nods.

I used to imagine those winged battles our legends speak of and picture creatures akin to dragons flying around, slamming together, and knocking each other out of the air with screams of pain and fury. I see one now in my mind's eye come crashing down on the roof, smashing the stone to bits before clambering back to its feet and launching itself into the air again. Considering the size of the Gryxen, I imagine the real battle didn't look much different from what I see in my head.

I look back at Caliborne, who's silently watching me, leaning against one of the remaining stone walls, and I remember I'm supposed to be starting a discussion.

"Right," I say as I turn away from the beauty of the fresh falling snow and focus on the issue—or issues—at hand. "I need to ask you a few questions, if you don't mind."

He bows his head to me and waits.

I start with the one that makes me the most anxious. "Something Fenmire said the other day bothered me, and… please don't take this the wrong way, but I have to know: do you only like me because I'm possibly the one who can break this spell? That's not the reason we've become close, is it?"

He pushes himself off the wall, his posture going rigid as he shakes his head with vigor. He beckons me close, and when he offers me his palm, I grasp his hand in both of mine as I lean my cheek into it.

At first, I see an image I've seen before, the one of myself scrambling backward across the ice of the pond the moment I first came face to face with a Gryxen. Again, I feel impressed and awed at this small creature's cunning then anger when I realize it's a female left out here to die by her people. That memory is quickly swept aside and replaced by another, this time of the same human huddled close to my chest as she lies in bed, her cheeks flushed with fever as she mumbles in her sleep.

"Father," she mutters with a whimper. "I want my father. Please. Will. Where's Will?"

In my chest, I feel an ache of regret that I didn't get her back to the castle faster coupled with hope that she survives. Her icy hand splays across my chest, seeking my warmth, and I squeeze her tighter.

What follows are a series of short memories that flash by one after the other, each featuring that same soft being: little heartbeat moments with her in my arms as she sleeps, the feel of her soft skin as I change her bandages, the smell of her hair once the taint of illness finally fades from her scent, all of which are surrounded by feelings of tenderness and affection that grow with each image.

The way their forehead crinkles as they tell their story about their names fascinates me. The way they look like one of the warrior priestesses when they step from the pool room for the first time takes my breath away. The sounds they make as I bring them pleasure stir my own desires. The sweet innocence of catching snowflakes on their tongue makes my chest squeeze around my heart until I can barely breathe. Their smile, their laughter, their pleasure, and their scent is intoxicating, and I'll never get enough.

My eyes burn when Caliborne finally takes back his hand. His feelings for me grew little by little through the moments we shared and not through the promise that I might someday liberate him from this snowy prison.

"I'm glad," I say softly. "I feel the same."

He strokes his thumb down my chin then leans back against his wall again with a nod for me to continue.

"Oh, right, my other questions." Now I'm nervous all over again. "I'm sure you've noticed Wexton is quite the flirt."

Caliborne snorts and nods.

"I was afraid that might upset you since we're together now, but he informs me your kind doesn't view such things like humans do. He says your kind often share partners and therefore don't feel jealousy in that way. Is that correct?"

I'm shocked when Caliborne nods. I'd expected him to tell me Wexton was playing some game, but this…

"You truly won't mind if I decide I also have feelings for Wexton?"

Caliborne shakes his head, and I blink up at him, dumbfounded.

The idea that I can enjoy the company of any or all of the Gryxen without feeling the slightest bit guilty feels like a weight has been lifted from my chest, a weight I never even knew was there. The thought that I can do whatever feels right to my heart and have the complete support of those who care about me feels almost too good to be true. Whether or not I can feel the same way for Wexton that I do for Caliborne remains to be seen, but knowing the option is there should I wish to find out is enticing.

Caliborne waves his hand to urge me to continue talking.

"I think that's everything," I say with surprise. He's effectively banished all my qualms. "Thank you for this. The talk and this." I indicate the snowy getaway around us with a smile. "This is beautiful."

I make to step around him toward the stairs to head back up into the intact parts of the castle, but he stops me with a hand on my shoulder. He takes the box out from under his arm and pats the top, beckoning me close once more.

"What is it?" I ask. When I reach for the latch on the front, he takes my hand, stopping me from touching it. "Caliborne?"

He sets his palm on my cheek.

I'm sitting at a table of gold bathed in bright sun in an outdoor seating area. I have a cup in my hands, but I haven't taken a drink in many minutes. There are two Gruxa—one male and one female—sitting at the table next to me, and I'm trying hard not to stare. The body language of the male is very telling, and I keep an eye on him, watching for the moment he makes his move. Finally, he shifts in his seat to take a small box from his pocket and slide it across the table to the female.

Her eyes widen at the sight of the box, and her hands shake a little as she takes it and plucks off the lid. I can't see what's in the box from this angle, but I can see the smile that forms on her face as she stares down at it. She looks at the male, who nervously awaits her reaction.

The female clutches the box. "It's lovely," she says. "Thank you."

The answering grin on the male's face is one of pure joy. She has accepted his gift—a courting gift—which means they are well on their way to becoming a mated pair, bonded for life. There is no greater joy, as long as they choose their mate, or mates, correctly. A bad pairing can destroy them both if they're not careful, but I can tell this couple is well-suited. They're both soft-spoken and have kind eyes. They will do well together.

The memory fades back to Caliborne's face as I stare up at him.

I look down at the box.

"For me?" I utter. "From you? A gift like the one in your memory?"

Caliborne nods.

"So this is like… like an engagement present?"

Caliborne tilts his head in confusion.

"It's akin to making a promise to someday get married."

He makes no reply as his eyes scan my face for my reaction.

"Can I see it?" I ask shyly.

Without delay, he flips open the latch and lifts the lid.

The box is simple in its design and is made from the recycled slats of crates from The Offering cart, but that doesn't detract from the beauty of the pieces I find within it. Along the bottom of the box, neatly aligned in a row, are three bracelets: one gold, one silver, and one bronze. They're each a weave of fine metal fibers woven into a braid that doesn't quite complete a full circle, and the centermost portions between each end of their crescents are hammered flat. I can just see the hint of letters etched into the flattened spaces, and I reach into the box to pick up the gold bracelet and inspect it more closely.

It reads *Evan* in stained black letters across its golden face. The silver bracelet reads *Eve*, and the bronze reads *Evangeline*.

This time, there's no stopping the tears as they well in my eyes and trickle down each of my cheeks. "Oh, Caliborne," I utter. With these, I'll no longer have to introduce myself from day to day to let others know which name to call me. No one has ever gifted me something so thoughtful or so beautiful in my life. "They're perfect."

I look up to find him slightly wide-eyed, and I remember how important this moment is. If I accept these, it's more than just a gift.

"To be clear," I say, still holding the gold bracelet. "Accepting these doesn't mean we *must* become mates, only that we're both seriously considering it, yes?"

He nods.

I smile. "Then I accept."

He lets loose a sigh that sounds ripped from his soul as he shuts the box with a snap, tucks it under his arm, and kneels on one knee in front of me. He takes the golden bracelet and slides it onto my wrist. It fits me perfectly. He takes my face between both his hands and kisses me, but what starts as a tender mating of lips quickly heats as I step into his arms and open my mouth. His plunging tongue makes my legs shake, and I realize there's something *I* want to give *him*. Something to show him, in my own small, human way, that this moment means as much to me as it clearly does to him.

"Make love to me," I whisper against his lips. "For a human, our first lover is something sacred, and I want that to be you. It's not a gift I can give twice, so if you'd rather not be the one who—"

He scoops me up into his arms, and I cling to him as he turns and heads back inside.

Chapter 16

Caliborne carries me straight to his room.

He kicks the door shut behind him and sits me on his bed, and I'm suddenly all anxious butterflies again as he sets my box of bracelets on his vanity and turns to face me. He crosses back to the bed and takes my hand, the one with the gold bracelet on the wrist. His finger hooks under the edge of my sleeve and slides it, ever so slowly, up my arm. As he does, he trails his forked tongue along my skin, humming slightly at the taste of me. When he reaches the end of where my sleeve will allow him to explore, he switches to my other arm and does it all again.

I would never have thought such a thing could be erotic, but at the feel of his hot, wet tongue gliding across my skin, I start to squirm. He tugs at the ties on the front of my shirt, and I let him loosen them before I strip the whole thing off over my head. His fingers trace the side of my neck, across my collar bone and shoulder, and I shiver. He gets down on both knees beside the bed and repeats that same path with his mouth, dusting kisses across my goosebumped skin. I sigh into his hair, but when he swipes a thumb over one of my nipples, that sigh turns into a choking gasp.

I make that sound all over again when he leans down and replaces his thumb with his tongue.

My face instantly begins to burn so hot my skin will surely melt right off. It seems scandalous to have anyone's tongue lapping at my chest, much less a demon, but it also feels like pure heaven. The pleasure wins out over the embarrassment, and I tip my head back to give him better access. He takes my whole nipple between his lips, bathing it in the heat from his mouth as well as the pressure from his tongue.

I moan.

He switches to my other breast.

My hips buck. "Caliborne."

Without taking his face from my chest, he reaches down and unfastens my pants, and I lift my hips enough for him to swipe them off me completely along with my boots. He even peels off my thick socks, leaving me naked on his duvet. His strong hands wrap around my bare backside and slide me closer to the edge of the bed, then he parts my legs. His mouth releases its teasing hold on my nipple and trails up my chest, my throat, and my chin, and just as his lips settle on mine again, his finger brushes over my clit.

I swear my eyes roll back so far I could see the inside of my skull if I tried. Caliborne's tongue probes my lips, asking for entry, and I give it willingly, plunging my own tongue into his mouth in rhythm with the circles his finger is now making between my legs. I throw an arm around his neck. He buries a hand in my hair. I break our kiss when his finger slips down through the wetness pooling where my body aches for him, and I gasp against his lips when he slides it inside me.

Again, he goes slow, allowing my body to set the pace, and I feel no pain even though his fingers are each at least three times the size of mine. The fingers on his other hand massage my scalp, and I tip my head back so that he's holding my head in his massive palm. That wicked forked tongue explores my throat as his finger works inside me to the hilt and starts thrusting, slowly at first, and then faster until the room is filled with the sounds of it and the smell of my arousal. I circle my hips, craving more pressure in that place he used to bring me apart before. He denies it, and I don't understand why until a second finger presses against my entrance.

"Oh, God," I utter, then I whimper as both fingers begin working inside me.

Caliborne chuckles as his tongue moves to my ear. One of his fangs brushes against my throat as he moves, and the thrill of such a deadly thing passing so close to vital places on my body makes me come alive in a way that I am definitely going to explore more fully in the future. Right now, though, my brain is mush as Caliborne makes love to me with two fingers, and I go so limp with pleasure that he soon lays me down on my back across the bed. I whimper sadly when his fingers draw out of me, but then I hold my breath as he stands and strips off his leather pants.

Both those beautiful cocks are rigid and begging for attention.

I blink up at him, unsure if he wants me to get up and go to him or…

He doesn't give me time to do anything at all as he leans between my legs. His blazing white eyes stare down at me with such intensity I'm momentarily stunned as he grabs my legs at the thighs and tugs me even further to the edge of the bed until I fear I might slip off. With one of my legs still held firmly in his grip, Caliborne reaches down and strokes his top shaft, the smaller of the two, and, without breaking eye contact, guides it inside me.

I clench at first, I can't help it, but Caliborne notices immediately and takes his time, coaxing me to relax with gentle rubs up my thighs and strokes across my clit that make me moan with each breath I take. Inch by glorious inch, my body accepts him until he buries himself as deeply as he can possibly go.

Caliborne arches his back and rolls his shoulders, and it's only then that I realize how much he's holding back right now. He's trying his hardest not to hurt me, and that makes the moment even more tender. When he starts thrusting, slowly, I feel my heart may burst, but it settles for tears, which I hastily wipe away.

Caliborne freezes.

"Don't stop," I say weepily. "I'm fine. It's normal." At least I think it's normal. I've never made love before, but this feels right.

Caliborne nods and moves again. As tall as he is, he can touch every inch of me, and touch he does, though one hand never comes out from between my legs as he goes on circling my clit. His hand runs through my hair, down my cheek, my throat, and my chest, around both nipples, down each peak and valley of my ribs, then across the dip of my belly before retracing that same path back up again. He seems mesmerized by my body, and he soon begins to grunt and moan between pants as if the sight of me is all it takes to unravel him.

He speeds his thrusts and settles his roaming hand, palm open, between my breasts.

That same flood of complete desire and unabated arousal sweeps over me, and I arch off the bed as I orgasm for the first time. I twitch and writhe beneath him as he goes on pumping himself into me, in time with the spasms wracking my entire body.

I barely still on the bed before the second one comes.

I grab Caliborne's wrist as he brings me pleasure again and again, and as one orgasm bleeds into the next and then the next, I wonder, morbidly, if one could die from too much pleasure. Thankfully, though, Caliborne eventually takes his hand from my chest. I'm limp as a noodle and making the most embarrassing noises with each thrust of his cock when he stiffens, growls low in his chest, then roars. His hands claw at the bedding, ripping the cloth in several places. His cock pulses inside me, growing even larger as he orgasms. When he finally stills, he leans down and holds my head between his massive hands as he nuzzles my face.

We're both sticky with sweat, but I couldn't care less about that as I tip my face up and kiss him over and over. Eventually, he taps me on the forehead with a searching look in his eyes.

"I'm fine," I say through dry lips and a hoarse throat. "Better than fine."

He takes a step back, and though there is a moment of discomfort as he slides out of me, I'm surprised by how painless losing my virginity was, probably due to the care in which Caliborne took it. I also notice there is no seed left behind, which again stokes my curiosity. I wonder if there's a reason other than size that he made love to me with one shaft and not the other. I want to ask but also don't want to ruin the moment with an anatomy lesson, especially when he scoops me up and tucks me close to his side in bed to continue kissing and petting me.

"Is this why you've been spending so much time in the forge?" I ask, shaking my wrist so that my new bracelet jingles a bit.

Caliborne nods.

"Does this mean you'll stop disappearing on me so much?"

I get a chuckle then a nod.

"Good. Both my days and my nights are lonely without you."

I stretch out under the blankets with a contented sigh and nestle my head on Caliborne's chest, peering up at him as he watches me with those glowing white eyes. They're fascinating. Everything about him is fascinating to me. The thought that there are infinite civilizations in the universe besides humans makes me feel so small. Not in a sad way, but in a way that makes me long to learn about as much of it as possible. There's more to life than the things I was taught were so important back in my little village, and that thought brings me peace. Things like marriage, manners, and status never mattered to me, and now I know why. It's as if my soul knew from the start that I was meant for bigger things.

And as I curl against the chest of a demon more than twice my size, I chuckle to myself.

"Caliborne?" I say with sudden inspiration. "Can you show me your world?"

He tilts his head.

"Wexton says it doesn't look so different from mine, and I'm deeply curious to know where it is you come from."

He nods and offers me his palm.

The first thing I see is dark red sand that stretches far into the horizon. There are rolling hills and the occasional bare tree that dot the land, but it's mostly just sand, and I can see heat waves rolling up off of it even though the light is dimmed as dusk falls, bringing a break from the scorching suns. I fly over the Vorisca Desert and crest a ridge, and a grand, golden city rises before me. The fading light shimmers on grand towers, vast bridges, and perfectly-kept streets. I've never seen anything like it in my life.

In the center, rising above all the other structures, sits the temple: a round, domed steeple with a long golden walkway jutting out from its eastern side that ends with a staircase leading down to the streets far below. Everything is made of gold from the tip of the temple's roof to the cobblestones of the smallest alley.

I slow my flight, taking extra time to enjoy the view as I head toward home.

The memory shifts, and I'm suddenly walking down one of the cobblestone streets. I keep my wings tucked in tight so as not to bump into others as I pass storefronts and cafes. A few call out greetings to me, and I bow my head to them as I pass. The structures here are all square. Each building is the same size and shape as its neighbor with no gaps in between for several blocks until a narrow alley breaks the pattern to allow foot traffic through to the next street. Everything is uniform and exact.

And gold. There is so much gold it almost hurts the eyes. But there are other colors too. Windows are draped with bright curtains, gardens overflow with greenery, and signage outside the various shops are painted or poured to catch the eye against so much dazzling gold. And the Gruxa. Where the four Gryxen I know are quite similar to each other besides their hair and eyes, Gruxa have a vast variety in not only shapes and sizes but also styles. The way they wear their hair, their jewelry, their clothing, it's all so different, not only from humans but from each other.

One female Gruxa walks down the street in a bright green dress that matches her eyes, but she has her hair cut down to but an inch of length. She wears silver bands around her neck, at least a dozen of them, and they jingle wildly as she walks by. Behind her, a male Gruxa tags along at her back, chatting to her as they make their way to what appears to be a bakery up the street. He's so short he's about the same height as a human, but his brown hair falls clear down to his waist. Both his eyes are covered by a cloth wrapped around his head, and yet he's able to see where he's going without hindrance. He's also wearing a dress, to my surprise, a long flowy one in the most gorgeous shade of purple. His ears twinkle, and I realize they're pierced along the entire outer edge with bright stones of all colors. They frame his face with tiny rainbows.

I continue on down the street and walk right out of the memory and into another. This time, I'm standing at the edge of a long rectangular pool carved right into the cobbled street. I'm surrounded by happy chatter, and I look around to find that every Gruxa bathing in the pool is naked. Males, females, and even children all bathe and converse without a hint of shame or bashfulness. Lovers wash each others' backs and feet, mothers scrub their children's hair, and in one corner, three younger males make a game of shoving and splashing each other until a few of the older Gruxa chastise them for ruining the peace.

I step down into the warm water and sigh as it soothes the ache in my feet. I sit down in water up to my chest, lean my back against the edge, and let my wings drift in the gentle ripples of the bath.

"Caliborne!" a young voice calls, and I look over as a small female with stark white hair splashes down into the pool. "You were supposed to wait for me."

I move closer to the stairs so she doesn't have to tread water to stand at the wall beside me. She tosses her wash bag on the floor at the edge of the pool then dunks her head under the water. A stream jets out of her mouth and up toward my face when she re-emerges. I know it's coming, though, and block it effortlessly with my arm.

"How long are you home for this time, brother?" she asks.

I hold up two fingers.

She stills in the water, her little face falling in heartbreak. "But that means you'll miss my celebration. You promised!"

I reach out my palm and reassure her I'll be here even if it means paying penance at the temple for skipping my duties. I wouldn't miss it for the world.

"Good," she says with a nod and a fresh smile. She takes her soap from her bag and begins to wash. "I'm thinking of coloring my hair sea blue. Mother just about had a fit when I first mentioned it, but I want to do something special for my party. What do you think?"

The young girl's face fades into one with similar eyes and hair as Caliborne takes his palm from my cheek.

"Was that your sister?" I ask.

Caliborne nods, and I realize that particular memory, while filled with joy and wonder like the rest, was also tinged with sadness and regret I didn't notice until it was over.

"You miss her."

He doesn't nod; he doesn't have to.

A sudden, heartbreaking thought occurs to me. "Was that the last time you saw her?"

This time, Caliborne hesitates before he nods.

"You didn't get to go to her celebration," I say, my heart aching for him. "You got stuck here before you could, didn't you?"

Another nod.

"I'm so sorry, Caliborne." I hug him around the neck. "I promise to do my best to give her back to you."

He merely strokes my chin and nestles me more comfortably under his wing with his arm curled around me.

"Are there any other cities from your world you can show me?"

He winks at me and sets his palm back against my cheek.

Chapter 17

I'm standing in the broken section of the castle, catching snowflakes on my tongue as the light slowly dims to dusk. The temperature begins to drop below what's comfortable for me, so I turn to head back inside, only the entrance to the rest of the castle is frozen over with a sheet of ice so thick I can't see through it.

I knock on the ice. "Hello?" I scream. "Can anyone hear me? Hello?"

I hear Reilanna's vicious laughter and start pounding on the ice with my fists. The wind picks up around me, and I shiver. My toes have gone numb. Snow now falls so heavily I can't see more than a few inches in front of my face, but I can feel the ice wall in front of me, and I kick it, screaming for someone to come rescue me before I freeze to death.

Frigid fingers grasp my shoulder and spin me around, and I'm suddenly standing at the edge of the crumbling floor of the castle, staring down at the whipping wind and snow that hides how far of a drop it is to the ground below. Those same fingers press against my back and try to push me over the ledge.

"No!" I scream, flailing my arms to keep from losing my balance as my toes slide over the edge. "Stop!"

Reilanna's breath is on my ear again as she whispers, "The Gate will claim payment."

Her fingers push harder.

I cling to a piece of broken wall to keep from falling.

From somewhere close by, some unseen creature roars, and though the sound is animalistic and full of rage, something about it banishes my fear and gives me hope. Reilanna hisses in frustration, and her fingers disappear.

The snow falls peacefully again, and when I turn around, there's no more ice wall blocking my path back inside the castle. Caliborne is leaning against the wall nearby and he raises his hand, pointing his palm at me to deliver a wave of peaceful calm that makes me smile.

I'm safe.

I'm not cold anymore either, so even though nothing is stopping me from going inside, I choose instead to go back to happily catching snowflakes under Caliborne's watchful stare.

When I wake up that morning, I find Caliborne's hand resting softly atop my head as he sleeps.

*****

Caliborne has patrol this afternoon, so I head upstairs in search of Wexton to ask him about something I'm still working up the courage to even bring up. I've decided a straightforward approach is likely best. It'll get his jeering out of the way so I can get to my answers faster. I find him in the study seated at the table where the abandoned card game was strewn, only it's abandoned no longer. Fenmire sits across from him, studying his cards intently until he sees me, then he rolls his eyes and puts them down in his lap.

"Great," he mumbles. "They've discovered the upper floors."

"Yes," Wexton says with a wink at me. "I gave them a tour."

Fenmire harrumphs and looks at me. "I suppose you'll be wanting us to teach you how to play."

"Maybe some other time," I say. "I'd actually like to talk to Wexton."

Without delay, Fenmire sets down his cards and rises from his chair. "Well, by all means, don't let me stop you." He strolls out of the study and turns right to head for his little library without another word.

I take Fenmire's empty chair—awkwardly, since it's comically tall compared to me—and smile at Wexton. "Can we talk?"

"It feels like that's all we ever do," he says with a smirk.

"If I'm bothering you, don't—"

He waves away my worries. "On the contrary. It's nice to have someone who enjoys chatting as much as I do. Fenmire clams up after a time, but you never seem to run out of questions to keep the conversation moving. I like that." He sets down his cards and leans back in his chair. "What is it you want to discuss this time? I fear I've reached the limits of my knowledge of religion, so if that's what you're—"

"You have two penises," I blurt far more forcefully than I mean to. I need to get it out or else I'll lose what little bravado I summoned on my way up here.

This is the first time I've ever seen him taken aback, and he blinks at me in shock before throwing his head back on a full-bellied laugh. I sigh and let him have his fun. Once he's calmed back down enough, he says, "Last I checked I did." He wipes moisture from his eye with another chuckle.

"Does each one have a separate… function?"

His face breaks into an infuriating grin. "I'd wondered how long it would be before such questions surfaced and whether or not you'd ask Caliborne or come to me instead."

"Yes, well," I say stiffly as my face begins to burn. "Here I am."

Wexton basks in my discomfort for a moment but thankfully doesn't comment on the blush. "Our cocks both function the same during love making, but only one can be used for breeding. The other is purely for pleasure."

"So, you only use the one unless you want to get a lover pregnant?"

"No. Impregnation is a whole other subject. Traditionally, our bottom shafts are reserved only for our mates. Many thousands of years ago, my kind considered mates to be the only ones worthy of our seed. The top shaft doesn't produce that, so we could use that one with anyone we wished, but it was considered highly inappropriate to use one's bottom shaft with anyone outside a mating bond."

"You say that like that's no longer common practice."

"It's not. Like I said, it's a tradition, one most don't adhere to anymore."

"Oh," I say thoughtfully. Is that why Caliborne only uses his top shaft with me? Because we're not a mated pair? But if his kind don't follow that rule anymore, then maybe the problem isn't his morals but something to do with me. I look up to find Wexton staring at me with one of his knowing little smirks on his face. "What?"

"Caliborne is the oldest of us," he explains. "He was born during a time when such traditions were still heavily practiced." He leans nearer to me. "There's nothing wrong with your union; he's just old-fashioned."

"How old is he?"

Wexton wrinkles his brow as he calculates. "I met him around thirty-five hundred years ago, and at that time, he was a well-known and highly decorated Gryxen. He was over twelve thousand at the time, so he'd be close to sixteen thousand years old now."

"Sixteen thousand?" I utter. My brain can't wrap itself around such an age. "And he's never mated with anyone before?"

Wexton shakes his head. "It wasn't from a lack of knowing what he wanted either. It took him no time at all to decide he wanted a bond with you."

"How old are you?"

"Seven thousand one hundred and fifty-two."

"What about the others?"

"I don't know their exact ages, but I'm the youngest. Fenmire and Drixus finished their training a couple thousand years before me, so they'll be closing in on ten thousand pretty soon, I think. They're close enough in age for the difference to be negligible, as I understand it."

"Can you tell me more about the mating bond? What exactly is it? I've been comparing it to a human marriage in my head."

"It's similar, I suppose, in that both parties agree to it and court beforehand, but that's where the similarities stop. A mating bond is something far more powerful than a piece of paper signed by a priest. It's the binding of two souls on a spiritual level. Once it's done, it can never be undone."

"A soulmate. That's what you're describing."

"One of our choosing, yes." He nods down at my wrist that's resting on the table between us, the one wearing my bronze bracelet today. "I see Caliborne gave you his courting gift. I hope you understand the significance of that."

"I do. He showed me how important it is."

"Good."

"He didn't show me how it will feel to become his mate, though; I guess because he has no memories to show me since he's never experienced it himself."

"I haven't either." He's thoughtfully silent for a moment then says, "Fenmire has, but I wouldn't ask him about it."

"Fenmire has a mate?"

Wexton nods. "I'm serious, though, Evangeline, don't bring it up. I shouldn't have mentioned it at all, but I don't want you asking him in passing thinking you'll get insight only to end up stumbling into a world of hurt."

"I won't, I promise. But is there anything about mating bonds you *can* tell me? Anything at all?"

He runs two fingers down his fangs thoughtfully. "The only thing I know is that mated pairs sometimes share their powers."

"You mean like Caliborne's control of emotions and memories?"

Wexton nods. "It's different for every pair, and some never experience it at all, but sometimes the mating bond connects us on a level deep enough our partners gain a sliver of our abilities."

"So, I could potentially control emotions and show my memories too?"

"You're human, so I don't know. You may get no powers at all. In fact, I'm willing to bet that's the more likely outcome considering your kind don't possess magical abilities yet."

I pout at the lost opportunity but quickly move on to my next inquiry. "How is a mating bond made?"

Wexton taps one of his impressive fangs with a bob of his brow.

"Through a bite?" I ask, my voice going a bit squeaky at the thought.

"Yes, but, like I said, both parties have to agree and want it equally. Otherwise, you just end up chewing on them, and no bond forms."

"Is there a ceremony?"

"Not in any official capacity, but it's pretty common for couples to perform it while fucking."

"Wexton!" I cry in shock.

"What? It's the truth."

"You're so… so…"

"Charming? Witty? Gorgeous?"

"Infuriating, crass, and incorrigible!"

He smiles. "As long as I can still make you blush, I'm alright with that."

I hadn't realized my cheeks were burning again.

"Did you ask him?"

I don't have to ask what he means. "He confirmed what you told me: your kind take multiple lovers and don't feel jealousy over it."

"So will you stop hiding that beautiful face from me whenever I say something scandalous enough to make it all rosy like it is now?"

My face gets hotter, but I tilt my chin up and ask, "Am I hiding it now?"

The smile that creeps across his face could only be described as wicked. "It's a start."

The implication makes my lips part in shock, but I don't say anything to deny it. I'm slightly panicked as my heart thumps like a drum in my ears, and I resist the urge to check the door for witnesses like some maiden without a chaperone.

It's alright to feel this way.

It's alright that I can picture myself strolling around the table and climbing up into his lap to see for myself just how wicked that mouth can be.

I bet it can be very, very wicked.

His smile widens as if he can read my thoughts.

My chest begins to vibrate with how hard my heart is beating.

No, wait… it's not me that's shaking.

Dust and rock rains down on top of the cards in front of me, but I have only a heartbeat to register what's happening before a pair of dark leather wings engulf me, and I'm suddenly crushed to Wexton's chest under his arm as the whole castle trembles. A bellowing wail echoes throughout the corridors, and I slam my hands over my ears as whatever creature that just crawled out of The Gate roars at the top of its lungs.

"It's alright," Wexton yells above the noise. "It'll pass in a minute."

"Caliborne's out there," I say fretfully.

"Yes, and he better wait until I show up before starting the fun part."

I give him one small nervous laugh.

The shaking stops, but the dust hasn't yet settled when Fenmire appears in the study doorway, weapons in hand.

"Let's go," he beckons.

Wexton still has his arm around me. He looks down at my face, gives me a wink, and lets me go. "Time to go to work. Flirt with you later, rosy cheeks." He taps me on the nose before running off down the hall with Fenmire.

*****

For the next week, my life falls into a pattern. I spend my days either helping in the kitchen or the stables or sitting in my room sewing more clothes. Sometimes Wexton finds me for a chat, and we spend hours talking, though we don't flirt as heavily as we did that day in the study. I get the feeling he's waiting, biding his time. Perhaps he wants to see how things between me and Caliborne progress before trying his own hand. I don't know. I like his company, though, almost as much as I enjoy Caliborne's.

I spend every night he's not on patrol in Caliborne's bed. I can't get enough of him and often catch myself daydreaming about the things we do together in the dark throughout the day. A few times, I rile myself up enough I have to excuse myself back to my room to take care of the ache in my middle, especially during the times Caliborne spends the night in The Deadwood on patrol. I've never had such a strong physical need before in my life, but now… now I find I'm cranky and tense without some form of release, whether by my own hand or Caliborne's various means.

As much as I look forward to the moments I spend bathed in pleasure, I crave the ones that come afterward just as much, the ones filled with nothing but the sound of the wind whipping outside Caliborne's window, the feel of his fingers brushing across my sensitive skin, and the taste of the kisses he can't stop giving. In those moments, I feel more at peace than I ever have in my life. And when I drift off to sleep in his arms, I know I'm safe, even from Reilanna, who can't break through the protective shield Caliborne puts between her and my dreams every night.

It's during one of those moments of blissful calm that I make my decision.

I'm ready to be his mate.

Chapter 18

I am so. damn. nervous.

I've decided that tonight, I will ask Caliborne to make us mates. Wexton and I discussed it again yesterday so I know what to expect. I asked if there was some sort of exchange of fluids, like venom or something, but the mating bond is apparently more complex even than that.

"It's not a chemical reaction," Wexton explained. "It's a bonding of souls, a blessing from Seerraf. Intent is all that's required, though I'm fairly certain you must break the skin. At least that's what my people still firmly believe."

We decided it should be Caliborne who performs the actual bite. Since I'm human, we're not sure if this will work at all, but for *me* to bite *him* would drastically reduce the likelihood since I don't think I could pierce that thick leather skin of his if I tried. Caliborne has the proper hardware, so it only makes sense. Plus, I want it to be him. I want him to claim me. He's earned that and so much more.

The only other thing to figure out is where the act itself will take place. Despite Wexton's previous declaration that most mated pairs form their bonds during love making, I'm not sure that's what Caliborne will want, and trying to find the nerve to ask him is slowly unraveling my sanity.

How in the hell does one ask their lover where they want to go so that they can bite you in the hopes that some soul-bonding will happen?

"This is madness," I mumble to myself as I finish bathing in the pool room.

Today is an Eve day, and I've decided to wash and brush my hair until it shines and wear the new dress I just finished stitching yesterday. It's some of my best work yet, a full-length creation with a dark blue bodice and baby blue skirt: the only one I'll be able to make that's all one color since those were the only two shirts in the whole pile that were the exact same shade. The rest of my dresses will either have to have a two-toned skirt or be made to fall no lower than the knee, which is not ideal in this drafty castle.

I've been clean for twenty minutes when I realize I'm stalling by continuing to float around the bath. I climb out and dry off then retire back to my room to dry my hair by the fire. Once it's dry enough, I count to one hundred strokes as I brush it to perfection, then I put on my new dress and my silver bracelet and go get my dinner. Levi has my meal already waiting on my tray in the kitchen, and he whistles when I walk in.

"Would you look at that," he says, eying my dress. "I don't think this castle has ever seen something that stunning." He motions for me to spin around, and I oblige. "Beautiful. Did you make that yourself?"

"Who else?" I ask cheekily.

"You're pretty talented, Eve. Perhaps you should've gone into fashion."

"Men's fashion, maybe. I only make the dresses out of necessity. Men's clothes are what I truly enjoy stitching."

"Is that so? Perhaps when you're done creating your own wardrobe, you can make a few creations for the rest of us. If you like, that is. I know I wouldn't mind a decent outfit or two for a change."

I blink at him in surprise. "I'd love to, Levi." I compare his frame to my own, seeing the measurements in my mind's eye. "If you can find me the cloth, I'll make you whatever you like."

"I'll see what I can dig up." He picks my tray up off the counter and brings it to me. As he hands it over, he says in a whisper, "I added something special." He nods down at the tray which has an extra lid this time.

I'm intrigued but don't ask and give away his secret. "Thank you."

He winks and promptly shoos me out of the kitchen.

I take my meal to the usual place, but as I walk in, I'm stunned to find not one, not two, but three Gryxen sitting around the table eating. Fenmire has been avoiding me like the plague, so it comes as quite a shock to see him sitting and laughing in the room where he knows I eat all my meals.

In my surprise, I forget about my new dress until all three Gryxen turn to stare at me.

Wexton's mouth falls open. "Where did you get that?"

I set my tray on the table across from him and climb up onto the stool as carefully as I can, tucking my skirt underneath me. "I made it." I look at Caliborne, who's staring at me with slightly wide eyes. "Do you like it?"

Caliborne nods with enthusiasm.

"Seerraf, yes!" Wexton exclaims. "You look great. Don't they, Fen?"

I glance uncertainly over at Fenmire, expecting to find nothing but hostility on his face, but am pleasantly surprised when he tilts his head in consideration then nods. "Very nice," he says simply, then he goes back to his dinner.

Wexton and I exchange twin looks of surprise.

Caliborne winks at me.

I pull the lids off my meal and find the 'something special' Levi slipped onto my tray. It's a pie no bigger than the palm of my hand. I pick up my fork and am about to break open the golden-brown top to see what kind of pie it is when it's snatched off my tray.

"Hey!" I cry as Wexton sniffs it.

"Seems Levi hoarded the last of the apples from The Offering," Wexton says. He locks eyes with me as he flicks that wicked forked tongue out, bringing it dangerously close to my golden prize.

"Wexton, give that back this instant!" I demand. "I haven't had a sweet in a month."

"You're supposed to eat dessert *after* the main course."

"I don't give a damn!"

"What will you give me for it?"

"I'm gonna give you a swift kick in the backside if you don't hand it over."

"Ooooo, I'm simply *terrified*."

Beside him, Caliborne growls.

"Oh, stop it," Wexton says with a roll of his eyes. "I won't hurt their precious sweet." He slides the pie back over to me. "There. Alright? You two aren't even bonded yet, so cool your protective tendencies."

There's a deafening clatter, and we all look over at Fenmire, who just dropped his fork onto his plate.

"Not bonded… *yet*?" he asks, and the barely-contained rage in his voice gives me chills. For the first time, he spies my bracelet, and the snort that comes out of him I swear should be accompanied by smoke. He snaps his head toward Caliborne. "You can't be serious!"

Caliborne growls again, only this time it's sinister. He's gone stiff, his ears are pulled back, and his eyes are narrowed at Fenmire, daring and hostile.

Fenmire stands up so fast his stool slams into the ground behind him. He pushes away from the table with a growl of his own and heads for the door but stops at the other end of the table to round on me.

"You have no idea what you're signing up for," he hisses.

"I do, actually," I reply, holding my head high.

"It can never be undone."

"I know, Fenmire."

"No, you don't know!" he yells, but then he closes his eyes, clearly trying to rein in his temper. He opens them again and fixes me with a piercing stare. "You don't know how it feels to choose wrong, to have everything you thought you knew about that other person ripped to shreds and stomped on, and to know that it doesn't matter what they've done to you, your soul is still tied to theirs, forever! You don't know about that part, Eve."

I get down off my stool and walk over to Fenmire, stopping with my toes just inches from his and peering up into his eyes.

"I hear you, and I know the risks," I say. "Wexton and I have discussed it at length. You say I don't know how it feels to have a mating bond go wrong, and that's true, I don't. But there's also something *you* don't know. You don't know what it's like to grow up thinking there's no one in this world who could possibly understand and accept you for who you are. You don't know the terror of having to choose between living a lie for the rest of your life or being exiled to a place where you're expected to suffer and die for just being yourself.

"I would've died back there," I say, pointing in the direction I'm pretty sure the village lies from here. "A death by a thousand tiny heartbreaks. I thought the best I could hope for was escaping to the city and living as a spinster with my best friend. But I came here instead. And I found understanding and acceptance and a whole lot more. I don't care if I live in this frozen wasteland for the rest of my life because… I'm happy. I've never been this happy in my entire life."

The entire room is deathly quiet around me, and Fenmire's intense, shimmering black eyes stare down at me while his hands ball into fists and relax at his sides over and over again.

"This feels right to me, Fenmire," I say softly. "I'm sorry if it upsets you, but just because your mating bond failed doesn't mean mine is doomed to as well."

Fenmire doesn't look angry anymore. He just looks sad.

"It's your life," he mutters.

"It is. And it's frighteningly short compared to yours."

Of everything I've said, this seems to affect him the most as he visibly starts and blinks a few times.

"Thank you for warning me," I say, then I smile. "It's nice to know you care enough to do that."

He snorts again, but some of the tension relaxes from his shoulders before he nods. He turns and leaves the room much more calmly than before.

I go back to my stool and pick up my pie.

"Not many speak to him so candidly," Wexton remarks.

"I don't know why," I say as I slice through crisp golden crust with my fork. "He seems like the type to appreciate candor."

"He does. But he's intimidating, so not many have the gall for it."

"He doesn't scare me." I take a bite of my pie, which is sweet and tart and absolutely delicious. "It takes more than some fangs and a foul temper to make a monster."

As the three of us continue our meal, I find my eyes drawn to Caliborne far more often than usual and am pleased when he not only notices but returns my frequent glances. Wexton, thankfully, seems to catch on that he's intruding and quickly cleans his plate, excusing himself much faster than usual. Once Caliborne and I are alone, the glances grow more heated. When I can't stand it anymore, I clear my throat.

"In case it wasn't clear enough after what I said to Fenmire," I say shyly, "I've made my decision about us."

Caliborne pauses with his fork halfway to his mouth.

I make myself meet his eyes even though the intimacy of it makes my heart thump painfully hard, and my face begins to burn. "In the weeks that I've been here, I've developed a fondness for you beyond simple desires. I feel bereft whenever we're apart and worry after you endlessly when you're out there fighting Reilanna's horrors. I'm not one to deny my heart anything it decides is as important as you've become to me. I would be honored to be your mate, Caliborne, and I'm ready to make that final leap with you if you are."

Caliborne sets his fork down and stands, and I watch with anxious eyes as he comes around the table to me. I yelp then laugh as he picks me up off the stool. I straddle his hips as his hands clutch me close by my backside, and I put my arms around his neck.

"I take that as a yes," I murmur.

His chest shakes with silent laughter before his lips are on mine, kissing me softly over and over. Up to this point, our displays of affection were subtle outside of the privacy of our own rooms, but now his tongue swipes across my lips, asking for entry right here in the dining room. I part my lips and moan when his forked tongue meets mine. He sits me on the edge of the table and clutches my face, and I tilt my head as his mouth slowly moves down my neck. His tongue licks up the curve of my jaw, and I shudder.

"What do you want, Caliborne?" I ask before the last of my coherent brain gives in to desire. "Where, when, and how do you want to become mates?"

He stops kissing my heated skin and meets my eyes. He considers my question for a moment before scooping me back up into his arms and carrying me from the room.

We go straight to his bedroom. I guess he really is nothing if not traditional.

This is the room where I got to know him, where he kept me alive and tended to me, where he showed me, day by day, that I wasn't alone anymore.

Yes, this room is fitting.

Caliborne runs one of his fingers under the collar of my dress.

"Do you really like it?" I ask. "It's my first attempt at a dress."

He sets his palm on my cheek and shows me two memories. The first is the moment I walked into the dining room earlier this evening. It's accompanied by an overwhelming feeling of awe, desire, and affection. The second is from just seconds ago when he first set me back on my feet. This one is accompanied by a question:

How do I get them out of that dress without ruining the beautiful creation they worked so hard on?

I'm laughing as Caliborne takes his hand from my face.

"Like this," I say, and I show him the ties that run down the front of my dress and the bows tucked under the waist of my skirt. I pluck the bows loose and untie the bodice, slipping it off over my shoulders once it's open in the front. I then show him the buttons holding my skirt closed and pop them open until it unravels from around my waist, taking with it the strip of material I installed around the waistline for extra support in keeping the skirt closed and up on my slim frame. It's the best dress I could make with the materials I had, and I'm quite proud of the simple design that will allow me to easily get dressed without assistance in tying up the bodice.

Caliborne takes each piece and lays it gently across the top of his dresser. Once I'm naked, he quickly shucks his own leather pants, almost tripping in his haste to get them off over his wide feet. I giggle and hop up on his bed. Caliborne follows me, taking my face between his massive hands again as I scoot myself back toward the pillows. His massive body covers mine two-fold, and that's without the wings. His shadow hides me from what little light comes in from the stormy window, and I hope that means he can't see the nerves on my face that are starting to creep up again.

Being the intuitive Gryxen he is, though, Caliborne senses my distress almost instantly and stills.

"Sorry," I say, though I know there's nothing I need to apologize for. "I don't know why I'm so nervous."

One minute, I'm lying on my back below him on the bed, the next, Caliborne grabs me and rolls, positioning me astride him with his back on the bed instead. He leans up on one arm enough that our chests touch, and I splay my hands on his shoulders as he softly brushes the loose hair from my face and tucks it behind my ear. I can feel his cocks underneath me, and I realize all I have to do to take one inside me is rise up on my legs a bit and…

"Oh," I say in pleasant surprise. "This is interesting."

Caliborne repositions his legs, and I move down his body enough to feel all his naughty parts pressing against mine. He sits up enough to free both his hands, and they hug me close as he leans down and captures my mouth again, but softly this time and without any tongue. His hands slide up my back as he holds me, and his mouth leaves mine to brush across my cheek, down the ridge of my ear, across my jaw, over my chin, and down the front of my throat. I lean back to give him even more access, and his mouth roams my neck and shoulder, then his tongue snakes into the soft valley between my breasts. I lean back even more, and his arms are all that hold me up as his forked tongue flicks across my right nipple.

"Caliborne!" I cry as my hips buck in response.

He moves to the other breast and does it again.

This time, I whimper, and the sound makes Caliborne's cock throb against my sex.

He peers up at me, and there's no mistaking the look in his eyes. He's asking for permission. To make love to me? To make the bond? I'm not sure, but the answer is the same regardless.

"Do it," I utter breathlessly.

Caliborne returns to licking my chest, his tongue making maddening circles around my left nipple until his arms tighten at my back and his mouth slides from my breast up my chest to a spot just over my heart… then he bites down.

I cry out, I can't help it, but the pain is a brief flash my body barely registers before a sweeping heat takes over, starting at the spot where Caliborne's fangs sank into my skin and quickly spreading over every inch of my body clear to the very tips of my fingers and toes. I'm lightheaded and feel like my body is floating in Caliborne's lap, like his arms are the only thing keeping me from flying right up to the ceiling. I thought my heart was hammering in my chest before, but now it's racing so fast I'm breathless.

Caliborne releases me, and he's panting, clearly as affected by what happened between us as I am. When his eyes meet mine, everything snaps into place.

Mate.

The word held little meaning for me before, but now… now I see my mate in those blazing white eyes, and the world shifts. Every choice I've made, every turn I've taken, every step I've walked has led me to this other soft soul who is now as much a part of me as my own limbs.

And he is breathtaking.

I throw my arms around his neck at the same time Caliborne makes a whining noise and crushes me to his chest in a hug so tight it's hard to breathe. He sets his forehead to mine.

Seerraf and the five… they are so painfully, wonderfully beautiful.

The thought is in my head, but it's not mine. The voice is deeper than Fenmire's or Wexton's and weighted with the wisdom of a Gryxen thousands of years older. I pull back and stare once more into Caliborne's eyes, fresh shock rendering me speechless.

Something's wrong. What is it, my love? Caliborne softly takes my chin between his finger and thumb. *Tell me.*

"I can hear you," I say as a twin pair of tears slide down my cheeks. "I can hear your voice in my head!"

Caliborne's brow crinkles. *This? You can hear this now?*

I nod.

Caliborne's eyes are wide with his own shock.

"Has anyone been able to hear your thoughts in their head before?"

No.

"Can you hear my thoughts?"

We're both quiet for a moment as Caliborne listens, and there's plenty to hear as my mind races with one thought after the other. Can I hear everyone's thoughts? Is this some power given to me or simply a new addition to Caliborne's? Perhaps he can simply share his thoughts with me like he does his memories. I'm not complaining either way. The thought that I can have full conversations with him now makes me elated. After a minute or two, Caliborne shakes his head.

I can't hear you.

He sounds sad.

"That's alright," I say, rushing to comfort him. "I'll tell you anything you want to know. You need only ask."

He doesn't ask me anything. Instead, he holds me tight and softly licks the blood from the bite on my chest I'd completely forgotten about. There are two vicious-looking puncture wounds above my left breast and a few smaller nicks from Caliborne's other teeth that barely broke the skin. The pain my body ignored earlier comes rushing back, and I grit my teeth as Caliborne cleans me with his tongue.

That can't be sanitary.

As soon as I think it, I laugh.

Caliborne looks up at me. *What's so funny?*

"I think my brain is still in shock."

I can distract it a bit more, if you like.

I'm suddenly flooded with an overwhelming urge to shove him down on his back and…

"Oh my…"

Caliborne laughs silently and recaptures my mouth.

His erection, which ebbed a bit during our shocking discovery, comes back in full force, and I feel both his shafts pulsing against my sex with every beat of his heart. I'm suddenly irritable that one of them isn't already inside me, but Caliborne is already gliding one of his hands between us to touch me. I push up off his lap with my legs, and one of his fingers teases me open and slips inside. I arch my back with a moan.

That sound. His voice contains the hint of a growl in my head. *It drives me wild.*

His thumb circles my clit, and I moan again.

Gods above…

"I want you inside me."

Gladly.

I push myself up higher, and Caliborne reaches down to hold his shaft up for me, the bottom one this time. It's considerably thicker than the one I'm used to, and my body protests briefly as his head pierces my entrance. I pull back and take my time. Caliborne is still and patient as I slowly lower myself onto him, and by the time I'm fully seated, I feel impossibly full. My orgasm threatens to slam into me at the mere thought of so much cock inside me.

This time, my moan comes out mixed with a whimper, but then I gasp as Caliborne thrusts his hips up. His top shaft sits at the perfect angle to rub across my clit when he moves.

It feels as good as I imagined it would.

That's when I remember Caliborne has never made love to anyone like this. I am the first, the only one to have this part of him inside of me. He's given me a gift much the same as the one I gave him the first time we made love.

I bury my hand in his hair. "I love you," I murmur.

And I love you, my stoferra. My mate.

We start to move together, me riding him with my legs while he thrusts his hips in time with me. Both his cocks together feel like heaven, so much so that when he puts his hand on my chest, I pull it off again.

"No," I say breathlessly. "Just keep... keep going... faster... yes!"

My fingers dig into his leathery skin as my legs lock, but he pushes me over the edge with one last hard thrust of his hips. My legs shake violently and my entire lower half clenches around Caliborne's hard length as my orgasm makes my entire body so stiff I struggle even to breathe.

Caliborne groans and stills, and I feel him come inside me, his seed noticeably hotter than his shaft still buried to the hilt between my thighs.

My stoferra! his voice roars in my mind, the word replaying over and over as he shudders under, around, and inside me.

He collapses onto his back, and I lie across him, exhausted, breathless, and aching in private places but also buzzing from head to toe. I lay my head against his chest to hear his heart racing beneath my ear as he gently runs his fingers through my hair, brushing it off my sweaty back and neck.

My mate. The words don't do this justice. 'My heart' is better, or perhaps 'my soul'.

I will never get enough of this.

"Me neither," I say, and Caliborne jumps in surprise. I laugh. "I can hear you now. You'll have to learn to control your thoughts around me if there are things you'd rather I not hear."

I have nothing to hide from you. Listen all you like. It might take me time to get used to it, though.

"That's fair," I say sleepily.

Caliborne shifts and pulls out of me, and I wince.

He freezes. *Did I hurt you?*

"Hurt? No. You were bigger this time, and that will likely make me sore for a bit, that's all."

I groan in protest as he moves me off of him and onto the bed. He gets up and pours fresh water into the wash basin on his vanity. He washes himself, rinses the rag, and offers it to me.

Emboldened by everything we've shared tonight, I part my legs and say, "Do the honors?"

I swear his lips twitch in a grin before he crawls up onto the bed and takes me up on the offer, gently washing me with the cool water that feels good on all my slightly-abused bits. When he's done, he tosses the rag into the bowl and climbs back into bed, settling on his back where he was before and dragging me right back up on top of him. He shuffles a sheet up over us both, and I hum with contentment as I find his heartbeat with my ear again.

Sleep well, my stoferra.

I manage no more than a hummed "Goodnight" before I fall off to sleep.

Chapter 19

I wake up to Caliborne's soft snoring, but it sounds different. I peek up at him from his chest and realize the only difference is that the snoring isn't being drowned out by the sound of the whipping wind outside like it usually is. I turn my head toward the window and see… sunlight? That's not possible. I must still be half asleep. I was dreaming of fishing in the stream at my parents' farm and haven't come back to reality yet. I close my eyes and go back to listening to Caliborne's breathing and heartbeat.

A bird chirps nearby.

This time, I push myself up off Caliborne's chest and look around.

That's definitely a bird. But where is it coming from?

I slide sideways off of Caliborne, who grumbles softly in his sleep as I scoot across the bed and get up. I cross to the window and pull back the thick purple curtains.

There's a tiny brown bird on the sill outside the window, and I have to block bright sunlight with my hand to see it. The bird is startled by my sudden appearance in the window and takes flight, and my eyes finally adjust enough for me to look out over The Deadwood, where not a single flake of snow is falling. The wind is gone, the snow has stopped, and the sun is out.

"Caliborne!" I cry. "Caliborne, wake up!"

He wakes with a startled snort and quickly jumps out of bed. He comes to the window too and stands behind me, blinking through the pain of sunlight in his eyes after two thousand years.

"The storm is over!" I say, hardly believing the words. "I'm not dreaming, am I?"

Caliborne touches my shoulder. *I don't understand.*

I turn my back to the window and face him. "Our mating bond. It must've affected Reilanna's spell. It…" The pieces snap into place in my mind. "*'One willing and eager to bind themselves to all four of you',*" I recite. "Bind. Soul-binding. Mate bonds. Caliborne!" I grip his arm. "In order to break Reilanna's spell, I must become a mate to all four of you."

Caliborne blinks down at me, clearly in shock since his thoughts are silent.

I turn back to the window. "Look at it, Caliborne," I say in awe. "We've brought the sun back to The Deadwood. We've broken a piece of Reilanna's spell."

I can't believe it.

I look down toward the ground in front of the castle, below the long staircase so covered in snow it looks like a small mountain of white instead of steps, and see people wandering through the powder. I can make out Levi's greying hair and Percival's hat, and the two of them come together, clapping each other on the back in celebration.

"I want to go out there," I say. "Let's go celebrate with the rest."

When I face him again, I find a troubled wrinkle in Caliborne's brow.

"What is it?" I ask, but I get only silence in response. "Caliborne?"

He blinks, confused, but then he looks at his hand and sets it back on my shoulder.

Can you hear me?

"Yes."

It seems we must be touching for you to hear my thoughts.

I consider the applications of this and nod. "I'm glad. You should have privacy in your own mind unless you wish to share your thoughts with me. But, what made you look so cross a moment ago?"

If you must become a mate to all four of us, that includes Drixus.

"Oh." I'd nearly forgotten about the fourth Gryxen whom I've yet to even meet. "That's right, he's a recluse."

That's putting it mildly. Drixus has been through a lot. More than any of us.

"Wexton said he was tortured."

Caliborne nods. *Reilanna might not have stolen his power, but she broke him. I don't know how you'll ever get close enough to him to form a mating bond.*

I smile up at him. "We'll figure it out. Have faith."

He touches my cheek affectionately and nods.

"In the meantime"—I take his hand—"come play in the snow with me?"

*****

Not twenty minutes later, Caliborne and I pick our way down the snowy front steps of the castle toward the gathered group of humans who all turn and call excited greetings to us as we join them in the clearing between the castle and the edge of The Deadwood.

"Can you believe it, Eve?" Levi calls. He closes his eyes as the sun beats down on his face, and he sighs happily. "This feels so nice."

The temperature is still quite chilly. It seems The Deadwood is still in the heart of winter, but the snow has stopped falling, and the sun is out in all its glory.

Percival comes over and wraps his arms around me, hauling me up and spinning me in a circle much like Will does when he's excited.

"You did this," he says as he sets me back down. "I just know you did."

"I hope to do much more," I tell him with a warm smile.

"The birds have all flown the coop, so to speak. As soon as we opened the doors to let the sun into the stables, they took off. All but Moon. It seems she's decided to stick around for now."

"She doesn't know anything else. But maybe now she'll find a mate and won't be the last of her kind after all."

"Maybe."

A shadow falls across us, and I look up to see a giant, winged beast pass across the sun and head straight for the castle.

"Caliborne?" I say in alarm even though no one else seems disturbed at all by its appearance.

Caliborne takes my hand. *It's alright. It's only Drixus.*

"What?" I study the beast more closely. It's easily twice the size of a horse with four legs and a long tail. It has two long feathered wings like an eagle. I can only see the underside of it as it flies overhead and up toward a high level of the castle. A piece of the outer wall has been broken open, and the beast flies up and into the hole, right into the castle. "Drixus is a beast?"

No. He rides one.

"Why does he need to ride a beast? Can't he fly like the rest of the Gryxen?"

No, he can't.

He doesn't explain further, and I don't ask.

The castle doors open again, and Fenmire and Wexton step outside. Wexton is dressed in his golden armor and carries his sword. He waves to me before taking off to start his patrol.

Fenmire, to my surprise, comes down the stairs and joins us. His eyes flick over Caliborne and I standing together and holding hands. "I suppose we have our answer about how you're meant to bind yourself to us. You've been mated, yes?"

"We have," I confirm.

Fenmire looks up at the sun. He closes his eyes and sighs, but it's not one of contentment like Levi's was. When he looks back at me, there's pain in his twinkling black eyes, and I realize what this means for him. In order to break the spell on him and his friends, he has to make another mating bond, the same thing that nearly destroyed him once. I suddenly understand why he's kept me at a distance since I arrived.

"I'm sorry," I say.

He doesn't say anything, he just turns and walks back up the steps toward the castle.

He'll be alright, Caliborne assures me.

"I don't want to hurt him."

You never could. Your heart is too pure.

I hope he's right.

*****

The next day is the full moon, and I wake up absolutely ecstatic.

Today is the day I get my best friend back.

"I need to tell you something," I say as Caliborne and I dress for the day. "You may not approve, but this is important to me."

Caliborne sits on the edge of his bed and waits for me to continue.

"I've told you about my best friend, Will, right?"

Caliborne nods.

"That day we went to the edge of The Deadwood to test if I could leave it, I found him on the other side trying to break in and find me. He has decided to join me here, and I promised to be waiting for him on our side of the arch when… when he jumps through after The Offering cart tonight."

Caliborne raises a brow.

"I know humans shouldn't be throwing themselves into The Deadwood," I rush to say before he can say no. "But Will's life in the village is… well, it's a lot like mine was, only he's been living the lie the others force him to, and it's slowly killing him from the inside. We were going to run away together, but then I got thrown in here, and now he's alone. I told him how I plan to destroy The Deadwood, and he trusts me to do it, so he wants to come here and be with me until I do."

Caliborne reaches for my hand, and I let him have it.

This person means a lot to you. You called for him during your fevered dreams.

"He means everything to me. Even more than my own family."

Are you involved? There's no judgment in the question, just genuine curiosity.

"No. Will likes men. Only men. That's why he's so miserable in the village."

I've never understood why your kind places such importance on sexuality.

"I take that to mean your kind doesn't?"

No. Our gods don't care who we choose to love. I find it hard to believe yours does.

"I've never understood it either. It's the same nonsense they used to spew at me when they tried convincing me I had to be a woman and nothing else."

If your friend wants to join us here, I have no qualms about it, though I'm confused why you're telling me this now.

"The Offering is tonight. Won't you be going after the cart like last time? I want to go with you so I can meet Will like I promised."

I have patrol tonight. Wexton will be retrieving the cart. You'll have to take that up with him.

I wrinkle my nose. "I'd hoped you'd be the first to meet Will, but I understand. Here's hoping Wexton doesn't make a bad first impression."

He'll try to.

I laugh because, of course, he's right.

War

And there went out another horse that was red:
and power was given to him that
sat thereon to take peace from the earth,
and that they should kill one another:
and there was given unto him a great sword.

-Revelation 6:4 KJV

Chapter 20

I meet Wexton at the front doors in the late afternoon when he comes in from patrol and Caliborne goes out. Caliborne leaves me with a deep kiss of apology that he won't be here tonight to chase Reilanna from my dreams.

"Be safe," I tell him before he disappears out into the dusk light.

It hurts to watch him leave, more so now than ever before. We stayed in bed all day today and even took meals in his room, so starved for each other's touch and company that we cuddled, talked, and made love up until the very last moment before he had to get ready and see to his duties. Watching him don his golden armor and take up his bow made me ache for him in private places all over again. Never before have I felt so lustful, and I refuse to let a single ounce of shame taint the experience. Caliborne is my mate, my partner in a far deeper way than a mere spouse.

I'll lust after his body all I like.

Wexton shuts the doors behind Caliborne and turns to me. "Mighty nice weather we're having," he says with a smirk I'm tempted to smack off his face.

"The start of many to come," I chime back.

"So mating bonds will break Reilanna's spell." He laughs. "Of course the witch would never think a human could care for us. She never did appreciate your kind."

"It doesn't bother you? The mating bonds part, not Reilanna."

"I already had a feeling this was the answer, but I kept it to myself since it was clear you and Caliborne were headed there anyway. If I was wrong, no harm done since it happened naturally between the two of you. And if I was right, well…" He winks at me.

I blush. "I might've gotten a power of my own from the bond."

"Might've?"

"I'm not sure if it's mine or something Caliborne can do now that we're mates."

"What is it?"

I beckon him over and hold out my hand.

He raises a brow but tucks his sword under his ravaged arm and gives me his good hand.

I hold it and simply wait.

What are they doing?

I smile. "Getting my answer."

Wexton rips his hand out of mine. "You heard that?"

"What's the matter? Afraid I'll hear all your naughty thoughts?"

"Yes! I quite like my depraved little mind and don't want to have to censor it."

"I can only hear it when we're touching. And even then, you don't have to censor it. I'm used to your filthy thoughts."

He laughs. "Oh, silly little human, you have no idea just how filthy my thoughts can get."

My blush deepens.

"I was just headed to the bath," he says, his voice low and deep. "Care to join me?"

"I thought you were getting The Offering cart."

"That won't be for several more hours. Why?"

"I'd like to go with you."

"It's still too cold out there for you to be walking through The Deadwood, and I can't fly you securely with only one arm."

"But I have to go with you," I argue.

Wexton frowns. "Why? Planning to make a break for it?"

I roll my eyes. "Don't be stupid. I have a friend who plans to come through the arch with The Offering."

"Plans? Since when do the humans sent with The Offering *plan* to go?"

"This is different. Will is my best friend. He hates the village as much as I did, so he's coming here. Willingly."

"Does Caliborne know about this?"

"He does."

"Fenmire will have a fit."

"Then don't tell him."

"That's not exactly how we do things around here."

"I thought you weren't one for following the rules."

He narrows his eyes at me.

I stick my tongue out at him.

"Fine," he relents, then he grins. "But only if you take a bath with me first."

Since I've already bathed with him once, it's not that outlandish of a request, but it's different now. Knowing what we do about the mating bonds, I'm afraid to trust that his invitation is genuine. As much as it hurts my heart to think it, what if he's only asking because he knows that us becoming mates is part of breaking the spell? Would he have asked regardless? Part of me thinks so since he's been an infuriating flirt since day one, but still, I question.

"What's wrong?" he asks.

"I don't know your motivations for asking, and that makes me anxious."

His brow wrinkles in a rare frown. "My motivations? I ask because I like your company and because you are a beautiful human and a good friend. Nothing more. I won't force myself on you if that's—"

"No! I'd never think that, Wexton. It's just that I don't want any of you to feel forced to become my mate because of—"

He raises his hand. "Let me stop you there. You're forgetting an important detail: the mating bond only forms when both parties want it equally. It won't form if one of the partners is hesitant in the slightest. And notice I said 'want' not 'are willing'. There has to be a genuine desire to be tied to another's soul. It can't be faked or coerced in any way." He takes a step forward and touches my chin. "I asked you to join me because I genuinely like you, Evan. I want to see how far that can take us, if that's something you want too."

Please say yes.

I smile. "Well, since you asked so nicely."

Wexton is taken aback until he realizes we're touching. He smirks. *This time, I hope you don't hide your body under the water. What I wouldn't give to bury my face between those perky breasts and—*

"Wexton!" I chastise as I step back out of his reach.

He laughs. "I told you. And that was tame."

I touch my burning cheeks, willing them to cool.

"I wonder what gifts you'll get from me if we form a mating bond."

"You've yet to tell me what powers you possess."

"I don't have powers. I have strength. I'm stronger than three Gryxen combined."

"Really?"

"Remember I told you I punched that first beast in the eye so hard it burst? None of the others could do that with their bare hands. It's a good thing too that I'm so strong or else I probably wouldn't be much use with only one arm."

"Don't say that. You'd adapt, I'm sure."

He merely shrugs. "So, bath then?"

"Let me get some clothes, and I'll meet you down there."

"Make sure they're warm. It's a three-hour walk to the arch, and it's still quite chilly outside, especially at night."

I go back to my room and round up the warmest outfit I can piece together. I grab a pair of pants that are nearly skintight on me and another, thicker pair that are a few sizes too big to wear overtop the first. I layer two shirts the same way, but even that I fear isn't thick enough to keep my core and arms warm in the winter chill. My thickest wool socks and Will's boots will do just fine for my feet, however. I pop into the kitchen before heading downstairs and ask if any of them have a jacket I could borrow.

"You're not going out in this chill, are you?" Levi frets.

"I'm helping Wexton retrieve The Offering tonight."

"Oh, well in that case…" He procures a jacket from a back room and hands it over. "Be sure to bring it back. It's the one we use to haul in the supplies from the cart through the service entrance."

"I'll bring it right back after, I promise."

I take my underlayers downstairs to the pool room, where Wexton is already soaking, leaning against the side of the bath just like last time.

"It's about time," he says as I set my clothes down by the wall and my washbag by the edge of the pool. "I thought you'd stood me up."

"I keep my promises," I say.

He nods. "So do I."

I almost tell him to turn around so I can undress, but then I change my mind. He likes to say and do shocking things to get me riled up. Two can play that game. As he watches, I meet his flaming red eyes, slowly strip off my boots and socks, and set them aside. Next come my pants, which I fold neatly before laying them on top of the boots. When all that's left is my shirt, I unlace the front and peel it off over my head, arching my back as my breasts are uncovered to air that's not quite warm enough to keep my nipples from hardening into two sensitive, peaked little buds. I fold that article of clothing too, this time with shaking hands, before stepping down into the pool and wading to the side across from Wexton. I keep my chest above the water this time.

Wexton chews his lip so hard I fear for that little strip of flesh. He doesn't bother hiding it as his eyes rake across my chest, and I swear they burn a little brighter. He finally stops to stare at a spot high up on the left side of my chest, and I peer down at the mating mark over my heart. It has already healed quite a bit thanks to the salve Caliborne insists I put on it twice a day.

"I have to admit," Wexton says, his eyes still locked onto the bite on my chest, "I was a bit jealous of Caliborne after he brought you home."

"Why's that?"

"Because he got to be your savior in The Deadwood that day. Afterward, you clung to him like he was life itself, and I didn't blame you. He showed us what you looked like on that pond, all beaten and bleeding and scared out of your wits. Afterward, you huddled to his chest and protested whenever he left your side. I wanted to know how it felt to be needed like that."

My chest hurts. "Is there no one waiting for you back in Michastiforo?"

Wexton hangs his head. "No."

"Not even family?"

"No one."

"I'm sorry," I say softly.

"I'm not telling you this to make you feel sorry for me. It's just that, even before I suspected the mating bond would break the spell, I got the feeling that you and I could easily be something more than we are. I've never met someone who doesn't mind my constant chatter much less seeks me out just to talk. It's got me hoping that, someday, you might look at me the same way you look at Caliborne. Maybe someday, you might need me too."

Well, damn.

"I already need you, Wexton," I say. "You're the first person I come to with a question. I know I can ask you anything and you won't judge me. Tease me endlessly, perhaps, but never judge me."

He smiles. "You're right about that. Especially the teasing part."

I splash him.

Conversation takes a back seat for a bit while we grab our respective bars of soap and start scrubbing. I'm nearly washed when I look over to see him yanking his fingers through his hair with a vengeance, doing his best to wash and rinse with one hand. After about the third snapping of strands I hear, I can't take it anymore.

"Stop, please stop." I wade over and hold out my hand for his soap. "Give it here."

"Why?"

"I can't watch you destroy that lovely hair a moment longer. Give me the soap and sit down."

With a snort, he slaps the soap into my palm then sits in the water while I stand behind him. This puts me at the perfect height to lather up his hair and scrub each strand from scalp to tip. As carefully as I can, I run my fingers through it, detangling the worst of the snarls. The rest will have to wait until I can tackle it with a comb. When I tell him to rinse, he dunks himself under the water and comes up shaking like a dog, spraying me with suds. I work the soap out between dunks until it's all squeaky clean and rinsed.

"Much better," I say.

"I used to braid it many moons ago," he tells me. "But I stopped for obvious reasons." He lifts his short arm.

I run my fingers through his hair again as I ask, "Would you like me to braid it for you?"

He's silent for a moment then says, "I would love that, actually."

We climb from the pool, and he passes me a sheet, no longer distracted by my naked body, it seems, as he focuses on patting the water off his own instead. We dress in silence that thankfully doesn't feel awkward.

"You'll want to dry that hair thoroughly before we go," he warns as we head back upstairs. "Wet hair is a recipe for pneumonia for you humans."

"I know that all too well." When we reach the foyer, I ask, "Do you want to dry yours by my fire? I can braid it for you afterward."

His notorious smirk is back. "Are you inviting me to your room?"

"Yes," I say without shame.

That seems to sober him a bit, and he nods, waving down the corridor for me to lead the way.

Back in my room, I move my favorite chair—a gift from Percival—away from the fire, where I usually sit sewing, to clear a spot large enough for a demon. Wexton plops down in front of the fireplace, and I add two large logs and stoke it up to make it hot enough to dry us out. With our backs to the fire, we sit and talk.

He tells me how he is an only child to a mother so old they were shocked she chose to have a baby when she did. They were even more shocked when he turned out to be a Gryxen.

"Do you know who your father is?" I ask.

"I figured it out, but my mother never officially named him. He doesn't know I know."

"Is he of the rotten sort?"

"Not at all. My mother wanted a child and chose someone she knew would breed good genes, and that was the end of it. There was no romantic interest there, so there was nothing to tell me about."

"So he wasn't her mate?"

"No. My mother was like me: very untraditional."

"Did she have your smart mouth as well?" I tease.

He grins at that. "On the contrary. She barely spoke. She didn't mind listening though. I guess that's where I picked up the habit of talking so much. I filled the silence enough for both of us, and she never minded."

"Is she still alive?"

"No. I was the only reason she stuck around for as long as she did. When I was assigned to The Gate and started leaving the city for weeks at a time, she saw I was moving on with my life and decided to do the same."

"Is it sad to have family pass on? I don't know your customs."

"We miss them like any other, but to pass on in the temple is an honor since it means you've lived a full life. Immediate family is allowed to go into the chamber with you, so I was with her until her last breath. I cried, but not necessarily out of grief."

"How old was she?"

"She was just over twenty-two thousand years old when she went to the temple."

I shake my head. "I can't fathom living to such an age. The sheer number of things she must've lived through…"

Wexton reaches up and brushes his hand over his hair. "I think it's dry now."

I touch it myself and confirm it is indeed dry enough to work out the last of the tangles. "I only have one comb. I hope you don't mind sharing."

He side-eyes me. "You don't have bugs, do you?"

I make a show of itching my head. "You know, now that you mention it…"

Wexton laughs, and I retrieve my comb and brush as well as a spare tie from the vanity. He spins around and I tackle his hair, starting at the ends and working my way up each little snag until my comb runs freely through it from root to tip. Then I brush it. I brush it to one hundred strokes like I do mine, and once it's smooth and shiny, I pet it just like I do Caliborne's.

Wexton's hair is finer and silky to the touch. I've never seen this shade of red in someone's hair before. We have a ginger or two in our village, but this is a deeper and more vibrant red. It shimmers in the light of the fire, and for a moment, I'm mesmerized.

Wexton loudly clears his throat. "Are you going to braid it or play with it all night?"

"Would you mind very much if it was the latter?" I ask.

"Truthfully? No. That feels nice."

I bury my fingers in to the scalp and run them clear through to the ends. I do this three times, and Wexton hums.

"If you keep doing that," he mumbles, "you'll put me to sleep, and we won't be able to go get your friend."

During our talking and joking, I'd completely forgotten about The Offering. I split Wexton's hair into equal thirds and braid it with deft fingers. I tie it off neatly with a bow of black fabric and pat it flat against his back.

"All set."

Wexton hefts himself up on his feet and goes to the vanity to check my handiwork in the mirror. He nods with satisfaction, but when he pulls the braid over his shoulder and inspects the tie, he narrows his eyes at me.

"A bow?" he says dryly.

I smirk at him. "Beggars can't be choosers." I get to work on my own hair and soon have it braided and tucked up under a spare hat I borrowed from Percival. "How soon until we go?"

"We should get going now. I don't want to risk leaving your friend in the cold."

I nod and start layering. Once I've got everything tucked, buttoned, and laced, I follow Wexton out and down the corridor. We're nearly through the foyer when I hear a chuckle from the stairs behind us. Fenmire is standing on the bottom step, watching us.

"It's about time someone tamed that mane," he teases with a nod at Wexton.

"Are you offering to help next time?" Wexton asks.

"What for? Looks like you've got your own personal stylist now."

"Jealous, Fenmire?" I ask. "I can check my schedule and pencil you in next."

Instead of rising to the taunt, Fenmire crosses his arms and levels me with an even stare. "Seems like you've selected your next conquest."

"Don't be like that, Fenmire," Wexton implores. "You know it's not like that."

"Isn't it?" Fenmire barks. "I love that you've all decided how this will end. Do you honestly think Reilanna would allow us all a happily ever after? Even you, Wexton, aren't that naïve."

"I believe that, when the time comes, we'll deal with whatever she throws at us like we always do."

Fenmire scoffs with a shake of his head.

"What else would you have us do?" I ask him. "Not try at all?"

"I would spend my time trying to find other ways for you to counteract her spell, not play right into her hands like you've been doing. This is what she wants, and it's unwise to continue to play her games by her rules."

I'm intrigued by this thought. "Do you have ideas for how I can try to counteract her spell?"

"A few. Come see me if you'd like to hear them. You know where I'll be." He turns and heads back upstairs.

Wexton ushers me toward the door. "Don't listen to him. We can handle Reilanna."

"Perhaps he's right, though," I insist. "Maybe I *should* be trying to find other ways to fight her. I can leave The Deadwood, which goes against the rules of her spell. There must be more that I can do."

"Have you considered how much she would love the opportunity to get rid of you entirely? You threaten to unlock the bonds she's placed on us. If we go playing with your safety, I doubt she would hesitate to hurt you in any way she could to keep you from freeing us. Perhaps *that* would be playing right into her hands."

I *hadn't* considered it, but it makes sense. I chew my lip fretfully, unsure who's right.

Wexton pulls the door open, and a rush of winter chill hits me even without the whipping winds from before. I huddle deeper in my borrowed jacket.

Wexton nods out into the darkness. "Let's go get your friend."

Chapter 21

The walk to the arch is uneventful, though we do have to stop a couple of times for me to warm my icy hands against Wexton's chest. The rest of the time, I keep them pulled up into my too-long sleeves. I wish I'd asked Will to bring me a pair of gloves and vow to make that the very next thing I stitch for myself. I hope Will thinks to dress warmly since we didn't bring any extra clothing with us. I'm saved from fretting too hard about such things, however, by Wexton and I's constant conversation.

"Did you and the others know each other before you were assigned to guard The Gate?" I ask.

"I knew Caliborne," Wexton says. "As I said before, he was a well-known Gryxen in Michastiforo. He taught at the training fields until The Gate popped up outside the city. He was selected by the temple priestesses to form the team that would guard the new Gate, and he chose me along with the others to be part of it." He laughs. "It caused a bit of a stir, actually. Many thought I was too young, but Caliborne vouched for me, so the assignment stuck."

"Is Caliborne your leader then?"

"Not really. We're a team, like I said. We make decisions by popular vote, but his opinion has always carried more weight because of his experience over the rest of us."

"What are the training fields?"

"Where young Gryxen go once we've matured so we can learn how to fight."

"Was Caliborne your instructor there too?"

Wexton smiles. "Yes. I confess I was a bit of a teacher's pet back then. We all held high respect for him and looked up to him as a mentor, but I knew the history of all his previous battles, where he'd been assigned throughout his life, and the commendations he'd received from various temples throughout our world. All of it."

"Why?"

"Our mothers were friends, so I'd heard of a few of his achievements as a child. The more I learned, the more I idolized him, so I learned all I could. When he came back to Michastiforo where he was born, the whole city was in a tizzy for a month before his arrival. It was like welcoming home our greatest hero. I was honored and a bit awestruck when I was assigned to his unit for training shortly after. He always showed a fondness for me too, I thought. But perhaps that was just delusions of grandeur. I was quite young at the time."

"Why did Caliborne come back to Michastiforo?"

"His parents had a second child. He came back to be in her life as she grew up."

"I saw her in a memory. The last one he has of her."

Wexton nods sadly. "Losing his sister hit Caliborne hard. He doted on her. She was about to have her fifteen-hundredth-year celebration. It's an important milestone for a Gruxa, especially for the females. It's considered the halfway point of adolescence. There's usually a grand party with dancing, drinking, and gambling; a little taste of adulthood, you could call it. Reilanna trapped us here a mere two days before her celebration. Caliborne spent that entire day by The Gate to be as close to her as he could possibly be."

That makes me want to cry for my mate. "What was her name?"

"Cecinora. We called her CeCe."

"You've met her?"

"Many times. She was stubborn and spoiled endlessly by her parents and her brother, but she was also smart and funny and had Caliborne's good heart. Our entire team watched her grow up. She was like a sister to all of us, but I was the closest to her besides Caliborne. I was to attend her celebration as well. I received invitations to a lot of their family events, more so than the rest of our team, probably because they had families of their own and I had no one. Caliborne's family became almost a second one to me after my mother passed."

"I'm glad you had them. I hope you'll have them back again someday."

He smiles down at me. "Me too."

We round one last bend, and I see the arch ahead.

"Looks like we beat The Offering," Wexton says, then he glances up at the full moon. "It should be any time now. This ought to be interesting. Usually, the humans can't see far enough into The Deadwood to see us waiting for the cart. It makes me want to wait around the bend until they leave, but your friend will be expecting you just inside the arch, and there's no way I'm leaving you up here by yourself."

As he's talking, I reach down in the lane and form a snowball with my sleeve-gloved hands. He's still rambling when I straighten and lob it at him. It smacks him on the side of the head, and he freezes mid-sentence. He turns, oh so slowly, in my direction and grins malevolently.

"This means war," he says, and he reaches down to form his own snowball with his one good hand by scooping up snow and packing it against his thigh.

I yelp and take off running down the lane. I vaguely remember the hole where I ducked into the brush away from Caliborne, and I dive into it just as Wexton throws his first shot. He misses me, and I quickly reach out into the lane and form my second projectile. When I lean out to throw it, he's already one step ahead of me and nails me in the chest with a snowball so hard it knocks the wind out of me.

"Take it easy, muscles," I wheeze.

"Learn how to dodge, short stuff," he calls back before he throws another.

I dive into the snow, and the snowball flies over me. I get up on my knees and take my second shot, but he blocks it with one of his massive wings.

"Cheater!" I yell, and he laughs from behind his shield. As soon as he lowers it, I throw another and this time hit my mark, smacking him right in the face.

"Ow!" he yells, and he clutches his eye.

I'm immediately filled with regret. "Are you alright?" I get to my feet and approach him. As soon as I'm close enough, he swipes a wing through the loose snow in the lane and hits me with a wave of white.

I stand there sputtering, covered head to toe in cold powder as he laughs.

"Gotcha!" he barks between fits of laughter as I shake the snow from my clothes.

"You're an absolute heathen!" I cry.

"You started it with a cheap shot. I ended it with one. We're even."

He kneels on one knee and pats the snow from my back. I return the favor by brushing it off his hair and shoulders. Our faces are just inches apart, and I freeze with my hand on his shoulder as our eyes lock.

I want to kiss them. Would that be appropriate? I should ask first. Or would that ruin the moment? Their cheeks are flushed. Is that from me, the cold, or the fight? How does Caliborne do this? I should ask him. That'll be nice and awkward.

I laugh.

"What's so funny?" he asks.

"Your mind is about as quiet as your mouth."

He looks at my hand still touching his shoulder, and for once, he looks bashful. "Sorry."

"I'm not," I say before I crush my lips to his.

Wexton's arm goes around me and tightens, pulling me closer, and I put an arm around his neck.

They're so small. I don't want to hurt them.

Wexton slides down to both knees in the snow and relaxes his arm around me.

I break our kiss. "Do you want me to stop?"

Oh, please don't do that.

I smile and bump my nose against his. "Yes, no, all of the above, and very carefully."

"What?" he asks, slightly breathless.

"The answers to your questions."

I hear him work it all out in his mind, and he smirks at me. "Wiseass."

"Look who's talking."

He chuckles and kisses me again, softer this time as he moves across my lips with tiny pecks as if exploring them. When I part my lips, he surprises me by pulling away.

"What is it?" I ask.

"Are you sure about this? I don't want you to feel like… like this is just some obligation on your part or mine."

I put my hand on the back of his head and pull him closer so that our faces are nearly nose to nose. My blood is already running hot from wanting Caliborne back at the castle, and Wexton's kisses have done nothing but fan the flames. I'm a bit breathless as I say, "You've been flirting mercilessly with that scandalous mouth for weeks. Are you going to give me a taste of it or not?"

Those red eyes smolder at me as an evil little grin spreads across his face. "As you wish, darling."

When we come together this time, his tongue thrusts into my mouth, and it laps across mine with a fervor far more intense than any of Caliborne's kisses. I'm momentarily stunned as he crushes me to his chest and ravages my mouth, the pure passion of it sending a jolt of desire straight to my groin.

What I wouldn't give to push them down in the snow, take their pants to their knees, and slide my tongue into that tight, wet—

I moan.

"Seerraf above, Evan," Wexton murmurs. "The things I'd like to do to you."

"I'm open to trying a few, but maybe not in the snow."

He chuckles against my lips before claiming them again. This time, the kiss is short-lived as a familiar creaking sound soon interrupts us. We look toward the arch where the vines are slowly parting. Wexton gets to his feet just before the first of the torches come into view. I take a step forward, eager to see if Will is among them, but Wexton puts his hand on my shoulder, holding me back.

Don't get any closer. I don't trust them.

I nod and remain where I am.

The last of the vines part, and a familiar face stares through the arch, only it's not the one I came here for. Elias stands just outside The Deadwood's border, his face illuminated by the torch he carries. He looks momentarily confused, no doubt by the lack of whipping winds and snow, but then his eyes find me, and his lip curls. It's a brief emotion since his eyes soon move on to the Gryxen at my side, and they widen as he takes a fearful step back.

"Demon!" Elias cries. "Push the cart through! Quickly, before it takes its vengeance out on us!"

I almost laugh as they trip over themselves to get the cart through the arch as fast as they can, but my enjoyment in their panic quickly gives way to panic of my own as the vines slowly start to recapture the arch, and I still don't see Will. Despite Wexton's request that I stay back, I run forward.

"Will?" I call. "Will!"

He doesn't appear, and the vines cover the arch and groan as they slide into their final positions.

I reach the cart and peer inside, thinking perhaps he hid himself away amongst The Offering, but I find nothing but crates. I turn again to the arch and take a step toward it, meaning to pass through and check if he was too late and got stuck on the other side, but again, Wexton's hand on my shoulder stops me.

"Wait a few moments for them to leave," he advises.

I wait on eager feet until Wexton decides enough time has passed, then I stick my head through the arch while holding on to his hand in case Elias is waiting on the other side. I see no one in the dark.

"Will?" I whisper. I hear no reply, so I call his name louder.

Silence.

I back out of the arch.

"Anything?" Wexton asks.

"I don't understand," I fret. "Will wouldn't leave me waiting with no word. Something must be wrong."

"Does he contribute to The Offering?"

"His family does. His father owns the general store."

"Perhaps he left you a message. Which crate comes from his father?"

Together, we move the crates around until we find the one filled with odds and ends from the general store. Wexton easily rips the top off, and I move aside candles, cloth, and coffee, looking for any clues as to what happened to my best friend. In the bottom of the crate, wrapped in a square of green fabric I recognize from one of Will's old shirts, I find a glass jar. It's full of my favorite peppermint candies, and there's a paper tucked along the edge. I quickly open the jar and fish it out.

Dearest Evangeline:

I'm sorry, but I couldn't come tonight. It's not that I've changed my mind; far from it. Remember I told you Elias has been watching me and Jacob ever since you left? Elias has apparently decided Jacob will be the next one he torments. Elias has gotten it in his head that Jacob must marry Elias' oldest sister. Pastor Elias has been talking to Jacob's father, who's keen on the idea as well.

Jacob is stalling them as much as he can, but he's miserable. I know that, if I were to leave him now, he would succumb to the pressure and marry the girl. You and I both know what kind of life he would have after that.

I hope you don't mind, but I told him about seeing you outside The Deadwood that day. I told him what you said about The Deadwood being so different from what we've been taught. I left out the part about you banishing it for good; I don't think he'd believe me anyway.

The point is, I almost have Jacob convinced to come with me, but I need more time. I'm hopeful that, by the next full moon, I can make him realize coming with me into The Deadwood is better than a life of misery here under Elias' thumb. If I fail, I will come alone with the next Offering, I promise.

Consider the peppermint candies my apology for making you wait another month. The whole jar cost me a month's wages from working at the store, so I figured it was fitting.

Stay safe, and I'll see you soon.

With love,
Will

"He's alright," I say with relief. "He plans to come with the next Offering instead."

"What kept him this time?"

"A boy," I say with a grin.

Wexton chuckles. "That'll do it."

He reaches up to help me off the cart, and once I'm on the ground, I pop a candy in my mouth, humming as it starts to melt on my tongue. I offer one to Wexton, who sniffs it curiously before sucking it out of my fingers in a way that makes me clench my thighs together.

He's smirking at me, but then as soon as the flavor of the candy hits him, his nose flares and his top lip curls before he spits it promptly out on the ground. I laugh as he dances a bit in place and scoops a handful of snow into his mouth to rinse it out.

"That's absolutely vile!" he cries.

"Good," I say as I screw on the top. "I won't have to worry about you stealing them then."

He huffs. "I won't be kissing you either with that flavor on your tongue."

I raise a brow at the threat. "Something tells me you don't have that kind of restraint."

He narrows his eyes at me.

I'm about to stick my tongue out at him when the ground begins to shake.

There are no raining rocks to protect me from this time, but Wexton still pulls me close as the next of Reilanna's beasts roars in the distance.

"Wexton!" I cry as we ride out the storm. "You don't have a weapon. How will you help Caliborne fight it?"

"Fenmire will bring me my sword, don't fret. This isn't the first time this has happened." The shaking soon stops, and Wexton directs me toward the cart. "Have a seat in the back. I'll go help the others and come right back for you afterward. Don't wander and—"

Just as I'm stepping up on the back of the cart, the ground begins to shake again. I nearly lose my balance as the cart rolls, but Wexton loops his arm around me and yanks me off, setting me back on the ground as a fresh roar cuts through the night. This quake lasts no longer than the first, but once it's over, we stand there dumbfounded for a moment, blinking at each other in shock.

"There are two," I utter in horror. "Has there ever been two before?"

Wexton straightens and looks in the direction of the castle. "No," he says, and the seriousness of his voice that's usually so light and full of laughter turns my blood to ice.

"Wexton?" I say, my voice wavering.

He touches my arm. "Everything is fine. We can handle this."

They know Evan and I came for The Offering, Wexton thinks to himself. *They'll know where to find me. Caliborne wouldn't want me to leave Evan. They'll divide between the beasts and—*

From nearby, so near I clutch Wexton's arm with a yelp of terror, one of the beasts screams into the night. I can hear it pounding through The Deadwood, the snapping of vines and the stomping of feet growing louder every second.

"Wexton, it's too close! It'll get out! The village—"

"It's not headed for the village," Wexton replies, and he moves me behind him with his arm.

"What…?" The question dies in my throat when I hear the beast's panting breath as it tears through The Deadwood, heading straight for us.

Straight for me.

"Have you considered how much she would love the opportunity to get rid of you entirely?"

Reilanna.

She's sent one of her beasts after me, and it's just me and Wexton here to fight it.

"You don't have a weapon," I say again, hating how small my voice sounds as I cower behind him.

Wexton looks down at me, and it relieves me a bit to see that he's smiling.

"I *am* a weapon," he says before there's an explosion of dead foliage down the lane as the beast smashes through the last of The Deadwood separating it from us.

Chapter 22

The beast lands in the snow, rights itself on its feet, snaps its head around to me and Wexton, and screeches in victory at having found its prey. Wexton keeps me behind him, holding tight to my arm and tugging me this way and that as he adjusts his stance in response to the beast's tiniest twitches. From around his back, I get short glimpses of the creature.

It's easily as tall as Wexton with a long, furry body and an extra long neck that moves in a figure S, like a snake. Its face is narrow and ends at a snout that gapes open with no less than four rows of pointed teeth. It snaps them together as it studies us, its yellow eyes moving independently from each other as it watches Wexton's every move. It has four long legs that end with massive claws tipped with talons similar to a Gryxen's. It stomps one foot impatiently and screams again.

Wexton pins back his ears and roars.

I clutch Wexton's arm fearfully.

"Let me go," he orders, his voice low but deathly serious.

I quickly oblige, and he lets go of me too a heartbeat before the creature leaps at us.

Wexton launches himself at the beast, the force of his jump knocking me on my backside. There's a sickening smack of flesh colliding with flesh as they slam together, and the force sends the beast tumbling back down the lane while Wexton regains his footing between us. As soon as the beast is back up on its own feet, it pounces again.

This time, Wexton punches it in the side of the head, and the beast staggers, knocked dizzy enough for Wexton to reach down and yank up one of its legs, knocking it onto its side. He places a foot on the creature's head, his talons piercing through fur and flesh, and yanks up on the captured leg, tearing the tendons in the beast's shoulder. It howls in pain and scrambles to get away, but it's caught under the Gryxen's massive foot as he goes on trying to tear its leg off.

The beast curves its body around and brings up its back leg to swipe at Wexton with those deadly talons. Wexton leans away from it, trying to avoid being clawed while also still trying to rip the beast to pieces. The shoulder finally gives with a loud snap, but the sudden slack makes Wexton lose his balance. The beast senses an opportunity and jerks up off the ground, throwing Wexton off, who falls back against a nearby tree.

The beast scrambles up to its feet, though only three of them are useful now. Rather than try to back away and regroup, the creature immediately lunges at Wexton, mouth gaping and aimed for his head. Wexton grabs it by the throat, holding it back as its teeth snap in front of his face. He tries to throw the beast back down the alley, but it hooks one of its back feet into his leg, digging its claws in to anchor itself to him. The weight of the creature topples Wexton onto his back in the snow, and the beast comes down on top of him.

Wexton screams in rage as he holds the creature back by the throat, but its mouth is slowly inching closer to his face. Wexton grimaces as he struggles to keep the creature at bay, and his arm begins to shake under the strain. It's only a matter of time before his strength gives out on him entirely.

"Hey, you!" I scream, but the creature ignores me. I fling the jar of sweets that's still in my hand, and it whacks the beast on the shoulder.

It snaps its head around at me with a snarl.

It must have remembered it's me it wants after all because it immediately lets go of Wexton and lurches toward me. Wexton rolls and grabs a back leg this time, holding it back as it claws at the snow and snarls, its crazed yellow eyes locked on me.

"I can't hold it!" Wexton screams, his whole body sliding in the snow as the beast slowly tugs him up the lane toward me.

The beast kicks out with its other back leg, hitting Wexton in the chest, who loses his grip, and that mouth full of razor-sharp teeth lunges for me.

"Evan!"

I scream.

A streak of gold comes crashing down on top of the beast with a deafening roar, crushing it into the snow. Caliborne stands up on the beast's back, bow up and arrow nocked. With lightning speed, he fires three arrows into the creature, and when it throws its head up to attack this new enemy, Caliborne tosses his bow, grabs the beast by the fur at the top of its head, draws a small dagger from his sleeve, and slits its throat.

Black blood gushes across the bright white snow, and the beast thrashes as its life slowly drains away with each pump of its heart. Only once it stills does Caliborne throw the head to the ground and climb off, replacing his knife in its hidden sheath as he marches my way.

I barely have time to hold my arms out before he scoops me up in his.

Please don't be hurt. Please.

"I'm alright," I say, hugging him tight around the neck. "Wexton protected me."

If anything had happened to you…

"Are they alright?" Wexton asks, and Caliborne gives him a nod. Wexton is bleeding down his leg profusely, and he limps as he walks around the carcass toward us.

"Put me down," I say with a gentle pat on Caliborne's arm. He hesitates at first but then relents and sets me back down in the snow. I go to Wexton and hug him around the middle. "Thank you. That thing would have eaten me alive!"

"Or worse," he says, slightly breathless. "You were a lifesaver yourself with that distraction. I guess this means we'll have to arm ourselves when we come for The Offering from now on. We'll all need to sit down and figure out how Reilanna managed to… how she… how…"

He starts to sway like Will did the first time we broke into his daddy's whiskey.

"Wexton?" I say in alarm as he runs his hand down his face, which glistens with sweat in the moonlight. A second later, he sinks down to one knee in the snow. "Caliborne! What's happening?"

Caliborne is beside me in an instant, kneeling in the snow with his hand on Wexton's shoulder to steady him.

Wexton waves a hand toward the carcass of the beast. "Check it," he mutters.

Caliborne goes to the body of the creature and inspects first its teeth then one of its claws. He takes his knife out again and cuts one of the long, curved talons off, holding it up to inspect in the moonlight. He touches the end to his tongue then promptly spits and tucks the talon in his pocket. When he comes back, he urges Wexton to sit in the snow and cuts his pant leg open over the wound left by the beast's claws. I gasp at the sight of it.

Where Gryxen skin is usually a dark blue color, I can tell even in the low light from the moon that deep black streaks have surrounded the punctures in Wexton's legs. Blood leaks from him in black rivers, and the smell… I have to plug my nose and breathe through my mouth at the smell coming from it.

"Damn witch sent a spitter," Wexton hisses between gritted teeth. He looks up at Caliborne. "Go get Fenmire. I'll be damned if I'm losing a leg too."

Caliborne nods but then looks at me.

"I'll stay with him," I say. "Hurry."

He doesn't need to be told twice.

Caliborne takes off, the force blasting me and Wexton with snow.

"Stay away from that blood," Wexton says, nodding toward the pool under the beast's body. "It's probably fine, but don't take any chances."

"Has this happened before?" I ask.

"Not since The Gate was sealed. Spitters can't wield spells, but they're natural alchemists, so they require more power to transport than the average beast." He winces with a groan. "They produce toxins that poison their prey."

I sit in the snow next to him. "How can Fenmire help?"

He grins at me, though it's forced. "This is Fenmire's specialty."

"Are you going to be alright?" I ask softly.

"Sure," he says. He sounds tired. "I'm just gonna..." He flops onto his back. "Just gonna lay here... for a minute."

I touch Wexton's arm.

Seerraf above, don't take the leg too. Kill me first. Don't let me wake up with one leg and one arm. I'd rather die.

I don't say anything as Wexton continues to pray, and I send up a prayer of my own when his thoughts eventually go silent. I continue to sit beside him in the snow, holding his hand and watching his breathing as I try not to fall apart.

I've never been so happy to see Fenmire when he lands in the snow beside me.

"Can you help him?" I ask as he kneels next to Wexton's blackening leg.

Caliborne lands near Wexton's head and opens one of Wexton's eyes to peer inside it.

Fenmire doesn't answer me. "How long was the spitter latched onto him?"

"I'm not sure. It all happened so fast, but... it had him pinned to the ground for a time, and its claws were in him until I drew it away."

Caliborne hands Fenmire the talon he took from the beast's corpse, and Fenmire touches it to his tongue as well. He makes a disgusted face, spits in the snow, and tosses the talon away with a huff.

Fenmire sets his shield and mace aside and hovers his hands over the wound on Wexton's leg, palms down toward the oozing punctures. A stream of green liquid starts trickling out along with the blood. It hisses when it hits the snow, where it pools into a green blob. Once every last drop is sucked from the wound, Fenmire scoops it up into a ball of snow and tosses it over his shoulder.

Fenmire looks gravely up at Caliborne. "It was a lot."

"Will he be alright?" I ask.

"I don't know. I can take out the poison, but I can't heal the damage it's already done." He touches Wexton's neck. "His pulse is strong. I don't think it reached his heart." He inspects the leg wounds more closely. "I don't like the look of these though. If it gets infected, he could lose the leg."

"I think that might break him," I say, remembering Wexton's prayers before he fell unconscious.

Caliborne taps Fenmire on the shoulder then points at the carcass.

"It's not edible," Fenmire says. "We should burn it. I'll need to inspect the other one, but we need to get Wexton home first. The faster the better." For some reason, he gives me a pointed look when he says this.

"What?" I ask.

"We need to fly him," Fenmire says. "He can't wait the time it would take to walk, and I can't carry him alone."

"So have Caliborne help you. I can wait here."

Caliborne touches my cheek.

I don't like leaving you here. What if The Gate opens again?

"We can't risk Wexton's life on a 'what if'. Take him home and come back for me."

Caliborne shakes his head.

"Yes," I insist. "There's no time to argue this, Caliborne. Please do this, for me if not for him."

Caliborne's shoulders sink, but he nods.

I pull him down into a quick kiss then say, "Go. Quickly."

They gather Wexton up from the snow and balance him between them, then they take off in unison. I watch their shadows fly across the moon as they head for the castle, and once they're out of sight, I hug myself as my bravado fades and I realize I'm alone in The Deadwood for the first time since I was thrown here against my will. Determined not to let it unhinge me, I go searching for my jar of sweets and find it, thankfully still whole and free of poisoned blood.

I climb up into the back of The Offering cart and pop the top off my sweets, huddling into my oversize jacket as I suck on peppermint candies and read Will's letter again.

As much as I wish for my best friend to be happy, I doubt very much he'll be able to convince Jacob to come with him into The Deadwood. Jacob won't even agree to go to the city. Why would he agree to come to the one place we've all been taught to fear since birth? It will all come down to how much Jacob trusts Will. Even I would've had a hard time believing him if he'd told me the truth about The Deadwood before I saw it for myself. I hope Will succeeds. He deserves to be happy, and he'll be anything but if he's forced to leave Jacob behind.

I'm on my third piece of candy when I hear a low whomping sound in the brush to my right as something lands in The Deadwood not too far from me. Caliborne wouldn't leave me here—no matter how much I insisted—if the other beast wasn't already dead, right? No, of course not. Then why do I hear snapping branches and crunching footsteps? I can even hear it breathing. I huddle behind the crates and try to be as still and quiet as possible. The noises stop, and I think perhaps whatever it is has moved on, so I chance a quick glance over the tops of the crates.

I can't see much, only a shadow, but there's definitely something staring at me through the dead vines and brambles. I hear the rustle of a branch and the stomp of a foot, then I see a single grey eye peer out at me.

It's glowing.

I sit up straighter.

"Hello?" I call.

I don't get an answer, but that grey eye continues to study me, and I know it knows I see it.

"Dr…Drixus? Is that you?"

The eye blinks in surprise, and it starts to move away, deeper into The Deadwood.

"No, wait!" I hop out of the cart. "Drixus, don't go!"

The eye disappears, and I know better than to try and follow him through The Deadwood's twisted underbrush. A moment later, I hear a warbling cry and the woosh of massive wings taking flight. The same creature I saw outside the castle flies over me and disappears in the distance. I'm still staring after it when Caliborne lands beside me, making me jump and swear.

"That was Drixus, wasn't it," I ask, pointing off in the direction he flew.

Caliborne nods.

"Why was he here?"

Caliborne takes my hand. *He must've known you were alone and came to watch over you. Or perhaps simply to see you with his own eye.*

"I wish he wouldn't have run away. I would've introduced myself."

He would rather see and not be seen. It's progress, though, that he cared enough to come here.

"If you say so. How's Wexton?"

I don't know. I helped Fenmire put him in his room then immediately left again to retrieve you.

"Let's go then." I stick my jar and letter into my jacket pocket.

What was that?

"A gift from Will."

Why didn't he come tonight?

"He's coming next month instead. That turned out to be a good thing since that beast attacked us. And now you can fly us home since it's just me."

Are you sure? It'll be a cold flight.

"I'd rather be cold for a few minutes than worry incessantly for the next few hours."

Caliborne scoops me up into his arms. *Tuck in close to me.*

I curl myself toward his chest and tuck my hands into my sleeves.

He wasn't kidding; it's a freezing flight. I manage to keep my face and hands warm against Caliborne's hot chest, which makes it bearable, but I'm more than a little glad when we land outside the castle doors again.

I head straight for Wexton's room.

Chapter 23

Caliborne shadows me as I make my way to Wexton's bedroom, the room right next to mine. I've never been in here, so I'm a little shy about stepping into his space uninvited, but, considering the circumstances, I don't think he'll mind.

When I first walk in, my eyes are immediately drawn to the walls where no less than a dozen pieces of art are hung. There are drawings of Michastiforo, of different Gruxa, one of the temple, and even one of all seven Gryxen standing together in a line. I am fascinated by the beauty around me, but I tear my eyes away to focus on the bed where Wexton is lying—still unconscious—with his ravaged leg stuck out of the blankets as Fenmire tends to his wounds.

I go to the bed, keeping a healthy distance from Fenmire as I don't wish to interrupt him. Wexton's breathing is ragged, and his face glistens with even more sweat now than before. I look at Fenmire with so many questions on my tongue, but I'm hesitant to ask, both because I don't want to distract him and because I'm not sure I'll like the answers.

As it turns out, I don't have to say anything as Fenmire starts talking, whether to me or to Caliborne, I'm not sure.

"The toxin spread to his organs before I could remove it. Several of them are failing now as a result. I'm doing all I can for the leg, but if his body doesn't have the strength to heal it, no amount of intervention from me will keep it from becoming infected." He looks sideways at me, and whatever look I have on my face makes him say, "As long as his heart doesn't give out, there's still hope. A Gryxen's organs can heal from a lot, but if his heart fails, there's nothing else we can do for him but help him pass peacefully."

I don't trust my voice enough to respond, so I look at Wexton, but seeing my usually carefree and laughing friend look so broken makes me want to cry. I swallow it back. I'm thankful when Fenmire fills the silence again.

"Reilanna sent that spitter after Evan," he says with a glance over his shoulder at Caliborne. "She knew where they were going to be tonight. The spitter didn't head straight for the village like the rest, but right for Evan at the arch. It was sent here for a purpose: to kill the one who would break this spell. If that beast had so much as scratched them, this toxin would've killed them in minutes. There would've been nothing I could do."

He looks at me. "You think you know why I keep you at arm's length, but you don't know the half of it. I know how Reilanna's twisted mind works. The closer you get to us, the closer you get to danger. You are *human*, Evan. You won't last in this war. By becoming Caliborne's mate, you've ended the blizzard outside, sure, but it seems you've also forced The Gate open enough for Reilanna to send not only two beasts through at once but a spitter, which we haven't had to deal with in over two thousand years.

"What happens when The Gate opens enough that we can no longer protect you from the horrors she pours through it? What will any of us gain if she kills you or us before the spell is broken?"

I don't know what to say, so I say nothing at all.

Caliborne steps forward and puts his hand on Fenmire's shoulder, and for once, Fenmire doesn't brush it away. After a moment, Fenmire closes his eyes with a sigh.

"I know," he says quietly. "I'm trying, alright? It's not easy, and I'm still not sure that's what I want."

Another silent moment passes, and Fenmire nods.

"I can do that," he says. "I offer no guarantees, though."

Caliborne lets him go and touches my cheek instead. *I'm going back for the cart and to help Drixus burn the carcass.*

"I'll be here," I say miserably.

Don't take his words to heart. Some wounds are more than skin deep. Give him time.

I only nod.

Once Caliborne leaves, an awkward silence falls in the room that's broken only by Wexton's wheezy breathing. To escape that horrible sound, I walk over to the nearest wall and examine the picture hanging there, the one of all seven Gryxen together. There's enough color in the drawing for me to pick six of them out—three of them being faces I know all too well and three others I recognize from the drawings in Fenmire's library—which leaves the seventh member of the team, a grey-haired and grey-eyed one, as the only one I've yet to meet, though I saw one of those eyes staring at me through The Deadwood not an hour ago.

Drixus is about Fenmire's height and stands next to his brother, Horthos, with his arm over his sibling's shoulders. He's smiling as widely as Wexton, which surprises me. This image was obviously drawn from a moment before Reilanna broke him, and this person I see laughing beside his brother looks nothing like the image the others have painted in my head. The detail in the picture is just as startling as the ones upstairs, and the life in all their eyes makes me sad.

The Gryxen in this drawing don't know the horrors that await them.

"You made this, didn't you?" I ask.

"Yes," Fenmire says rather coolly. "Am I to take that to mean you've been snooping through my papers?"

"Not snooping. I was simply admiring your work and spotted the drawings. They're very good." I touch the sketch in front of me. "The way you capture each of their personalities is remarkable. Caliborne's stance and solemn expression. Wexton's crossed arms and cocky grin. You even captured yourself perfectly." I chuckle. "You look as if you just rolled your eyes at one of Wexton's jests."

I look again at Drixus. His stance is so relaxed, his face soft, his eyes warm, and his smile welcoming. So unlike his brother beside him, who looks like he just sucked on a lemon. Fenmire is drawn on Drixus' other side, though Fenmire has his back turned toward him.

I move on to the next drawing, and I recognize this face too. "This is Caliborne's sister."

Fenmire's tone lightens when he says, "Yes, that's CeCe. She and Wexton were close."

There is only one other drawing of a person, and this time, I don't recognize the face. It's a female Gruxa with long, wavy dark brown hair and eyes similar to Caliborne's, full of old wisdom. "Who's this?"

"Wexton's mother. Caliborne showed me what she looked like. Apparently, he knew her before Wexton was even born."

"Did Wexton ask you to draw these?"

"No. I like to draw, and I thought…" He sighs in exasperation. "I thought they'd make him happy, at least while we're stuck here."

"Don't worry, your secret is safe with me."

"What secret?"

"That you have a soft heart too under that gruff exterior."

He snorts at me.

I turn away from the drawings and face him. "I know you think I'm some succubus determined to collect you all like a bunch of freakish mate trophies or something, but—"

To my utter surprise, he laughs. "That paints quite a picture."

"I just want to help. However I can. I'm willing to try anything you can think of to see if there are other ways I can help you defeat Reilanna."

Fenmire nods thoughtfully. "Let's get him back on his feet"—he nods down at Wexton—"then you and I will discuss it."

I wander over and sit on the foot of Wexton's bed. "Be honest with me. What are his chances?"

Fenmire stares down at Wexton, and we both listen to him breathe for a moment before he looks gravely back up at me. "Fifty-fifty. And that's being generous."

"Is there anything I can do to help improve them?"

"It sounds like you already have. You drew the spitter off him. If it had pumped even a drop more toxin into his system, he'd be worse off than he is. You've got gumption. For a human."

"Thanks. I think."

"You're welcome. I guess."

*****

I sit with Fenmire at Wexton's bedside until Caliborne comes back. It's nearly dawn, and I'm exhausted, so both Gryxen insist I get some sleep. I'm so tired I don't have the strength to even think about lovemaking and end up falling asleep nearly the moment my head hits the pillow—or rather Caliborne's chest—in his bed. We sleep until early afternoon when Caliborne has to get up and relieve Drixus. Since Wexton is hurt and Fenmire is caring for him, that leaves just Drixus and Caliborne to take over patrols for the time being. It's going to be an exhausting time for everyone for a while, it seems, and that's made even more apparent when I find Fenmire half-asleep in a chair at Wexton's bedside.

"How is he?" I ask.

"No change," Fenmire mutters.

"Perhaps you should rest. I can watch over him and get you if anything happens."

"It's too precarious a time. If he wakes up, I'll relax. But right now, I'm all that's keeping infection from wreaking havoc on his already-overloaded system."

"How did you draw the poison out of him like that?"

"My powers. I can summon blight and disease. I can also control poisons and contain infection since I can differentiate between naturally-occurring substances from foreign ones in the body and isolate and remove those that don't belong while encouraging ones that do to continue to function under duress."

"So, you're a healer."

"I'm a killer who can manipulate my powers to help rather than hurt. I can keep people alive through some of the worst sicknesses and injuries, but their bodies have to do the healing themselves."

"Good thing you're on our side then," I joke.

Fenmire doesn't even smile. "I suppose so."

The seriousness with which he says it doesn't bother me, but the sadness in his eyes does. "Do you regret not siding with Reilanna?"

He raises a brow at me. "That's quite a candid question."

"I see no point in vagueness. I never have."

"I can respect that." Fenmire settles more comfortably in his chair. "Enslaving your people would've been wrong; it goes against everything we stand for as Gryxen. I don't regret standing against Reilanna. My regrets run far deeper than that and begin long before I ever heard her name. It just so happens she was the catalyst that made me regret my past."

"If you knew then what you know now, how it all would turn out, would you choose differently?"

"With Reilanna or before?"

"I meant with Reilanna, but let's say both."

He thinks about it for a moment then says, "No. This outcome isn't ideal, but who's to say another wouldn't be worse?"

"Better the devil you know than the devil you don't."

Fenmire cocks his head. "That's one I haven't heard yet. I like it."

I distract myself with tidying Wexton's space a bit, gathering pairs of dirty pants and various weapons from the floor, cleaning trash and dirty dishes from surfaces, just to have something to do so I don't bother Fenmire with constant chatter. After a time, he chuckles.

"He'll just mess it all up again in a day," he says.

"I need something to do with my hands."

"I thought you spent your free time sewing."

"It gets tedious after a while."

"This whole place is tedious."

"I asked you to teach me to fight. That would've been something different."

"I trained for thousands of years. I've no desire to do it again."

"Well, the offer still stands if you—"

"Will the two of you shut up, already?" Wexton turns his head with a groan. "You're making my head hurt."

"Wexton!" I exclaim.

Fenmire hops up from his chair. "How do you feel?"

"My head is throbbing," Wexton says with a grimace. "My leg burns like someone's stabbed me with a hot poker. I guess that means it's still there?"

"You've still got two legs," I say with a happy smile. "For now, at least."

"Evangeline," Fenmire says, "go to the kitchen and ask for fresh water, as much as you can carry, as well as a bowl of hot broth."

Wexton glares at him. "Ask them nicely, Fen."

Fenmire rolls his eyes. "Please," he says dryly.

I barely contain my smirk. "Sure." I pat Wexton on his good foot. "I'll be right back."

"I'll be here," Wexton says. "Something tells me he's not going to let me out of this bed anytime soon." He jerks his chin at Fenmire.

"You're right about that," Fenmire says sternly. "You're still not safe from complete system failure. Your liver and kidneys—"

"Spare me the details, would you? Just let me know when I can go back to swinging my sword."

I let myself out while they continue to bicker, and the fact that my friend is well enough to run his smart mouth again makes me smile clear to the kitchen.

"I hope that look means Wexton is on the mend," Levi comments when I walk in.

"He's awake, so that's a good sign, I think. Fenmire sent me for water and hot broth."

"If it's for Wexton, the broth will take a bit. Have a seat." He waves me toward the low stone beside one of the large furnaces.

I sit as he pours a jar of black liquid into a pot. While that heats over one of the fires, he fetches a dripping pitcher of water and the largest bowl I've ever seen, which is gold like the Gryxens' plates. Once the 'broth' is steaming, he pours it into the bowl and sets it on the counter.

"All set," he says. "Mind you don't spill any of that on your skin. It causes a chemical burn. Not fun."

I'm extra cautious as I walk the bowl back down the hall, but when I head back into Wexton's room, I walk into utter chaos.

Fenmire is kneeling up on the mattress with Wexton on his side as he jerks so violently the whole bed shakes.

"What's happened?" I ask in a panic as I put the water and broth down on a dresser I only just cleaned off.

Fenmire doesn't answer me; he just starts barking orders. "Come around the bed. Quickly! Hand me that pillow. Pull that blanket off his legs. No, don't try to hold him down, you'll only hurt him. We have to let it run its course."

"What is it?"

"A seizure."

I've heard about them, but I'm not prepared for how terrifying it is. Wexton looks possessed with his eyes rolled back in his head so far I can barely see their red light anymore. His talons rip at the bedding as his whole body bucks and shakes, and all I can do is watch as Fenmire keeps his head from slamming into the headboard.

"Is he in pain?" I ask.

"No. He likely doesn't feel anything."

Eventually, it fades until Wexton finally stills on the bed with his eyes closed, unconscious once more. Fenmire puts his hands out over Wexton's body, running his palms over his head, torso, and injured leg.

"Is he alright?" I ask.

"I think so. His body has been through a lot. He's dehydrated and needs nutrients, but I don't sense any further damage."

It's only a few minutes before Wexton's eyes flutter open again, and without asking if it's alright, I crawl up onto the bed and sit beside him. Wexton studies me, grunts, then flops his arm over my lap, pulling me closer until his face is nestled into my side. I run my fingers through his hair, tucking flyaways back into his braid.

"You scared us there," I tell him softly. "You have to stop being so dramatic, or I'll end up feeling sorry for you."

That earns me a snort from both Gryxen.

Can't talk. Too tired.

"Oh, good. We'll get a break from that mouth a bit longer then."

Wexton snorts again and tightens his arm around me. *Stay?*

"I'm not going anywhere."

I go on petting his hair as he falls back to sleep, willingly this time. He looks so sweet in sleep with his cheek pressed against me that I can't help but lean down and plant a soft kiss on the top of his head.

From beside the bed, Fenmire watches with a look of embarrassment tinged with sadness and longing.

Regret.

Chapter 24

Wexton has two more seizures throughout the day, and by dinner time, he's running a fever so high I can barely stand to have his skin touch mine. Despite all of this, Fenmire tells me not to worry, that the temperature is normal and means his body has started healing at last. I don't know if he's being truthful or if he just doesn't want to deal with me worrying myself sick on top of everything else. I spend the night in Wexton's room because I can't stand the thought of not being here if something happens. Caliborne brings the chair from my room, and I fall asleep in it at the bedside opposite Fenmire.

This time, my dreams are full of spitters as they chase and poison everyone I care about, even my parents as well as every animal on their farm. The last one chases me down the lane in The Deadwood, its teeth snapping in my ear as I scream for help I know won't come because everyone else is already dead.

I wake up with a gasp to find Fenmire watching me, his finger circling his chin thoughtfully as he does.

"Did no one ever teach you it's rude to stare?" I grumble as I rub my face. Judging by how quiet the castle is, it's not yet dawn. I touch Wexton's hand on the bed in front of me.

It's cooler to the touch than it was last night.

I stand and touch his face, which is free of sweat at last.

"He'll be fine," Fenmire says, and he sounds utterly exhausted. "There wasn't a hint of a seizure in the night, and his fever broke not an hour ago. His organs are well on their way to healing, and the leg is fine. I bandaged it with some salve." He stands up with a heavy sigh and cracks his back. "Let me know if anything changes and keep him in bed for a few days at least." He turns to leave the room.

"Thank you, Fenmire," I say with tears of relief burning in my eyes.

Fenmire stops, and his head turns my way, though he avoids my eyes. "I didn't do it for you," he mutters, but then those shimmering eyes finally meet mine, and he softens as his shoulders slump. "But you're welcome anyway."

He stalks from the room.

I sit on the edge of Wexton's bed and take his hand between both of my own. I'm so relieved that he's on the mend that I start singing, softly. It's just an old nursery rhyme my father used to sing when I was little, but it makes my heart so happy I start it over once I finish it the first time. After a few minutes, I hear Wexton's thoughts as he starts to wake up.

What is that? Evangeline. Don't open your eyes or they'll stop. Don't move. Don't even breathe funny. Just listen. It's so beautiful.

I finish the song a second time then say, "Don't get used to it. I don't like singing with an audience."

Wexton's face splits into a grin, and he opens his eyes. "Haven't I earned a serenade or two? I did save your life after all."

"I probably saved yours back, so I say we're even."

"Ah, come on. I must have earned a little something extra for my efforts."

I slide up the bed and lean over him, my hair falling around both our faces as I take his chin in my hand and kiss him once on the lips. "How's that for a reward?"

His hand clutches the back of my head and pulls me down so he can steal another, much longer and more passionate kiss. When we break apart this time, we're both breathless.

"Now that's a reward," he murmurs.

I set my forehead to his. "You scared me," I whisper. "I thought for sure I'd lose you."

His hand slides around to rub my cheek with his thumb. "Silly human. It'll take more than a spitter to take me down for good."

I close my eyes briefly at his touch. "Remember when you said you hope someday I might need you like I need Caliborne?"

His smile slips a little, and his fiery eyes dart back and forth between mine as he says, "Yes."

I set my hand against his and lean my cheek into his palm. "I think I already do."

Wexton sits up abruptly, and I yelp as he hooks his arm around me and hauls me into his lap.

"Take it easy," I protest, and I try to push him back down, but of course, he doesn't budge. "You still need rest to—"

He crushes his mouth to mine, silencing me. With his hand buried in my hair, he ravages my mouth, that wicked, forked tongue thrusting with that same passion I got barely a taste of in The Deadwood. I moan as I pull him even closer, craving more. He spins me so that my back is to his chest, then his fingers pluck the bottom of my shirt from my pants before sliding under the waistband. He nips my ear hard enough to make me suck in a startled breath.

"Spread your legs for me?" he requests in a heady whisper.

I throw an arm up and loop it around the back of his neck as I comply.

His hand slides further south, and his touch is much firmer than Caliborne's when his finger finds my clit. Everything about him is more intense, and he quickly has my hips bucking against his hand. He slides two fingers inside me, and I cry out softly.

"Oh, that sound does things to me," he murmurs in my ear. "Do it again."

He thrusts his fingers deep, ripping another soft cry from me.

His cocks grow hard under my backside.

"Look at me," he says.

I turn and look up at him, and he captures my mouth again, his tongue and fingers falling into a rhythm that makes me moan and writhe against him.

I'm already close when he says, "Say my name when you come. Scream it and show me how much you need me."

Holy God above do I ever scream it. I come apart so hard it brings tears to my eyes, that dirty mouth pushing me over the edge like nothing I've experienced before. And he keeps talking as I buck and whine in his lap.

"You got another one in there for me?" he asks as he nuzzles and kisses my throat. "I want to taste your orgasm on my fingers for days. I bet you're sweet and dripping down there. Let's see if we can make you even wetter."

He sucks on a spot under my ear at the same time his thumb finds my clit. I whimper as my whole body twitches under his touch.

"Tell me you need me," he murmurs against my skin.

"I need you," I choke out between gasping breaths.

"Again."

"I need you, Wex...Wexton!" I cry out pitifully as I orgasm a second time.

"Beautiful," he says, his hand still wringing every last twitch from me that he can. Once I finally still, breathless and slightly lightheaded, he takes his hand from my pants and sticks both his glistening fingers in his mouth, sucking them clean with a moan. *Mmm, delicious too. I knew they would be.*

"Jesus Christ, Wexton," I mutter, my face so hot it feels as if I've started running a fever myself.

His fingers come out of his mouth with a small pop. "That's just the beginning, darling, a mere taste"—he wiggles his wet fingers at me—"of what's to come."

I swing my legs to one side so I'm in no danger of kicking him where he's still healing, then I lean into him again and plant a kiss on his collarbone.

I could get used to that.

"Used to what?"

"I don't know if I should say. It might taint your opinion of me."

"It would have to be something pretty egregious for that to happen."

He hums to himself and runs his mouth back and forth across the top of my head, savoring the feel of my hair on his lips as he considers. "I've never had a mate either," he finally admits. "Mostly because I was quite... generous with my lovemaking and rarely bedded the same partner twice. I was hesitant to commit to anyone long-term, so I didn't stay put long enough to try. The result was a lot of hot sex, and I mean a *lot* of hot sex. Like there was a time when I—"

"Move on to the point, you heathen."

"Right... The problem was that, since I didn't hang around, there was never any feeling behind it, no emotions. It was hot, but it was also lonely. None of them needed me, and by the time I was ready to be needed by someone, we were stuck here, and I had no one." His arm tightens around me. "But now you're here, with your tender kisses and a mouth as smart as mine."

"That's a stretch."

He huffs into my hair, and I laugh.

He leans down to my ear again. "The last thing I want to do is run from you, Evangeline."

"You wouldn't get far if you tried anyway," I tease.

He chuckles. "Wiseass."

"Look who's talking."

He's back to sucking on my neck, and my eyes roll up in my head despite the fact that I'm still a limp noodle from his previous pleasures. "You should… eat something. Something other than me, that is."

"But you're so tasty," he murmurs, but that's quickly followed by a growl from his stomach so fierce it vibrates through me as well.

"Food now. The more carnal stuff later. *Much* later. Fenmire says you have to rest for a few days."

"How have the two of you been getting along?" he asks, but the attempt at conversation turns out to merely be a distraction as his hand starts inching back into my pants.

I slap it away. "Stop that now." I scoot off his lap and hop from the bed.

Wexton flops back onto his pillows with a huff. "Spoilsport."

I stick my tongue out at him and head for the door. "Stay put," I order sternly. "You better be in that very spot when I come back from the kitchen."

"And just what will you do if I'm not?"

"I'll wake up Fenmire. He hasn't slept in days, so you can guess about how well that would go."

He narrows his eyes at me. "That's playing dirty."

"As dirty as your mouth."

I leave him laughing, the sound carrying me down the hall toward the kitchen.

*****

I spend the next three days using every threat and promise in my arsenal to keep Wexton in bed. Fenmire checks on him once on the second day, proclaims him well on his way to fine health, and tells me, in a much less flattering choice of words, that he's my problem now.

"No walking or bathing until that wound stops seeping," Fenmire barks as he stalks out of the room.

So it is that I become Wexton's personal servant with the goal of keeping him immobile for as long as I possibly can, though he never asks me for a thing. I gladly fetch and wash bedpans, bring his meals to his room, help him change his bandages, and, most importantly of all, keep him company so he doesn't hobble out of bed out of sheer boredom. We sit and talk for hours, though it's mostly one-sided since he has so many more stories to tell than I do.

Though his flirting does nothing but pick up steam as he heals, I refuse to give in to my desires and join him in bed again. It's not for a lack of wanting either. He knows exactly what to say and how to say it to make my entire body hot all over to the point where I'm aching to take our intimacy to the next level, which is why I refuse him every time he invites me close for so much as a cuddle. I don't trust myself or his impulse control not to take things past what he can handle right now. Thankfully, I have a mate who's all too eager to handle the pent-up sexual frustration I feel every evening after listening to Wexton's not-so-subtle innuendoes and graphic thoughts all day.

Every day after dinner, I bid Wexton goodnight and cross the hall to spend my evenings with Caliborne. And while the conversation is still a bit one-sided, it's me who gets to do most of the talking this time as I tell him about my day and unwind with a cup of tea before he ultimately takes me to bed, where I get my fill of pleasure and affection I've denied myself all day. True to their word, neither Gryxen have a negative thing to say about the fact that I'm technically pursuing a relationship with both of them. Wexton makes the occasional joke but never at my expense.

"How will you ever handle us both?" he asks when he catches me yawning for the fourth time the morning after a particularly exuberant night with Caliborne during which I got little sleep.

He has a point. I'll have to find a balance somewhere if I'm serious about mating with both of them, and the more time goes on, the more I consider it. I look forward to my mornings bounding into Wexton's room just as much as I look forward to shuffling my tired feet into Caliborne's at day's end. And the way Wexton's face brightens each time he sees me tells me he feels the same.

It's not just my choice to make, though. Wexton says he's anything but traditional, so I have no idea if he follows the same courting rituals Caliborne does. Will he give me a courting gift too? Does he even want to be mates? He says I'm more to him than all the ones who came before, the ones he slept with only once then never saw again, but words are pretty and mean very little.

In the end, I decide to focus solely on getting him healthy and deal with the rest later, but as the wounds in his leg slowly seal, and his restlessness mounts, so do his intentions. I can hear them in his thoughts, but I don't have to read those to know what's on his mind. He tells me clear as day the things he wants to do to me, with me, in me...

I honestly can't wait.

Chapter 25

On the fourth morning of Wexton's recovery, his bandages come off clean.

The glint in his eye is unmistakable, but he surprises me by announcing the first thing he wants is a bath.

"Will you join me?" he asks.

There it is.

I raise one brow to let him know I'm on to him but end up nodding, regardless. "I could use a good soak."

He throws the blankets back and hops his backside across the bed, but when he stands, he teeters. I put both hands on his chest and shove him back down to sit on the edge of the mattress.

"Easy, muscles," I say. "Let's take it slow."

"Any slower and I'll start growing moss," he grumbles.

"It'll add to your charm."

I yelp when he grabs me by the arm and hauls me close between his knees. I'm overly conscious of his nakedness but refuse to let it phase me as I stare up into his eyes.

"You don't like me charming," he says. "You like me crass and filthy."

I bite the inside of my lip. Don't smile. Don't—

"Your cheeks are giving you away, silly human."

My face feels like it's on fire. "You smell."

Wexton throws his head back on a hearty laugh. "That'll happen when you're stuck in bed for days, as I'm sure you know." He releases me and stands—more slowly this time—and manages not to topple over. "Let's go clean me up then."

He's still as naked as the day he was born when he heads for the door.

"Wexton."

"What?" he asks, his hand already on the knob.

"Let's not traumatize the staff." I go to his dresser, fish out a pair of clean pants, and throw them to him.

He tugs them on but doesn't bother tying them up before letting himself into the hall.

We stop at my room long enough to grab my wash bag and dress—somewhere this morning, the day shifted from an Evangeline day to an Eve one—before heading down to the bath. Wexton walks slower than usual and still has a bit of a limp, but he's all smiles as he follows me down the winding staircase and into the pool room. I know from experience how good it feels to come here after spending so long in bed, so I don't fault him a bit when he immediately shucks his pants again and wades into the water. He sighs in contentment as he sits with his back to the edge of the pool in his favorite spot.

I follow suit, not the least bit shy of being naked around him anymore as I step down into the water. I *am* shy, though, when it comes to deciding where to go once I'm in. Do I stand across the pool from him like I normally do? Should I be brave and swim over to him? Perhaps he'd rather just get cleaned up. I know I wouldn't have appreciated someone in my space while I washed after my recovery. I avoid making the decision at all by taking out my soap and lathering up, washing every inch of myself while Wexton watches.

"If you're done teasing me with that pretty little body," he says as I'm putting my soap away again, "care to come over here and let me play with it?"

His words are like a caress down my spine, and I shiver.

I smile at him but swim only halfway across the pool toward him. "On one condition."

"What's that?"

"You let me wash your hair again."

"Deal. I like when you pamper me." He pushes away from the wall and turns to give me his back.

I swim over and untie the bow I placed at the end of his braid what feels like forever ago and unwind the strands. Since they've been braided this whole time, they're relatively free of tangles, and I easily smooth them out as I scrub them. He hums as my fingers knead across his scalp.

"Oh yes, I can definitely get used to this," he says sleepily. *Is this the sort of stuff I've been missing out on all this time?*

"About that," I say, and my nerves roar to life.

"Yes?" Wexton prompts when I'm silent too long.

I'm no longer paying attention to cleaning his hair; my fingers merely play with the suds as I ask, "What assurance do I have that you won't change your mind about us, once you've... once we've..."

His scalp disappears from under my hand as he dunks himself under the water and comes up facing me instead. He looks hurt.

"I wouldn't do that to you," he says. "I think I explained it poorly before. It wasn't that I slept with others after making false promises only to run away when the sun rose. I made it clear to each of them that I wasn't looking for anything else. Most of them agreed and wanted the same. It was mutual. I didn't lie or manipulate to get what I wanted, and I don't plan to start now.

"I genuinely want more with you, Eve. Have I ruined my chances by telling you about my past? Should I have—"

"No," I say firmly, and I briefly touch his arm in reassurance. "You've ruined nothing, and I appreciate your honesty. I merely wanted to voice my concerns. Sometimes, just speaking them aloud takes away their power over you."

He's quiet as his eyes bore into mine.

"What?" I ask.

"I'd like to give you more than words to reassure you."

"What did you have in mind?"

"I don't know yet, but I'll come up with something."

"Does that mean you no longer want to play?" Disappointment settles in my stomach like a ball of lead.

Wexton's wicked smile banishes it. "Oh, I intend to play, but I think we'll hold off on a few things until I've proven to you I'm not going anywhere."

His arm snakes around my back, and he pulls me closer, so close I can feel his hardening cocks against my thigh. There's still soap in his hair, and a stream of it trickles down his forehead. I wipe it away before it can run into his eyes.

Tender and sweet, just like they taste. I'd love to have that hand wrapped around my cock.

"Which one?" I ask.

Wexton laughs again. "Whichever one you please, darling."

It takes my brain a second to realize that's an invitation, and I lick my lips nervously as I peer down into the water between us. I have experience with this, so I'm not going in blind, but I only have Caliborne to compare, and maybe Wexton is different, which—

They're adorable when they're flustered.

I huff, throw an arm around his neck, and wrap my fingers around his top cock, stroking firmly.

Wexton's eyes close, and he moans softly. *Seerraf and the five... A little harder... All the way down... palm the head...* His fingers flex against my back, and he arches into me.

I lean up on my toes to whisper, "You know what that dirty mouth of yours does to me. But what, pray tell, does dirty talk do to you?" I keep stroking, and judging by his thoughts, the feel of my hand gliding up and down his shaft has rendered him speechless for the moment, which is no easy feat. I kiss his collarbone. "I haven't tasted a Gryxen yet," I confess. "I wonder what you'd taste like."

Wexton's arm twitches at my back, and his hips buck his cock into my hand.

I chuckle and kiss him again, higher up his collar. "You say I'm tender and sweet, just like I taste. If that's the case, I bet you'll be all pepper and spice on my tongue." Another kiss, at the base of his throat this time. "Would you like that?"

The laugh that escapes him is primal. It crawls up his throat and whispers out between gritted teeth at the same time his hand slides up my back and into my wet hair. He cups the back of my head as he leans down not an inch from my face.

"You have no idea the sorts of things I'd like to do with that mouth," he growls. I lose my grip on him as he spins us around and backs me against the side of the pool, but I find him again in the water at the same time his hand dives between my thighs. "But, for right now, I want to hear it scream my name so loud it echoes off the cave walls."

A single finger thrusts inside me, and I gasp, my hand stilling momentarily on his cock as I adjust my stance, spreading my legs to give him more access.

"That's right, darling, open up for me."

He looms over me, pinning me between his massive torso and the rock wall at my back. It makes me feel trapped, vulnerable, and I bite my lip against a groan that quickly turns into a stifled cry of pleasure when Wexton doubles the fingers inside me.

"Let go of that lip," he says, his voice quivering with his own arousal. "I want to hear you."

His fingers curl inside of me, and his thumb runs softly up and down my clit, rubbing that sensitive spot from both inside and out. It's all I can do to pay attention to my own hand and continue pleasing him as my legs start to shake. His hand falters for a second, and a muscle in his neck pops out as he clenches his jaw.

"Very close now," he murmurs. "But I want to hear you first." His fingers start moving, petting that spot inside me while his thumb continues to drive me wild. I thrust my hips, matching his pace and taking him deeper. "Tell me you love the feel of my fingers fucking you."

"Wexton," I whimper, my orgasm so close I can barely breathe. His thumb stops, and the orgasm ebbs away. I growl in frustration.

"Is that too crass for you?" he asks. "How about 'I love the feel of you inside me'? Say it, and I'll make you scream for me."

"Wexton…" His fingers stop moving too, and I give him what he wants. "I love the feel of you inside me." I squeeze my hand around his cock, making him gasp. "Now finish what you started."

He smiles. "My pleasure."

His fingers and thumb start working me, fast and hard, and I go up on my toes with a whimper.

His cock throbs in my hand, and his lips part as he starts to pant.

I hold on to the edge of the pool with my free hand as my whole body tenses.

"Come for me," Wexton growls.

And I do. My nails rake across the stone, and I shout incoherent babble mixed with his name as I arch and thrash in the water. Under my palm, his cock grows even harder before he cries out with a snarl and a curse. At least I think it's a curse. It's in his tongue, so I can't be sure. I let go of him when he withdraws his fingers. He lifts his hand from the water and sniffs them.

"Pity." He licks his fingers and pouts. "I was looking forward to another taste. I suppose I'll simply have to make a whole meal of you soon."

"What does that mean?" I ask breathlessly.

He merely winks at me before leaning down and stealing a kiss, his tongue dancing across my lips as he pulls away. "That'll have to do. For now."

*****

The walk back upstairs is considerably slower. He denies it, but I can tell Wexton is in pain with every step. He overdid it, but he'll never admit it. We go to my room where we sit on the floor like before, drying our hair by my fire, only this time he has his arm around me, and I lean against him as we talk.

"What do you mean you've never seen a snowman?" I ask. Somehow, we've gotten on the subject of winters in the village and the various activities humans enjoy in the snow.

"The Deadwood has been stuck in a never-ending blizzard for as long as humans have lived here," he says with a shrug. "I've rarely seen them go out at all, much less for the fun of it. It never snows in Michastiforo, so…"

"We should definitely build one sometime then. You roll the snow up into large balls and stack them on top of each other, then you place rocks or lumps of coal in the topmost ball to create a face, place two long sticks in the second ball for arms, and set a hat on the top of his head. Snowman."

"I'd love to see you make a snow Gryxen."

I tilt my head in consideration. "Challenge accepted. Once Will gets here, he'll help me figure it out, wings and all." I think back at my many winters with Will, remembering the mischief we got into over the years. "There's also icicle sword fighting. Fenmire already saw that first-hand."

Wexton laughs. "I would've loved to see that. He needs to have more fun instead of spending so much time with nothing but his books for company."

"Is that a recent change or was he like that even before Reilanna trapped you here?"

"He was always a bookworm, but it got much worse when he got stuck here with nothing much else to do. I try not to judge. The war affected us all differently, and I think I came out of it the most unscathed. Caliborne lost CeCe, Fenmire lost his mate, and Drixus—"

I sit up so straight I bump my head against his shoulder. "Fenmire lost his mate in the war? Did Reilanna kill them? But she… she killed…" A horrifying thought occurs to me. "Wexton… was Fenmire's mate one of the Gryxen who betrayed you?"

I can't imagine the pain of having my mate side with my enemy and fight to kill me only to then have my heart broken a second time by watching them die at the hands of that same enemy. Suddenly, Fenmire's moods and unwillingness to even call me a friend make so much more sense. I think back through all my interactions with him, seeing them through a new light.

Wexton sighs. "I didn't mean to say that. Listen, it's really not my story to tell you, Eve. I'm sorry. Maybe Fenmire will share that with you himself one day."

I scoff. "Knowing what I know now, it's a miracle I've exchanged as many words with him as I have over the past month."

"Fenmire is my best friend," Wexton says. "I know he seems like nothing but a grouch who hates the world, but I promise you, under that gruff exterior lies a Gryxen who cares a lot more than he'll ever let on. He already likes you or else he wouldn't be so grumpy around you."

"That seems rather backward."

"You'll understand someday. I'm sure of it." He adjusts his arm around me, wincing as he moves his injured leg against the stiffness of sitting on the floor. "What other things does your kind like to do in the winter?"

I decide to play along with his casual change of subject and humor him. "Well, there's ice skating, I suppose, but we rarely got the chance to do that since the lake is a three-hour ride north of the village. I don't suppose you've heard of that before either?"

"No, what is it?"

"You strap thin strips of metal to the undersides of your shoes and go out on a large icy surface, like a frozen lake or pond, and you glide across the ice. It takes some practice to balance on the skates, but once you get the hang of it, it's like dancing. Some of the girls in my village can skate like the wind. It's beautiful to watch."

Wexton's arm disappears from around me. I look up in alarm, but he's merely checking if his hair is dry.

"Will you braid this for me again?" he asks.

I climb to my feet. "Of course." He's silent as I brush and braid his long hair and tie it off with a fresh strip of cloth—another bow, to his dismay.

"What should we do now?" I ask. "I'd suggest a walk, but I can tell you've already taken too many steps today. Don't bother denying it or I'll fetch Fenmire to lecture you instead. I could run upstairs and grab a deck of cards from the study. You could teach me that game you and Fenmire are always playing."

"Actually…" He won't meet my eyes. "There's something I—"

Someone knocks softly on my bedroom door.

"Come in," I beckon.

It's Caliborne. Since Fenmire rejoined the patrol rotation a few days ago, I've been getting both afternoons and evenings with my mate again. I greet him with a happy hug and kiss.

"Is all still quiet out there?" I ask him. Since the spitter came through The Gate, it's been suspiciously dormant, though the others tell me that's normal. It takes time for The Gate to recharge, and the more power it expels, the more time it takes for that to happen.

Quiet and peaceful. I see Wexton is up.

I give Wexton a stern look. "Yes, but he should return to his bed for the rest of the afternoon if he knows what's good for him."

"I didn't hear you complaining about that an hour ago, darling," Wexton replies with a smirk. "Quite the contrary."

I blush as I look up at Caliborne.

I feel his silent, shaky laughter. *Is he behaving himself?*

"Does he ever?"

More shaky laughter. *Good. He must truly be on the mend then.*

I sigh in pretend exasperation. "Yes, it seems we're still stuck with him."

Wexton hefts himself up off the floor. "I have something I need to take care of. Eve here was just saying they'd like to go for a walk, Caliborne. Why don't you escort them, and I'll go tend to my own business."

"Oh no you don't," I object. "You need to go rest."

"How do you know that's not exactly what I plan to do?"

"Because I know you, so I know better."

He laughs a little evil, mischievous laugh. "You would be unwise to think you know me well enough that I can no longer surprise you." He heads for the still-open door, blowing me a kiss as he steps through it. "Take them out and have them show you what a snowman is, Cal," he says before disappearing down the hall.

"His bed is the last place I'll find him today, isn't it?" I grumble.

Without a doubt. You should've seen him after he lost the arm. Fenmire threatened to tie him down for the number of times we caught him wandering, so weak he had to lean against the wall for balance as he raided the kitchen or attempted to fix his broken armor in the forge.

"I suppose it's a good thing he's so stubborn. It probably saved his life. He'd likely mock the reaper if it came for him."

Caliborne strokes my cheek with his thumb. *Shall we walk, then? What's this I hear about a snowman?*

I smile. "Why don't I show you?"

Chapter 26

After my somewhat exuberant bath with Wexton, I'm a little sore, the good kind that makes me blush when I move just right and remember all the naughty things he whispered in my ear with his fingers inside of me. It means, though, that I have to tell Caliborne I'm not up for much by way of lovemaking tonight after we retire to his room. He doesn't so much as utter a word of complaint, not that he ever would.

Am I right in assuming, then, that things between you and Wexton are becoming more intimate? Caliborne is seated on the edge of his bed with me between his knees as he brushes the hair from my face and caresses the side of my neck between soft kisses on my cheek.

I stiffen. "That's still alright, isn't it?"

Yes, of course. It's just that… there's something I think you should know. I probably should've mentioned it before, but… Wexton is—

"Your son," I say, and I smile. "I know."

Caliborne blinks at me in surprise, his hand stilling on my neck. *How?*

"The others gave me the pieces, I just had to put them together. Fenmire told me you knew Wexton's mother before he was born. That's how you showed Fenmire what she looked like for the drawing in Wexton's bedroom. Wexton said your mothers were friends, so that's no doubt how you met her. Wexton also said his mother chose his father for whom she thought would breed the strongest child, and I can think of no one better for that than Michastiforo's greatest hero. Wexton was assigned to your unit in training as soon as you came back to the city, which I assume was done by your urging, and then you chose him to be part of your team to protect The Gate despite his young age. You even vouched for him when others doubted his capabilities. That sounds like the actions of a father going above and beyond for his child."

Caliborne blinks some more, his mind utterly blank in shock.

I smile. "And then there are the less obvious things, like the fact that you both have a good heart and accepted me with open arms from the day I first arrived here. You're both fierce warriors and love to please others. And you both have the same tiny dimple just at the base of your—"

Please don't finish that sentence. I don't want to know.

I laugh softly then touch Caliborne's cheek. "Have you and Wexton spoken about this?"

No.

"Why not?"

His mother made it clear I was to have no part in his life. She approached me with her desire to have a child because she had no one else and wasn't ready to go to the temple yet. I'd known her most of my life. She was a wise and caring Gruxa. I knew she would be a good mother, so I gave her my seed. We were not mates nor even lovers, and I left the city again shortly after that, so I didn't even know if she conceived successfully. It wasn't until I came back after CeCe was born that I learned she'd indeed birthed a child, but she never confirmed he was mine. I suspected so, of course, but she never brought it up and I didn't either.

"So then why did you have him assigned to you at the training fields?"

Caliborne hangs his head. *Like I said, I suspected he was mine. The timeline for his birth fit. I wanted to know him, so I went against what his mother and I agreed upon and asked for him to be assigned to me. His mother never objected, so I assumed she didn't mind. We grew close, so close that, when I was chosen to form our team, I picked him to come with us and fought whoever objected. It was selfish and wrong of me.*

I tilt his chin up. "Why was it wrong to want to be near your child?"

Caliborne's blazing white eyes close softly for a moment then look at me gravely. *Because I'm the reason he's stuck here like the rest of us. I'm the reason he lost his arm when the first of Reilanna's beasts came through The Gate. I'm the reason he nearly died protecting you from that spitter. I'm the only one to blame for everything Reilanna and her spell has done to him because I drew him into this whole mess for my own selfish desires.*

"Oh, Caliborne," I say, and I touch my forehead to his. "I don't think that's a fair assessment at all. You should talk to him. Perhaps it would put your guilt to rest."

How would it do that?

"Because I doubt very much Wexton holds a single grudge for any of it. And if he holds no grudges, what reason do you have to feel guilty?"

I still dragged him into this.

"The way he tells it, you gave him fantastic opportunities and made his dreams come true. I believe the word he used to describe how he felt to get to train with you was 'awestruck'."

He was one of my best charges, a hard worker and a good listener. I'm quite proud of him.

"And he adores you. You should tell him. I think that conversation might surprise you, in a good way."

Caliborne furrows his brow, but I simply smile and give nothing away.

*****

Wexton is suspiciously hard to find for the next week. He pops up so randomly, I get whiplash whenever he turns a corner and is suddenly in front of me. Once Fenmire declares him fit for patrol again, he's even harder to pin down, though he makes a point of seeing me at least once every day, even if just for a minute.

Considering Caliborne once did the same—added to Wexton's promise to prove he won't abandon me—I have a good idea where he keeps whisking off too. I ask Caliborne once to show me the forge only to receive the same answer I got from Wexton before.

Humans aren't allowed. That's a Gryxen-only space.

I huff. "But I'm your mate. Doesn't that make me like… an *honorary* Gryxen or something?"

I get only his laughter and a final shake of his head for an answer.

I pout but try to understand. This is their custom, their ritual to show their partners how much they care. I must respect it and wait for Wexton to be done with whatever he's creating.

So, in the meantime, fueled by both boredom and a promise I made, I seek out Fenmire.

I find him in the library, because where else would I find him?

I knock lightly on the open door before walking in. "Hello?"

Fenmire looks up from his desk with a blue pencil stuck in his mouth and a brown one clutched in his hand, poised over a paper. He drops the pencil from his mouth into his open hand and sets them both on the desk, shuffling papers to cover whatever it is he's working on.

"Yes?" he asks.

"You told me to seek you out when I'm ready to explore other ways to break Reilanna's spell."

He pushes his chair back from his desk. "I was starting to think you wouldn't come."

"I had to find a time when Wexton and Caliborne wouldn't see me slip up here. I don't know what you're planning, so I didn't know if they'd protest."

Fenmire raises a brow. "Sneaking behind your mates' backs to see me, are you?"

"Wexton isn't my mate yet."

"Yet." He pounces on the word, studying me the same way he did when I woke in my chair at Wexton's bedside. "I wonder, have you come here truly seeking knowledge, or have you merely fingered me as your next conquest?"

I roll my eyes in exasperation. "Do you want me to leave? Because I didn't come here to fight with you."

Those shrewd eyes study me, their gaze so piercing my heart kicks up a notch.

"Fine," he says at last. "I stand by what I said before: I think we should take you to The Gate and observe."

"Just observe?"

"Of course." He tilts his head at me. "Or are you afraid I'll try to throw you in?"

"I'm not afraid of you, Fenmire," I say with conviction. "I think it's *you* who's afraid of *me*."

He scoffs and adjusts in his seat, giving me a bored look. "That's quite a theory."

I could say more, like the fact that two of his brothers-in-arms pursuing me as their mate has clearly unnerved him. He's proven that with his own actions. Or that it must make his heart ache to know the one thing that nearly destroyed him is the key to their freedom. Or perhaps that I know his mate was one of the ones Reilanna not only turned against him but tortured and killed. My mere presence here must pick at those old wounds. I could say any of that and prove my point, but I don't. I let my eyes tell him as much as his shrewd ones can glean before I change the subject.

"So, to The Gate then?"

"Right now?" he asks.

"Unless you've more important things to do with your day."

Fenmire rises from his chair and straightens his desk, stacking papers in neat piles and tucking books into columns before stepping away and waving toward the door behind me. I turn and precede him down the corridor and stairs to the foyer.

"I need to borrow the jacket from the kitchen," I say. "I'll meet you out front."

"Meet me in the stables."

"Why the stables?"

"It's closer to The Gate."

Fifteen minutes later, I enter the stables bundled into my borrowed jacket and the new gloves I finished stitching yesterday. I even have a scarf now made of layered pajama bottoms and stuffed with some loose rabbit fur Percival gave me. Fenmire is standing on the far side of the stables near the large wooden doors, which are closed right now to keep the heat in since it's a rather overcast, dreary day.

"Evangeline!" Percival calls happily. "You're just in time. One of the foxes is laboring. We're expecting a litter of pups any time now." When he notices my attire, his face falls a bit. "Oh, are you going out?"

"With Fenmire, yes." I touch his arm apologetically. "I'll be back soon, though, and I'll come right down to watch all the excitement."

Percival peers over his shoulder at Fenmire, who's watching us with his usual scowl on his face.

Where is he taking them? Fenmire never goes out with anyone. He doesn't even look happy about it. Not that he ever looks happy about anything, but…

"Where are the two of you off to?" Percival asks, trying and failing to sound casual.

"Just for a walk," I lie as I take back my hand. "I want to get to know him better." At least that part is true.

Percival nods, but I can tell his worries haven't been quelled.

"Is something the matter?" I ask.

"Oh, no, nothing. Just be careful. The weather could turn sour quickly."

"I will, and I'll be back later this afternoon."

"Sure," he says with another nod, and he walks me to the doors.

"Ready?" Fenmire asks. He grips the knob on a smaller, Gryxen-sized door that's been cut into the larger, ceiling high ones for easier comings and goings.

"Ready," I say, and I pull my scarf tighter around my neck and face.

We step together out into the frigid air. I've never been out on this side of the castle, so I turn around and peer up to get a good look. Off to the left, I can see the broken section of the castle where I stood catching snowflakes weeks ago. From here, it looks like something massive swept a whole section clean off of it, like a spoon through Mother's tapioca pudding.

"Caliborne says that happened during The Great War," I say. "I assume it was after Horthos sided with Reilanna, or he could've fixed it."

"It happened during the final battle," Fenmire says, "the one that ended when we sealed Reilanna on the other side. She commanded many flying beasts with the powers she stole from Jothrik. Wexton ripped the wings off of one in the air, and it crashed into the castle as it fell."

"Since Horthos created the castle, does that mean he controlled stone?"

"He controlled earth in all its forms: dirt, stone, and even lava. That's how the bathing pool is heated, you know. There's molten rock not far below the surface down there that keeps the water warm. It's also the source of the smell."

"And Jothrik's powers had something to do with plants and animals? Wexton says he grew The Deadwood, but you just said his power allowed Reilanna to command flying beasts."

"Jothrik's power is why we must fight against the beasts she constantly sends to torment us. He couldn't create life, but he could control it."

"I don't understand."

Fenmire searches around for inspiration on how best to explain it to me, and the snow crunches under his feet as he swivels in place. He points toward the base of a gnarled vine nearby. "Think of a seed and how long it takes for it to grow into a tall tree or a bush full of ripe berries. It could take weeks, months, maybe even years. Jothrik could coax that seed to grow to its final form in seconds. He could raise a freshly-birthed creature to adulthood in minutes then control its mind to do whatever he wanted. Reilanna uses those powers to send her horrors after us."

"So the beasts she sends are ones that occur naturally in your world? She merely commands them?"

"No. Reilanna had powers of her own before she stole the others'. She is a sorceress. She can wield many forms of magic, but her specialty is shapeshifting. She can take an innocent creature as small as a rabbit, turn it into the most horrific form of beast, then, with Jothrik's powers, send it through The Gate with a thirst for our blood or a hunger for human bones."

I try to ignore the picture that paints and ask, "And Breklen controlled the weather?"

"Yes. He could strike his enemies from the sky with a bolt of lightning, freeze them solid with a gust of glacial wind, or drown them in a downpour so thick the water seeped into their noses and mouths with each breath they took."

I gauge Fenmire's reaction to each of his fallen comrades, trying to guess which of them was the mate that broke his heart, but his face remains neutral as he talks, giving nothing away. I don't pry any deeper. Instead, I turn and look out over the frozen wasteland before us.

"Where's The Gate from here?" I ask.

"Not far," Fenmire says, and he steps closer to me. "It's easier to fly, but if you'd rather walk…"

I'm honestly surprised he's offering. I've only ever flown with Caliborne, and though I'm not nervous about the idea of doing so with Fenmire, I know it's a rather intimate thing to be held so close in a Gryxen's arms. Fenmire and I haven't even touched since I got my powers from my mating bond. Oh, the thoughts that must go on in that mind.

I take a welcome step toward him. "We can fly."

He bobs one brow at me before scooping me up into his arms. I listen intently for the thoughts to come only to be immediately disappointed when I can't understand a single word of them. He's thinking in his mother tongue. Is he doing that on purpose? I look up to find the faintest hint of a smirk on his face. Oh yes, he's definitely doing that on purpose.

"What's the matter?" he asks innocently.

"Absolutely nothing," I say, and I burrow into my jacket, gloves, and scarf against his warm chest.

I swear I hear a chuckle a heartbeat before we launch into the sky.

Chapter 27

The Gate is not at all how I'd imagined it.

I'd pictured swirling colors, perhaps an arch with carved runes around its edges, or some other evidence of the magic and power this place possesses.

We land at the edge of a clearing, and the only thing odd about it is that it's free of snow. In its center is a circle about five feet wide made of plain grey stones. Fenmire sets me down, and I take a step toward the circle.

He grabs my arm. "Wait just a moment."

We wait, and we watch, and we listen.

Nothing happens.

Fenmire gives me a nod, and we walk together toward the circle. I'm still in awe that this is all there is to see. The ground on the inside of the stones looks the same as the outside, just plain, bare earth.

"What would happen if I stepped inside the circle?" I ask.

"Nothing. The Gate is closed right now."

"What would it look like if it was open?"

"You would see my world in the space between the rocks. It's like looking through a window at the red sands and rolling hills of the Vorisca Desert."

"It's so small." I remember the size of the spitter and compare it to the space inside the circle. How did something so large come through such a tiny space? And didn't Wexton say a beast the size of a mountain came through once? Impossible.

"Size means nothing to The Gate," Fenmire says. "A being's passage isn't measured in inches or feet."

Wexton told me this too, but I wasn't quite sure what he meant. I still don't completely understand, if I'm honest. All I can picture are massive creatures squeezing themselves through comically-small spaces the way the kittens in papa's barn do through knotholes and gaps in the floors.

I kneel next to the stones.

"What are you doing?" Fenmire asks.

"We came to see if my presence has any effect on it, right?"

"Right."

"Seems only logical that I should touch it to find out for sure."

Fenmire tilts his chin up as he considers, then he nods once. "Be careful."

I place my hand on one of the stones.

Ah… the one who would free me.

The voice startles me so badly that I yelp and jump backward, falling on my backside.

In an instant, Fenmire is kneeling beside me with a hand on my arm. "What happened?"

"It… it spoke to me."

"That's impossible. The Gate isn't sentient."

"Then whose thought did I hear in my head just now?"

Fenmire's eyes flick from me down to the rock by my leg then back up again. He looks around the clearing as if indeed searching for some other party who might be responsible.

I get up onto my knees and reach for the stone again.

Fenmire grabs my hand to stop me.

"This is what we came here for, isn't it?" I ask. "Maybe it can help us."

Fenmire looks torn and nervous, which is quite a change from the cold indifference he usually projects. He touches the stone himself, passing his palm over the surface a few times before finally letting me go.

I touch the stone again.

They are quite protective of you. That's good. The sound isn't a voice, but it speaks, nonetheless. It sounds like rocks tumbling together, or sand being poured against glass, or pebbles crunching beneath a boot, more mechanical than biological.

"Why is that good?" I ask.

You are the one who would free me, are you not?

"I am," I reply.

"What's it saying?" Fenmire asks.

"It asked if I'm the one who wants to free it."

"Can it hear you as well?"

"I think so."

I hear and see everything.

I nod up at Fenmire before asking, "Are we in danger? Will one of Reilanna's beasts come through soon?"

Another Earthen dusk and dawn will pass before I have the strength again for that.

"Tomorrow, Fenmire. There will be more beasts tomorrow."

I'm pleased to meet the one who will finally free me from that witch's tethers. I can't stand them. They're like chains around my jaws, ripping my mouth open whenever it suits her. I can taste them, like bitter poison on my tongue.

"How can I sever them?"

At this, The Gate laughs. *You already know.*

"Is there no other way?"

No. Reilanna was crafty when she cast her spell. You must mate with each of the four Gryxen and then come to me.

I swallow. "Then what will happen?"

I will accept payment.

"What does that mean?"

I think you already know the answer to that too, human. You'll have to pass through me to break the spell completely. Reilanna no doubt means for me to take your life in the process, but…

"But?" I prod.

I don't have the power to take or give life, so how Reilanna expects me to take yours is a mystery even to me, but when the moment comes and you pass through, I promise to spare you, if I can.

"What's happening, Evangeline?" Fenmire asks.

I ignore him. "Why should I believe you?"

You don't have to. You'll come to me regardless to save the ones you love. It's only a matter of time. If Reilanna doesn't kill you first, that is.

"Do you know what she's planning?"

I can't see the future, but I can see the present. The golden city, the one they call Michastiforo, is golden no longer. Now it is black and filled with evil. The sun never rises upon it, and a piece of it caves with each quake when she shoves her foul beasts through me.

"What happened to the people who used to live there?"

The day Reilanna was trapped on the other side, she turned her fury toward the city. Many escaped. Many more did not. The ones who took up arms against her died. The temple priestesses, along with their warriors, were all slaughtered, and the temple was crushed to rubble. All trade stopped. Those who are left live in the shadows and step lightly so as not to anger her. They bring her creatures she can twist into her beasts as tribute for peace. They are a starving, dying people. Michastiforo is no more.

Tears burn in my eyes at the picture it paints, so different from the one Caliborne has shown me in his memories. This will crush them all to hear.

"What is it?" Fenmire asks.

I shake my head, mostly to clear it. I must focus and think. What else should I ask? What else do I need to know?

"Is there anything else you can tell me that will help us?"

There is nothing, human. You know what you must do. Come to me once you've finished your task.

I feel rather than hear The Gate go silent. A vibration I hadn't noticed until it stops was rumbling under my hand the whole time. Its absence makes my arm feel funny, and I shake the feeling away.

"What did it say?" Fenmire asks, and for once his tone is free of any judgment or hostility.

"Becoming a mate to all four of you is the only way to break the spell," I say. "And Reilanna has taken over and destroyed Michastiforo. It's gone."

Fenmire hangs his head. "I'd feared as much. How else would she have such constant access to The Gate? What did it say about what happens after you mate with us?"

"I have to pass through The Gate."

"That's it?" Fenmire narrows his eyes skeptically. "There has to be more to it than that."

"It thinks so too, but it doesn't know what Reilanna plans for me after that."

"Nothing good." He runs his hand down his chin thoughtfully. "There has to be something we're missing. The Gate is a doorway, nothing more. If a doorway is all that's required to break the spell, there must be a way to—"

"Fenmire," I say, and when those shimmering eyes meet mine, I touch his arm. "I need you to make me a promise. You're the only one I can trust to keep it."

"What is it?" he asks carefully, not promising anything until he hears my request.

"When the time comes, *if* it comes, I need you to promise to send me through The Gate. No matter what that means. No matter the outcome or the cost. When it comes time to break the spell, send me through. Can you promise me that?"

Fenmire's eyes are wide with shock, and I still can't understand his thoughts to know what he's thinking as he stands there in silence. I expect him to deny me and tell me that I'm being ridiculous, that he has a dozen other things for me to try before we resort to that.

He says none of those things.

His shoulders sag, and he bows his head at me. "I promise."

"No matter what?" I ask.

"When the time comes, I'll make sure you go through The Gate. No matter what."

I can't resist. I hug him. "Thank you, Fenmire."

At first, I don't think he's going to hug me back, but then a hand finally rests on my back.

I won't survive this.

"You will," I say, and he jumps. He must not have realized his thoughts slipped into my language. "We both will. We just have to have faith."

"I'm in short supply of that nowadays."

"I'll simply have to find enough for both of us then."

I earn another chuckle, the second in the same day.

I feel honored.

*****

Fenmire flies us to the front door on the way back since it's lunchtime and that's closer to the kitchen. As soon as we walk in, Wexton enters the foyer from the staircase, the one that leads down to the pool room, though he doesn't look fresh from a bath.

"There you are," he says as soon as he sees me. "I've been looking for you." He glances at Fenmire at my side. "Where've you been?"

Fenmire looks down at me, no doubt waiting for whatever story I'll come up with to explain our whereabouts, but now that we've done what we needed to, I see no reason to lie to Wexton.

"We were at The Gate," I say.

Wexton's face falls, and his eyes turn accusatory as he glares at Fenmire. "Why?" he asks simply, his voice one of simmering rage.

Fenmire shrugs. "Call it an experiment."

"If you want to experiment with your own health and safety, Fenmire, be my guest, but leave Evangeline out of your mad schemes."

"I *wanted* to go," I say. "I sought out Fenmire myself and asked him to take me."

"Why?" Wexton asks, more gently this time.

"To learn if there are other ways for me to break Reilanna's spell."

Wexton's shoulders slump a bit. "Do you not wish to mate with… us?"

I know what he was about to ask instead.

I walk over to him and meet his eyes, holding his gaze as I say, "That's not at all how I feel. It's not fair that the four of you have no choice in the matter. If I mate with any or all of you, I'd rather it be out of desire and not necessity. That's all."

Wexton kneels down on one knee. "It's not out of necessity for me."

I smile. "I know." I drop my voice to a whisper and say, "You weren't the one I was referring to."

Wexton's eyes flick briefly up over my shoulder at Fenmire.

I bob my brows instead of nodding.

Wexton takes my hand. *It won't be out of necessity for him either. He already has feelings for you, you know that right?*

Another bob of my brows.

Please be careful. I understand your desire to protect him, but don't sacrifice your safety in exchange.

"We were safe. That was the first thing I asked The Gate."

"*Asked*? You *spoke* to it?"

"It seems The Gate is capable of conscious thought," Fenmire says.

"What did you learn?"

"The mating bonds are the only thing that can break the spell," I say, then I hang my head. "And Michastiforo has been destroyed."

"Destroyed? By Reilanna?"

"Yes. The Gate said it's no longer a golden city but a black one. The sun never rises there, and the people are either dead or dying."

"The temple?"

"The priestesses were all killed when Reilanna sacked the city. The temple was toppled shortly after." At the horror in Wexton's eyes, I say softly, "I'm sorry."

I'll tear her to pieces. The evil, heinous witch.

I take his face between my hands. "You'll free your people. You'll bring the peace back to Michastiforo. Have faith."

Behind me, Fenmire sniffs.

Wexton's hand settles over one of mine. "*We* will liberate the golden city. All of us, together."

I smile and nod, but secretly, I doubt very much I'll be there to see Michastiforo shine golden once more. "You said you were looking for me?"

"Yes. I have a surprise for you, but it will have to wait until after lunch now." He gets to his feet. "Care to join me?"

"I'd love to. Will you join us too, Fenmire?"

"No thank you," he says, though his tone is far warmer than it usually is. It seems our excursion today yielded a cease fire between him and I, if nothing else. "You two enjoy your meal. I've work to get back to." He quickly takes to the stairs and disappears.

Once he's out of earshot, Wexton asks, "Did you two enjoy each other's company today at least?"

"'Tolerated' would be a better word, but it wasn't an unpleasant adventure. He told me you're responsible for the crushed portion of the castle."

"That doesn't sound like me," he says with a smirk as he starts down the corridor toward the kitchen.

I laugh and trail after him. "That sounds *exactly* like you."

Chapter 28

Caliborne is eating when Wexton and I enter the dining room. I sit across the table from him like I usually do, but Wexton takes the seat to my left instead of beside Caliborne where he normally sits. I eye him curiously, but he ignores me as he tears into his food.

"Oh, Cal," Wexton says with his mouth full of black meat. "Ask your mate what they were up to with Fenmire this morning." He elbows me so hard I drop my spoon into my stew, flinging a piece of potato out onto my tray. "Go on, tell him."

I load the runaway potato back onto my spoon and fling it at him. It smacks him on the cheek.

"That mouth of yours will be your end one of these days," I grumble. I look sheepishly up at Caliborne. "I went with Fenmire to The Gate."

Caliborne tilts his head, waiting for me to go on.

So I do. I tell him everything The Gate told me, though I don't bring up the promise Fenmire made me afterward.

"Can you believe it, Cal?" Wexton asks. "They're trying to find a way out of mating with us." He looks down at me. "Little do they know, we're far too charming to resist, spell or no spell."

"I thought we've established you're anything but charming."

Wexton's wicked little grin is back. "And you like it that way."

I look at Caliborne and try to gauge his reaction to my trip to The Gate. For the first time in a while, he uses his palm to tell me how he's feeling, and I experience a wave of worry, intrigue, and a bit of anger.

"We were safe," I say to alleviate the worry. "You know I just want to help, however I can. I don't feel there's any harm in trying other things. It doesn't mean I don't want to have mates," I say with a caustic look at Wexton. "It's just good to know all the ways I'm useful, is all. I'm angry and sad to hear what's become of Michastiforo. I hope it can all be undone after the spell is broken."

"The city can be rebuilt," Wexton says. "Even the temple can be replaced. I'm the most upset about the priestesses. Seerraf and the five must've wept that day. All that pointless bloodshed." He shakes his head.

"Who are 'the five'? I hear them mentioned regularly."

"The five are Seerraf's most loyal acolytes. They've each done him a great service to earn their place at his side."

"So, they aren't gods?"

"Not gods, no. They were once just everyday folk, followers of Seerraf and his teachings. They each did something that proved they were pure of heart in a way beyond simple goodness."

"They're heroes then?"

Caliborne nods.

"That's something you could ask Fenmire about, if you need topics of discussion," Wexton says. "Ask him to tell you each of the five's heroic acts that earned them their place at Seerraf's side. He no doubt has those tales memorized."

The conversation dies down to silent chewing for a while, and about the time I scoop the last spoonful of my stew into my mouth, Wexton pushes his plate away. It's still half full of food.

"Since when do you leave a meal on your plate?" I ask. "Are you feeling alright?"

"Just fine. I'm simply not in the mood for meat today."

"What else is there?" I mean it to be rhetorical, but he leans down near my ear and answers anyway.

"I'd like to delve my tongue into something sweeter, something much more tender, warm, and wet."

Caliborne, who's mid-drink, snorts into his cup.

I smack Wexton on the arm.

"Ooo, you want to put up a bit of a fight first?" Wexton asks. "I can oblige, darling, as long as you understand your loss is inevitable. I'll even chase you up and down the halls if that'll sweeten your flavor beforehand."

I groan, mostly because he's absolutely ridiculous, but also because a part of me—and I don't know how big that part is—finds the thought of him chasing me down and taking what he wants highly alluring. I go one step further and picture him holding my wrists together above my head as he enters me. In this fantasy, we're not even in bed but sprawled out on the stone floor.

I don't realize I'm staring at him until he grins and winks at me.

Of course my face is on fire again. I should carry a fan around with me all day like the girls in my village. Was that why they were constantly fanning themselves? To save them the embarrassment of burning cheeks whenever their thoughts ran away with them? I doubt any of them had to deal with a dirty-talking demon whispering all manner of indecent things in their ears all damn day.

Not that I'm complaining about that part.

Caliborne coughs conspicuously and stands from his stool.

"You don't have to go," I say.

He comes around the table with his plate and kisses me on the cheek.

Douse his fires, my stoferra. You clearly want to. I'll see you tonight.

"I love you."

He takes my chin in his hand and kisses me again then claps Wexton on the shoulder on his way out.

Caliborne is barely out of the room when I'm whisked off my stool and set up on the table in front of Wexton.

"What on earth are you—" His tongue in my mouth cuts me off.

"I told you I'd make you a meal," he murmurs against my lips. "Or have you forgotten?"

"We're in the *dining room.*"

"What better place for a meal than a room made entirely for eating?"

I can't help but laugh, but then I glance over at the open door. "What if someone walks in?"

"Does the thought of getting caught bother you?"

Bother me? No. Excite me? I give him a mischievous grin of my own.

"I didn't think so," he says, then he captures my mouth again.

My arms loop around his neck as that wicked mouth and tongue turn my brain to mush. His hand inches up under my shirt, his calloused fingers scratching lightly over the soft skin of my belly as they head for my chest. His palm grazes across one of my breasts, and the nipple hardens into a sensitive little bud. He takes it between his finger and thumb, rolling it lightly before pinching it hard enough to make me jump with a moan.

"Oh, you like that," he whispers. "How about this?"

His head dives under my shirt, and I lean back on my arms to give him room as he replaces his hand with his mouth. That forked tongue swipes across the same nipple, then he sucks it. I bite my lip so hard it hurts to keep from crying out as his arm goes behind my back, holding me up as he switches to my other breast. This time, he rolls my nipple between his teeth, slowly increasing the pressure until I whimper.

He relinquishes my breast and starts kissing a slow trail down my stomach. He knocks my arms out from under me and lowers me to my back on the table. His face emerges from under my shirt, and he peers up at me as his forked tongue flicks into my belly button.

I laugh, but the sound dies away when he starts unbuttoning my pants.

He stops. "I don't like that crinkle in your brow. What's wrong?"

"I've never had someone's mouth… down there before," I say truthfully.

"Do you want me to stop?"

"I haven't bathed today."

He grins again. "Good. You'll taste even sweeter."

I bite my lip against fresh desire.

He continues to wait for me to choose.

I reach down and unbutton the rest of my pants, inching them out from under me until my bare backside hits the chilly table.

Wexton continues to kiss my lower belly, his eyes never leaving mine. "I want to hear it."

"Hear what?"

"That you want me."

I close my eyes as my cheeks burn. "I want you," I mumble.

He chuckles. "Louder, darling. I couldn't quite hear you."

I swear up at the ceiling, look him in the eyes, and say, "You better put that salacious mouth to good use between my thighs or I'll get up from this table and go find someone who will."

His tongue flicks down toward the patch of dark curls near his chin. "You're not going anywhere until I've finished my meal."

He takes my pants down to my ankles and sets my feet in his lap before parting my knees. His kisses start again, just on the inside of my knee, and trail up the inside of my thighs toward where I'm aching. And wet. My damp arousal chills where it's exposed to the air, and it reminds me we're still in the middle of the dining room. I'm now on full display for anyone who walks in here. I rub my face against the fresh burn at the thought.

Part of me hopes someone walks in.

Wexton's face brushes against my pubic hair as he works his way up my thigh, but just before he reaches his final destination, he stops.

"Right here," he says softly, tracing a circle on my thigh just below my sex.

"What?" I ask, already breathless at the thought of having a demon's face between my legs.

"This is where my mate mark will go."

He doesn't give me a chance to refute him as he parts me wide open with his fingers and licks me, that wicked tongue of his dipping into me before flicking up over my clit.

A second later, he sucks on it just like he did my nipple.

The moan that comes out of me makes me cover my face with both of my hands, but I drop them again to slap the table as his finger joins the fun, sliding deep inside me. He pulls it right back out again and licks it clean with a moan of his own.

"Gods, Evangeline," he mutters. "Tender and sweet doesn't come close to how you taste." He licks me again and hums. "I want every drop of your cum on my tongue."

My heart kicks into overdrive. "You're an absolute heathen," I hiss.

He chuckles. "I know." And then his mouth is on me again, only with far more vigor than before. His tongue slides deep inside me, lapping at me like I'm a feast to save a dying soul with the occasional suck on my clit that makes me buck my hips, grinding myself against his face.

I toss my head from side to side, lost in pleasure. I'm begging, though I'm not sure for what exactly. My hips flex up on instinct as my first orgasm builds, and Wexton throws his arm over me, holding me down as he thrusts his tongue in and out of me. I come apart with a cry I try to keep soft, but I know I fail. My nails scrape across the tabletop as he rides out the storm with his tongue still deep inside me, and once the twitching stops, he pulls back enough to breathe in deep and let it out on a growl.

"That smells heavenly," he murmurs. He reaches down and pets the wet curls between my legs. "You got any more of that sweet nectar in there for me?"

He yanks my boots and pants off and throws each of my legs over his shoulder, then he drags me to the edge of the table before diving right back in. My thighs clench around his face, and he moans, the vibration of it driving me wild as he sucks my clit again. He peppers every inch of my sex with kisses, and when his tongue flicks out again, it swipes down across my backside.

"Wexton!" I cry out as I jump.

"I bet that hole tastes just as good."

I'm going to pass away. Right here, right now, I'm going to melt into a puddle and disappear from how hot my entire body is burning.

"Are we not ready for that yet?" he asks sweetly.

"Yet?" I ask, my voice as high and squeaky as a barn mouse.

"There's plenty of fun to be had back there as well, darling. Soon," he promises, though I don't know if he's talking to himself, me, or my ass.

Probably all three.

I hear footsteps in the hall, and I tense with a gasp as someone rounds the corner and walks in. It's Fenmire. He has one massive golden plate in one hand and an open book in the other, and when he glances up from the pages, he freezes just inside the door, his eyes going wide as he sees me splayed out on the table. Wexton doesn't seem to notice him as he doesn't stop licking and sucking and delving into all my naughty bits. It's not until Fenmire clears his throat that Wexton pauses and peers over my thigh toward the door.

There's a long moment of silence as Wexton and I look at Fenmire, whose eyes flick back and forth between us as he continues to stand there, still as stone and staring.

My heart is thundering in my chest, and yet my greatest wish in that moment is for Wexton's mouth to go back to sucking on my clit.

Wexton is unfazed, and he proves as much by replacing his mouth with his hand, his fingers teasing and thrusting as he watches Fenmire.

Despite the audience—or perhaps because of it—I moan.

Fenmire swallows, and his eyes lock onto me and only me.

I don't break that contact as I audibly moan again.

Fenmire snaps his book shut, and a look crosses his face that makes me feel like prey caught in a predator's gaze. It sends a delicious shiver down my spine right to the place where Wexton's hand is pleasuring me.

"Are you going to keep standing there watching, Fen?" Wexton asks. "Or would you rather join us?" He looks at me. "What do you think, darling? You think you can handle two filthy demons making a meal out of you? Would you like that?"

He adds a second finger inside me, and I gasp and bite my lip, not trusting my voice to give him an answer yet. I'm doomed even more when his thumb starts circling my clit.

"Oh, God," I mutter.

"That wasn't a no, Fen," Wexton says. He leans down and kisses my belly just above my pubic hair, and his tongue snakes down to circle my clit in place of his thumb. "You should taste this." His fingers slide out of me, and he holds them up for Fenmire to see my glistening juices before sucking them into his mouth. "Mmm, delicious."

Fenmire is still staring at me, his eyes roaming over all my exposed bits before locking onto mine.

"Is that what you want, Evangeline?" he asks, his voice low and deadly. "You want two beasts to eat you until you beg them to stop?"

The fact that those words come from Fenmire makes them ten times more potent. Add in the fact that Wexton is back between my legs in full force, and I almost orgasm again right there.

"Please," I whimper pitifully.

Wexton knows I'm close, and his tongue moves faster, determined to make me come while Fenmire watches. It won't take much convincing on his part. A wave of heat is already gathering throughout my entire body, heading for my center where Wexton's tongue is buried to the hilt inside me.

Fenmire licks his lips. "I like being begged," he says. "But that wasn't quite enough. Do it again. Do it harder."

I swallow and close my eyes. "Pl—"

"Look at me!"

The sharpness of his voice freezes my lungs in my chest. Nothing else matters except making my eyes stare directly into his. It's as if he's reached right into my soul to command my every move.

"Beg," he orders.

"Please," I say obediently.

"Harder."

"Please, Fenmire!" I cry. My hips buck against Wexton's face, and my legs start to shake, but all I can focus on are those shimmering black eyes as the moment stretches on and on. My orgasm is locked behind a wall I can't break, and I whimper again, desperate for release.

Fenmire nods. "That's very good, pet." His chin tilts up and his eyes narrow. "Now come on his face."

Do I ever.

My orgasm shoots straight through me like a lightning strike. Tears burn in my eyes as I twitch and flop on the table, my legs clutching Wexton's head so tight it's a miracle he can even breathe, though he's certainly not complaining.

Fenmire never looks away. "Looks like this meal has already been claimed," he says once I finally go still. "Maybe next time." He tucks his book under his arm, inclines his head at me, and leaves Wexton and I alone in the dining room once again.

That just happened.

I peek down at Wexton, and he winks up at me.

"Told you he'd come around," he says.

"I didn't think you meant literally."

"Neither did I."

He offers me his hand to sit up, which I appreciate since my limbs are no use to me right now. Once we're face to face again, I realize his is glistening wet.

"Would you like a napkin?" I tease.

His eyes get an evil little glint.

"No!" I scream, but it's too late.

He buries his face against my chest and wipes it dry on my shirt.

"You are every inch the beast I was warned about growing up!" I declare, then I pout. "Now I'll have to change before I go down to the stables."

Wexton's face falls. "You're going to the stables?"

"Yes, Percival says one of the foxes is about to give birth. He invited me to watch."

"Oh. Alright."

The disappointment on his face confuses me.

"You can come too, of course. Or are you still busy in the forge?"

"Who told you I was in the forge?"

"No one. I guessed. There aren't many places in the castle for you to disappear to."

He clears his throat. "Yes, well, my armor needed some maintenance. It's a big job to tear it all apart, fix it up, and put it back together again."

I play along. "Have you finished fixing it, then?"

"I have."

My stomach flutters. "I can't wait to see it. Was that the surprise you wanted to show me?"

"No. That's… outside."

"Outside?" What could he have possibly made for me outside?

"Yes, but it's getting late enough in the day it will have to wait until tomorrow. Or, I suppose the next day would be better since you said The Gate will open again tomorrow, right?"

"That's what it told me. Are you sure you don't mind waiting, though? We could stop by the stables for a moment then head out the back door to your surprise."

He pats my bare thigh. "Don't fret. It will wait for another day. It's not your fault you've already made plans, and I don't expect you to drop what you're doing at the snap of my fingers."

"That's good because if I end up mating with all four of you, you're all going to have to have some patience when it comes to sharing my time."

"Exactly. So, to the stables then?"

I point down at my pants and boots on the floor. "Can I have those back first?"

"Are you sure? I'd love nothing more than to watch your bare backside all the way to the stables."

"We're not supposed to be traumatizing the staff, remember?"

He snorts. "You humans place way too much importance on modesty." He plucks my pants up from the floor and starts threading one of my legs into them.

"Wrong leg," I say. "Turn them around. And you can thank Adam and Eve for the modesty."

He takes the pantleg back off and swaps it for the other. "You and who?"

"Not me. A different Eve. The first man and woman were called Adam and Eve. They lived happily naked until they defied God and ate fruit from the tree of knowledge. Then they suddenly realized they were naked and ran to cover themselves in embarrassment."

Wexton wrinkles his brow. "That's a horrible story. The pursuit of knowledge should be encouraged. Why would your God forbid his beings from seeking it?"

"Because in seeking knowledge it destroyed their innocence."

"Why would the pursuit of knowledge destroy their innocence?" he asks as he starts threading my other leg into my pants.

"Everything they knew before eating from the tree was good and pure. They weren't ashamed of their nakedness because they didn't know what it was to feel ashamed. Eating from the tree woke shame and guilt and other evils inside them."

"That seems rather backward," he argues. "True knowledge would say there is no reason to be ashamed of one's body. It's all just flesh, blood, and bones, nothing to be ashamed of."

"I think it had more to do with testing their faith and obedience. God told them not to touch that tree and only that tree, but they did so anyway. Their punishment was full knowledge of sin. And being thrown out of the garden, of course."

"Sounds like an awfully manipulative and moody God," Wexton grumbles. With my pants finally on and pulled up to my thighs, he slips one of my boots back on and retrieves the other from across the room. "That's like setting a toy in front of a child and telling them not to touch it then getting angry when they do it anyway. It's like he wanted them to fail."

I smile at him. "It's only a story, Wexton, one of many to help teach us God's will."

He slides my other boot on then helps me down from the table. "I think they're teaching you all the wrong lessons."

I pull up my pants and work the buttons closed before smoothing my shirt back down. "What sorts of things does Seerraf teach?"

Wexton counts them out on his fingers as he lists them. "Loyalty, kindness, charity, honesty, forgiveness, acceptance… I think that's all the most important ones, anyway."

"Obedience isn't one of them?"

"No. Obedience isn't a virtue. Seerraf doesn't order us, he shows us the kinds of people we should be by being all of those things himself. Our scriptures are filled with stories of Seerraf's acts of virtue, stories like "The Beggar and the Coin" and "The Brothers' Oath." They're all told from Seerraf's point of view and describe what he would do in a given situation. He leads by example through such stories. Some of them are quite entertaining; others are heartwarming. A few make me cry every time I hear them."

"I would love to read those."

"Ask Fenmire. He no doubt has them all written down somewhere."

"It might be a while before I can face him again."

Wexton grins. "If I were you, I'd skip off to the library right now, still covered in my own juices"—he plucks at the front of my slightly damp shirt—"just to see what he'd do."

I shake my head, my face burning again at the mere memory of it all.

Wexton tosses my hair over my shoulder and sets his hand on the back of my neck, pulling me nearer as he stares down into my eyes. "Don't you dare feel embarrassed about what happened here, not for a second," he says with conviction. "You have nothing to feel ashamed of. You ate no forbidden fruit, Evangeline." He leans down and sets his forehead against mine. "This fruit is ripe and willing and begging to be eaten." *Still curious to know how I taste?*

"Yes, but I don't want to do that here. I've never done it before and am nervous enough about trying it."

He touches my chin. *You let me know when you're ready, darling. I'm not going anywhere.*

Even without a courting gift, I'm starting to believe him.

Chapter 29

It's four days before Wexton and I can venture outside.

The Gate does indeed open when it said it would, and again, Reilanna sends one spitter and one of her regular, simple beasts. It seems, for now, that's all The Gate can handle, but at least it takes longer for it to recharge enough for each attack. Longer stretches of peace in exchange for more dangerous battles; I can't decide if I prefer this arrangement over our previous one or vice versa.

The day after that, it does nothing but snow.

On the third morning, it's bright and sunny, so I go looking for Wexton only to discover he's disappeared again. He spends the day off somewhere before showing up just before dusk.

"Tomorrow," he declares. "Tomorrow, first thing, I give you your surprise."

So it is that, as soon as the sun rises that fourth morning, Wexton comes banging on Caliborne's bedroom door, demanding we get up and dress and meet him promptly in the foyer. When I remind him about breakfast, he sits impatiently on the stool beside me in the dining room and watches every bite travel from my plate to my mouth until I give up halfway through my porridge and let him haul me to my room.

"Dress warmly, but… not too warmly," he says.

I laugh. "What does that even mean?"

He leaves me to figure it out on my own as he goes to retrieve something from his own room. Both he and Caliborne are waiting for me in the foyer once I'm dressed and ready to go. Wexton has a wooden box under his arm as he stands impatiently at the door with his hand on the knob.

"Finally," he grumbles, and he yanks the door open. "Let's go!"

"Are we flying?" I ask as Caliborne and I follow him out.

"It's a long walk otherwise."

I reach for my mate, and Caliborne scoops me up into his arms.

"Do you know what he's up to?" I ask.

I don't, but I wouldn't tell you even if I did.

"If I ask the right questions, your mind might."

I'm sixteen thousand years old. I think I can control my thoughts better than that.

"Not if last night was any judge."

He blows a puff of air in my face, and I jump and laugh before we shoot up into the sky. It's a bright, sunny day, so the flight isn't as cold this time, but I still hide my face against Caliborne's chest to keep my cheeks from burning in the wind. We land at the edge of a pond.

Wait.

I know this place.

"Is this where we first met?" I ask Caliborne.

It is indeed.

The space has changed a bit since I was here last, and not just because of the nicer weather. The pond that was once covered in windswept snow is clear now. In fact, it's smooth as glass. That's when I notice the piles of shoveled snow all around the edges as well as the hole where the ice has recently been broken to access the water underneath. That must be how the surface is so flawlessly smooth. Wexton spread a layer of water out across the ice yesterday, which froze overnight to create…

"An ice rink," I say in awe. "Wexton—"

I turn to find the Gryxen in question down on one knee with the wooden box balanced on his palm between us.

"Eve," he says. He looks a bit nervous, the poor thing. "I promised to show you how serious I am about you, about us, and there isn't a more serious act of devotion and commitment for my people than this."

He nods down at the box, and I open my hands for him to pass it to me so he can open the lid. Inside sits two golden ice skates. Their bases are large flat slabs where the bottoms of my boots sit above long, shiny golden blades. There are leather straps attached to the sides and backs to strap them securely around my boots. Along the sides of the blades, wildlife scenes are carved in vivid detail. I recognize every creature—from the large elk down to the tiny mice—as each of the ones housed in the stables. A giant letter E is carved into the center of each skate, marking them as mine no matter which name I'm using for the day.

"A courting gift," Wexton says. "To show you I am truly yours and to officially ask if you would consider becoming my mate."

I touch one of the skates, running my finger along the elk's impressive antlers before softly closing the box and hugging it to my chest. I'm a bit breathless with emotion as I reply, "I accept."

Wexton smiles. "Good. Because I really want to see you skate like the wind."

I laugh and wipe my wet eyes.

Caliborne touches my shoulder.

I turn and open the box again to show him the skates.

What are those for? he asks.

"Let me show you."

Wexton lets me sit on his drawn-up leg with his arm behind me so I don't fall as I lace up the skates, then Caliborne picks me up to carry me over the snow to the edge of the ice. He sets me gently down on the skates. It's been so long since I've done this, and the ice is so smooth that I almost immediately fall on my backside. The only reason I don't is because Caliborne is still standing right behind me and catches me.

Are you sure this is safe? he frets.

"I just need to get my bearings."

Beside us, Wexton steps out onto the ice, his claws digging in with each step to keep him from sliding. When he holds out his hand to me, I give him both of mine, and he pulls me slowly out of Caliborne's arms and out onto the pond with him.

"How did you know how to create a rink?" I ask. "Do people skate in your world?"

"I'm afraid our feet aren't quite designed for such sports," Wexton says. "Fenmire helped me. Once I explained it to him, he knew just what to do to make the perfect surface for it."

I test my balance with a few tentative swipes of my new blades and let go of him with one hand. While he still holds the other, I circle him, and he pivots with me, allowing me to safely get a feel for the ice. Once I'm confident I won't fall on my face, I let go of him and push off over the pond. I've never skated so smoothly before, and I have to pace myself so I don't go too fast too quickly, but soon enough, my body remembers what to do, and I sail and spin over the ice, making figure eights and laughing as a familiar childhood happiness washes over me.

The sunshine, the click and swoosh of the skates, the feel of the wind in my face as I pick up speed, and the grace in my movements I can never find anywhere else… All that's missing is Will, and it would all be perfect. I try not to let his absence ruin the moment and instead circle back around to Wexton, who pulls me close under his arm.

"You look so free," he says in awe. "I understand why your kind enjoys this."

"It's as close to flying as we can get."

"If I had both my arms, I'd get you closer."

"You don't need both your arms to make me happy, Wexton." I hold his hand and spin underneath it as if we're dancing. I point down at my skates. "These are beautiful." I wave an arm behind me at the pond. "This is beautiful." I beckon him back down on one knee and take his face between my hands. "Thank you."

He thumbs my chin. "You're welcome, darling. Is this proof enough of my loyalty then?"

I kiss him once, softly. "Your word is proof enough. I told you that already."

His eyes bore into mine, and his arm tightens around me. "I don't deserve you. I'm not sure that any of us do. Maybe Caliborne, but—"

"I'm nothing special. I just happen to fit the requirements of Reilanna's spell."

"I don't think that's true. I think she knew exactly what she was doing. She knew what kind of soul it would take to free us, and she never thought we'd find one."

"What kind of soul is that?"

"A pure one."

I start to argue all the reasons I'm anything but a pure soul, but I'm interrupted when a giant snowball strikes Wexton in the back of the head, explodes, and dusts us both in icy white. We sputter and shake the snow from our hair and face and round on Caliborne, who's already forming his next projectile by one of the shoveled piles of snow.

"To war!" Wexton cries.

I shriek with laughter as we both bolt to a nearby snow pile, ducking as Caliborne keeps up the assault on us both. I use Wexton as a shield and pop around his massive body to throw snowballs at Caliborne, but then I move away to my own bank and form no less than a dozen balls of my own before launching an attack on Wexton from behind.

"Treachery!" Wexton yells as he's pummeled from both sides. "Treachery within the ranks!" He flaps his massive wings to give him speed as he darts across the pond, his claws raking the ice as he skids to a stop on the other side.

It's a three-way battle now, every man for himself, though the two Gryxen target each other far more than they target me as I lob balls at them both. I'm so consumed in our game, that it takes me a moment to hear the subtle flap of wings from somewhere nearby. I look up, and at first, the beast in the sky terrifies me as I think Reilanna must've sent something through The Gate, but then I recognize Drixus' mount as it flies overhead, though I've never seen it this close before. I still can't see its rider, but I can see the feathers on the beast's underbelly as well as its beaked mouth and long, tapered tail. It looks like an eagle, a horse, and a dragon combined into one.

"Drixus!" I shout, and I wave to get his attention.

A hand touches my shoulder. *Don't be disappointed if he doesn't come down,* Caliborne tells me.

"I don't expect him to, but I want him to know the invitation is open."

Wexton joins us on my other side. "He's not on patrol today. He came to watch."

"It seems he does that a lot."

"What do you mean?" Wexton asks.

"Oh, I don't think I told you about that." I describe my encounter with Drixus at the arch after the spitter attack.

"That's good, Eve. Even if he's merely curious, it's better than the cold indifference we've gotten from him these past two thousand years."

We all watch Drixus circle a couple more times then fly off back toward the castle.

"It's a start," I say thoughtfully.

Chapter 30

I skate until the temperature drops enough that the exercise can't keep me warm anymore. Once my cheeks and nose begin to burn, I sit on Wexton's leg again as Caliborne plucks the straps loose from around my boots, dusts the snow and water from my skates, and sets them back in their box. Our flight back to the castle is a bit more uncomfortable, but the kiss on the neck Caliborne gives me as he sets me down helps bring some heat back to my face afterward.

I have patrol again tonight, he reminds me as we head inside. *I need to take over for Fenmire soon.*

"I know. Don't worry. I think I might have plans."

Caliborne looks across the foyer as Wexton pauses at the end of the hall to wink back at me before heading to his room.

Ah, yes, I see.

"I'm sure he just plans to teach me how to play cards."

He laughs that silent, shaky laugh of his. *Absolutely. Without a doubt, that's what he's planning.*

I give my box of skates a shake. "I'm going to put these in my room then I'll come help you with your armor, if you like."

I'd rather you go take a bath. You were in the cold an awfully long time today.

Hmm, tempting.

We both know what Wexton really has planned for tonight, and it isn't cards. Perhaps a bath is a good idea since I've been sweating most of the day.

"You're right."

I usually am.

"I still want to help you get dressed, though."

Whatever makes you happy, my stoferra.

Ten minutes later, with my skates tucked away in my room, I'm standing on Caliborne's bed so I can reach to help him buckle on his shoulder and chest plates. Once those are secured, he sits on the side of the bed so I can brush his hair, and when I'm done, I hop down to stand in front of him between his knees so he can brush mine. It's something we started doing about a week ago, a small, intimate thing we do to care for each other. Sometimes we talk, and sometimes, like tonight, we sit in silence broken only by the sound of the bristles working through the tangles.

When my hair brushes soft and smooth, Caliborne leans in and kisses me on the side of my neck, and I lean my cheek against him.

My heart is so full and happy that it makes me wonder, when I take another mate, if this feeling will only intensify, or if I will feel a little empty whenever I'm with one of them and not the other. I would ask but, considering none of them have had more than one mate before, they wouldn't be able to tell me from experience. In the end, it doesn't matter. I plan to mate with Wexton regardless. If not tonight, then soon.

*****

After my bath, as I'm headed back to my room to drop off my laundry and wash bag, I run into Percival as we both enter the foyer from the stairs, him from the upper floors and me from the lower one.

"Good evening, Percival," I say.

"Good evening, Eve," he greets happily.

"What were you doing upstairs?"

"I was helping… um…"

"Fenmire?"

"No."

"Drixus?" I ask in disbelief.

"Sort of? He has a companion. I was helping her more than him, really."

"You mean that flying beast Drixus rides? That companion?"

He nods. "She has an irritated feather making her quite uncomfortable. Drixus asked me to help him take care of it since I'm the most knowledgeable when it comes to feathered friends."

"Will she be alright?"

"Oh, sure. It's a common ailment for her since Drixus occasionally upsets a feather or two while fighting from her back. It's inevitable in their line of work."

"Does she have a name?"

"Drixus calls her Mara."

"Where did she come from?"

"Where do all beasts in The Deadwood come from?"

"Drixus caught and tamed one of Reilanna's horrors?"

"'Tamed' is a bit of a stretch, but yes, Mara was one of the creatures sent through The Gate by the sorceress. From what I understand, Caliborne knocked her from the sky, and when Drixus went to finish her off on the ground, he chose to spare her instead."

"I'm surprised the others allowed it, all things considered."

"She allows him to fight in the air again, so I suppose they thought the benefits outweighed the risks."

I grunt thoughtfully.

"I need to get back to the stables for feeding time. Do you want to join me?"

"I'm sorry, I can't this time. I have plans for this evening and still haven't had my own dinner."

He gives me a kind smile. "Until next time, then."

I wait until Percival is far enough down the hall that he can't see me, then I dart silently up the stairs to the third floor.

The first thing I notice is how cold it is up here. Cold and dark. The sconces in this hall aren't lit, so the only light comes from a window all the way at the end. It's dusk now, so even that is muted. All the doors are closed, and the air feels heavy and stale.

I shiver, and it's not from the cold.

There's a layer of dust on the floor with fresh prints leading off to the left, a single set that leads both away and back again. I follow them down the hall to a door on the left, the second from the end of the hall. I lean near the wood and listen.

At first, there's no sound, and my feet start to ache for how long I stand there, back stiff and ear pressed to the door, but then I hear a scuff, like the scrape of Gryxen talons on stone. That's when the muttering starts. I listen for a moment, but it's far too quiet to understand any of it.

I gather my courage, lift my hand, and knock. "Drixus?"

The silence that immediately falls on the other side of the door makes my heart thump loudly in my ears.

"Drixus, it's Evangeline." Have the others explained about my names yet? I don't know how much he knows about me. "I saw you today, and I just came to introduce myself. I haven't had the chance yet, and I'd love to meet you face to face sometime, if you'd like. If not, that's alright. The invitation is open."

I wait, but there's no response.

"I tell you what: I'll come back in a week. Same day, same time. If you want to meet me, simply leave your door open. If not, I understand."

I still don't get a reply, but I'm no longer expecting one. I push away from the door and head back downstairs.

*****

With my dinner in hand, I go to the dining room expecting to find Wexton there. I'm surprised instead to find Fenmire sitting at the table. Considering the last time I saw him in here, Wexton had me sprawled out across the tabletop, I'm tempted to turn and flee the moment his eyes look up from his plate and lock on to me.

I take my usual seat instead. "Hello," I greet, and I nod at the book he has propped open in one hand. "What are you reading?"

"It's one of the tomes on the history of Michastiforo. The first of five."

"Isn't it boring reading the same books over and over?"

"I have plenty to choose from and am always adding to my collection, so no."

"Did you really write all the books in the library yourself?"

"I'm not their original author; I simply transcribed them. When we were trapped on this side of The Gate, I lost access to the temple libraries. Rather than mourn the loss, I decided to recreate my favorites here to the best of my ability."

"You mean you rewrote all those books from memory?" I ask in awe.

He nods. "It's not perfect, and I occasionally leave out details I remember later, so I'm constantly rewriting them, but it gives me something to do in this wasteland."

I take a sip of tea and say over the rim of my cup, "A few are in my language."

"Sometimes it helps me remember more when I translate them from our tongue into yours. Again, just something I do to pass the time."

"I've been meaning to go up there and borrow one. I had a small collection myself back at my parents' farm."

"I don't have any fairytales."

I smirk at him. "Do you have any books on math?"

He blinks in surprise. "Your kind's math or mine?"

"What's the difference?"

"Humans haven't yet discovered the more advanced mathematics. Your math is far simpler."

"Can your books teach me your math?"

He considers this for a moment. "I'd have to translate one of my books into your tongue and provide you with notes to bridge the gap, but yes, I think so."

This request went much better than when I asked him to teach me how to fight. "I'd like that. I studied the work of Sir Isaac Newton before I was sent here."

"Who's that?"

"A mathematician as well as many other things. I've long wished I could be as smart as he was and talked about him a lot. Will found a copy of his book in a shop in the city a few years ago and begged his aunt to buy it for him. Of course, Will would rather eat a cow pie than read about math. He gave it to me for my birthday that year. I've probably read it three times now."

Fenmire closes his book and sets it aside. "You studied a mathematician's work for fun?"

"Why does that come as such a shock?"

"From what I understand of your village, it's mostly full of simple folk. There's nothing wrong with that, of course. It's just surprising to me that someone raised in such an environment would strive for further education, particularly one raised their whole life as a female. Don't your kind tend to dissuade women from educating themselves?"

"They do, but I love to learn. That's why I ask so many questions. And yes, that was quite an annoyance for me growing up.

My mother thought books would ruin my chances of finding a husband." I roll my eyes as I take a bite of my dinner.

Fenmire stares and says nothing.

"So when can I borrow that book?" I ask, trying not to sound too pushy.

He shakes himself and finally breaks his stare. "Give me a week or so to translate the first couple chapters and write up some notes."

I nod, and we both go back to our food, but I don't let the silence stretch on for long before I ask, "Do you have family back in Michastiforo?"

"I don't know."

I tilt my head. "You don't know if you have family?"

"I'm sure I do, or did, somewhere, but I don't know them."

"Why not? If you don't mind me asking, of course."

"I am a *vauncidi*—a child born outside a blessed conception—so I was raised by the temple priestesses."

I don't understand half of what he just said, so I laugh. "Alright…"

"Pregnancies for our kind don't usually occur naturally," he explains. "They require intervention from Seerraf himself to induce conception. Usually, couples wishing to have a child go to the temple together, and the priestesses call upon Seerraf to bless them and allow conception. The couple is then given a tea they both drink for four days, and then, on the fifth day, conception *might* occur. It often takes more than one try.

"Due to how involved the process is to have a child, our kind don't worry about pregnancies occurring outside of a blessed conception. But, very, very rarely, conception happens anyway. When it does, that child is called a *vauncidi*: a fate child. It's surmised that *vauncidi* births are sacred, chosen by fate to occur with or without Seerraf's involvement. I was such a child. *Vauncidi* are always given to the temple to be raised by the priestesses."

"That doesn't seem fair. What if your mother wanted to keep you?"

"It's not that she didn't want to or couldn't keep me. It's considered a privilege to give birth to a *vauncidi*. My mother was honored to carry me in her womb and give me to the temple. I was born there. Both my parents participated in the ceremony afterward when the priestesses named me. It was a happy, celebrated occasion."

"But you weren't allowed to know your family? Their names? If you had siblings?"

Fenmire shrugs. "I didn't care to know. My childhood lacked nothing, so I saw no point in asking. I was cared for at the temple, and I got to grow up in a house of Seerraf, surrounded by his light and love. My love of learning and reading was welcomed and encouraged, so I was given unfettered access to the temple libraries and scholars. As a result, I was one of the most well-educated Gryxen in Michastiforo by the time I went to the training fields. My love of art was also fostered. Several talented artists volunteered their time to give me lessons on drawing and painting throughout the years."

"Weren't you ever lonely?"

"Not really. When I lived at the temple, the priestesses were always around for company whenever I wanted it. When I went to the training fields, I was surrounded by my comrades. Then I met Wexton," he says with a grin. "He's been a welcome thorn in my backside ever since. He's lively enough for three Gryxen, so he's more than enough of a companion for me."

I grin too. "He's a lot sometimes."

"Yes. Yes, he is."

"I wouldn't want him any other way, though."

Fenmire takes a long breath in and says on the longest sigh I've ever heard, "Me neither." He bobs one brow. "Speaking of which, I saw him duck into your room as I was on my way here."

"*My* room?"

He nods. "I don't know what he's planning, but if I were you, I'd finish the rest of that meal without any more chatter so as not to leave him unattended long in there."

I narrow my eyes. "Is this your way of getting out of talking to me?"

"On the contrary. I enjoyed this conversation."

"Really?"

Fenmire sighs. "Yes, Eve. Despite your obvious beliefs otherwise, I don't hate you or your company. I'm simply more wary than the others, more realistic."

"I understand that, Fenmire. And I understand why you're so cautious."

He doesn't meet my eyes as he runs one finger down the edge of his book's cover. "You understand, I'm sure, that in order to fulfil the promise I made to you the other day at The Gate, we'd have to...?"

I nod.

"Then you understand the weight of the thought you overheard after I made that promise?"

"I do."

He takes a deep breath in and lets it out slowly. "I'll keep that promise, but I'll do it under one condition."

"What condition?"

He finally meets my eyes. "I'm going through The Gate with you."

That isn't at all what I expected. "But we have no idea what will happen when—"

"I don't care. If the rest of the spell's conditions are met, and I have to send you through The Gate, I won't send you alone. Whatever waits for you on the other side, I'll face it with you, even if it's death."

I'm speechless and teary-eyed. "Fenmire..."

"Do you accept my condition?"

I swallow and say softly, "Yes."

"Good."

We both finish our meals in silence.

Chapter 31

My thoughts are buzzing after my conversation with Fenmire as I take my dishes back to the kitchen and head for my room, but when I open my door, my mind goes completely blank as I freeze and stare, slack-jawed, at what's waiting for me on my bed.

"There you are," Wexton says. "I was worried I'd have to take care of things all on my own if you kept me waiting any longer."

He's naked.

Sprawled out on his back on my bed.

And stroking himself.

My entire body combusts, and I start panting, completely forgetting I'm standing in the open doorway until he smiles and asks, "Are you just going to watch, darling? Or do you want to come in here and let me show you what these beautiful cocks can do for you?"

I try to laugh, but I'm so breathless and shaky that it comes out as a snort. I shuffle into the room and shut the door, but then I go right back to staring. And what a sight he is. He's lounged back on my pillows, turned slightly onto his side with one leg drawn up as his fist moves up and down his cock, the top one. He closes his eyes briefly on a moan.

"Just the thought of you drives me wild now, you know," he says. "I've been laying here thinking of my tongue between your legs, remembering your taste and the sounds you make as you come… I couldn't help but touch myself. Hope you don't mind."

The sheer audacity of him, the unbridled sexuality and wicked mouth, drives me wild too. So wild, in fact, that it pushes me to do something just as risqué as he did. Without thinking too much about it so as not to lose my nerve, I cross the room, crawl up onto the bed, shove him onto his back, straddle his legs, and take the cock he was stroking into my mouth instead.

Wexton gasps then swears in both his language and mine.

I've never done this before, but I'm familiar enough with Gryxen anatomy by now to know where the most sensitive places are, and I bathe them with my tongue as I adjust to the feel of having something so hot and thick in my mouth. I focus on pleasing the length of him I can fit comfortably over taking any more of him than I can handle. I suck, I lick, I nip, and I listen for his little groans and gasps to learn what works and what doesn't.

His thicker, bottom cock rubs against my jaw as my head bobs up and down. I'm tempted to stroke it with my hand, but I don't know how Wexton would feel about that. Despite his assurances he's anything but traditional, I don't want to cross that boundary without invitation.

"Just like that," Wexton utters between moans. "Your mouth feels amazing on my cock. Oh… I like that. Do that again. That's fantastic." I peek up at him, and he rubs his hand down his face. "I'm going to come if you keep looking at me like that." He doesn't break eye contact, and neither do I as I pick up speed. "Oh, Eve… I'm going to… I'm…"

His back arches off the bed, and he cries my name as his whole body shudders with his orgasm. The fact that I can make a demon come does unspeakable things to me. I'm half tempted to reach under my dress and touch myself, but I'm confident he'll see to that as soon as he catches his breath.

At least he will if I have anything to say about it.

He peeks over at me through one half-open eye. "You have entirely too much clothing on," he mutters.

I absolutely agree and start unfastening my dress to rectify that. He sits up and helps me until I'm naked. I'm still straddling his legs, and I reach down to stroke his cock again. He takes my hand from the top shaft and wraps my fingers around his bottom one.

"Go slow," he requests. "I don't want to come again until I'm inside you."

I stroke him from base to tip, slowly, like he asked.

He flops back down on the bed. "How do you want me? You wanna ride me from up there? You want me on top? Want me to bend you over and take you from behind?"

I bite my lip at his last suggestion, picturing myself on my hands and knees while he pumps himself against my backside. My nerves can't bring me to say that's what I want, but thankfully, I don't have to.

"Oh, you like that idea, don't you?" he says with a wicked grin. "My Eve wants to get a bit carnal this evening. I can oblige."

Before I know it, I'm flipped over onto my back as Wexton rolls me under him. I yelp and giggle as I bounce on the mattress. Wexton leans down and kisses me, his forked tongue sweeping through my mouth as he hums.

"I'll never get enough of you," he mutters. "I could eat you forever and still die hungry for you."

"I can't be so different from the others you've tasted."

They have no idea how special they are. "You're the sweetest by far. That story you told me before, the one about the forbidden fruit, if all humans taste like you, I can understand the origins of such a tale." He kisses me again, his tongue delving and thrusting with a passion until he pulls away again. "How could any human resist such sweet nectar? I refuse to believe it's wrong to devour you, not when you seem designed for just such a thing."

"Devour me then. And, for the record, I don't believe it's wrong either. Not anymore."

"Good. Now roll over."

I'm grinning like a fool and blushing like a maiden as I do as he asks, settling on my belly underneath him. Wexton brushes the hair from my back before kissing my shoulder and swiping his tongue up my neck under my ear. When his fangs brush my skin, I shiver.

"Not yet, darling," he murmurs. "And not there. Soon, but between your legs." *My favorite place.*

"It's not that," I whisper.

Wexton pauses. *Oh, I see.* "You wish to be like prey caught by the beast, is that it?"

"Maybe."

Wexton chuckles as he goes back to dusting my neck and shoulder with kisses. "That's not my specialty, but there's one here who could bring those fantasies to life for you if you asked him." *Or begged him.*

"How do you know? Have you and Fenmire ever…?"

"No. We were always better suited as friends, but that doesn't mean I don't know what he likes. We lived under the same roof as him and his mate for centuries, after all."

I hum thoughtfully then groan as Wexton swipes his hot tongue down the top of my spine.

"Up on your knees, darling," Wexton murmurs, and he tugs on my hips to spur me to lift them up off the bed. As soon as I do, he reaches around my leg to stroke my clit as his rigid cocks bump against my backside and thighs. He pulls his wings in around us, blocking the rest of the room from view.

I'm cocooned by dark leather and his scent, and the rest of the world disappears with nothing to focus on but the feel of his hot breath on my neck and his fingers between my legs.

"Wexton…" I mumble as pure, unbridled feeling sweeps through me. I've never been in such a vulnerable position before, and yet I've never felt so safe. When his fingers glide inside me, I reach over my shoulder to bury mine in his hair.

"I'm here, darling. Always."

I lift my head from the blankets. "Then take me."

"Gladly." *Finally.*

His hand disappears, and I sigh softly at the empty feeling they leave behind. I'm not empty long. The head of his cock nudges against my entrance, and when it slides inside, I call his name again.

Wexton coaxes me up onto my hands and knees, and once I'm there, his hand slides across the bed to rest over mine. I weave my fingers between his as he starts thrusting. As big as he is, the curve of his body gives mine plenty of room to move underneath him, and I rock back into him with every thrust, taking him as hard and deep as I can. His bottom shaft rubs my clit each time, and I'm soon mewling with each plunge.

"The day I claim you as mine, I'll take you on your back with your feet on my chest," he says. "I'll fill you with my seed then lick you clean before sinking my fangs into you."

"Oh, God… Oh, *God*!"

Wexton speeds his thrusts, and a long whine escapes me that's interrupted a bit with each slam of his hips against mine.

I still plan to taste that other hole soon as well.

My body begins to tense as his dirty thoughts send jolts of desire straight through my core. I throw my head back, and Wexton licks my cheek then nips my ear.

"Come for me," he says. *I want to feel that sweet cunt clench around my cock.*

I cry out as I orgasm, and Wexton slams his cock inside me to the hilt. My body tightens around his hard length, squeezing him as the spasms wrack through me.

"Keep milking my cock, darling," Wexton says breathlessly. "That feels so good. Just like that."

Once my orgasm settles, I clench my lower body around him as tight as I can myself and squeeze my thighs together for good measure. The sound he makes as a result leaves me breathless.

"Do it again," he says in my ear, and his voice is raw and full of feeling. "Please."

I squeeze him inside me over and over, and his hot breath puffs against my throat as he starts to pant.

"Oh, Eve," he mewls. "Eve. Please. Oh, Gods…" He swears as his fingers tighten around mine, and a moment later he convulses and cries out into my neck.

I let go of his hand to touch his face instead, clutching him close as he comes apart. His thoughts are a jumbled mess of his language mixed with mine, and I can't keep up. I don't need to hear what he's thinking to know how he feels. Once his orgasm fades, he turns and sets his cheek against mine.

"You're the sweetest, softest, most precious creature in this world," he murmurs. "Never let anyone tell you otherwise."

"Oh, Wexton," I whisper.

He pulls out of me, which makes me groan, then he rolls onto his back. He beckons me over and tugs me up across his chest before draping his wings over us again, blocking out everything but me and him as he pulls me into a kiss, a long and soft one with no tongue.

"I can't wait to be your mate," he says.

I smile and touch one of his fangs, stroking it with a single finger. "About that. I'm ready whenever you are."

He bobs a brow and fights a grin. "Are you now?"

I kiss him. "Yes."

"Soon." He slides his hand up my back and into my hair, and his fingers start massaging lightly across my scalp. "There's just one small thing I'm waiting for."

I frown. "Is something the matter?"

"Not in the slightest. Don't worry, I'm not going anywhere."

"I'm not worried," I mumble. His fingers are sending delicious tingles down my spine, making me sleepy. I yawn loudly.

"Sleep now, darling." He pulls his wings a little tighter around us.

I hum and close my eyes. "Mmkay…"

*****

I'm running down the lane in The Deadwood, but I'm not moving fast enough to escape the smoke billowing around me or the crackling roar of the fire that's devouring the vines and brambles behind me, racing through the dead underbrush to reach me before I clear the arch. I turn a corner and see it in the distance just as a vine whips out and trips me, and I land painfully hard in the snow. I scramble to get back to my feet, but that same vine wraps around my ankle, yanking my leg out from under me and dragging me back down the lane toward the fire.

"No!" I scream. I dig my fingers into the snow, searching desperately for something to hold onto as I kick out at the vine, but it continues to pull me toward the flames. "Help me! Someone help!"

"Eve!"

I recognize the voice. "Wexton! I'm here! Help me, please!"

Another vine wraps around my other ankle and they drag me faster together.

"Help! Wexton!"

"Eve, wake up."

I can feel the heat of the flames on my back.

"Please," I utter as I start to sob.

There's vicious laughter on the wind, and it swirls around me like the smoke in the air, black and poisonous.

"Go away, you witch!" I yell, then I scream as the vines tighten painfully around my ankles, threatening to break the bones.

"Eve!" Wexton calls again, but his voice is nearly drowned out by the roar of the fire.

The vines twist and flip me to my back, and I scream. There's a wall of fire in front of me. The heat of it makes my face instantly start to sweat. The smoke chokes me, and I thrash and cough as the vines tug me closer.

"Wexton!" I holler, then I scream as the flames start licking up my legs.

Reilanna laughs in my ear. "They can't save you. You know that. I'll claim your soul for my own, sooner than you expect."

I cover my face with my arms as the fire chars my flesh and boils my blood, and I cry as I accept my fate and wait for the end.

"Eve!"

Someone is shaking me so hard it's making my head hurt. I open my eyes and see blazing red, and at first, I think it's the fire still turning me to ash. I blink the nightmare away and focus on Wexton's face, on those red eyes full of such concern I'm instantly on high alert.

"What's wrong?" I ask.

"I couldn't wake you," he says. "You were crying and thrashing in your sleep, and no matter what I did, you wouldn't wake up."

I touch my face, which is wet with sweat and tears. "I heard you calling to me."

"Was it Reilanna?"

I nod.

He brushes the hair from my damp face. "I'm sorry."

"It's alright. Caliborne usually keeps her away at night. I rarely have to deal with the dreams anymore."

"What do you mean?"

"Somehow Caliborne's powers block Reilanna from my dreams. We're not sure how exactly, but as long as he's touching me, I don't have nightmares."

If that's true, maybe they shouldn't sleep away from him.

I tilt my head. "Are you trying to kick me out of your bed?" I glance around and realize we're still in my room. "Or… *my* bed, I guess."

Wexton smiles. "Not at all, darling. I just think it's foolish to let Reilanna continue to torture you this way if there's a perfectly reasonable solution."

"I already spend most of my nights with Caliborne. I'm only away from him when he has patrol."

"We can adjust our schedules so he doesn't have night patrols at all anymore."

"I don't want others out in the cold just so I can sleep soundly an extra night or two. That's not fair."

"Eve—"

I put a finger over his lips. "No. You all already do too much for me. You almost died protecting me for Christ's sake, Wexton. Consider this my price to pay for that."

Stubborn little thing. Wexton curls his tongue around my finger and sucks it into his mouth. He takes my hand and pulls it back out with a pop to kiss my wrist instead. "You don't owe me a thing." His lips move slowly up my arm, inch by inch and kiss by kiss. "You're a gift from Seerraf himself." He sucks lightly on the inside of my elbow then sits up to continue kissing up my upper arm. "And I'll protect you 'till my last breath."

I believe him.

I also believe he's trying to start something with those wandering kisses.

"Can I help you?" I ask sweetly.

He hums as his lips touch my shoulder. *Oh, you can help me alright.*

I chuckle then sigh softly as his kisses dust up my neck under my ear. My arms break out in goosebumps, and I throw a leg over his. He reaches down and hauls me up on top of him. I push him down onto his back, and he peers up at me with that wicked smile on his face I know so well.

"Wanna take me, darling?" he asks. "I'd love to see you ride me."

"I just bet you would," I quip. "But can you lie still and keep your hand to yourself while I do?"

He frowns. *Where's the fun in that?*

"The fun would be me watching you try to control yourself."

He narrows his eyes at me. "A challenge, is it?" He tucks his hand under his head. "Fine. I can be good."

I laugh so hard I have to steady myself on top of him with both my hands on his chest. "You? Be good?" I laugh some more.

Wexton bucks his hips and almost unseats me.

I yelp and go on laughing until his hard cock brushes against me.

Wexton grins at me. "I'm all yours."

I lift myself up and reach behind me for his top shaft, stroking it a few times with my hand before pressing it between my legs. When the head nudges against my entrance, I slowly sink down onto it.

Wexton rolls his shoulders and settles his head deeper into the pillow. *Stay still. Don't move or touch.*

"What's the matter?" I ask cheekily. I move up and lower myself further onto his cock, painfully slow. "Wishing you could take control right now?"

He growls low in his throat. "Tease."

I giggle. No one has ever called me that before. I feel like such a vixen as I withdraw and take him again and again. His lips slowly part and his eyes roll up a little further in his head each time. When he buries to the hilt inside me, I stop, and his eyes lock on mine. While he watches, I lick two of my fingers and slide them between my legs to touch myself.

A snarl erupts from him followed by a string of words I don't understand and probably don't want to. *I wish it were my tongue, or my finger, or my shaft. I wanna bury myself in both your holes and—*

I gasp softly.

"Oh, you like that idea?"

"I… I've never thought about it."

"You know how two men make love, don't you?"

I nod.

He shrugs. "Your anatomy is no different in that regard."

I consider what it must feel like to have someone inside me… back there. The thought makes me hot all over. The Gryxen have two cocks. Any one of them could bury themselves in both places at once. I'm shocked when the thought makes me moan.

Wexton grins, and suddenly, I'm flipped over onto my back.

"What are you doing?" I cry as his cock slips out of me.

"I've decided I can't wait to taste that precious little bud."

"You're going to lick me… there?"

"Unless you tell me not to."

Stopping him is the furthest thing from my mind, so I remain silent.

Wexton grins again and slides his arm under both my knees, shoving my legs up as far as they'll go. It tilts my lower body up toward him, and I'm suddenly self-conscious about how open and exposed I am.

"Wexton?" I say in uncertainty.

He freezes. "Tell me no, and I'll stop. No questions asked."

"Have you done this before?"

He chuckles. "Many times."

"Will it hurt?"

"No, darling. I'll be so gentle, all you'll feel is pleasure."

I nod for him to go ahead.

His face disappears below his arm.

His tongue slides across my clit as he first explores the places his mouth has already been. It dips inside me a few times until I relax.

You taste so good. I could make a meal of you forever and die a happy Gryxen.

When a small groan escapes me, his mouth stays where it is, but his tongue flicks down across my backside. I jump at the feel of it, but when he does it again, I lie still and soak in the sensation.

Oh gods…

He takes his arm off my legs, and I grab my knees myself, holding them back the same way he did. His mouth disappears and is replaced by two of his fingers, which work around my clit then slide inside me where his cock was just moments ago. I close my eyes as they slip in and out of me and his thumb finds my clit, making slow, maddening circles at the same time. When his mouth comes back, it's on my backside. This time, his tongue circles that hole, and I clench without meaning to.

I can only imagine how good it would feel to have that sweet little hole clench like that around my cock.

"Wexton," I murmur.

His tongue presses harder against my backside in response.

The combination of his fingers and his tongue are starting to make me writhe, and I can't help but buck my hips against his hand, begging for more.

I wanna slip my tongue inside you.

"Please," I utter, but I'm not entirely sure what I'm begging for. I just know his dirty thoughts are sending jolts of pure desire straight down my spine.

"That wasn't a no, darling," Wexton says. He licks my hole again, and that wicked forked tongue presses against me until my body begins to open for it.

I gasp at both the feeling and the thought of a demon's tongue in my…

Wexton is as slow as he promised to be, and I know no pain as his tongue slides inside, only an odd pressure and heat in a place no one has ever touched before, not even me. The sheer thought of what's happening has me panting, and soon enough, my body begins to tense.

"Wexton," I utter, and his tongue plunges deeper. "Oh *God*, Wexton!"

If I had my other arm, I'd be stroking myself right now.

I orgasm with a cry, and both my holes convulse around him.

Wexton groans and goes on touching and tasting me until I'm so limp and exhausted I can barely hold my legs up anymore. He sits up on his knees and lowers both my legs to the bed for me.

"Watch me," he says breathlessly, and I lift my head enough to watch him wrap his fingers around his top shaft and begin stroking himself. He stares straight into my eyes as he does, his breathing becoming more labored and erratic as his fist slides up and down his hard length. "Tell me when you want me to come."

"What?" I ask in disbelief.

"I won't do it until you tell me to." He closes his eyes for a second, groaning against his imminent orgasm. "I'm completely at your mercy."

It's my turn to flash an evil grin. I watch, and I wait, and I let him continue pleasuring himself. His breathing turns downright frantic, and he lets out a low, whining moan.

"Not yet," I say.

He growls and strokes himself faster, still not breaking eye contact.

"A little more."

His lips part in a gasp for air as his whole body tenses. He's shaking, vibrating the whole bed.

"Now!"

A visceral snarl rips from him and his whole body shudders as he orgasms, his eyes still locked on mine as he twitches and shakes from the force of it. "Yours," he declares. "My pleasure, my body, my heart… all yours."

I open my arms, and he flops down over top of me, holding himself back from crushing me with his elbow as our faces nearly touch.

I kiss the tip of his nose. "You're crazy, you know that?"

"Absolutely," he murmurs, brushing his nose against mine. "Crazy for you, darling. Completely crazy for you."

Chapter 32

Over the next week, I spend most mornings skating, most afternoons helping either in the kitchen or the stables, and my evenings alternating between Caliborne's bed and Wexton's. If I'm craving soft and sensual love-making, I seek out the former; if it's passion and depravity I want, the latter.

Neither leaves me wanting, and both make me feel equally loved.

Some mornings when he has nothing more pressing to do, Caliborne flies me to the pond, on others, Wexton and I walk there together. He carries my skates and helps clear any snow that's blown over the ice in the night, then he holds my hand as I skate around him, dance under his arm or spin myself dizzy. More than once, we end up on our backs together on the ice, watching the clouds and soaking up the winter sun while I catch my breath.

A few times, we do more carnal things on that ice, and the thought that whoever is on patrol could fly over us at any given moment makes it that much more tantalizing.

Bit by bit and day by day, Wexton unearths my deepest, filthiest desires, opens them up wide, and brings them to life. At first, the thoughts of the things we do make my heart skip frantically in my chest, but after a while, any shame I have fades away and is replaced by a small, secret smile that creeps across my face whenever I remember the feel of him on or inside me, whether it's his cock, fingers, or tongue…

"What are you thinking about?" Wexton asks as I brake hard and come to a stop in front of him, spraying him with ice.

"Nothing. Why do you ask?"

"You're a terrible liar. You've got that little grin on your face again, the one you get right before you shove me on the bed and have your way with me."

"I haven't had my way with you once. You keep taking over and having *your* way instead."

"I haven't heard you complain yet."

I turn to give some smart remark and teeter on my skates. My feet slide out from under me, and I almost fall flat on my back, but Wexton catches me effortlessly, lifting me in his strong arm. He doesn't set me back on my skates, though. He hauls me to his chest and leans down toward my face with that wicked grin of his.

"Allow me to offer my sincerest apologies," he murmurs. "I don't mean to keep stealing your moment."

"Sure you don't," I reply with a bob of my brow. "But you're right that I've had zero complaints so far."

"I'm glad to hear my services have been satisfactory."

I bite my lip trying so hard not to smile and end up failing anyway.

Our faces are mere inches apart and growing closer when a shadow passes over us and is gone so fast I know it wasn't just a cloud drifting past on the breeze. I block the sun with my hand as I peer up and see Fenmire soaring high above the pond. I tap Wexton on the chest, and he sets me down.

"Fenmire!" I call.

Fenmire slows and spins in midair to look back at us since he's well past the pond by now, and he hovers there over the trees.

I wave him down. "Come here!"

Fenmire tucks in his wings and shoots straight down toward the ground, pulling up just in time to plant his feet on the ice in front of us, his claws digging in to keep him from sliding as his wings blast us with loose snow. He's dressed in his golden armor and carries his golden shield and mace.

"What is it?" he asks. "Is something wrong?"

"No. I just wanted to say hello. I've seen very little of you this week." I haven't seen Fenmire since our talk, and I get the distinct feeling he's avoiding me again.

"I'm on patrol," he says dismissively.

"The Gate won't open for two more days," Wexton chimes. "Caliborne and I took Evan out there yesterday morning to make sure they were safe to be out of the castle so much."

"And you trust it?"

Wexton shrugs. "It hasn't lied to them yet."

Fenmire sniffs and glances around the sunlit pond, his eyes scanning across the tree line before flicking over to me. He quickly looks away again and wanders to the side of the pond, mumbling the whole way. I think I hear the word "distractions" mixed with a few huffs and curses. At the bank, he slams first his shield then his spiked mace into the ice. They both stay stuck in place when he lets go and turns back to me.

"I'll spare a few moments," he says. "But no more."

I skate slowly over to him. "It's occurred to me that I never thanked you before."

He eyes me suspiciously. "For what?"

"For helping Wexton with this." I wave my hand around at the pond and its smooth, crystal-clear ice.

"Oh," he replies, and his shoulders relax a bit in obvious relief. "You're welcome. Though, I only came up with the idea. I wasn't involved with its execution."

"No, that was my job," Wexton chimes. "I had to borrow one of Drixus' axes to chop through all that ice."

"You borrowed *one* of his axes?" I ask. "How many does he have?"

"Two. He dual wields."

I picture a Gryxen sitting astride some dragon-sized flying beast with an axe in each hand. "Fascinating."

"Are you trying to make me jealous?" Wexton teases. "Gonna leave me for a Gryxen with two arms?"

Before I can reply, Fenmire huffs then says stiffly, "I should go."

"No, Fenmire, wait," I implore, and I take his hand to stop him from walking away.

He stares down at my fingers clutching his as his thoughts race, but they're not in my language, so I have no idea what he's thinking.

I scramble for something to say that will make him stay a little longer. "Wexton told me earlier that he flies faster than you."

"Hey!" Wexton says indignantly.

I stick my tongue out at him and turn back to Fenmire. "I told him if he feels the need to brag about it, then it must not be true."

Fenmire cocks one brow, his eyes narrowing as he studies me. He no doubt sees this conversation for the bait that it is, but he must decide to humor me and take it. "There's only one way to settle it," he declares. "Let's have a race."

"Yes!" Wexton cheers. "Right now!"

"No, not right now," I say. "It wouldn't be fair with Fenmire carrying all that armor. Who has patrol tomorrow morning?"

"Drixus," they both answer in unison.

"Perfect. We'll have it then. Caliborne and I will watch to make sure it stays fair." I give Wexton a pointed look.

"Me, cheat?" he says, touching his hand to his chest in dramatic fashion. "Never."

"I might just let you cheat to make it fair," Fenmire says with a small smile.

"Ohhh, cocky are we?" Wexton says with his hand on his hip. "Perhaps we should make a wager on this race."

Fenmire crosses his arms. "Perhaps we should."

"If I win, you have to draw me a portrait of Evan and I together naked."

"What?" I exclaim.

"With your permission, of course, darling," Wexton adds.

I try to cool my burning cheeks with my chilly hands and look to see Fenmire's reaction.

After a moment's consideration, Fenmire says, "Agreed. But if *I* win, the portrait will be of you alone, only you'll still be nude and posing on the roof."

Wexton bursts out laughing so hard he has to wipe tears from his eyes as he replies, "There's the fun-loving Fen I used to know. Deal." He sticks his hand out to Fenmire, who shakes it.

Fenmire grins wickedly. "I'll make sure you have an admiring audience when you pose for me."

Wexton laughs again. "All you need to worry about is how to perfectly capture the pleasure on my mate's face when you draw them with my cock buried inside them."

I groan and cover more of my face as the burning intensifies.

Fenmire's smile slips a bit. "Mate. Has that happened, then?"

"Not yet," I say behind my hands.

"Soon," Wexton promises with a wink at me.

Fenmire walks over and yanks his weapons from the ice. "You should warn us before it does so we can prepare for whatever surprises might come through The Gate afterward."

That sobers the smile on Wexton's face. "I'll make sure you all know beforehand."

Fenmire nods and looks at me. "I've finished translating the first few chapters of that book you asked to borrow. You can come by the library for them any time."

"Thank you. I will. But before you go…" I step closer to him. "What did you think I was thanking you for earlier?"

"What?"

"When I said I failed to thank you before now, you looked uncomfortable until I explained what I was thanking you for. What did you think it was about?"

Fenmire hesitates, and I look at Wexton who merely shrugs with a small shake of his head.

Fenmire stares at me so hard I frown in concern. "Fenmire?"

He adjusts his grip on his mace, shrugs his shield higher on his arm, and says, "I thought you were thanking me for saving your life."

I shake my head, confused, but when I start to ask him what he means, he takes off before I can finish my question. I shield my face from the blast of icy wind his wings kick up as he launches into the sky.

"What's he talking about, Wexton?" I ask, brushing snow from my jacket.

"He asked us not to talk about it."

"He did save my life, then? When?"

Wexton chews his lip in uncertainty. "When you first came to the castle. I don't know much more than that."

We both look up at the sky again, but Fenmire is already long gone.

*****

Once we return from skating and I've soaked the chill from my bones in the bath, I sneak up to the third floor. The footprints from a week ago are covered with a fresh layer of dust that hasn't been disturbed since the last time I was up here. As I approach Drixus' door, I'm disappointed but not at all surprised to see that it is closed. They all warned me this wouldn't be easy, which is why I don't walk away but instead march right up to that door and knock again.

"Drixus?" I call through the wood. "Are you there?"

At first, I hear nothing, but then I hear footsteps, and they sound like they're getting closer. I hold my breath as they come all the way to the door, and I stare at the handle, waiting for it to turn, but it never does.

"Drixus?"

Though I know he's right on the other side of the door, he still refuses to open it. I consider it progress anyway. If he wants to keep us separated by a door, I will grant him that comfort for as long as he needs it. I sit cross-legged in front of it and imagine myself sitting down for tea with a new friend in my parents' house.

"It's awfully drafty up here," I say. "Good thing your kind doesn't get cold. I wish I had that skill whenever I had to do my chores in the dead of winter. The animals always had to be fed, even when the snow was blowing so hard we had to tie a guide rope from the house to the barn so we didn't get lost.

"That happened to a farmer's wife several years ago, you know. She headed out to the barn to milk the cow right before a storm, and by the time she was ready to go back inside, it was a white out from all the blowing snow. She got lost walking back to the house and froze to death. She was from the city originally, so she didn't know any better. If it'd been me, I would've slept with the cow until the storm passed. It might've been a bit uncomfortable, but I would've been warm. And alive.

"I almost froze to death myself when the village tossed me into The Deadwood, I don't know if the others told you. The bastards who dragged me out of bed didn't let me put proper clothes on, and it was raining that night, so I was drenched by the time I was tossed into the snow. Caliborne saved my life. Or at least, he rescued me from the storm. I don't remember very much about those first few days after I got here. I was pretty sick, as you can imagine."

I slide closer to the door, leaving a streak in the dust on the floor with my backside as I do. I listen closely and hear a small shuffle as Drixus moves closer on his side as well.

"I know I told you before that my name is Evangeline, but it's a bit more complicated than that. I don't know if Caliborne has explained it to you or not, but I actually have three names. Today, my name is Evan. Sometimes it's Eve, and others it's Evangeline. You can just call me Evangeline until we get to know each other better though, alright?"

I don't get an answer, but he also hasn't moved away from the door, which I consider a good sign. Not wanting to overstay my welcome, I get to my feet.

"I'm going to go for now, but I'll be back in another week like last time. If you want to meet face-to-face, just leave your door open that day, but if not, that's alright. I'll sit and talk to you a bit anyway." I put my hand flat on the door in farewell. "Until then."

Chapter 33

By the time the next morning rolls around, the entire castle has heard the news of Fenmire and Wexton's race, and the whole staff wanders out in the snow to watch. I hear more than one bet made between them on who they think will win.

"Who has your vote?" I ask Caliborne as we land in the open patch of yard between the castle's front steps and the edge of The Deadwood.

Fenmire, he replies without hesitation. *We all know Fenmire is the fastest.*

"Then why would Wexton agree to a race?"

Wexton never backs down from a challenge. Besides, I'm sure he's planning on cheating.

"That's what I said!" I say with a laugh.

The Gryxen in question comes out of nowhere and slams into the ground a few feet away. He's all cocky smiles and puffed out chest when he stands up.

"Good morning," he says to me. "I was looking for you, but you were already out and about this morning."

"Caliborne and I were setting up for the race. Was there something you needed?"

"A good luck kiss."

I raise a brow. "Just a kiss?"

"I'll take all the *luck* you're willing to give me, darling. But what do you mean you were setting up for the race? Setting up what?"

I wink at him. "You'll see."

Fenmire steps out of the castle and glides over to us.

"Got your pencils sharpened for the drawing you'll be making for me soon, Fen?" Wexton jeers when his best friend lands beside him.

"Sure, I do," Fenmire replies with the hint of a smile on his face. "I've already picked the perfect place on the roof for you when you pose for me. The whole Deadwood will be able to see you in all your glory."

"Ha! 'Tis a pity they'll miss the show since I'll be the one winning today."

"We'll just see about that."

I clap my hands to break up the snark. "Right, so, Caliborne and I took a trip to the arch this morning, and I left something behind. Two somethings, actually." I show them my ungloved hands. "To keep things fair, rather than have a timed race someone could cheat by taking shortcuts,"—I look sideways at Wexton—"you'll both start at the bottom of the castle steps, fly to the arch, and retrieve one of my gloves. Whoever brings it back to me first will be the winner. To ensure even that can't be tampered with, each glove is a different color. Wexton, you are to bring back the red one; Fenmire, yours is the black one. If you bring me back the other's glove, you'll be disqualified, so no stealing."

Fenmire snorts. "They know you well, Wexton."

"Both of you stand side-by-side at the bottom of the steps," I order, and Wexton pats me on the butt as he walks past me toward the stairs. I stand a short distance away and nod to Caliborne, who walks a dozen or so steps toward The Deadwood and faces Wexton and Fenmire.

Wexton is flexing his wings and running in place to warm up.

Fenmire watches him with a shake of his head, obviously not worried in the slightest about his chances.

Caliborne lifts both his arms above his head.

"By the way, Fen," Wexton says with a grin, "when I say you'll be drawing us in the nude, I mean for you to be naked as well."

Fenmire glances over at Wexton in disbelief just as Caliborne throws down his arms. Wexton takes off, leaving Fenmire on the ground, who realizes a split second later what Wexton has done and launches into the sky himself with a snarl. I hear Wexton's distant laugh as he flies over the tops of the trees with Fenmire hot on his heels. The staff on the ground all laugh and cheer as both Gryxen disappear from sight.

Caliborne comes and picks me up.

"I guess that wasn't *technically* cheating," I say.

Caliborne's chest shakes with his silent laughter before he takes to the sky himself, and we fly up so far above the castle I hug him tighter around the neck.

Are you scared, my stoferra? You needn't be with me.

I relax my arms and kiss his cheek. "I know. It's just pesky human instinct."

I look out over The Deadwood and see two dark flying figures in the distance. From here, it looks like they're flying side-by-side, and only when they overlap do my eyes finally see one is most definitely in front of the other, though it's impossible to tell which one's which. A moment later, one dips down and disappears into the trees, presumably to retrieve my glove from the arch. Only seconds later, he's back in the sky again and headed this way only to clash into the second figure in midair.

The two Gryxen tumble together in the sky before one dives back down into The Deadwood. The other flies away only to dip down into the trees himself shortly after. One reappears and begins his flight back toward the castle, and it's some time before the other pops back up out of the trees behind him. I can tell one has a fairly large lead on the other, and when I spot a shimmer of red on the one in front, I realize Wexton is winning.

Fenmire isn't about to let him win that easily though, and the black-haired Gryxen is gaining on Wexton fast. The humans on the ground cheer when they see Wexton reappear over the trees, and he has but a few seconds of flight left before he reaches me, but Fenmire is flying so fast behind him it's impossible to tell which of them will reach me first.

When there is but a few yards left between us, I reach out my hand, and so does Wexton, offering me his red glove.

Fenmire dives toward the ground.

Just a few more feet and Wexton's red glove will land in my outstretched hand.

He smiles at me, already basking in his victory.

A figure shoots up in front of me, and a glove is slapped into my palm with such force I almost drop it. I curl my fingers around the black fabric with a laugh.

Wexton pulls up hard, his wings beating backward to keep from crashing into me and Caliborne as he swears like a sailor.

"Language, Wexton," Fenmire says with a grin as he glides over beside him. "No one likes a sore loser, especially one who loses despite trying to sabotage his opponent."

"What did you do?" I ask Wexton.

"Evened the odds," he says with a shrug.

"I was first to the arch," Fenmire explained. "On my way back, he flew into me, stole my glove, and threw it into The Deadwood. I had to search for it in the underbrush. It was a miracle I found it at all."

I roll my eyes over to Wexton.

"Like I said, I evened the odds," he says with a grin.

We all fly down to the ground where I show the staff the black glove I'm holding. There's an equal amount of cheers and groans throughout the crowd as winnings are collected.

Caliborne sets me back on my feet, and Wexton hands me my other glove.

"I knew it was a long shot," Wexton says. "Fenmire has always had the fastest wings. I just wanted to have some fun."

"Did you?" I ask.

He winks at me. "I would've had more if I'd beaten him. I'd hoped you'd throw your arms around my neck—with that glowing smile of yours on your face—and declare your love for me as my grand prize."

"Oh, well, in that case…" I motion him down with a bend of a finger, and he drops to one knee in front of me. I put my arms around his neck, kiss him once passionately on the lips, and say, "I love you, Wexton. You don't need to win any race to earn that."

His answering smile is breathtaking. "Finally," he utters, and he kisses me again.

"Finally?" I ask once our lips part. "Is that why you've been waiting to make us mates? You were waiting for me to tell you I love you?"

"Yes," he admits. "No lover has ever told me that before, and I wanted to hear it born from your true feelings and not those created by the bond."

I touch my forehead to his. "Well, consider it born. I love you." I lean close to his ear and say in a whisper, "And I want to become your mate. Tonight."

"I have patrol tonight."

My shoulders sag, and I pout.

Wexton laughs. "I'm kidding."

"You're a heathen."

"I'm *your* heathen."

"Yes, you are."

"And tonight, I'll make you my mate. At last."

*****

On the way back to the castle, Wexton is all flirtatious suggestions and wandering eyes, but when we arrive back home, I beg my leave of both him and Caliborne and head up to the second floor. I don't know what will happen after Wexton and I create our mating bond, and that makes me nervous. I love Wexton to pieces just like I love Caliborne, but the last time I mated with one of them, Reilanna started sending even more horrible beasts through The Gate.

What will she have in store for us this time?

I don't want thoughts of Reilanna anywhere near my mind when Wexton and I become mates, so I seek out the best distraction I can think of.

I knock lightly on the library door and wait for Fenmire's invitation before letting myself in. He's already seated at his desk with a pencil in one hand and an open book in the other. When he sees it's me who's disturbed his peace, he tucks the pencil into the book and sets both aside.

"Yes?" he asks.

"I came for those chapters you promised me."

Fenmire leans back in his chair. "It seemed to me like you had other, more important plans for your day than studying numbers."

"I need to clear my head first."

"Clear it or fill it with enough noise to push unpleasantries out?"

I shrug. "Take your pick."

His inky eyes slide up and down my entire body, studying me. "This is exactly what she wants, you know. She wants to sow doubt and grief. That's why she chose the mating bond as the condition for her spell. She means to poison what's supposed to be one of the happiest occasions of our lives."

He leans toward me. "Don't let her. Even Reilanna's spell can't change what a mating bond is at its core. She can try to taint it with her magic, but at its conception, a mating bond is pure, honest love. Don't let her get in the way of that."

"But what about The Gate and what she might send through it afterward?" I ask.

Fenmire waves the question away. "We can handle anything she tries to throw at us. She caught us off guard last time, but that won't happen again. Nothing she squeezes through The Gate now can come close to the things we fought in our war with her before. The true battle will be when the spell is broken and we rush back through The Gate to end her once and for all."

"You speak as if that's a certainty."

Fenmire gives me a pointed look but doesn't comment. He reaches into a drawer in his desk and takes out another book with a few folded papers stuck under the front cover.

"This should get you started on learning our math," he says, holding the book out to me. "Let me know if you get stuck, otherwise, return the book to me when you're done with what's here so I can continue my translation."

I take the book and flip through a few of the pages. Fenmire's neat but cramped writing takes up every free inch of space around the illustrations and equations in the book, and the sheets of notes he's included are every bit as detailed. This will certainly leave very little room in my head for worrying.

I smile at him. "Thank you." I tuck the book under my arm but don't turn to leave. "You won the race today," I say matter-of-factly.

A smirk teases the corner of his mouth. "I know. I was there."

"You and Wexton had your own wager, but I'd like to reward the winner myself as well."

Fenmire crosses his arms. "And just how do you plan to reward me?"

I shrug. "What do you want?"

I expect him to declare he wants nothing at all or perhaps chastise me for my silliness, but he doesn't. He considers my question carefully before rising from his chair.

"Come with me," he says. He leads me between the shelves and plucks a book down from one on his right. "This tome is full of everything we know about The Gates and their origins, which is frighteningly little, I'm afraid. I would love to add to it. Our last trip to The Gate got me thinking that, since you are the only one I know of who has ever communicated with one before, perhaps you could help me do that."

"You want to question The Gate again?"

"If you don't mind acting as an interpreter, then yes."

"I don't mind at all. I'd love to help."

Fenmire nods, regards the book in his hands, and almost puts it back on the shelf before changing his mind. "I think, while you have the book I was in the middle of translating,"—he nods toward the one tucked under my arm—"I'll begin translating this one as well. That way you can read about what we already know."

"I'd like that. Thank you."

"It's too bad you had to leave behind that book by the mathematician… what was his name?"

"Newton."

"I would've liked to read it."

"Perhaps someday you will."

"I wish I had your optimism."

I shake my head. "It's not optimism. It's accepting that I don't know what the future holds, which means everything is a possibility."

"Does that mean you don't believe in fate?"

"Not in any predetermined sense, no. I think perhaps there are places we're meant to go in our lives, but how we get there or even if we get there at all is up to us. There may be forces that help guide us, but it's our choice where we end up, in the end. Who knows, maybe there would have been a whole other life for me in the city if Will and I had left as we'd planned. Perhaps some other human capable of breaking the spell would've ended up here eventually instead."

"Do you wish that had been the case?"

"Not at all," I say with a smile. "I'm happy here, happier than I've ever been in my life. My only regret is leaving Will behind."

Fenmire leans down toward me. "And you plan to fix that soon, don't you?"

My eyes widen. "You know about that?" He chuckles, and I grimace. "I just told on myself, didn't I?"

"I'd already guessed the truth. After that spitter attacked you and Wexton, I wondered why you were with him at the arch. Considering the fact that you've talked about that boy non-stop since you got here—even during your fevered sleep those first few days—it wasn't hard to guess the reason."

"Will has just as miserable a life in the village as I did," I rush to say. "He's just better at hiding—"

Fenmire raises his hand, and I fall silent.

"Does he understand he can never leave again?" he asks.

"He does."

"Then it makes no difference to me. If it'll make you happy to have him here, bring him."

"I wasn't seeking your approval," I say with a bob of my brow. "But it's nice to know I have it, nonetheless."

To my surprise, he smiles at me. "If there is one thing I admire most about you, it's your candor."

"If that's what you admire *most*, then there must be other things you admire about me as well."

The low chuckle I get sounds downright devilish. He motions toward the door. "Be gone with you. As much as I'd enjoy a battle of wits, I have work to do."

"All you do is work, Fenmire." I wave my arm around at the shelves full of books surrounding us. "It seems to me you've spent the last two-thousand years searching for a distraction yourself."

"You're right," he replies, taking me off guard. "Care to let me get back to it?"

I immediately turn for the door, and he walks me to it.

"Enjoy your distraction, Evangeline," Fenmire says as I step into the hall.

"You too," I say before he softly shuts the door.

Chapter 34

I take my new book back to my room and sit in front of my fire as I pour over the pages. A few of the papers Fenmire stuck inside are blank, and I use them to work through equations as I read. I've always been good with numbers, but even I struggle to understand the complex calculations Fenmire has broken down into steps for me. And this is just introductory work? I can't imagine what their advanced mathematics must look like. As difficult as it is, it has the desired effect of wiping anything else from my mind as I sit reading and working until dinnertime.

I take the meal in my room, wishing for a few more hours of solitude. The delightful crackle of my fire coupled with the smell of the book in my one hand and the hot cup of tea in the other settles what little anxiety there is left inside me until I finally put the book away in my desk, set my empty cup on the tray with the rest of my dinner dishes, and gather my washbag and a change of clothes. I take the tray back to the kitchen before heading downstairs for a bath.

I've barely got my feet wet in the pool when I hear the clomp, clomp, clomp of Gryxen feet on the stairs. I already have a sneaking suspicion about who it is, but even so, I chuckle to myself that the thought of being caught naked by any of them no longer bothers me in the slightest. I slide into the warm water and turn as Wexton strolls into the room.

"You're avoiding me," he says softly. "Have you changed your mind about tonight?"

Instead of an answer, I motion him down into the pool. He wastes no time in dropping his washbag and shucking his pants to join me. Once he's in the water, I tug him down to sit and straddle his lap, wrapping my arms around his neck and kissing him silently, over and over, until the worried crease in his brow disappears.

"I haven't changed my mind," I say. "As much as I love your company, I've barely had a moment to myself since I came here that wasn't filled with pacing and worrying over you all as you fight Reilanna's beasts. I just needed some time to myself."

"Am I disturbing that now?"

I pull his braid over his shoulder and pluck the tie from the end, unraveling it until I can run my fingers through it. "No. You showed up at the perfect time. I was just thinking about you."

I hope they were the sordid sort of thoughts.

I lick one of his fangs. "Maybe."

He growls low in his throat. "I could spend eternity in your bed and still hunger for you. I'll never tire of your company, darling, so if you need time for yourself from now on, don't hesitate to tell me. I know I'm a bit much sometimes—"

"No," I say with a finger to his lips. "You're just enough."

His answering smile makes my heart sing. *I love you. I love you so much I can't think of anything else. I wake up thinking of you, I fall asleep doing the same, and all the moments in between are spent wondering where you are, what you're doing, what you're thinking, and how I can spend the rest of my life making you happy.*

I laugh tearfully and kiss him.

The moment heats as it always does, and I part my lips, inviting him in. His tongue sweeps across mine, and his arm tightens on my back, pulling me closer. His cocks are hardening underneath me, so without breaking our kiss, I reach down and take the thicker of the two in my hand. He groans in my mouth.

"I want this inside me," I murmur as I stroke him.

"Not like this," he replies.

I still my hand. "No?"

Without warning, he stands up, and I yelp as he drags me up with him, turns, and deposits me on the side of the pool.

"What are you doing?" I ask.

"Wrap your legs around me," he says.

I do, and when he presses firmly on my chest, I lay down across the stone on my back. Wexton's fingers trace the round mound of my breast before sliding across my nipple. He rolls it between his finger and thumb, drawing a soft moan from me.

"Do you remember what I said I'd do the night we become mates?" he asks.

"Yes," I say breathlessly.

"If you've any complaints, now would be the time to voice them, darling."

"The only complaint I have is that you're not inside me yet."

Wexton barks with laughter as his hand slides down to my groin. His fingers swipe across my sex that's wet with more than just pool water, and two slide inside me as his thumb circles my clit, softly. He takes his time, plunging his fingers in and out of me at an agonizing pace. When a third one joins in, I wiggle on the stone, tilting my hips up to take them deeper. Wexton obliges immediately, thrusting them in as far as the digits can reach inside me. I moan again.

"You want me right here?" Wexton asks. "Where anyone could walk in and see you spread out like this for me?"

Part of me will be disappointed if no one walks in, but I bite my lip against the urge to blurt that out.

Wexton grins down at me. *I can read your face as easily as you can read my mind, you know.*

I put his theory to the test and look down at his swollen cocks, licking my lips at the thought of him plunging deep inside me. When I peek back up at his face, he laughs.

"Alright, darling," he says, and his fingers disappear. "I know what you want."

The head of his cock starts to enter me.

"Wexton," I say.

He freezes and looks me in the eyes.

"Don't you dare hold back."

The wicked grin I get in reply sends a shiver down my spine before he thrusts inside me, hard. Every nerve from the waist down fires at once as his thick length spears deep inside me, and I cry out. Wexton is still, his eyes searching mine for my reaction, and I nod.

"Just like that," I utter.

Wexton growls low in his throat, wraps his arm around one of my legs, and gives me everything I'm asking for. His hips slam against my backside over and over, and the only thing keeping me from sliding across the wet stone is his arm that tugs me closer by the leg with every thrust. The head of his cock rams inside me. It hurts a little, and yet I want more. I wrap my legs tighter around him, pulling him close with my feet on his backside, rocking him deeper. His other cock slaps against my clit each time, driving me wild.

"Yes," I murmur. "Yes, yes… Yes!"

I'm going to fill you up then lick you clean. I want to taste your sweet cunt mixed with my seed before sinking my fangs into you and making you mine.

I lift my head and watch his body slide in and out of mine. It looks impossible that something so large would fit inside someone as small as me. My lower belly bulges a bit every time he thrusts inside me, and I put my hand over the spot to feel it.

"You like watching yourself take me?" he asks. "I should have brought a mirror and given you a proper show." He pulls out of me, and I whimper, but then I groan when he taps his wet, hot cock against my clit a few times.

"Put that back," I order.

He laughs as he does, and when he's back inside me, he speeds his thrusts until I find it hard to breathe. His cocks stroke all my sensitive places at a punishing pace, and my orgasm rushes up so fast it startles me. I gasp and shudder as it slams into me, making me shake from head to toe. I lose control of every muscle in my body as I twitch and writhe on the stone, and with Wexton's cock still slamming inside me, it doesn't stop. It's not until I'm slapping the stone for mercy that he finally slows and I can breathe again. I stare up at the ceiling, seeing stars.

My body is still clinging to him, my muscles contracting around his cock so tight they protest every time he pushes inside me.

Wexton arches his back with a groan. "You squeeze me so tight. I've never felt anything so good in my life." After another lazy thrust, he looks down at me. "I can't wait to see you dripping with my seed."

I whimper, and my body clenches around him.

Wexton closes his eyes with a moan. *I'm so close.* His eyes flutter open again. *Ask me to come inside you. Please. Ask me, beg me, order me, I don't care which.*

I push myself up on shaky elbows and stare up at him. "Come inside me," I say sternly. "Right now."

Without breaking eye contact, Wexton tightens his grip on my leg and thrusts inside me twice more. His lips part on a strangled sort of whimper before he buries himself to the hilt and shudders as his warm seed bursts inside me. He rocks back and forth, milking himself of every drop. He's still quivering when he tugs me closer to the edge of the pool, pulls out, and immediately kneels in the water. My face heats as his eyes widen.

"Gods, Evangeline…" he whispers.

His fingers gently part my sex, and I feel a warm drop of his seed slide out of me.

He sighs as if it's the most beautiful thing he's ever seen before he leans in and puts his mouth to me.

I drop to my back on the stone again. If I watch any more, I'll burst into flames, but that only means I have nothing to focus on but the feel of him licking me clean. His tongue slides through my folds and plunges inside me, and the noises he's making soon have me panting with fresh desire.

I'm adding this meal to the menu permanently.

I cover my heated face with both hands only to drop them to the stone again with a moan as his fingers join the fun, sliding inside me and holding me open to let his tongue delve deeper.

"Wexton," I mutter.

He hums in response, not willing to pause his meal to give a proper answer.

"Do it now." I'm more than ready.

In a minute. I want to hear you come again first.

His tongue slides up across my clit, and I whimper again.

"That's right, darling," he murmurs. He slides his fingers inside me then curls them, probing a spot that makes my hips buck of their own accord. "It's your turn to come for me now." He flicks his tongue across my clit a few times quickly, and that coupled with whatever his fingers are doing sends me over the edge.

My back arches off the floor and my nails scrape across the stone as I orgasm again, and it voids my mind of anything but the feel of him touching and licking my most sensitive places. It's not until both his fingers and his mouth disappear that I remember what's coming next. I choose not to look and resist the urge to tense as his lips softly kiss my inner thigh.

Now?

"Yes."

His fangs sink into me, and I bite my lip against the pain, but it's quickly swept away again by an intense wave of heat that washes over my entire body. The lightheaded and floaty feeling I had the first time is back again, and tears spring to my eyes as my chest tightens with so much feeling I'm suddenly heartbroken to be lying alone on the stone floor.

Wexton must feel the same way because he stands up and reaches for me at the same time I sit up and reach for him. I throw my arms around his neck and slide into the pool with him, and he sits in the water and hugs me close.

I'd worried I would feel torn or like my heart was stretched thinner with each new mating bond, but that's not at all how I feel.

I feel like my heart has grown.

There's the love and connection I have with Caliborne, but there is also this new one with Wexton, and they are equal parts of me now. I nuzzle my nose against Wexton's cheek and kiss him there.

"I love you," I whisper. He turns his face into my neck but doesn't reply, and even his thoughts are silent. "Wexton?"

He shakes his head, and I freeze. It's only when his shoulders start to shake that I realize what's happening.

He's crying.

At first, I'm shocked that such a deadly, powerful being is falling to tears on my shoulder, but considering the overwhelming feelings flowing through my own heart at the moment, I can understand why.

Even a demon can be overcome with emotion, after all.

Tears of my own trickle down my cheeks as I squeeze him. "I know," I say, my voice shaking and breaking with every word. "You're stuck with me forever now. I'd cry too."

He finally lifts his head from my shoulder with a shaky laugh and touches his forehead to mine. I wash the tears from his face with a wet hand.

"I didn't know it was possible to love anything as much as I love you," he whispers. "I knew the mating bond was powerful, but I hadn't expected… this. I feel so full. And happy."

"I know what you mean." I kiss him softly on the lips. "Welcome to forever."

*****

I get very little sleep throughout the night. In fact, I sleep so little and so lightly that I don't dream even once, which gives Reilanna no chance to torment me. Wexton is insatiable, and I don't utter a word of complaint as he rouses me again and again with his teasing touches, dirty thoughts, and hard body. When dawn finally breaks, I'm sore and tired but utterly blissed. Neither of us are in any hurry to get out of bed, and it seems the entire castle has guessed why. Levi stops thrice throughout the day to bring us meals with a small, knowing smile on his face.

"I'm happy for you, Evangeline," he says to me after dropping off our dinner, and it's only then that I realize what this is.

This is the Gryxen equivalent of a honeymoon, or at least as close to one as we'll get in The Deadwood.

When I close the door and turn around with the dinner tray in my hands, I find my mate sprawled on his back across my bed just like the day I found him there before. And just like the last time, he's stroking himself and staring at me as if I'm the only meal he wants or needs. The smile he gives me both melts my heart and makes me clench my thighs together.

I quickly set the tray aside and join him, and by the time we eat our dinner, it's stone cold but no less delicious. We're just discussing whether we should have… dessert, or if we should take a bath first when there's another knock on my door.

"Who is it?" I call.

All I get in response are a few taps of a knuckle on the wood in a tune I don't recognize.

Wexton grunts as he sits up. "It's Caliborne." He scoots across the bed and stands, but then he swivels in a circle twice, searching the floor for his pants.

"Behind the chair," I tell him as I get up and start to dress.

It's an Evan day today, so I choose a dark brown button up and the only clean pair of pants I have left. I tuck up my hair and slip on my gold bracelet before following Wexton out into the hall.

Caliborne is leaning against the wall a short distance away dressed in his golden armor. At the sound of my bedroom door closing, he pushes off the wall and walks over to me, his white, blazing eyes studying me from head to toe.

I smile at him, and he palms my cheek.

You're glowing.

"I'm happy," I tell him.

He only nods because, of course, he knows the feeling himself. He turns to Wexton and claps him on the shoulder. A silent moment goes by during which Caliborne conveys whatever it is he feels the need to say to his son in this moment, then Wexton grins.

"I love you too, old man," Wexton says.

Only once they've parted do I ask, "What's going on, Caliborne?"

He takes my hand and starts walking us down the hall toward the foyer. *I think you should see it for yourself.*

"Are we going outside? I don't have my jacket."

He leads us all the way to the front doors before he replies, *You won't need one.*

Caliborne opens both doors up wide, and Wexton and I step out onto the landing next to Fenmire, who's also dressed in his armor, having just finished his patrol. Once my eyes adjust to the bright sunlight after being shut up in my room for so long, I look around and barely recognize the landscape staring back at me.

Most of the snow is gone, and what little is left in shoveled piles is melting in tiny rivers. It's so warm I'm a bit overheated in my long-sleeve shirt. The Deadwood is still brown and lifeless, but there's grass peeking through the snow between the castle's massive stone steps and the edge of the vines and brambles. Already, there's a hint of green life where there hasn't been in over two-thousand years.

I take Wexton's hand. "We brought summer to The Deadwood," I say with a smile up at him.

"Damn right we did," he replies. He squats and tugs me to sit on one of his legs with his arm around me. "Reilanna made a grave mistake when she made you the key to breaking her spell. She underestimated your kind." He strokes my cheek. "We'll make her regret that."

"Damn right we will."

Chapter 35

Caliborne takes off to begin his patrol as Fenmire follows Wexton and I back inside the castle. I'm giddy and feeling playful, so I turn to Fenmire and ask, "Can I hold your mace?"

"Absolutely not," he says with a scoff.

I frown. "What about your shield?"

Fenmire sighs with a roll of his eyes and removes his shield from his arm, holding it out to me.

I slide my arm through the straps on the back, but as soon as Fenmire lets go of it, the weight of the shield nearly topples me. I'm saved from falling over completely by Wexton's strong grip as he grabs me by the other arm.

Both Gryxen are laughing.

"You're *both* heathens," I jest as I take back my arm. My grip on the shield fails, and it falls over onto the floor with a loud clatter.

Fenmire kicks the shield up with his foot and snatches it out of the air, mounting it effortlessly back onto his arm in one fluid motion.

"Show off," I tease.

"Now aren't you glad I didn't let you have the mace?" Fenmire asks with a smirk. "You might've—"

The castle begins to shake, and Wexton pulls me protectively close with a wing over us both as little rocks rain down on top of us. The quake is short, thankfully, and once it passes, Wexton kisses me on the cheek.

"I've got to go to work, darling," he says sadly. "But I'll be back soon for that dessert we talked about bef—"

A horrible crash reverberates throughout the entire castle as the whole thing begins to shake again, only this time, the quake is so violent it knocks all three of us off our feet.

"Wexton!" I scream as even larger stones crash to the floor and explode into shards.

Both Gryxen grab me by the arms and huddle close, one on each side of me, and Fenmire holds his shield above us all in time to block one of the rocks from slamming down on our heads. Down the hall, one of the hanging baskets breaks from its chain and crashes into the ground in a burst of fiery embers, ash, and smoke. I scream, but Wexton holds my head protectively close to his chest.

"It's alright," he reassures me, but I hear concern in the voice of one who's usually nothing but jovial.

That scares me more than crashing stone and flame.

This quake goes on and on for so long I'm sure nothing will be left of the castle when it's over, but when it finally fades away, the castle still stands, though obviously battered. The floor is riddled with stone, and there are cracks in the walls. Wexton lets go of my head, and Fenmire lowers his shield.

"We need to go," Fenmire says. "Now. Whatever just came through The Gate… it's powerful."

Wexton nods, and the Gryxen get to their feet. I take Wexton's offered hand, but as soon as I'm back on my own feet, the front doors of the castle slam open, and a burst of wind whips down the hallway. It's so strong it puts the fires out in the remaining baskets and sconces. I sidestep closer to Wexton in fright as a large figure walks in and stops in the foyer. It spins in a small circle until it spots us, then it faces us with its arms held at its sides, its hands splayed, and its feet spread. It leers down the hallway at us, breathing heavy but not saying a word.

The creature has stark white hair and two glowing white eyes, and though the face is much older than the one I've seen in Caliborne's memories, I still recognize it.

"CeCe?" I say in awe.

"Look again," says Wexton. It comes out like a growl.

I study the creature anew. She's at least a foot taller than Caliborne and much broader in the shoulder. In fact, her whole body looks disproportionally larger than her head. Her chest, arms, and legs are half again as thick with muscles as any of the other Gryxen.

CeCe isn't a Gryxen, and yet this creature has two large, black wings.

"Who is it?" I ask, taking a cautious step back.

Fenmire shakes his head. "I wouldn't worry so much about the 'who'."

"What do you want?" Wexton calls to the creature.

She opens her mouth, and I believe at first she means to answer, but then she jerks forward with a screaming wail that makes me slam my hands over my ears and cry out as a wave of pain hits my entire body. Suddenly, Fenmire's shield is in front of me, and the pain stops.

"It's a wailer!" he screams, his face twisting with pain as he struggles to hold his shield up against some invisible force.

Wexton tugs me behind Fenmire and ducks so we're hidden from the creature's magic, but the sound still makes me whimper and press my hands harder over my ears. Even Wexton is desperately trying to plug his ears with his hand and shoulder. A horrible cracking sound rises over the creature's screams, and Fenmire cries out, gripping the arm that's threaded through the straps on his shield. It's broken. I can see the bulge of bone against his taut leather skin.

I put both my hands over my mouth in horror. If this creature's screams can break Gryxen bones, what will it do to me?

Fenmire looks at Wexton and I and yells, "Run!"

Wexton sweeps me in front of him as we turn and start running down the hall.

"Fenmire!" I scream.

"I'll be right behind you," he calls after us.

The screaming stops, but Wexton and I don't slow down. We seem to be in silent agreement where we're going as we head together toward the open kitchen door at the end of the hall. I can see Levi peeking out from around the doorframe.

"Go, go, go!" I call to him, waving my arms. "Out the back!"

He ushers the other two cooks from the kitchen, and they all run for the delivery entrance.

I hear pounding feet behind us, and I hope that means Fenmire is running as well, but just as Wexton and I reach the kitchen doorway, another scream erupts. I look back, and the force of the creature's scream slams into Fenmire, sending him tumbling down the hall. He lands on his back and immediately raises his shield to protect himself as he crawls backward toward the kitchen.

Wexton and I rush through the door and set our backs to the wall by the frame, neither of us daring to peek around the corner. Even with a wall of stone between us and the wailer, its screams still make my body hurt.

"Fenmire?" Wexton calls out.

A second later, Fenmire emerges, scrambling across the floor on his back with his shield held aloft as he crawls the last few feet into the kitchen. Wexton reaches down and grasps his arm, yanking him forcefully out of the doorway. Fenmire's nose and both his eyes are bleeding, but he wipes it hastily away and joins Wexton in slamming the door shut. They start flipping counters and tables over and stacking them against the door as well.

"Evan," Wexton calls, and he holds his hand out to me. I take it, and he begins leading me toward the service entrance where Levi and the others fled.

We don't make it even two steps.

Another scream, even louder than before, reverberates through the door and furniture stacked against it. I hold my head in my hands and scream from the pain. My brain feels like it's about to burst. A series of loud snaps, like whipcracks, make us all turn toward the door, and we all watch, helplessly, as the door, the furniture, and even the stone wall to either side begin to fracture under the assault.

Fenmire cries out in pain as he pulls his shield off his broken arm. "It's no use. It'll only give chase if we run." He holds the shield out to Wexton. "Make them some cover!"

Wexton holds tight to one of the straps, holds the shield high above his head, and slams it down at the floor so hard the shield imbeds itself several inches into the stone. "Evan!" he calls again, and I rush to him. He shoves me down behind the shield, and the pain in my head eases, though I can taste blood in my mouth.

"Stay behind it," Fenmire orders. "No matter what."

"What about you?" I fret.

"His armor will protect him from the worst of it," Wexton says.

"And you?"

"Strong as three Gryxen, remember?" he says with a wink. "I doubt very much she can break my bones."

"The others will come," Fenmire says. "As soon as they've dealt with the other one, they'll—"

An explosion of wood and stone bursts into the room, and I duck down lower behind Fenmire's shield as rocks and splinters rain over us. The screaming stops and everything goes quiet for a moment, though my ears are ringing so loud it's as if the whole room is filled with angry cicadas. I wipe a trickle of blood from under my nose and look for Wexton. He's not beside me anymore. I peek around the side of the shield.

The room is still clouded, and the only light in here comes from the two sconces that haven't been blown out yet, but I can still see the pair of glowing white eyes that peer through the darkness and dust as the creature steps over the threshold, stomping on debris that crunches under her feet with every step. As the air clears enough for me to see her hulking form, those white eyes lock on me, and the creature leans forward, opens her mouth, and…

A wailing yelp is all she's able to produce before Fenmire's mace slams against the side of her face, the sharp barbs on the sides digging into her skin and getting stuck in the cheekbones. She jerks back with an angry cry and dislodges Fenmire's weapon before Wexton attacks from her other side, stabbing her with one of Levi's long carving knives. It sinks hilt-deep into her back, but their attacks only seem to anger her more. She throws her arms out, knocking them both back a bit. Fenmire recovers first and swings again with his mace, only this time, she grabs it by the head, turns, and unleashes another of her wails.

Wexton silences her again by stabbing her repeatedly in the chest until she spins on him instead, giving Fenmire the moment he needs to plant his feet and rip his weapon free of her grasp. They go back and forth this way, each landing a blow or two and catching her attention in turns when the other falters. Eventually, the creature becomes frustrated and stops, throws out her arms, and sucks in a massive breath. I hide back behind my shield before a deafening blast of her magic detonates around the room, sending all the broken pieces of wood and stone flying and putting out the last two fires, pitching the room into total darkness.

I'm afraid to breathe as I huddle down behind the shield. I can't hear any movement, and I can't see to check if the others are still standing. I hear the scrape of talons on stone to my left and turn my head.

And peer directly into a pair of glowing white eyes.

I hear groaning and scrambling and the scrape of metal on stone as the others get up, but the creature strikes at me first, wrapping her massive hand around my neck and lifting me up off the floor.

I kick and choke and dig my nails into her arm, but her hold never slackens.

I hear a click, click, click sound, then the room is lit up with flickering firelight as someone re-lights one of the sconces, and I can suddenly see the creature holding me.

This close, she looks like something from one of my nightmares. Her skin is inky black and oozing blood everywhere, not just where the Gryxen have injured her. Her eyes, though glowing white like Caliborne's, are oddly inverted pits instead of domes, and her hair is streaked with black throughout the stark white strands. Her fangs are longer than normal and curved so harshly they bite into her chin, but that doesn't stop her from snapping her teeth at me, driving those fangs into her own flesh with every clack.

I look into those white eyes as my own fill with tears.

Fenmire warned me Reilanna would never let me break her spell. But as I look my own death in the face, I know in my heart it wouldn't have mattered if I'd known this would be the outcome.

I wouldn't trade any of it for a different ending.

My lungs are burning, and I'm starting to panic. I grab onto the creature's wrists, willing for her to let me go.

Her fingers around my throat twitch and loosen. A little air slips through my burning windpipe, but my eyes are watering so badly I can no longer see her face.

Let. Me. Go!

Her fingers slacken even further, and she screeches and shakes me as if the move was involuntary on her part. Her grip is loose enough I can breathe again, and a second later, it falters completely, and she drops me.

I hit the ground and scramble backward, gasping and coughing as Wexton vaults over the shield, knife in hand. He has black blood dripping from both his ears and his nose, but he stands up tall between me and the creature. She takes a swipe at him, which he blocks easily with his weapon. Fenmire rushes her from the side, and they're back at it, attacking and distracting her in turns, but she's beyond frustrated with both of them now and keeps knocking them back with wide sweeps of her long arms and claws. Wexton gets knocked into the shield that's still stuck in the ground and topples over it, holding his borrowed knife above him to block her claws from ripping him to shreds as he struggles to get back to his feet. She takes Fenmire by the hair and throws him against the wall, which knocks the wind out of him, and she grabs his broken arm and twists.

Fenmire's cry of agony is almost worse than the wailer's vile screams.

Wexton gets back up on his feet and attempts to strike her in the back while her attention is fixed on Fenmire.

She turns with unnatural speed, grabs onto his knife mid-strike, and refuses to let go. With Fenmire's broken arm still held in her grasp, she takes a deep breath and opens her mouth to scream right into Wexton's face.

A sharp whistling sound is quickly followed by a dull thud and a screech of pain, and the creature frantically drops both Gryxen to bat and dig at her face where an arrow is now stuck in her right eye. Fenmire's good arm loops around her neck, yanking her to the side and slamming her to the floor in front of the fireplace.

Caliborne strolls into the room from the service entrance, his next arrow already nocked, but when he sees the creature on the floor, he freezes, his eyes widening in shock. I'm still coughing and choking on air and can't tell him the beast in front of him isn't his sister. Wexton pins her to the floor with a foot on her neck as Fenmire walks over, raising his mace to strike her down for good.

Caliborne roars, but neither of the other Gryxen hesitate. Wexton and Fenmire strike down at her with their weapons, carving and caving in her blackened chest as her arms and legs flail and she tries to scream, but no sound slips through the pressure of the foot holding her to the ground by the throat. Black blood arches off their weapons as they go on mangling her torso until she finally stills, the last of the air leaving her lungs in a whine that almost makes me feel bad for her.

Wexton yanks the knife free and tosses it aside before lifting his foot at last, and the head of the creature rolls sideways so that the one remaining eye peers across the room toward Caliborne and I.

Caliborne tosses aside his bow and stalks across the room toward the body.

Wexton meets him halfway, slamming his hand into Caliborne's shoulder to stop him. "It's not her."

Caliborne doesn't seem to hear him. His eyes are locked onto the creature on the ground as Fenmire kneels beside it, clutching his broken arm to his chest as he runs his good hand over the body to examine it.

"Caliborne, stop," Wexton says as Caliborne tries and fails to shove him aside. "Father!" Wexton screams, and Caliborne finally stills, his eyes going wide with shock as he gives Wexton his attention at last. "It's not her! CeCe isn't a Gryxen. She doesn't have wings. It's just some shape-shifted beast made to look like her to unnerve us. Right, Fenmire?"

When he doesn't reply, we all look at Fenmire. He's still kneeling next to the body, but his hand is no longer running over it as he stares at it, his expression blank.

"Fenmire?" I say, though it comes out all croaky and makes my throat ache horribly.

"She's been shifted to give her the wings," Fenmire says, and his voice is emotionless. "She's also been given increased muscle mass, and her brain is little more than mush, but…"

"But what?" Wexton asks, and the panic in his voice makes me instantly sick to my stomach.

Fenmire looks up at us all, and his voice breaks as he says, "I'm sorry."

"No…" I utter in horror.

The noise Caliborne makes breaks my heart.

"You're wrong!" Wexton yells. "Check again."

Caliborne finally breaks from Wexton's grip and drops to his knees beside the body.

"I checked twice," Fenmire tells him. "A lot has been done, but at her core… it's CeCe."

I'm shell shocked and one wrong move away from being sick.

Beside me, Wexton whimpers. "That's not true," he says tearfully, searching all our faces as if one of us will provide him the evidence he needs to deny all of this. "It can't be."

Caliborne sits on the stone floor and gathers his sister into his lap.

Wexton walks over and kneels beside him, his eyes scanning over the body in disbelief. "CeCe," he says softly. "How? How did

Reilanna…?" He looks at Fenmire for answers, but Fenmire shakes his head with a glance at Caliborne.

Caliborne closes his eyes and starts to sob, his shoulders shaking as he puts his forehead to CeCe's and holds her close.

My family is in terrible pain. I can feel it in my stomach as if it's my own. It *is* my own. My mates' loss is my loss. I want to go to them and touch both their shoulders to let them know they're not alone, but I don't move. They deserve privacy in their minds right now. I stand a short distance away, trying not to fall apart and wishing I could wring Reilanna's neck.

Fenmire moves away from the others and joins me. Without saying a word, he pulls me close with his good arm.

"Is this my fault?" I ask softly enough I know he's the only one who can hear me. My voice breaks twice, and my throat feels like it's on fire.

No. It took a long time for Reilanna to twist CeCe into the beast she is now. It started long before you were ever in the picture.

"Did she suffer?"

There's a long pause before Fenmire answers, *Yes.*

"I'm going to be sick," I croak.

Fenmire spins me around in time for me to throw up on the floor near the wall as he holds back my hair.

If anything, you helped end her suffering. You and Wexton opened The Gate enough for Reilanna to release her and send her through. She's with Seerraf now and no longer in pain.

It's not much, but it's enough for me to be able to breathe and calm my heaving stomach. "I'm going to end her," I vow shakily. I spit some blood on the floor and wipe my mouth. "I swear to my God and yours I'll make her pay for this."

"I'll help you," Fenmire says, and he meets my eyes as I stand upright again. "I believe in you, Evan. It may take me time, but… I'm with you."

"You mean…?"

I've never seen so much feeling in Fenmire's eyes before. He looks heartbroken and terrified all at once, and it makes the tears I've been fighting this whole time finally spill over and run down my cheeks. His throat bobs as he swallows, and he wipes one of my cheeks dry.

I truly don't know if I can do this again.

"It's alright," I say. "We'll find out together."

"Evan," Wexton calls tearfully. He holds his hand out to me, and I leave Fenmire's side to go to my mate, who tugs me into his lap and buries his face into my neck.

Beside us, Caliborne takes my hand.

"I'm sorry," I whisper.

Me too.

I squeeze Caliborne's hand and put my arm around Wexton's neck, holding them both the best I can as I stare down at CeCe's lifeless face and mourn the loss of the sister I never met but loved all the same.

Famine

And when he had opened the third seal,
I heard the third beast say,
Come and see.
And I beheld, and lo a black horse;
And he that sat on him had
a pair of balances in his hand.

-Revelation 6:5 KJV

Chapter 36

We bury CeCe near The Gate. Caliborne and Wexton spend several days building her coffin together in the forge, and Fenmire and I join them as they dig a grave at the edge of the clearing. They won't let either of us help, though, so we stand a short distance away in silent solidarity. Fenmire's arm is still bandaged, but the splint and sling he wore for the first couple of days are gone. He wasn't kidding about the Gryxen's extraordinary healing capabilities.

"She'll be safe here until we can take her home again," Wexton says once they've lowered the box inside the hole. "Once Reilanna's spell is broken, we'll take her back to Michastiforo and lay her beside the rest of the family."

Caliborne shakes his head.

"No?" Wexton says. "Why not?"

"Michastiforo is gone, Wexton," Fenmire says, gently but still matter-of-factly. "There's nothing left to take her back to. It's more peaceful here. And beautiful. She's better off staying where she is."

"But that's her home."

"It's also where she suffered a fate worse than death."

Wexton falls silent at that and looks down into the grave at the coffin. After a moment, he nods sadly.

There's a heavy silence in the air that makes my heart feel like it's creeping up into my throat, and just when I think I can't take it anymore, it's broken by a song.

We all look over in shock as Fenmire sings softly in his own language. I don't understand the words, but the low and soft tone of his voice and the emotion that crosses the other Gryxen's faces tells me plenty. For several minutes, we stand there gazing down at the golden box and listening to Fenmire's song. When he falls silent, Caliborne takes up his shovel and tosses the first scoop of dirt onto the box.

"What was that?" I ask.

"A hymn," says Fenmire. "The one the priestesses sing to bless those who choose to pass on in the temple."

Wexton takes up his shovel too, and he joins Caliborne in covering the coffin with dirt.

"Does your kind believe in heaven?" I ask.

"No. We believe a person's soul moves from one life into another."

"What, like reincarnation?"

"That's right."

"What happens to wicked souls after death?"

"That is a subject of much speculation and turmoil. There are those who believe there is no such thing as a soul that's born wicked. They believe every soul at its core is something pure, like a blank canvas. What it becomes as it ages is determined by what is added to that canvas throughout its life. If a soul ends up wicked, it still passes on to the next life and is born pure once more.

"Then there are those who believe there are moments in our lives that change our souls forever and that certain decisions made from one life to the next alter the very essence of who we are. Like mating bonds, for example. Since mates bind their souls together, that bond carries over into the next life. It's a choice that affects your soul for this life and all the ones that come after."

"Do mates find each other more than once?"

"Many believe so," Wexton answers between shovelfuls. "They also believe there are consequences if you fail to find your mate again. There are those who never feel satisfied with life. Regardless of the many blessings they receive, it always feels like something is missing, like their heart isn't quite whole. That's how it feels to miss a mate you bonded with in a previous life. Or so they say."

Fenmire nods in agreement. "Such a thing brought countless Gruxa to the temple seeking to pass on during the years I lived there. They describe it as a feeling of deep grief they can't explain. They may have never lost a loved one, but it feels like they did, and the pain of that loss is unbearable."

"Do the priestesses let them pass on?" I ask.

"It depends. If the feeling has drained any joy left in life, then yes. If they have other things to live for—living mates or children, for example—things that make the pain bearable, then they usually deny the request the first time or two. If they come repeatedly to the temple seeking relief from their pain, the priestesses will eventually allow it. No one should be forced to live if they no longer wish to."

I want to ask him if he's ever considered doing that himself since he lost his mate, but I bite my tongue. This is neither the time nor the place for such a personal question. We stand in silence once more as Wexton and Caliborne finish covering the coffin with earth. They ring the mound with stones, then Wexton snaps a dried twig from a nearby tree and hands it to Caliborne, who draws several symbols in the dirt over his sister.

"What are those for?" I ask Fenmire quietly.

"Protection from grave robbers," he explains. "Anyone who breaks the runes runs afoul of Seerraf himself. Disturbing someone's final resting place is considered one of our most grievous sins."

"Humans don't take kindly to it either."

A shadow passes over us, and we all look up as Drixus flies overhead.

No one is on patrol today. With sadness hanging heavy in the air and The Gate's promise nothing will be coming through for a good long while, all the Gryxen are taking a day of rest to grieve, which means Drixus is here for nothing but CeCe. He and his mount circle us high in the air as Wexton and Caliborne gather their shovels and join Fenmire and I across the clearing.

I take Caliborne's hand and lean my head against Wexton's side. We all stand together there, staring at the grave in silent respect until Mara screeches as she and Drixus turn and fly away. The rest of us take that as our cue to leave as well, and Caliborne scoops me up in his arms before the three Gryxen launch into flight, and we all head back home.

*****

My emotions are a mess when we arrive back at the castle, so I beg my leave of the others, feigning the desire to take a nap, which I really should do anyway since tonight is The Offering. I'll be up late tonight for a trip to the arch, but instead of catching up on the sleep I'll miss doing so, I make my way up to the third floor to Drixus' door instead. It's closed, which no longer surprises or disappoints me. I take my seat in front of it, and when I call his name, I hear him shuffle closer, though he still doesn't speak a word.

"Thank you for coming to lay CeCe to rest today," I tell him. "I doubt the others will say anything, but it means a lot that you did that. It meant you loved her too and that you still care."

I pick at a spot on my dress as I gather my thoughts, choosing words that best fit my misgivings. "I feel selfish showing the others how sad her death makes me feel. She wasn't mine to lose, and they're in far more pain than I am, I know. I don't want them to think they have to comfort me through their own grief."

I sniffle back tears. "But I was looking forward to having a sister," I say sadly. "I've always secretly wanted one, you know. My parents couldn't have any more children after me, so it was never going to happen, but I used to ask God every night if he could somehow give me one anyway. Maybe that's why I asked Caliborne so many questions about CeCe. I thought those prayers would finally be answered, and I feel like I got to know her through his memories. It breaks my heart to know that she will never know me like I knew her."

I wipe my face with both hands. "I'm sorry. I don't mean to dump my sorrows on your doorstep. Despite what's happened, there is reason to celebrate today. Tonight is The Offering. My best friend, Will, has decided to join me here in The Deadwood. He promised he would be at the arch tonight when the village delivers the cart. Will and I have barely gone a day without seeing each other since we were just five years old. These last two months have felt like an eternity without him.

"I hope the others like him. Will is funny, caring, and protective. Kind of like Wexton, now that I think about it. I think they'll get along the best. I suppose that means he'll get along fine with Fenmire too, since he and Wexton are so close."

Drixus shifts. It sounds as if he's moved away from the door and further into the room, so I get to my feet, taking that as my sign to leave him be.

"I'll talk to you next week, Drixus. I hope someday you'll agree to meet me properly, but if not, I do enjoy coming up here and talking to you. I hope you do as well. Until next time."

I knock once on the door before making my way back downstairs to my room to take that nap after all.

*****

The moon is full and bright as I step out into the chilly evening air, all but tugging Caliborne along with me.

I haven't seen you this excited in a while, he comments.

"I've missed Will so much," I say. "I can't wait to see him."

"Does he understand there is no going back if he comes here?" Wexton asks as he joins us, shutting the castle doors behind him.

"He does. Even if we fail to break the spell, he'd much rather live here with me and Jacob over staying in the village where he could never be truly happy."

"We'll gladly be a safe haven for those who are otherwise unwanted or don't feel safe amongst your people. It's sad that we have to provide that at all."

I nod in agreement. "I wonder, what will happen to The Deadwood once the spell is broken?"

I assume it will go back to how it used to be, says Caliborne.

"So, just a normal forest?"

"Not exactly. What Jothrik created isn't your typical forest. It's enchanted to keep the humans away from The Gate."

"How does it do that?"

"By herding anyone who comes into the forest away from its center. Strategically placed trees, logs, streams, and thickets direct them around and away from The Gate."

"You're saying it *moves*?"

"Sure does. It's subtle and unseen magic, but your kind has enough intuition to know something isn't quite right. Few wandered into the forest back then. It made humans uncomfortable, so they usually stayed away on their own."

"And it can still do all of that even now that Jothrik is gone?"

"If it goes back to what it was before the spell, then yes. Jothrik gave the forest its own will so it could function on its own without his constant supervision."

"I hope I get the chance to see that someday."

Caliborne's hand tightens on mine. *Of course you will.*

Our flight is short, and we land in the lane near the first bend, within sight of the arch.

I'm nervous. Not about seeing Will again but rather *for* him. What if they catch him trying to come through the arch? What if they try to stop him? I want to move closer so I can help him if he needs me, but the Gryxen won't move up the lane so they don't scare the humans out of leaving the cart, and there's no way they'd let me wait up there on my own.

An hour goes by with no sign of The Offering.

"What's taking them so long?" I wonder out loud.

Wexton answers. "Whenever The Offering has been this late in the past, it usually means…" He gives me a sideways glance.

I hug my jacket tighter. "They plan to send someone through with the cart."

Caliborne nods.

I wonder who it will be this time as I fidget with my jacket sleeve. "I should greet them first. I know how scared I was when I first encountered a Gryxen. Maybe it won't be so upsetting if—"

The sound of creaking vines and groaning brambles stops me as the arch begins to open. I'm dying to walk toward it, and I squeeze Caliborne's hand to stop myself.

Don't get closer until they're gone, he cautions.

"I won't."

The cart starts moving through the arch, and I can see the flickering light of torches behind it. Orders are being shouted above grunts of exertion, and the cart is finally heaved through the hole. I lean around Caliborne so I can see the arch more clearly, and I put a hand over my mouth as a bound and lifeless figure is tossed through it into the dirt. Standing just outside The Deadwood again is Elias, and when his eyes meet mine, the look he gives me chills my blood to ice.

He's smiling. He even gives me a little wave as the vines begin to close over the arch again.

Something is dreadfully wrong.

I take a step forward, but Caliborne holds on tight to my hand.

Not yet.

As soon as the vines cover the opening, I lurch forward up the lane. The figure lying behind the cart isn't moving, and the closer I get, the more unnerved I become. He's the right size and height, and I think I recognize the color of his hair.

"Will?" I call as I round the back of the cart. I kneel at his head. If Elias has hurt him, I'll…

The man on the ground groans as he turns his head, but the person who looks up at me isn't Will after all.

It's Jacob.

Chapter 37

"Jacob?" I say in shock. "What's happened? Where's Will?"

"Eve," Jacob mutters. "I knew Will was telling the truth."

I start working the knots loose on his wrists. His skin is rubbed so raw he's bleeding underneath the rope. "Why did they bring you here, Jacob?" I ask even though I already suspect the answer.

"Elias caught Will and I together," Jacob says. He rolls over to face me, wincing and gasping in pain as he does. "I knew we should've come here at the last full moon, but—"

"What do you mean? Will told me you were still unsure about coming here and that he needed another month to convince you."

"No. When Will told me you survived and asked me to come here with him, I was fully prepared to do so. But Will's father fell very ill, and Will didn't have the heart to leave him like that." I finally have the ropes free, and he tosses them aside and sits up. "Will didn't want to tell you. He knew you'd try to be there for him, and he was afraid Elias would get his hands on you.

"Ever since you left, Elias has been insufferable. It felt like he was around every corner, spying on everyone. He's started whipping people in the square for petty crimes, and he's taken his father's place in the church even though he's still unmarried. We'd hoped another month might see Will's father on the mend and we'd get away for good, but..."

Jacob's eyes flick up over my shoulder, and he stiffens.

I don't have to look to know what he's seen that's frightened him. "It's alright." I put a comforting hand on his shoulder. "They're with me." I look back at my mates who are slowly approaching the cart, but when I raise my hand, they both stop and wait where they are. "So, Will's father got sick. Did he get better like you hoped?"

Jacob hangs his head. "No, Eve, he didn't."

I close my eyes. Poor Will. He's lost both his parents now.

"It gets worse," Jacob says miserably. "After the funeral, Will and I met up in that old, abandoned sugar house. You know the one?"

"Sure. Will and I used to take picnics up there in the summer."

"Yes, well, Elias must've been watching our houses after dark, because when Will and I snuck out and met up there to be alone and discuss our plans, Elias and a group of men from the village surrounded the sugar house. They dragged us out and threw us in the dirt in front of Elias. He said we'd both stepped off the path of God and needed punished."

"That sounds familiar," I grumble sourly.

"My father was there. He begged Elias to give me another chance, so Elias gave me a choice: marry his oldest sister and never see or speak to Will ever again or be exiled here in The Deadwood. I thought he meant to send us here together. That was our goal anyway, so I gladly refused to marry the girl. It wasn't until afterward he told us I would be the only one sent here. It seems Elias knows you've survived. He refuses to send Will here because, now that he's seen you're alive and well, he's afraid we'll all survive and be happy here together instead of suffering and dying like we're supposed to."

"What have they done with Will instead?"

"Elias kept us in the church cellar until The Offering. Will was still there when they came for me, but they plan to send him into the city in the morning. He's being sent to a facility for sinners of the flesh. I've heard of it before, Eve. It's nothing but a place of torture for people like us. They shock and beat and drug us to try and make us into what they want us to be. Few survive, even fewer yet ever get released. We can't let them do that to him."

"Don't worry, we won't." I help him sit up more comfortably with his back against the cart. "I'm going to call the others over now. Don't be afraid. They mean you no harm."

"It's true then? You walk with demons now?"

I nod. "It's true, but the demons of The Deadwood are nothing like what we've been taught. Here, let me introduce you." I wave to my mates, who approach the back of the cart as slowly as before. When they round the corner, Jacob's eyes widen, but he doesn't cower or move away. "This is Caliborne and Wexton. There are two others but they're not here right now."

Caliborne bows his head.

Wexton kneels beside me. "You are a friend of Eve's?"

Jacob looks at me for reassurance, and when I nod again, he clears his throat and says simply, "Yes."

"A friend of our mate is a friend of ours. Welcome to The Deadwood."

"Mate?" Jacob asks, his eyes flicking between Wexton and I.

"It's a long story," I say, "and we don't have the time right now to tell it." I touch Wexton on the shoulder. "Can the arch open more than once during the full moon?"

"Yes," Wexton says. "I've seen it myself when the village took too long sending a human through behind the cart. It opened a second time so they could push him through."

"The ones who sent me here, they've taken Will. They plan to send him away to the city to a place where they abuse people like us."

Wexton bristles.

Behind him, Caliborne growls.

"I need to go get him," I say.

I expect an argument, but Wexton looks over his shoulder at his father, who sends some feeling back through his palm before they both look at me.

"You can't go alone," Wexton says.

"I don't have a choice. No one else can leave The Deadwood. Unless…" I look at the arch then back at my mates as a hopeful thought occurs to me. I think back to the last time we were here during the last full moon. None of the Gryxen touched the arch that night. I never thought to have them try. "Come with me." I take Wexton by the hand and tug him over to the arch. "Please, God or Seerraf—whoever might be listening—please, let this work," I mutter before sticking my hand through the arch.

My hand disappears through the vines like they're not even there. I nod to Wexton.

He reaches out toward them as well… and his hand passes straight through.

I whoop with joy. "Caliborne! Come quickly!"

Wexton sidesteps to let Caliborne try, and his hand passes through the arch just as easily.

My mates can leave The Deadwood. Binding their souls to mine has released them from this part of Reilanna's spell.

"Come with me!" I cry. "Help me rescue Will. Both of you. Please."

The two Gryxen look at each other again.

"The humans will panic when they see us," Wexton says. "We'll likely be attacked."

"The church sits outside the northeastern corner of the village," I explain. "We could fly around and sneak up to the back of the church and through the back door. The hatch to the cellar is just across the hall. We could be in and out before anyone notices we're there."

"Eve," Jacob calls. "Elias had men guarding us day and night to be sure no one tries what you're suggesting."

"Are they armed?" Wexton asks.

"Yes, with clubs."

"We can handle that," Wexton says.

Caliborne nods in agreement.

"You'll help me then?" I ask.

Wexton gives me an odd look. "Of course we'll help you. That was never a question, darling. It was just a matter of how."

"Will you be alright here for a bit?" I ask Jacob.

"Are there beasts roaming these woods?" he asks.

"Not at the moment," Wexton replies. "You'll be safe here until we return, but we could call our friend to sit with you, if you'd prefer company."

I try not to laugh at the thought of Fenmire sitting with a strange human, making small talk.

"I think I'd rather be alone until you come back," says Jacob. "No offense."

"That's likely a wise choice," Wexton mutters so quietly Jacob can't hear him.

I stifle a giggle.

Caliborne touches my shoulder. *Stay close to us. I don't trust these humans not to hurt you.*

"Neither do I anymore," I say. "That's why we have to get Will. Elias will make his life a living hell if we don't."

"We'll get him, don't worry," Wexton assures me. "I'll go inform Fenmire."

"Be quick," I tell him fretfully.

When Wexton launches into the air, Jacob whistles.

"I'm glad they're on our side," he comments.

Caliborne kneels at Jacob's feet and takes him gently by the chin, turning his battered face one way then the other.

"I'm alright," Jacob says shyly. "It's mostly just scrapes."

"From rocks?" I ask.

Jacob nods. "And maybe a bruise or two from a few cheap shots they took before they threw me through the arch."

Caliborne growls.

I touch his shoulder. "They'll get theirs. Someday they'll face judgment for their sins."

"Do you truly believe that?" Jacob asks bitterly.

"I have to. Otherwise, the wicked suffer no consequences and the good reap no rewards. What would be the point of that?"

"I'm beginning to believe the only point to life is living it. What we get out of it is what we put in and nothing more."

"Maybe you're right, Jacob. I guess we'll never know until we pass on from this life and face whatever awaits us afterward."

"If there is a heaven, you'll get there some day," he says with confidence. "You've been nothing but kind to everyone you meet, and I've never seen an ounce of judgment in your eyes. Not even the day you caught me and Will behind the schoolhouse. You just winked and offered to keep watch for us. I'll never forget that."

Wexton lands in the lane past the cart, and Jacob and I jump. He's not alone as Fenmire lands beside him a heartbeat later.

I step away from Jacob toward the two Gryxen. "You didn't have to—"

I shut my mouth as Fenmire stalks toward me. He sets aside his mace and shield and kneels in front of me, sliding a golden dagger from the sleeve of his armor and holding it out to me.

"Take it," he orders.

"Me?" I ask, bewildered. "But I've never—"

He grabs my hand, opens it, and plops the hilt into my palm. It's much heavier than I would expect a knife of this size to be. He rolls it in my hand to reveal a row of runes carved up the side of the hilt and brushes his finger across them. "This will protect you should you have to defend yourself."

"It's going to be alright, Fenmire," I say, but my heart is beating so wildly in my chest the words come out a bit strained.

"I'm not taking any chances."

I curl my fingers around the dagger, lean forward, and kiss him on the cheek. "Thank you."

His eyes bore into mine until he finally nods, stands, takes up his weapons, and flies off without another word.

I'm staring at the knife in my hand when Wexton says, "I doubt he'll ever explain this to you, so allow me: That blade was a gift from the temple priestesses the day he left them to go to the training grounds. It's one of his most prized possessions."

"Why didn't he entrust *you* with it then?" I ask.

"Because I'm not the one he's afraid to lose." Wexton takes the blade from me, running his thumb along the runes just like Fenmire did. "This weapon holds great power. The blade has been blessed by each of the temple priestesses. They carved their names into the handle and prayed for Seerraf to protect their *vauncidi* as he guarded The Gate. I've seen it work its magic a few times over the years when Fenmire drew it to protect himself. That's the key, you know. If you wield it for your own gain, it's just a regular blade. But if drawn to save yourself…" He holds it back out to me. "He's right, it'll protect you. Keep it close."

I'm stunned as I take the dagger back, and I take his words to heart, clutching it to my chest before securing it in the slender belt around the waist of my dress.

"Time to go," Wexton says, and he takes my shoulder and steers me toward the arch.

Caliborne is already standing beside it, waiting.

I look down at Jacob as we walk past. "We'll be back," I tell him. "With Will."

"I'll be here," he says.

Chapter 38

As much as I love the home I've found with the Gryxen, I can't help but stare up at the bright, moonlit sky and breathe deep of the scent of fresh grass and wildflowers when I step out of The Deadwood. Caliborne comes through the arch a step behind me, and his eyes sweep across the horizon.

It looks so different.

Wexton steps out next, and he whistles. "It's so green out here. And what's that smell?"

"Wild lavender," I say. "It grows in the field between the south road and the edge of the village."

Wexton kneels and runs his hand across the tops of the long grass at his feet. It's been two thousand years since he's had the chance to do that, which is why it breaks my heart to take him by the arm and tug him to his feet.

"Later," I say regretfully. "Will needs us."

He nods and shakes his shoulders. "With you, darling."

Caliborne scoops me up in his arms, and we all take to the sky.

"Follow the south road," I tell him. "It ends just before the church driveway. We can fly to the right before the turn off and circle the thicket at the back of the church. There's a footpath from the back door to a small stream on the other side of the trees. It may be wide enough for a Gryxen."

"I'll make it wide enough," Wexton chimes from beside us.

"We should stay quiet."

This will be anything but quiet, Caliborne chimes. *If there are guards watching your friend, they'll raise an alarm immediately. This will be more about getting in and out as fast as we can over staying silent.*

I'm all nerves when the village comes into view. We keep our distance even though it's so late it's doubtful anyone is outside right now. The Gryxen fly low to the ground at the end of the south road and curve around the thick grove of trees, flying down the hillside that marks the northeastern edge of the village until they reach the little creek at the bottom.

"Right here," I tell Caliborne, who lands much more softly than usual on the northern bank of the creek.

Wexton lands far less gracefully, kicking up rocks and weeds as he skids in the dirt and splashes down into water up to his ankles. He barely keeps from toppling over onto his backside in the creek.

I shake my head but can barely contain my laughter at the same time as I say, "Beautiful landing. Truly inspiring. Can you teach me how to do that?"

He reaches out and scoops me up with his arm, hugging me to his chest as he wades across the creek. "You're lucky we've a job to do, or else I'd drop you in this water right now." He sets me on the opposite bank near the tree line.

I grin mischievously as the perfect response blooms on my tongue. "I suppose that's one way to make me wet."

Wexton has to physically squeeze his lips shut so as not to burst out laughing, which only causes me to fall into hysterical giggles myself.

Caliborne splashes past us, gives us both an exasperated eye roll, and shakes his head.

That doesn't help with the laughter.

I point out the footpath, but it's much smaller than I remember it. The Gryxen duck, scoot, and weave between the trees, but despite their best efforts, Wexton does in fact have to break a few branches and in one case nearly uproot an entire tree in order for them to make it up the hill. I worry about how much noise we're making, but the church soon comes into view without incident. The back of the church is a few yards from the tree line, and I can see the stained-glass window that looks in over the main room from behind the pulpit. There is a pane missing in the bottom right-hand corner that a fallen tree branch broke out years ago.

"Wait here," I whisper to my companions before I tiptoe out from the trees to the wall of the church.

"Eve!" Wexton hisses at me, but he stays behind like I asked. I can feel both their stares boring into my back as I put my eye to the hole in the window.

There are two men inside, sitting at two separate pews. The hallway to my left is pitch black, the only light in the church coming from a row of candles burning on the steps in front of the pulpit. Hopefully that means these two are the only ones here.

I sneak back to the trees and tell the others what I can see.

"Where is the hatch to the cellar?" Wexton asks.

I point to the back door of the church. "That leads to a short and narrow hallway." I draw a small map in the dirt at my feet to better show them what I mean. "Once we get inside, there's a door to the right that leads to the main room where the two guards are, one to the left that leads to the pastor's office, and then the cellar hatch at the other end of the hall."

Were the guards armed? Caliborne asks.

"They weren't holding anything that I could see, but I'm sure they have something nearby to scare people off with."

"What if I just burst in there and run those two off?" Wexton asks. "They're not going to take on a demon with a couple clubs. I'll chase them out the front door and bar it behind them. We can grab Will and scoot out the back before they even know what's happening."

I look at Caliborne, who shrugs.

"I guess that could work," I admit apprehensively.

"Great," Wexton says gleefully, then he darts out of the trees toward the door.

Caliborne and I follow him at a distance.

"Who's out there?" one of the men inside calls.

"You better announce yourself," says the other. "Or we'll—"

Wexton rears back his foot and kicks the church door so hard it splits in two and crashes in on the hallway floor. He roars in the doorway before dashing inside, and the terrified screams of the two guards soon follow.

"I suppose that's one way to do it," I say.

Caliborne holds me back by the shoulder as he peeks in the door. *You should know by now he'd never miss a chance to make a scene.*

A fresh roar provokes a second chorus of screams from inside.

"And to think both his parents were the soft and silent type," I comment.

Caliborne winks at me before ushering me inside ahead of him.

I take exactly one step into the church before the bell begins to ring.

"That's going to wake up the whole village!" I say in a panic.

Caliborne looks around thoughtfully as he steps inside the church, ducking his head through the doorway that's barely wide enough to fit his massive frame. He waves me on, more focused on the task at hand than the crowd we'll no doubt gather soon.

I lead him down the hall past the pastor's office. There's no light here, so I guide myself forward with a hand on the wall. This hall is so narrow Caliborne's wings scrape against the sides.

"I can't see," I say as I kneel down and run my hand across the floor, searching blindly for the hatch.

There's a tap, tap, tapping sound behind me, and a second later, the hallway is illuminated by a soft white light. I search for its source and find Caliborne holding a small crystal that's glowing brightly. He hands it to me.

"Whoa," I say in awe as I take it. It's warm to the touch and perfectly smooth on all sides, but upon closer inspection, I find a large crack through the middle where the light seems to originate from. "Fascinating."

I go back to the task at hand and find the cellar hatch a few feet away. I kneel in front of it but am immediately disheartened when I see a large iron lock on it. I pick it up and give it a tug to confirm it's actually closed, then I rattle the hatch to check for any weak spots I might be able to break open, but everything is sturdy and locked up tight.

"Caliborne?" I call.

My mate reaches over me, wraps his long fingers around the lock, and pulls. The nails and wood groan under the strain until the whole latch pops off. I throw the hatch open, which bangs against the floor on the other side.

I stick my head down into the pitch black hole above the spindly wooden ladder, holding my glowing crystal out in front of me to peer into the dirt cellar. There are shelves of dry goods down here as well as a few maintenance supplies for the church, but otherwise, this place is empty, dark, and cold, definitely not a place suitable for a human regardless of their crimes. I don't see Will, but my light doesn't reach the back of the room to tell for sure it's empty.

"Will?" I shout. Please let him be here. He has to still be here, right? Elias wouldn't have men guarding the church if—

"Evangeline?" Will steps out of the darkness, shielding his eyes from my light as he squints up toward my face. "Is that you?" He's filthy, smeared head to toe in dirt from the floor with his hair sticking up in odd angles. He has a black eye and is holding his side, likely nursing bruised or broken ribs.

I reach down for my friend, and he takes my hand. His fingers are like ice, and I can't get him up the ladder fast enough so I can wrap him in my arms. His feet have barely settled on the landing when I give in and yank him into a hug, taking care to avoid his injured side.

"Eve," he utters into my shoulder as he holds me so tight I can feel his relief in my bones.

I pull away and take his face in my hands. "Are you alright?" I ask tearfully. "Did they hurt you bad?"

"A few cheap hits, but I'm fine. Jacob? Did he—"

"He's waiting for us, in The Deadwood. We have to go, quickly."

I raise my crystal to light up the hallway, and at the sight of Caliborne, Will starts so hard he nearly topples back into the hole behind him. I grab his arm to steady him and smile.

"I came with friends," I say. "I'll make introductions later, but you're safe. You'll have to take my word on that, alright?"

Will gives me a half-hearted nod, his eyes wide and locked on Caliborne, who's moved back down the hall a ways to give us some space. "Is that one of the demons?" he asks quietly.

"Yes."

He's shaking, and I have a feeling it's from more than just the chill of the cellar.

"Will?"

He finally takes his eyes off Caliborne to look at me.

"They won't hurt you, I promise, but we have to go. Elias will be here shortly."

That seems to shake him out of his stupor. He nods again, and I take his hand to lead him back down the hall toward the door. We're a few feet away from freedom when Wexton bursts into the hall with a pew tucked under his arm. Will, Caliborne, and I all jump back to keep from getting smacked as the pew swings around the corner into the tight little hallway.

"Wexton!" I cry. "What on Earth are you doing?"

Wexton kicks the broken pieces of the back door into its frame and wedges the pew up against it to hold it in place. "We have a problem."

I'm about to ask for clarification when a voice from outside makes us all freeze and fall silent.

"They've barricaded the doors! Bring the torches!"

"That's Elias," I say quietly.

"Throw those broken branches up against the wall. Light it! Send the demons back to hell."

"Do they mean to burn their own church?" Wexton asks.

The scrapes and thuds as wood is stacked up against the walls of the church are answer enough.

"There are people in here!" I scream out. "Please!"

"Don't listen to her," Elias orders. "She walks with demons now, remember? She would call to your good nature to save her and her beasts only to walk you right through the gates of hell with them. We can rebuild our house of faith, but if we let those demons leave here, they'll slaughter us all in the name of their lord, Satan."

"Ignorant fool," Wexton hisses.

"Will is still in there," one of the villagers responds.

"One life to safeguard the rest of the village is a trade God himself will understand," Elias replies.

Will scoffs. "You abandoned God's path long ago, Elias!" he yells. "Stop pretending you're doing this for anything more than your own selfish gains. You can't control the masses unless they're scared, but the real demon here is you!"

After a brief moment of silence, Elias says, "There are dozens of our women and children huddled in their houses relying on us to protect them. Are we to trust their lives in the hands of demons and sinners we've condemned to exile? Stack the wood and burn the wicked back to hell! For our wives, sisters, and daughters!"

The men outside cheer, and the banging of wood on wood starts up again. A moment later, I smell smoke.

"Time to go," Wexton chimes. "Is there a way to the roof?"

"There's a ladder up to the bell tower," Will says. "But I don't think you'll fit through the hatch."

"We'll have to make our own way out then."

We all file into the main room where Wexton stares up at the ceiling, spinning in place as he searches for the perfect spot. When he finds it, he takes flight, nearly knocking Will and I on our backsides since we're both standing beside him. He latches onto a support beam with his back claws, anchoring himself there as he punches and tears at the wooden roof. Bits of wood rain down around us, and Caliborne spreads his wings over Will and I to shield us from the worst of it.

Smoke begins to fill the room, making my eyes water.

Will starts to cough.

Caliborne whistles.

"Nearly there," Wexton yells down. "Another minute."

A crash of breaking glass makes me yelp, and a torch bounces off the top of the pulpit and lands on the floor in front of us. Caliborne kicks it away with a growl, and it slides under a nearby pew, setting it ablaze.

"Wexton!" I scream as we all step back away from the growing flames.

The Gryxen in question lands beside me so hard he cracks several of the boards in the floor under his feet. Caliborne gathers me up in his arms, and Wexton taps Will on the shoulder.

"This won't be a comfortable flight," Wexton says with a smirk. "But it'll beat burning to death."

Without waiting for a response, Wexton picks Will up in his one arm and tosses him over his shoulder like a sack of potatoes.

Caliborne wraps his wings in tight around us, bends his knees, and shoots up toward the new hole in the roof through which I can see a patch of starry sky. We land on the sloped roof, and Caliborne digs his talons in to keep from sliding down as we wait for Wexton and Will to join us.

"Demon!" Elias screams from the ground.

Wexton's flaming red hair appears a second later, and he doesn't bother landing on the roof at all. As soon as he's clear of the hole, his wings pop out and he swoops into flight, barely missing the bell tower as he glides toward the woods.

"Don't let them escape!"

Caliborne turns and runs across the roof in the direction of Elias' screams. When he reaches the edge, I barely register Elias' shocked face from atop his chestnut mare before Caliborne leaps off the roof, right toward him. Elias screams along with half a dozen of his posse at the sight of a demon headed right for them, but at the last second, Caliborne spreads his wings, and we curve up into flight just inches away from Elias who tumbles backward off his horse in terror.

I can't contain my laughter as we turn and fly over the trees, retracing our steps back toward home.

Chapter 39

We all land in the grass beside the arch. The Gryxen set us humans down on our feet, and Will groans.

"You weren't kidding about the uncomfortable part," he says, rubbing his aching side.

"It *was* better than burning to death, though, wasn't it?" Wexton asks with a wink.

"Will, this wiseass is Wexton," I say with an affectionate pat on Wexton's chest. "And the big and silent one here is Caliborne. They're my mates."

"Your what?" Will asks.

"It's a long story."

"Eve has told us a lot about you," Wexton says.

Caliborne offers Will his hand, and when he takes it—apprehensively at first—some of the tension melts from Will's shoulders. I bite my lip to hide my smile as my mate calms my best friend's nerves.

"Nice to meet you," Will says, and he sounds much more at ease now.

I hug Will again, properly this time. "Oh, how I've missed you."

Will hugs me back and kisses the top of my head. "Not as much as I've missed you. I'm sorry I didn't come last month. My father fell ill, and I couldn't leave him. I was the only one still living at home, so I was all he had, and—"

"It's alright, Will. You did the right thing. You didn't have to lie to me though."

Will scoffs. "Would you have stayed put in The Deadwood if I'd told you the truth?"

I chuckle. "Probably not."

"Exactly."

I pull away and take him by the arms. "Are you sure about this? Remember what I said before? Once you step through that arch, you can't step back out again, not until I break this spell."

"I have nothing left in the village. Everything I love is in The Deadwood now, so yes, I'm sure."

I rub my hands up and down his arms with a smile. "Alright."

I turn to my mates as Wexton flops down on his back on the ground with a large sigh. He spreads his wings and arm out wide and stares up at the stars as he runs his hand softly over the tops of the grass.

I laugh and walk over to him.

He gazes up at me with a smile so content it melts my heart. When he pats the ground under his arm, I crawl down into the grass to lie beside him. His hand brushes my shoulder.

One of these days, I'm bringing you out here and making love to you in this very spot.

I roll and throw an arm over him. "Deal." When he wraps his arm around me, I see his hand is swollen and every knuckle is raw and bleeding from punching his way through the church roof. I carefully slide my fingers between his and give them a gentle, affectionate squeeze. "Thank you."

"It's nothing, darling. They'll heal in a day or two." He tugs me up across his chest until we're nose to nose. "I'd fight my way through a thousand ceilings for your happiness."

I lean up until our lips are nearly touching. "Good to know," I murmur.

Will clears his throat. "I don't mean to ruin the moment, but… Jacob."

I snort against Wexton's lips and give him one chaste kiss before I get to my feet. I offer him my hand, but it's mostly just to be polite as my meager strength does nothing to help him up. We all gather near the arch, and I loop my arm around Will's as we face it together.

"Let's try this again, shall we?" I say.

We walk arm in arm toward the arch, and the vines groan as they slide apart. There, just on the other side by The Offering cart, stands Jacob. His face twists into a look of pure agony, and he reaches for Will, who immediately abandons my arm to launch himself through the arch into his lover's.

"I didn't let myself hope until I saw you with my own eyes," Jacob says as I cross through the arch myself.

"It's alright, love," Will says softly, taking Jacob's face in his hands. "I'm here, and we're both safe now."

"This isn't exactly how I pictured we'd get here," Jacob says with a small laugh.

Will laughs too. "No, it's not."

"I love you."

Will kisses Jacob tenderly then says, "I love you too, so, so much. We're free now. Free and together."

"Well," Wexton chimes as he and Caliborne file through the arch, which is already closed over again. "There are too many of you to fly this time. Or would you like me to flag Fenmire down again?"

"We humans can ride in the cart," I say. "Care to pull us home?"

"Turning me into a pack animal, are we?"

"Are you good for much else?" I tease.

He hums under his breath and gives me a look that says there are a thousand comebacks on the tip of his tongue he's only barely holding back.

I smirk at him.

He heads for the front of the cart, and as he passes me, he leans down and whispers, "You'll pay for that later."

"Promises, promises," I quip as Caliborne gently picks me up and sets me in the cart over the side.

The boys both clamor in the back, and we all sit together in a cramped little huddle amongst The Offering. Wexton takes up the hitch, and the cart lurches into motion.

"Where are we going?" Will asks.

"The castle," I say happily.

"It's real then?" Jacob asks.

"Oh, it's real. But that's pretty much where the truth in our legends ends. The Deadwood, the demons, and even hell are nothing like what we've been taught all our lives."

As the cart slowly bumps along the lane, I tell them what I've learned about The Deadwood and the warriors who've dwelled within it for the past two thousand years.

*****

I fall asleep on the ride back home and wake up hours later in bed. The arms around me are familiar and comforting, but everything that happened tonight comes rushing back to me, and I jolt upright.

"Will and Jacob?" I ask.

They're tucked in for the night in the room beside yours, Caliborne answers. *Go back to sleep, my stoferra.*

I check my waist for Fenmire's knife, and when I can't find it, I start to panic.

It's on the nightstand.

I look and find it, safe and sound, on the table by my side of the bed.

"I should give it back to him."

You can do that in the morning.

As if in silent support, the sun crests the trees at that moment, sending a single, bright beam of light into the room. Dawn means Fenmire will have just gotten back from patrol.

"There, see, it's morning now," I say with a smirk.

Caliborne sighs into my shoulder and uncurls his arm from around me. *Very well. If you're adamant about it, then go. Hurry back, though. I'd hoped to spend a few hours bathing you in pleasure this morning since I have patrol tonight.*

I bob my brows and give him a quick kiss. "I'll be right back, then."

I scoop the knife up off the nightstand and pad out into the hallway in my nightgown. Fenmire's room is only one door down from Caliborne's, and I knock lightly on it in case he's already asleep. I soon hear the scrape of a chair across stone and heavy footsteps before the door opens. He's not only still awake but alert.

I smile at him. "I just wanted to let you know we're back."

"Did you find your friend?" he asks.

"We did."

"Good."

I hold his knife out to him. "I didn't need it tonight, but thanks for letting me borrow it all the same."

He chews his lip thoughtfully as he regards the weapon. "Keep it."

"Oh, no, I couldn't."

"Not forever but for now," he insists.

He turns and walks deeper into his room, leaving the door open. I'm not sure if he means for me to follow him or not, so I step awkwardly just inside the door but go no further. I've never seen Fenmire's bedroom, and knowing how reserved and guarded he is, stepping into his personal space feels surreal.

There's another desk in here, like the one in the library, as well as the biggest bed I've seen in the castle yet. It dominates the left wall, taking up well over half the room. Every remaining inch of wall is full of bookcases, and my eyes sweep across each shelf. It's as if I've stepped back into my old bedroom, or at least what my room could have been had I not been forced to mitigate my hobbies and interests all my life.

Along Fenmire's shelves, there are books, of course, but there are also rocks, wood, clumps of different ores, and bones. There's a large green egg, a fossil the size of my head, and even a jar with a perfectly-preserved serpent floating in clear liquid. There are gems the size of my fist in every color I can name and a few I can't all lined up neatly around a golden statue of a Gryxen with four arms.

My fingers ache to pluck each item down and inspect it, but I don't move from my spot by the door. Maybe someday I'll be invited to explore this space, but this doesn't feel like the time.

Fenmire goes to the one small dresser in the room—it's tucked up against the side of his desk since there's no other place for it—and opens the bottom drawer. He takes out a delicately-carved leather sheath and brings it to me.

"Here," he says, laying it in my hand. "Find yourself a sturdy belt and keep my blade close. I'm sure Wexton already explained how it works."

"He did."

He tilts his chin up. "What else did he tell you about it?"

I shrug and slide the knife into its sheath. "Everything?"

Fenmire breathes in deeply through his nose. "Perhaps that's for the best," he says on the exhale. "You deserve to know the truth."

I see an opportunity I may not get again for a while, and I take it. "If that's the case, will you tell me why you fought so hard to save me when I came to the castle? I know you agreed to try because Caliborne asked you to, I remember that much, but when the others thought I wouldn't make it, you refused to give up. Why?"

A long silence follows during which we stare at each other, neither willing to blink or look away first. After a while, Fenmire's shoulders sag a bit, as if it releases some weight from them to say, "I almost did give up. There was a moment where I lost hope for you and took my hands from your chest, intending to let nature take its course. I watched your breathing slow to small, painful gasps and considered ending your suffering myself. As I sat there in indecision, you reached out in your fevered sleep, and your hand found mine on the bed beside you. You squeezed my fingers so tight…"

He lifts said hand and flexes his fingers, remembering my grip on them. "Having grown up in the temple, I know what a spiritual presence feels like. I've felt Seerraf touch my shoulder during prayer, I've seen his hands reach through existence to heal a suffering soul, and I've watched his golden light dawn on a battlefield to lead us to victory. But, ever since we've been stuck here in your world, I haven't felt Seerraf's presence here. Not once. There's been a chill in my bones these past two thousand years that wasn't caused by the weather."

Fenmire looks into my eyes. "But when you grabbed my hand, Evangeline, I felt Seerraf in the room with me that day, and I knew what I needed to do as clearly as if he'd whispered it in my ear. I knew at that moment you were important. I didn't know why yet, but I knew Seerraf sent you to us for a reason. Letting you die wasn't an option." His hand comes up to cradle mine, the one holding his knife. "I made a promise that day to you, myself, and both our gods that I would do everything in my power to keep you alive. I like to think I've succeeded so far."

My mouth opens and closes twice as my mind forms a question I don't want to ask but must know the answer to. "Knowing what we know now, everything that we know, do you regret saving me?"

Fenmire's answer is immediate and resolute. "Not one bit."

I don't know what I was expecting, but his answer makes me teary eyed. I blink the sting away, determined not to cry in front of him.

I nod down at the knife in my hand and hug it to my chest. "Thank you for this," I say, though my voice wavers a bit. "I'll take good care of it."

"You do that," he says softly. "It'll take care of you too if the day ever comes when I can't."

I turn and leave his room, no longer trusting myself not to cry.

Before I step into Caliborne's room, I look back down the hall toward Fenmire's door and find him standing in it, watching me. The look in his eyes is one of intense indecision, like my name is on the tip of his tongue and he's fighting the urge to call me back. I count to three, and when he remains silent, I step back into Caliborne's room and shut the door.

Chapter 40

I spend the afternoon showing Will and Jacob around the castle. I introduce them to Levi in the kitchen and Percival in the stables: a place that fascinates Jacob to no end. He has a hundred questions for Percival as we walk the aisles and meet all the animals.

"You can come help Percival down here any time you like, Jacob," I say as I pass him a rabbit to cuddle. "We're all free to lend a helping hand wherever brings us the most joy."

"Where do you work?" Will asks.

"The kitchen sometimes, but I rarely have time anymore."

"Why? What do you do instead?"

"Um…" I say shyly, then I laugh. "I do some sewing and reading, but the Gryxen usually keep me pretty busy otherwise."

Will raises a brow then touches Jacob on the shoulder. "I'll be right back."

Jacob is all smiles with his arms full of rabbit, and he nods that he heard Will before firing his next question at Percival.

"Walk with me?" Will requests.

I give the fluff ball in Jacob's arms one final scratch and follow Will down the aisle until we're well out of earshot of the others.

"You haven't explained how exactly you're supposed to break this spell," Will says quietly. "You said those two from last night, the Gryxen? Is that what they're called?"

"That's right."

"You said they were your mates."

"I did," I say vaguely.

Will isn't about to let me off that easy. "Care to explain?"

"I will if you can promise to keep an open mind about it."

He gives me a pointed look. "You honestly think I would judge you? You know me better than that, Eve."

"This goes beyond anything we've discussed or experienced before, and it directly contradicts everything we've been taught in church and by our families all our lives."

"At this point, after everything that's happened to you, to Jacob, and to me at their hands, I care very little for anything the village may have taught us. You said our legends were wrong. So teach me the truth. Please."

I nod. "Not far from here is a gateway to another world, a world our people have long thought was a realm of fire and brimstone where the wicked are sent to suffer for eternity."

"You mean Hell."

"That's right, only that's not what's on the other side at all. It's a doorway to a world that's a lot like ours. I've seen it. It's rich with colors and people and religion just like Earth. Humans have vilified what they don't understand. The Gryxen are what their kind calls 'Gate Guardians'. They protect both our world and theirs from unwanted travel between them.

"About two thousand years ago, a sorceress tried to come through The Gate and take over our world. The Gryxen stopped her, but she cast a spell that created The Deadwood and sealed The Gate. The Gryxen have been trapped here ever since. But the spell speaks of a human, one who is neither a woman nor a man, who can free the Gryxen and open The Gate again."

"And you think that human is you?"

"I don't think. I know. Every time I mate with another of the Gryxen, the spell loses more of its hold on them. Caliborne and Wexton were able to step out of The Deadwood last night and help rescue you because they are my mates. They haven't been able to do that in two thousand years."

"You're telling me they're over two thousand years old?"

"Gryxen live forever unless killed by injury or disease."

Will runs his hands through his hair, taking a brief moment to absorb all of this before he says, "Alright, so you're their mate. What exactly does that mean?"

"It means I've bound my soul to theirs."

Will blinks at me. "You've bound your soul to *demons*?"

"They're not demons, Will. They're Gryxen. What our people call them and everything we've learned about them isn't real. They're warriors, not evil spirits."

Will takes a step closer and lowers his voice. "What if they're just telling you all of this to gain your trust? What if they really are evil?"

"I don't believe that," I say with confidence. "And I think once you spend some time getting to know them, you won't believe it either."

Will falls into thoughtful silence. His eyes slide past me to Jacob, who's still happily chatting with Percival, only they've moved down the aisle to the fox pens. Jacob is laughing and playing fetch with one of the younger male foxes, and when he sees Will watching, he waves.

Will sighs. "This is the happiest I've seen him in months." When I don't say anything, he looks at me again. "You seem happy too."

"I'm more than happy. I'm in love."

"Is that what happens when you become their mate?"

"Not in my experience. Love comes first. The mating bond has to be wanted by both parties in order to form."

"So they didn't force you?"

"Not at all. Even if the mating bond allowed such a thing, the spell specifies the human has to be willing and eager. I love them, and I want to help. The rest just sort of fell into place on its own."

"If you've already mated with two, how many more are there?"

"There are four Gryxen in total."

"And they all want to mate with you?"

"That part is complicated, but I'm working on it."

"What happens when you break the spell?"

"We don't know for sure, but it's probable they'll have to fight the sorceress again. She destroyed the city on their side of The Gate and made it her fortress. She cast her magic on Caliborne's sister and sent her to kill us all. It was awful."

"She *sent* her? What do you mean?"

"Ever since she cast the spell, Reilanna—that's the sorceress—has sent beasts through The Gate to torment the Gryxen. They've been fighting her beasts and keeping our village safe since the spell was cast. Those legends we have of great beasts sent to punish us for refusing to send The Offering? They were actually the few beasts that managed to slip past the Gryxen over the years. It doesn't happen often."

"So we didn't even have to send The Offering at all?"

"No, but it's a good thing we did. It's what's been feeding all the people the village sends here. The Gryxen eat Reilanna's beasts, but The Offering feeds the humans who live here now."

Will shakes his head in bemusement. "This is all so unbelievable."

"It's a lot to take in," I concur. "But the important thing is that we're safe here. Better than safe. We have the chance to just be us." I touch his arm. "You and Jacob can hold hands, kiss, share a room, or even get married here. The Gryxen don't share the same views as our elders do about such things, and the humans here, you'd be amazed how many of them are like us. Not one of them batted an eye when I told them I wasn't a woman or a man and that I go by three different names. It'll be no different for you and Jacob, I'm sure of it."

Will's eyes glaze over and drift away from mine. "Marriage?" he says in awe.

"Sure. Why not?"

"I just… never thought of that as an option. Even if we'd managed to escape together into the city, there are no churches that offer to let two men get married. I was more worried about getting us both out alive."

"Well, you're both out now and most definitely alive. We don't have a church or even a pastor, but does formality really matter in here? We could simply witness you promise yourselves to each other and celebrate your love and union. Isn't that what's most important?"

"I…I don't even know if Jacob would want that."

"You should ask him."

Will nods absentmindedly. "Perhaps."

"Did you have any more questions?"

Will breaks from his stupor with a start. "What? Oh, no, I don't think so. As long as you're happy and they treat you right."

I smile. "I am, and they do."

"Good."

"Will!" Jacob calls. He and Percival have moved to the left wall of the room by the long wire cages, and when we look over, Jacob holds up some small rodent for Will to see.

"Is that a rat?" I ask.

Will laughs. "He was constantly trying to keep one as a pet when we were kids. His mother always caught him and let them go again."

We make our way back over to Jacob and Percival, and it is indeed a large fat rat Jacob is fawning over.

"Will," Jacob says in an excited rush, "Percival says when the next litter is born, I can have one for my own if I want!"

Will eyes Percival. "He'll hold you to that, you know."

"Oh, I mean every word," Percival assures him. "He can have a pair, if he wants."

Jacob scratches the rat in his hands between the ears. "Would you mind very much sharing our room with two tiny critters?" He holds the rat up for Will's inspection. "Isn't she such a sweet thing?"

Will sighs and puts his arm around Jacob, pulling him closer. "Whatever makes you happy, love." He kisses Jacob on the cheek.

Jacob looks at Will in disbelief then glances anxiously at both Percival and I. When neither of us react in any way to Will's display of affection, Jacob laughs with relief and visibly relaxes into Will's side, who runs a tentative finger down the rat's back.

"Here," Jacob says, and he hands the rat over to Will, who goes wide eyed as he wraps his hands around the rodent. "I'll get another." Jacob dives into the rat cage.

I snort at the look on Will's face as he struggles to find the proper way to hold the animal.

Will sticks his tongue out at me.

I return the gesture.

I'm so happy I could cry.

Chapter 41

The next day, I spend every free moment I have working through all the problems and notes Fenmire gave me, but for the life of me, I can't figure out the last equation. No matter how I go about it, I keep getting the wrong answer. I get the *same* answer each time but the wrong one, nonetheless. I'm about ready to tear my hair out when I finally admit defeat and make my way up to the second floor.

The library door is open, but Fenmire doesn't hear me approach it. He's leaned over his desk, drawing in a notebook with a pencil in each hand, one tucked behind his ear, and one in his mouth. He squints in concentration as he makes short, rapid strokes with his pencil. I'm so fascinated by his work that I stand there in the doorway, content to watch him for a bit.

It's several minutes later when he finally glances over and sees me, and when he does, he promptly sticks one of his pencils in his book and flips it closed. He doesn't say anything, he just raises a questioning brow and waits for me to speak first.

"I'm stuck," I say, and I lean dejectedly against the door frame as I wave the book he gave me in the air like a white flag.

Fenmire turns his chair to face me, and the hint of a smile twitches at the corner of his mouth. "Are you now?"

"On the last problem."

His smile widens. "Ah, yes, that one."

"Why don't you look the least bit surprised?"

He shrugs. "Because I'm not."

I narrow my eyes. "It's impossible, isn't it?"

Fenmire snorts.

"You cheeky little devil. You gave me a problem I can't solve!"

"You *can* solve it. You just don't have the proper notes to do so."

I shake my head, mourning the loss of the hours I spent trying to solve a problem I was doomed to fail again and again. I push off the door frame and walk toward his desk. "Well, give me the proper notes then, you fiend."

He takes a piece of paper from his desk drawer and offers it to me, but when I try to take it, he yanks it back out of my grasp. He moves his book aside and sets the paper on the desk in front of him.

"Work it out here," he says. "I want to watch your mind work."

"Do you have a spare chair?"

Fenmire rises and retrieves one from behind his shelves, setting it beside his. We both take our seats, and I launch into the problem, writing the complicated equation across the top of a fresh sheet before studying the new notes he gave me. A symbol I mistook for a wonky subtraction sign is actually a new function altogether. I read the notes about its operation three times but still can't understand what they mean.

"This doesn't make sense," I complain. "Five minus two is three in any language—that's just how numbers work—but this new symbol makes the answer two. That's not possible."

Fenmire is grinning at me.

I sigh. "There are more notes, aren't there?"

He chuckles and sets another sheet on the table in front of me.

This one is a list of numbers from one to ten, but next to each of them is another number, a twin to its neighbor, only with that weird subtraction symbol underneath it.

"What are these?" I ask, touching the numbers with the symbols.

"They are called spares. They are used only when using this symbol, which is called a *decrot.* When using a *decrot,* the number immediately to the right of it becomes a spare. Spares are interchangeable but all affect the equation in different ways."

"How are they interchangeable? Each would change the answer to the problem."

"Precisely."

"That doesn't make sense, Fenmire. That would mean there is no correct answer to the problem at all."

"That's right."

"What is the point of such a problem then?"

"To give a mathematical understanding to things that are either ever changing or infinite. Let me give you an example. How much oxygen is currently in your lungs?"

I focus on my breathing, on the never-ending in and out of air through my nose, and I shrug.

"Alright, now hold your breath."

I do.

"Even now the oxygen stored in your lungs is not a fixed value, is it?"

I shake my head as I release my breath.

"Oxygen consumption in the body is determined by dozens of factors that are constantly changing. How about this one: how big is the universe?"

"It goes on forever."

"Does it? Things are not created out of nothing. You must first have a seed to grow a plant, and that logic can be applied to anything and everything. So if you must first have something to create something else, logic would say the universe doesn't go on forever, for that would mean it is always being created where before there was nothing." He taps the equation on the paper in front of me. "This problem has an answer and yet no answer at the same time. The universe is infinite as we understand it, but the laws of creation say that is not possible, so it both goes on forever and it doesn't at the same time."

I sit back in my chair, blinking and trying to wrap my mind around this logic. "This equation is attempting to find the size of the universe?"

"Not attempting. It found it, because the problem goes on forever but also doesn't at the same time, just like the universe. It has infinite answers, but answers it does have."

"Why wouldn't you just use the infinity symbol?"

"Because that symbol suggests there is no limit, but we both know there is a limit to everything in life."

I nod, accepting that as fact.

"Would you like to try something easier? I confess it was highly unfair of me to select this equation as your first." He gives me a cocky smile. "I wanted to see what you'd do with it."

"Sure," I say, sitting upright again.

A full hour goes by during which Fenmire gives me problems and I work them out, occasionally hitting a new stumbling block that turns out to be another chunk of missing notes that he gives me to add to what I've already learned. Knowing Fenmire's brooding ways, I never expected him to be a patient tutor, but as I make mistake after mistake, sometimes erasing a problem half a dozen times before getting even close to solving it, he never once gets frustrated with me or makes me feel stupid. Quite the contrary. The longer we work, the more relaxed he becomes and the more excited he gets to give me the next problem. My head starts to hurt after a while, but he's enjoying teaching me so much, I don't have the heart to stop the lesson.

I finish the last problem with a final stroke of my pencil, and Fenmire leans forward to inspect my work more closely.

"Perfect," he says with a grin.

Our faces are mere inches apart as we both stare down at the paper, every free centimeter of which is full of my work. We've both slowly scooted closer to each other throughout our lesson, but I only just realized our legs are brushing together and Fenmire's arm is draped over the back of my chair. His hand lightly touches my back whenever I move.

He turns to me, bringing our faces that much closer together. "I must admit, I was skeptical you'd ever be able to understand this stuff. I know you said you studied math and science on your own, but… I doubted you. I'm sorry for that. You've exceeded my expectations by leaps and bounds."

"Well, you're not a bad teacher. You've helped me understand all of this more efficiently than my human teachers taught me my first one two threes."

He silently studies my face for a moment before he says, "I think I know why your village turned on you, and I don't think it had much to do with what names you chose for yourself, how you dressed, or who you married."

I tilt my head. "Why then, do you think?"

"They felt threatened by you. You are beautiful, intelligent, and independent. You have an air of someone who could change the world, and I've no doubt you would've started in your little village. The ones in power couldn't very well let you do that, could they? So they sought to tame you, through either threats or promises, and when neither worked, they chose to get rid of you instead."

Fenmire turns in his chair toward me, and my breath catches in my chest when he reaches out and softly takes my chin between his thumb and finger.

"But there's no getting rid of you, is there, pet?" he asks quietly. "You're too powerful to simply be thrown away."

"Pet?" I whisper.

He lets go of my chin and leans closer. His breath feathers across my cheek as he says, "It was something Wexton said when you first arrived at the castle. While we were discussing what to do with you or if you'd even survive, I made a comment to Caliborne, something along the lines of, 'you rescued them, so they're all yours', to which Wexton replied that you are not a pet for one of us to claim. He was right, of course, but the longer you're here, the stronger grows the urge to claim you as mine anyway."

I must be dreaming.

This is Fenmire, the one who shows restraint, who hides his thoughts behind a language I can't understand because heaven forbid someone hear how he truly feels.

"Would you like that, Evangeline?" he asks.

I only nod because I know if I speak right now, it will come out as a choked croak.

"Are you sure?" he presses. "I'm not soft like Caliborne or a dirty talker like Wexton. I'm the one who'll make you get on your knees and beg me for what you want, and even then, I might not give it to you. Or maybe I'll tell you to run so I can hunt you, pin you down, and take what I want. Can you handle that, pet? Can you handle me?"

"There's only one way to find out," I reply with far more bravado than I feel.

Fenmire chuckles. "Come here."

"I am here."

"No. Here." He pats his lap.

I tentatively slide from my chair, and Fenmire leans back in his to give me room to crawl up onto his lap.

"On your knees," he orders, and my legs shake as I comply, straddling his lap with my knees on the seat of his chair. His arms wrap around me and pull me close so fast I give a little yelp of surprise. We're nose to nose now, and Fenmire brushes the end of his against mine so lightly it tickles. "What do you want, Evangeline?"

"I…" I swallow. "I want you to kiss me."

"Beg me."

I close my eyes as my skin warms in a full flush, much like the way it used to at Wexton's flirty words. This is different, much more intense, because it's Fenmire.

I sit taller in his lap. "Please kiss me."

He hums as he studies me. "You can do better, I think." One of his hands slides around my body and up to my throat. I gasp when his fingers wrap around my neck. He doesn't squeeze, but part of me wishes he would, and that scares me for a moment. "Try again."

"Please," I utter, my voice breaking from the pure adrenaline racing through my veins. My heart is beating so hard and fast I'm breathless. "Please, kiss me. Please."

He grins. "That's better." He pulls me nearer by the neck until our lips are so close I can feel the heat of his on mine. "You have no idea how long I've wanted to do this."

"Then do it already," I challenge.

He chuckles wickedly then kisses me.

Never in a thousand years would I have guessed Fenmire would kiss me like this. Part of me never expected he'd kiss me at all, but the way his lips roam over mine, demanding and taking while I'm held captive by the throat in his powerful grip… this is beyond anything I've imagined. When his tongue thrusts into my mouth, it's every bit as hard and unyielding, forcing my tongue to kiss him back just how he wants it to and never giving me the chance to take control. It even ends when he decides it's over, and he pulls me away from his lips with the same hand wrapped around my neck.

I blink up at him, shocked by the audacity and barely-contained passion I got merely a taste of in that kiss.

"Like I said," he murmurs, and I'm pleased to note he's as breathless as I am, "I'm no soft dirty talker. I'm the hard, demanding one. I'll bend you until you think you might break, but I won't let you. I'll take until you think you have nothing left to give me then ask you to give me more. If you want me, pet, that's what you'll get because I don't do things halfway. It's all of me or none of me."

"I want all of you," I say with confidence.

I'm shell-shocked when he lets go of my neck and deflates, his shoulders slumping as his smile fades.

"Then you have me," he says, but he sounds sad. "Or at least, what's left of me."

I put an arm around his neck, burying my hand in his hair as I lean close and kiss him once, softly, on the lips.

"I know the one that came before me broke something inside you," I whisper. "I won't promise to fix it, I don't think anyone has that power, but I will promise to handle what's left of you with the care it deserves." I palm his cheek and stare into those dark eyes, hoping they can see the sincerity in mine. "I won't break any more of you, Fenmire. I already care about you too much for that."

He takes my hand from his face and leans his forehead against mine. "Go ahead and break me, pet. Maybe I'll heal right this time."

Chapter 42

My interactions with Fenmire leave me in a state of shock for the rest of the day. I go to bed that night in Caliborne's arms, and when we wake up the next morning, I sit quietly on the side of his bed, remembering the feel of Fenmire's fingers around my throat and the way my heart raced when he made me beg him to kiss me.

Caliborne brushes my cheek with his thumb. *What are you thinking that's bringing that color to your face?*

I smile shyly. "Are you sure you want to know?"

Is it something to do with Wexton?

"No, it's Fenmire," I say, still in awe that something has finally happened between us to even prompt this conversation.

Caliborne blinks at me. *Oh?*

"Yesterday, in the library, we kissed."

We told you he'd come around eventually.

"I guess a part of me never believed it."

He strokes my cheek again. *That must've been some kiss to make you blush like this. That usually doesn't happen unless I'm inside you.*

"Caliborne!" I chastise with a giggle.

He laughs silently then kneels in front of me to kiss me softly on the lips. *Please remember that this is all by your choice. Nothing happens without your consent.*

"I know. I wanted Fenmire to kiss me. I asked him to." I can't quite work up the courage to say I begged for it, but something in the way Caliborne's eyes crinkle at the sides makes me think he already suspects the truth. I change the subject to keep him from asking any questions. "When do you have patrol again?"

Not until tomorrow morning.

"If I asked you to do something crazy with me today, would you?"

Well now, that depends. Just how crazy are we talking?

"I'd like to leave The Deadwood this morning. As soon as possible, in fact."

And go where?

"To my parents' farm. It's Sunday, so they'll be at church this morning, and there's a few items I left behind I'd like to have back."

You say no one will be there?

"Even the hands my father hires don't show up until after church on Sundays."

But the church burned down.

"That won't matter. They'll still hold service, just somewhere else in the village for the time being."

Where is the farm?

"At the end of the south road, about a mile out of town."

Caliborne nods thoughtfully. *Since it's so far away from the village, I see no harm in going. As long as we're careful.*

I smile and take his hands in mine. "We could make it an adventure, just for you and me. Other than in bed at night, I feel like we haven't had time alone together in a while."

You're right. We should make a point to do something together regularly. I don't mind sharing you, but I want my time with you too.

"And you should have it. We'll have to work out a system so that everyone gets time alone with me. I don't want any of my mates to feel left out."

Your happiness is my primary concern. As long as you're happy, I'm happy. I'm sure the others would agree.

I slide my arms around his neck. "I love you."

He kisses me and rubs my arms. *We should go if we want to get there and leave again before your family returns.*

"We'll save this for later then," I whisper against his lips.

He winks at me.

I hop out of bed and get dressed. It's an Evan day, so I choose a shirt, pants, and Will's old clunky boots. It's warm outside now that summer has come to The Deadwood, so I roll up the sleeves of my shirt and the legs of my pants. I tuck my hair up into my hat, slip on my gold bracelet, and wrap the belt with Fenmire's knife around my waist. When I look at myself in the mirror above Caliborne's vanity, I nod in approval.

Caliborne steps up behind me in the mirror and puts a hand on my shoulder. *Handsome, as always.*

I can't help the beaming smile that spreads across my face.

*****

We manage to slip out of the castle without running into any of the others. We fly over The Deadwood toward the arch, and before we land in the lane, we test out to see if Caliborne can simply keep flying out of the trees. When he reaches the edge of The Deadwood, he hits an invisible barrier that keeps him inside the perimeter. Even I can't stick my hand through it, and it's like pushing against a brick wall when I try. It seems the only way for anyone to get in and out of The Deadwood is through the arch.

We land and file through the arch out into the long grass between the woods and the road, then we take to the air again, following the south road in the opposite direction as the last time we were here. It's daylight now, so we keep even lower to the ground and further away from the road as we travel. Within minutes, the farm comes into view, and Caliborne circles around it, giving the buildings a wide berth in case we're not alone. He lands in the field by the woods next to the river where I used to fish, and we walk the tree line together toward the back of the barn.

"My room is that one," I tell him, pointing to the window at the top left corner of the house. "I hope my mother hasn't thrown all my things away already."

Would she really do that?

I shrug. "They don't think I'm coming back, so they're bound to eventually. My mother thinks the pastor and his family walk on water, so she'll do whatever Elias feels is right."

He's the one they tried to make you marry, right?

"Yes. Jacob says he's the head of the church now. I guess his father let him take his place without marrying someone first after all."

Caliborne shakes his head. *The hatefulness of human men will ruin your god's following before he ever gains the power to put it right. False prophets are the biggest threat to any religion, especially one as new as yours.*

"How do you tell the difference between a false prophet and a genuine one?"

False prophets very rarely teach about things that don't favor their own. A genuine one preaches the truth, whether it benefits him or not. 'False be the words of a holy man who sits atop a throne while his people beg for their supper'. That's from one of Seerraf's teachings.

"Your god seems very wise."

He is, but he also admits that he can make mistakes too. No one is perfect, not even a god. Your village would do well to remember that.

We both fall silent as we approach the back of the barn. I can hear the horses shuffling around in their stalls, but no human sounds stand out to me, and when I peek in the window, there's no one in the aisle. All is still and quiet, so we round the back corner of the building. Our wagon is gone, which is all the evidence I need that my parents are off to church and we're alone.

"You're not going to fit in the doors," I say as we start across the yard toward the house. "Do you want to wait for me on the—"

The screen door flies open and slams against the side of the house.

Caliborne and I freeze a few feet from the front steps as my father steps out onto the porch. His eyes are as wide as saucers as he slowly comes to the top of the steps. He stops and puts an arm around the wooden beam of the porch as if he needs its support to keep from toppling down the stairs.

"Evan?" he utters.

Caliborne takes my arm and pulls me closer to him. He ruffles his wings, preparing to take flight.

"Wait!" I cry with a hand to Caliborne's chest.

Who is it?

"My father," I say tearfully. Now that I've seen him, I want nothing more than to wrap my arms around him, if only to give him the proper goodbye I was denied before.

Ask if he's alone.

"Is Mother here too?"

He shakes his head. "Your mother would never miss a service. Especially not now. Elias has his claws in her deep. She worships him, as does half the village."

"Why aren't you with her?"

My father hangs his head. "After that night… when they took you from us…" He comes halfway down the steps, and Caliborne tenses beside me. "I couldn't pretend to believe anymore. I couldn't understand how sending you to that awful place was the right thing to do, for God… My God would never ask for such a thing." He walks down the last of the steps to the ground and stops.

Caliborne takes one large step back, drawing me back with him.

"I'm so sorry, Evan," my father continues. "We failed you. *I* failed you." He sniffles. "I should've stood in front of you and told them they'd have to kill me first if they wanted to take you away. I should've bundled you up in the wagon and snuck you out of the village as soon as I heard their plans. I should've *killed* Elias for ever suggesting you were some damned beast of the devil. My own daughter…"

My father—the man who raised me to know nothing but kindness and love, the one who taught me to have a gentle hand with all living creatures, who was one of the few to accept me no matter what the others whispered behind my back—starts to sob.

"I'm so sorry," he says brokenly.

"Let me go, Caliborne," I order, and he immediately releases me. I dart across the yard into my father's arms.

He hugs me so tight his arms shake, and he continues to cry big broken sobs that make me start crying right along with him.

"It's alright, Papa," I tell him tearfully, rubbing his back. "Everything is alright."

"It's not," he says angrily. "It's not alright. None of this is alright. Not what they did to you or to Jacob or to Will, none of it. When I heard you stole Will away, I was so relieved. Not only were you alive, but you rescued him too. I was proud of you for defying them. I only wish your mother could see the truth like I do now."

"Maybe she will someday."

My father pulls away and takes my face in his hands. "I thought I'd lost you forever."

"It was a close call at first. Caliborne saved me." I wave my hand toward the Gryxen behind me, who has moved much closer now, likely so he can intervene if he needs to.

For the first time, my father regards my demon lover, and he swallows. His eyes flick to me in uncertainty.

"Don't worry, he doesn't bite," I tease with a smile at Caliborne, who rolls his eyes. "Caliborne, this is my father."

Caliborne bows his head in respect.

"You saved them?" my father asks.

Caliborne nods.

"I almost froze to death in The Deadwood," I explain. "But Caliborne found me and took me to their castle."

"Are you… a demon?"

"A Gryxen," I correct him. "They aren't from our world."

My father nods, still staring at Caliborne. "Elias said you and two demons made off with Will and lit the church on fire as you escaped."

"What a lying snake! We didn't burn the church. He did! He tried to burn us alive inside it. What was it he said, Caliborne? Something about killing us being a trade God himself would understand?"

Papa shakes his head. "Elias is lost. He'll lead us all to hell in time."

"Not you," I say with a squeeze of my hand on his. "Do you want to get away from all of this, Papa? You could join me, Will, and Jacob in The Deadwood at the next full moon. Just say the word and I'll be waiting for you on the other side of the arch."

He palms my cheek. "I can't. If I left, there would be no one to run this farm. Your mother would likely give it to Elias. This land is my life. I belong here."

I nod sadly. I didn't expect any other answer, but I had to offer. "I understand."

He kisses me on the forehead. "I'm so happy to see you again, but I know you didn't come here to see me, so what brought you back?"

"I wanted to get a few of my things. Is my room still…?"

He nods. "Your mother wanted to have a sale and donate the funds to the church, but I wouldn't let her. I put a lock on your room to keep her out." He fishes a key from his pocket and hands it to me.

I take it and kiss him on the cheek. "Thank you."

"Take anything that's important to you. I can only keep your mother at bay for so long."

"I'll be quick," I tell them both before I dart into the house and up the stairs.

I remove the massive lock Papa has on my door with a shake of my head. My mother was likely furious at him for this, but I'm so grateful that he did it. My room is exactly how I left it right down to the messy bed I was dragged from over two months ago. It feels very odd to be back in this space after everything that has happened. This doesn't feel like home anymore, and I'm suddenly eager to get the things I came for and get back to my real one.

I take an old sack from my closet and move around the room, plucking things from shelves and drawers and haphazardly stuffing them in. I grab a few of my favorite clothes—especially the ones I bought for church that I only wore the once—Will's hat and letters, a few knick-knacks from my shelves, and, last but not least, the thing that brought me here above all else: my book on Newton's teachings. I smile as I tuck it nicely into the side of my bag so as not to crinkle the pages. I can't wait to show Fenmire. I take a couple of my other books as well, just my favorites, and close the flap on my bag.

I stand in the doorway and take one last look around. If I had the time to sit and sort through the rest of the stuff in this room, I wouldn't salvage a single thing in here beyond what I've stuffed in this sack. This room isn't me anymore. I'm not sure it ever was. I happily close the door and lock it back up.

I walk slowly down the hall and back down the stairs, my eyes drifting around this house filled with so many memories, very few of them worth remembering. I've had more happy moments over the past two months in a castle of stone filled with demons than I have in this house over the last twenty years. When I head back out to the porch, I'm more than ready to say goodbye forever.

Saying goodbye to the man who turns and smiles at me as I walk down the front steps, however, is a different story.

"Did you get everything?" Papa asks.

I give him back his key. "I did. You can go ahead and let Mother do as she likes with the rest. It should buy some peace between you for a while if nothing else."

He pockets the key and nods his head toward Caliborne. "Does he ever talk?"

"No, not a word."

"He seems rather intense. I swear he tracked your every step through the house just now."

I bite my lip to hide my smirk. "Yes, I'm sure he did."

"You're not… They aren't keeping you… prisoner or anything, right?"

"No, Papa. It's not like that. I'm safe and happy, I promise."

"And Will is with you now, right?"

I smile. "Will and Jacob are both at the castle now. Together," I say with a pointed look that makes Papa nod in understanding.

"Good. Those two boys never hurt anyone. They didn't deserve what Elias did to them. He wanted to send Will away, you know."

"I do. Jacob told me."

Papa shakes his head, but then he smiles at me and takes me by the shoulders. "You'll come again, won't you? It's just me here every Sunday. You could come back. I've missed you so much."

I want to. Gods, do I ever. I look over at Caliborne.

He shrugs, leaving the choice up to me.

"I can try, Papa, but if I don't make it, don't worry over me, alright?"

He hugs me tightly. "I'll always worry, but I get your meaning. I love you, Evan."

"I love you too, so, so much. I didn't get to say goodbye before, so I'll do it now, even if it's only for a week. Take care of yourself, please."

"I will. See you next week, hopefully."

Chapter 43

Caliborne and I are even more cautious on our way back to the arch since it's nearly time for service to be over and we don't want to run into anyone on the road, least of all my mother, who would no doubt make my father's life a living hell if she knew he'd seen me. We land in front of the arch and pass through it without incident.

Once we're in the air again, I ask Caliborne, "How did it feel to meet my father?"

Quite pleasant. He seems like a kind and gentle man. I see now where you get that.

"What did he say to you while I was in the house?"

He asked me if I was truly in the service of the devil. Since Seerraf is nothing like the entity your people believe him to be, I wasn't sure how to respond. In the end, I shook my head because, no, I am not some servant sent to steal humans' souls or to torment them like your people claim. That was what he was truly asking, after all.

"It was," I concur. "My father is a smart man. He likely already suspected the truth. He's said many times in my life that the way the village treated me went against the true word of God. I think that's why he never once tried to change me."

I'm sorry your mother is not so open-minded.

"Me too."

I know it's not the same as a parent's love and approval, but you are *loved, Evan. I love you deeply, as does Wexton and even Fenmire, in his way. We would never ask you to change for us.*

I kiss him lovingly on the cheek. "You're right, it's not the same, but I appreciate it, nonetheless."

We land in front of the castle and head inside, and we're no more than a few steps over the threshold when Wexton finds us.

"There you are," he says. "I've looked all over for you two." He spies the bag on my shoulder and loses his smile. "What's going on?"

"Nothing that needs you to look so concerned, Wexton," I say. "Caliborne helped me retrieve some of my things this morning, that's all."

"You went out of The Deadwood?" Wexton pouts. "Why didn't you ask me to come too?"

"I asked Caliborne to take me because I wanted to spend some time alone with him. It's important to me that each of my mates gets that equally from time to time. I hope you understand."

"Of course. That's a reasonable request. I just thought you'd want us both to go with you to better protect you."

"Oh, that wasn't a problem. I chose today because the farm was supposed to be empty as my family would be at church."

"*Supposed* to be empty?"

I smile sheepishly. "My father was there."

Wexton looks at Caliborne. "You met their father?"

Caliborne nods.

"Would you like to meet him too?" I ask. "I told him I would try to come back next week. You and I could go together then."

"Do you want me to meet him?"

"I'd love that. I'd like you all to meet him eventually. You're as important to me as he is. It's only fitting the people I love get to know each other."

That makes Wexton smile. "In that case, I would be honored." His smile shifts into something more wicked as his eyes slide up and down my frame. "Since you had your excursion with Caliborne this morning, does that mean you're free for the rest of the day? I don't have patrol until tonight."

I glance up at Caliborne.

He laughs, leans down, and kisses me on the forehead. *Go with him, my stoferra. I will see you tonight.*

Caliborne continues down the hall to his room.

I give Wexton a pointed look. "I mean it, Wexton, you have to let me have time alone with the others, uninterrupted."

Wexton puts his hand up in surrender. "I don't mind that, truly, but Caliborne gets you in his bed most nights, darling." He slides a step closer. "That just leaves the daylight hours for me to have you in mine."

"You are an absolute heathen," I say, struggling not to laugh.

"Oh, I know. And you like it."

I clear my throat, finally bringing myself under control. "I do. But if you want my company this afternoon, you can have it anywhere *but* your bed." He opens his mouth to ask the obvious question, but I cut him off. "No, that doesn't mean you can have your way with me somewhere else around the castle. You'll have to come up with some other activity to enjoy with me today. Unless my body is the only thing you love about me."

He immediately looks so wounded I almost regret the comment. "That's not true, Evan. You don't really believe that, do you?"

"I don't, but I would love if you'd put aside your physical desires for a day and show me some other ways you'd like to spend time with me."

He nods. "I can do that. How about I teach you the card game Fenmire and I are always playing? You're smart enough you can probably best him easily. I rarely win, and when I do, I think half the time it's because he lets me."

I laugh. "I can try. Why don't I meet you in the study? I'd like to go unpack my things first."

"What sorts of things did you get?"

"Would you like to see?"

"Yes."

Do we eventually end up in the study playing cards? Yes.

Do I decide I physically want my mate as much as he always wants me and let him have his way with me first? Also yes.

Do I feel the slightest bit bad about that?

Not at all.

*****

It's not until the next day that I get the chance to return to the library. When I left it last time, Fenmire sent me off with the other book he's been translating for me, the one about The Gates and their origins. I've finished reading the chapters he's translated so far, which he tells me is about half of the entire book. He's right, there is frighteningly little even the Gryxen know about them. They have a basic understanding of how The Gates work but who created them, how long ago, and why are all mysteries yet to be solved. I hope I can help solve them.

I knock on the library door, but there's no answer, and when I let myself in, I'm surprised to find it empty. Fenmire usually spends every waking minute he's not on patrol up here.

"Fenmire?"

There's no reply, but I walk in anyway, though it feels almost eerie to be up here alone, akin to walking into Fenmire's bedroom uninvited. I go to his desk, intending to have a seat and wait for him, but when I get closer, I freeze at the sight of a drawing left on the tabletop. It's half-finished, but there's no question who the person outlined in dark charcoal is.

It's a drawing of me. My hair is braided and draped over my shoulder, an Evangeline day, but my face is downcast as I stare at something just out of the frame. Even though the background is blank, either by choice or because he simply hasn't gotten around to it yet, I can tell by the look on my face and the outfit I'm wearing that this is me the day we buried CeCe. Though the finer details have yet to be filled in, the drawing is already exquisite, and I pick it up to admire it better.

The bang of the library door closing makes me jump so hard I drop the paper on the floor. Fenmire is standing there with his hand still on the knob.

"I see I'll have to start locking my desk when I leave the room from now on," he says moodily.

"I'm sorry," I rush to say. I pick the drawing up and put it back where I found it. "I meant to wait here for you, and it was just sitting there, and… well, it's gorgeous. I couldn't help but look."

Fenmire crosses the room and sits heavily in his chair at the desk. He plops a chunk of charcoal on a blank, crumpled piece of parchment off to the side that's already smeared almost black.

"It's alright, Eve," he says, and he sounds tired and a little sad. "I didn't mean to bark at you."

"Is everything alright?"

He looks sideways at me but doesn't answer. Instead, he nods to the books I'm holding. "What have you got there?"

I take both books from under my arm and set the book about The Gates on the desk beside his drawing. "The one I borrowed." I set my book on Newton on top of the other with a smile. "And something extra."

He picks my book up and opens it in the palm of his hand, and his eyes slowly widen with each flip of a page. "Did you go back to the village for this?"

"For a few other things too but mostly for this, yes. You said you wanted to read it."

"Did someone go with you?" he asks with deep concern.

"Caliborne."

He relaxes a bit and turns back to the book, leafing through a few more pages. "These are impressive advances for your kind. I didn't realize just how far humans have come in their understanding of mathematics."

"These are all very recent discoveries."

He flips to the front of the book to the page with the year of publication. "Oh, I see. Within the last century." He snaps the book shut. "May I borrow this?"

"Be my guest."

He sets the book in his lap and studies me. "Thank you for thinking of me, though I wish you hadn't wandered into danger just to satisfy my curiosity."

"I didn't really. I chose the safest opportunity to go, and I didn't do so alone."

"That's good, at least."

I take a step closer to him. "You're drawing me," I say, but it's more of a question than a statement.

The tiniest hint of a grin twitches at the corner of his mouth. "You caught me."

"Why me?"

He runs a finger thoughtfully across his lips before answering. "I'm an artist. Capturing beauty on paper is my specialty. With someone as beautiful as you walking these halls day after day, it would be a crime not to capture you too."

I blink in surprise. "Was that a compliment, Fenmire?"

"I've been known to bestow those from time to time."

"Will you show me the final drawing when you're done?"

"If you wish."

"Please." I nod down at the other book. "In the meantime, do you have more for me to read? More math for me to study?"

"I don't. I've been… preoccupied." He sighs, leans back in his chair, and turns it toward his desk, setting my book on top of his drawing with a scowl on his face.

"What's wrong?"

He says nothing.

"Don't you trust me?"

"Trust is not the issue." He puts his hands together on top of the book and stares down at them, avoiding my eyes. "Today is the anniversary of a day I wish I could forget forever. It always sours my mood whenever it rolls around each year."

I don't know which anniversary he's talking about since there are several nasty moments in his past I can think of off the top of my head, but I don't ask for clarification. "Is there anything I can do to help?" I ask instead.

He turns his head toward me, though he still avoids my eyes. "I'm afraid not, pet," he says quietly. "In fact, it's better if you left me alone right now. Not that I don't enjoy your company, but…"

"I understand. I hope your day improves."

He taps a finger on my book. "It already has."

I give him my warmest smile then leave him to his thoughts.

*****

I steer clear of the library for a few days to give Fenmire space. The others don't see much of him either as he skips most of his meals and only comes out of the library to sleep or go on patrol.

"Don't worry," Wexton tells me over breakfast on the third day. "This happens every year. He'll snap out of it soon."

"He seems awfully moody no matter the day," Will comments. He and Jacob have taken to eating their meals in the Gryxen dining room with me rather than with the other humans.

"We've all been through a lot," Wexton replies. "And we all handle it in different ways. Drixus isolates, Fenmire broods, and Caliborne makes the best of it."

"What about you?" Jacob asks.

"Me?" Wexton leans back on his stool so far it's a miracle he doesn't topple backward. "I'm the funny one."

Caliborne reaches over and gives him a shove, and Wexton flails in midair, grabbing the edge of the table just in time to keep from crashing to the floor.

The rest of us howl with laughter.

"What did I miss?"

Everyone goes silent as we all look over at Fenmire, who's standing in the doorway with his usual plate in one hand and book in the other.

I recover first and smile at him. "Just Wexton being the butt of the joke."

"Ah, so business as usual then."

The rest of the room chuckles, breaking the tension.

Fenmire strolls to the table and waves his plate toward the empty spot next to me. "May I?"

"Sure."

He plops his plate and book down and slides onto the stool next to mine, and he's so close his elbow brushes my arm as he starts cutting his meat. He takes several bites of his food before glancing around the room, which has fallen silent again.

Rather than let it grow even more awkward, I turn to Will on my other side. "What plans do you and Jacob have for today?"

Jacob perks up a seat away. "I was just telling Will this morning how much I'd like to go swimming. Do you know of a place we can do that here?"

"You mean besides the bathing pool?"

"I mean outside." He leans over to me across Will's empty plate. "Somewhere we can take a dip and let the sun kiss our more private places, if you catch my drift."

My mouth falls open in feigned horror. "Jacob, you scoundrel," I say with a snort.

He laughs and pops the last bite of his breakfast in his mouth.

"There's a pond," Wexton says. "It's the only body of water in The Deadwood that's big enough for decent swimming. It's quite a trek from here though."

"I can take you," Fenmire offers.

We all turn to him in shock.

He stops mid-chew and looks around at each of us. "What? Caliborne has patrol this afternoon and flying with Wexton is less than ideal."

Will grimaces and rubs his ribs, no doubt remembering how it feels to fly thrown over a Gryxen's shoulder. "You sure you don't mind?"

Fenmire shrugs. "I don't have any other plans for my day." He slides his book toward me. "I finished translating the rest of the book about The Gates for you."

"Thank you," I say as I pick it up. "I'll finish the reading this afternoon then."

"Don't you want to come swimming with us?" Will asks.

"I didn't realize I was invited."

"Oh, yes," Jacob says with excitement. "Do come with us, Evangeline… er… It is Evangeline today, isn't it?"

"It is indeed," I reply, shaking my bronze bracelet around my wrist.

"I've always wanted to join you and Will in your mischief growing up but always had to keep my distance, for obvious reasons." He gives Will a loving smile before turning back to me. "Will you help me make up for lost time?"

"Aww, that's sweet, Jacob. Of course I will."

"What about you, Wexton?" Will asks. "Do you want to come too?"

"I wish I could, but I'm spending the afternoon in the forge today. I broke a buckle off my armor several days ago and have put off fixing it for too long now."

"There's a forge here?"

"Yes, but the Gryxen keep it hidden from us humans," I grumble. "It's a Gryxen-only space, apparently."

Will chews the inside of his lip as his eyes glaze over in deep thought. When I raise a suspicious brow, he snaps himself out of it with a small shake of his head. "So it's settled then?" he asks a little too nonchalantly. "The four of us are making a day of it?"

"We should pack a lunch," I say. "I can ask Levi to throw something together. And we'll need to grab some sheets from the pool room downstairs."

"On it," Jacob announces, and he jumps from his chair, gathering both his and Will's dirty dishes before giving Will a quick peck on the lips. "I'll meet you in the foyer."

Chapter 44

Before the others can convene in the foyer, I quickly throw on a light, flowy dress and braid my hair back out of my face, then I dart up to the third floor to Drixus' door. I knock and call his name, but of course, there's no answer. I know he's there, though, since Caliborne just left to relieve him from patrol. I don't sit on the floor since I can't stay very long this time, but I put my hand on the door when I hear his shuffling footsteps on the other side.

"I don't know if the others told you, but not only has Will joined us in the castle but his partner Jacob has as well. The night of The Offering was utter chaos. We discovered Caliborne and Wexton can leave The Deadwood now that they're my mates, which is good because we had to go rescue Will. The village threw Jacob through the arch but were keeping Will hostage. We got him out safely, though, and now he and Jacob can live here together, and they never have to hide their love for each other ever again.

"We're going swimming at the pond today. If you want, you could join us. Though, be prepared to be scandalized. I think the boys plan to swim nude. Maybe I'll join them. It's something I've always wanted to do, but women aren't allowed to do that in my village. If I'd ever tried, my mother likely would've locked me in my room for life out of shame.

"Oh, I saw my father! Caliborne took me home so I could get a few of my things, and Papa was there. It was so nice to see him again. Everyone else I care about is here in The Deadwood with me. I worry about him and miss him terribly, but I know he'd never be happy here.

"It still makes my head spin when I think about my life before The Deadwood compared to now. It's as if I was dreaming for the first twenty years of my life and finally woke up the day I was thrown through the arch. Going back there, even for a few minutes, feels like walking back into that dream, only now I know I'm dreaming. It makes my skin crawl. I hope that's not what it feels like for you and the others to be stuck on this side of The Gate."

I wait to see if he might comment on this, but I hear nothing but the usual silence. "The others are probably waiting for me," I say regretfully. I wish so badly to open this door and meet the Gryxen on the other side, but it's not my choice to make. I tap my finger against the wood. "I'll be back next week. Until then."

I head back downstairs and find Will and Jacob already gathered in the foyer. Jacob has a stack of neatly folded sheets in his arms and Will has a sack and a large basket sitting on the floor by his feet.

"There you are," Will says. "Levi sent these." He indicates the sack and the basket. "There's food and water as well as"—he leans toward me with a wink—"a couple bottles of wine Levi dug out of the pantry just for us."

"Ooo, yum." I pick up the basket. "Are we ready then?"

Fenmire comes down the stairs with another book tucked under his arm and a slim leather case in his hand. I consider teasing him on the fact that he can never go anywhere without a book, but I honestly considered bringing the one about The Gates with me today to possibly read later myself, so I stay quiet.

"I can only take you one at a time," Fenmire says as we step out into the bright sunlight. He touches my arm. "I'll take you last, if you don't mind."

I don't, so I merely give him a smile and a nod.

He takes Jacob first, who cries out in both fright and excitement when Fenmire takes off with him in his arms. Fenmire is gone only a few minutes before he comes back for Will, who is much more at ease climbing into Fenmire's arms than his lover was.

"At least I'm not thrown over your shoulder like a sack of potatoes," Will says as he secures his bag, tucking it tightly between him and Fenmire's chest. They're soon soaring over The Deadwood toward the pond, leaving me alone at the top of the steps.

I'm staring out across the endless spans of The Deadwood when a screech from above startles me. I look up as Mara slips out of the hole in the castle wall. I try to catch a better glimpse of her rider, but Drixus is very good at keeping himself out of sight. Mara tucks her wings in tight and shoves off the castle wall, diving toward the ground at an alarming speed before spreading her wings and curving up through the air. They soon fly out of sight, not toward the pond, I note with disappointment, but in the opposite direction.

I glance at the hole in the wall where they came from and do a quick mental walkthrough of the castle. If my calculations are correct, that hole is awfully close to Drixus' bedroom. He doesn't share a room with that creature, does he?

Fenmire lands beside me with a slam, startling me out of my musings. He grabs my arm to keep me from falling down the steps as I jump backward.

"Easy there, pet," he says as he steadies me. "Is everything alright?"

"Sure, sure, I just didn't see you coming is all."

"What were you…?" He looks up toward the spot I was staring at, and his lips thin. He picks me up, and I hold on tightly to both him and my basket as he launches into the air. He's silent as we fly, and I'm afraid I may have spoiled his mood again until he says, "Fair warning: your friends were already stripping when I left them mere moments ago."

"The horror," I say with a snort. "Thank you for bringing us out here. Will you be staying with us or venturing off on your own?"

"I thought I'd hang around, if you're alright with that."

"Why wouldn't I be?"

He clears his throat. "I'm not your mate yet, Evangeline. I don't want to overstep my bounds or make you uncomfortable."

The 'yet' surprises me, though I'm not entirely sure why. He already said he's ready to try for just such a thing with me, and yet part of me still can't believe it's true. We've kissed, but even that feels like a dream.

"I want you to stay," I say softly as we descend toward the pond.

Fenmire lands on the bank beside the water and carefully sets me on my feet. "Then I'll stay." He's still holding my hand, and his thoughts are racing in his language. I wish I could understand them, and as if in answer to my silent request, one thought slips through.

I need you to help me feel again.

I blink up at him and refuse to give back his hand when he tries to tug it out of mine.

"Evangeline!"

I jump and look out over the water at the two bobbing bodies nearby.

Fenmire uses this opportunity to take back his hand.

"Come on!" Will urges with a wave.

I set the basket by the tree line where it's in no danger from splashing water and slip off my boots and socks. My dress is all one piece—little more than a nightgown really—and I easily slip it off over my head. The sun feels like heaven on my bare skin, and a light breeze keeps the heat from becoming unbearable. The two boys neither stare nor say a word about my nudity as I wade into the pond.

"You too, Fenmire!" Will calls. "No dry bodies allowed."

"No clothes either," Jacob adds.

"Fenmire doesn't know how to have fun, boys," I say with a sideways peek at the Gryxen in question.

"You think I won't do it?" Fenmire asks.

I shrug my shoulders. "Care to prove me wrong?"

"Yes, I do." He marches over to the basket and sets his book and case on top, and the three humans cheer as he starts stripping. When he rips his pants down, however, Will and Jacob stare in shocked awe at their first glimpse of Gryxen anatomy.

Me? I stare for a whole different reason.

Both of Fenmire's cocks are the biggest I've seen yet. It never occurred to me Gryxen genitalia would have variety, but of course that makes sense considering even humans come in all shapes and sizes.

The first thing I think is how good it would feel to have them inside me.

I'm immediately mortified by my own runaway thoughts, and I duck my head under the water to cool my heating cheeks. When I come back up, Fenmire has waded into water up to his chest. He swims lazily toward me.

"Why the sudden shyness, pet?" he asks quietly enough only I can hear him as the other two laugh and splash together several yards away. "Am I not quite what you were expecting?"

I close my eyes and pray for sanity as my face gets even hotter. "I honestly didn't know what to expect at all. I never thought about it."

Fenmire hums and swims closer. "You've *never* thought about me? Not once?"

The truth is I've dreamt up a few different fantasies about what our time together might be like. "Maybe once," I concede.

"Maybe twice?" he asks, swimming closer still.

"Maybe."

"I'd love for you to tell me the details of such thoughts."

"I bet you would."

He starts swimming in circles around me. "Don't want to tell me? I promise you can't dream up anything wild enough to make me say no."

I believe him, which is why I'm just not ready to tell him yet. We've had exactly one intimate moment together, so it feels a little too soon to start telling him my darkest, most carnal desires, the ones so wicked I can't even bring myself to tell Wexton about them.

"It's alright, Evangeline," Fenmire says, stopping his circling to tread water in the deepest portion of the pond. "We haven't gotten there yet, and that's fine." He holds a hand out to me. "Come here."

I peek over at Will and Jacob to find them entangled near the bank, kissing passionately. I swim to Fenmire and take his hand. He pulls me to him and holds me up in the water so I don't have to kick my legs anymore. His hands grip my backside and tug me closer, and with us both bobbing in the deep water, we're nose to nose.

I smile at him. "Hello."

"Hello, pet." His fingers flex on my backside as he grips it tighter in both hands. "Is this alright?"

"Yes, I think so."

He leans his face toward mine until the tips of our noses brush together. "And this?"

"Yes," I say breathlessly.

"Would you like me to kiss you, Evangeline?"

"Do I have to beg this time?"

"No. This one is a gift."

"Then yes, please."

He captures my lips with his, and he doesn't mold my mouth with the force of his kiss this time. This time, he's soft and gentle. I splay my hands across his chest and tilt my head to better kiss him back around his fangs, and he hums softly before pulling away.

"I owe you an apology," he says, taking me completely by surprise.

"What for?"

"I've been nothing but short and distant with you since you arrived here. I was callous and uncaring even after I knew how important you are. I just want you to know that's not who I really am. Words are hollow and meaningless, so I plan to show you myself in time, but please, accept my apology in the meantime. Or don't until I've proven myself, I don't mind, but I offer it all the same."

"I don't begrudge you for being cautious with your heart, Fenmire. I understand completely why you held me at a distance and reacted as you did when you learned I was the one to break the spell, even more so after we discovered the key to doing so was through mating bonds. I can't imagine how that must've felt after everything you've been through." I set my cheek against his and add in a whisper, "And I know that's not who you really are. I look forward to getting to know the real you."

"I meant what I said before." His voice deepens, and it makes me shiver. "I'm not soft with a wicked mouth. I'm hard and demanding." He lets go of my backside to put a hand on the back of my head instead, yanking me so close our lips brush as he continues. "I like to chase, and take, and own. I like pleasurable pain and torturous rapture. I like begging, sure, but I also like to hear my lovers cry my name as a plea for mercy while they're tied to my bed."

I gasp and clench my thighs together.

"Oh," he says with a grin. "You like that thought, don't you, pet?"

"I… I don't know."

"That's alright. We'll find out exactly what you like. Together. Would you like that?"

"Yes," I utter.

He kisses me again, and that hard, demanding mouth is back, forcing my lips to part to let in his tongue. I moan, and he grips my hair in his fingers so tightly my scalp burns.

I wish he'd do it harder.

Again, he breaks the kiss himself, pulling my face away so I can't even sneak an extra taste of him on my own terms. His other hand lets go of my backside and slides to my lower back. He pulls my body against his, and the thick, hard length of his cocks press against my lower belly.

"Do you feel what you do to me?" he asks.

I only nod, my voice lost in the buzz of pure desire racing throughout my entire body.

"Do you want to know how many times I've thought about *you* these past two months?"

Again, I only nod.

"Dozens. So many I lost count. I've thought about all the ways I could please you, tease you, and fuck you senseless as I stroked my cocks under the covers, Evangeline."

"Jesus Christ," I murmur breathlessly. "You're going to make me burst into flames if you keep talking."

"Well now, we don't want that, do we? I wanna see you burn in my bed where you belong."

Who is this Gryxen?

This can't be the Fenmire who glared daggers at me for nearly the entire first month I lived here.

There's no way this is the same person who threw a fit when he found out I was planning to mate with Caliborne.

The one who turned down the chance to join us in the dining room when he found me half naked and sprawled across the table with Wexton's head between my thighs.

I muster my bravery, tilt up my chin, and flash him a mischievous smile. "It's nice to meet you at last, Fenmire."

"Make no mistake, pet, there's still much to learn about me. You've only scratched the surface."

I press my nails into the thick leather skin of his chest. "I can't wait to scratch deeper."

Fenmire laughs, and it's the first genuine, deep-belly laugh I've ever heard from him. It's a wonderful sound, and it helps me understand the thought he let me overhear earlier.

'I need you to help me feel again.'

Perhaps it's a fool's errand to think I can soothe this warrior's wounded heart, but I have to try. That he's even willing to *let* me try is progress.

"Hey, you two!" Jacob yells, breaking me and Fenmire apart as we look over at the bank. "Will is already breaking into the wine, so you better come have some before he drinks it all."

"You make me sound like a drunk," Will complains as he works the cork out of the first bottle.

"Do you like wine?" I ask Fenmire.

"Human wine is tasty enough, I suppose," he says. "But its alcohol content is far too small to have any effect on a Gryxen. It's little more than juice to us."

"Well, I plan to enjoy a glass of that juice myself." I push out of his arms and start treading water again. "Care to join me?"

"In a moment," he says with a smirk. "Unless you'd like your friends to know what you do to me as well."

I bite my lip and shake my head as I swim away toward the shore.

*****

I'm lying across one of the sheets on the shore of the pond with my head on Will's shoulder as we both stare up at the sky and watch the clouds. He has his arm around me, his fingers softly running across my upper arm as we talk. He and Fenmire put their pants back on while we ate our lunch, but Jacob and I chose to remain nude. The sun feels far too good to cover up right now. Of course, Will doesn't pay my naked body a bit of mind, not even in his thoughts.

"Can you imagine what our families would say if they could see us right now?" I ask.

Will laughs. "Their closed little minds would implode."

"Any regrets about coming here?"

"Are you kidding me? I keep thinking I'm going to wake up back in the village and realize I dreamt this place up. It feels too good to be true."

"I felt that way too at first, but there are downsides to living in The Deadwood. Reilanna still sends her beasts through The Gate to torment the Gryxen, but you and Jacob won't ever have to deal with that."

"Have you ever seen one?"

"Yes. One attacked me and Wexton before we learned I can talk to The Gate and—"

"You can *talk* to it?"

I haven't gotten around to telling Will about the powers I've gained from my Gryxen mates, or mate, I suppose, since I have yet to see any power from my mating bond with Wexton. Jacob is preoccupied digging around in the basket for more food, and Fenmire is perched on a large rock a ways down the bank, drawing in his book. Now is as good a time as any. "It's a bit of a trick I picked up from Caliborne. I can sort of… read minds."

Will laughs again. "Very funny, Evangeline."

"Think of a color."

They can't be serious.

"Humor me, please."

Will snorts. "Fine." *Green.*

"Green."

"Lucky guess."

"Alright. Pick another."

Yellow.

"Yellow."

Will's hand stops rubbing my arm. *Pink.*

"Pink."

Red, blue, orange.

"Red, blue, and orange."

He sits up, his eyes wide and mouth agape. "Evangeline…"

I prop myself up on one arm. "It's nothing really, just a byproduct of my mating bond with Caliborne."

"It's amazing!" Will says in awe. "A gift straight from God."

I snort. "I think you're giving him far too much credit."

Will's smile fades. "Do you no longer have faith in him?"

"I don't think he has the power to do half of what we pray to him for."

"So prayer is worthless?"

"Not worthless, no, but you have to be realistic in your expectations. I've learned a lot about gods in the last couple of months. The truth is both enraging and mind-boggling."

"Where, then, do you feel this gift of yours came from?"

I shrug. "Seerraf perhaps."

"That's the Gryxen's god?"

"That's right."

"And he's… the devil, right?"

"That's what our people call him, yes."

Will shakes his head and lays down on the sheet again, pulling me back onto his shoulder. His fingers go back to stroking my arm as he says, "If it were anyone else claiming they were gifted by the devil, laying with demons, and planning to break magic spells, I'd call a doctor and discredit every word as crazy talk. But it's you. You've always been bigger than life, Evangeline—bigger than *this* life, anyway—and I know you to be as sane as I am, saner even. You're the only one who could make me believe the devil and his demons are anything but evil."

"Don't take my word for it. Get to know them and decide for yourself."

"About that…" Will lifts his head enough to check on Jacob, who has wandered down the bank to Fenmire.

"What are you drawing?" Jacob asks him.

As Fenmire shows him the book, Will brings his mouth to my ear.

"You mentioned a forge before," he whispers.

"What about it?"

"Do you think the Gryxen would make something for me?"

"That depends on what it is, I suppose."

"A wedding ring."

I squeal a little, and Will shooshes me, glancing nervously down the bank at Jacob, who is now offering Fenmire a swig of his wine.

"I have no doubt they'd gladly make one for you," I say.

"I'd like a matching pair, if they can manage it. Who do you think I should ask?"

"Caliborne. He made my bracelets."

"Alright. I'll ask him. Pray he says yes for me, would you."

"What are you two whispering about?" Jacob asks as he saunters up to the sheet. He lays down on Will's other side, corks his wine, and rolls over onto Will's shoulder as well. He kisses Will on the cheek then hums. "You smell good, love."

I giggle. "I don't think you have to worry about that, Will."

"Worry about what?" Jacob asks.

"Nothing," Will and I reply in unison, and for reasons unknown, we all laugh.

I'll carry this day in my heart forever.

*****

I wake up when something soft is laid on top of me, and I roll over, shielding my eyes from the sun as I blink up at the figure leaning over me.

"Your skin is turning red," Fenmire says as he finishes draping my dress over me. "I'm no expert, but I think you're sensitive to the sun."

"Oh, no…" I mutter miserably. I can already feel the burn. It's protesting even the soft touch of my dress. "How long have I been sleeping?"

"A couple of hours."

I groan. I fell asleep on the sheet next to Will, but Will is back in the pond now, swimming laps with Jacob. In my slumber, I rolled onto my belly and let the sun scorch my poor back, bottom, and legs. My skin feels like it'll split open at the smallest movement.

"What is it, Evangeline?" Fenmire asks.

"Sunburn. A bad one by the feel of it."

Fenmire kneels beside me and lifts the edge of my dress to touch my back. I hiss at the contact, and his face shifts from slightly worried to deeply concerned.

"It's alright," I assure him. "It's normal. I was in the sun too long, that's all."

Will starts splashing his way toward us. "What's wrong?"

"They've been burned by the sun," Fenmire explains.

Will kneels beside me and lifts my dress too. "Oh God…"

"Is it bad?" I ask.

"Um… it's…"

Jacob joins us too, and he peers at my back over Will's shoulder and whistles. "That's pretty bad. I saw a burn like that once. My uncle worked his fences an entire afternoon with his shirt off after a summer shower soaked him to the bone. He was sick in bed for a whole week from it."

"Sick how?" Fenmire asks.

"A terrible headache, fevers and chills, and he threw up a few times, stuff like that. His skin blistered something awful."

I whimper, my misery mounting with each passing minute.

Fenmire stands up. "Stay here," he barks, then he takes off.

"Where's he going?" Will asks.

"I don't know," I say through gritted teeth. "I feel like my back is on fire."

"I can help that," Jacob says, and he gathers up one of the sheets and takes it to the water. He tosses it in and shoves it under the surface until it's soaked, then he wrings out the excess and brings it back. "This might hurt for a second."

Will takes off my dress, and Jacob lays the sheet over me instead. The second the wet cloth touches me, I yelp. It's so cold against my overheated skin that it hurts, but soon the burn begins to fade, and I relax with a soft sigh.

"Better?" Jacob asks.

"Much. Thank you."

Will retrieves one of our water skins and hands it to me. "Here, you should drink something other than wine."

I've taken no more than a swig when two Gryxen land beside the pond, one dressed head-to-toe in shining gold armor.

"You didn't have to bother Caliborne on patrol," I say. I try to sit up, but my backside immediately protests, so I lay right back down with a grunt.

Caliborne sets his bow aside and comes to me, kneeling and peering at my back like the others did.

"I'm alright," I insist. "Foolish, but alright."

Are you in pain?

I don't want to lie to him, but I also don't want to worry him too much. "A little." I give him a smile so forced I know it won't fool anyone.

Caliborne places his hand, palm down, on my back.

I jump, I can't help it. The metal of his gloves is like ice against my red-hot skin.

He looks up at Fenmire and conveys some message with his palm I can't overhear.

"I should be able to help," Fenmire says in response. "I'll take them home and do all I can."

"I'm sorry, Evangeline," Will says. "When I got back in the water, I should have covered you up. I didn't even think about it."

The boys don't look burned at all since their skin is already protected by a series of dark summer tans.

"It's alright, Will," I assure him. "It's no one's fault."

Fenmire scoops me into his arms as gently as he can, but I still moan and groan through the whole thing. He keeps me wrapped in the wet sheet, but the press of his arms under my back and legs is pure hell, regardless.

"Caliborne will take you back," Fenmire tells Will and Jacob.

"Will, come here," I beckon. I wince as I lean down near his ear. "Now is the perfect time to ask Caliborne about what we discussed."

Will nods and gives me a wink. "See you back home."

The fact that he considers the castle his home now too makes me smile.

I nod to Fenmire, and we take off. The wind feels nice as it chills the damp sheet around me, but it also makes me shiver as the chills set in. By the time we land in front of the castle, my teeth are chattering and my skin is covered in goosebumps.

Fenmire moves as softly as he can as he opens the castle door. "I knew your kind's skin changed color under prolonged sun exposure, but I didn't know it could hurt you like this."

"To be fair, you haven't had much sunny weather in the last two thousand years."

He snorts. "No, we haven't."

We walk down the hall, and I think he's taking me to my room until we walk right past my door. He takes me to his instead, and the awe I felt before about stepping into his personal space is overshadowed by the pain across the back half of my body, which is quickly heating again with no breeze to keep it cool. Fenmire sets me gently on the bed, detangling me from the damp sheet as he positions me on my belly across the softest bedding I've ever felt.

"This is nice," I say, patting the fluffy comforter.

"It better be. It took me years to collect all those feathers from the stables."

"You made this yourself?"

"You're not the only one who's handy with a needle."

He takes a mortar and pestle from a drawer and snatches bottles and vials down from his shelves, lining it all up on his desk, then he starts pouring and mixing and throwing things into the bowl without measuring any of it.

"What are you making?" I ask.

"A salve."

He excuses himself from the room and comes back with a bottle of oil from the kitchen. He adds a few drops to his concoction and starts grinding it all together, spinning the mortar in one hand while rhythmically working the pestle with the other. When he's done, he scoops the mixture out and pats it into a round gold tin, then he starts the process over. He does this three times before he finally comes to the side of the bed.

"This stuff may tingle on contact, but it shouldn't hurt," he says.

I feel like I'm roasting, and my head is starting to throb, so I only nod.

He smears the salve across my skin, starting at the back of my neck and working his way down. It's cool and soothes the burn even more than the wet sheet, though I break out in even stronger goosebumps that make me shiver. When he reaches my backside, I tense, but Fenmire doesn't even hesitate as he coats that with his medicine too. His fingers don't miss a single dip or curve, and he continues down the backs of my legs. He even dabs it on my feet wherever they've turned red.

"There," he says as he caps the tin. "That should keep you from blistering and dull the burn." He sets the tin aside and kneels beside me to run the backs of his fingers across my forehead. "You're already warm. Does your head hurt?"

"Very much."

He goes back to his shelves, picking up a bottle here and there, shaking one or two, and sliding others to the side completely until, finally, he finds what he's looking for: a bottle of some dark, almost black swirling liquid that reminds me of his eyes.

"Drink this," he says, uncorking the bottle and handing it to me. "Just one little swig."

"What is it?"

"Your typical pain reliever. Or, at least, typical for a Gryxen. It's safe for human consumption, but you only need a taste, and it will probably knock you out cold."

I sniff it tentatively. It smells alright, so I take a sip. It's spicy on my tongue, like my peppermint candies, and also fruity, like a berry of some sort, but it's also so sickening sweet I shake my head and make a face as I swallow it.

Fenmire takes back the bottle, recorks it, and sets it on his bedside table. From his tiny dresser he takes out a clean, dark brown sheet, shakes it out, and drapes it over me.

"It's gonna get dirty," I say, but the words come out all garbled.

"Don't worry about it," Fenmire says sternly. "Close your eyes and get some rest."

"That's what got me in trouble in the first place," I grumble.

He chuckles. "Don't worry. This isn't the first time I've nursed you through a fever."

My head is spinning now, but at least the headache is gone. I'm just conscious enough to feel Fenmire's fingers brush my cheek before whatever was in that black bottle yanks me into a deep, dreamless sleep.

Chapter 45

When I wake up, it takes me a moment to remember where I am. Why am I naked? I'm so stiff. I groan as I turn my head and see a body sprawled out on the bed beside me. At first, my muddy brain thinks it's Caliborne, but then I blink him into focus and see the black hair and slightly more angular face.

"Fenmire?" I'm croaky, and when I lift my head, I realize with horror that I've drooled on my arm a bit.

"Good evening," Fenmire bids. He's lounging back against the headboard with a book open on his chest, the one I let him borrow.

"It's nighttime?"

"Not only is it night, but it's the *next* night. You've slept for over a day."

The details slowly trickle back to me. "Did your salve work?" I roll my shoulders under the sheet with little discomfort.

"You're considerably less pink now, so I believe so. I washed the first coat off and reapplied it this morning, which probably helped."

"You washed me?"

Fenmire tilts his head. "Does that bother you?"

"No. It's just that no one's ever done that for me before."

He sets his book down on his chest. "That's not true. I washed you before, during your fevered sleep when you first arrived here. You were caked with mud and blood and covered in gashes. I didn't want you to get an infection, so I cleaned you the best I could."

"Oh. Well, thank you. For that and for this."

He nods and sets the book aside on the nightstand. "Would you like something from the kitchen?"

"Yes, please."

He swings his legs out of bed. "Stay put. I'll be right back."

Despite his request, nearly as soon as the door shuts behind him, I sit up. My backside certainly feels better, and my legs don't protest when I bend them anymore. I sit on the edge of the bed and stretch life back into my limbs before wrapping the sheet around me and standing up. I cross the room to Fenmire's shelves to admire his collection more closely, and I pluck down one of his books. It's in the Gryxen language, so I can't read a single word. I wonder if Fenmire would teach me to read this if I asked him. Something tells me he would, and that makes me smile as I slip the book back in place.

I pull the sheet tighter around myself and move down the shelves. There's a stone the size of my head, but when I pick it up with both hands, it's lighter than I expect. At first, I think it's black, but when I turn it in my hand and it catches the light, I can see that it's actually a very deep purple. I hold it up to the light of a nearby sconce to see its color more clearly.

Something moves inside.

It's not a rock but an egg.

I inspect it more closely and see a creature with four legs and a tail swimming around inside. It makes a few lazy figure eights and stills until I move the egg again, then it goes back to swimming.

"It's called a quaheitan." Fenmire is standing in the doorway with a plate of cold cuts and a cup of steaming hot tea. He crosses the room and sets both on the bedside table at my side of the bed. "They're large, bird-like reptiles from our world."

"Why do you have one?"

"It's not viable. It's little more than a fossil."

"But it's moving," I say as the creature makes another figure eight.

"It's alive, but it'll never hatch. If it did, it would die almost immediately. Inside its egg, it has its own, perfect little ecosystem. It can live forever in there as long as the shell never breaks."

He comes and takes the egg from me, and I relinquish it as softly as I can. He chuckles and knocks it against the side of the shelf as if he means to break it open, but the shell remains as solid as ever.

"Nothing can break this except the mother who laid it," he explains. "Quaheitan teeth are the only thing hard enough to get through the shell." He sets the egg back on the shelf. "I think she knew this one wouldn't make it. That's how I ended up with it; it was left in a nest thousands of years before I was born, thousands of years before Caliborne even. It's a rare find. Most of the time, the mothers break them open and let the healthy babies eat the ones that don't survive."

"That's a bit barbaric."

"I don't think so. It's nature making use of every resource it can. Otherwise, it would rot and go to waste. I think that would be worse, don't you?"

"I guess so."

"Would you like to see what they look like?"

I smile. "Yes."

Fenmire plucks a book down from the top shelf, flips quickly through the pages, and hands it to me.

The left page is filled with his cramped handwriting, but the right page is dominated by a detailed sketch of a scaly creature with a long body, four thick legs, a spiked tail, and wings made of dark leather with ridges of bone, like a Gryxen's. It has a pointed snout with fangs on both the top and the bottom of its mouth and a long, curved neck. Its eyes feel like it can see into my soul as it stares at me from the page, and I swear that deadly mouth is smiling at me.

I touch the drawing in awe. "It's a dragon."

Fenmire looks taken aback. "You've seen this creature before?"

"Only in fairytales. Dragons are a myth, at least in our world."

"Most myths grow from some kernel of truth. If you consider how many worlds there must be in the universe, I think it's safe to assume just about anything your mind can dream up exists in some capacity on at least one of them."

"I would love to see a real-life dragon."

"My kind are forbidden from interacting with them unless we're sent by the temple with official business. Quaheitans are vastly intelligent and dangerous creatures. They can wield magic like we can, and have their own tight-knit communities, leaders, and religions. They are their own people in our world. They rarely get along with us though."

"How come?"

"Our kind hunted theirs for many millennia, almost to extinction. It took them a long time to rebuild their population, and even now very few of them exist compared to the numbers there used to be."

"Why did your people hunt them?"

"We used to consider them little more than beasts. Their bones, talons, and eyes were used in alchemy, their teeth were coveted by warriors who wore them as trophies, and their eggs and meat were considered a delicacy."

"But you've stopped hunting them?"

"Seerraf's fifth acolyte, Orikmory, befriended a den of quaheitans. They spent years in the company of the quaheitans, learning their ways and language, and were the first to realize quaheitans are as intelligent and sentient as us. Our people refused to believe them, though. A war broke out between Orikmory's home city and the den, and Orikmory lost their life defending the quaheitans in a bloody battle. Upon their death, Seerraf added Orikmory to the hall of acolytes and deemed the hunting of quaheitans immoral. As a result, we passed laws to protect the quaheitans, and the hunting stopped, though there's still the occasional poacher. Usually, the quaheitans have no trouble defending themselves from one or two with ill intentions."

"Have you ever met one?"

"Once. The temple had some business with a den not far from Michastiforo many years ago, and I asked to tag along. Not many get the chance to see a den, and I wasn't about to let such an opportunity pass me by."

I close the book and hand it back to him. "I envy you."

"Why?"

"Your love of learning was never squashed throughout your life. How I would've loved free reign to learn about the things that interested me as a youth. My shelves no doubt would've looked a lot like yours." I wave my arm around at his vast collection of books and oddities.

"It's not too late, you know."

I tug the sheet back up on my shoulders, avoiding his eyes. "Over the past week, ever since Will joined me here, I've come to realize something. This happiness I feel now, it's overwhelming and complete, and I think there's a reason for that. I think it's because some higher power knows how this will end, and they're allowing me to experience a lifetime's worth of happiness in what little time I have left." I dare a glance up at him, and I'm relieved to see his face is not one of derision or even horror. He's simply listening without judgment. "I think it may be too late after all, Fenmire."

Fenmire puts his hand on the side of my neck with his thumb on my throat, which he strokes lightly. "I wish I were an optimistic one who could tell you you're wrong and that we'll figure something out. But that's just not me."

"I don't want pretty lies," I say softly. "I want to be prepared for the worst then be pleasantly surprised if things work out in our favor."

One side of his mouth turns up in a half grin. "I think you and I are more alike than I thought."

"I think maybe you're right."

His thumb is still making circles on my throat, giving me goosebumps. He's staring at me, his eyes sliding across every inch of my face as he swallows. He finally lets go of my neck and takes my chin in his hand instead, tilting my face up until my eyes bore into his.

"I prayed for you," he says. "I prayed every day for two thousand years for someone to come and end my pain, either through another mating bond or with my death. Why do I get the feeling that, with you, it'll be both?"

I want to tell him not to say that and assure him it won't be that way, but even I know our chances aren't good.

And he doesn't want pretty lies either.

Since placations he doesn't need are all my brain can think of right now, I choose not to respond at all, and a silence falls between us that would probably be awkward in the company of anyone else. Instead of awkwardness, I feel heat and longing grow in the pit of my stomach. There's a predatory look in his eyes that calls to something inside me, and I feel my hesitation ebb away as my deepest, most carnal desires growl impatiently from the back of my mind where I've kept them hidden for the past twenty years. That look has me craving his hand around my throat again, ropes around my wrists, his grip on my body so tight it aches as he takes what he wants.

My lips part as my breathing speeds up, and Fenmire smiles.

"Your tea is getting cold," he says in a low voice.

"I don't mind cold tea."

That's all it takes. Those five little words break the wall between us, and I drop my sheet at the same time Fenmire leans down and yanks me into a kiss. The same needy, dominating mouth molds mine as both his hands grip my face, holding me in place until he breaks the kiss to breathe.

"What do you want, Evangeline?" he asks.

"Eve..." I utter.

"Eve," Fenmire whispers against my lips. "I want to take you back to bed, tie your hands above your head, push you up on your knees, and explore every inch of your most private, sensual places."

I brush my lips across his. "I think I want that too."

Fenmire pulls away and gives me a stern look. "Maybe you do. But you might decide you don't once we're in the moment. If that happens, I want you to tell me. I like taking control of my lovers, but only so far as they're willing to give me control. If you say 'stop', I stop. If you say 'no', nothing happens. Understand?"

"Yes."

"Say only what you mean and don't be coy."

"I understand."

Fenmire nods and steps back away from me. "Then lie down on the bed, face down."

I reach down for the sheet I dropped.

Fenmire gently takes it from my hands. "You won't be needing that anymore."

"Don't I still have salve all over me?"

"You won't for long."

I hop back into Fenmire's massive bed and lie on my belly across his fluffy comforter. I'm not sure what to do with my hands, though, since he said he plans to...

I opt for simply tucking them under my head, confident he'll tell me what to do when the time comes.

Fenmire goes to his dresser and pours fresh water from a pitcher into his wash basin, which he brings to the bed along with a clean rag. I expect him to start at the top and work his way down, but he surprises me by starting at my feet.

He quickly and efficiently wipes the old salve off, washes it into the basin, and pats me dry with the clean sections of the sheet I recently relinquished to him. As he works up my body, he straddles me and inches his way northward, slowly covering me with his much larger frame. When he reaches the back of my neck, he sweeps my hair aside, which I realize has been freed from the braid I wore swimming. Once I'm clean and dry from head to toe, he tosses the rag in the basin, leans down, and kisses the side of my neck, suckling on my skin and biting the bottom of my ear hard enough to make me gasp.

"Put your hands together above your head," he orders, and he guides my arms up above me. "You want to see why I love this bed so much?"

I nod, and he climbs off me to open a drawer in the bedside table. He takes out a length of rope and reaches for my hands. Within seconds, my arms are expertly bound at the wrists. Though the rope isn't tight, the way in which Fenmire has tied it leaves no room to wiggle free even if I wanted to.

He presses the mattress down near the headboard so I can see as he loops the rope through a metal ring drilled into the wood. When he pulls the rope taut, my arms are stretched above my head until he ties it off. He fingers a loop sticking out from the knot.

"See this?" he asks. "With one pull, the knot instantly releases." He demonstrates, and the rope immediately falls slack. "Should you ever tell me to stop, you'll be freed in seconds. That's a promise."

"That's not giving you true control though, is it?" I dare to ask.

"Is it not? Make no mistake, Eve, I can take exactly what I want while also ensuring I never cross your boundaries. I wouldn't be a very good lover if I couldn't."

He reties the rope and moves the wash basin back to the dresser, then he's back on top of me with his hard cocks pressing against my backside through his leather pants as he kisses my neck some more. His fingers tickle down my sides which make me jerk and laugh, but then I groan softly as he drags his nails up my still slightly sunburnt back, sending intense shivers throughout my entire body.

"You'll tremble for a whole different reason soon enough," Fenmire murmurs in my ear.

He slides down my back, dusting kisses down my spine clear to my tailbone. His legs part mine as he moves between them and kneels, then he tugs up on my hips, moving me up on my own knees. This angle prevents me from lifting my head comfortably, so I keep my cheek pressed to the bed.

"Arch that back for me, pet," Fenmire says with a firm press of his hand to my spine. "I want every one of your little curves and folds on full display."

I hide my burning cheeks in the bedding as I do as he asks, arching my back until my backside sticks out toward him. He parts my legs more, opening me wide.

The vulnerability of my position right now hits me hard, and my heart kicks into overdrive. I'm tied up, naked, and pinned beneath a demon who could do whatever he wants to me with little effort on his part.

And the last thing I want is to tell him to stop.

"It's too bad the sun got to this beautiful backside first," Fenmire says, palming both my cheeks. "I would love to redden it with my hand instead."

"What?" I say in shock. "You mean…?"

Fenmire taps his hand against one cheek hard enough to produce a faint sting. "That's exactly what I mean. Someday."

I have no doubts that he'll live up to that promise.

His finger slides across a spot on my inner thigh, close to my sex. "I see Wexton staked his claim on his favorite spot."

I laugh into the sheets, but the sound turns into a gasping moan when Fenmire leans down and swipes his tongue over the mating mark. His thumbs slide slowly up my inner thighs, and they don't stop when they reach my groin. Fenmire fingers my sex, parting me wide open before swiping a single finger through my slit.

"So wet for me," he murmurs. "But this isn't the hole I'm interested in tonight."

A slight whimper escapes me when I realize what that means, and a moment later, I jump when that same finger—now wet with my own arousal—touches the place only Wexton has explored in the past. Fenmire's finger circles that hole, and his palm slaps my ass again, a little harder this time.

I cry out softly, but then Fenmire's finger increases the pressure to the point I'm sure he means to slide it inside me. I tense without meaning to.

"Relax, pet," Fenmire says. "Let me sink my finger in that sweet little bud. Someday, it will be my cock."

"It'll never fit," I say.

"Oh, you'll take it. You'll take all of me, and I'll make you cry out for mercy as you come with my cock in your ass."

The moan his words draw from me is raw and primal, and I melt against the bedding. Fenmire's finger disappears, and he spits, his warm saliva landing between my cheeks. He swirls it over my hole then slides inside me.

It's not the first time I've had something in my ass, heaven knows Wexton has explored that place with his tongue enough to prepare me for this, but Fenmire's finger is harder and more demanding. He pushes inside me, pumping his finger in and out as he slides his thumb down to stroke my clit with each thrust. I'm overcome with sensation and catch myself arching my back even more. He spanks me again, and I cry out. My body clenches around his finger, making things that much more intense.

Fenmire suddenly shifts. While not removing his hand from between my legs, he reaches up with the other and grasps my hair. At first, he just weaves his fingers through the strands, gripping them firmly, but when he gives an experimental little tug, I gasp and groan, wishing he'd do it harder.

He immediately obliges.

His fingers tighten in my hair and pull so hard my scalp burns. My head is yanked back so that I can no longer hide my cries and moans in the bedding as Fenmire's finger moves in and out of me at a punishing pace, his thumb still stroking my clit with every plunge. I'm soon mewling with each thrust and pumping my hips in rhythm with his hand, seeking more.

"What a greedy little pet," Fenmire says near my ear. "You like my finger in your ass?"

"Yes," I say, my voice heavy with arousal.

"Want me to make it two?"

"Yes."

"Beg me."

I whimper again, and Fenmire responds by taking his finger out entirely to spank my ass hard enough my breath catches in my chest.

"I said beg," he orders sternly.

I don't know what comes over me, but my will to do as he says overrides all shame as I utter the words, "Please, Fenmire, stick two fingers in my ass."

He leans to the side of the bed, opening another drawer in the table and rummaging around for a small blue bottle. He rips the cork out with his teeth and drizzles a liquid between my cheeks. It's cool and thick but quickly warms as he spreads it with his fingers. Two of them press against me and slip easily inside, aided by the slick liquid. Fenmire's other hand is still in my hair, and he tugs my head to the side so he can lean down and whisper in my ear.

"Just imagine it, pet, imagine how it will feel the day I tie you up, bend you over, and slide one cock deep inside you here." He plunges his fingers deep inside me, and I gasp. "While my other cock fucks you here." His thumb slides inside my wet cunt.

My legs start to shake, and he chuckles. He pulls my hair even harder, and I cry out, my breath puffing in and out so fast I don't know how much more I can take. Tears of pain sting in my eyes, and I'm straining against the ropes involuntarily. Every muscle from my waist down is tense, preparing for the orgasm I know is coming.

Fenmire stops, takes his fingers and thumb out of me, and slaps me on the clit.

I cry out sharply.

"I want you to come like this," he says, and he slaps the same spot again.

This time, my cry is tearful. I'm poised perfectly on the edge of pain and pleasure, both in agony and bliss. Another slap, and I'm crying, but my whole body is shaking now.

"Again?" he asks.

"Yes," I utter, then I start to sob when he hits me again. "Please," I babble. My body is so tense and ready to burst, but the pain is almost too much.

"You can do it, pet," Fenmire says. "Relax and let it sweep you away."

I release the tension in my body, first in my arms, which makes the rope go slack around my wrists, then my neck and shoulders, my back, my legs, everywhere. Once I'm like putty under Fenmire's hands, he releases my hair and shoves my head to the bed, which takes the pressure off my scalp. He slaps my clit again and again, softly at first then harder and harder. The heat from his strikes warms the spot, and that heat builds and spreads throughout my entire lower half until, finally, I come with a scream of victory, my entire body locking up under the spasms. Fenmire continues to slap my clit, which makes me jerk and writhe and cry out as I come apart.

When he stops, my body stills, though it twitches now and then in the aftermath of one of the most intense orgasms of my life. Fenmire gently slides each of my legs out until I'm lying flat on my belly again, then he tugs the loop on the rope to free my wrists before sliding up to sit with his back to the headboard. He hauls me between his legs so that I'm sitting on the bed with my head on his chest, then he wraps his legs around me and pets my hair, massaging my scalp where his grip from before made it ache.

"Calm down now, pet," he says softly. "Let it all wash away."

I'm not sure what he means at first, but I scoot closer to him and close my eyes. My body hurts in delicious ways, and my muscles are still contracting, but after a while, a peaceful haze falls over me, and everything else melts away. I can hear Fenmire's heartbeat and feel his chest softly rising and falling under my head. I breathe deep and let out the longest sigh of my life.

"How did all of that feel?" he asks, running his fingers up and down my bare arm. "Was it too much, not enough, or just right?"

I wet my lips and clear my throat before responding. "Just right, I think. There was a moment where I thought I'd have to stop you, but then you let go of my hair, and I was fine again."

"I sensed you might be reaching your limit. Next time, let me know when you get to that point. I want to push you only as hard as you need to be pushed, not to the point where you're uncomfortable."

"Next time?" I ask with a grin.

He grins wickedly back at me. "Oh yes. Next time I fully plan to redden that ass, like I said."

"You truly mean to spank me?" I ask shyly.

He nods. "Until you're all soft and limp with carnal pleasure like you were just now. Then maybe I'll tie your hands, put you down on your knees, and fuck both your tight little holes."

I swallow down a groan. "You may have a dirtier mouth than Wexton."

He snorts. "You have no idea." He takes both my hands in one of his and inspects my wrists, which are red-ringed from the rope, and starts gently massaging them. "Do you mind if I tend to the other places I abused?"

"You mean my…?"

"That's what I mean, yes," he says in amusement.

"How do you plan to tend to that?"

He slides me from his lap and goes to the water pitcher, dampening a fresh cloth in the clean water, then he returns to the bed and tugs me back into his arms, only this time, he lays me down more horizontally across his lap.

"Open up," he orders with a nudge to my knee.

I shyly part my legs.

He lays the cool, wet cloth against my sex, and it instantly soothes the burn where he'd slapped me over and over.

"Better?" he asks.

"Much. Thank you."

He leaves the rag in place and waves a hand over my chest with his palm a mere inch from my skin. He stops at a spot between my breasts and tilts his head as if listening to something.

"What are you doing?" I ask.

"Checking your heart. I've never done these things with a human before. I want to be sure your system can handle it."

I stay quiet so he can focus, and he lowers his arm a moment later, seemingly satisfied with my condition. He flips the cloth over so the cooler side is against me, and I'm suddenly so comfortable and tired that I yawn loudly. I close my eyes and rest my head against his chest again.

"Don't you want your tea?" Fenmire asks, and I can tell by his voice that he's smiling.

"Later," I say sleepily.

I think he says something about me needing to eat, but I'm already half asleep and merely hum in response.

Chapter 46

I'm walking down the castle hallway with Fenmire on one side and Wexton on the other. Fenmire and I laugh at some ridiculous thing Wexton says, but our mirth is cut short by a howling scream and the castle doors crashing open. A burst of wind ushers in a figure with stark white hair and pitch-black wings that stands at the end of the hallway, staring us down.

When I look at my companions, I find not only Fenmire and Wexton with me, but also Caliborne, Will, Jacob, Percival, and even Levi. They all stand around me in silent solidarity, their eyes locked onto CeCe who stomps one foot, her eyes narrowing and her wings twitching as she regards us all.

I take a step back then another and another, and I don't understand why the others continue to stand there. I open my mouth to suggest we all flee, but CeCe opens hers at the same time, and a deafening scream erupts, shaking the entire castle as hard as The Gate's tremors. Everyone cries out in pain, all except for me. I don't feel anything. Her screams don't even hurt my ears, and yet my friends and loved ones all go down to their knees, clutching their heads and curling in on themselves.

"Stop!" I scream, and I step between them and CeCe. It does no good. Her screams continue without pause, as if she has no need to breathe.

I hear a horrible snapping sound and turn to the others. They're all sprawled out on the floor, groaning and crying out in agony as their limbs jerk and bend in odd angles, breaking under the strain and piercing through their skin and clothes. Blood trickles from their ears and mouths, and one of Will's eyes bursts.

"CeCe, stop!" I scream. "Please stop! Please!"

My begging does nothing.

Over the sound of CeCe's relentless howl comes laughter, and it's a voice I know too well by now.

"You evil witch!" I yell at the walls since I can't see where the voice is coming from. "Show yourself!"

Fenmire cries out in fresh horror as one of his wings fold up into a bloody ball on his back. Beside him, Wexton's does the same, then Caliborne's.

Jacob's head jerks around with a sickening snap as his neck breaks. He lies lifeless on the stone as the others continue to writhe.

I go down on my knees and start to sob. I want to be sick, I want to help, I want to murder Reilanna and free the ones I love from her forever, but I can do nothing but kneel there and cry and watch them die one by one.

"Evangeline!" *It's Fenmire's voice, but it's not coming from the figure with the black hair and eyes on the ground before me. It's all around me, like an echo.* "Evangeline, it's a dream. She's in your—"

Reilanna's laughter and CeCe's screams intensify, blocking him out.

"Fenmire!" I yell so loud my voice cracks.

"She's in your head, Evangeline. It's not real!"

I look around me. "Not real?"

The blood smeared across my friends' bodies looks real enough, and I can smell the metallic tang of it as it pools across the stone.

"It's a dream. Reilanna's in your head, but it's *your* mind. Fight back!"

A dream. In my head. Reilanna…

That's right. She invades my dreams.

Is this a dream?

I look around, and now that I'm paying attention to the details, I can see the flaws. The castle walls are moving, warping and bending like a sheet in the wind. I look back down at my friends and realize their faces are wrong, like someone drew them from only the vaguest descriptions. Even their voices are wrong as they shout my name.

"You're not real," I mutter as I stand up. "None of this is real."

"Fight back, Evangeline! Push her out."

Surely it can't be that simple.

I face CeCe and raise my hand, holding it out in front of me like a shield.

"I said stop!" I cry, and all at once, the screaming dies. CeCe's mouth is still open, but no sound is coming out now. "Get out!" With a swipe of my hand, I push her out the front doors and slam them shut behind her.

"Would you look at this," Reilanna says, though I still can't see her. "The human has learned a new trick. Now we can have some fun."

The floor under my feet suddenly tips, and I go sliding, falling onto my back as I'm swept down an endless stone chute. Eventually, I'm dumped out into a grassy field, the one just outside The Deadwood's arch. Will is running toward me with his axe in his hand and his arms outstretched.

"Will, stop!" I scream, but it's too late. Vines from The Deadwood whip out and snake around his wrists and ankles, lifting him up and stretching him out, spread-eagle, in the air. The vines pull taut, and I see pain on my best friend's face as they pull his limbs so hard they threaten to tear off his body.

Faced with this fresh horror, I forget myself, but only for a moment.

"Push her out."

"You're not real!" I yell angrily at the figure who is definitely not Will. This person looks nothing like him. I turn away from the illusion. "Why won't you face me?" I scream at the sky. "Are you such a coward you refuse to fight a mere human face to face?"

"It's not you I wish to fight."

Her voice comes from right behind me, and I whirl around, clenched fist flying at the spot I know she was standing a second ago, but all I catch is a glimpse of black shadows that dance off to the left, out of my sight. The sun and the grass are gone now. It's a pitch-black night, and I'm standing at the edge of the pond where we swam just days ago, looking out over the water, only the place looks completely different, wrong. The pond is bubbling, the trees groan and sway though there's no wind, and there's a stench in the air, like something rotten.

"Psst," says a voice behind me, and when I turn around, I cover my mouth to stifle my scream.

The entire village lies dead in a heap at the edge of the trees. The carcasses are bloated with flies buzzing loudly overhead. At the very front and center of this mountain of death sits my father, who looks up at me through bloodshot eyes from beside my mother's corpse.

"Look what you've done," he says. "So much pain…" He waves a hand over the endless bodies behind him then reaches down to stroke my mother's hair. His eyes turn suddenly hostile, and his lip turns up in a sneer as he says, "I should have killed you in the cradle, you wretch."

His words cut straight through my heart, and I take a step back, splashing one foot down into water up to my ankle. My father starts to laugh, then he takes a knife from his belt and slits his own throat just before a hand bursts out of the pond and grabs me by the ankle. With impossible strength, it rips me into the water and drags me under.

I kick and thrash and pump my arms and legs as hard as I can, but the hand on my ankle is too strong, its grip so tight it hurts. It continues to pull me down, down, down until I can no longer see the surface. I'm dragged into the cold, inky depths, and my lungs start to burn, begging for air. I panic and suck in water instead, which immediately chokes me. I cough and sputter and thrash until my muscles eventually give up, and I feel death creep in. For reasons unknown, the only thing I can think of is the little stillborn foal Papa's mare gave birth to.

I hope I get to see him in heaven.

A burst of white light cuts through the water, blinding me, and I think at first that it's God come to take me to the afterlife, but then I see wings and talons and two strong arms reaching for me, and I recognize the one who's come to save me. With the last of my consciousness, I reach for Caliborne's hand, and I barely feel the warmth of his fingers close over mine.

I wake up gasping for breath with my chest aching as if I was really drowning just seconds ago. I have a death grip on Caliborne's fingers, and his face is inches away from mine. There's nothing but worry in his glowing white eyes, and the urge to comfort him trumps my panic enough to slow my breathing.

"I'm… alright…" I bite out between breaths. "It was just… one of Reilanna's tricks."

Fenmire is suddenly beside me, his hands roaming over my body as he checks for himself that I'm unharmed. His eyes are nearly as worried as Caliborne's.

We couldn't wake you, Caliborne says.

"I know. It's… it's happened before."

"What?" Fenmire fumes. "How many times?"

"Just once, with Wexton, but he was eventually able to wake me up."

"Why didn't you tell us the dreams were getting this bad?"

"I thought I could handle it," I say, though I hear how foolish that sounds now that I'm saying it out loud.

It's not shameful to ask for help.

"I know, I just didn't want to give her the satisfaction of seeing me hide."

"I watched your heartrate drop just now, Evangeline," Fenmire says. "Another minute, and you'd have been dead. For your safety, you must allow Caliborne to shield your dreams from now on. Whenever you're sleeping, he must be nearby."

I nod sullenly. "I understand. I'm sorry I worried you both."

Caliborne touches my cheek. *Now I get to spend every night with you in my arms. I'm honored, my stoferra.*

"Here," Fenmire says, handing me my stone-cold tea. "You should drink something."

"What time is it?" I ask as I take the cup.

"Around midnight."

I sip my tea, which is still good despite the temperature. "I heard you," I tell Fenmire. "You made me realize it was all in my head. I tried to fight back like you said. I did fight a little bit, but she kept changing the dream, and every time she did, I'd forget that's what it was. Maybe with practice I could keep her out myself."

That's not a risk I'm willing to take, Caliborne says.

At the same time, Fenmire says, "Absolutely not!"

I huff at them both. "I'm not some scared damsel."

"But you *are* human," Fenmire says, matter-of-factly. "You're the last I'd call weak, but there are limits to what you can do and what your body can endure. No amount of bravery can change that. And Reilanna wouldn't pass up the chance to kill you before you can break her spell. Like I said, she came far too close to doing so just now. If Caliborne had been out on patrol tonight..."

I shiver and swallow a gulp of my tea, remembering the feel of death's chill washing over me as I drowned in my dreams.

Caliborne bumps his shoulder against Fenmire's with a small nod down at me.

Fenmire clears his throat. "I don't mean to scare you, of course, but—"

"You don't have to shield me from the truth either," I say with a pointed look at both of them. I toss the blankets back, scoot to the edge of the bed, gulp down the last of my tea, and set the cup on the bedside table. I hold my arms out to Caliborne. "To bed then?"

He scoops me up without delay.

"I hope the rest of your night is filled with better dreams," Fenmire bids.

"Goodnight, Fenmire."

Caliborne carries me down the hall to his own bedroom, and once we're tucked in tight in his bed, he nuzzles my neck and says, *I heard you yelling earlier. Before the dreams, I mean.*

"I'm surprised you didn't bust down the door," I tease.

He snorts one short puff of laughter against my skin. *I am very familiar with your cries of passion, my stoferra. I wasn't about to interrupt what I suspect was a moment of intimacy between you and Fenmire.*

I smile. "You suspect correctly."

That's going well then?

"It's *going*. I'll let you know how well it is or isn't once it's had time to grow."

I'm proud of you.

I burst out laughing and immediately explain why so as not to hurt his feelings. "Forgive me. It's just that I never thought in my wildest dreams someone would be proud of me for my promiscuity. If I had behaved this way before coming to The Deadwood, I would've been labeled a whore."

Caliborne clicks his teeth together. *I don't like that label.*

"Don't worry, I don't think of myself that way."

Good. His hand moves under the covers to my chest, and he traces the soft skin between my breasts with a single finger, making me shiver. *I would love to hear those sounds you made before uttered while I bring you pleasure. Or are you too tired and sore?*

I smile sleepily. "I'm never too tired to want you. Just be gentle with me."

Caliborne spends the next hour showing me just how gentle he can be.

*****

The next morning, Caliborne and I sleep in long past sunrise, only getting up when my stomach grumbles so loudly it makes him laugh. When we leave the bedroom to head for the kitchen, we both pause together at the sight of Fenmire standing across the hall, waiting for us.

"Good morning," he bids. He gives me a small bow of his head. "Might I have a word?"

Caliborne shuts the bedroom door and gives my shoulder a squeeze. *I'll see you at breakfast,* he says before making himself scarce.

"Is something wrong?" I ask Fenmire once we're alone.

"Not at all. I just wanted to ask how you were feeling this morning."

"Quite well, actually. I caught up on my rest thanks to Caliborne."

He smirks. "I'm glad to hear that, but I was actually asking if you're sore." His eyes flick down to my groin and back up again.

I try not to grin, truly I do, but I fail miserably. "A little, but it's the good kind of sore."

"What makes it good?" he asks, but his tone is more of a dare. He knows the answer, he just wants to hear me say it.

I look him right in his eyes and say, "It's the kind of pain that makes me want to clench my thighs together to remember how good it felt."

Fenmire runs his tongue along his bottom lip in a way that makes me consider skipping breakfast all together. He pushes off the wall and approaches me, and I'm mentally preparing myself for what he might have in store when he holds out a book, the one I let him borrow.

"I finished it last night," he explains.

I push it back toward him. "Keep it. Add it to the library."

He hums and nods. "It'll be nice to see a proper printed book on the shelves instead of just my hand-bound tomes."

"You bind your own books?" I ask in awe.

"Of course. Where else would I get them?"

"Right, yes, that makes sense."

He tucks the book under his arm and takes a step closer. "Care to join me on an adventure tomorrow morning?"

Our flirting from before emboldens me, so I reply, "I'm free right now. What sort of *adventure* did you have in mind?"

He bobs one brow. "The sort that requires you to not be sore and that I have a full night's rest beforehand. Besides, I have patrol this morning."

"Isn't patrol change usually earlier than this?"

"Usually."

"Shirking your duties to see me, are you?"

He smiles. "Maybe." He takes another step closer, forcing me to back up against the door behind me, which he sets his hand on above my head as he leans over me. His other hand tilts my face up by the chin. "Maybe I couldn't stand the thought of leaving without seeing how wrecked I left my pet last night."

"Wrecked?" I laugh softly. "You'll have to try harder than that to wreck me, Fenmire."

Fenmire growls, and his hand goes from my chin to my throat, his fingers wrapping around and tightening enough to make me gasp. He leans down until our faces are only an inch or two apart.

"Challenge accepted," he murmurs.

I swallow but don't break eye contact.

Fenmire crushes his lips to mine, taking everything he wants like he usually does until I'm breathless and flushed and about half a second away from demanding he take the morning off and wreck me right now, soreness, sleep, and patrol all be damned.

"Meet me in the stables tomorrow morning," he orders.

"The stables?" I ask, my brain only half registering the words.

"That's right."

"Wait, tomorrow morning?" I force myself to clear my head. Tomorrow is Sunday. "I can't tomorrow. I already have plans with Wexton."

"Wexton has patrol tomorrow morning."

My shoulders sag. "Oh." I'd hoped to introduce him to my father tomorrow, and I mentally kick myself for not checking ahead of time that the patrol schedule didn't get in the way of that.

"I tell you what," Fenmire says, "I'll switch with him. That'll free me up for the morning after next. Are you free then?"

I grin. "I'll check my schedule."

Fenmire chuckles. "Don't keep me waiting, pet, or I'll double my wrecking efforts when I get my hands on you again."

He lets me go, shoves off the door, and walks away, leaving me breathless and overwhelmed with desire. I giggle to myself as I head off in the opposite direction.

I'm going to leave him waiting as long as possible.

Chapter 47

Sunday morning, I burst into Wexton's room as soon as he bids me to enter when I knock.

"Are you ready to meet my father today?" I ask excitedly, bouncing up onto the bed on my knees beside him.

"Is that why you asked Fenmire to switch patrols with me?"

"Did you forget what day it was?"

"You tend to stop keeping track of the days after a few centuries."

"That makes sense, I suppose. But I haven't stopped keeping track yet. It's Sunday, the day you're to meet my family, or half of it, anyway."

"Do you think your father will like me?" Wexton asks nervously.

"Of course he will. You make me happy." I lean down and give him a quick peck on the lips. When I move to slide back off the bed, he rolls and throws his arm around me, yanking me back.

I yelp and laugh as he settles me on his chest and wraps his wings around us.

"Where are you going so soon, darling?" he purrs. "You think you can just bound in and out of my bed that fast? You ought to know better by now."

"Oh, I do, but we don't have time for much else this morning. My mother will be on her way to church soon, and I want as much time as I can get with Papa."

Wexton sighs. "I suppose my desires can wait. I'll drink my fill of your sweet nectar later then."

I touch my nose to his. "Promise?"

He puts his hand on the back of my head and pulls me into a deep kiss, his tongue dancing across mine and thrusting into my mouth until I'm breathless and flushed. He bucks his hips, pressing the hardened bulge of his erections against my groin.

"I'll be in utter misery until I can sink my cock into you," he mutters against my lips.

"You're an absolute heathen." I kiss him on the lips again. "I love it."

He laughs as he unfolds his wings and releases me. I lounge on his bed, watch him get dressed, and imagine the things I'd like to do to him later. He catches me staring and winks at me.

Gods, I am the luckiest human in this world.

*****

Wexton and I run into Will and Jacob on our way out of the castle, and since very few know about my Sunday journeys to my old home, I simply tell them we're on our way out for a walk. Will doesn't buy it, I can see it in his eyes, but he doesn't comment. I'll no doubt have some questions to answer later, though.

It's overcast today, which brings the heat down to a more pleasant temperature. I do hope it doesn't storm though. Caliborne has agreed to fly me to the arch this morning to cut down on our travel time, but there's still a bit of a walk to the farm from there and then of course the whole trip home afterward, none of which will be much fun in the rain.

Caliborne lands in front of the arch and sets me on my feet. *Be careful.*

"I always am," I say as I adjust my skirts. It's an Eve day, so I'm wearing the blue dress I made and my silver bracelet. I've left my hair down, and I smooth down the flyaways from our flight before kissing Caliborne goodbye.

Caliborne touches Wexton's arm for a moment, conveying a message Wexton replies to with only a brisk nod.

After Caliborne takes off back toward the castle, I ask, "What did he say?"

"That I'd better bring you back whole or he'll relieve me of another limb."

I put a finger to my chin thoughtfully. "Do you think he'd let me choose which limb? I don't want to risk you losing one I'm partial to."

His lips twitch in an effort not to smile. "And here I thought you were partial to all of me, darling."

"Am I?" I tease with a tilt of my head.

He loops his arm around my back and pulls me close. "You better be, because not a single inch of me will be anything but yours for the rest of my existence."

"So I'm stuck with you then?"

"Indefinitely, I'm afraid."

I sigh dramatically. "I'll just have to learn to live with that."

"Oh, woe is you that you must live bathed in my pleasures."

"It's a sacrifice I'm willing to make for the greater good."

Wexton laughs.

I spin out from under his arm, take his hand, and tug him along through the arch. I keep hold of his hand as we walk through the knee-high grass along the edge of The Deadwood.

It really is beautiful out here, Wexton thinks as he peers around at the trees and wildflowers. *Everything is so alive, so vivid.*

"Your world is just as vivid, is it not? I've walked jungles and prairies full of colors I've never seen before in Caliborne's memories."

"I wouldn't know. I've never been away from Michastiforo to see such things."

"Why not?"

He shrugs. "I am a Gryxen, so I always knew I would end up going to the training grounds. Leaving for a few years just to come right back seemed like a waste of effort, so I stayed where I was. Then, after my training, Caliborne added me to his team, and my job of protecting The Gate was paramount to anything else."

"If there was nothing and no one to stop you, where would you choose to go first?"

He ponders that for a while, and I hear the names of many places pop into his mind before he eventually settles on one. "The Isles of Aorresik. They are said to be made of pure crystal. I would very much like to see that."

I try to imagine the beauty of crystal islands, but I know the picture I paint in my mind doesn't do them justice. "I think, once Reilanna's spell is broken and we've defeated her at last, we will all have earned a long vacation. Perhaps we can go see your islands then, together."

Wexton squeezes my hand. *I would like that very much.*

I smile as we continue walking, but in the privacy of my own thoughts, I'm a little sad and worried I won't be able to follow through on these plans. But spending every minute thinking I'm going to die so there's no point in planning a future seems silly and depressing. So I smile and picture islands of crystal and squeeze Wexton's hand.

I choose hope and happiness.

*****

We follow the edge of The Deadwood even after the road curves and cuts across the fields toward my family's farm. The grass here grows so tall it's hard for me to continue walking through it in my dress, so Wexton kneels on the ground and pats his shoulder.

"Climb up here," he says.

It takes some careful maneuvering since Wexton only has one hand to help guide me, but I eventually end up sitting astride his shoulders with my dress bunched behind his neck. He crosses my ankles across his chest and holds them tightly in his one large hand as he stands up and keeps on walking.

I drape his braid across my leg and run my fingers through the tufts at the end. "I wish I could fly. Too bad I can't grow wings from a mating bond."

"Speaking of which, have you noticed any additional powers since we were joined?"

"No. Though truthfully, I haven't fully tested it. I'm not sure what to even look for."

"You haven't noticed you're stronger than you used to be?"

"I helped move some crates in the kitchen's storage room for Levi a few days ago. The task wasn't any easier than it's been in the past."

Wexton hums thoughtfully. "I find it hard to believe you'd gain powers from Caliborne and not from me, but maybe your human body can't handle feats of extreme strength. Perhaps you've gained my powers in some other form."

"You think that since Caliborne's powers are of the mind I was better able to absorb them?"

"Perhaps. Your body might be limited in its capabilities, but I daresay your mind is as sharp and powerful as a Gryxen's."

It's then that I remember a moment I've been actively trying to forget since it happened. I remember the feel of blackened fingers wrapping around my neck, lifting me high in the air, and squeezing so hard I can't breathe. The memory makes me rub my throat with a grimace, but then I also remember those fingers losing their grip on me, the frustration on CeCe's face as if her hand was refusing to listen to her, and the thought that slammed through my mind in that moment.

Let. Me. Go!

"Wexton?" I say thoughtfully. "Wexton, stop."

He does. "What is it?"

I wave at the ground, and he slides me off his shoulders back onto my feet.

"Give me your hand," I say.

He wrinkles his brow but offers me his hand regardless.

I take it. "Now squeeze. Not hard, just enough to keep me from pulling my hand away."

He wraps his fingers around my hand, and they're long enough to encompass it entirely. He grips tightly, and I give a test tug to try and take my hand back. It doesn't budge.

I focus on his hand and will it to release me.

At first, nothing changes, but then I feel a twitch from Wexton's fingers just like I felt from CeCe's.

What…?

I keep focusing.

Wexton's fingers start to relax.

"That feels… unsettling," Wexton says. "It's as if my muscles aren't strong enough to hold on to you." The muscles in his upper arm bulge as he tries to squeeze my hand again, but his grip only gets looser until I'm able to pull free with a small shout of victory. Wexton flexes his fingers, balling them into a tight fist. "What did you do?"

"I just kept picturing your hand letting me go," I say with a shrug.

Wexton grasps my hand. "Do it again."

We repeat the process twice more, and each time, Wexton grunts and strains as he attempts to maintain control, but each time, his grip relaxes against his will.

"Weakness," he says in awe. "You didn't gain strength from me. You gained the ability to inflict weakness! Or rather, you strip strength instead."

I look at my hand. "Caliborne can send memories and emotions from his mind into someone else's, but I can pull thoughts from other's minds into my own. You have strength, but I can take strength away. It's as if I've gained the *reverse* of both your powers."

Wexton tilts his head then nods. "It seems so."

"Is that what usually happens with a mating bond?"

"I'm not sure. I just know sometimes powers are shared between mates." He touches my chin. "I knew you had to have gotten something from me."

"It saved my life. I used it without even knowing it. The day she attacked us, I made CeCe drop me."

"I wondered what made her do that." He looks away. "I thought maybe some sliver of who she used to be made her realize what she was doing in that moment, like a brief flash of sanity. I can't decide if it makes me feel worse or better to know she was already truly gone that day."

I touch his arm. "I'm sorry," I say quietly. "I shouldn't have brought it up."

He smiles sadly at me. "Nonsense. It happened. There's no point pretending it didn't. I just wish… I wish I'd told her we were family. I mean, she was already family to me, but I regret not telling her I knew Caliborne was my father."

"She knew," I say with certainty. "Or at least, some part of her did."

"You think so?"

"She grew up with you, Wexton. You said yourself Caliborne's family took you in like you were already one of their own. You think Caliborne's mother didn't know he had a child with her friend? You don't think that's why they included you in everything they did? They knew. And if they didn't, it didn't matter, because they loved you all the same."

He sniffles, avoiding my eyes, then he nods and kneels down in the grass, patting his shoulder again. "Come on. We should get moving."

I climb back up on his shoulders and point off to our right. "Head down that little hill there. There's a creek that runs through a small gully at the bottom. We'll follow that down into the lower pastures to my fishing spot."

"What sorts of fish do you catch down here?" Wexton asks as he starts down over the hill. I can hear the creek gurgling in the distance.

"Chub mostly, though I've caught the occasional perch, which made my mother much happier since they're easier to fillet. I actually think chub are tastier, but that's just me."

"Is fish something humans have to cook like other meats in order to eat it?"

"You don't have to, no, but not everyone likes it raw. I like it baked. Papa likes it pan-fried. I remember Will's mother used to make the most delicious fish I've ever tasted. She made this sauce I used to lick off my plate it was so good."

Wexton laughs. "How unladylike."

"You have no idea."

Wexton steps carefully down the steepest section of the hillside and splashes down into the creek. Rather than cross to the flatter shore, he wades through the water downstream.

"How far?" he asks.

"Just around that far bend there. There's a large flat rock on the shore I like to sit on. The back pasture is through these trees, and Will and I used to build a fire at the edge of it, near the tree line. We'd spend all day out here, catching fish, roasting them over the fire, and eating them right off the sticks."

Wexton lifts his head and sniffs. "I smell smoke. I think someone has a fire built there right now."

"It must be Papa. Oh, I hope he brought my pole. It would be nice to catch a few before we go home."

"You should bring it back with you. The pond has fish, though I don't know what kinds."

"I bet Fenmire knows."

We both laugh, because of course he does.

We round the bend and find my rock on the bank. There's a footpath through the trees behind it that leads to the pasture, though I have to duck my head as we walk up it since the trees here are thicker and their lower branches threaten to knock me off Wexton's shoulders. When we break through the tree line, we find a fire ring made of stones Will and I placed in another life. There are large logs set around the ring for seating, and on top of one sits my father with one leg crossed over the other, a piece of straw in his mouth, and a stick in his hand he's using to stir up the fire he's built in the ring. He jumps from his seat when he sees us with an excited wave that nearly brings tears to my eyes.

Gods, do I love this man and his unconditional love.

"Let me down, Wexton," I request, and he immediately kneels and guides me to the ground.

I run to my father and giggle with glee like a child many years younger when he scoops me into a tight hug.

"You came," he says with relief.

"I did. And I brought someone with me like last time."

I turn and wave Wexton closer, who's stayed at a distance until now. My father, to his credit, doesn't back away when Wexton approaches, though he does tense a little at my side.

"Papa, this is Wexton. Wexton, I'd like you to meet my father."

"How do you do?" Wexton asks.

My father jumps. "Oh, this one speaks."

"Does he ever," I mutter.

Wexton winks at me.

My father takes one tentative step closer and holds out his hand.

Wexton takes it, and he moves as slow and gentle as I've ever seen him.

"You look quite a bit different from the one I met before," Papa says.

Wexton smiles. "Right you are. I'm much more handsome."

Papa barks with laughter.

I can't get the silly grin off my face at the sight.

"Did you have any trouble getting away?" I ask once introductions are complete.

"I told your mother I'm spending the day fishing. I even packed a lunch so she wouldn't come down here to bring me one."

"So you can stay even after…?"

He nods. "We have all day."

I hug him again. "I'm selfishly glad for your white lies. I've missed you."

"What white lies?" He pulls away with a smirk on his face and reaches behind the log he was sitting on, producing both our fishing poles. "I fully plan to spend the day by the water."

I laugh with delight as I take my pole. "You read my mind."

Papa turns to Wexton. "Care to help us find some bait?"

"I'd love to," Wexton replies. "Um… How do I do that, exactly?"

Under Papa's guidance, Wexton lifts old logs and rocks for us to dig under until the old tin Papa brought is full of wriggling bait. Papa and I sit side by side on my flat rock and slide the fattest of the worms on our hooks.

"I would have brought a pole for you too," Papa says to Wexton, "but we've only got the pair."

"I don't need one," Wexton says. He wades into the water, to the deepest spot nearby, then he goes still, though his eyes continuously flick back and forth, searching the water. All of a sudden, he slams his hand in the water and pulls it back out again a second later with a fat chub caught in his fist.

I clap and cheer when Wexton holds up his catch. "That was amazing!"

"It was," Papa agrees. "Though I fear we'll catch very little ourselves if you scare the rest away."

"It was a one-time performance, promise," Wexton says as he wades back to the shore. He sits in the dirt beside our rock and promptly bites the head off his fish, crunching away until he catches us staring. "What?"

"You eat those bones and all?" Papa asks.

"Bones, scales, eyes…" He takes another bite and shrugs. "It's all good eating."

Papa gives me a perplexed look then casts his line. "Waste not, want not, I suppose."

I cast my own line before leaning my head against Papa's shoulder.

He puts his arm around me and kisses the top of my head. "I miss you, kid."

"We have today, Papa," I say as our cork floats bob softly side by side in the water. "Let's make the best of it."

Chapter 48

Papa, Wexton, and I spend the morning fishing and the early afternoon sitting around the fire as we humans roast our catches and the Gryxen cracks jokes. My father ends up laughing so hard tears fill his eyes. Once the fish are cooked, I give Wexton a bite of mine to try, and though he admits the seasonings Papa brought in a drawstring pouch are nice, he still insists he prefers them raw.

As dinner time rolls around, the sky begins to darken, and Papa looks up at it with a frown.

"You better get going soon," he says. "It looks like it might rain, and your mama will be hollering for me to come get cleaned up any minute."

"Do you mind if I take my fishing pole with me?" I ask.

"It's your pole," he says, handing it over. "You don't gotta ask my permission."

Leaving Papa behind kills me, but I know he's better off here. This farm is his home. It always was and always will be. My home is in The Deadwood, in the arms of the demons who've captured my heart. Our worlds are just too different, but that's alright. I'll cross over into his as often as I can to see him.

As if reading my thoughts, Papa asks, "You can come back next week, right?"

"I'll try my best."

"Do bring this one back sometime," he says with a pat on Wexton's arm. "It's been too long since I've laughed like this."

Wexton bows his head. "It would be my pleasure."

"Your lot have better manners than some humans I know."

"From what Eve has told us of your village, that's not hard to believe at all."

Papa frowns. "They're mostly good people. They're just scared. We're all used to following the head of our church's example. No one is willing to stand up against Elias, though I've heard several others have stopped going to church, so perhaps something is brewing. I hope so."

"I will pray your people see sense soon," Wexton says.

Papa nods. "Appreciate that, friend."

I hug my father. "Goodbye. Be safe."

"You too. I'll see you next week. Hopefully."

Wexton and I wave at the tree line before heading back down the footpath. We stop at my rock so I can climb up on Wexton's shoulder before we start wading back up the creek.

We don't even make it to the edge of The Deadwood before it starts to rain. At first, it's just a light drizzle, but by the time we're back in the waist-high grass beside the twisted brambles of our home, it's pouring. Wexton curves one wing up over his back like an umbrella to shield me from the worst of it, but by the time we arrive at the arch, I'm soaked anyway. Wexton lets me down, but when I head for the arch, he takes my hand and tugs me to a stop.

"What is it?" I ask.

He smirks at me. "I believe we had plans for something special in this very spot." He motions to the grass nearby where we lay looking at the stars after rescuing Will.

"But… it's raining."

He shrugs. "We're already wet."

I bite my lip. The temptation to let him have his way with me right here in the grass and the rain is overwhelming. But it's broad daylight. I couldn't.

Could I?

Wexton's eyes twinkle with mischief, and when I smile, he growls a little as he flops down into the wet grass on his back.

He motions me closer with the bend of a finger. "I want you to get over here, straddle my head, and sit that delicious cunt on my face."

It's amazing that his dirty mouth still has such an effect on me. My heart instantly starts to race, and my stomach jumps up into my throat even as a jolt of pure lust shoots straight for my groin, making me clench my thighs.

"How will you breathe?" I ask even as I come closer. I can't help it. I'm drawn to his every dirty thought as if they're my own.

"Don't worry about that. All I want you to think about is riding my face until you come on it."

"Jesus Christ, Wexton," I mutter as I step up beside his head.

He reaches out, grabs me by one ankle, and tugs, guiding my foot over his head until I'm straddling him. Thunder rumbles in the distance.

He reaches up under my dress and tears my panties to shreds until they fall off in the grass. "Now sit down so I can feast."

I toss my fishing pole in the grass and lower myself onto him, and he guides me down so my most sensitive bits are right where he wants them. He hums with delight, and the vibration makes me bite my lip against a moan. With my legs parted around his head, I'm spread wide open for him, and he takes full advantage, bathing me with his tongue and suckling my clit with a vengeance. He can't talk with me sitting on his face like this, but his thoughts are as dirty as his mouth has ever been.

I could die happy right here with your sweet cunt dripping all over me. It weeps for me like this. Pump your hips. Fuck yourself on my tongue. His tongue thrusts deep inside me.

"Wexton," I whimper. I move my hips, driving myself down onto his stiff tongue. I tip my head back, letting the rain cool the flush on my face. A flash of lightning cuts across the sky and is followed a second or two later by a loud crack of thunder.

Do you like riding my face, darling? Next time, I'll turn you around and eat from that other hole instead.

I'm moaning with every pump of my hips now. I move faster. He presses his tongue against a spot deep inside me that makes me cry out. Every strand of hair on my body stands on end, and my limbs start to tingle.

Come for me.

I yell his name in release just as a bolt of lightning strikes the halfway tree beside us. The deafening crack of thunder and breaking wood covers up my screams as I come and cry out his name again and again. Fire begins lapping up the tree.

I want to sink my cock into you.

I push myself up off his face with shaking legs. He sits up so abruptly he knocks me backward, but he catches me with his arm looped behind my back and lowers me to his lap.

"Lie back down," I say.

"Why?"

"I'm not done riding you."

He raises a brow but does as I ask with that familiar cocky smile on his face.

I straddle him again, work open his pants, and sink down onto his hard cock, taking his thicker shaft as deep inside me as I can. When I start moving, I reach down and press his smaller one against me so that it rubs my clit harder than ever. It's already sensitive from my previous orgasm, and the friction makes my legs shake violently.

Wexton bucks his hips, ramming his cock inside me.

I cry out in surprise, but then I angle my hips and plant my hands on his chest.

"Do it again," I demand.

He starts pumping into me from below at the same time I rock my hips in time with his thrusts. He's so deep and ramming inside me so hard it hurts, but in a way that drives me crazy. I dig my nails into his chest until he hisses.

Start saying my name and don't stop until you come again.

"Wexton," I say, and at first, it's barely more than a whisper. But as our furious lovemaking continues, my voice gets more and more carnal and desperate until I end up screaming his name with every slam of him inside me. A few prayers join the mix along with a swear word or two until my entire body stiffens and shakes from head to toe as I come again, and this time, no amount of thunder or lightning in this world could drown out my screams.

My turn.

"Wha—whoa!"

I'm suddenly flipped over onto my back in the tall grass with a demon hovering over me.

Wexton taps one of my knees. "Spread those legs nice and wide for me, would you, darling?"

I giggle as I oblige, and the feel of the rain and the breeze on all my private places when I hike up my dress makes me feel like a complete vixen.

I love it.

Wexton takes one of my feet in his hand and kisses my ankle, then my calf, then the side of my knee, working his way slowly northward while never breaking eye contact.

You're so fucking beautiful it hurts.

"Oh, Wexton," I say with a sigh.

Grab your legs at the knees and pull them up toward your chest.

I do as he asks, and he gives me a mischievous wink before leaning down and pressing his slick, wicked tongue against my ass until my body opens up and lets him inside.

A flaming branch on the halfway tree breaks off and lands with a crash in the grass, sending up a cloud of bright red embers that hiss in the rain and light the twilight sky behind Wexton with a fiery glow. He's never looked more like a being from hell while his tongue brings me nothing but sinful pleasure. He's impossibly deep inside me in a place I never dreamt anyone would ever touch, much less a demon. And I've had *two* inside me there now.

Someday, I'll fill this hole with my seed as well.

I reach down and grab him by the hair, pulling his head up until his eyes meet mine.

"Why don't you fill the other in the meantime," I say breathlessly.

He grins at me. "Pull it harder and say that with more bite."

I yank his hair so hard a small snarl escapes him, and that makes my heart beat wildly in my chest, spurring me on as I hiss between gritted teeth, "Fuck me and come inside me, now!"

He doesn't need told twice. Wexton grabs one of my legs, shoves it up higher, and thrusts inside me. His eyes bore into mine as his hips buck hard and fast and his breaths puffing out in ragged gasps.

"Now!" I yell sternly.

His fingers tighten on my leg so hard they'll leave bruises, and he stops breathing entirely as he slams himself to the hilt inside me. His entire body quivers, then he gasps as the heat of his seed fills me. He collapses down on his arm, blocking me from the rain as he captures my mouth in a deep, passionate kiss he only breaks to catch his breath. His face smells like my arousal, and it's glistening from more than just rain.

"Good boy," I murmur.

He laughs and nuzzles my nose. "That was even better than I imagined." He looks over at the tree and startles. "Shit. Did we do that?"

"Not unless you can control the weather."

Someone shouts in the distance, and I spin around to look up the road. Several people on horseback are heading our way followed by a cart loaded with rain barrels. They must be coming to put out the fire so it doesn't spread.

"Time to go," Wexton says, then he hops up, buttons up his pants, and grabs my hand, yanking me up on my feet as well.

I can see the rider leading the group more clearly now. It's Elias. Out of pure pettiness and spite, I wave to him before snatching up my fishing pole and dashing to the arch, hand in hand with my demon lover who laughs and spins me under his arm as if we're dancing as we step through the vines. I laugh too once we're safely back within The Deadwood.

"I would've loved to see the look on his face," I say gleefully.

"The only face I concern myself with is yours," Wexton replies.

I smile and shake my head at him, but with a bend of a finger, I urge him down to one knee in front of me and put my arms around his neck, kissing him just as deeply as I did before we were interrupted as the rain continues to pour down on us both. When I pull away, I touch his lips with one finger.

"Oh, how I love this mouth," I say softly. "Such sweet and naughty things come out of it."

He pulls me closer. "Those words are for you and you alone from this day forward, Eve. You're my mate, and you'll be my only one. I've no desire to ever show another the affection I wish to shower on you for the rest of my life."

I laugh to keep from crying and kiss him again.

We both jump when a body lands beside us with a slam. It's Caliborne.

He strokes a thumb down my wet cheek. *I've been watching for you. I didn't want you to have to walk in the rain.*

The air has grown uncomfortably chilly now that the sun is setting, so I reach for him eagerly, and he scoops me into his warm arms.

"Race you home?" I say to Wexton.

His wings jolt out to either side of him, crushing the vines and brambles that get in the way. "You're on."

There's no countdown as Caliborne immediately launches into flight, but that doesn't save us as Wexton quickly overtakes us and lands at the castle's front doors a good ten seconds before we do. He's as smug about that as one would expect as Caliborne carries me inside, insisting he take me downstairs to the bathing pool right away to warm up as I'm now shivering in his arms.

I spend the rest of the evening bathing with my mates and recounting my day to Caliborne over supper until it's time to bid Wexton goodnight as he leaves for his patrol. As Caliborne and I are heading to bed, Fenmire comes in the castle front doors, stopping just inside to shake the rain from his wings. He sees us, and before I follow Caliborne into the bedroom, Fenmire catches my eye and gives me a wink, reminding me, no doubt, that he has plans for me for the next day.

I smirk back at him.

I have plans for him as well.

Chapter 49

I keep Fenmire waiting as long as possible the next morning as I take my sweet time dressing, seeing Caliborne off, and eating my breakfast. I even linger in the kitchen to talk to Levi and the others for a few minutes before finally relenting and heading for the stables, where I find Fenmire leaned casually against the door of the elk's pen, absentmindedly scratching the animal's nose as he reads from one of his books. When he hears my footsteps, he glances up, cocking one brow as he snaps the book shut.

"It seems someone took the bait of my dare," he says. "You humans are so predictable."

"Are you saying you *wanted* me to disobey you?"

He smirks. "There is pleasure to be found in disobedience from time to time."

I don't know what he means by that, but I have a feeling he'll show me very soon.

"How were your plans with Wexton yesterday?" Fenmire asks, and one of his brows bobs just a bit.

I smirk at him. "Just fine, thank you."

"You realize I know what the two of you were up to, don't you?"

"No, I never would have guessed you'd have the slightest idea," I reply with sarcasm dripping from every word.

Fenmire narrows his eyes and smacks his lips, but I can tell he's fighting a smile by the little dimple that appears in his cheek. "Are you ready to go?"

"Where are we going?"

"To talk to The Gate."

"Oh." I try my best not to sound disappointed, but Fenmire hears it in my voice anyway.

"Don't worry, pet, I fully plan to make good on my promise for making me wait."

I smile. "Good."

He shakes his head as he ushers me out the stable door into the sunshine.

"I brought this," he says, showing me his book. It's the one he had me read about everything we know about The Gates. "There are plenty of blank pages left to take notes."

"What am I supposed to ask it?"

"Anything you want. We still don't know how they were created, when, or by whom. Thanks to you, we now know they have conscious thought, but have they always had that, or was there evolution over time? Can they all communicate with each other? What determines when and where they are created? How—"

I laugh. "Why don't I let you ask the questions and I'll report back the answers?"

Fenmire nods thoughtfully. "That may save us some time." He's silent for a moment then shakes his head and peers around at the trees. "Would you like to walk or fly?"

I look up at the bright, beautiful sun and close my eyes as the heat of it kisses my face. I'm dressed in light pants and a thin, billowy shirt that lets the breeze ripple pleasantly through the fabric. "Let's walk."

It's not nearly as far to The Gate as it is to the arch. We walk through The Deadwood, picking our way through trees and around patches of underbrush and veils of vines for about thirty minutes. At one point, I catch my foot on a tree root and almost fall flat on my face, but Fenmire catches me.

"Seems you're not very good at hiking through the forest," Fenmire comments.

"Can't say I've had much experience trekking through this place in my lifetime," I reply.

As he sets me back on my feet, I barely catch it as he mutters a single word under his breath. "Pity."

Why is it a pity that I'm no good at hiking? I almost ask the question out loud but choke it back at the last second. As with anything with Fenmire, I'm sure he won't tell me the answer, but he'll show me eventually if he wants me to know.

We arrive at the clearing and cross the open space, taking a moment to stop and pay respects to CeCe before approaching The Gate. The simple circle of plain stones is still a shock to me. Such an ordinary sight for such an extraordinary phenomenon.

"Check that it's safe for us to be here," Fenmire says.

I kneel and touch one of the stones.

Hello again.

"Hello. Will there be any surprises coming through anytime soon?"

The creatures Reilanna sends now are different. They possess power of their own. They take more effort on my part to send here, so it takes longer to recover after each one sent. I won't be strong enough to send the next for several more days. If, however, she chooses to send one of the mindless beasts she did before, I have the ability to do that now.

I swallow and relay this information to Fenmire.

"Can it warn us before something comes through?" Fenmire asks.

I will alert you should Reilanna head this way.

"Great," Fenmire says cheerfully once I repeat The Gate's words. He opens his book, flips through a couple of pages, then looks at me. "Ready?"

"Do you mind if we ask you some questions?" I ask the stones. "Since I'm the first to be able to communicate with you, there's a lot we can learn."

You are by no means the first to communicate with me, human, but you may ask your questions.

"Oh… It says I'm not the first."

Fenmire stares in shock, his pencil poised, unmoving, on his paper. "Does it mean you're not the first to communicate with *this* Gate, or…?"

The Gate laughs in my head, and the sound is odd in its grainy, rock tumbling voice. *He suspects correctly. My thoughts are not solely tied to this gateway. I am a collective consciousness shared across the universe with every Gate between every world.*

When I tell Fenmire this, he breaks from his stupor and starts writing frantically in his book. "How old is it?"

That is not a number either of you can comprehend. I have watched the birth of every living species that has ever existed. And I've watched the extinction of most of them as well.

"Who created you?" I ask.

No one. I was born of… necessity. Curiosity. Energy. I'm not entirely sure. One day, I merely was. My earliest memory is of a bright light and heat, like an explosion, then suddenly, I had thought, and I had will, but I was alone.

I sit next to the stone, and Fenmire wanders over and follows suit, plopping down in the grass beside me with his legs crossed and his book open on one knee.

"You were born before any other living creature?" Fenmire asks.

Yes.

"Are you a god?" I ask.

No. Gods are born and grow powerful through the masses who worship them. At the time my powers were born, there was no one alive to worship me.

"Why did you start placing gateways between worlds?" Fenmire asks.

The universe is a lonely place, winged one. I should know. I spent an eternity in it before the first breath of life was taken. So many worlds hold intelligent life but believe they are alone in the great expanse. My gateways are meant to alleviate that feeling.

"You wanted to connect people," I say.

Yes. Once a species is advanced enough to ask if they are alone amongst the stars, I answer their question.

"What if they never ask?"

They always ask, sooner or later.

"How do you decide which worlds connect with which?" Fenmire asks.

Compatibility. Life that relies on oxygen, for example, can only be connected with worlds that contain such a thing. Worlds that contain poisons can't be connected to ones that would be harmed by such substances, but if another world flourishes with those same toxins, they can be connected.

"But what about the people?" I ask. "What happens if the creatures from these connected worlds don't get along?"

That has happened, I will admit, but I don't let it stop me. There are such risks to every connection made between living beings, even within their own species. Two cities joined by a road may some day go to war, but that's not the road's fault.

"Yes, well," Fenmire says rather stiffly, "roads are usually built at the will of the creatures who travel them. *You* choose where to place the gates without input from the ones they will affect."

I try my best to make connections where I think the worlds' beings can coexist peacefully. Similar civilizations and values are the goal. It usually works out fine, in the end. Many form lasting bonds of allyship and cooperation. They trade, they love, they mingle. That tends to be the natural state of life, in my experience.

"What about beings like Reilanna? How often do things like this happen?"

Not often. Reilanna is a special breed of evil I've experienced only a few times in my existence.

Fenmire snorts with a nod of agreement as he continues taking notes. "Am I correct in assuming you are omnipresent?"

You are.

"Can you read people's thoughts?"

I can not see into others' minds. I can only hear those thoughts they choose to speak aloud. You would be surprised how many thoughts are not kept private.

"What about gods? Can you see and hear them too?"

No. I see them when they choose to interact with the beings who worship them, but when they are not in direct contact with the living, they disappear from my sight.

"Have any of them spoken to you directly?"

Never. I believe they fear me, or at least they are wary. They mostly ignore me.

"Do you worship any of them?" I ask out of pure curiosity.

I have no need to worship. I know of them and believe in their existence, but I never will my thoughts to their ears.

"How many gateways do you command?" Fenmire asks.

Countless. The number constantly changes as connections are made and broken.

"Broken? Gates disappear?"

Not disappear. They are removed. Once one or both worlds connected by my gateways no longer contains intelligent life, I sever the connection between them. The Gates are meant to connect the living, after all, and life is constantly born and extinguished with every passing moment. My pathways are constantly in motion, shifting between worlds to join new life as the old dies away.

"That's sort of beautiful," I say.

I think so too.

Fenmire's pencil goes still, and he frowns. "If we asked you to sever the connection between this world and ours, would you?"

Reilanna controls this gateway. There is nothing I can do to stop her, or I would have already.

"I don't mean it as a way to stop Reilanna; I mean after."

My stomach does a nervous little flip. "That would make it so you could never go back. Or do you mean...?" The thought of my Gryxen disappearing through The Gate back into their world and leaving me here with no way to ever see them again makes my mouth dry.

"It's just a question," Fenmire says quietly. "I don't mean that we'd actually do it."

It makes little difference what you meant, winged one. I would not remove this gateway simply because you asked. Just like a city would never remove a road for one citizen. The one does not choose for the many.

"But the many don't know they have a choice."

It's not their choice at all. It's mine. The Gate stays.

Fenmire purses his lips, but he goes back to writing without further comment.

We sit here for another thirty minutes or so as Fenmire starts to ask more specific questions on how exactly the gateways work, the specific process of transferring a living being from one place to another. There are even a few equations thrown in the mix that I don't understand yet, and one even stumps Fenmire, who asks The Gate to repeat it three times in order to get it written down correctly. Fenmire's questions run out as he's absorbed in his notes, and he starts mumbling to himself as he starts working the numbers.

I decide to ask a few questions of my own. "If I asked you to, could you send me to a different world through this gateway instead of the Gryxen homeworld?"

No. This path only connects your worlds.

"Is it true that the universe is always expanding?"

Yes. New life is constantly born at the edges of existence, pushing it farther and farther. New worlds are created through violent explosions that send out seeds of matter that eventually grow into new planets, though it takes a long time for them to sustain life, if they ever do.

"Where's the closest world with intelligent life?"

Far, far away, human. The distance is incalculable.

That answer makes me sad, though only briefly, but for that split second, I can understand why The Gate chose to connect us all.

"Are you still lonely?"

With this question, The Gate spends a quiet moment considering before it responds. *No. I am in the company of an infinite number of beings at all times. I am no longer alone and never will be again.*

"Do you have a name?"

I have so many it would fill your lover's book hundreds of times over.

"Do you have a favorite?"

Another quiet moment of reflection passes, and then it says, *I do not. I have no favored name because I have no favored beings. I value all life the same, and thus I treasure each name they give me equally.*

"I wish we could all love like you."

Love?

"Of course. It was love that made you want to bring us all together, wasn't it? You didn't want us to suffer the loneliness you experienced in your early years, so you made sure we were never alone. That sounds like something one of my mates would do for me."

The Gate doesn't respond.

"Did I offend you?"

I take no offense. But you are unlike any human I've met before.

"Have you spoken to other humans in the past?"

Yes.

It doesn't elaborate, and I don't ask it to.

Fenmire snaps his book shut. "Well, this has certainly been enlightening." He peers down at the stone still under my hand. "Do you mind if I share this knowledge? A book like this hasn't been published in my lifetime, nor, I daresay, in many that came before mine."

The Gate chuckles. *Publish your books, winged one. Write my tale. It will be interesting to watch your kind's reaction.*

The smile that stretches across Fenmire's face is one of pure delight and excitement. He looks up at me. "Are we done, or do you have more questions?"

"I can't think of anything else right now."

Fenmire stands and offers me a hand.

"Thank you for speaking with us," I say to the stone.

It's my pleasure, human. Do come back and entertain me with your inquiries again in the future.

"Knowing Fenmire, that's pretty much a certainty."

The last thing I hear is stony laughter before I take my hand away and take Fenmire's, who pulls me up onto my feet. One of my legs is asleep, so I hop around a bit to bring back the blood flow, wincing as my foot fills with little needles.

"Did you get everything you wanted?" I ask.

"I think so. It's hard to believe some of it, but I suppose it makes sense that something as powerful as The Gates would be controlled by something primordial. I'm not sure I entirely agree with its methods, but who am I to disagree with something that's been around since the dawn of time?"

I chuckle incredulously. "Fenmire, you'd disagree with a god with nary a qualm and likely tell them so to their face if given the chance."

Fenmire snorts. "Perhaps."

We begin our trek back through the trees toward home, but we go just far enough that the clearing is out of sight before Fenmire stops and turns to me. I stop with a raised brow, glancing around at the surrounding thickets and vines for what caused him to pause.

"Is something wrong?" I ask.

"You kept me waiting this morning," he says, and his tone is deadly though his lips perk up into a half smirk. His eyes narrow a bit and slide up and down my body like a hungry beast sizing up his prey. "I believe I warned you not to do that, didn't I?"

Though I know I'm in no real danger, my pulse quickens anyway. "You did," I say, tilting my chin up stubbornly. I cross my arms. "What do you plan to do about it?"

The laugh that bubbles out of him sounds more like a growl, and he leans closer, stooping so we're face to face. "I'm going to give you five minutes to run as far and as fast as you can," he murmurs. "Then I'm going to come after you. If I catch you, *when* I catch you, I'll hold you down across my lap, bare your backside, and take a switch to it. Once I feel you've learned your lesson, I'm going to… Well, perhaps we'll leave the rest as a surprise."

I swallow as my face heats. "What if you don't catch me?"

He smiles. "Something tells me you would be very disappointed if that happened."

I bite my lip to keep from smiling back. "Is this why you said it's a pity I'm not a better hiker?"

"I prefer a bit of a challenge. It gets the blood flowing." He straightens his shoulders and loses his smile as he turns suddenly serious. "It goes without saying, but say it I will, regardless: if you tell me to stop, it's done, no questions asked."

"I know." I've never felt anything but safe with Fenmire, and now is no exception. This new game he's proposing may be carnal, but it's something I've imagined for quite some time, and I want nothing more than to play.

Fenmire leans down, tips up my chin, and kisses me on the lips in his usual hard and demanding way, then he whispers, "Run, pet."

I turn and flee into the trees.

Chapter 50

At first, I pick my way somewhat carefully through the trees, around clumps of bushes, and over fallen logs, but as time ticks by, I imagine what it would feel like to run from a true beast, one with a hunger for my flesh. Safe inside the game Fenmire has created for us, I let myself become prey and pretend I'm truly afraid for my life. Eventually, my body reacts as if that fear is real, and when adrenaline kicks in, I run more frantically. My breaths puff out in painful gasps as I leap and weave, and thorny brambles scrape across my clothes, grabbing at me like the night I ran from Caliborne. I try to remember how terrified I was then, and I tell myself I can't let the beast catch me or he'll do unthinkable things to me.

My heart hammers from far more than fear.

Suddenly, a terrifying, snarling howl erupts from deep in The Deadwood behind me. I stop to catch my breath as the sound sends a chill down my spine.

I'm officially being hunted.

With a small yelp, I start running again and reach a grove of trees so thick I doubt Fenmire could maneuver between them. I pause in the small shelter they provide, listening intently. I don't hear anything, and somehow that's worse than hearing the clomp of heavy footsteps in the underbrush or giant wings flapping overhead. I don't know where he is, how close he's come, how accurately he's tracking me. He could be right behind me, his fangs inches from the back of my head, just waiting for me to turn around. I whirl, scared by my own imagination, but there's nothing there but more trees.

I move on and come across a small stream. I try to jump over it only to splash down into a couple inches of mud and water on the other side. Thank the gods I chose to wear pants today. Moving around, under, and over the thick trees and logs and keeping myself from getting snagged in the thorny underbrush would've been much harder in a dress. I'm about to take off running again when I pause and look down at the little gurgling stream.

My feet are already wet, and the water could help cover my tracks for a while. I'm not even sure if Fenmire's tracking me by footprints or if he's following my scent, but I decide to give myself the best chance to lose him and wade back into the stream, right into the middle where the water has washed away the leaves and dirt to create a somewhat rocky bed. I wander and splash up the stream for maybe a hundred feet or so then wade up onto the opposite shore again, trying my best to avoid the mud and step up onto dry, solid land where I'm less likely to leave a footprint.

Another howl, much closer this time, rises up in the distance, only it's in front of me now instead of behind. I stand there in confusion for a moment. Did I get turned around or did he fly over me at some point? I hop the stream again and run back in the other direction.

I'm starting to run out of energy, and I have to slow my pace to keep from tripping over obstacles I was leaping over just moments ago. My breathing is so labored I fear he'll hear me long before I hear or see him. I slow even further to bring it back under control.

A loud snap of a branch off to my left makes me stop and listen. I can't tell how far away the sound was, but I don't see anything. Was it an animal?

Or is it the beast who means to bend my body to his will when he catches me?

I swallow down the moan that thought threatens to unleash and start walking again, as quietly as I can. I dart from tree to tree, bush to bush, seeking cover and stopping to listen every minute or so.

A snarling growl makes all the hairs on my arms stand up.

He's just on the other side of a thick grove of trees ahead of me.

I duck down behind the thickest trunk and cover my mouth with my hand to keep from panting as my heart kicks into overdrive.

"Evaaaan," Fenmire calls in a sing-song voice. "I will find you, pet. And when I do, I'm going to bend you over the nearest stump and take everything I want."

I inch backward and try to turn and head in the opposite direction, but my boot hits a tree root with a loud thump.

Knowing my cover has been blown, I take off running, but I don't go very far before I find another hiding place—a fallen log—and duck down as far as I can.

A second later, the ground shakes as a heavy body lands on the other side of the log a few yards away.

I close my eyes and focus on breathing as quietly as I can through my mouth. I'm shaking from adrenaline, and it's hard to resist the urge to run again. I can hear his footsteps now, and it sounds like he's getting closer.

"Where are you, pet?" Fenmire asks, and his voice is low and growly. "The longer you run, the redder your ass will be when I'm through with you."

I squeeze my eyes shut and stifle a groan.

"I'll snap a switch off the nearest tree, something nice and flexible so I can leave a welt or two. Don't worry, though, I'll make you beg for it first."

His voice is getting quieter as he moves away, and eventually I don't hear his footsteps at all anymore. When I think I'm in the clear, I peek over the log. I don't see him anywhere, so I slowly stand up from my hiding place, throw a leg over the log, and attempt to hop over and head back toward the grove of trees. Just as my foot touches the ground on the other side and I lean over, a voice from above makes me scream and jump so hard I fall over the log onto my back on the ground.

"There you are."

Fenmire is perched about halfway up a tree to my right. How he managed to get up there and move around behind me again without making a sound, I don't know. I have no chance to recover myself before he leaps down off the tree and slams into the ground, pinning me on my back beneath him with an arm on either side of my head. He leans down until his face is nearly touching mine.

"What a naughty little pet," he says. "Shall I show you who you belong to so you never forget again?"

I'm at a loss for what to say. The temptation to stoke his ire is overwhelming, but I'm not sure what things said here are to be taken at face value or as a part we're both playing in this game. I swallow and try three times to find the right words, but I'm frozen in indecision between what Evan would say in this moment and what prey would say to the predator who finally caught them.

"Come now, pet," Fenmire murmurs, and he takes my chin in his hand hard enough to make me squeak. "Show me your claws."

That's all the encouragement I need. "Let me go, you foul beast!"

Fenmire laughs, and it sends a chill down my spine. "I'll let you go once I'm done using you for my pleasure. And right now, it would please me greatly to hear you cry out as I take a switch to your backside for keeping me waiting this morning."

He grabs me by the front of my shirt and hauls me to my feet only to take a seat himself on the fallen log. He draws a length of cord from his pants pocket and puts my wrists together in front of me, tying them together. He strips off my shirt. It gets caught at my wrists, of course, but Fenmire doesn't seem the least bit concerned about that as he leaves the fabric hanging there. I'm topless now, and the breeze kisses my nipples, hardening them. Fenmire pinches one.

I cry out and try to pull away.

He yanks me back and over his lap on my belly. He ties the sleeves of my shirt to one of the thicker branches on the side of the fallen log, locking me in place over his lap unless I want to roll off into the dirt.

"There now," he says. "Are you comfortable?"

I yank my arms up, struggling against the bonds, but not too hard. The last thing I want, after all, is freedom.

Fenmire tugs down my pants, and I still as the breeze hits my bare backside. He strips my pants down to my knees then breaks a branch off the nearest tree. He waves it back and forth a few times, and it makes a whistling sound as it moves through the air.

"Perfect," he says with glee. "Now, beg me to spank your ass."

I jerk and writhe and almost fall out of his lap. He yanks my pants to my ankles then steps on them, wedging his massive foot between mine to hold me in place.

"Now, now," he says. "Manners." He grabs me by the hair but doesn't pull, merely holding it to keep me from moving. "Beg!" he snarls.

I whimper. "P...please."

"Harder."

"Please, Fenmire."

"Please what? You will ask for it, pet. Say the words."

"Please spank me!" I cry, my chest heaving with anticipation and fright. I yelp when the switch lands on my ass, even if the strike wasn't very hard. Yet.

"Again."

"Please spank me."

There's more bite this time when the switch connects, and a slight burn rises up on my skin following the strike.

"Keep going. You will beg after each and every hit until I'm satisfied you've learned your lesson."

So I do. I beg Fenmire to smack my ass with the stick each time, and each time, he hits a little harder. What starts as a slight burn turns downright unbearable until my eyes start to water and I have to wait longer and longer between hits to catch my breath before I can form the words to ask for another. Despite the pain, my body is hot all over, and my thighs clench together against a desire so overwhelming it makes my legs shake. After a while, I realize the pain is fading altogether, which confuses me since the sound of Fenmire's switch hitting my flesh definitely hasn't dulled. A blanket of calm euphoria settles over me, and my voice gets all dreamy as I continue to beg. After a while, I don't even have to think about it, the words roll off my tongue, welcoming the next burst of pain that sends little ripples of pleasure throughout my entire body.

I'm so out of it, it takes me a moment to notice Fenmire has stopped.

He throws the stick away and palms my abused backside, making me jump at the contact.

"Beautiful," he murmurs. His fingers slip lower, between my thighs. "And so wet. Are you ready to feel my cock inside you at last, pet?" One finger slips inside me, and I moan. "I can't wait to feel that heated skin bouncing against my hips as I drive into you over and over."

Fenmire stands and shoves me over the log. The bark flakes and crumbles beneath me, smearing me with dirt and rotten wood as he bends me over. He removes his foot from my pants and yanks one leg and one boot off so he can spread my legs. His hand is still fisted in my hair, holding me down across the log as he steps up behind me. I hear the buckle of his belt and the pop of buttons as he opens his pants.

"Beg for my cock," he orders. "I'd love to stick them both inside you, one in each hole, or perhaps both in your cunt at once, but for now, you'll only get one."

"Please…" I utter. My voice is barely more than a broken whisper, and I don't have the energy for anything else. "I want your cock."

"And I want to fill you with my seed, but you haven't earned that quite yet. Have you earned my cock, pet?" He smacks my ass hard enough to make me whimper. "Want me to fuck you so hard you'll think my cock is splitting you in half?"

"Yes…" I murmur. "Please."

Fenmire plunges two fingers inside me, and I arch my back, opening myself up as much as I can as he fucks me with them, driving them inside me over and over until the wetness of my arousal drips down my inner thigh.

He takes back his fingers and reaches around me, holding them up in front of my face. "Want to know what you taste like?" He wriggles the glistening digits at me. "Open up."

I open my mouth and suck his fingers, tasting myself. My eyes roll up in my head, and I moan, completely enthralled by my carnal desires.

Who is this person sucking their own juices from a demon's fingers? I've never felt as vulnerable nor as free as I am in this moment. I can call this off with a simple word, but all I want is for this wicked creature to make good on his promise.

"Fuck me," I say, and it comes out so desperate and pleading that I don't even recognize my own voice. "Fenmire, please… fuck me."

He laughs again. "There's my pet. So wanton and ready for me." He steps closer, and the head of his cock presses against my opening. I push back against him, craving him inside me, but he pulls back, denying me.

"Please!" I yell in frustration, but then I cry out sharply as he slams into me.

He bucks against me a few times, and my ass burns with each slap of his hips. "Like this?" he asks. "Or like this?"

He grabs my shirt and yanks it so hard it tears in half, freeing me from the branch, then he takes me by the throat as he thrusts inside me so hard I nearly go flying headfirst over the log. I hold the hand at my throat with both of my own, more for balance than actual concern for my safety. He's not squeezing, just holding my neck in his massive grasp as he rams into me from behind, and yet the fact that his strong fingers are wrapped clear around my neck, one twitch away from snapping it like the branch he took from the tree moments ago makes me shudder.

Fenmire's other arm wraps around my belly, and he reaches between my legs to rub my clit as he leans down near my ear.

"Your cunt hugs my cock so perfectly, pet. I can only imagine how good your ass will feel when I fuck that instead."

I'm too wrecked to respond, and Fenmire doesn't wait for me to. He speeds his thrusts and circles my clit faster as his breath huffs against my neck.

"Come for me," he says, and the way his voice breaks in pleasure when he says it is my undoing.

I start to cry as I orgasm. My emotions and body have been pushed to their very limits, and I don't try to hide my response to everything that just happened as I sob and babble and come.

Fenmire shudders and stiffens a second later, and he tightens his grip on my throat enough to make me gasp as he groans in my ear. The little gasps and groans he makes as he twitches from his orgasm enthrall me. "Good, little pet," he says breathlessly. "You did so well." He loosens his grip and slides his cock out of me.

I hiss in pain. My sex is swollen and sore, and my ass is burning.

"You're alright," Fenmire says softly, and he quickly works the cord loose from my wrists and removes it along with my ruined shirt. He frees my other leg from my pants and boot as well then hauls me up into his arms. He walks away from the log and finds a spot not far away that's flat and open and sits with me in his lap, facing him.

"Breathe with me," he says, and I don't understand why until I try to match his slow and even pace and realize my breaths are coming out in hitched little gasps. I'm still crying as well. He wipes my tears from my cheeks with his thumbs. "You're alright, I promise. Calm down."

It takes a bit, but eventually, my breathing calms and my heart slows, and as the adrenaline fades, a heavy blanket of exhaustion settles over me instead. I end up slumped against Fenmire's chest with my head on his shoulder as he softly pets my hair and whispers sweet words to me.

"How do you feel?" he asks once I stop shaking.

"Tired," I reply, and my tone only supports my answer. "Sore. Hungry."

"All normal. You ran far more than I expected. It took me nearly an hour to find you."

"That long?" It didn't feel like an hour to me.

"Did you enjoy this?"

I smirk. "Yes."

"Good," he says diabolically. "Because now that I've had a taste, I'll always crave the thrill of chasing, catching, and taking you however and whenever I please."

My already ravaged body warms all over again at his wicked words. "You truly are a beast, aren't you?"

"You have no idea."

Chapter 51

Now that the excitement is over and my temperature is returning to normal, the breeze feels chilly on my skin, causing me to shiver in Fenmire's arms.

He urges me off his lap and lies down on his side instead, stretching his wing out across the ground. "Come here," he says, patting his wing.

"Won't that hurt you? Your wings are quite thin, and I wouldn't want to—"

"They're sturdier than they look," he insists with another pat. "Now stop arguing and get down here."

I roll my eyes at him but oblige and lie down across his leathery wing. He rolls close to me and brings his other wing up over us, tucking the edge against my back and pulling the bottoms of both wings together under my feet to create a cocoon. His body heat and soft breath warm the space, and I'm so comfortable I know I'm going to hate getting up to go back to the castle later. I curl up against his chest, and it feels unreal to me that I'm cuddling with Fenmire the same way I do Caliborne and Wexton. I suppose part of me thought we'd never overcome our differences enough for this, but now that I'm here, it feels as natural as it does with my mates.

Or perhaps that's just the aftereffects of what we did together today.

It does feel like something has changed between us, though. I can feel it in his soft touches and the occasional kiss he lays upon my hair. My body hurts in all the places he abused it, and yet I've never felt so cared for.

"Tell me a story?" I request.

"What kind of story?"

"How about another of Seerraf's acolytes? The others said you know those tales well."

Fenmire nods with a small smile. "I likely know them better than most considering I grew up listening to the priestesses repeat them as lessons of morality. 'Doing right isn't always the easiest path, just ask Divnamar,' or 'Sometimes, Seerraf's miracles ask us to give far more than we expect them to. That didn't stop Kliotay, so it shouldn't stop you'."

"Which was the first acolyte?"

"That would be Vorilai."

"Will you tell me Vorilai's story?"

He shifts beside me, getting comfortable on the hard forest floor. He throws his arm over me and places his palm against my backside where it hurts the worst, and as his palm heats with his powers—either to help heal or simply inspect the marks, I'm not sure which—he tells me the tale.

"Vorilai was a temple priestess. She dedicated her life to Seerraf by guarding his holy places and keeping the peace. She was many thousands of years old when a quake struck the city where her temple resided. It was a catastrophic event that leveled a good portion of the city. The rest saw varying levels of damage, but many of the buildings toppled in the minutes and even hours following the great shake.

"One of the buildings that was struck unstable was a school not a block or two away from the temple. The quake struck in the middle of the day, so the building was full of children. The temple priestesses acted quickly, but even so, by the time they arrived, the building was already crumbling. With every passing second, beams fell from ceilings, walls toppled over, glass shattered, and above it all rang the screams of the children still trapped inside.

"Vorilai didn't hesitate as the others did. She ran full speed into the building and called to each living soul inside, searching them out by the sound of their screams through the dust and smoke. Each body she found that was still breathing, she rushed out the front door, then she would dash back inside for the next. She took countless blows from falling debris as well as burns from the spreading fire, but she refused to stop going back into the school and carrying out each child she found as well as several of the teachers.

"Eventually, her luck ran out, and the building gave way, but not before she tossed the last living child through an open second-story window into the arms of another priestess waiting on the ground below. Vorilai was buried alive as the building collapsed on top of her. Her body was pulled from the rubble days later. They say she died when the building fell, a painless and instantaneous death."

When Fenmire falls silent, I ask, "What lesson did the priestesses teach about her story?"

"Perseverance. Vorilai kept pushing back into the rubble though she knew it could fall at any second. Because of her persistence, dozens of children were saved from a tragic fate."

"I can't imagine how scared she was," I whisper.

Fenmire looks down at me. "I don't think she was scared at all. I believe that all she thought in that moment was that those kids needed her. There was no time for fear. Even as the walls caved in around her, all she thought about was getting that last child to safety. The last thing she saw was him passing through a window, and she knew her temple sisters would help him land safely. After that, she felt nothing but peace."

"And then Seerraf named her an acolyte?"

"Yes. A day or two later, Seerraf himself materialized in each of his temples, added a wing, and carved Vorilai's story into the walls. Then he looked to the priestesses and said, 'Make Vorilai's story part of your teachings from this day forward. Make it known that her tale is one we should all look upon with eyes eager to see the impact a single life can have on us all. You've wept, you've prayed, you've sent your thanks. Now study and learn and emulate.' They say he cried."

"Why, do you think?"

Fenmire sighs. "I think he was so very proud to know a soul that pure that he mourned her loss as hard as we did, maybe even harder. Where some gods grow cruel and indifferent toward the beings who worship them, Seerraf has always been deeply involved with and loyal to his followers. He truly loves us all, and to see a bright a star as Vorilai snuffed out made even a god's heart ache."

"Can gods take mates?"

Fenmire seems slightly taken aback by my question as he blinks down at me for a moment. "I don't know. I suppose so, though there are no texts that mention Seerraf's mates if he has any. Why?"

I shrug. "Only curious. If his acolytes meant so much to him, I wonder if he ever considered making them his mates."

Fenmire presses his lips into a thin line and bobs his brows. "Hmm. It's possible, I suppose, though if he has, he's never made it known."

"What was the second acolyte's name?"

"Divnamar. But I think it's *your* turn to tell a story, pet."

"I doubt very much I have any tales worth telling a being who's been alive hundreds of times longer than I have."

"Tell me about the pastor's boy. The one they cast you to The Deadwood for refusing to marry."

I scrunch my face. "Why do you want to know about *him*?"

"You said you refused to marry him because he wanted you to pretend to be something you're not."

"A woman, yes."

"What about you did he find unsavory for a potential spouse?"

"My clothes, my names, my mannerisms, the fact that I go by 'they' instead of 'she'. Elias saw me as a conquest, a beast to be tamed to show the strength of his faith as a man of God and help bolster his image in the village."

Fenmire harumphs. "He didn't want a partner. He wanted a pretty doll to place on his arm. His kind are not tolerated by my kind."

"What do you mean?"

"Men like that, they see their partners as property or slaves. They like obedience and worship and are often vindictive when they're denied either."

"How does your kind deal with such men?"

"The temple priestesses bring them to justice. Allegations of abuse are treated very seriously. Anyone found mistreating partners, spouses, mates, or their children are punished, often quite extensively. Abusing a loved one is considered one of the most heinous things you can do amongst my kind. It's a deep violation of trust and respect that goes against Seerraf's teachings."

"What sorts of punishments do they receive?"

"That depends on the severity of the abuse. Sometimes it's a simple dissolvement of the partnership or marriage with strict orders to stay away from the victim. Other times it's imprisonment for months or even years. But if the abuse is excessively atrocious, especially if it impacts the victim's future quality of life, they may be banished from the city entirely after their imprisonment is over. They also must pay heavy sums of coin to their victim so that they have the best chance to start their life over for the better."

I picture what such a system might have done to Elias after our altercation behind the church and cuddle closer to my demon lover, thankful that, even here on the human side of The Gate, I live by his world's rules now.

"He abused you, didn't he?" Fenmire asks, and though his tone is a quiet one, it's laced with something deadly that makes me shiver. "You don't have to answer if you don't want to."

I consider staying quiet, for what good could come from discussing something that feels so far in my past it's practically part of a different life altogether? But then I remember the tragedy that befell Fenmire's mating bond and how vulnerable he must feel even to have me lying here with him like this. He deserves nothing but the truth.

"Once," I say softly. "Will intervened."

I expect anger, which is usually Fenmire's default emotion, but he surprises me this time by nodding and saying calmly, "I like Will. He seems like the kind of friend you meet only once in a lifetime."

"Yes," I concur. "I don't know that I'd have any sanity left without him."

"I know the feeling."

I look up at him. "Wexton?"

His lips twitch in a grin. "There was a time when I wanted nothing more than to just… cease to be. But on the days when that black cloud of hopelessness and regret threatened to swallow me whole and never let me go, Wexton would burst into my room and declare I looked like shit, and he wouldn't leave until I'd dragged my backside out of bed. No matter the insults I spat at him or the projectiles I threw, he'd simply laugh and tell me to move my ass or he'd carry me out of the room himself. We even traded blows a time or two, and yet he never stopped rescuing me from my own darkness."

"He certainly has a knack for—"

I've always thought the phrase 'speak of the devil and he doth appear' held little truth, but when the very demon who's the topic of discussion lands with a slam a few feet away from us at that moment, I question if the saying carries more weight than that of a simple idiom.

Fenmire and I jump and jerk our heads up to peer out of the gap in Fenmire's wings at the obnoxious, smiling face we both know and love.

"There you two are," Wexton says as he stoops to stare into our leathery cocoon. "I've been flying around looking for you for an hour at least."

"Well, now that you've found us, you can shove off again," Fenmire grumbles.

"Sorry, friend, but no," Wexton replies sweetly. "You absconded with my mate this morning, and they've missed both lunch and dinner. Evan would usually be getting ready to tuck in with Caliborne for the night right about now, and he's done nothing but fret harder and harder the later it's gotten."

"Oh, no," I say miserably. "I didn't mean to worry him. Was he truly upset or—"

"Don't listen to him," Fenmire says with a snort. "Caliborne knows you're safe with me."

"Yes, well," Wexton continues, "you better get them home soon or Caliborne really will take a chunk out of your hide."

"I am pretty hungry," I say apologetically.

"Go home and get Evan a shirt, would you?" Fenmire says with a glance up at Wexton. "I made a mess of the one they were wearing."

"Oh sure," Wexton says, his tone dripping with sarcasm. "You want me to bring you dinner in bed as well?"

Fenmire swipes a rock off the ground and hurls it at him, but Wexton takes flight, and the rock slams into a tree instead. He laughs as he flies away.

"Insufferable ass," Fenmire mutters.

"Yes," I say. "But you love him as much as I do."

Fenmire snorts in exasperation and buries his nose in my neck, breathing deeply. This must please him, because he does it twice more. "You have no idea how long I've imagined what you smell like." He kisses my neck. "What you taste like." He pinches my sore backside, making me yelp. "What you sound like. I confess, I imagined those things long before I had any business doing so."

I touch his face, marveling yet again that I can lie here like this with him and not have him flinch away from me. "I'm sorry about the one who broke your heart before," I whisper as I trace a finger across his lips. "I don't know what's going to happen, in the end, but I promise never to make you regret me."

He seizes my hand with his own and kisses my fingers, my palm, my wrist, then finally my lips, and for the first time, his kiss is soft and gentle and not the least bit demanding as he presses his lips to mine over and over. His arm slides up my back, and his hand buries into my hair, pulling me closer, and yet his kiss doesn't harden. When I open my lips in welcome, his tongue explores my mouth in small, tentative thrusts as if he's afraid to take too much and ruin the moment.

"Evan…" he murmurs, and I hum softly against his lips.

I wrap my leg around his, pulling his hips closer to mine in welcome, but before he can take me up on the offer, a rumbling slam makes us both jump again.

"You two aren't dressed yet?" Wexton asks once the dust from his landing settles. "You better get a move on. I asked Levi to make Evan a plate."

Fenmire groans and rests his forehead against mine.

I laugh and kiss his nose. "Tomorrow," I promise softly.

"Actually… I'm busy tomorrow," he says. "But I'll be around. I'll find you."

The look on his face makes me narrow my eyes, but when Wexton barks again for us to get moving, Fenmire detangles himself from me and sets me up on my feet, effectively squashing the conversation.

Once we're back at the castle, Fenmire bids me good night and disappears upstairs without joining us for a late dinner.

"What's he up to?" I ask as Wexton and I head for the kitchen.

Wexton scoffs. "You realize it's *Fenmire* you're asking that about, right? He could be up to anything from rewriting the same boring tome for the fourth time to… Actually, no, that's more than likely exactly what he's up to."

I laugh and walk with my mate toward the kitchen, eager for a meal to satisfy my grumbling stomach.

Chapter 52

Fenmire is impossible to find the next two days. I'm used to this pattern by now, so it doesn't concern me, though I am a bit nervous, more so than I was with Caliborne and Wexton. What will Fenmire give me for a courting gift? Where will he choose to mark me as his? What power will I get from him, if any at all? But most of all, I think my nerves come from a place of concern for his well-being. This hasn't been easy for him, and now he's about to tie his soul to another when the last one nearly killed him.

I'm terrified I'll hurt him too.

It's a foolish thing to worry about, at least that's what Caliborne and Wexton tell me, but Fenmire means enough to me already that the weight of his heart in my hands makes me question if he's right to trust me with it.

On my way to dinner on the second day, I stop by my room and find a note on my bed, and though the butterflies are definitely still there, I smile at the sight of Fenmire's cramped handwriting when I unfold it.

Come to my room this evening?

I can barely eat my dinner, but I force down every bite to keep my mates from worrying. My best friend, though, isn't fooled a bit.

"What's the matter with you?" Will asks about halfway through the meal.

"What do you mean?" I ask innocently.

"You love stew, and that little apple pie has been sitting on your tray, untouched, for this entire meal."

"Maybe I want to save it for last."

"You never eat dessert last."

I roll my eyes at him.

He crosses his arms.

"I'm fine," I insist.

Caliborne and Wexton are looking at me now too, their eyes roaming over both me and my plate, searching for whatever it is they've missed that Will has somehow picked up on.

"I'm fine!" I say again, more forcefully this time.

"You *have* been quieter than usual this evening," Wexton remarks. He tilts his head with narrowed eyes. "Fenmire?"

I don't offer any explanation over a simple nod.

"Ah," Wexton says, then he winks at me and mouths, *good luck*.

I smile at him, and that seems to soothe everyone's worries besides Will, who continues to stare at me for the remainder of the meal.

After I drop off my dishes in the kitchen and change into more comfortable clothes—a new, soft cotton dress since today is an Eve day—I find myself standing in front of Fenmire's door, staring at the wood. Why do I suddenly feel like *I'm* the beast about to pounce on their prey this time? If it weren't for Reilanna, this wouldn't be happening, and though my previous two mating bonds were made under the same circumstances, this one feels different. In the end, I remind myself that a mating bond can't form unless both parties want it equally, and that gives me the last bit of courage I need to knock on the door.

"It's open," Fenmire calls.

He's sitting at his desk when I walk in, and the smile he gives me when he looks up from his work calms my nerves more than anything else has for the past two days. He turns his chair away from the desk and holds out his hand. I shut the door and hurry across the room to take it. He tugs me between his knees.

"Thank you for coming," he says softly.

"Of course," I say with a smile. "Why wouldn't I?"

"I didn't know if you already had plans with one of the others."

"I've kept my days pretty open. I… well, I didn't know if you'd… when you'd…"

He takes my chin between his finger and thumb. "You don't have to wait for me, Eve. I'd rather run to catch up with you than watch you miss opportunities on my behalf."

"I'll remember that."

He smirks. "Be sure you do, or I'll take you over my knee. Which reminds me…" He puts an arm around me and gently squeezes my backside. "How does this feel?"

I bite my lip. "It twinged a bit to sit for a day, but I'd nearly forgotten about it until I saw the marks in the mirror as I dressed this morning."

"And how did the sight of them make you feel?"

My smirk breaks free of my teeth. "Naughty."

Fenmire laughs and pulls me close. "Good." He crushes his lips to mine, and his hand fists the fabric of my dress at my back as his tongue invades my mouth, taking and claiming like it usually does. He's as breathless as I am when he pulls away. He sets his forehead to mine and rubs his hands up my arms for a moment before sitting up straight and motioning toward the bed.

There's no wooden box but a square parcel wrapped in fabric sitting on the foot of the mattress.

"For you," he says.

With a nod of encouragement from him, I step over to the bed and run a hand down the parcel. It's hard under the fabric. I pluck the knots holding the corners together at the center and peel back the cloth to reveal… a book. I almost laugh because, of course it's a book, what else would it be? The cover is pure gold with hinges at the edges of the spine, which is drilled with holes and sewn down its length with a thick golden thread. It's held shut by a golden clasp, and when I pop it open and leaf through the pages, I gasp.

It's filled with drawings in Fenmire's usual, breathtaking style.

They're of me. Every single one of them.

I turn to the beginning and start flipping through them. The first shows me in Caliborne's arms as he carries me through the castle's front doors. I'm in my tattered nightgown and am clinging to Caliborne's neck. I can see every scrape and bruise on my body as well as the deep concern in Caliborne's eyes for my well-being. A single sentence is written at the bottom in Fenmire's cramped but elegant writing.

'The moment everything changed.'

The second drawing is of me in Caliborne's bed—I recognize the purple blankets—tucked in clear to my chin with my hair fanned across the pillow beside me. The line at the bottom of this one reads, *'The moment I knew you'd survive.'* The next is me holding my icicle sword out in front of me. *'My ice warrior.'* I laugh as I flip the page to see me sitting with the three of them in the dining room. *'Fate's council.'* Me in my blue dress. *'The first time my heart skipped a beat in over two thousand years.'* Sleeping in my chair at Wexton's bedside. *'An angel's vigil.'* Ice skating. *'Racing the wind.'* Dozens of moments, some of which I had no idea he even witnessed, are perfectly captured on paper. Some are charcoal, some are in full color, others are mere shadows…

I stop on one that makes me blush. It's two whole pages of me lying naked in the sun next to the pond. *'Sun-kissed and god-touched.'* There's one of me tied to Fenmire's bed with his hands on me, his fingers slipping inside me. *'A pet's embrace.'* The last few in the collection are of our time in The Deadwood just days ago, and the final one is of me lying naked across a leathery wing with a look of pure, blissful happiness and calm on my face.

'A mate's smile.'

I'm teary-eyed as I close and latch the book. "This is breathtaking." I turn to face him. "How long have you been working on these?"

"Since the day you arrived," he admits.

A tear breaks free and trickles down my cheek. "Really?"

This time, when he holds his hand out to me, he tugs me clear into his lap with my knees straddling his legs in his chair. He holds me by the hips and looks me deep in the eyes. "I was captivated by you the moment I saw you in Caliborne's arms the night he brought you to the castle. Somehow, I knew your arrival would change everything, and that terrified me. I could sense your god-touched soul and knew you were the answer to our prayers, but I didn't know what I'd have to give up in exchange for our freedom. When I started caring for you"—he looks away shamefully—"I desperately tried to distance myself from you out of fear. But that didn't stop the feelings. It didn't change my fate, *our* fate."

He looks at me again and takes my face between his massive hands. When he speaks again, he's breathless and on the verge of tears of his own. "My heart's been shattered, pet. But you can have what's left of it, every little piece, for as long as Seerraf grants us in this life. That is, of course, if you choose to accept it."

I hug him so tight around his neck I'm probably cutting off his air supply. "I accept, Fenmire," I say through my tears. "I accept all of you, broken or not."

The next thing I know, we're kissing again, only softly now like we did on the forest floor. One of his hands buries into my hair as the other touches my cheek then my neck. He breaks our kiss as his finger catches the collar of my dress and tugs it down. He runs his fingers lightly across the bare skin of my shoulder and searches my face for… something.

"There?" I ask softly.

He nods.

I nod too.

This is happening. Tonight. Right now.

A shiver runs through my entire body as I kiss him again, but his lips soon break away from mine and trail down my cheek, neck, and shoulder. He kisses that spot tenderly then rests his mouth there. I hold him tighter and brace myself for the ache of those fangs sinking into my skin…

Fenmire lets a breath out on the most guttural sigh I've ever heard, and he shakes his head. "I can't," he whispers. "I'm sorry… but I can't do this." He tries to pull away.

I don't let him. "Fenmire—"

"I can't, Eve. I'm sor—"

I put a finger over his lips. "Don't apologize. It's alright."

He turns away, avoiding my eyes.

"Fenmire?"

He looks miserably back at me. "It's not that I don't care for you. I care so much it scares me. You *scare* me, Eve. I'm just… I'm not ready."

"And that's alright," I say again. "I'm not going anywhere."

"I have no idea how long it will take."

"I don't care. You warned me. I don't want it if you don't, Reilanna's rules or not."

"It's selfish of me," he says bitterly. "The others—"

"Would agree with me. It wouldn't matter even if they didn't. For this, all that matters is you and me." I put my hand on his chest, palm down over his heart. "You don't scare me, Fenmire. I know you'll never hurt me, not my body or my heart, and I'll wait as long as you need me to, to prove I won't hurt you either."

We kiss, softly at first but soon with much more passion, though Fenmire remains soft and tender where he's usually hard and demanding. He stands up, holding me on his hips as he walks to the bed and crawls up on it on his knees. He lays me down underneath him.

"If I can't claim you as my mate tonight," he says, "I'd like to claim you in a far more carnal way, if you'll let me."

I grin. "What did you have in mind?"

"Both my cocks inside you at once, one filling each of your holes."

I swallow down a groan. "I haven't done that yet."

"I'd hoped not. I want my cock to be the first to fuck your ass."

I gasp at his depravity, and he smiles wickedly at me.

"Will it hurt?" I ask.

"Not if we go slow, and I'm prepared to go as slow as you need me to."

I pull him down into another kiss then whisper against his lips, "Then claim me."

I'm surprised that, instead of immediately ravishing me like I expect him to, he rolls and climbs off the bed. He goes to his vanity and pours clean water from his pitcher into the wash basin, grabs a washrag from one drawer and his small blue bottle of oil from another, and brings everything to the table beside the bed, lining it all up neatly.

He beckons to me, and I rise up on my knees and shuffle to the side of the bed. He slips my dress off between kisses then pushes me down to my back before dusting more kisses across my thighs, knees, and shins clear down to my feet. He wraps his arms around my thighs, hauls me to the side of the bed, and parts my legs. He catches my eyes and holds my gaze as he bends down and buries his mouth between my legs, licking, kissing, and nipping me as I giggle. With a jerk of his arm, he suddenly flips me over onto my belly and smacks my ass, making me yelp.

"Up on the bed," he orders, his voice low and lethal.

I shiver as I oblige and crawl to the center of the bed where I was before.

Fenmire takes off his pants, picks up the blue bottle, and follows me up onto the bed. "On your hands and knees."

I get on all fours in front of him, my face already burning at the thought of what he's about to do to me. I'm already clenching my thighs in anticipation.

Fenmire grabs my legs and slides them apart across the bedspread. Another smack to my ass makes me cry out softly, but he's not striking with near the intensity he did the other day in the forest. It does make my skin heat pleasantly, however, and I get goosebumps from the thought of what's to come. When he leans down and licks my backside, I bite my lip and close my eyes against the urge to feel ashamed.

I am allowed to like this.

I am allowed to give my body to whomever I want however I want.

I want this and am allowed to have it.

"You taste so good, pet," Fenmire croons. "You'll taste even better filled with my seed, but that will have to wait. This beautiful little bud will just be taking my top cock tonight. Someday, though…" He tongues me again and this time presses against my hole until it opens and lets him in.

I arch my back as his tongue plunges inside me. His hand cups my sex then slaps my clit, and I jump with a whining whimper. His tongue flicks in and out of me a few times before it disappears entirely, and cool liquid drips between my cheeks. Fenmire corks his oil and tosses it across his bed, then he circles my hole with his finger, spreading the oil with increasing pressure until that too slides deep inside me.

Another slap to my clit makes my legs shake.

"More?" he growls.

"Yes."

He hits me harder, and I cry out.

He moves his finger quickly in and out of me, going deeper with each thrust until it's as deep as it can go.

"Ready for another?" he asks.

"Yes, please."

He retrieves his bottle and slicks two of his fingers with oil before tossing it back across the bed and entering me again. My ass stretches to accommodate him, and I rock my hips back, taking him deeper.

"That's right, pet," Fenmire mutters. "Fuck yourself on my fingers. Harder. That's right. Good."

I rock back and forth, spearing myself on his fingers until he shoves them deep inside me. He turns his hand and splays his fingers, stretching me more than ever before. When he pulls out of me, I feel empty. With one final pour from the bottle, Fenmire fists his cock with oil. I look over my shoulder to watch him stroke himself. He's hard as a rock, and yet he touches himself with a grip so firm I don't know how he hasn't lost all control already.

"I won't be rough, not this time," he says. "But I will own you, and you'll know it. If ever you want me to stop, just say the word."

"Just fuck me already," I bark breathlessly.

He lurches forward and grabs my hair, shoving my head down to the bed. He doesn't pull, but his grip is firm, holding me down as he kneels between my legs. First, his lower cock brushes my sex, which is plenty wet enough for him to enter me without resistance, but then that smaller top cock touches my ass, and I jump. The head presses against me, and my already-open body takes it. The most intense stretch yet makes me hold my breath.

"Breathe, pet," Fenmire murmurs, and I do. "Good." He presses his hips forward, and both cocks inch deeper inside me.

I gasp into the bedding. This is far more overwhelming than I anticipated, and I've never felt so vulnerable. I whimper, and he stops, pulls out a bit, and thrusts again, taking me slowly and without pain, just as he promised. The feel of him in my ass makes my cunt clench around his other cock, and I can feel my heartbeat in my clit for how turned on I am right now. It takes time, but Fenmire doesn't rush, and soon enough, he's buried to the hilt in both places in my body at once.

Fenmire arches his back. "You feel perfect. Your body hugs me so tight I can feel you quivering." He pulls out and thrusts back in again.

"Fenmire…" I gasp out.

"You'll get real good at this with time," he promises. "Someday, I'll rope you down on this bed and fuck you so hard you'll have trouble walking the next day." He thrusts again, a little harder. "You'll think of me and my cock with every step you take." Another thrust. "And you'll beg me on your knees to fuck you like that again." He thrusts twice in rapid succession, and I moan.

He lets go of my hair and grabs my throat instead, hauling me up onto my knees with his body still buried inside me. He holds me hard to his chest with his fingers wrapped around my neck and tilts my chin up so I'm staring into his eyes.

"Mine," he growls, pumping his hips against my ass, driving himself into me. "Say it."

"Yours," I say tearfully. "I'm yours." I can't help the crying, not this time. I feel so emotional and vulnerable and yet safe in his arms, as demanding as they are. I want more of him. I want all of him.

I want to be his mate.

A tear trickles down my cheek.

He wipes it away with his free hand then touches me between my legs, circling my clit with his fingers. I gasp softly with each thrust of his hips and cling to his arm at my throat.

"Please," I utter.

"Please, what?"

I tap the hand on my throat.

His eyes widen. "Are you sure?"

I nod.

He squeezes.

My eyes roll up in my head, and I moan. I can still breathe, but the simple thought of such a powerful creature literally holding my life in his hand makes my body ache in private places, places his cocks are currently filling. My fingers grip his arm so hard my nails dig into his leathery skin, and he hisses and hardens his thrusts in response.

He loosens his grip on my throat, and I relax against him. "Come with me," he orders sternly, then he squeezes again, harder this time.

I whimper and claw at his arm as he thrusts faster, and my entire body shakes until he stiffens and slams deep inside me with a snarl. At the feel of his hot seed spilling inside me, I come too, just as he ordered me to, and I start to sob.

He lets go of my throat and lowers us to the bed, and, with his cocks still deep inside me, he covers me, brushes my hair from my face, and holds both my hands as he kisses my neck and shoulder.

"Beautiful human," he murmurs. "You're simply too perfect for this world." He nuzzles my cheek. "Breathe, pet. You're safe and cherished."

My mind is reeling over what we just did, what I asked him to do. I lie there in shock, staring at the headboard as my heart thumps so hard I can barely hear Fenmire's soft words. Eventually, he pulls out of me, and I'm left aching and empty in his absence. He goes to the side table and wets the washrag.

"Up on your knees again for me, pet," he requests.

I struggle to get my limp legs to obey. Once I finally manage it, he cleans me with the damp cloth, and the cool water feels good on all my overheated, sensitive bits. Afterward, he gathers me to his chest in our wing cocoon like he did in The Deadwood, and he pets my hair, strokes my arms, and plants tender kisses on my face as my breathing returns to normal.

We're staring into each other's eyes when a truth tumbles from my lips I see no point in hiding. "I love you, Fenmire."

The sound that escapes him is something akin to a whimpered gasp, as if hearing the words both breaks and mends something inside him at the same time. He kisses me, pets me, and hugs me close, and it's not until later that I realize.

He never says it back.

*****

Going back to Caliborne's room for the night feels wrong. After what happened between me and Fenmire, it feels like I ought to have a new mate. It feels as if the bond was there, ready to join our souls together, but it was never consummated, leaving me feeling empty and fractured.

The next day is no different. I dress in a state of shock and eat my breakfast in a daze, both of which make Caliborne watch me with cautious eyes, though he doesn't pry. I don't see Fenmire, and I don't go looking for him. I think we both need some space right now. I love him, that hasn't changed, but there's a part of me that's not only heartbroken he's not my mate, but that my declaration of love went unreturned. I tell myself it's not a matter of want and that he's dealing with his own trauma. If I'm patient, he will come around, I know that, but I also know this sadness I feel is genuine and deserves time and space to heal. My hurt doesn't erase his nor does his invalidate mine.

We both knew this wouldn't be easy.

I spend most of the day in my room, and after my third cup of hot tea, I start to feel a bit better. Will sits with me for a while, and though I spare him most of the details, I explain to him why I seem so sad today. He can't offer me more than pleasant platitudes, of course, but it's nice to have my best friend to confide in again like old times. When Jacob comes and rounds Will up to go for a walk before dinner, I decide I should get out of my room too, and it's only then that I remember what day it is.

I perk up as I make my way to the third floor. Perhaps chatting with Drixus, no matter how one-sided the conversation might be, will help cheer me up. I turn the corner into the hall from the staircase, following my well-beaten path through the dust, and when I look up, I freeze in my tracks with a startled little jump.

Drixus' door is open.

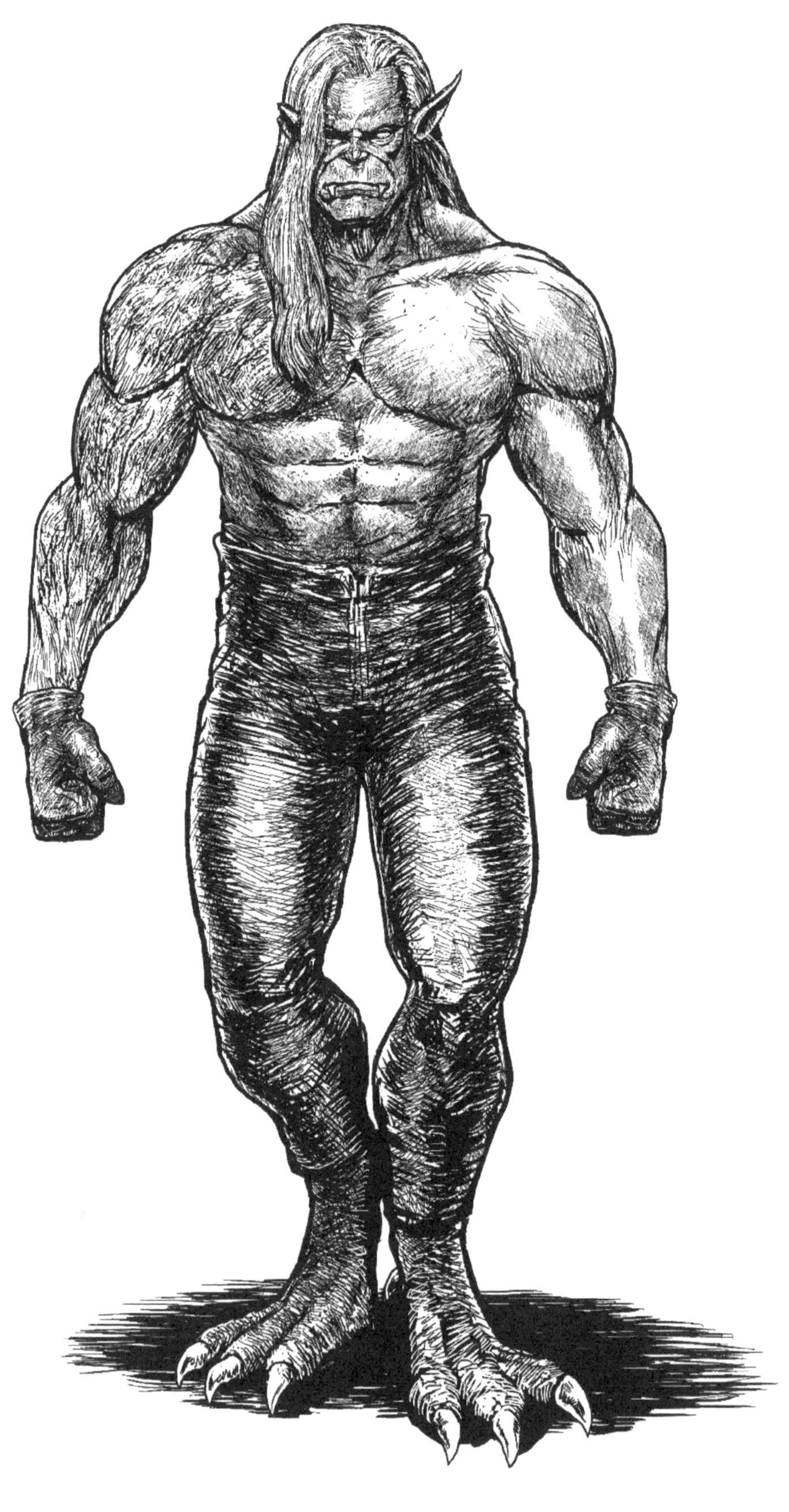

Death

And I looked, and behold a pale horse:
and his name that sat on him was Death,
and Hell followed with him.

-Revelation 6:8 KJV

Chapter 53

I stand blinking at the void where Drixus' door usually is while I try to decide what this means. Could it have been left open on accident? Perhaps Percival was up here earlier and forgot to close it as he left. Or perhaps Drixus left it open himself as he left his room and he's not even in there right now.

Or perhaps he really does want to meet me.

I'm shaking as I step up to the open doorway. It's even darker in the room beyond than it is in the hall, so I can't see much. The smell of stale sweat and manure wafts out on a light breeze. I wrinkle my nose against it as I knock one knuckle on the door frame.

"Hello?" I call softly. "Drixus?"

My eyes adjust to the light, allowing me to see a bit more of the room. There's a bed on the left-hand wall, but there's not much else by way of furniture. A figure, more like a shadow, is standing toward the back with one glowing grey eye. It moves, and there's a whisper of sound as it does, like the tap of a fingernail against stone.

Or a claw.

"Drixus?" I say again, and I take one tentative step into the room. "Is that you?"

The smell intensifies as I walk in, but I try not to show any reaction to it. There's a horrible draft, though it brings a hint of fresh air into the space. It's coming from a hole in the wall to my right that leads into the next room. I can see daylight through it, though very little of it filters into this room to penetrate the darkness. I take another step forward then another.

"Is this alright?" I ask, regarding the shadow that is definitely a Gryxen, though I can't see more than an outline. "How close do you want me to—"

When I'm about halfway between him and the door, he growls and shuffles further back toward the wall.

I immediately stop in my tracks. "This close. Got it. Not one more step, I promise."

I can see the room more clearly now, but there's little to see. The bed is in shambles, and not just because it's unmade. The bare mattress is sliced open in several places and the sheets and blankets on top are nothing more than a pile of shreds. The smell is horrendous, and the floor is so filthy the bottoms of my boots stick with every step. I can't imagine an animal living this way, much less a person.

I slowly lift my hand and give him a little wave. "Hello. I'm Evangeline. I'm very happy to finally get to meet you."

He doesn't reply.

"Don't you want to introduce yourself?"

Silence.

Maybe he doesn't speak my language. That doesn't seem right since Percival says Drixus speaks to him on occasion. Part of me is tempted to sit down and start talking to him like I did when the door was closed between us, but at the condition of this floor, I dismiss the idea immediately.

"Would you like me to leave?" I ask. "We don't have to do this if you don't—"

"You already know who I am," he says, and the sound of his voice startles me at first. It's deep—so much deeper than any of the others—and it rumbles straight through my core as he speaks. "Don't pretend the others haven't told you everything you need to know about me."

"They've told me very little about you, actually. They like to let me get to know each of you myself."

"Why would you want to know me?"

"Well for one thing, I don't know if you've heard, but I'm the one who can break Reilanna's spell."

At mention of the name, he shifts uncomfortably.

"Sorry," I say softly before I continue. "If I'm to free you, I have to… become close to all four of you."

"Become our *stoferra*, you mean to say."

"It seems so. That's not the only reason I'm here though."

"You don't want to be my mate, human. And yes, that's the only reason you're here."

"It's not."

"What other reason do you have then?"

"Curiosity? Friendship? Compassion?"

"I don't want friends, and I need no compassion from you. But the curiosity perhaps I might entertain, if only because I believe you'll leave me alone once you realize what I am."

"What are you?"

"A beast."

"I've met a few of those in my time."

"I don't mean the kind with sharp teeth and claws."

"Neither do I."

He's silent for a moment as he studies me. I can see now that his arms are crossed, and I can just make out the features of his face, though it's still too dark to see his expression below that one glowing eye.

The screech of an animal—Mara presumably—comes from the next room, and I glance through the hole in the wall. All I can see is another empty and dirty room, though that one is better lit. I turn back to Drixus. He hasn't moved an inch.

"Won't you come into the light where I can see you?" I ask.

"Why?"

I shrug. "Like I said, I'm curious."

He falls silent again, and I leave him alone as he considers. I stand there so long I get bored and start to fidget with my shirtsleeves before he heaves a grunting sigh and takes a shuffling step forward. I stiffen, barely breathing as he comes closer, and when he steps into the soft light from the hole in the wall, it takes every ounce of my self-control not to gasp.

Drixus' entire right side is covered in scars. Burn scars, I realize. The right side of his head has been burned so badly the top of his right ear is gone as well as a fairly large patch of hair on that side. His right eye is gone as well, hence the single glowing grey orb. The scars continue down his entire right arm, the right side of his torso, and his right hip and disappear under his leather pants, which are full of holes and tears. His hair is matted, and now that he's this close, I realize the smell in the room is mostly coming from him.

I'm so focused on the scars that it takes me a moment to realize…

He has no wings.

The others told me he can't fly anymore, but I hadn't considered he'd have no wings at all.

I take it all in as he watches me with his good eye narrowed and his lip slightly curled in disgust.

I smile. "Hello." I hold out my hand even though he's still several steps away from me.

He regards it suspiciously.

"I promise I don't bite."

He indignantly blows a puff of air through his nose, and it reminds me so much of Caliborne that I laugh.

One small, shuffling step at a time, he crosses those last few feet between us and reaches for my hand, pausing just inches away from it as if he might change his mind before finally taking it.

This time, I audibly gasp.

His fingers are colder than ice. I've never felt skin so cold. I can only hold on for a few seconds before I have to let go and stick my freezing hand under my other arm to warm it.

His arm slowly lowers to his side.

The smell of him is nearly overwhelming now. It's making my eyes water, so I breathe through my mouth. Does he ever bathe? Clearly not considering the condition of his hair and clothing much less the room.

In the next room, there's a bang and another screech from Mara.

"You should go now," Drixus says.

I don't take it personally, or at least I try not to. I don't want to overstay my welcome and push him too far, so I nod. "It was a pleasure to meet you."

He scoffs. "No, it wasn't."

"It was. In fact, I'd like to come back sometime, if you're alright with that."

He stares at me and doesn't reply or move as I back away toward the door.

"In a week?" I ask.

"Tomorrow."

The request surprises me. I smile. "Tomorrow then. Same time."

Drixus nods once.

I step out into the hall and give him a cheerful little wave before closing the door behind me.

Holy Mother of God… fresh air.

I take several cleansing breaths in through my nose and out my mouth as I fight not to gag. Something must be done about this. No one deserves to live in such filth no matter what sins they've committed. I should talk to Caliborne or Wexton about it. For now, though, I'm ecstatic that Drixus not only invited me into his space but had a whole conversation with me, be it a short one.

It's a start.

I dart down the hall, down the stairs, through the foyer, and out the front doors into the setting sunlight. I look around for Will and Jacob and spot them wandering across the lawn toward the front steps on their way back from their walk. I run to them.

"I met Drixus!" I exclaim as I skid to a stop before them. "Just now!"

"The recluse?" Jacob asks.

"How did you manage that?" asks Will.

I tell them about my weekly trips to Drixus' room and how I sat in front of his door to talk to him and left each time with the invitation to open his door should he ever want to meet me in person. "And it worked!" I say with a giddy clap of my hands. "I went upstairs, and his door was open, and he let me come in and introduce myself."

"What's he like?" Jacob asks.

"Um…" How should I describe Drixus' condition? Should I tell them about the horrible smell and matted hair? "He's… reserved and kind of gruff. He thinks I only wanted to meet him to break the spell."

"Well…" Will says with a small tilt of his head. "Isn't that sort of true?"

"If that's the outcome, then that's great, but I think even if the spell didn't require me to meet him at all, I still would've tried."

Will smiles. "I think so too. It's just your nature."

"He wants me to go back tomorrow."

Jacob frowns. "Can I ask you something?"

Will touches his arm. "Don't."

My excitement vanishes. "What is it?" The boys stare at each other with knowing looks that carry on—or possibly continue—a conversation I'm not privy to. "You can tell me."

Jacob turns to me. "What happens to all of this"—he waves his arm at The Deadwood and the castle—"when you break the spell? What happens to us?"

"Nothing will happen to you, Jacob. The castle and the forest were here before Reilanna's spell and will be here after as well. This is your home for as long as you want it to be, only you'd have the option to leave if you wanted."

"But that would mean the village could come here too, right? They could come for us?"

I take both Jacob's hands. "We would never let that happen. I was told the forest has a way of protecting this place. It keeps humans away who don't belong. I doubt they'd ever find us, and even if they did, we have four Gryxen warriors on our side who would protect us."

"They'd protect *you,*" Jacob says. "They don't owe us anything."

Will huffs. "I'm sorry. I asked him not to—"

I wave him to silence. "After everything we've been through, Jacob's questions and concerns are valid." I hold tight to one of Jacob's hands and tug. "Come with me."

Jacob hesitates with a look at Will, who shrugs, but then both boys follow me back inside and down the hall to Wexton's door.

"It's open," Wexton calls when I knock.

"It's always open," I say back. "But are you decent for once?"

A few seconds later, the door opens to a Gryxen half-dressed in his golden armor. His eyes pass over all three of us on his doorstep. "Yes?"

"Can we talk to you for a moment?" I ask.

Wexton pushes his door open wide and steps back into his room. "Sure, if you help me with this first." He motions to the leather strap of his chest plate. "It's stuck again."

I climb up onto his bed and attack the strap like I've done half a dozen times before. "You really need to fix this. What would you do if I wasn't here?"

"Ask Fenmire."

I feel a pang of sadness in my stomach at the mention of his name. In the excitement of meeting Drixus at last, I'd almost forgotten all about that mess. I help Wexton strip off the rest of his armor in silence, and once he's free of it, he rolls his shoulders with a sigh of relief.

"Much better," he says, and he smiles. "What can I do for you?"

"Jacob is afraid the village will come for us here once the spell is broken," I say. "I told him you and the others would never let them, but he needs some reassurance."

"It's not that I don't think you're good people," Jacob says in a rush. "It's just that… we're not your responsibility. I won't underestimate how far Elias and his sheep will go to hurt us, and you have no obligation to protect us once the spell is broken."

Wexton nods. "All fair points, and unfortunately, I can offer you nothing more than my word on the matter. You say we have no obligation to protect you, but that's not true. Your village has thrown many humans on our doorstep, and we've accepted you all without question. This is your home now as much as it is ours, and we protect our own. Should anyone from the village come here to harm you in any way, we would handle it. We wouldn't leave you to fend for yourselves."

I hop down off the bed, smile at Jacob, and loop my arm around his. "See? I told you so. Now, will you stop worrying? Everything is going to be fine, I promise."

Jacob slumps his shoulders. "I'm sorry. I'm just happy, and whenever I'm happy, I'm usually one step away from losing everything. I've been taught since I was a child that life is supposed to be hard and painful, but since we came here, everything has been easy and wonderful, and I feel like I can't breathe because I'm terrified it'll all go away." He hastily wipes his eyes. "I'm sorry."

Will takes Jacob by the shoulders and tugs him into his arms. "It's alright, baby." He kisses Jacob on the top of his head and rubs his back. "That life is over. You can breathe now."

Wexton touches my shoulder. *Did I make it worse?*

I shake my head and tug him down for a kiss on the cheek.

Jacob recovers himself quickly. "I'm sorry," he says as he backs out of Will's hug.

"Stop apologizing, Jacob," I say. "You've done nothing wrong. Don't carry the weight of others' sins."

He nods. "I've let Elias scare me for too long. No more," he vows with a glance at Will.

Will smiles and takes Jacob's hand. "To hell with Elias. He can't touch us here." He looks at Wexton. "Right?"

"Right," Wexton replies with a definitive nod.

Will holds his hand out to Wexton. "Thank you."

Wexton shakes it. "Anytime."

"See you at dinner," Will says as he leads Jacob out of the room.

I go and close the door behind them then turn to Wexton. "Thank you for that. I knew you'd know just what to say."

He smirks. "I'm anything if not good with my mouth."

I groan. "That one was bad."

He laughs and takes my hand, tugging me in for a kiss. When we break apart, he asks, "How did it go with Fenmire last night?" My smile is instantly wiped away, and Wexton frowns. "What happened?"

I pull out of his arm to sit on the edge of his bed. "Nothing. I mean… not nothing, but we aren't mates."

He sits beside me. "Do you want to talk about it?"

"There's nothing to talk about. He's just not ready. We both want it, but…"

"He'll come around."

I nod.

He bumps my shoulder with his own. "Want to go to the library and use Fenmire's fancy colored pencils to draw lude sketches and leave them on his desk?"

I burst out laughing. "That's oddly specific. Have you done that before?"

He smiles. "Many times. It drives him *crazy*."

"You're a terrible influence." I hop down off the bed. "Let's do it."

Chapter 54

I'm a bundle of nerves as I climb up to the third floor the following afternoon. Will the door be open? Or has Drixus changed his mind and decided I'm not welcome after all? What will we talk about? How can I get him out of that room? Should I even try?

I duck quickly past the second-floor landing so as not to be spotted by Fenmire. We've still not spoken a word to each other, and since he doesn't seem in any hurry to break our silence, I'm not either.

Something has got to give at some point, though.

My stomach is all anxious butterflies as I round the corner into the third-floor hallway, and I take a deep breath to calm myself when I see the open door on the left. I'm prepared this time, but the smell still takes my breath away when I step into the doorway.

"Drixus?" I call into the darkness.

"Why do you call my name each time as if you expect me to be anywhere else?" he grumbles from the shadows.

"Habit, I guess," I say as I enter the room. The lighting is as low as last time if not even more so since the sun is setting a little earlier each day now. Drixus is standing at the back of the room again, and I give him a friendly wave. "Hello."

All I get is a grunt in response.

I squint my eyes as they adjust to the light, but I still struggle to see more than an outline of him. "Do you always sit in the dark up here?"

"Yes."

"How come?"

He doesn't answer.

"Would you mind if I lit a torch or—"

"Yes," he barks.

"Alright. I won't." I wander over to the bed and search the mattress for a spot that's clean enough I might possibly sit down. "Do you mind if I…" I wave toward my chosen perch. When he says nothing, I sit.

Drixus shifts in the dark so that he's standing more in front of me than to my side now that I'm seated.

"What do you do up here all day?" I ask.

Again, I get no answer.

I chew my lip as I search for a topic he might actually engage with. From the next room comes another screech, providing me a possible answer.

"That's Mara, right? Percival told me about her. Is she friendly?"

At first, I think he means to ignore me again, but then he says, "When I ask her to be."

"How long have you had her?"

"A long time."

"She must have a long lifespan like your kind does then."

"Something like that."

"It's incredible that you were able to train one of Reilanna's beasts. I've seen one first-hand." I shiver. "It was awful."

"The spitter."

"That's right. I saw you that night, in The Deadwood. Why didn't you introduce yourself then?"

"I don't talk to people."

"Why not?"

"They don't want to talk to me."

"I do."

He harumphs. "Clearly."

"Am I bothering you?"

He ponders this question for a moment. "I don't know."

"Is there anything you'd like to ask *me*? Anything at all?"

"You said you have three names."

"That's right."

"Why?"

"Didn't Caliborne explain it? I asked him to tell everyone."

"He offered. I declined."

I consider it a good sign that he is now interested enough to ask when before he didn't care to know. I draw my legs up and cross them underneath me as I explain. "It has to do with why I'm the one to break Reilanna's spell. You know the 'neither a man nor a woman' bit? Well, I don't call myself a woman or a man. There are days when I feel more feminine, days when I feel masculine, and days when neither feels right. So, I have three names: Eve, Evan, and Evangeline."

He grunts. "What name do you use today?"

"Today is an Evangeline day."

Another grunt. "You can't outsmart her, you know."

"I don't mean to. I'm playing by her rules."

"You can't play by the rules if you don't understand the game. She'll play with you like she does us, and she always wins."

I cross my arms. "Not this time."

He crosses his arms too. "I can't tell if that's confidence or arrogance. Either way, it'll probably get you killed."

I think of Fenmire and the vow we made about The Gate, and my stomach swirls with nerves so badly I fail to come up with a response.

Drixus stands up straighter. "Perhaps you understand the game better than I thought."

I dry my clammy palms on the legs of my pants. "I understand that to win, we actually have to lose. I'm prepared for that."

The silence that falls between us hangs heavy in my heart, and I'm thankful when he breaks it again.

"I was thrown through The Gate before the spell was cast, and the witch never mentioned her plan for it beforehand, but I can tell you this: none of the powers she stole from the others nor the ones she possessed naturally could've trapped us here or sealed The Gate. The storm, The Deadwood, her shifted beasts, that can all be explained, but the magic barrier around the forest and her control of The Gate cannot."

I tilt my head. "Are you saying she has powers we don't know about?"

"Or she had help. Either way, breaking the spell is likely not as simple as it seems, and she no doubt has more tricks up her sleeves than we know. Have you dreamt of her?"

"Many times."

He nods. "The ability to invade another's mind in that way is yet another skill she shouldn't possess. The dreams didn't start for us for several years after The Gate was sealed."

"She stole that power from someone else after she took over Michastiforo?"

"Most likely."

I consider how many new powers Reilanna might have acquired over the past two thousand years. "Can a spell be altered after it's cast?"

"I don't know the finer details of casting. My powers are spread through touch."

I remember how cold his hand was when I shook it yesterday. "What powers do you have?"

He doesn't answer.

I glance around the bare, filthy room and shake my head angrily. "Drixus, you can't keep living like this."

He snorts. "Watch me."

"When is the last time you had a bath?"

"I don't remember." He sounds bored.

"Would you like to take one? With me?"

"No."

"Are you sure? We could go down at night when everyone else is asleep."

Silence.

"You don't have to make up your mind right now. I can meet you downstairs tonight if you decide that's what you want."

"Why?" he asks, and his voice is as chilly as his hands. "Why do you care?"

"I don't like it when people suffer. No decent person does. I want to help you."

"I didn't ask for your help."

"No, you didn't, which is why it's entirely up to you. I can only offer. It's your choice whether you accept or not." I slide down off the bed. "But something tells me you do want my help, at least some part of you does. Why else did you show up that night by the arch or come to watch me skate or open your door for me yesterday? You could've ignored my existence in this castle and barred me out forever, but you didn't. I'm here now, and you aren't ordering me away. So why am I here, Drixus, if not to help you?"

I expect only silence again, and at first that's all I get, but then he sighs softly and says, "I don't know."

I smile. "That's alright. Just let me know when you do." I head for the door, but I stop in the doorway with my hand on the knob and look back. "I'll be in the pool room tonight, around midnight. If you decide you want to join me, the invitation is open."

He doesn't say anything, so I softly close the door and walk away.

*****

After dinner—which is, yet again, missing one moody, black-haired Gryxen—I go immediately to Caliborne's door and bound into his room when he lets me in.

"You'll never guess who I've finally met!" I exclaim.

The look he gives me says he already has guessed, because, honestly, who else would I be referring to, but I still announce Drixus' name as if revealing the juiciest morsel of gossip to a room full of busybodies.

Caliborne bobs his brows.

"He's let me go in his room and talk with him not once but *twice*. Can you believe it?"

He touches my shoulder. *I won't tell you what to do, but I will ask you to be careful with him.*

"Are you afraid he'll hurt me?"

Not physically.

I smile. "Don't worry. I'll wrap my heart in armor."

Just don't expect much, then you won't be disappointed.

"You really don't think I can get close to him?"

Another long, considering pause follows before he says, *I think Drixus has been through a lot, so I don't know if he's capable of that, with anyone. It's nothing against you.*

"I understand. Truthfully, that's not why I'm doing this anyway. I can't stand to see him living like that. That room… gods above." I wrinkle my nose against the memory of the smell.

Caliborne nods in understanding. *It's not pretty. Wexton has tried many times to include him in things and get him out of his room, but he refuses every time. I think he feels he deserves to live in filth and misery.*

"You mean like he can't forgive himself?"

Precisely.

"I'll try to work on that, but first, let's get him clean. Can I borrow a pair of your pants?"

Caliborne goes to his dresser, riffles in a drawer for a moment, then tosses a pair of leather pants to me.

I fold them up neatly and set them aside before standing up on the bed and beckoning him over with a bend of a finger. When he comes, I wrap my arms around his neck and kiss him on the cheek. "Thank you."

He puts an arm around me. *You're welcome.*

"I'll be late to bed tonight. I'm meeting Drixus downstairs at midnight. Well, hopefully, if he decides to show up."

Caliborne takes my chin in his hand. *If anyone can get through to him, it's you. Just be careful. Not just with him, but…*

"But what?"

No, nothing. It's not my place.

"Alright," I say with a suspicious raise of a brow. "Keep your secrets, you fiend." I kiss him on the nose. "Wish me luck?"

Caliborne tugs me close and kisses me on the lips, sweeping his tongue across mine in a quick and passionate frenzy that makes me giggle when he pulls away.

I wish you all the luck in your world and mine, though I doubt you'll need it.

Chapter 55

Hours after everyone else is asleep, Caliborne gives me a quick kiss before I slip out of his room and down the darkened hall toward the foyer. I have the pants he gave me, my wash bag, extra soap and rags, and a hairbrush… which is definitely not the right tool for this job, I think to myself as I make my way downstairs. I've never been down here so late before, so I never considered how the sconces get lit every day. They're not, I quickly realize as I walk into the pool room. The fires around the room are burning as bright as ever down here. It must be magic, for I never see anyone maintain the sconces throughout the castle. I should ask Fenmire how—

There's the sound of footsteps behind me, and I turn as Drixus descends the last few steps. He stops at the bottom, that one grey eye wide and flicking about the hall and room beyond in obvious discomfort. I set my things by the side of the pool and give him a wave as I start undressing. I don't approach him or beckon him in, giving him time to make the choice himself to join me.

I'm no longer the least bit bashful as I strip and set my clothes aside—neatly, as I plan to wear them again afterward—then I step down into the pool and swim a good distance away to give Drixus space. I try not to look at him too often, but I can't help but glance up occasionally as he comes tentatively to the doorway and watches me swim for so long I'm afraid he doesn't plan to get in after all. I dunk my head under the water and loosely braid my hair back out of my face. As I'm standing there tying it off, I see movement out of the corner of my eye and peek over as Drixus comes to the edge of the pool.

In the brighter lights of the fires about this room, his scars stand out much more starkly against his dark blue skin. There are raised patches covering his right side that look almost webbed, their tendrils pulled taut over muscle and bone. His eye is sunken and covered with more scarred skin, and his scalp is burned bare along the entire right side of his head. His hair is swept to the left and matted tight against the other side of his head where it hangs off him in long coils that sway as he walks. The top of his right ear ends in jagged ridges, like a row of teeth, and his right cheek is marred enough to tease that corner of his mouth back in a permanent smirk. There are other scars too, hundreds of them of varying sizes and shapes that cover his entire torso in dark lines.

I don't stare. I merely take it all in with one quick glance then lock my eyes on his one remaining grey one.

"Hello," I greet cheerfully. "I'm glad you decided to join me."

He pokes the leather pants on the floor with his foot. "What are these for?" His rumbling voice sounds even more intimidating as it reverberates throughout this large space.

"For you. If you want them. If not, that's fine too."

"Who?"

"Who what?"

"Who did you take them from?"

"I didn't take them. Caliborne gave them to me."

"He knows? That I'm…?"

"Yes, but he won't bother us."

Drixus stares down at the pants just like he stared at me before, and the sadness on his face makes my heart ache for him.

I wade closer, but at the panicked look he gives me, I stop again. "Do you want to come in?"

He looks out across the water, and I can tell he wants to, but still, he hesitates.

"Why don't you sit down on the edge and stick your feet in? If that feels good, you can just slide in the rest of the way."

This must be acceptable to him, because he slowly lowers himself to the side of the pool, though he doesn't take off his pants as he plops his legs into the water. He kicks his feet a little, like a child testing the temperature before taking the big plunge.

To keep from staring, I swim back and forth from one side of the pool to the other, being careful not to move any closer to him as I do. After a few laps, I stand back up and point to my bag beside him.

"Can you throw me my soap and rag?" I ask.

He regards my bag and fumbles with the flap as he searches inside for the things I asked for. Eventually, he tosses the soap to me, which lands right in front of me without issue, but the rag that follows only comes about halfway across the pool to me, forcing me to swim closer to retrieve it. I take a chance and choose to stay there instead of backing up again. There's now only a half dozen or so feet between us.

I skip washing my hair since I did that yesterday, but I soap up and scrub my face, neck, chest and arms, making little noises of contentment as I do. When I look over at Drixus, his eye is narrowed. He's on to me but doesn't comment or leave. I rinse off and tread water up to my chin.

"Coming?" I ask.

Drixus swallows, regards the rags and soap sitting on top of the leather pants, and looks at me again.

I shrug. "It's up to you."

He heaves one long, sad sigh before pushing off the edge and sliding into the water, his long, matted hair falling in behind him with a splash.

I want to cheer but offer him a beaming smile instead.

He doesn't move away from the edge, but he does sit down, letting the water reach up past his waist.

I take one small step toward him. "How does that feel?"

A nod is all I get for an answer.

"Do your scars hurt?"

"Sometimes."

"Does the warm water help?"

He looks away as if ashamed as he says, "Yes."

I frown at the thought that Drixus thinks he doesn't deserve even this basic comfort. I take another step toward him. "I'd like to help you wash up. Would you like that?"

"I'm not a child," he barks.

"I know that, Drixus. I just want to be close to you."

He huffs. "No, you don't."

"I do." I take another step to prove it. He's only a few feet away from me now. "If you'd like me to leave, I will, no questions asked. But I would rather take that soap over there and wash your hair for you. All of it from scalp to tip."

He touches the mats on the side of his head. "It's a lost cause."

"Maybe. I'd like to wash it regardless."

My request is met with stillness and silence and one narrowed grey eye that sweeps me up and down as if it can find an ulterior motive written on my skin. I stand there patiently while he considers, and when he finally nods, I'm giddy with excitement as I take those last couple steps toward him. I go to the edge of the pool and swap my soap for the bar I brought for him, breathing through my mouth to avoid smelling anything until I can get him cleaned up.

"Take a dip down under the water and wet your hair," I request.

He does, and I'm horrified by the color of the water running off of him when he comes back up. I hope the pool can handle this as I lather up my hands and start applying suds to his scalp, or as close to it as I can, then I set the soap aside and dive in with my fingers, massaging as I break up the gunk the best I can. When the soap loses its lather, I have him dunk and rinse, and then we start again, working slowly down his hair in small sections.

It takes forever. My fingers are beyond pruney and ache terribly by the time I rinse out the ends of his hair, but the water is washing clear, and I count that as a major victory.

"Much better," I say as I hold his hair above the water. It's much lighter now, which has to be a relief on his poor scalp. It should be cut and brushed, because he's right, detangling matting clear to the floor would take forever, but I have to take this one step at a time. I grab one of the spare rags I brought and lather it up, holding it out toward his face. "May I?"

Rather than let me do it, he takes the rag and washes his face, neck, chest, and arms himself, taking time to re-lather when the soap turns foul. When he glances over his shoulder at his back, I hold out my hand. He gives me the rag—which is ice cold now—but then he hesitates to turn around.

"What is it?" I ask.

His throat bobs as he swallows. "Nothing," he mutters, then he relents and turns his back to me.

I see immediately why he was hesitant to do so.

Drixus' back is burned on his right side, and the same small marks cover his back just as they do his front, but what draw my eyes above that are the two large, mounded and jagged scars where his wings used to be. It gives me chills to imagine what it must have felt like to have the limbs cleaved off. It makes me want to cry, but more than that, it makes me angry. When I first discovered the condition in which Drixus lives, I thought there was no being who deserved such a life.

I was wrong.

Reilanna deserves such misery for the horrors she's committed, and not just against Drixus. For the lives she's ruined and the ones she's taken, I would gladly lock her in such a place forever.

I lather the rag and move Drixus' hair aside to softly clean the back of his neck then work my way lower, washing the dirt and grime of centuries away in brown rivers. When I'm done, I tap him on the shoulder and give back the rag.

"Don't you want to wash the lower half?" I ask. "I won't watch, I promise."

"I don't care if you watch, human." Though his words are as sharp as before, his tone has softened considerably.

I move a short distance away as he stands, strips off the ruined pants, and tosses them out of the pool. I lean my back against the wall as he scrubs the rest of himself down. He even washes between his toes. I'm shocked that the water around him is clear when he's finished. I never considered it before, but there must be some sort of natural current keeping the water fresh or else it would've gone brown years ago from so many bodies bathing in it. For the first time since he got in the water, I breathe through my nose, and though the smell is still there a bit, likely permanently soaked into his hair, it doesn't make my eyes water.

Drixus wrings out the rag and tosses it over with his ruined pants before turning back to me. His eye refuses to meet mine as he mumbles, "Thank you."

I smile at him. "You're welcome. If you like, I can cut your hair and try to detangle as much as I can."

He sighs. "You're truly not going to leave me be, are you?"

"No, I don't think I will."

"I won't make you any promises."

"I don't want you to. I don't want you to do anything you don't want to."

He nods before hefting himself out of the pool and grabbing one of the sheets from the wall, wrapping it around himself like a blanket. He looks at his ruined, soaked pants on the floor then over at the clean ones at the edge of the pool. I swim over and pick up the clean ones, holding them out to him.

"Take them," I beseech. "I'll get rid of the others. If you like," I add to reinforce that this is all up to him. Everything we do, every moment we spend together, is all by his choice.

To my surprise, he doesn't hesitate to come take the new pants from me, but then he leaves without getting dressed and without a goodbye. He must've reached his limit for today.

Once his footsteps have faded away up the staircase, I giggle to myself and spin in a circle in the water, splashing a wave around me in celebration of what I achieved here tonight.

I not only got Drixus out of his room for the first time in centuries, but I got him to take a bath, which hasn't happened in just as long. I want to shout about it from the rooftops. I want to tell…

My laughter and smile fades, and a wave of sadness washes over me.

I want to tell Fenmire.

I want to celebrate this victory with the Gryxen who never smiles but would for me and my happiness.

The one who should be my mate but isn't.

I burst into tears.

I lean over the edge of the pool and sob into my arms as the rejection I've been avoiding for days slams into me so hard it's physically painful.

"I can't. I'm sorry… but I can't do this."

Something is wrong, something beyond my mere hurt feelings. This pain is illogical. I know it's only a matter of time before Fenmire and I bond our souls together. I'm every bit as confident in that fact today as I was two days ago, so why does my chest feel like someone has punched me so hard my lungs ache to breathe? I was right there with him; I was ready. I could feel his breath on my skin and his fangs on my flesh. I'd held my breath and closed my eyes and prepared to feel my heart swell with the same love and passion I've felt twice before, only it never happened, and now I feel as if my heart made room for a mate that just… never came.

I wonder if he feels this way too.

"Evangeline?"

I gasp and whip my head up.

Wexton enters the room, marches to the pool, and jumps down into the water with his pants still on. He wades over to me and tugs on my arm. "Come here."

I relent with a small whimper and crush him in a hug.

"What's happened, darling?" he asks softly as he holds me. *Please talk to me.*

I don't have the strength to hide my pain from my mate. "It's Fenmire. We… tried to become mates only he… couldn't do it, and now I feel… I'm…" I cry against his chest.

Wexton snarls. *I'll kill him.*

"No!" I look up at him. "It's not his fault. I'm not angry with him. He wasn't ready, but I was, and I think something went wrong. I feel like I became his mate that night, only he never became mine, and it hurts."

Wexton frowns. "I've never heard of that, but if that's truly what happened then we need to fix it. We need to tell Fenmire and have him—"

"No. I won't force him. We can't anyway, you know that. Please don't say anything, Wexton. Promise me."

"Evangeline…"

"Promise me!"

He grimaces as he stares down at me, but then he sighs softly and pulls me close, kissing me on the top of my head. "I promise not to tell Fenmire, but you need to tell Caliborne so he can be here for you too until Fenmire makes this right."

I wipe my eyes. "I'm sorry. I shouldn't be crying to you about this."

"I'm exactly the one to cry to about it," he says sternly. "No jealousy, remember? If you're hurting, I'm hurting. That's what being mates is all about: sharing both your brightest and your darkest moments with someone who would never dim your light or add to your darkness."

"It feels a bit wrong to complain to one mate about the woes of taking another."

"That's just your pesky human morals talking."

I snort. "My mistake. I thought I exchanged them for the Gryxen set. I must've missed some."

He chuckles and rubs my back. "I'm sorry Fenmire is being difficult."

"Would he still be Fenmire if he was anything but?"

Wexton places his arm under my backside and hefts me out of the pool to sit on the edge while he stands in front of me. "It kills me to see you in pain. It's not fair that you have to do this for us. I want to wring Reilanna's neck for it."

"There's a price for everything, and this is mine to pay." I stand up. "What are you doing down here this late?"

Wexton hops up out of the pool himself. "Oh, um… nothing. Just taking a walk is all."

I laugh. "You're a horrible liar."

He walks to the wall and takes two sheets from the shelf, throwing one to me. "Who, me?" He points at his face. "Completely unreadable. You can't…" His eyes land on a ball of wet, balled up leather a few feet away, and he walks over and picks up Drixus' ruined pants, inspecting them for a good long moment before looking up at me with both eyebrows raised comically high.

"Was he here?" he asks.

"He was."

Wexton blinks at me, seemingly lost for words.

"It's not what you think, though."

"Oh? You didn't get the single most reclusive Gryxen of all time to leave his room *and* take his first bath in two thousand years?"

"Alright, perhaps it is what you think."

Wexton shakes his head in disbelief. "You're unbelievable, you know that?"

"He deserves the credit, not me. All I did was encourage him a little."

"Two. Thousand. Years, Evangeline." He shakes the pants. "This is amazing, and don't sit here and pretend like it wasn't all your doing."

I shake my head but don't bother trying to argue with him. I march over and snatch the pants away from him. "You be quiet about this too, understand me?" I say sternly, brandishing the pants at him. "Drixus has taken a single step toward freeing himself from his self-constructed prison, and I don't want to give him any reason to lock himself away again."

Wexton holds up his hand. "I'll take it to the grave, darling, you have my word."

"Good." I wave toward the stairs. "Now go back to bed."

He smirks. "I love it when you're bossy." He wraps the sheet around himself, bows, and motions toward the stairs. "After you."

I precede him up to the first floor and kiss him goodnight before going to my room, alone, despite his obvious desires otherwise. I'm just not in the mood. I toss Drixus' disgusting pants into my fire along with a couple more logs and stand in front of the flames for a long time, watching them slowly burn away. It takes longer than I expect, and while I'm standing there with nothing but my thoughts for company again, I decide the only way I'm going to make it through whatever is happening between me and Fenmire is to keep busy and distracted.

And I know just the project to help me with that.

Chapter 56

The next morning, I stop in the kitchen as well as run all the way to the stables to gather the supplies I need before making the trek back up to the third floor.

"Good morning!" I greet cheerfully as I walk into Drixus' room yet again. Now that Drixus has had a bath and his door is being left open so often, the smell in here is starting to dissipate, but I fear there's no getting rid of it entirely. It's likely permanently soaked into the bed, walls, and floor.

That's a problem for another day.

"Ready to tackle that hair?" I ask. I line up my supplies on the bottom of his bed. "I have this comb, and I borrowed these heavy shears from Percival and this bottle of oil from Levi," I say, holding each item up for his inspection.

Drixus steps forward out of the shadows to see the items for himself. "Who's Levi?"

"He works in the kitchen. He's kind of the boss down there."

He grunts. "I forgot you humans have to cook your food."

"Our bodies are a lot pickier than a Gryxen's."

"Pickier, smaller, softer, paler, weaker…"

I laugh. "All true things. Does that mean you don't care for humans much?"

"I haven't met many to tell." After a pause, he adds, "I like Percival. He's kind to Mara."

"Percival is a very kind man."

"I suppose you're not so bad either."

"Was that an attempt at a compliment, Drixus?"

He tilts his head, considering. "I suppose so, yes."

"Well then, thank you. You're not so bad yourself."

He sniffs and nods down at the things on his bed. "I see you're determined to do this."

"I am, but only if you're alright with it."

"How? Where?"

"I usually stand on the bed when I brush the others' hair."

"You brush their hair?"

"All the time. I braid Wexton's too."

"He always did like it braided," he says thoughtfully.

It's the first time he's mentioned one of his friends, or former friends, I suppose. I don't bring attention to it, not wanting to ruin the moment with my fussing. Instead, I climb up onto the bed and stand at the foot. When I beckon him over, Drixus no longer hesitates to approach me, and I spin him by the shoulder until I can reach his hair.

"How short do you want me to go?" I ask.

"I don't care."

"You don't have any preference at all?"

This time, he considers before answering. "Can you keep it below my shoulders?"

"I can certainly try."

I pick up the shears and straighten his hair as much as I can with how matted it is. There's a massive knot about halfway down his back, so I pick a spot just above it and start cutting. It's slow going, and my hand starts to cramp before I finally get through the thick matting, but once I get through the last little chunk, the rest of it falls to the floor with a thump.

"I bet that feels so much better already," I say.

He merely grunts in response.

I set the shears aside and hope I won't need them again as I take up the bottle of oil instead. I soak the matted ends with it clear across the bottom before taking up my comb.

"Ready?"

He shrugs.

I dive in.

I've detangled the tails of Papa's horses enough times to know what I'm doing, but they were never this bad. I pull apart the clumps and slowly pick out the tangles as carefully as I can to keep from ripping the strands. As I work, I talk. Drixus offers responses where prompted, but for the most part he's silent. It's like being on the other side of the door again as I tell him stories about my childhood, about the people in the village, about holidays and what it was like growing up as an only child. Drixus rarely responds, and when he does it's with a grunt or a single word. After a few hours, I fall quiet too, fearing I might be bothering him with my constant chatter.

When the silence grows so loud it starts ringing in my ears, Drixus breaks it.

"What's wrong?" he asks.

"Nothing. Why do you ask?"

"You stopped talking."

"Do you like when I talk?"

"It's been a long time since anyone talked to me. It's nice."

"Why do you avoid the others if you miss talking to people?"

"They don't want to see me," he grumbles.

"That's not true. I'm told Wexton has tried to get you to come downstairs several times before."

"Inviting me to be polite is not the same as wanting my company."

"That's true, I suppose, but I don't think Wexton has ever done anything just to be polite in his life."

A laugh, an actual, genuine laugh, barks out of him.

I'm so happily surprised by the sound that I laugh too.

"I wish we had some music while we worked," I say. "Do you like music?"

"Back in Michastiforo, when we were still at the training fields, we used to throw parties to celebrate both new trainees joining our ranks and those who were leaving us to go on assignment. There was always singing at those. Through the constant flux of Gryxen who came and went, the songs never changed. We passed them down to the new recruits to carry on singing once the older ones were gone." He hesitates as if he's not sure he should say anymore, but then he adds, "I sometimes sing them to myself when I'm on patrol."

"Will you sing me one?"

He's quiet again, and I don't break the silence as he considers. Maybe I asked too much, pushed too hard. If that's the case, I hope he can forgive me. The last thing I want to do is hurt the delicate balance we've formed between us.

Drixus takes a deep breath and lets it out slowly. When he starts to sing, it sends a chill down my spine. His voice is so deep—even deeper when he sings than when he speaks—and it rumbles through the room as well as my chest. He sings in his mother tongue, so I have no idea what the words mean, but I shiver more than once at the sheer power in his voice. Whatever this song is, it sounds beautiful coming from him. His voice rises and falls in perfect pitch, and I close my eyes whenever it bottoms out on notes I've never heard anyone hit before. When it's over, I'm sad.

I wish he'd sing forever.

"That was beautiful," I say once I'm sure I won't cry. "What was it about?"

"Death."

"It didn't sound like a sad song."

"That's because it's not. Not all death is a tragedy."

"Wexton told me your people sometimes go to the temple to die, or pass on, as your kind calls it. Is that what the song is about?"

"No. It's about a warrior who finds death in battle, an honorable death. Seerraf allows him to stay and watch the rest of the battle before passing on. His friends win, so he finds peace in the fact that he helped them rise victorious, that his death wasn't in vain. A warrior at heart couldn't ask for more."

"It's still sad that his friends have to go on without him."

"I suppose that depends on the quality of the friendships."

"Well, they wouldn't call him a friend at all if they wouldn't miss him, I don't think."

"Just because he calls them friends doesn't mean they call him one back."

I see where this is going, and I know I should tread carefully, but if he's willing to have this conversation, then I'll go as far as he'll let me. "By that logic, how do we know if anyone truly considers us a friend?"

"Their actions."

I nod in agreement. "Actions do speak louder than words, this is true. But, in the end, which matters more: that the warrior was as true a friend as he could be toward the others, or the others' opinions of him as a friend?"

This one stumps him for a moment. "I don't know."

"I think it's the former. As long as one truly does his best unto others, their opinions of him would be good if they're truly his friends. And if their opinions of him are that he isn't a good friend, that's them expecting more from him than he's able or willing to give. That's not true friendship, that's greed."

"How does one know if you've truly given your best?"

"When you go as far for another as you can go without causing yourself undue harm in the process."

"What if, in one's attempt to give their best, they make a horrible mistake instead?"

That one is like a punch to my gut, and at first, I don't have a good answer for him. Several quiet moments go by as I pick at knots, both in my hands and in my mind. "That would be hard," I admit. "But I suppose, if it were me, I would trust my friends to hear my side. Even if the friendship isn't salvageable, I'd explain my actions and ask for forgiveness without expectations and hope we could both start to let go of the pain my mistake caused. If there is a friendship to be salvaged after that, we could work together to rebuild it, piece by piece. But forgiveness must come first."

"Some mistakes can't be forgiven."

"Maybe. But you never know until you try."

Drixus falls silent, and I'm about to change the subject when he says, "I see why the others like you."

"Why's that?"

"You're kind like Caliborne, witty like Wexton, and articulate like… Fenmire."

"More compliments, Drixus? You're good for my ego."

I get another bark of laughter.

I take a break to rub my tired hands, and my stomach growls loudly.

"You're hungry," Drixus comments.

"It must be close to dinnertime."

He looks over at the hole in the wall and the fading light trickling in from it. "About an hour past it, actually."

"Oh." I've missed both lunch and dinner. No wonder my stomach is complaining. "Perhaps we should stop for today." I assess my work. I've made a decent dent on the right side, freeing up about a four-inch square section. The left side hasn't even been touched yet.

"I'll braid what I've freed up so far to keep it from tangling again until tomorrow."

"Tomorrow?"

"Is that alright?" I split the combed hair into three sections and do a quick braid, then I pluck the tie from my own hair, rip it in half with my teeth, and secure Drixus' mini braid with one piece, tucking the other half in my pocket for later.

"I have patrol tomorrow."

"So you'll be back at sundown?"

"That's right."

"Do you mind if I bring a couple of candles with me then? I can come after dinner and work until—"

"Why are you doing all of this?" he asks, turning to face me. We're nearly nose to nose since I'm still standing on the bed.

I stare into that intense grey eye. "Because that's what friends do."

"Are we friends?"

"I think so. Or at least, we're well on our way to becoming friends. Don't you think?"

"You don't want me as your friend."

"Yes, I—"

"No, you don't!" he rages. He spins with a huff and stalks across the room to the farthest wall, puts his back to it, and slides down to sit on the grungy floor.

I hop down off the bed and approach him, slowly, and when he doesn't growl or order me to leave, I come close enough our feet nearly touch. He looks at me, and in the dusk light, I can barely see his face, but the pain on it burns as bright as a beacon.

"I hurt my friends," he says bitterly. "If you stay, I'll only hurt you too."

"Maybe," I reply. "But maybe not. That's a risk I'm willing to take."

"Why?" he asks, his voice breaking on the single word.

"Because I think you deserve to find peace. You've been punishing yourself for a long time, but I think you might be ready to forgive yourself and move on. I want to help you, but only if that's what you want. I can't help if you're not ready."

He hangs his head and doesn't say anything.

"I'll come back tomorrow after dinner. If you want me to come, leave your door open."

He doesn't make any indication that he heard me, and I don't push him. As much as it pains me to do it, I go to the bed, gather up my things, and leave his room, shutting the door behind me.

I don't go back downstairs right away. Instead, I cross the hall and open the doors to the rooms across from Drixus and Mara's. The first two are completely empty, but the third, the one directly across from Mara's door, is another bedroom. There's a bed and a dresser and even a window in here, though the entire room is covered in a thick layer of dust.

Dust I can deal with.

Knots as well.

The rest I'm not so sure about.

Chapter 57

Sunday morning sees Caliborne, Wexton, and I flying to the arch for my weekly visit with my father, and since neither of them has patrol today, they both get to come with me this time. We fly for most of the trip but land and walk the last leg through the woods so as not to startle my poor father, who we find in his usual place: lounged back on one of his log seats by the fire with a fish already roasting over the flames.

"Oh, hello," he says as we all emerge from the trees. He stands and wraps me in a hug. "I don't know that I'll ever get used to the sheer size of your companions."

I kiss him on the cheek. "Papa…" The smell of him, the feel of his familiar arms around me, and the love he pours into an extra tight squeeze before he pulls away nearly brings me to tears, which doesn't take much these days. His thoughts are filled with nothing but joy at my visit. No matter what happens, I will always cherish this little link to my past, the only one worth keeping.

Papa regards my mates, oblivious to the fact that I'm wiping my damp eyes behind his back as he says, "Wexton and… Caliborne, right?"

Caliborne gives a polite bow of his head, but Wexton marches up for a handshake that turns into a one-armed hug that leaves my father sputtering in surprise.

"It's good to see you again," Wexton says.

"You… you as well," Papa replies.

Though the fishing poles wait at the tree line, we all gather by the fire as we wait for my father to enjoy his first catch. And as we wait, we talk, at first about nothing in particular, but, soon enough, the topic switches to the village and the latest turmoil.

"Elias has decreed that any ladies in the village who wish to marry must subject themselves to a purity test beforehand," Papa says, his tone dripping with contempt. "Any potential bride found attempting to 'deceive their grooms', as he puts it, will not only be barred from marrying but excommunicated from the church." He looks up at me. "I'll let you guess who you think gets to perform these tests."

"Elias," I say miserably.

My father nods.

"What do the grooms have to say about that?" Wexton asks.

"There are a few who staunchly agree with the new rule, but most seem hesitant at best. They dare not speak up on the matter or face possible excommunication themselves. A few have already stepped on too many of Elias' toes and found themselves barred from service, but it's so much worse than that. Elias' oldest sister now owns the general store since Will and his father are gone and none of Will's brothers wished to take it on. If you're excommunicated from the church, you're no longer welcome at the store, the feed mill, or the tavern, all of which are owned by Elias' family now. Excommunication from the church means losing your way of life for most. The few affected have fled to the city, and Elias quickly swooped in to take over their properties as well, furthering his reach and influence throughout the village."

"How has the village not recognized this is exactly what he wants?" I ask angrily. "The general store, the feed mill… those are places owned by people Elias' family have thrown into The Deadwood. They're making themselves irreplaceable and calling it God's will."

"The village *has* recognized it. That's why a few have started gathering for a whole different reason." He bobs a brow.

"They're organizing?" Wexton asks. "Have any plans been made?"

"I don't know. I haven't officially been invited yet. I only heard something about it from Oren on my last trip to town."

"Old man Oren?" I ask in surprise. "The gossip?"

Papa leans forward. "Oren is far more than a mere gossip. He knows everything about everyone. You'd think someone like that would be invaluable to Elias, but they can't stand each other. Oren hasn't been to church since his son, Roderick, moved to the city a couple of years ago. Oren has been helping to organize those of us who see Elias and his family for who they truly are, and Elias can do nothing about it since Oren is almost entirely self-sufficient. What he doesn't grow himself at his little homestead he now gets sent to him in small care packages from his son. He has no need for the places Elias bars to those who don't agree with his rulings, so Oren can say and do what he pleases with little fear of retaliation. He's cautious, though, so as not to provoke Elias."

"And you plan to get involved with this Oren?" Wexton asks.

"I expressed my interest in attending one of these meetings. Whether or not I'll receive an invitation is yet to be seen. It's certainly no secret how I feel about Elias and his ways, so I'm hopeful."

I take my father's hand. "Please be careful." I won't tell him to sit idle while others wage this war on our behalf, but the temptation is strong. Elias grows bolder by the day, and I won't underestimate his malice.

Papa pats my hand. "Don't worry about me," he says sternly. "The fate of the village isn't your concern. You were the victim of a problem we let fester for far too long. It's up to us to put that right. I aim to help however I can, and I'll deal with any consequences that arise from my involvement. It's the least I can do."

"Just don't do it for me, Papa. I'm happy and wouldn't go back and change any of it for the world. Do it so no one else suffers at Elias' hand."

Papa searches my face. "*Are* you truly happy? Don't just say that for my benefit. I want the truth."

Caliborne rises and circles the fire to sit at my father's side. He holds his hand out to Papa, who looks at me. When I nod, he sets his hand in Caliborne's massive palm, but Caliborne takes my hand as well and places it on top of my father's before curling his fingers around us both.

Papa gasps slightly as the images fill his mind, but he doesn't pull away, and since my hand is clasped with his, I see everything he sees.

Caliborne shows my father the castle, from the bustling kitchen to the crowded stables. He even shows him my room with its twin armoires and crackling fireplace. He shows Papa my bracelets with my names engraved in each, he shows me flying across the pond like the wind on my skates, me playing with the foxes with Percival and helping Levi in the kitchen, fighting playfully with Wexton over apple pie, the snowball fight, the blue dress I made, my happy reunion with Will… Just about every smile and every laugh that's occurred since I arrived in The Deadwood is showcased for my father, who sits grinning like a fool with tears in his eyes.

Even I'm emotional when Caliborne pulls his hand away.

I have been so incredibly blessed.

Papa clears his throat and nods. "You've found yourself a beautiful life. I'm glad. You deserve nothing less."

I put my arm around him and lean my head against his shoulder. "How about I'll promise not to worry about you if you promise not to worry about me."

He chuckles. "Deal."

A kiss on the cheek seals it.

*****

We visit with my father until dinnertime and leave him with the same promise I always make to see him in a week so long as all goes to plan. Caliborne, Wexton, and I end up missing dinner by the time we make it back, but Levi supplies us with a quickly-prepared meal anyway. Afterward, with my arms laden with the same things as yesterday as well as a few candles, I make my way upstairs, but when I turn the corner at the third-floor landing, I stop with a sad sigh, my shoulders sinking in defeat.

Drixus' door is closed.

I knew I pushed too hard. He wasn't ready, and now we're right back where we started. I set my things down on the floor by the stairs and go to the door. I don't hear anything at first, but when I knock and call his name, Drixus shuffles closer like he always does.

"I'm sorry," I tell him. "I'm sorry if I invaded your safe space and made it no longer safe with me in it. You have every right to place this door back between us if I overstepped."

He doesn't respond.

"I didn't mean to upset you, but intent doesn't erase the harm. I'll leave you alone now. I hope you can forgive me."

I wait a moment, and when there's no reply, I go back to the stairs, gather my things, and head back downstairs.

I go back to my room with a heavy heart. I'm disappointed, mostly in myself. I have no right to meddle in things that were broken thousands of years before my birth, and yet what else am I expected to do? I'm here to help the Gryxen, one way or another, and I've done my best to do so. I comb back through all my interactions with Drixus and search for a place where I did or said anything wrong. I can find none, though I recall how upset he seemed yesterday when I left him.

He must truly believe I'm only helping him for my own selfish gain, which considering everything he's done and been through, I don't exactly blame him. The only way to prove to him that's not the case is to take a step back. If I push myself back in where I'm not wanted, he'll always believe I have some other, nefarious motives, but if I stop and respect that closed door, perhaps he'll realize I truly want nothing more than to see him be happy again.

And he knows where to find me if that day ever comes.

A soft knock on my door interrupts my dreary thoughts, and it's only then that I realize I'm merely standing in the middle of my bedroom in a daze with my arms still full of oil, scissors, combs, and candles.

"Just a minute," I call as I toss it all down on the vanity. When I turn to the door, however, I find a piece of paper on the floor in front of it that someone slipped through the crack underneath. I pick it up and open the door, but there's no one there. I close the door again and sit on my bed as I unfold the paper.

It's a charcoal sketch of me lying at Fenmire's side under his arm with my hair spilling across his leather wing and pillows. His hand is softly brushing my hair as I stare up into his eyes with a look of such longing and love on my face that I instantly start to cry.

This picture, like the others, has a single sentence written along the bottom.

'The moment you owned me, body, heart, and soul.'

There's a letter as well, written on a separate sheet of paper and folded up in the drawing.

E,

I owe you an apology—more than one, actually—the first being for my absence lately. I want you to know, my distance isn't born from any ill feelings toward you. Quite the contrary. You see, when you said those three words to me the night we should have become mates, I thought I was prepared to hear them again.

Oh, how wrong I was, pet.

I thought I was afraid to fall for you out of fear of getting hurt a second time, but the moment you told me you love me, I realized what I'm most afraid of is hurting you. My heart has been shattered, Evangeline, and its edges are sharp. I saw you as a being of tender flesh and bone, and the last thing I want is to bleed you dry.

But during my recent self-reflection, I've realized something.

You said you doubt anyone has the power to fix what's been broken inside me, and I think you may be right about that, but over these past few days, I've discovered those pieces I feared might pierce and bleed you, they're not so sharp anymore. I think, rather than my heart cutting yours to ribbons, yours has worn down my sharp edges, like ocean sand against broken glass. You've never once pulled away from me. You're constant and reliable and tender and warm, which is something I've only experienced once before in my life. I never thought I'd find that again.

And thus, we arrive at my second apology, pet. I'm sorry I underestimated you yet again. I really ought to have learned my lesson by now, but perhaps it is a good thing that you keep exceeding my expectations by leaps and bounds. If you can surprise me, of all people, then you can surprise and overcome our enemies who no doubt underestimate you even more than I have.

You are, without a doubt, the highest blessing I've ever been given, and I'm a vauncidi, a child whose very birth is said to be a blessing straight from Seerraf.

I love you with every shard of my shattered heart, and someday soon, I will be your mate, though all I can do is promise you this and hope your faith in me carries us through until then.

With love,
Fenmire

P.S. My door is open to you, night and day, and I stand ready to make amends for my recent absence any way you see fit.

I'm equal parts crying and laughing when I finish reading. I hug the drawing to my chest then fold it and the letter up and tuck them inside my golden book. Without much thought toward what I'll say or do when I get there, I head for Fenmire's room. When I knock, he bids me entry, and I find him sitting in his chair with his back to his desk, one leg casually crossed over the other, and his hands clasped together on his drawn-up knee, waiting for me. He doesn't say anything as I enter the room and softly shut the door behind me.

"Hello," I say quietly.

"Hello, pet," he replies. He uncrosses his legs and rests his hands on the arms of his chair but doesn't make a move toward me nor speak again as he watches me expectantly.

"The drawing is beautiful, as always," I say. "Though I have to wonder what those artists who taught you to draw would think if they saw you using your skills to draw me naked."

He barks in laughter. "They'd no doubt praise the pieces like any other. Do you think a single one of them hasn't drawn their lovers before in all their glory? No doubt a few of them pursued the craft for just such a purpose from the start."

I swallow. "Your letter was beautiful too."

He leans forward, placing his elbows on his knees as he continues to stare at me. "I'm glad you liked it. Since you're here now, am I free to make amends for my recent behavior?"

"There's no need for that, Fenm—"

He waves me to silence. "You bared your heart to me, and I crawled away into my books and brooded like I always do. You deserve better. You deserve everything. I will make it right." He looks me in the eyes. "What do you want, Evangeline? What price do you see as fair for the pain I've caused these past few days?"

The thought that occurs to me at this moment makes my heart skip a beat. I dare not ask, and yet the longer I consider, the more my heart is set on it. I bite my lip as I consider it.

"Tell me," Fenmire orders, and though his voice is low, his tone is stern.

I tilt up my chin. "We both know how much you like being begged, but how do you feel about being the beggar?"

I don't know what to expect. Laughter? A look of shocked horror, perhaps?

But that's not what happens.

Fenmire sits still as stone for a few terrifying seconds, but then he slides from his chair and drops to his knees on the floor before me. At first, his eyes are locked on a spot below my chin, and his lips part on ragged breaths. When he finally looks up at me, there's so much pure feeling in his eyes it takes my breath away.

"Please forgive me," he says in a breathless whisper. "I love you. I've loved you from the start, and I was a coward not to admit it. But I'm yours now, Evangeline. I'll never doubt or underestimate you again."

I've heard enough. I lurch forward, wrap my arms around his neck, and burst into tears. "I love you," I utter. "It felt like my heart was fractured without you these past few days."

"I needed time to get my head straight," he says. "Never again, I promise. I love you."

He repeats those words many more times throughout the evening as we kiss, shed our clothes, and make love right there on the floor.

I don't tell him my suspicions about our mating bond. I still have no desire to force him, and just being back in his arms alleviates the ache in my chest enough I can bear it until he's ready.

His love is enough to soothe my soul for the time being.

Afterward, we lie on the cool stone, soaking up each other's warmth for as long as we can before I have to go to Caliborne's bed once again. Fenmire is on his back with one arm tucked under his head and the other buried in my hair, his fingers softly petting my scalp as he stares at me.

"What?" I ask with a shy grin.

He shakes his head. "Just thinking."

"About what?"

"One of Seerraf's acolytes, Divnamar. I've always struggled with the lesson their story was meant to teach, even more so after… But I think I understand it better now. I don't know that I could do what they did, but I get it."

"Will you tell me the story?"

He settles more comfortably on the floor, stretching his legs and staring up at the ceiling as he begins the tale. "Divnamar was a Gruxa soldier who joined the army only to drop back out after a few decades to travel the world as a sellsword instead. They traveled alone for several thousand years, taking only those contracts that suited them and spending coin as fast as they earned it. Eventually, they found a companion, a Gruxa named Tordeeron, who joined Divnamar in their travels. After a time, the two became a renowned team. They were often sent for by major cities to deal with situations where failure was far more catastrophic than some petty criminal walking free, usually things involving assassination attempts on people in positions of power, though no matter the job they took, they never stayed in one place for long."

"Were they lovers?" I ask with a smirk.

Fenmire chuckles. "Yes."

"Did they become mates?"

"They didn't get that far."

"What happened?"

"One day during their travels, the duo came across a camp of traveling merchants who were down on their luck with a couple of broken carts. Divnamar and their partner offered aid, but the merchants were well on their way to fixing their vehicles and turned them down. Divnamar and Tordeeron moved on and made camp about an hour later.

"Sometime in the night, Divnamar woke alone in their camp. Thinking their companion merely stepped away to relieve himself, they thought little of it until the next morning when they discovered fresh blood on Tordeeron's equipment. When confronted, Tordeeron admitted to doubling back to the merchants' camp with the intent of stealing some of their coin. 'For our travels', he said, only it all went wrong when one of the merchants woke and caught him picking pockets and bags. Tordeeron was forced to kill the merchant to get away with his own life.

"Divnamar was shocked by this confession because they weren't hurting for coin enough to result to thievery much less murder, but Tordeeron made his case, begged Divnamar's forgiveness, and promised it wouldn't happen again. The two packed up camp and continued into the nearest city where they stayed for several days to restock their gear and earn a few hot meals. During their time in the city, news spread about a traveling band of merchants, all of whom were slaughtered just a few hours travel from the city gates.

"When news of this reached Divnamar's ears, they confronted Tordeeron again, who confessed the full truth: that he'd not just slain a single merchant but the whole camp. This broke Divnamar's heart, for they knew what needed to be done. They gave Tordeeron a choice: either turn himself in to the authorities and pay the price for his crimes, or the two would have to go their separate ways, and Divnamar would spend the rest of their life hunting Tordeeron to bring him to justice. Tordeeron chose to turn himself in to spare them both the hurt of becoming mortal enemies. They held a trial, and Tordeeron admitted his guilt, which saved his life. He was sentenced to three thousand years' imprisonment for each life he took, which totaled twenty-four thousand years."

I wince, not able to imagine a life that long much less an imprisonment.

"Tordeeron went to prison there in that city," Fenmire continues, "leaving Divnamar alone once again. Divnamar didn't regret their choice to turn Tordeeron over to the authorities, it was the right thing to do, but Tordeeron's guilt didn't erase the loyalty Divnamar still felt for him. So, they joined the very authorities who imprisoned their lover and pledged themselves to the safety of the city where he was held. For those twenty-four thousand years, Divnamar paid their own debt to those his lover had harmed as they waited for Tordeeron to be set free.

"After those twenty-four thousand years were up, Divnamar was there the day Tordeeron was released, and they were reunited. Witnesses of that reunion spoke of two souls deeply in love, neither the least bit bitter about the past. They were both quite old by that point, so they lived together in that same city for a few hundred more years before going to the local temple where they were permitted to pass on, hand in hand."

"What lesson does Seerraf wish us to take from such a tale?" I ask sleepily.

"The temple priestesses called it a 'lesson of love, loyalty, and morality'. Sometimes, our love for others might attempt to cloud our judgment, but we can't let it, no matter how badly it hurts. Divnamar knew they would lose the love of their life, but they did the right thing and made him atone for his crime. Divnamar was the only one who knew of Tordeeron's guilt. They could have easily moved on from that place and continued their lives as sellswords like nothing had happened, but Divnamar sacrificed that life and his love instead. Not only that, but they stayed close for Tordeeron's entire imprisonment and were there with open arms and heart the day his debt was paid and he was released. They forgave Tordeeron for his sins and waited for the day when they could be reunited in life and love. The strength it must've taken for them to wait, alone and lonely, for that long." Fenmire shakes his head.

"Twenty-four thousand years," I mutter. That's twelve hundred times the life I've already lived. "I can't imagine that." I look up at Fenmire. "I can see why that story would bother you."

He nods. "The idea that someone can show such loyalty… I confess it struck a nerve for many years. But that story has always bothered me for another reason."

"What reason?"

"I don't understand how Divnamar still loved Tordeeron after what he did. How were they not utterly devastated to learn their lover was not who they appeared to be? After such a grievous sin, how did they find it within themself to forgive Tordeeron?" He shakes his head. "I don't know that I could ever do that."

"I don't think we could ever know for sure what we'd decide unless we're put in such a position ourselves."

"I think I finally understand why I struggled with the story before. I always placed myself in Divnamar's shoes. Of course I did, because we all wish to be the hero of every story. But lying here with you just now, I realized my place in the story isn't Divnamar's. It's Tordeeron's."

"Fenmire—"

"No, let me finish. Tordeeron did something horrible, and he saw in his lover's eyes the weight of his sin. He admitted his guilt and atoned and held no grudge against Divnamar for convincing him to do so. It's not just Divnamar's story of loyalty and morals, it's also Tordeeron's story of accepting our flaws and the repercussions that arise from them without turning on the ones we love, who often can show us our faults better than we can see them within ourselves. That's a lesson I can appreciate."

I peer up at him with a smile. "If you ever murder a band of traveling merchants, I promise to hold you accountable."

He touches my cheek. "I don't think you have to worry about that, but I'll gladly beg at your feet for forgiveness whenever you feel it's owed. Don't hesitate to tell me if or when I make a mistake, pet. Not many are willing to do that."

"No? But you're so approachable."

He laughs.

I squeeze him in a hug. "I'll tell you. I've never been afraid of you, Fenmire. You can always expect the truth from me, no matter how much it hurts."

He pulls me up onto his chest until we're nose to nose. "Good."

Then he kisses me.

Chapter 58

For the next few days, I fall into a pattern of sorts where my time is spread across all three of my Gryxen lovers who, without needing my help or input most of the time, work out schedules so they all receive equal hours with me between their patrol duties. It's wholesome, really, watching them negotiate meals, baths, and… other activities amongst themselves while deferring to me for the final say.

I remind them I'd like time for myself as well, but the few times I sequester myself away in my room alone, I end up bored and lonely and seeking one of them out anyway to keep myself from slipping up to the third floor to Drixus' door. Despite the temptation, I've kept well away from Drixus' space, afraid even hearing my footsteps in the hallway might make him think I'm just waiting for the opportunity to overstep the new boundary he's placed between us.

Besides, there's another Gryxen who's begging for my help in every way but words.

I've never seen Fenmire so needy. Every moment he gets with me, he's touching me, either with a hand on my back, soft caresses on my arms and hair, or his body wrapped around mine in bed. When we're in the library studying, he's usually got me sitting in his lap with our books and notes strewn across the desk in front of us and his arms around me as we take turns working out math problems or transcribing his notes on The Gate into his bound tomes. He thinks much more in my language now than his own, which allows me to hear his thoughts far more often, and the further he pulls back that curtain, the more I understand why he kept it drawn for so long.

So many times, I catch him comparing what we have to what he had with the one who hurt him, though he never uses his mate's name, not even in his thoughts. The damage this other soul's betrayal has caused is far deeper than I anticipated, and on several occasions, I have to stop whatever we're doing, take his face in my hands, and look him in the eyes as I assure him that, this love between us, it's safe and reliable and neither of us will come to regret it. No, I'm not afraid he'll hurt me. No, I won't stop loving him if we're never anything more than what we are now. No, I don't think he's weak. Yes, I do still very much want to be his mate.

This sudden shift from sullen, broody Fenmire to this anxious, self-doubting one is quite a shock at first, but I find it endearing that he now trusts me enough to show this more vulnerable side of himself.

The one thing that hasn't changed? The way he can discover my deepest, darkest desires and live them out in the flesh until I'm a wrecked, wobbly mess of a human who can barely walk the next day. I often catch myself daydreaming about the things we do to the point my heartbeat spikes and my whole body starts to shiver. I seem to have finally found the perfect balance: Wexton and his wicked mouth during the day, Fenmire and his domineering passion in the evening, and at night, calm and sensual touches with Caliborne.

But I still haven't broken Reilanna's spell.

Drixus no longer wants to see me, and I'm not sure that will ever change. I could be perfectly content with my three mates—once Fenmire and I get to that point, that is—but then what? Is it enough to live a full life here in The Deadwood with the ones I love? What will they do once I'm gone? As I once told Fenmire, my life is frighteningly short compared to a Gryxen's. Once I die, they'll all be right back where we started, only they'll also have to live with the pain of my loss. What then? Do they merely wait for another human to come along who fits the requirements of the spell so they can try again?

That seems morbid.

We've come this far. Giving up now feels wrong. But when I bring it up to any of them and ask for their input, their answers are always some variation of the same response.

"Everything we've done up till now and whatever we do from this point forward is contingent on your feelings, pet."

"Your wants and desires trump all, darling."

If this is where you want to stop, it stops.

I have to admit, it's rather tempting. All three of my lovers go above and beyond every single day to make me happy. I have my best friend here with me, and he's well on his way to finding his own happily ever after. I still have my father in my life as well. And I never have to lie or pretend about who I am ever again.

And all of that would be enough… only Reilanna doesn't plan to let any of us live in peace and happiness that easily.

Weeks have passed since CeCe came through The Gate when I'm woken by a deafening crash and the whole castle shaking so violently Caliborne's dressers and cabinets start falling over, the window shatters, and the raining rocks are large enough they smash and splinter the furniture they land on. Caliborne immediately scoops me up and shields me under his hardier frame. We huddle in the bed as the quake goes on and on, and I watch from under Caliborne's arm as great cracks rip through the walls. I scream, terrified the castle will crumble and bury us alive.

It's alright. I've got you.

What will come through The Gate this time? Will it come to the castle? Will and Jacob! They won't know what to do.

When the shaking finally stops, Caliborne pats me all over. *Are you hurt?*

"I'm fine," I say in a rush. "You need to go!"

With shaking hands, I yank on some clothes, help Caliborne put on his armor, toss him his bow, and watch from his bedroom door as he runs down the hall with an arrow already nocked and ready to fire. A second later, Fenmire's door slams as he too rushes off toward the castle's front doors.

"Be careful!" I call as they disappear together through the foyer.

Will and Jacob open their door and peer out, both half-dressed and wide-eyed.

"Are you two alright?" I ask.

"I think so," Jacob says. "The room is a mess, though."

"What the hell was that?" Will asks.

"Something came through The Gate. We should stay in our rooms until the Gryxen deal with whatever it is."

"Care to join us then?" He beckons with his hand. "Surely it'd be better if we stuck together."

After a mere second's consideration, I scurry across the hall and into the boys' shared bedroom. It's every bit as destroyed as Caliborne's with toppled furniture and rocky rubble littering the floor.

"Let's clean this up while we wait," I suggest, and all three of us start righting dressers and desks, gathering chunks of rock, and shaking dust from the bedding.

Cleaning serves as a decent distraction, even if we do most of it in tense silence. When we finish the boys' room, we move together down the hall into mine and tidy it as well. With nothing else to do, we also fix Caliborne's and Wexton's rooms next, though we decide not to even venture into Fenmire's. That's a whole level of chaos I can't even begin to put right.

Eventually, Levi rounds us up for a meal once they get the kitchen running again, and we all have a quick brunch in there, none of us even bothering to take trays and eat in the dining room.

"Does that happen every time something comes through The Gate?" Will asks.

Levi and I exchange knowing looks.

"The Gate and the spell are closely related," I explain. "The closer we get to breaking the spell, the more powerful the beasts are that come through The Gate, and the worse the ground shakes when they do."

"But the Gryxen can handle it, right?" Jacob frets.

"Absolutely," I say with confidence. "They've trained for hundreds of years for this. They know what they're doing. And the good news? While the beasts might get more powerful, they appear less often. When I first came here, one of Reilanna's creatures came through The Gate every three days or so."

Just then, Wexton shuffles into the kitchen, and all the humans stand up straighter. He's splattered in blood, and his sword is black clear to the hilt.

"Is everyone alright?" I ask.

He comes to the counter where we're all eating, picks up a pitcher of water, and drinks from it in deep gulps until he has to stop to breathe. "Everyone's fine," he says breathlessly. "Fenmire took a swipe to the back, but the weapon wasn't poisoned, so…" He takes another deep drink, more slowly this time. "It was two Gruxa. They came through together and were shifted just like CeCe. One carried a sword. She was a temple priestess. Fenmire recognized her. The other was a spitter. We think it might've been one of our old instructors from the training grounds, but he was shifted too much to identify him properly."

I reach to touch his arm but change my mind when I see how filthy it is. "I'm sorry."

"They're dead?" Jacob asks.

Wexton nods and places the empty pitcher down on the counter with a heavy thud. "We buried them near The Gate." He looks at me. "Caliborne, Fenmire, and I are heading downstairs to get cleaned up. You're welcome to join us." He doesn't wait for a reply before he turns and walks back out of the kitchen.

"I've never seen him so serious," Will comments.

"I should go with him," I say, and I shove the last few bites of my food in my mouth and wash it all down with a swig of tea. I kiss Will on the cheek on my way by. "I'll see you later."

I rush down the hall to catch up to Wexton, and when I do, I don't say a word, I just take his hand and walk at his side down the hall toward the stairwell.

He squeezes my hand but stays silent.

We walk together down to the pool room where we find Caliborne and Fenmire in various stages of dress. Caliborne seems to have forgone taking his armor off completely and jumped in the water fully dressed. Fenmire is sitting at the side of the pool, struggling to remove his chest piece, which is buckled and sliced open in the back. Still without uttering a word, Wexton and I walk up and help him work the armor off over the deep gash across his back. We all strip and hop down into the water with Caliborne who sits against the edge of the pool with his eyes closed.

I'm the first to break the silence. "Was it that bad?"

"We could handle the fight," Fenmire explains. "But we didn't know *who* we were fighting, which is what made it hard."

"It could've been anyone," Wexton comments. "Our friends, families, mentors.... No one is safe."

I nod. "I can't imagine how that felt. I'm sorry."

"Stop apologizing," Wexton says, and it's the first time I've ever heard him be stern.

I grab one of the rags they've brought with them and help Wexton clean the blood from his face and hair. After that, I help

Fenmire clean the wound on his back. It's already starting to close, so I doubt it'll need stitches. When I approach Caliborne, he takes the rag from my hand, tosses it out of the pool, and pulls me into his arms. I lean my head on his armored shoulder with a sigh.

"Fenmire," I say softly. "Tell a story. Please." Anything to lift this blanket of regretful silence that's fallen over us all.

Fenmire sits down and stretches his wings out, hissing as the water burns his back. "I've told you about the first, second, and fifth of Seerraf's acolytes. I'll tell you my favorite of the tales next."

"Let me guess which is your favorite," Wexton says with a raised brow. "Kliotay, right?"

Fenmire rolls his eyes at him. "Kliotay, the fourth acolyte, was a reeshro: a special kind of healer who specializes in treating the brain. You know how I can detect illnesses and injuries in the body? Reeshro can do that in the mind. They can detect and treat things like trauma, psychosis, and catatonia. They can't cure these things, necessarily, but they can lessen the symptoms and help heal the brain after physical trauma from things like blows to the head. It's a very rare form of magic, so rare there's never more than one reeshro in existence at one time in our world, if any at all.

"Kliotay not only practiced her craft but spent centuries researching new ways to use her powers to heal. One of her theories, her most controversial and ambitious one, was full brain transplants. She theorized that, with the proper time and conditions, she could take a functioning brain from a dysfunctional body and place it in a functioning one. The conditions for such a procedure were so complex, however, that she very rarely got the chance to test her theory much less put it into practice.

"But then, one day, a pair of Gruxa came to the clinic, both having been injured in a horrible accident. They were both female, of similar age and body types, and it just so happened that one sustained extensive injuries to her body while the other was brain dead. The one whose brain was injured was beyond even what a reeshro could save and would die as soon as the healers stopped keeping her alive. The other's body was failing and would also die once the healers stopped their emergency measures.

"The conditions couldn't have been more perfect, so Kliotay requested permission to attempt her procedure, and the families of both Gruxa gave it. Unfortunately, the procedure proved to be even more complex and difficult than Kliotay predicted. It took her over 30 hours, but she successfully took the brain from the failing body and transplanted it into the one that would heal from a few minor injuries, but she had to spend untold amounts of her own energy and powers to keep the brain from dying in the process. There was a whole team of healers and priestesses aiding her who came and went in shifts during the whole thing. Nearly the moment the procedure was deemed a success, Kliotay collapsed and died from pure exhaustion and shock."

"Did the woman survive?" I ask.

"She did. The remaining female Gruxa, who was both a mate and a mother, went on to live a long, happy, and healthy life."

"Why is that story your favorite?"

"Because Kliotay no doubt knew at some point during that procedure that she was pushing herself too far, but she kept going anyway. She knew the chances of her getting to try again were slim, and if she was ever going to prove her theory—a theory many told her was outrageous and impossible—then this procedure had to succeed. And since her procedure was a success, many reeshro have since studied and expanded upon her notes, and several other procedures have been done, most of which were successful."

"Have other reeshro died?"

"No. They were better prepared and were able to improve the procedure so that it's no longer deadly for the reeshro."

I give Caliborne a kiss on the cheek then push away from him to swim to Fenmire instead who tugs me down to sit in his lap as he holds me.

"I see why you like that story," I say. "Kliotay made the ultimate sacrifice for knowledge she knew would save many more lives in the future."

"Exactly. She knew she was probably going to die, but to her, failure wasn't an option, so she did what she had to do."

Fenmire and I exchange a look of deep understanding, and at that moment, surrounded by my lovers who look as tired and broken as I've ever seen them, I make a decision.

Failure isn't an option.

Chapter 59

After our group bath, I continue helping others put things back together throughout the castle, though there's little to be done about the cracks in the walls. They're yet more evidence that we can't go on like this forever. Reilanna will continue her assault on us until she drives the Gryxen mad or buries us in stone. As the hours go by, I grow more and more resolved.

I must break the spell. That's what I am here to do, and I will see it done.

After dinner, I go back to my room with the intention of gathering my things and going upstairs to knock on Drixus' door in hopes of repairing what's been broken between us, but when I enter my bedroom, I'm surprised to find a tall, wingless figure standing in the shadows in the back corner.

"Drixus?" I say in surprise. I quickly shut the door behind me. "What are you doing here?"

"You didn't come back," he says.

"Your door was shut."

"I know, but I thought you'd come back."

"I thought you needed some space."

"I suppose I did, but..." His hands at his sides close into fists and open again, over and over, and I see they're now covered in a pair of brown leather gloves. "I've thought about what you said."

"About forgiving yourself and moving on?"

"Yes." He takes an uncertain step closer. "I want that, Evangeline, but… I'm…" He swallows. "I don't know if I'm ready, and I'm afraid to try. I don't want to disappoint you."

"You can't disappoint me, Drixus. And that's not me showing an unrealistic amount of faith in you, that's me telling you this isn't about my wants and desires. This is about you and only you. I want to help you, but only so far as you want to help yourself. It's impossible for you to disappoint me if I have no expectations."

"That sounds good in theory, but I'm not convinced I won't end up hurting you somehow."

"If you came here hoping I'd convince you, I'm sorry to disappoint you, but I won't do that. It's your choice and yours alone."

He hangs his head. "I've made some notoriously bad choices in the past."

"Perhaps that's the first thing you should forgive yourself for. It won't matter how many others forgive you if you can't let go of your past mistakes and move on. I think two thousand years' worth of guilt is enough, don't you?"

"I don't know." He turns away and walks over to my fireplace, which isn't lit now that it's summer in The Deadwood. "I—"

Someone knocks on my door.

Drixus and I both jerk our heads toward it.

"Evangeline?" Fenmire calls from the other side.

Drixus backs up two steps as if Fenmire might burst through the door and turn him to ash on the spot.

I put a hand up to calm him. "It's alright," I say softly. "I'll see what he wants and send him away." I cross the room to the door and crack it open with a quick, reassuring smile back at Drixus before I peek out at Fenmire. "Hello."

"Hello," he says. He puts a hand on the doorframe beside me. "I just wanted to make sure you were alright. That story I told earlier, I didn't mean for it to sound as if I'm pressuring you to do something you're not ready or willing to—"

"I didn't take it that way. It did provide me with some motivation I was missing, though."

He studies me, chewing his lip in deep thought for a moment before dropping his hand from the doorframe and standing up tall. "I never want you to feel scared, Evangeline. I keep flipping back and forth between telling you to forget about all of this—the spell, mating bonds, fate, everything—and praising you for being so dedicated to us and this fight you never signed up for but threw your whole self into nonetheless." He shakes his head. "I constantly pivot between awe and terror at the thought of what we've accomplished and what's still to come, and I just want you to know you're not alone in it."

"I know that, Fenmire. But thank you for the reminder."

He nods then smiles. "Want some company this evening? My room is a disaster, and I have zero desire to fix it right now."

"Oh, um… now's not a good time."

Fenmire cocks a brow. "Wexton beat me here, didn't he?"

I chuckle. "That's not it, but I do already have plans for this evening. I'm sorry."

Fenmire's eyes glance over my shoulder into my room, but I only have the door open enough to show him the side of my bed and nothing more. Those shrewd eyes narrow a bit, but he doesn't contradict me.

"Next time, then," he says.

"Next time," I say with a smile. "Good night."

He backs away from the door, but I can tell he wants to do anything but.

I shut the door before he can change his mind and turn back to Drixus. "There, see. Everything is fine."

"I don't mean to intrude," he says softly.

"It's alright. They all understand my time is limited. They're used to sharing me." I clap my hands together. "Since you're here, and I have no other plans for this evening, would you like to work on some more of your hair?"

"If it pleases you."

"Would it please *you*, Drixus?"

He regards me silently for a moment then nods.

I smile. "I have everything we need. Why don't you sit on the floor this time, and I'll sit behind you in my chair?"

We sit together in front of the dark fireplace, and I work in silence this time with the bottle of oil propped between my legs. It's not until the third hour or so that I realize Drixus has fallen asleep at my feet. His head lolls toward his chest, so I sit taller so I can reach his hair without waking him. He no doubt needs the rest, and I'm flattered he feels comfortable enough to sleep around me. I've almost doubled the area in his hair that's free of tangles when I start to yawn, and at the sound of a rather enthusiastic one, Drixus snorts awake. He peers around the room then over his shoulder, and he starts at the sight of me.

"It's alright," I say, raising my hands. "It's just me."

"Just you," he says with a small harumph. "You're a lot all by yourself."

I giggle. "Sorry?"

"Don't be. It'll take one exceptional human to deal with all of us." He stretches his arms out wide, rolling the muscles in his back and shoulders to work out the kinks from sitting still so long. "I don't envy you."

"It's not so bad. I'm much happier here than back in the village, due mostly to the company I keep now."

"The others have told me very little about how you came to be here. I didn't care to know the details before."

"Do you want to hear them now?"

"Only if you don't mind telling them."

I tell him everything, the same story I told Caliborne when we first met months ago. Drixus is quiet through it all as I go on combing his hair.

"And now I have these bracelets Caliborne made me," I say as I conclude my tale, and I shake the bracelet on my wrist over his shoulder. "So everyone knows what name to call me."

He reaches up and touches it. "Very nice. Caliborne chose his courting gift wisely."

"He did," I say as I lovingly touch the bronze band. I go back to combing.

"I see what you mean by the company you keep now in comparison to before in the village. If it's any consolation, those things that made you an outcast amongst your people wouldn't earn you a second glance amongst mine."

"Perhaps I was meant to be a Gryxen and ended up born in the wrong body."

"That's not how Seerraf operates. You're right where you're meant to be."

"I didn't even know Seerraf existed until a couple of months ago."

"He knew you. If you'd been born a Gryxen, you wouldn't be here to save us now."

"You think I was fated to find you?"

"Is that not what you believe? Reilanna's spell was far too specific for it to be mere chance someone like you would find their way to our doorstep. The conditions were too perfect. And what better place for a human like you than with us: a race of beings who would never judge or damn you for simply being who you are."

"You think it was Seerraf who did that?"

"It certainly wasn't your puny God… No offense."

"None taken," I mutter absentmindedly as my fingers work loose another snarl. His words stir up a whole nest of questions, and I go silent again as I consider them.

Have I been praying to the wrong god my entire life? Have I been asking for guidance and begging forgiveness from a being that had no control over my fate while remaining ignorant to the one who was actually pulling the strings? If so, is Seerraf angry at me for it? And if not, would he mind very much if I chose to pray to him from now on instead? I don't know the finer details of switching religions.

"I've upset you," Drixus says.

"No, no, not at all. You've given me some things to think about, that's all." I don't even notice I've worked a section of his hair free of tangles clear to his scalp until he reaches up and touches it, running his fingers through it from root to tip. "What do you think?"

"I haven't been able to do that in so long," he says in wonder, and he does it again. His fingers come away coated in loose hair.

I clean them off. "You'll lose a lot more before we're done. I'm being as gentle as I can be, but your hair has been through a lot. There's going to be some breakage no matter what."

He continues to touch his hair regardless, passing me the loose strands after each pass. "I just realized I've never properly thanked you," he says quietly. "When I was first told you were here, I feigned indifference, but, from the first time I saw you with the others, I've been secretly fascinated by you.

"That day you knocked on my door for the first time, I was terrified. You would've thought some horror waited for me on the other side for how badly I shook and how hard my heart raced. And yet, as soon as I heard your footsteps fade away, I regretted not opening the door."

I touch his shoulder. "But you finally did. You faced your fears and let me in."

He stares down at my hand. "I won't make you any promises."

"I don't expect any."

He nods.

I've had very few opportunities to touch him, so I keep my hand on his shoulder, waiting to hear his thoughts, but there's only silence.

I jump when he says, "You won't hear anything."

I take back my hand, quickly, like a child caught touching something they ought not to be. "What do you mean?"

"My thoughts. You won't hear them."

"You know about that?"

He nods.

"Why won't I hear them?"

"Because I don't think like the others."

"What does that mean?"

"When you think, is it like a voice is speaking in your head?"

"Yes."

"I don't have that."

"At all?"

"No."

I've never heard of such a thing before and am instantly fascinated. "If there's no voice in your head, what is there instead?"

"Emotions. It's like there's a river of feelings in my head, and depending on what's going on around me, the river changes in response. Sometimes it's difficult to describe in words."

"That's a beautiful way to describe it. How is that river now?"

He's quiet for a moment then says, "Content and resolved, but a bit anxious."

I nod and go back to combing. "What are you anxious about, if you don't mind me asking."

His hand is resting atop his knee, and it balls into a fist, making the leather gloves creak before he relaxes it again. "Have the others told you about my powers?"

"No. Like I said, they leave me to learn about you all at the source."

Another fist, another creak of old leather. "I'm anxious because I'm afraid you'll fear me when you learn what I can do."

"That's unlikely. It's not about the powers but rather how you use them. Just look at Fenmire."

He grunts, unconvinced.

"You don't have to tell me if you don't want to."

"I know." There's one more creak from his glove before he reaches over, unbuckles the strap at his wrist, and pulls it off. He holds up his hand, but it doesn't look any different from the other Gryxens'. "The day you met me, you shook my hand. Do you remember how that felt?"

"It felt like grasping ice."

He nods. "Death's touch." He flexes his hand. "If you'd continued to hold on, I would've drained you of life until your heart eventually stopped."

My fingers still in his hair. "How long would it have taken for that to happen?"

"For a being as delicate as you? Ten seconds, at most."

I blink in surprise. "Is that why you're wearing gloves now?"

He pulls the glove back on and straps it tight around his wrist. "Yes. It has to be skin to skin contact with my palms. You're safe as long as there's a barrier."

"So you don't get to choose when you use your powers?"

"That's right."

I grunt thoughtfully. "That sounds powerful but complicated. I can't imagine not being able to touch the ones you love."

"That's why the gloves are fingerless." He wiggles his fingers.

I chuckle. "That's smart."

"You're not afraid I'll accidentally kill you?"

The candidness of his question makes me laugh, but I appreciate the direct approach. "No, Drixus, I'm not. I certainly hope in the past… however many thousands of years you've been alive, that you've learned not to accidentally kill your friends."

He snorts. "It hasn't happened yet."

With my hands still buried in his hair, I lean over his shoulder, and he turns his head enough to look me in the eye.

I give him a smile. "I'm not afraid of you or your powers, so you can tell your river it needn't feel anxious anymore, alright?"

He looks away but also nods with the smallest hint of a smile on his face.

"Alright then," I say, then I go back to detangling.

Over the next hour, I get another small section done before I have to stop to crack my back and stretch out my shoulders. I yawn again.

"I should go," Drixus says.

"Are you sure? I could do this another hour at least."

"I would rather continue tomorrow."

I take his hair tie from my pants pocket and start braiding. "Do you want me to come upstairs after dinner again?"

"I'd rather meet you here. This room is… comforting."

I glance around my room, at the odds and ends I've collected in the short time I've been here. It feels more like me than the room I lived in the first twenty years of my life. "It is, isn't it?"

It feels like home.

It's well after dark when I walk Drixus to my door. Everyone else has long-ago gone to bed, which is why I'm startled to find a figure standing in the hallway, leaning against the wall across from my bedroom door when I open it. I freeze when I realize who it is.

"Fenmire? What are you…?"

Fenmire's not looking at me. His eyes are narrowed and hostile as they glare at a spot several feet above my head. I look over my shoulder at Drixus, who stepped up behind me in the open doorway before he realized we weren't alone.

"You," Fenmire sneers.

"Fenmire," I say again, sternly this time.

He ignores me. "What are you doing with them?"

"Fenmire," Drixus says softly, and the fear in his voice makes me angry. "I… I'm…"

"It's alright, Drixus," I say with a pointed look at Fenmire. "You haven't done anything wrong."

Fenmire pushes off the wall and stalks closer.

I don't move, but I hear Drixus take several steps back.

"You can't trust him," Fenmire says to me.

"Do *you* trust *me*?" I ask.

Fenmire scoffs, snorts, and stares me right in the eyes. "You know I do."

"Then you have to trust I know what I'm doing. Trust my judgment, please."

Fenmire growls and turns away, stomping back toward his room. He stops halfway down the hall and turns back. "He's going to *hurt* you, Evangeline!" he yells. "Maybe not today or tomorrow, but he will hurt you. That's what he does!"

"I won't." Drixus gently moves me aside with a hand on my shoulder and steps into the hall. "I won't hurt them, Fenmire, you have my word."

Fenmire's face turns murderous. "Your word, Drixus? *Your word*? Your word means nothing. Not after what you did!"

A door opens and Wexton's sleepy face pokes out of his room, taking in the whole spectacle. I shake my head at him with a finger to my lips to tell him to be quiet. I step around Drixus and position myself between them again where I can quickly intervene if I have to.

"Horthos was my brother," Drixus says, his voice breathless with emotion. "You know how much he meant to me. What was I supposed to do?"

Fenmire takes a threatening step forward, points to his own chest, and screams, "You were supposed to choose me, Drixus!" He's shaking and breathing so hard it's coming out in ragged puffs. "You were supposed to choose your mate."

I gasp and look at Drixus. "You're his…?"

Of course. It all makes sense now. How did I miss it?

Drixus looks at my shocked face then back at Fenmire. "You didn't tell them."

"Perhaps I should have," Fenmire barks. "They should have been warned what kind of Gryxen you are."

"Fenmire, I'm so—"

"Don't! Don't you offer your apologies now. Don't you dare."

Wexton steps out of his room and walks over to Fenmire, setting his hand on his best friend's shoulder. "Leave him, Fen."

When Fenmire doesn't break his glare, Wexton shakes him a little. Finally, Fenmire turns away, pushes Wexton's hand off, and stalks into his room, slamming the door behind him.

Drixus heaves a shaky sigh, and when I turn to him, the pained look on his face makes my stomach hurt.

"Drixus?" I say softly.

He shakes his head and walks away down the hall toward the staircase.

"Drixus, wait!" I call after him, but he waves me off and keeps walking.

Wexton is suddenly beside me. "That went about as well as I suspected it would."

"Thanks for warning me, ass," I snap.

He raises his hand in surrender. "Not my story, remember?"

"I know, but this"—I wave my hand up and down the hall after both hurt Gryxen—"could have all been avoided."

"No, it couldn't have. These two need to clear the air, and it's not going to be pretty or happen overnight. This is just the start. The fact that they even spoke at all is progress. There's been two thousand years of nothing but hurt and anger between them. No amount of preparation would've helped that go any smoother."

I look at Fenmire's closed bedroom door then down the hall toward the staircase. "Who do I go after?"

"Drixus," Wexton says with a nod of certainty. "Fenmire is likely far too heated for company, and if you ever want Drixus to come out of his room again, you should go help him face whatever he's feeling right now."

"Fair point." I turn and pull him down for a kiss. "I'm sorry for calling you an ass."

"You can make it up to me later, darling."

He smacks *my* ass as I walk away.

Chapter 60

I head up to the third floor and knock on Drixus' door. "Drixus?" I call through the wood. "Are you in there?"

He doesn't answer.

"Drixus, please let me in."

After another moment of silence, he responds, "It's open."

I open the door and step back into that dark place, wrinkling my nose against the smell as I cross the room toward the dark figure standing at the far wall where I found him the day we first met. "Do you want to talk about it?"

"There's nothing to talk about," he says. "You know what I've done."

"But I don't know why."

"Does it matter?"

"You tell me."

He goes quiet and turns to stare at the wall, and I think he's dismissing me until he finally says, "Fenmire doesn't understand, and after everything that's happened, I can't ask him to try."

"You can ask me. I want to understand. Will you explain it to me?"

"You won't believe me."

"I might."

This time, I wait out his silence until he's ready to tell me the story I know is poised at the tip of his tongue.

"Horthos was my little brother," he says. "I was supposed to protect him. We lost both our parents when he was a few hundred years old, so I raised him. He usually followed my lead wherever we went, but when Reilanna got her claws into him, he told me he was leaving with her and there was nothing I could do or say to stop him. He asked me to go with him, begged me, so I had to choose: my brother or my mate. I chose to go with Horthos.

"What the others don't know, though, is that I didn't choose my brother, Evangeline. I chose Fenmire."

I frown. "I don't understand."

"I went with Horthos to take Reilanna down from within. I didn't choose my brother, I *used* him. I used him to get close to her and end her, end all of this. But she figured it out, and she panicked, thinking the others might be in on my plans. So she killed them. She killed them all and made me watch.

"She saved my brother for last," he says softly. "And she made him linger and suffer for as long as she could to punish me. I held him as he died begging for the end to come."

I put a hand over my mouth to hide my horror, but Drixus isn't done yet.

"When she finally turned that agony on me," he continues, "I wanted to die. I prayed for it. But I… couldn't. All I could think about as she tore off my wings, gouged out my eye, and burned off my skin was the fact that Fenmire was still out there, and he'd have to fight that witch after I was gone, only then, she'd have my powers too. I was scared he might be next to suffer at her hands, and I couldn't let go."

"Your mating bond," I say tearfully.

He nods. "Our bond kept me alive when I wished for death. When Reilanna gave up and threw me through The Gate, I thought I might get the chance to explain everything to him. But once I'd recovered enough to try, I saw how deeply Fenmire hated me. And I didn't blame him. I hated myself enough to understand. I still do.

"I failed him. I failed my brother *and* my mate and lost them both."

I take a few steps closer to him. "Drixus," I call softly, and after a few heartbeats' hesitation, he turns again to face me. "I believe you."

"Why?" he asks. "Why would you blindly believe everything I've told you?"

"Because I trust you."

"Then you're a fool!"

I shake my head. "I learned long ago to trust my heart when it comes to judging others. My heart tells me yours is a genuine soul. What reason now do you have to lie?"

"I could still be working for Reilanna. Perhaps this is all a ruse to help bring about the fall of your world."

"And she ripped your wings off, took your eye, and burned you to sell that lie, did she?"

His face twitches in a near grimace. "Your beliefs don't change things between me and the others. Fenmire will never believe my story."

"Don't you think he deserves the chance to make that choice for himself?" I take another couple steps toward him. "I get it, Drixus. You're scared to tell him your side because once you do, you can't control the outcome or his reaction. Right now, by letting him believe you're a traitor, you know what to expect, but look what it costs you every single day." I wave my hand about the filthy room. "You don't deserve this, and Fenmire deserves to hear the truth, whether he believes it or not."

Drixus hangs and shakes his head.

"He misses you too."

His eye snaps back up to mine.

"He doesn't say it, but I can see the pain in his eyes. He thinks you don't care enough about him to choose him. He no doubt feels he failed you too somehow to make you choose Reilanna over him. I know I would."

"That's not true," Drixus utters.

"Then you should tell him. Maybe then you can forgive yourself. And you never know, maybe he'll forgive you too, someday."

Drixus walks over to the bed and sits on the edge of the grungy mattress. "What if he won't listen?" he asks, regarding me with a pleading look. "You saw him just now. He doesn't even want my apologies."

I walk over to stand in front of him. "He'll listen. He's spent the last two thousand years wondering why you did what you did. He'll hear your story, if for nothing else but to get some answers after all this time."

Drixus reaches out, slowly, and his fingers pluck timidly at my sleeve, inviting me closer. I step between his legs so our faces are mere inches apart. His eye roams over my face, and the look of sadness on his makes my chest feel very tight, like I can feel the weight of his worries and fears pressing down on me as well.

"It's going to be alright," I tell him softly.

"I haven't believed that in two thousand years," he whispers.

I reach out to him, making my intentions known before taking his face in both my hands. "You beautiful, broken boy. It's alright to let the past go."

He's shaking under my hands. "I should never have gone with Horthos. I should've knocked him over the head the moment he suggested it. I thought I'd be a bigger help on the other side and that, if I could just get close enough to Reilanna, just once, I could end it all. I thought Fenmire would understand eventually. I thought we were strong enough to survive this. I've never been so wrong or felt so much regret in all my thousands of years, Evangeline. Every mistake I've made feels like a dagger straight through my chest, and I can't breathe. I can't breathe."

He starts to sob.

I pull his head to my chest and hold him. "It's not too late to fix it, Drixus. Let it all go and make a better, brighter future for yourself. I'll help however I can, I promise."

He hugs me tightly and continues to cry into my shirt, and I let him, nearly falling to tears myself at the sound of so much pain and regret finally being released. I can't imagine living with all of that for one year much less two thousand.

I hope Fenmire is willing to listen. They both deserve to clear the air, even if it doesn't fix what's been broken between them.

After a time, Drixus calms in my arms and picks his head up. "I'm sorry," he murmurs.

"Don't be," I say sweetly. "That sounded cathartic."

"I feel very tired now."

I nod. "I often do myself after a good cry."

His one grey eye glances shyly up at mine then away. "Will you… Umm…?"

"Will I?" I prompt.

"Stay with me tonight?"

My face falls. "I'd love to, but I can't. I have to sleep with Caliborne. He keeps Reilanna out of my dreams."

He grunts in understanding then leans his forehead against mine.

"I can stay for a little while, though." I glance around the dirty room. "But how would you feel about moving somewhere cleaner?"

"You mean like your room?"

"No, I mean like your own space, a new space where you can start over. I don't think there's any saving this room."

He looks around the dark and dirty place himself. "What did you have in mind?"

I take his hand and tug him to his feet. "Come with me." I lead him to the door and check that the hall is empty before taking him across to the bedroom I found before. It's just as dark in here right now since the sun has set, but the smell is gone, and besides the thin coat of dust on the floor, it's clean.

"What do you think?" I ask. "You'd still be close to Mara and would remain undisturbed up here on the third floor."

Drixus peers about the room but doesn't say anything as his eye locks onto each piece of furniture then finally lands on the window, which he stares at so long his face becomes blank.

"Drixus?"

He jumps and swallows. "This was Horthos' room."

Oh shit. "I'm sorry. I didn't know."

"No, it's alright." He walks to the bed and rips off the dust sheet to reveal perfectly-made dark orange and red bedding, fall and sunset colors. "I harbor no grudges against this room." He runs his hand across the blanket then sits on the edge of the bed. He holds his hand out to me, and I cross the room and retake my place between his legs, facing him.

"Are you sure?" I ask. "I can look for another room."

He shakes his head. "I can think of no better place to start over. I have many happy memories in this room of the Gryxen my brother was before Reilanna poisoned him. Perhaps they will help me remember what we fight for."

I brush back the braid he's let fall in front of his face, tucking it behind his ear and revealing his ravaged eye. "You don't have to hide from me," I say softly. "Not your scars or your past. I promise not to judge."

"In that case, there's something I should tell you."

"What is it?"

"I know your relationship with the others is… passionate. I don't know where things will go between us, but I need you to know, I don't do that."

I tilt my head. "Do what?"

"Make love."

"At all?"

"No. I tried to when I was younger and always hated it, so now I just… don't."

"Should I…?" I take a step back.

"No," he says with a slight panic, and he tightens his hand around mine. "I like this."

So, I stay. I set my forehead to his again, and a silence falls between us that's so calm and peaceful I jump a bit when he breaks it.

"I believe Seerraf did send you," Drixus murmurs. "And if he sent you here to us, that must mean he has plans for me as well. I trust you and Seerraf, Evangeline. I'll tell Fenmire everything in the morning."

I lift my head. "I don't know about Seerraf or what he has planned for us all, but I'm here for you, Drixus. Spell or not, I want to help you. I want to see you smile again."

He flashes me a smile so ridiculously forced it makes me burst out laughing.

I'm shocked when he laughs with me.

"That's a lovely sound," I say.

"I haven't heard it in a long time."

"Let's make more reasons to hear it. Together."

He nods, and silence falls once more.

*****

An hour or so later, I slip silently into Caliborne's room, tiptoe to the bed, and try to peel back the covers without waking him. When I slide in between the sheets, he stirs anyway and reaches for me.

There you are. I almost came looking for you.

"Sorry," I whisper. "I was with Drixus."

What was all the commotion earlier?

"Drixus and Fenmire had an… altercation."

Hmm, the first of many, I fear.

I settle into Caliborne's arms, close to his chest.

He sets his chin on the top of my head. *What's the matter?*

"What do you mean?"

He gently squeezes me up my back and across one shoulder. *You're stiff as a board.*

I tilt my face up and nuzzle his throat. "Drixus shared some things with me tonight, troubling things, about his past. He carries so much darkness, it's scary just how much."

Yes, it is. And we know only pieces of it, that which he chooses to share. I'm sure there is much he chooses to keep to himself.

I shiver.

What can I do to help?

I take his hand and place it on the side of my face. "Show me more of your world," I request. "Take me on an adventure."

Caliborne kisses me on the forehead then floods my mind with another of the beautiful places he's seen.

I see a vivid green jungle filled with the strangest little animals and flowers blooming in colors I can't name. I can smell the earth beneath my feet and feel the sun on my face. A creature akin to a monkey with curly blue fur hops from one tree to another over my head. When it sees me, it scurries away, tittering back at me for disrupting its peace.

I fall asleep listening to birds sing around me and the steady clomp, clomp, clomp of Caliborne's feet on leaves and moss.

Chapter 61

I go back to Drixus' room before sunrise the next morning. He's already awake when I knock on the door. In fact, he looks like he didn't sleep at all.

"Are you ready?" I ask. "Fenmire is in the library. I heard him walking around and muttering when I put my ear to the door moments ago."

Drixus nods and steps into the hallway with me. As we start toward the staircase, I take his hand. He's shaking like a leaf.

I tug him to a stop in the middle of the hall. "Look at me." He does. "It's going to be alright. I'll be right beside you the whole time."

"No," he says. "I need to do this alone. Help me get him to listen, but if he does, I want to tell him everything in private."

"Understood," I say with a nod. I raise his hand to my lips and softly kiss the back. "For luck."

To my surprise, he smiles a little.

We walk down to the second floor and start down the long hall toward the library, and even my chest starts to feel tight with anxiety as we march ever closer to the door. We're nearly there when it opens, and Drixus freezes as Fenmire steps out, sees us, and glares. He turns to go back inside.

"Fenmire, wait," I call.

He stops but doesn't turn around.

"He just asks that you listen for a few minutes," I say. "You don't even have to say anything in return."

Fenmire looks back over his shoulder, his eyes burning into Drixus, who stiffens at my side. "It's been two thousand years—"

"Two thousand, one hundred, and forty-nine," Drixus mutters.

Fenmire's eye twitches. "What could you possibly have to say to me after so long?"

"I…" Drixus swallows and lets go of my hand. "I want to tell you the truth about what happened."

"I already know what happened. I was there. I don't need to live it twice."

"You don't know why I went. You don't know why Reilanna killed the others when she did. And you don't know why she failed to kill me."

Fenmire's nose flares, and he finally turns around with his arms crossed and his lips pulled up in a sneer. "How can I trust you to tell the truth about any of it?"

"I don't expect you to. I just want the chance to tell my side. I need it. Afterward, I'll never speak to you again, if that's what you want, and you can go back to pretending I'm dead."

Fenmire stares at Drixus so long the silence grows unbearable. Eventually, his eyes flick down to me at Drixus' side, and I give him the smallest of nods. He grits his teeth so hard in response that his jaw pops from the strain.

I don't break eye contact.

His sneer fades, and he looks back up at Drixus. "Fine."

Drixus swallows again and nods. "Can we speak in private?"

Fenmire rolls his eyes with a snort and walks back into the library, leaving the door open behind him.

Drixus looks down at me, and I give him a smile of encouragement.

He rolls his shoulders, stands up straighter, and walks into the library too, closing the door behind him.

And then I wait.

I walk about halfway down the hall so as not to overhear, but I do listen for the sounds of shouting or smashing bodies. I don't hear anything, which I consider a good sign. They aren't fighting at least. It's almost an hour before the door opens again, and Drixus strolls out. I don't see Fenmire.

"Well?" I ask.

He shrugs. "He listened, asked a couple of questions, then asked me to leave when I was done. I don't know what that means."

"Did he seem angry?"

"No, just indifferent."

I nod thoughtfully and look again at the library door. Fenmire still doesn't appear.

"I'm going back upstairs," Drixus says. "Will you... do you want to join me?"

"I'd love to work on your hair some more if you're willing, but I think I should check on Fenmire first. Meet you up there in a bit?"

Drixus nods and heads for the stairs.

I head for the library and knock before entering.

Fenmire is sitting in his chair, but he's not working; he's merely staring down at the desk in front of him with empty eyes. He doesn't react when I walk in. I cross the room and gently put an arm around him and lean my head against his shoulder.

After several moments of silence, I ask softly, "Do you believe him?"

"Do you?" he asks. He sounds like his usual, broody self.

"I do."

He runs both his hands down his face. "I'm afraid to."

"Because you think he's lying?"

"No. Because of what it would mean if he's not."

"Will you explain it to me?"

He finally looks at me, and the broken look in his eyes makes my heart hurt.

"If it's true"—he shakes his head—"it means I failed him. Even more than I thought he failed me."

"You didn't know. What more could you have done?"

"I could've had more faith in him than that. The moment he left, I considered him a traitor, and when he came back..." He winces. "When he came back, I wanted to kill him. I would have if the others hadn't intervened. I never thought for a second that he did it for any other reason than he's selfish and a fool. Why did it never cross my mind that Drixus wouldn't do what it looked like he did? I'm his mate. I'm supposed to know him better than anyone, better even than his own blood, and I immediately accepted that he'd betrayed me, like it wasn't even a question. Why did I never question it?"

"I have a theory if you'd like to hear it."

He nods for me to continue.

"You've never had a family, Fenmire. Your mother gave birth to you because you were a *vauncidi,* not because she wanted a child. Then she gave you to the temple priestesses who raised you out of obligation, not out of love. Of course you thought Drixus betrayed you. You've never been shown true love in your life to expect anything different."

"I see it now, between us."

"Do you?" I challenge. "Or do you see it as yet another product of circumstances beyond your control since a mating bond between us is crucial to breaking the spell?"

He opens his mouth but snaps it right back shut again without a reply.

"That's what I thought."

"It doesn't change how I feel about you," he rushes to say. "It's just that I know it never would have happened without Reilanna and her spell. I hate her for that. I want to love you and have you love me because it was meant to happen, not because of some obligation, as you say."

"Not a single one of you are an obligation to me," I declare. "I lose nothing by refusing to mate with any of you. I could leave The Deadwood tomorrow if I wished, mating bonds be damned. I could have run off with Will when I first stepped outside the arch that day with Caliborne and never looked back, but I didn't. I walked right back through it because I *want* to be here. I *want* to be with you. I love you." I kiss him on the lips. "Reilanna has no control over that. That's between you and me and no one else.

"I love you, Caliborne, and Wexton because you make me happy. You make me whole. Is that not how you feel about me?"

"It is. On Seerraf and the five, I swear it is."

I take his face in my hands. "Then forget about Reilanna. Her end is coming, and afterward, it'll still just be you and me."

He pulls me into his lap, tucking me to his chest under his chin as he holds me tight.

I don't know what to think or do.

"I think you know what your heart's telling you; you're just afraid to listen."

He growls under his breath. *I hate that you're right.*

"Everything else aside, can you imagine how good it would feel to let go of over two thousand years' worth of bitterness and resentment?"

He rubs his chin across the top of my head then buries his nose in my hair, breathing deeply. *There hasn't been a day since the spell was cast that I didn't wake up angry.*

"Maybe tomorrow you won't."

*****

I spend the day with Drixus and manage to detangle over half his hair. It's long enough now that I can braid it close to the scalp the way mother used to braid mine to keep it out of my face. Drixus is even quieter than usual, and instead of filling the silence with my own voice, I let it be.

That night, when I tell Caliborne about everything that happened, he's hopefully optimistic, but he also warns me not to get my hopes up.

Those two broke each other. Regardless of the reasons or the intent, that's not something that can be healed overnight.

"I know. Drixus was so nervous, the poor thing. I hope Fenmire appreciates how much it took for him to do that."

He knows. Drixus was always the softest spoken and the slowest to anger. He never argued with anyone. In fact, whenever there were disagreements amongst our team, he usually acted as a mediator of sorts to help resolve things between both parties. He hated turmoil amongst friends. I think that's what drew him and Fenmire together. Fenmire has always been broody and choleric whereas Drixus was calm and peaceful. They complimented each other, balanced the scales.

It was no small shock when we discovered Drixus had gone with Reilanna. It went against his nature. But then again, his brother had gone, and Horthos' well-being was always Drixus' number one concern. He knew Fenmire could take care of himself, but Drixus was always watching out for his brother as if he feared Horthos was constantly one step away from self-destruction. Turns out he was right.

"Did you know he raised Horthos?"

We all knew. Drixus and Horthos went to the training grounds together. Drixus was far older than was typical for a Gryxen just starting training. He requested permission to wait to train until Horthos was also of age so that he could raise his brother after their parents died.

I shake my head. "I can't imagine having to choose between my mate and someone I spent my entire life protecting."

At some point, you have to let others walk on their own. Drixus learned the hard way the consequences of always catching someone when they so much as stumble. Horthos knew his brother would be there to save him from even the smallest mistakes, which gave him far too much confidence in making bigger ones. Unfortunately, he eventually made one big enough Drixus couldn't fix it.

"Did you know that's why Drixus went with Reilanna? Is that why you and Wexton wouldn't let Fenmire kill him afterward?"

We didn't let Fenmire kill Drixus because it went against Seerraf's teachings. Drixus surrendered to us without a fight and vowed to help us defeat Reilanna. Seerraf teaches us to allow others the opportunity to right their own wrongs, and we knew we'd need his help. We planned to present him to the temple afterward and allow them to pass final judgment. At the time, we didn't know the real reason Drixus did what he did, but Wexton and I guessed it had something to do with Horthos. It didn't excuse what we still considered a betrayal, but we understood the weight of that choice and how hard it must've been for Drixus to make it. Fenmire was in so much pain we knew he wasn't thinking straight, and we feared he'd do something he'd only come to regret.

"Well, I hope they can both find some peace now, even if it's not with each other."

Forgive me for prying, but are you and Drixus… growing closer?

"As close as one can expect, given the situation. I like to think we're friends, but I still fear we're one misstep away from him slamming his door in my face and slinking back into his shadows forever."

I only ask because, no matter what happens between Drixus and Fenmire or even between you and Drixus, he still must be taken to the temple once this is over. I want you to be prepared for that. As much as Drixus works to help us defeat Reilanna and her beasts now, he still helped her rise to power and was instrumental in Michastiforo's eventual downfall. They might decide he hasn't atoned enough for that and sentence him to an extended imprisonment.

My stomach rolls. "Would they lock him away knowing my life isn't eternal like yours? That would be unnaturally cruel to both of us, wouldn't it? If we were mates, I mean."

They would look at the entire situation as a whole and make what they feel is the fairest judgment for all. I can't say with any certainty what they would decide.

"Would they let me speak on his behalf?"

Oh, yes. We'd all get to give testimony.

I sit with that for a moment then say, "I suppose we'll tackle that problem when it comes. There's no use dwelling on it now."

I just don't want you to be unpleasantly surprised by what could happen.

"I know." I scoot further up his chest and kiss him. "Thank you."

He strokes my cheek. *No matter the outcome, I am so unbelievably proud of you. You've already accomplished so much I thought impossible only months ago. You're the highest blessing from Seerraf and deserve the world. When this is over, I want to show you mine. With your own eyes, not just as mere memories.*

I smile. "You'll have to wait your turn, dearest. Wexton already plans to take me to The Isles of Aorresik."

Ah. I've heard they are magnificent.

"You've never been?"

I have not. Perhaps we could all go together. That is if Wexton doesn't mind sharing the occasion.

I smile and kiss him again, but secretly, I'm anxious and a little heart-broken.

Seerraf, please, let me live to see islands of crystal with the ones I love.

Chapter 62

Breakfast the next morning is a somewhat quiet affair. Wexton has patrol today, so his usual chatting is missing, and since Caliborne never says anything, that leaves Fenmire and the three humans as the only remaining sources of conversation. Fenmire spends the meal in thoughtful silence, and though I try not to worry about it, I catch myself glancing over at him far more often than usual. To my surprise, Jacob is the one to fill most of the silence.

"Percival says I can have my rats soon," he announces excitedly. "He's coming to Will and I's room today to help me set up a hutch for them. I do worry, though, about the earthquakes. Will and I talked, and we think we've come up with a way to anchor the box to the wall so that..."

As Jacob continues to talk, Will nudges my knee, and I look down to find his closed fist in my lap. I'm mid-drink when he opens it to reveal two identical golden bands. I briefly choke on my tea, which earns me a curious glance from both Gryxen, but I wave away their concern and pluck the rings from Will's palm, twirling them in my lap to get a better look. When I put them back, I give Will an inconspicuous wink.

"Will?" Jacob says.

Will jumps so hard he slams his leg on the underside of the table. "Ow! Yes? What is it?" he asks nervously, rubbing his abused knee.

Jacob gives him an odd look. "I asked if you have a preference on gender. For the rats. Percival says there are plenty of both, so we can have our pick."

"Oh, um… No, I don't have a preference, love. You pick."

I take a large bite of my breakfast to hide the grin on my face.

When everyone is finished eating and starts gathering their dishes, Fenmire touches my arm.

"Wait here with me?" he asks.

"Of course," I say, and I wave my friends and Caliborne out the door with promises to see them later. Once we're alone, I ask, "Is everything alright?"

"I'd like you to come with me upstairs… to the third floor."

"Oh? Are you sure you want me to come?"

"I thought perhaps you could see if Drixus is willing to hear what I have to say… You know, before I… If not, we can try another time… I don't…" He huffs. "Oh, fuck it. Emotional support. That's why I want you there."

I'm trying not to smile, but I know I'm failing. "Is Drixus going to like what you have to say?"

Fenmire leans on his arms on the table. "I don't know. I was up all night thinking about it. I wrote down everything he told me and studied it, looking for holes in his story. A lot of things that didn't make sense before do now, but he knows enough to be able to spin a convincing lie. I bounced it back and forth for hours, but I eventually realized exactly what you said yesterday: my heart has already made up its mind. I can either accept that and move on or continue to wake up angry every morning."

I smile. "I'm proud of you."

"You don't even know what I've decided yet."

I shrug. "It doesn't matter. You listened, didn't immediately react, took time to process all the information you were given, and arrived at a calm and collected conclusion." I hop down off my stool. "But now here comes the hard part: let's go tell Drixus what you've decided."

We head together up to the third floor, and Fenmire stops at the landing with a frown as he peers around the corridor. "It's filthy up here."

I grimace because he really has no idea. "How long has it been since you've been up here?"

He gives me a pointed look. "Two thousand, one hundred, and forty-nine years."

I shake my head and follow him down the hall, but when he stops outside Drixus' old bedroom, I touch his arm. "He's not in there anymore." I go to his new door and hold up my hand for Fenmire to wait where he is while I knock. "Drixus? It's me." Drixus opens the door, and I beam at him. "Good morning. There's someone who wants to speak with you. Is this a good time?"

Drixus gives me a flabbergasted look then leans his head out the door to see Fenmire waiting down the hall. He chews his lip, steps out of his room, and shuts the door. He faces Fenmire, but his eye stares down at the floor near the other Gryxen's feet, and he crosses his arms as if to make himself smaller while keeping his body half turned toward his bedroom door as if preparing for a hasty escape.

I give Fenmire a wink then step to the side, disconnecting myself from the conversation while still staying near enough for the support he asked for.

"What is it?" Drixus asks.

"Look at me," Fenmire says, his tone gentle yet firm.

Drixus closes his good eye in a wince, but when he opens it again, it's looking up at Fenmire's face.

Fenmire stands up tall, takes a deep breath, and says, "I believe you."

Drixus blinks and drops his arms. "Really?"

Fenmire interlaces his fingers in front of him. "Yes. Your story answered questions I've been asking myself for over two thousand years. Not to mention, I've known you long enough to know you're a terrible liar, and you seemed nothing but genuine in everything you told me yesterday. Plus, I trust Evangeline, and they trust you, so…"

Drixus seems momentarily stunned, and he shakes his head in disbelief. "I honestly wasn't expecting… Thank you."

Fenmire holds up his hand. "There's a 'but'."

Drixus swallows and nods for Fenmire to continue.

"I believe you, but that doesn't mean I want to pick up where we left off. So much has happened. Part of me wishes you'd told me the truth sooner, but a bigger part of me knows I wouldn't have believed you if you tried. Trust was broken on both sides, and I apologize for my part in that, but I'm not ready to forgive and forget.

I'll need time for that, Drixus, probably a lot of it, and even then, I won't promise things will ever be the same."

"I don't ask for that," Drixus said. "*I'm* not the same, and I doubt you are either. I just want peace between us."

Fenmire considers this then nods. "I can do that."

I give them two celebratory claps and a little squeal of delight. "You guys…" I palm both my cheeks. "I'm so happy I could cry."

Drixus looks away nervously, but Fenmire rolls his eyes over to me. "You ought to be," he says. "You're responsible for this."

I raise my chin. "I sure am, and proud of it."

Drixus snorts. "If I'd known we'd end up here, I would've answered my door sooner."

"You answered when you were ready. Everything happened just as it was supposed to." I touch them both on their arms. "I bet Seerraf is smiling right now."

Fenmire clears his throat uncomfortably. "Yes, well… I've said all I needed." He regards Drixus again, hesitantly, but then he offers him his hand. "To burying hostilities and moving forward, not quite as friends, not yet, but allies against a mutual evil."

Drixus stares down at Fenmire's offered hand and swallows again before taking it in his gloved one.

The moment stretches beyond a simple handshake, and I look at each Gryxen's face as they stare at each other. There's an intensity in their eyes, and they seem unable to look away. That is until Fenmire shakes himself, yanks back his hand, and takes one large step back.

"Good day," he says a bit breathlessly, then he turns on his heel and marches away.

Drixus and I continue to stand there until he disappears down the stairs.

"What was that about?" I ask.

"That," Drixus says with a small sigh, "was two mates touching for the first time in over two thousand years." He looks at his hand as he flexes it. "As much hurt as there is between us, our souls still crave each other. That's partly why I haven't tried to make amends with him until now. Being near him but unable to touch him is like starving next to a feast I'm not allowed to eat."

"And what does a handshake feel like?"

He looks at me. "Like putting my face over that feast and breathing in its delicious scent but still denying myself a bite."

I grimace.

He nods. "Exactly."

"Do you regret telling him?"

His answer is immediate and resolute. "No. He was in pain. I hope the truth eases some of that."

"What about *your* pain?"

He smiles sadly at me. "I'm used to it."

"Drixus," I chastise.

"I hurt while he thought me a traitor, and I'll hurt while he heals from learning I wasn't one. It makes little difference to me, but it makes all the difference for him. I can live with that."

My heart hurts. I touch his arm. "How can I help you?"

His smile this time is soft and welcoming. "Help me fix more of my hair?"

"Happily," I say with a grin.

*****

A few hours later, I head to the second floor to see Fenmire, but on my way down the hall to the library, I stop short at an open door I've only seen open once before, the day I took my initial tour of the castle with Wexton. Fenmire's workshop. Inside are the same bins of water, buckets, and grates I saw before, but bustling among them this time is Fenmire.

I tap lightly on the doorframe. "What are you up to in here?"

Fenmire picks up a wooden frame with a thin cloth stretched taut across it and dips the whole thing into a large bin of water. He shakes it a bit before lifting it out again. The water drains away, leaving a thin layer of sediment behind on the fabric.

"I'm making paper," Fenmire says as he carries the frame to a bench and sponges away the excess water, then he turns the frame over and pops the sheet of sediment onto the bench beside a row of others he's already made.

"Really?" I say with interest, and I come closer to inspect his work.

"Where else do you think I get all my books from?"

"I never thought about it, truth be told. You bind the books yourself too, then?"

"I do."

"Can you teach me?"

Fenmire carries the frame back to the bin and sets it on the side as he regards me. "You've asked me to teach you to fight, to understand our math, to read our language, and now this. Is there no end to your interests?"

I shrug. "Not really. I like to learn. The subject doesn't matter much. Though, I always hated learning to cook, but perhaps that's because my mother forced it on me as a task I had to master to be a proper wife and mother, neither of which I've ever wanted to be."

"What *did* you want to be?"

I smile sadly. "I never got the chance to find out. I was too busy fighting just to be myself."

He holds his hand out to me. "Come here." I do, and he picks me up and sets me on the dry side of his workbench. He puts his arms around me and nuzzles my hair. "I wish I could give you a Gryxen's lifetime to experience all the things you deserve to."

"Me too," I say softly. "But there's no use thinking of all the things I'll miss in my short life. Help me fill it with everything I possibly can until it's over."

He tilts my face up toward his. "I can do that."

He kisses me, softly this time, and at first, I think that's as far as it will go, but when I tilt my head and open my mouth in invitation, his tongue thrusts inside, and all at once, the kiss changes. Fenmire's hands tighten in my shirt at my back, and he steps closer, looming over me as his lips harden against mine. I wrap my legs around his waist, yanking him closer, and he thrusts his hips once against mine.

I moan into his mouth.

He growls into mine.

He buries a hand in my hair and tugs, forcing my head back, and I gasp then moan again when he licks my throat.

"Precious pet," he murmurs. "*Delicious* pet."

He tips my head to the side and kisses my neck, then he nips my earlobe hard enough to make me jump. He sucks the pain away then kisses down the side of my neck. His grip on my hair loosens as he reaches the spot where my neck and shoulder meet, and he licks up the length of my collar bone, dampening my skin. I turn my head away as far as I can to give him room as his mouth slides across my shoulder, and his other hand tugs the fabric of my shirt to the side. The feel of his lips on the spot he's chosen for our mating mark makes me shudder, but when his fangs brush my skin there, my heart explodes, each intense beat slamming a single word through my mind.

Mate. Mate. Mate…?

Fenmire freezes, and I stop breathing entirely.

Please.

He pulls away.

My heart shatters, and without meaning to, I choke out a single cry of agony. I slam my mouth shut on it, but it's too late.

"Evan?"

I turn my face away as tears well in my eyes.

"Look at me."

I don't.

"Evan, talk to me," Fenmire pleads.

I can't. If I open my mouth right now, he'll hear the pain in my voice no matter what words I choose to say.

He takes me by the chin and turns my face toward his. He searches my eyes, and I hear his shrewd mind work through the clues he finds in them. *They're in pain. Is it because I…? because we haven't…? Are they already…? No. No, no, no. What have I done?*

"It's not… I'm…" I can't say it; I know he'll know it's a lie.

A series of emotions flash across his face: horror, sadness, anger, then finally, determination. One second, he's staring into my eyes, the next, he's yanking my shirt down at the shoulder and sinking his fangs into my flesh.

I gasp and cling to him as a familiar heat spreads throughout my body, only this time it's so hot it's borderline painful.

And yet I want more.

As if he can read my thoughts, Fenmire bites down even harder. *Mine!*

I cry out tearfully and dig my nails into his back, scratching down his leather skin as hard as I can in repayment.

He growls again and lets me go.

I shove him—which is like pushing against a boulder—but he takes a couple of steps back anyway. He's panting through blood-covered lips, and nothing has ever looked so alluring in my entire life.

"Take me," I say breathlessly. "Hard."

Fenmire doesn't hesitate. He grabs me by the front of the shirt and hauls me across the room, out the door, and down the hall. He throws the library door open, tosses me inside, and slams it shut again. When he looks at me, he's all ruthless predator, and my heart skips a beat with anticipation of being his prey.

Chapter 63

Fenmire grabs me by the shirt again, only this time, he rips the fabric to shreds until it falls completely off me. He grabs me by the throat and marches me backward toward his desk, which he clears off with one swipe of his massive arm, sending papers, books, and pencils scattering across the floor. He backs me against the wood then unbuckles his belt with his free hand, ripping it through the loops of his pants. The sound makes me shudder, and I jump with a gasp when he whips it down across the desktop right beside me, making the leather snap menacingly. He leans down until our faces are an inch apart.

"I want to spank your ass with this"—he brandishes the belt—"then fuck it until it's dripping with my seed."

My entire body quivers.

Fenmire tilts his head. "Yes or no?"

"Yes," I utter.

"I'm going to do what you asked, but if you ever want me to stop—"

"Don't you dare," I hiss.

He chuckles wickedly. "I won't unless you tell me to, pet." He turns me by the shoulder and shoves me down on my belly across his desk. "Grab onto the wood. Spread your arms more. That's right. Hold onto the edge. Head down. Good, pet. Stay just like that."

He yanks my pants to my ankles but doesn't remove them entirely, which leaves me feeling even more vulnerable than if he had. I'm shaking but in anticipation, not fear. My body is still warm and buzzing from our mating bond, so much so that the first strike from

Fenmire's belt barely stings, but maybe that's him easing me into it. The next has more bite, but I still want more. I want red hot, blistering pain then pleasure as his cock fills me.

The next hit of the belt makes me grunt, and the one after that makes me pant. My bottom is warmer than the rest of me now, and the burn intensifies with each slap against my skin. I arch my back, begging for more, and Fenmire gives it to me, hitting me twice in rapid succession, making me cry out. He reaches in a drawer to my right and sets a bottle on the desk beside me, a bottle of the same oil we used before in his bedroom.

He sets both his hands against the desk, one on either side of me, and leans over to lick the blood from the bite on my shoulder. "Good thing I'm always prepared," he murmurs in my ear, then he stands up and spanks me with the belt again, the hardest he has yet. It sends me up on my toes with a hiss. "Breathe, pet. I want your ass cherry red before I fuck it." Another strike, and the pain has changed from red hot to white and takes a second to register, and when it does, my legs shake from the intensity. Tears sting in my eyes, and at the next strike, I scream and start crying.

Fenmire touches my back, running his palm across my skin from tailbone to neck. "Are you still with me?"

"Yes," I say through pitiful tears.

"More?"

As painful as it is, I don't want him to stop, not yet. "Yes, please. More."

The sharp crack of leather on skin precedes the pain which shoots throughout my entire body when it hits, making me shake so violently I suddenly understand why Fenmire insisted I hold on to the tabletop. He hits me three more times before dropping the belt and palming my ass, one hand on each cheek. They're so warmed by his strikes his heated hands feel cool to the touch.

"I fucking love you," Fenmire says, squeezing my abused flesh with both hands. "But I'm going to fuck you like I don't. Do you understand?"

"Yes," I whisper.

He picks up the bottle of oil and slicks three of his fingers with it, though only one slides inside me at first. The sensation barely registers around the heat and sting of my ass, and it's not until the third finger slides inside me that the pleasure overrides the pain.

Fenmire works those three fingers inside me for a while, slowly stretching me until he's sure I can take his cock instead. He palms some more oil and groans as he strokes himself with it. The head of his cock touches me, and we moan in unison when he enters me.

Gods, he's big. The stretch immediately overwhelms me, and I almost panic, but Fenmire goes slow, working himself inside me one fraction of an inch at a time. With every thrust, I gasp at the feel of him burying deeper and deeper.

Fenmire buries his hand in my hair again, holding me down as he slowly pumps himself inside me. "You have no idea how long I've wanted to feel this hole clench around my cock," he growls. "And it's every bit as glorious as I imagined." He pulls out of me then glides right back in, deeper than ever.

I whimper.

When his hips bump against my tender cheeks, I know he's buried himself completely inside me, and I sigh with both pleasure and relief.

He leans over me again, still holding on to my hair, and says, "Give me your hands, pet."

I let go of the wood. My knuckles are stiff from how hard I was gripping it. I bring my arms behind my back, and Fenmire holds them together at the wrist in one of his massive hands. With my arms pinned behind me and my head held down by the hair, I'm completely at his mercy, and with my backside speared by his hard, long cock, there's no escape. I don't know what comes over me, but at that moment, I relax against the wood with another soft sigh, completely at ease despite the situation.

Fenmire chuckles. "That's right, pet. Melt for me."

He starts moving, but gone is the slow and gentle Gryxen who stretched and opened me up to this point. The predator is back, and he bucks his hips against mine with so much force the desk screeches across the stone floor with every thrust. His hips slam into my ass over and over, bringing the burn and sting back with each impact. He takes me fast and rough and hard, just like I asked.

And I love it.

I'm mewling with every plunge of his cock in my ass, and even though he's fucking me exactly like he said he would, he still continues to praise me.

"You feel so good, pet. I love hearing you whimper. Every time I sit down to work at this desk from now on, I'll remember the feel of your ass milking my cock."

I'm floating, no longer one with my own body but an observer from above. I can feel Fenmire's cock, my burning ass, his fingers gripping painfully in my hair, but that's not me. I'm somewhere else, wrapped up in the pretty words Fenmire never stops uttering.

"You're so beautiful. And mine. My mate."

That word makes me cry again. My heart ached for this, and now it's so full I might burst.

"I want you to come for me, pet. I want to feel your body convulse around mine."

I don't even have to try. It's as if Fenmire has reached inside my soul and taken over, which, all things considered, is a pretty accurate depiction of recent events. At his request, my body tightens, and I moan.

"Come for me," Fenmire orders with an extra hard slam of his hips.

And I do. My body shakes and jerks but there's nowhere for me to go, caught in Fenmire's grip like I am. My eyes roll up in my head, and that floaty feeling intensifies until I can no longer comprehend what Fenmire is saying. I do notice, though, when he stiffens and leans over me, covering my body with his own, and I feel the heat of his seed burst inside me as he nuzzles my neck. He's still talking, and I can tell by the tone of his voice that his words are just as pretty even if I can't understand them. He presses his hips against my backside, burying himself as deep as he possibly can as he jerks and shakes overtop of me, and he kisses and licks the bite on my shoulder as I slowly float back down inside my body.

I lie across the wood, breathing heavily and slowly gaining consciousness again. My breasts are pressed beneath me so hard they hurt but not as badly as my ass which throbs with every beat of my heart. Fenmire pulls out of me, and I gasp in pain. My body has been used and abused to its limits, and yet I don't regret a single bit of it. His seed is running down my legs, and it makes me snort as I press my sweat-slick forehead against the desktop.

"We're a mess," Fenmire murmurs. "Let's fix that."

He pulls his pants off then helps me step out of mine without toppling over. Once we're both naked, he picks me up and carries me out of the library, down the hall, down the stairs, and into the pool room.

We slide into the pool together, and even in the water, we don't leave each other's arms.

The water feels good on all my abused bits, and Fenmire washes both me and himself before settling against the pool wall with me in his lap on my knees, facing him.

"Why did you do it?" I ask, knowing I don't have to explain what I'm talking about. "You weren't ready."

"I was. If I wasn't, it wouldn't have worked. I've wanted it for a while, but I was afraid. Each time I was there with your skin under my teeth, my heart would race in anticipation, but then I'd remember the mess and the pain of my previous mating bond, and I'd freeze. But when I saw you were in pain, the need to fix it squashed my fears. Why didn't you tell me?"

"Because I knew you'd only punish yourself even more than you already do. Telling you would've put you in an impossible position, and I didn't want you to do something you weren't ready for out of some self-imposed obligation."

"What happened to you, it's called *ihnrohada*. Usually, when one partner is ready and willing but the other isn't, a bond doesn't form, but, very rarely, it *does* form but only for the person who truly wanted it. It's said to be even more painful than losing a mate, for the one you've bonded with is alive and well but doesn't want you. Thankfully, it happens so infrequently that lovers usually never worry about it. A bite normally has to happen, though. I've never heard of *ihnrohada* between two partners who didn't get that far."

"Perhaps me being human has something to do with it. I can't bite you, so perhaps the mating bond doesn't require that step for me."

Fenmire blinks down at me in surprise. "That's a very good observation. I bet you're right." He cups some water in his hand and splashes it onto my shoulder, rinsing the bite.

I hiss and look down at it for the first time. "Oh my…" It's worse than the other mating bites I've had so far. Since Fenmire bit much harder, many more of his teeth broke the skin besides his fangs, which left quite sizable holes that are still weeping red.

"I got a little carried away, I'm sorry."

"I'm not. It suits you."

He smirks then moves me from his lap so he can stand up. "Come on. We should put something on that so it doesn't get infected." He climbs out of the pool and offers me a hand out. I dunk under the water one last time before taking it.

"What powers do you think I'll get from you?" I ask as he yanks me out of the pool beside him.

He hands me a sheet. "I have a theory."

"Don't you always?" I ask with a snort. "Care to share?"

"We'll find out tonight."

"What happens tonight?"

"We're going to do an experiment," he says with a wink. He wraps a sheet around his shoulders and suddenly drops to his knees in front of me.

"What are you doing?" I ask with a laugh.

He goes down on his hands and knees and leans his face down to my feet, licking at the rivers of water running across the top of one of them. His tongue follows the water up my ankle, my calf, my knee, and my thigh. He buries his face into my groin with a groan, probing his tongue between my thighs for a moment before continuing his path up my belly, between my breasts, and up my throat to my mouth, which he seizes in a kiss so instantly heated I groan.

His arms wrap around me, and his fingers dig into my welted backside, making me whimper.

"I might take what I want from this body," he says in a low voice against my lips. "But I need you to understand that every moment of every day, both between and during the times you surrender to me, I am utterly and completely at your mercy. This body might be mine"—he yanks me closer in his arms—"but this one is yours as well." He takes my hand and places it, palm down, on his chest. "As well as every ounce of my devotion. Do you understand, pet?"

I touch my nose to his. "Perfectly. I love you."

"I love you too."

The slightest sound, like a pebble bouncing on stone, makes us both turn toward the door where Drixus is standing, wide-eyed and staring at us.

"Drixus," I say in surprise. I look at Fenmire, gauging his reaction, but his face is emotionless as he stares right back at Drixus without blinking.

Drixus takes a step back. "I… I'm…" He's holding a washrag and a clean pair of pants. To see him come down here during the day is nothing short of a miracle, and I hate that we might've ruined that.

"It's alright," I say. "We were just leaving. You don't have to—"

Drixus shakes his head and backs up another step.

"Stop," Fenmire orders, and Drixus freezes, his eye going so wide this time it looks ready to pop out of his head. Fenmire stands and wraps my sheet around me, then he puts a hand on my back, ushering me toward the door. "It's all yours," he says as we walk past Drixus.

Drixus doesn't move, he doesn't even turn his head, he stays in the doorway and stares at the spot where Fenmire and I were just standing as we start up the stairs.

We're almost to the foyer when Fenmire says softly, "He looks good."

"We're still working on it."

"How are you fixing his hair?"

I tell him about my experience detangling the tails of Papa's horses.

"It's impressive."

"It's a lot of work, but we're almost done."

He nods and goes silent as he leads me through the foyer and down the hall to his room where he sits me on his bed and retrieves one of his many golden tins from his shelves. He wipes away the blood still running down my wet skin with a corner of my sheet then smears a generous dab of the salve from his tin across the bite. The salve burns on contact, and I hiss.

"Sorry," he says, and he blows lightly on it to soothe the burn.

With his mouth so close to mine, I can't resist leaning in and stealing a kiss or two. He returns my kiss with a groan then takes my face by the chin and pushes me sternly away.

"Let me cover this before you seduce me again, would you?" he murmurs.

"You better get a move on, then," I reply. "I've got another hole aching for you to fill with your seed."

Fenmire tilts his head and closes his eyes as if my words cause him physical pain. "You don't take prisoners, do you?"

"Where's the fun in that?" I shrug the sheet off, lean back on his bed on one arm, spread my legs, and touch myself, all while staring into his eyes.

"Seerraf and the five, Evan…" Fenmire utters between gritted teeth. He tosses the tin aside, crawls up on the bed overtop of me, and grabs me by the throat, shoving me flat on my back.

I wrap my legs around his, tugging him closer. "Take me again? Fuck me like you hate me while you talk to me like you love me."

And he does.

*****

After dinner, Fenmire asks for Wexton and I to wait in the dining room while he retrieves something. A few minutes later, he comes back with his hands clutched together, holding something still between his palms. He sits back down at the table, and we lean closer as he opens his hands enough for us to get a peek. It's a mouse so small and delicate it looks comical between Fenmire's massive hands.

"I borrowed him from the stables," Fenmire says, running one of his massive fingers across the top of the little creature's head. "He's going to help us find out what powers you got from me, if any. So far, your powers have been the reverse of that of your mates'. My powers allow me to infect living things with disease. If my theory is correct, you should be able to do the opposite. This little guy will allow us to test that theory."

"You don't mean to infect him with some disease, do you?" I ask in a slight panic.

"I do," Fenmire says with a nod. "Then you'll try to cure him."

"But what if I can't?"

"I'll try my best to keep it mild. He should recover on his own in time."

The little mouse closes his eyes under Fenmire's stroking finger, completely at ease and oblivious to his fate.

"I don't know," I say uncertainly.

"We should know the extent of your powers if you're to help us fight Reilanna."

"Evan will never have to face Reilanna," Wexton declares.

"If you truly believe it won't come to that, then you're a fool," Fenmire barks. "Reilanna has already tried several times to kill our mate. Would you rather give them false assurances and hope for the best or be as prepared as possible for when Reilanna tries again. And she *will* try again. We all know it."

I put my hand on Wexton's. "It's alright. I want to try. I want to know."

Wexton nods and stays silent.

Fenmire closes his hands around the mouse again and closes his eyes to focus, and after less than a minute, he holds his hands out to me. I cup mine together, and he deposits the mouse into my palms.

The difference in the little creature is heart-breaking. He's squeaking softly and shivering. He can barely open his eyes to look at me.

"It's alright, little guy," I tell him softly as I hold him between my palms. "I'm going to fix it. It's alright."

I don't close my eyes like Fenmire did. I look into that tiny face and watch his nose twitch, his whiskers dancing wildly as he smells me. I focus on his body, on the bones of the little feet gripping my skin, on the soft fur beneath my fingers, then I move my focus inward. When I do, I hear his little heart racing, the soft gurgling of his stomach, and his lungs drawing ragged breaths. I can feel those things as if I've reached inside and touched each organ individually, feeling the life flowing through them under my fingers. I keep going, searching for the sickness I know Fenmire has placed inside the tiny creature. I focus on the brain.

There. There is the infection. I can feel it. I can *taste* it, like something sour on my tongue. I make a face.

"Can you sense it?" Fenmire asks.

"Yes."

"Good. Now, can you control it?"

Feeling the mouse struggling to breathe has me on edge. I want to do more than control it. I want to make his pain go away. This time, I do close my eyes as I focus on that sickness. I find its edges, feeling how far it has spread in his tiny body, and will it away.

The palms of my hands grow incredibly warm, so warm I'm afraid it might hurt the mouse, but I can still feel his heartbeat and nothing else in his body feels to me like it's in distress, so I keep going. I focus my intentions on that sourness in his head, squeezing it and forcing it smaller and smaller until there's little more than a hint of it left, then it's gone completely.

I open my eyes and smile at Fenmire, parting my hands to show the wriggling mouse in my palms. He's slightly sweaty but otherwise unharmed and much livelier than he was a moment ago.

Fenmire holds his hands out and silently accepts the mouse from me. He waves a palm over the animal to check it for injury or sickness. I already know he won't find any, so I'm not surprised when he smiles up at me. I *am* surprised, however, by the tears in his eyes.

"Fenmire?" I say in concern.

He glances briefly at Wexton. "Give us a moment?"

"Did it not work?" Wexton asks.

"It worked just fine," Fenmire says, holding the mouse out to Wexton, who holds it carefully between his hand and chest. "Take him back to the stables for me, would you?"

"Alright," he says uncertainly, but at a nod from me, he leaves.

As soon as we're alone, Fenmire stands and rounds the table to me, dropping down on both knees in front of my stool.

I put my hands on his face. "What is it? What's wrong?"

He takes both my hands from his face and turns them, palms up. He rubs his thumbs down them softly, lovingly. "Once we suspected your powers are the antithesis of our own, I couldn't help but wonder… to hope that would be the case with me as well.

"All my life, I've been treated like a miracle. My conception, my birth as a Gryxen, my genius, my drive, everything that made me who and what I am was seen as a gift straight from Seerraf and the five. But my powers, they never felt like a gift to me. You once called me a healer. Do you remember my reply?"

"You said you were a killer who can sometimes use his powers for good."

"That's right. I was given the power to take life and create misery. I can make a man live for days, weeks even, in a body that's failing him. I bring suffering and heartache and death. It was only through years of experimentation that I learned how to manipulate my powers to do a shred of good amongst the pain I caused, but I never felt it was enough. But now…"

He locks eyes with me, and the feeling I find in those wells of inky black makes it nearly impossible to breathe.

"You have the power to truly heal the sick, to end others' pain," he says. "You will bring nothing but good into this world. And those powers were born from mine." He squeezes my hands as if desperate to make me understand.

I understand perfectly.

"Your powers *are* a gift, Fenmire, like the rest of you. I could've told you that from the start."

He's quiet for a moment before he says, "I lost faith in Seerraf those years we were stuck here with no help and no hope. I'm ashamed to admit that now. He sent you to us, to me, and I'll spend the rest of my life trying to make up for ever doubting either of you."

Chapter 64

Fenmire has patrol tonight, so I go back to his room with him after our experiment to help him dress in his armor. It's an unspoken ritual of mine with all of my mates, one that comes completely natural to me after the mating bond but never before. Fenmire is quieter than usual as I help him buckle and strap in.

"What's the matter?" I ask.

He surprises me with a straight answer. "I don't want to go out tonight. Maybe it's the protectiveness that comes with a new bond, but I feel like I shouldn't be away from you right now."

I smile. "It wouldn't matter if you stayed since I have to spend my nights with Caliborne."

"No, I know that. I don't mean that I want to… Well, I mean, I *do* want to, but—"

I laugh. "I was only teasing. I know what you meant. But you technically protect me more on patrol than you do here in the castle."

He smirks. "Except that one time."

"Except that one time," I agree with another laugh.

He palms my face. "My icicle warrior," he murmurs. "Now that your heart and soul are bound to mine, I regret not teaching you how to fight to better protect them when I'm not around."

"You're never not around," I say, drawing the knife from my belt that never leaves my side.

He lunges and grabs me by the throat. "It won't protect you from me though," he growls.

"Oh, no," I say dramatically. "Whatever shall I do?"

He kisses me and nips my bottom lip hard enough to make me gasp.

"You'll do whatever I tell you to," he murmurs.

I put his knife to his middle, the tip pressing just under his ribcage.

He chuckles. "There's my warrior, and they're wielding something far more deadly than an icicle this time." Suddenly, the knife is knocked away, and I'm spun around and held against his chest like that day in Caliborne's bedroom. "As I said, pet," he growls in my ear, "it won't protect you from me." He rips the knife from my hand and throws it, and the blade sticks into one of his shelves with a thud. "If I hadn't already used both your holes this afternoon, I'd bend you over my bed and—"

There's a knock on his door: three taps followed by a break then three more taps.

"I hear you," Fenmire calls. He kisses me on the cheek. "I have to go."

"That's too bad," I say as he releases me. "Because I have one hole you haven't used today."

Fenmire shakes his head when he understands. "Do you have any idea what that thought is going to do to me all night?"

I smirk at him. "I do, actually." I retrieve his knife and replace it on my belt. I turn to him, grab the bottom of my shirt, and lift it above my breasts. "Picture this too," I say with a shimmy. "All. Night. Long."

He snarls and lunges at me.

I scream and fling his door open, fleeing down the hall while tugging my shirt down and cackling insanely. I almost run into Caliborne's back, but he spins and catches me with one arm just in time.

What in the—

Fenmire skids into the hall, stops when he sees we're not alone, stands up straight, and runs his hand through his hair. He chuckles and sniffs. "Caliborne," he says with a nod of his head. He reaches in his bedroom door for his shield and mace then heads off toward the foyer. When he passes me, he leans down and whispers, "You'll pay for that tomorrow."

"Promise?" I whisper back.

He walks away, and a wicked smile spreads across my face at the thought of how he'll make me pay.

Caliborne clears his throat.

I smile sheepishly up at him. "Hello."

He raises a brow. *Hello. Have something to tell me, my stoferra?*

I tug my shirt down at the collar to show him the bandage on my shoulder.

It happened at last?

"It did," I say happily.

He opens his bedroom door. *Help me out of this armor while you tell me all about it?*

"Gladly."

*****

I'm running through The Deadwood, weaving between trees and leaping over logs and streams to escape the beast I can hear chasing me.

"Evaaaangeline," Fenmire calls in a sing-song voice. "I will find you, pet. And when I do, I'm going to bend you over the nearest stump and take everything I want."

I giggle as I run harder. I think I'm losing him as I can no longer hear his massive footfalls behind me. It's starting to get dark, but I don't realize just how fast the light is fading until I almost run headlong into a tree. I slow and look up to see great, black clouds rolling across the sky, slowly blocking out the sun.

I stop.

The forest is silent. There isn't a single rustle of leaves in the breeze, no bird calls, no gurgle of water, nothing. It's growing darker still, and shadows are beginning to press in around me. I swear I see one move out of the corner of my eye, and I whirl. There's nothing there, and yet I can't shake the feeling I'm being watched.

"Fenmire?" I call.

There's no answer.

The shadows move again, and this time there's the snap of a twig as well. It's deafening in the silence, and I jump and spin to face the source of the sound. There's something watching me from the darkness. I can't see it, but I can sense it's there. Fresh fear ripples through me but not the fun kind.

"Fenmire?" I call again, and when there's still no reply, I take a step back. "Stop, Fenmire. You're scaring me."

The silence that meets me this time terrifies me.

Fenmire would never keep playing if I asked him to stop.

I take another step back. "Who are you?"

A low, rumbling growl answers me, and a glowing pair of yellow eyes appear in the nearby brush.

I turn and run the other way, but I can't see where I'm going. I take no more than a couple steps before my boot catches a tree root and I go sprawling across the forest floor. I hear thundering steps behind me, and I roll onto my back to see those glowing eyes getting closer and closer, moving at an impossible speed. I scramble backward, but a massive mouth lined with rows of dripping, razor-sharp teeth lunges at me. I cover my face and scream.

Nothing happens.

I lower my arms. I'm sitting next to the pond, but the water is inky black and rippling unnaturally as if something massive lies just below the surface. I stand and back away. The smell of rot hangs heavy in the air, and my boots squish into a stream of something wet that's trickling down the bank into the water. I turn to find the source.

The entire village lies dead in a heap at the edge of the woods, and my father sits in front of it with my dead mother's head in his lap.

"Look what you've done," he says. "So much pain…" He glares at me. "I should have killed you in the cradle, you wretch."

I narrow my eyes.

My father would never say that to me.

I take a step forward and study him. This man looks nothing like my father. And the body in his lap, that's not my mother.

I peer around me. Though this is the bank of some body of water, it's not the one where I've made many cherished memories during my time in The Deadwood. I look at the black water, remembering the feel of a dead hand wrapping around my ankle and pulling me below the surface. This may not be my pond, but I've been here before.

I almost drowned here once.

Caliborne saved me… he saved me from a dream.

A dream.

Reilanna.

"You witch," I sneer. I back even further away from the water. "Get out of my head!"

With a wave of my hand, I send the entire pond rushing through the forest, emptying it to nothing but a pit of mud with a wriggling creature in its center made entirely of arms, like a morbid ball of human snakes. It tries to crawl up out of the pit, its fingers digging into the mud as it slips and slides through the muck. I turn my back on it.

"Where are you?" I scream at the sky.

"Right here."

The voice is in my ear, so I whirl.

I'm no longer beside a pond but standing in the lane, facing the arch. I turn around, ready to strike at… something, I can't remember what. I freeze with a cry of horror instead.

All three of my mates are in the trees at the side of the lane, their flesh rotten and dripping from their bones, which hang from ropes strung around their necks. Drixus stands in front of them, and he turns to me with a look of bitter hatred on his face.

"You were supposed to fucking save them!" he yells.

Something's not right.

This Gryxen, though he lacks wings and an eye, doesn't look like Drixus, not really. He's missing most of the scars besides the ones caused by Reilanna's torturous fires, and his hair is different. I look at the others hanging in the trees. The one with red hair has two arms instead of one.

"You don't know what they look like anymore," I mumble. "This is just a dream."

Reilanna's laughter echoes down the lane on the wind.

"This is just a dream," I whisper to myself, and I keep whispering it, over and over. I can't let her distract me again.

"It may be a dream," Reilanna says, "but if you die here, you die in your bed, and this time, your lover can't save you."

"This is just a dream. This is just a dream."

The ground under my feet begins to shake.

"No!" I scream, and I stomp my foot, willing the earth beneath it to be still.

The quake stops.

I snap my fingers and banish the bodies and Drixus.

"You are not the one in control here," Reilanna says. Her voice is behind me again, but I know if I turn around, she'll only change the dream and force me to continue playing her game.

I lurch backward and grab with both my hands, and I'm shocked when they connect with a warm, solid body. "Neither are you." I close my eyes and picture the clearing by The Gate. Reilanna slips from my grasp, but when I open my eyes, I'm standing in that space next to the circle of grey stones. I kneel and touch one. "Help me! Please!"

There's no answer, mostly because the stone disappears from beneath my hand before I can hear one. When I look up, the woods are on fire. I spin in place. I'm surrounded by flames, and the smoke slowly billows toward me, slamming into me from all sides and making me choke. Something moves to my left, but my eyes are burning, so I can't tell what it is.

"This is a dream. This is a dream. This is a dream." I chant the words to myself as I wave my hand and dispel the smoke.

This is getting me nowhere. I can't keep reacting to her horrors.

I must become a horror myself.

I close my eyes and imagine a form that could fight her, and as I do, I feel my body become heavy, starting at my feet and gradually moving up to the very top of my head. My hand is suddenly filled with a hard piece of metal, and my stance corrects as a great weight is added to my back near my shoulder blades on both sides. I open my eyes and glance down at my body that's now adorned with a full set of golden armor identical to the kind the Gryxen wear. I lift my arm and admire the sword gripped in my hand. It's made of solid ice so cold it's smoking, but my hand isn't cold at all. I catch a glimpse of gold out of the corner of my eye and look over my shoulder at the pair of beautiful, gold-feathered wings sprouting from my back, fluttering softly in the breeze.

I draw Fenmire's blade from my belt and spin in a circle. "Fight me!" I scream. "We've played your game long enough. Now play mine! Or are you afraid you'll lose?"

The handle of Fenmire's knife grows warm, almost too warm for me to hold on to.

I feel the heat of Reilanna's breath on my ear as she laughs beside it. "Deal."

As if pulled by the weapon clutched in my hand, my arm jerks around, spinning me on my heel so hard and fast, I nearly fall over as the blade of Fenmire's knife connects in a near-deafening clang with the head of a giant spear that had been only inches from driving into my back, and for the first time, I come face to face with the witch who's haunted my dreams since I arrived in The Deadwood.

Reilanna is shorter than my Gryxen mates but no less intimidating. She has four arms instead of two, though the two extras are spindlier than the others and pure black, having obviously been added by her shapeshifting abilities. She has wings, but they're also black and unnatural like the pair CeCe had when she came through The Gate. Her hair is short and patchy as if she's ripped bits of it out, and the color is a sort of dirty orange that's not consistent throughout the strands. Her eyes are yellow with black slits in their centers, and her teeth are all black when she smiles at me, though many are chipped or missing.

Her tongue clicks as she hisses at me like some giant insect. "Little human," she sneers. "You may look impressive in your armor with your weapon of ice, but that doesn't mean you have what it takes to fight me." She whips the butt of her spear toward me, and though Fenmire's knife moves to defend me, injuring me wasn't the purpose of her strike. The force of her blow knocks me off my feet and backward across the clearing, and I land with a clatter by the trees, so close to the fire the heat of it burns my back. I scramble away with a cry of pain, dropping my knife.

Reilanna marches toward me, and I do the only thing I know I can do.

I use my imagination.

With a wave of my hand, I summon a wall of stone between us that stretches across the entire clearing. I snatch up my knife and get to my feet with my eyes to the sky, expecting her to fly over it, but I throw up both my arms to protect my face from flying bits of rock a second later when the wall explodes toward me. Reilanna steps through it.

"Tricks of the mind won't save you tonight," she tells me. With her palms pointed at the ground, she summons a series of stone spears that jut out of the dirt, one after the other, headed straight for me.

I watch them come, but just before the last one skewers me from below, I scream and punch the ground, cracking the earth in a massive fissure that snakes toward Reilanna along her line of stone spears, each of which crack and shatter into hundreds of pieces. When my fissure reaches her, she steps aside and looks at me rather boredly.

"You can't beat me," she says matter-of-factly. "I can do everything you can, and I have years' more experience. Why fight the inevitable?"

I know she's right. I'm on my knees, panting and holding my head that's screaming in pain. I'm suddenly exhausted. What little I've managed to do has already taken its toll on me. How can I possibly beat a witch who's made a hobby of invading people's minds and torturing them with her games?

She starts walking toward me again, and I watch her come with a sinking feeling of dread and defeat.

A sudden break in the black clouds above lets a single ray of bright golden light through, which strikes the chest of my armor, warming it instantly. That warmth spreads throughout my entire body, and I feel a wave of blissful calm wash over me. Reilanna's steps slow until she's barely moving, and I look up, directly into the light, as a voice speaks in my head the same way my mates' thoughts do when I'm touching them.

'Fight with the strength of the five that came before you, my champion.'

Champion? What does—

Five voices—three feminine, two masculine—speak in my head in turns.

'We'll stand with you against this evil.'

'You're not alone.'

'We fight as one.'

'Lift that blade!'

'Be ready to strike.'

I stand up. The armor around me feels familiar now, so does the weight of the weapon in my hand, as if I've touched these things a thousand times before. I wrap both hands around the hilt of my sword and correct my stance, and I look up at Reilanna as time rights itself, and she starts walking toward me again at a normal pace. I let her come and smile as she rears back her spear.

My body reacts on instinct, and I swing up with my sword with unnatural speed, knocking away her strike. My fingers flex around my weapon, eager for a fight, and I peer up into the face of my enemy, still smiling. Reilanna narrows her eyes, then she strikes again. And again. And again. My movements are fluid perfection as I meet each blow with one of my own. My feet dance across the ground, each of my muscles honed and guided by the experience of the warriors whose very essence I can feel inside me. Their thoughts swirl inside my head, urging me on, and they feel so familiar there, like they're not intruders in my mind at all but part of me.

I can anticipate her blows now, and I realize she's actually not that experienced a fighter. She uses the weight and length of her weapon to keep her opponent at a distance, which means…

I need to get closer.

I roll under a swipe from her spear and deliver the first true blow of my own: a punch, right to her middle. I'm not very strong, so it does little more than startle her, but the swipe of my sword I follow it with certainly leaves a mark as my blade runs up the length of her bare chest. She staggers back with a cry of pain, clutching the bleeding spot in shock. The wound heals beneath her hand in seconds, but her eyes narrow again as they stare me down.

"Who are you?" Reilanna snarls.

When I answer, it's in my voice, but there are other voices as well, five of them, all speaking in perfect synchrony with me. "I am the one who will make you pay for all the pain you've caused. I am your end, Reilanna, and I'm coming for you."

Reilanna's lip curls back, showing her black, rotted teeth, but when she speaks, it's not to me. "Seerraf!" she screams in utter disgust. "What have you done?"

Laughter bubbles out of me that's not my own, and I feel that warm touch on my chest again.

'Cast her out of your mind forever, my champion.'

With pleasure.

I strike, which she immediately blocks with her spear held out in front of her between two hands, but I hit again and again, faster and harder, until finally, with a massive overswing, I bring my sword down on the wooden length of her spear and snap it in half. She rears back and takes flight, but I give her no rest. I jump into the air and continue my onslaught, raining blow after blow upon her, and though she manages to block them all with the broken bits of her weapon, she's slowing down and becoming more and more unsteady. I scream in rage with every swing, never missing an opportunity as I push forward. With the flat part of my blade, I hit one of her hands hard enough she drops one half of her spear.

I can see The Gate below us, and the ground between the stones begins to shimmer. As I keep up my assault, The Gate opens, and the red sand of the Vorisca Desert appears in that window into the Gryxen homeworld.

Reilanna's homeworld.

I charge and tackle her middle, shoving her toward that gateway I know will send her out of my head forever. I summon a wind stronger than her black wings that pushes her toward the ground, and we plummet. I let her go before we hit the ground, and she lands on her back, sprawled out across The Gate. She throws her arms and legs out wide, clutching its edges to keep from falling through.

"You are not in control here!" she screams again. "I will not let you release them. You have to know, even if you succeed, I will win. I will win!"

My wind holds her down, but her grip on the edges of the gateway keeps her from falling through. I take Fenmire's blade from my belt again and approach her, and the voices in my head all speak at once.

'Yes.'

'It's time.'

'She wins nothing today.'

'Take the kill.'

'She's yours.'

I throw my sword aside, take Fenmire's knife in both hands, and plunge it into the center of her chest.

Reilanna cries out and stills, but her grip doesn't loosen. She pulls herself up toward me, her lips curling back over her rotten teeth as she screeches her hot, angry breath in my face.

We lock eyes.

"I'm coming for you," I say again, and the five echo me in turns.

A flicker of fear crosses Reilanna's face before I yank back Fenmire's blade, and bury it, hilt deep, into her chin instead.

Reilanna's eyes fall out of focus, and her grip finally relaxes. Her body folds and falls, plummeting toward the desert sands below. It never lands, though, as she explodes into black dust long before she reaches the ground. The Gate shimmers again, and the forest floor slowly forms between the stones, sealing her on the other side.

I sit on the ground beside The Gate to catch my breath. The black clouds immediately begin breaking apart, and the sun pokes through, sending beams of light to the ground like golden pillars. One lands on my chest again, and the warmth returns, only this time, it's accompanied by a feeling of victory, pride, and…

And love.

I look up into that ray of golden sunshine as it slowly grows to encompass me entirely. I'm entranced by the light, even more so when I feel a touch on my face as if a palm has landed softly on my cheek. A wave of emotions swells inside me that's so intense a single tear spills down the opposite cheek.

"Don't go," I plead, though I have no idea why.

'I never do. Go back to your lovers now, my champion. I will see you again very soon.'

A hand, a real, corporeal one, grips mine, and the sudden contact makes me jump. I turn away from the light to find Caliborne standing beside me. My armor and wings are gone, and it's just me and him standing alone in The Deadwood.

Wake up, my stoferra.

My eyes blink open to a plain stone ceiling. I look around and find Wexton and Fenmire standing around Caliborne's bed, staring down at me. Caliborne has his head bowed and eyes closed as he holds my hand between both of his at the side of the bed.

"I killed her," I say in disbelief.

Caliborne's head shoots up, and Fenmire and Wexton step closer to the bed.

"What did you say?" Fenmire asks.

"Reilanna. I killed her. In my dream." My voice cracks, and my throat is so dry it hurts to swallow. I'm very tired, and my body feels sluggish and sore.

I couldn't wake you, Caliborne says. He brushes the hair from my face. *She snuck right past me and wouldn't give you up. I'm sorry.*

"It's not your fault. I don't think we have to worry about her anymore. Not when it comes to my dreams, anyway."

"You killed her?" Wexton asks.

"Yes. I realized it was a dream and kept myself focused until she had no choice but to face me." I sit up a bit and look more closely at my mates. Fenmire is dressed in his armor, which helps me remember… "You were on patrol."

"Wexton came and got me when Caliborne couldn't wake you up," Fenmire says.

"You should go back. I love you, but I'm fine. Someone needs to be watching The Gate. Reilanna is probably angry, and I don't want her to catch us off guard when she chooses to retaliate."

Fenmire starts to argue, but Wexton puts his hand on his shoulder. "I'll go." He comes around the side of the bed, leans down, and kisses me on the forehead. "I'll watch The Gate. Let Fenmire make sure you're alright. And don't fuss about it."

"Deal," I say.

Wexton leaves and Fenmire takes his place beside the bed. His hands begin their usual sweep over my body.

"How do you feel?" he asks.

"Tired. Thirsty. My head hurts."

"They're dehydrated," Fenmire says. "Caliborne?"

Caliborne nods and immediately leaves the room.

"I don't think lack of water is what's making my head hurt like this," I say, touching my palm to my forehead with a wince.

Fenmire scoots closer and raises his hand an inch from my temple. "I don't feel anything unusual. Why do you think something else is wrong?"

"I don't think there's anything wrong, necessarily. It's just that, in my dream, I was preparing myself to fight Reilanna, so I chose a form I thought might be up to the task. But then, someone spoke to me in my head. They had a deep and powerful voice, not one I've heard before, and yet I knew immediately who it was."

"Do I even have to ask?" Fenmire says with a hint of a grin.

I smile too. "Seerraf told me to 'fight with the strength of the five who came before me', and then I heard them in my head too."

"The five?" Fenmire asks in surprise. "What did they say?"

"It wasn't so much what they said. It was as if they weren't just speaking in my head, but they were *in* my head. I heard their voices sure, but I also felt like their years of experience were flowing through my body. Suddenly, I could fight! I fought so well it took Reilanna by surprise, and I was able to overtake her."

"You say you killed her. How, exactly?"

"I drove your knife into her chin," I say, still shocked at my heroics, even if it was only a dream. "She fell through The Gate and burst into black dust. The five cheered me on as I struck her down, but the moment Seerraf summoned them to my aid, he called me something. He called me his champion. He said it almost lovingly, as if he knew me. Have you heard of this name before in your studies?"

Fenmire's brow crinkles as he frowns in deep thought. "Not that I recall. There's the five, of course, but I don't remember any reference to a champion. Are you sure Seerraf's voice and your embodiment of the five weren't just tools your own mind used to give you the power you needed in your dream to strike Reilanna down?"

"I don't think so. It felt like they were there with me, inside my head and body. It almost felt like they belonged there. The moment I woke up, I was relieved to see all your faces gathered around me, but there was also a painful longing, like I had to say goodbye to old friends. And my headache, it doesn't feel like anything I've experienced before. It's almost as if my brain is protesting their absence. I know that likely sounds very strange and foolish, but—"

"Evangeline," Fenmire interrupts softly. "You just slew Reilanna in your dreams, and I have a feeling that, by doing so, you've banished her from your mind for good. I have no doubts that what you say you experienced is true. And if Seerraf did in fact send the five to help you, then he's obviously watching over you. I don't know exactly what he meant by calling you his champion, but having a god on your side is a blessing we'll take right now, all things considered."

"Agreed. I just..." I rub my face, trying to find the words to explain this hollow ache in my chest that rivals the one in my head at the moment. "Being host to the five, it felt so right, like I was whole and confident and strong. Now, I feel like I've been fractured. I feel... lonely."

Fenmire considers this a moment. "You've been touched by a god. However brief that touch might've been, it's bound to leave you feeling bereft for a time afterward, I'm sure. It sounds like he gave you quite a gift, be it only temporary. The whole experience was likely far more than a human's mind is used to dealing with."

This explanation satisfies me, and I nod. "You're right." I touch my cheek where I know I felt Seerraf's palm on my skin in my dream.

There's a soft knock on the door a second before Caliborne lets himself back in carrying a tray with a few dishes, a cup of tea, and a mug on it. He sets the tray on the bedside table and hands me the mug. It's water.

I carefully sit up with my back to the headboard, closing one eye against the throbbing pain in my head as I take a sip. I swallow and moan a little at the feel of the water running down my dry, burning throat. "Thank you."

Caliborne touches my knee. *I'm sorry I couldn't save you this time.*

"Stop apologizing," I say softly. "I'm fine."

He looks at Fenmire for confirmation.

"They'll live," Fenmire says with a grin.

Caliborne sits beside me on the bed and hands me cups and plates from the tray while Fenmire sprawls out on his side across the bottom of the mattress near my feet. They talk and laugh and watch me closely as I drink and eat and eventually nod off again into a much calmer sleep filled with normal dreams for the first time in months.

Chapter 65

My mates don't want me to get out of bed in the morning, but I don't want to lie around. Since Drixus has patrol today, I can't finish his hair right now, so I decide to take a walk to the stables instead.

Wexton tags along.

"I don't need a babysitter," I grumble as we head down the long, covered walkway.

"Can you blame us for being extra cautious right now?" Wexton asks. "Last night stressed us all out."

I grunt. "Well, I killed the witch. Problem solved."

"You killed her *in your dreams*. There are still plenty of ways for her to cause trouble for us."

It's not that I actually think killing her in my dreams killed her in real life, I've just been avoiding thinking about her at all since Fenmire and I became mates, not wanting her to ruin a moment we both fought so hard for. But I can't avoid it forever. As victorious as I was last night, there's still whatever punishment she means to send through The Gate next, and we must be prepared for that. Last night's victory doesn't erase that danger.

"I didn't mean to upset you," Wexton says at my silence. "We can handle whatever she's planning, don't worry."

I don't reply. I'm irritable today and unwilling to put on a brave face to assure him I'm fine. Perhaps I should've stayed in bed after all. Thankfully, my mood lightens a bit when we walk into the stables and I'm met with the happy sounds of the animals and my name being called joyfully from across the room.

"Evangeline!" Percival rushes up the aisle to us. "I haven't seen your face down here in a while."

"I'm sorry about that. I've been so busy. I'm here now though."

"And I have the most exciting thing to show you. Come here!"

Percival loops his arm around mine and tugs me about the stables, showing me all the new babies and enclosures and updates they've made to the space since the weather turned. I'm right in the middle of cuddling a new family of baby bunnies when Fenmire appears seemingly out of nowhere beside the enclosure.

"Evangeline," he calls, and he motions urgently for me to join him.

"What's wrong?" I ask as I step over little fluff balls and hop over the fence to his side.

"You need to see this," he says, motioning me toward the door, which is already open with workers pouring out of it, calling back at the others to come see whatever has drawn everyone's attention outside.

"What's all that about?" Percival asks as he joins Fenmire and I.

Fenmire takes my hand. "Come see."

Fenmire, Wexton, Percival, and I follow the others down the aisle. I hurry ahead of Fenmire out the door and through the gathered crowd until I step into bright sunlight.

"Whoa," I utter as I spin in a circle, taking in the sight around me.

Everything is green. The trees, the vines, the forest floor, it's all green and alive and vibrant. The trees aren't like anything I've seen before. Their leaves are a shape unfamiliar to me and a shade of green far darker than the trees outside The Deadwood. The trunks are twisted and bent, leaning toward and away from each other in a way no other forest grows. Every inch of the forest floor is coated in moss, like a blanket has been thrown over the entire Deadwood, and strings of deep green ivy hang between the trees like ancient ropes.

I turn to Fenmire as he steps up beside me. "We brought the forest back to life!"

Fenmire closes his eyes and breathes in deep. "Gods, I've missed that smell."

I breathe it in too. It's an old, woodsy scent that's much more potent than anything I've experienced.

This is how the forest was meant to be, the way Jothrik created it.

I start to ask Wexton a question, but the words die unspoken as the ground lurches beneath me, sending me sprawling onto my back. I'm surrounded by cries of surprise and pain, and I can barely get my limbs beneath me enough to sit up as the ground rumbles and shakes.

Everyone is yelling, but above that comes a sharp cracking sound from back toward the stables. A fracture forms in the stone above the massive wooden door. It starts out small but quickly widens and expands. Another crack forms. And another. The stone around the door begins to crumble and the door wobbles.

"Everyone move!" Wexton yells.

I'm suddenly hauled up into Fenmire's arms, and he starts running. Workers scramble to stay on their feet as they run for the woods. Percival trips, but Wexton hauls him back onto his feet as he herds the stragglers. With one last loud crack, the door comes loose from the stone and begins to fall. The last of the workers scream and trip and crawl to get out of the way. Wexton grabs the last one under his arm and launches into flight, barely sliding under the door as it crashes to the ground, blasting a cloud of dust, leaves, and rocks over us all.

The ground is still shaking, but we're all standing at the tree line now, holding onto trunks and branches to stay on our feet. I cough and cover my mouth with my sleeve to keep from breathing in the dust as Fenmire checks I'm unharmed.

A fox runs past my legs.

Then a rabbit.

A deer whips past Fenmire, nearly running into him as it streaks into the forest.

As the dust settles, a wave of feathers and fur rushes out of the stables as animals, big and small, soar, bound, and race into the forest.

Percival slams into the tree next to me, out of breath and struggling to stay on his feet through the quake.

"They're all getting away!" I call to him.

"Let them," he replies. He jumps to my tree and grabs my arms. "The forest is ready for them. They can go home now."

The shaking finally stops, and everyone looks around in shock at everything that just happened as the last of the animals disappear into the trees. A few linger at the edge of the forest, tamed to the point the nearby humans don't bother them.

Wexton joins Fenmire and I. "Are you both al—"

A mighty, shrieking roar cuts him off, and Fenmire and I look at each other.

What did the witch send this time?

We all step away from the trees and look in the direction of The Gate, and more than one terrified cry erupts at the sight of the beast that flies up over the nearby treetops. The drawing in Fenmire's book didn't do the sheer size of this creature justice. It's easily as large as ten Gryxen with a body covered in scaly green skin, though black, oozing cracks now streak through its hide, evidence of Reilanna's poisonous magic. Two massive wings beat the air with a deep whomping sound broken by another screech that reveals a mouth full of sharp fangs. Its long neck whips back and forth as it searches the sky with eyes far shrewder than the ones on the mindless beasts the witch has sent before. There's rage and intelligence in this creature's stare that instantly terrifies me when its eyes land on all of us.

I'm likely the only human who knows what the Gryxen call this creature, but I know what the others must be calling it in their minds right now.

Dragon.

"She sent a fucking quaheitan," Wexton hisses. "Fuck, fuck, fuck!"

Another screech, one I recognize this time, comes from behind us a second before another beast flies overhead, one with a rider armed with a pair of twin axes. Mara and Drixus head straight toward the quaheitan, which immediately turns its full attention on the duo with a cry of challenge.

"Everyone back inside!" Wexton orders. "Get to the castle!"

Percival leads the charge back inside the stables.

I don't follow.

"Evangeline!" Wexton calls, motioning me toward the gaping stable entrance.

"No," I reply as Drixus and Mara slam into the quaheitan. "I'm staying."

Wexton takes me by the arm. "You'll be safer in the—"

I rip my arm free. "I can help!"

"There's no time to argue!" Fenmire yells. "We need to—"

The quaheitan screams again and rears back its massive head. Its body turns in midair as it watches Drixus and Mara fly around its left side.

"Drixus, it's tracking you!" Wexton screams.

The quaheitan opens its mouth and fires a lightning bolt Mara is too slow to dodge. The bolt strikes her in the chest, and she jerks and screams in agony. She freezes in midair, stunned, and, as if in slow motion, she tips backward and begins to fall. Drixus hangs from her back for a moment, but either his grip fails or the feathers he's holding onto rip out, and he falls off as they both plummet toward the ground.

"No!" I scream at the same time Fenmire takes off, streaking toward Drixus as fast as his wings can carry him.

Wexton takes me by the arm again and pulls me protectively close as we watch.

"Will he reach him in time?" I ask in a panic.

"He's the only one who has a fighting chance," Wexton replies.

Mara wakes up in midair, flaps her wings desperately to slow her descent, and crashes into the trees. At the same time, Fenmire slams into Drixus, and they careen out of control as Fenmire fights and fails to hold them both in the air. They eventually disappear below the tree line as well.

The quaheitan stretches its wings and gives a cry of victory before it turns and starts flying toward the arch.

"It's headed for the village!" I cry.

I jump with a scream when something lands beside us, but it's only Caliborne with his arms full of the others' weapons. He tosses Wexton his sword then grabs me by the shoulder.

You should be inside!

"You need to take me to Fenmire and Drixus. They could be hurt."

"Can you heal those types of wounds?" Wexton asks.

"We're going to find out."

It's not safe.

"Fenmire is right. I'll have to fight eventually. So take me where I'm the most useful."

Both Gryxen hesitate.

"Nothing against my will, remember?" I say heatedly. "Are you going to leave me behind when I'm asking you not to?"

At that, Caliborne hands Fenmire's weapons to Wexton, straps his bow across his chest, and picks me up.

Where are they?

I point in the direction Fenmire and Drixus fell.

We fly over the trees, and I can see the quaheitan headed in the opposite direction. We need to be fast or else it will level the village before we ever get there to help. Fortunately, we find the other two Gryxen fairly quickly.

Not so fortunately, they're both not moving.

Drixus is slumped over a tangle of roots at the base of a tree, and Fenmire is sprawled out on his back nearby with one of his wings bent underneath him at an odd angle. We land between them, and I go to Fenmire first, kneeling beside him while Caliborne kneels beside Drixus.

I call Fenmire's name and touch his face, which is smeared with black blood from a cut above his eye. I touch his wing, assessing the damage, and Wexton sets his load of weapons aside to help me roll him off the limb.

It's broken. I can see the bone along the top is snapped and pressing against the leathery skin. I freeze in horrified shock, but Wexton doesn't. He plants his foot at the base of Fenmire's wing and tugs, yanking the bone back into place.

Fenmire wakes up with a sharp inhale of breath and promptly punches Wexton in the leg. "Get off!"

"Stay still," Wexton barks at him. "I need to stabilize this."

Fenmire sees the break and swears. "This is the last thing we need."

"Let me try to help," I say, scooting closer.

Wexton looks at Fenmire.

"Let them," Fenmire says.

Wexton keeps his foot and hand on the wing, holding the bone in place as I cover the break with my palms.

And I focus.

My hands heat up like they did with the mouse, and I feel the bone under Fenmire's skin. But it's more than that. I can see the fracture in my mind, the jagged edges of two bones that should be one. I feel the swelling and the blood pooling around the wound, desperate to heal it. I will the bones to mend back into one solid piece, and I gasp when they respond. The edges shift and line up, and the space between them grows smaller and smaller until they begin to fuse. Muscles and tissue warp and right themselves, and blood flows freely again as the fracture disappears entirely, leaving behind one smooth, intact bone. I take my hands away. The wing looks good as new.

"By the five…" Wexton mumbles as he lets go.

Fenmire sits up and flexes the wing without pain. He grabs me by the face and kisses me quickly on the lips. "You're a fucking angel."

I laugh with delight.

"Fenmire…?" Drixus wakes up with a disoriented groan, but as soon as his eye focuses on all of us standing nearby, he sits up with a hand from Caliborne and looks to the sky. "The quaheitan! It must be nearly to the village by now." He starts to stand only to stumble and lean heavily against the nearest tree with a hiss of pain, clutching his middle.

Fenmire takes a single step toward him but then stops with a small shake of his head.

"You all need to… to go," Drixus says through gritted teeth. "Now!"

"What about you?" I ask. "Let me look at—"

"Later. I'm going to look for Mara. You all need to get moving! The humans won't be able to stop this creature. It'll rip through your village and move on to the next. A quaheitan is too dangerous for this world."

"He's right," Fenmire says. He picks up his shield and mace from where Wexton discarded them. "The three of us will be hard pressed to bring it down. The humans will be little more than fodder."

"Then let's go," I say.

"Evangeline…" Wexton says with a pleading look.

"No. I'm coming. No arguments."

"Told you so," Fenmire says with a smirk at Wexton.

Wexton barks back something in their language and snatches his sword up from the ground.

Caliborne snorts as he picks me up again.

"What did he say?" I ask.

You don't want to know.

Drixus leans even harder against the tree.

"I'll help you when I get back," I promise.

He only nods.

My mates and I take flight and fly over the forest toward the arch.

The quaheitan is nowhere in sight.

We all land in the lane, but it's little more than a slide across the threshold as we dart through the arch and take flight again on the other side all while barely slowing down.

"When we get there, put me down at the edge of town," I tell Caliborne. "I'll help get people to safety."

Be sure to look out for your own safety above all else. You're too important.

"I'll be careful."

The village finally comes into view, but the quaheitan has already started its rampage, as is evident from the smoke in the sky and the sound of distant screams. Fenmire reaches the village first, and as such, he's the first to draw the beast's attention. The quaheitan climbs up on top of the roof of the closest building and opens its mouth, readying an attack at Fenmire, but the quick-winged Gryxen rolls away from the bolt of electric energy the quaheitan fires at him with ease.

Fenmire bangs his mace against his shield. "Come on, you ugly brute," he jeers.

Wexton joins the fray a heartbeat later, and he flies up behind the creature, daring a swipe across its back with his sword that makes the quaheitan twist its neck around, turning its attention away from Fenmire, who moves in quickly to strike with an attack of his own. I've seen the two of them use this method before with CeCe. I only hope it works with bigger prey.

Caliborne lands at the edge of the village behind the last row of buildings and sets me on my feet, but he keeps ahold of my hand.

Usher people inside and out of the streets. Avoid open areas that might draw its attention. And for Seerraf's sake, don't try to help us fight it.

"Got it." I yank him down for a quick kiss. "For luck."

He takes off toward the sounds of battle while I dart down an alley toward the sounds of running feet and terrified screams.

Chapter 66

I skid out of the alley into the main street to find humans running every which way, slamming into and pushing each other as they scramble away from falling rubble and flames. Several of the buildings are on fire, which yet more people are struggling to put out while keeping an eye on the quaheitan still fighting my mates on a nearby rooftop.

"Leave it and run!" I shout to the nearest man holding a dripping bucket. "It's not worth your life!"

This must be all the encouragement he needs because he immediately drops the bucket with a splash and takes off running down the street. A young woman trips on her dress and falls in the middle of the street, and I run for her.

"Come on," I say as I tug her to her feet. "You have to get inside!"

She looks at me, and I recognize her as one of the ladies who sneered at me in town, the one with the sour look on her face when I told them good morning.

"Evangeline?" she says in awe.

The quaheitan roars, and she screams and jumps into my arms.

"This way!" I yell, and we run arm in arm to the nearest open doorway, which just happens to be the general store. I do little more than usher her over the threshold before dashing back into the street. "Inside! Inside!" I holler, waving my arms toward the store. As people file in past me, I shout, "Stay away from the windows! Move toward the back. Be as quiet as possible."

A man with blood trailing down the side of his face runs inside screaming, "Abigail? Abigail!" He steps back outside, pushing through the bodies rushing in the opposite direction. "Abigail!"

"You should go inside," I tell him. I take out Fenmire's knife and cut a strip of cloth from the bottom of my shirt, ball it up, and put it in his hand, but he's too busy frantically searching the street behind me to notice. I guide his hand to his bleeding face and press, and the pain finally makes him look at me. "Who are you looking for?"

"My daughter. She was playing behind the tavern when the beast attacked."

"How old is she?"

"Only eight."

I nod. "Go back inside. I'll look for her."

He's hesitant, but I give him a push, and he finally follows the others back inside the store.

The tavern is down the street, away from the quaheitan, so I start running, keeping to the store fronts and alleys as much as possible while directing everyone I meet into open doors. The street is almost empty when I reach the tavern, and there's no sign of the girl, so I'm about to check if she went in the building when a deafening screech stops me in my tracks. The quaheitan has taken flight in an attempt to shake my mates, but they continue their assault as the beast flies over the village, headed my way. I call to the last few stragglers in the street and all but shove them into the tavern. I mean to follow them, but a tiny voice calls out from nearby, definitely not from the safety of the tavern.

"Papa?"

I see the child. She's across the street at the edge of old man Oren's garden, clutching the fence in fright as she searches for her father. I swear under my breath, but the sound is swept away by another cry from the quaheitan before a bolt of electricity cracks down on the roof of the house beside Oren's. The roof shatters, and the house immediately catches on fire. The girl barely manages to avoid being hit by falling wood and stone as she cowers by the fence.

I jump off the tavern porch and dash across the street. A great shadow passes over me as the quaheitan flies overhead, following the street. I reach the girl just as the ground shakes so hard I nearly fall over. The Gryxen have knocked the quaheitan out of the air and into the village square on the other side of the tavern. Its landing obliterated the stone fountain and several farmers' stands, and it destroys another with a vicious swipe of its tail as it scrambles back up on its feet.

I gather the girl in my arms. "Hold on to me!"

The child sobs as she clings to my neck. "Where's Papa?"

The quaheitan is too focused on the three Gryxen flying around it in circles to pay any attention to us, but we're so close to the fighting that bits of wood and stone roll across the street at my feet as I head for the tavern. The beast spins with another electric blast up toward Wexton, who rolls out of the way at the last second, but the quaheitan's tail whips around and slams into the side of the tavern, caving in a section of the wall.

Screams erupt from inside, and several people flee the building. The sudden appearance of so many running bodies draws the quaheitan's attention, and it roars, preparing to fire its electricity right down the middle of the street. I turn on my heels and run back toward the garden, hopping the fence the moment the quaheitan lets loose its deadly electric breath. I hit the ground and cover the child with my body. My skin tingles and all my hair stands up as the air becomes so charged it crackles. Stone and wood go flying, but I huddle with the girl in the garden behind the fence which, miraculously, remains whole enough to protect us from the worst of it.

The ground rumbles again as the quaheitan takes flight. It swoops across the sky above us and lands in the street in front of the few who fled the tavern and managed to escape the blast. They stop with screams of terror as the quaheitan faces them, and it readies for another attack, which will hit us as well if I stay where I am. I get up and scramble back over the fence a second time, but three blue figures streak past us up the street and slam into the beast, attacking together in a coordinated strike at its head.

Fenmire brings his mace down on one of the quaheitan's eyes, which bursts under his spiked weapon. When it screams in pain and rage, Caliborne shoots it in the mouth with several quickly-fired arrows. The beast's scream this time is more panicked, and it throws its head back, spitting arrows and black blood. Wexton darts in and flies across in front of the creature, just under its head, and at first, I don't understand why, but then the quaheitan lets out a sad, gurgling wail, and a river of black blood begins running down its scaly neck from where Wexton slit its throat open.

It takes them several more strikes, but between the three of them, they overwhelm the quaheitan until, with a final blow from Fenmire's mace to the top of its head so hard the weapon becomes lodged in the skull, the quaheitan stills and staggers then falls. Those who were nearly electrified a moment ago now run with fresh screams to avoid being squashed as the beast slumps across the stone, its wings scraping across the fronts of stores and houses, shattering glass and tearing off porches as it collapses in the middle of the street.

I look at the girl in my arms. "Are you alright?"

She nods through her tears. Her face is smeared with dirt, but she seems unharmed.

Everything is so still and quiet in the aftermath. After a moment, heads start popping out of doors and windows, and the crying begins. Men run for water barrels and start putting out fires while the women call to lovers and children. I wave to my mates, all of whom land near the quaheitan and direct the humans well away from it since it's still twitching with the occasional crackle of electricity from its gaping mouth.

"I'm returning her to her father," I call to them. "At the general store just up the street."

"Be quick," Fenmire advises. "We shouldn't linger in case Reilanna has any more surprises for us back home."

I nod and break into a jog. When I arrive at the general store, I find most of the people have already left and are having tearful reunions in the street. The father isn't hard to spot though. He's still bleeding and calling his daughter's name into the crowd.

"Papa!" she calls when she hears him.

He pushes his way through the few people separating us and takes the child from my arms.

"Oh, my girl," he says tearfully, hugging her tight. "Oh, thank god." He looks at me. "And thank you, Evangeline."

"You know who I am?" I ask.

The look he gives me is one of shameful regret. "I was there the night we banished you to The Deadwood." He sets his daughter down, holding her against his leg with one arm as he touches my shoulder with the other. "Please forgive me. I can't ever give enough to repay you for what you did for me today, and after what I… what we…"

"You owe me nothing, friend. But perhaps take this as a lesson of loyalty and morals. Elias has become a blight in our village. Something must be done about it."

You have no idea, he thinks to himself, but he only nods, accepting my words of warning without a response.

A crowd has gathered, all eyes locked onto the massive body of the beast currently blocking main street and the three demons who just saved all their lives. People are murmuring and pointing at my mates. Children are wide-eyed with wonder while the adults are more cautious, though they look more bewildered than fearful.

"Move aside!" A familiar voice orders. "Out of the way!" Elias bursts through the crowd and takes in the whole scene, his eyes dancing across the destruction, the few bodies in the street that didn't make it to safety, and the quaheitan's carcass before finally landing on me. His face turns murderous. "You," he sneers. "Of course you're involved in this. You no doubt summoned this beast to punish us!"

I hear a telltale slam, and the ground rumbles beneath my feet as a Gryxen lands in the street right behind me. He's quickly joined by a second then a third.

The crowd takes a few steps back, all but Elias whose eyes scan across my mates. His lip curls. "So it's true. You stand with demons now, do you?"

I smile at him. "Yes, I do."

"Witch," he sneers.

From behind me comes more than one low growl.

"I would be very careful how you speak to me right now if I were you," I say.

Elias holds his bible high in the air. "*'And I saw a woman sit upon a scarlet-coloured beast, full of names of blasphemy, having seven heads and ten horns. And the woman was—'*"

"Your words hold no power over me," I shout above his ranting.

"They are God's words!"

"That book holds very few of God's words, if any at all. They are the words of men like you, Elias, men who know neither God's words nor God's will nor even what it truly means to be a man of God. What you hold is a book of fairytales, nothing more."

Elias sputters, his rage rendering him momentarily speechless.

Fenmire steps up beside me and drops to one knee, leaning down near my ear to ask, "Is it safe to assume this is the pastor's son who put his hands on you?" He's sure to say it loud enough for everyone gathered around to hear, and more than one voice murmurs in surprise.

"It is," I confirm.

Elias' eyes go wide.

"Want me to send him to meet his god?" Fenmire asks sweetly.

Elias takes a fearful step back.

I tilt my head, pretending to consider it and letting the fear fester in Elias' eyes for a moment before I say, "Not today."

"Pity. I'd love nothing more than to rip those offending hands from his body and gift them to you."

I reach over and set my palm lovingly against Fenmire's cheek, pulling his head closer to mine. Intimately close.

Elias looks like *his* head might explode.

I mean it. I'll make his hands into trophies for you. Just say the word.

"He's not worth the effort," I say, then I kiss Fenmire on the cheek. "But thank you for the offer."

He doesn't deserve your mercy.

"*I* don't deserve to carry the weight of his death on my conscience."

At this, Fenmire nods, understanding better than anyone the pain of a heavy conscience.

I turn to the gathered crowd, scanning their faces. Some I used to call friends, some are merely acquaintances, and a few more I recognize from the night I was thrown into The Deadwood.

'They're mostly good people. They're just scared.'

Spurred by Papa's words, I take a step forward. "It breaks my heart to see so many of you following Elias' hateful teachings. You all condone public beatings and murder as he sees fit, do you?"

The silence that follows my question is fraught with tension, and many eyes flick nervously to Elias then back to me. It's clear not many are comfortable with these things at all, but none are willing to speak out against it publicly.

"So many lies have been told under the guise of holy guidance," I continue. "But I think more than a few of you have realized things have gotten out of hand. I pray you all stand up for what's right and correct your paths. This is not holiness. No god worth worshipping would wish for such violence and hate.

"I will tell you one piece of truth though: there *is* a great evil working in The Deadwood, a true malevolent force that wishes nothing but death and destruction, but it's not us." I wave my arm to indicate myself and my mates.

"Don't listen to her!" Elias cries. "She and her beasts burned our holy place; or have you forgotten?"

"*You* burned the church, Elias, while we were inside trying to right *your* wrong."

"You were freeing a sinner!"

"Love that's different from yours is not a sin."

"Do you see?" Elias yells, waving his arm toward me while regarding the crowd around him. "She'll lead us right to—"

"Let her speak!" cries a voice from the masses.

"Are we in danger?" asks the father still standing nearby with his daughter clutching his leg.

"We fight to protect you," I say. "Like we did today. But things will likely get worse before they improve."

"What do we do?" asks another voice.

"You should set up watch on the highest rooftop in the village," Fenmire replies. "Keep your eyes pointed toward The Deadwood. If you see any beasts headed your way, either by sky or on foot, raise the alarm. Take shelter, board your doors and windows, and don't try to fight them yourselves."

"We've fought these horrors for centuries to keep you safe," Wexton adds. "We'll continue to do so, but you should take steps to protect yourselves as much as you're able."

"If you're such honest and noble protectors," Elias spits venomously, "why have you never come to help us when beasts have charged out of The Deadwood to ravage our home in the past?"

"We didn't have Evangeline," Fenmire says. "They are the reason we could be here today. If it weren't for them, your village would be destroyed and everyone in it, dead. You'd be wise to heed their words and ours."

"Lies!" Elias screams. "All lies to lead us off the path of God."

"Believe what you want, Elias," I say. "But the dead don't get to pray, regardless which god they worship."

Elias' mouth moves but no words come out.

I'm so tired of hearing his voice, I don't wait for him to find it. "Take me home," I request.

Not a heartbeat later, I'm in Fenmire's arms, and he launches us into the air.

*****

We find no unpleasant surprises waiting for us back at the castle, but the place is a mess once again. Though the structure seems sound, the destruction within it is staggering. Many pieces of furniture have been destroyed entirely, and the staff are already moving pieces beyond salvaging into empty rooms or breaking it into firewood. Most of my things made it. One armoire took a beating, but Wexton and Caliborne help me rope and nail it back together temporarily. It won't last another quake, though.

I find Drixus upstairs in his room, and when he answers the door, he's clutching his side in obvious distress.

"Let me see," I insist.

"It's fine," he says stubbornly as he sits on his bed with a wince. "It's probably just a bruise."

I put my hands on my hips. "Drixus, I can help, so let me help."

He groans but relents and lies on his back across his bed as my palms settle over where he feels the most pain. Through my powers, I find no less than three broken ribs. I click my tongue at him as I will them right again. "Just a bruise indeed," I mutter.

He gives me a small, bemused smile. "Are you angry with me?"

"No… well, perhaps a little." I look up at him as the last rib mends and the swelling subsides. "It angers me to see you suffer, and to see you do so willingly, knowing there's a quick and easy way to fix it…" The wound is healed, so I move my hands to his face instead. "I don't want to see you punish yourself anymore. I thought we ended that when we moved you out of that room, cleaned you up, and fixed your hair?"

His smile widens. "My hair isn't fixed yet."

I roll my eyes.

He sits up and takes my hands, tugging me between his knees. "I'm sorry. Old habits and all that."

I rub my hands up his arms and settle them on his shoulders. "I haven't asked you for anything, I want nothing from you, but I want this for you. Will you try to look out for yourself better? For me?"

His eye darts shyly away, but he replies, "I'll try."

I change the subject to save him from becoming embarrassed. "How's Mara?"

"She's fine. She managed to land with only a few upset feathers. Percival looked in on her already."

"I'm glad." I run my fingers down his braided hair. "Would you like me to work on more of this? I should be able to detangle the rest by dinnertime."

"If it pleases… I mean, I'd like that."

I chuckle and take his hand. "Would you like to come to my room?"

At this, he smiles. "I'd love to."

Chapter 67

Now that Reilanna has been driven out of my dreams, I'm free to sleep with any of my mates I see fit. This time, I choose to spend the night with Fenmire. I check with Wexton to be sure Fenmire doesn't have patrol the next day, so when dawn breaks and we come to consciousness Sunday morning, I put my arms around his neck before he can slip away and make his own plans.

"I want you to meet my father today," I whisper.

There's no surprise in Fenmire's eyes. I know he guessed what I've been up to every Sunday some time ago, but I didn't know how he'd feel once the invitation was extended to him.

He grunts and strokes a finger down my cheek. "Are you sure?"

"Yes."

"He may not like me. I'm nothing like Caliborne or Wexton."

"You love me and make me happy. That's all Papa will care about."

Fenmire nods. "Then let's go."

*****

We slip quietly out of the castle before the others wake up, and when we land and pass through the arch, I ask, "How does it feel to step out of The Deadwood?"

He shrugs, glancing around. "Your world is pretty enough, but—and forgive me for saying so—it's nothing but another prison for us. This isn't where we belong either."

I nod in understanding. "You'll get to go home soon."

We take flight again, and I direct him toward my parents' farm.

He's silent for a bit before he asks, "Am I to take that to mean that you and Drixus are…?"

"We're friends, but we haven't discussed a mating bond yet."

He grunts.

"When the quaheitan knocked Drixus out of the sky, I was moved at how hard you fought to save him from serious injury."

Another grunt.

"Was that the result of instinct or some residual feelings between you?"

Fenmire sniffs and avoids my eyes. "There's nothing *residual* about my feelings. Drixus and I are mates, whether we wish to be or not. The loyalty, protectiveness, and concern that come with that bond will never be broken, no matter how much betrayal or pain occurs between us."

"So if he hadn't told you the truth…"

"I would've reacted the same to seeing him fall."

"Even if you hated him?"

"Yes."

"Has that sort of thing happened bef—"

Fenmire stops abruptly and hovers in the air. "Eve…"

I follow his eyes south and see a large plume of billowing smoke in the distance, right in the direction of…

"Oh, no," I mutter.

"Is that—"

"Yes!"

Fenmire flies straight toward the smoke, no longer the least bit concerned about being seen. We fly over the woods, and when the farm comes into view, we find the barn engulfed in flames. We fly wide to avoid the smoke and land in the yard between the barn and the house, which looks safe for now. Not a soul is fighting the flames or even watching them to be sure they don't spread. Papa's mare is in the paddock attached to the barn, screaming and running around the enclosure in a panic. As soon as Fenmire and I land, I dash to the gate and fling it open.

"Go on, git!" I holler as I run around behind her, flapping my arms and herding her toward freedom. She doesn't need much convincing and takes off, fleeing across the yard to safety.

"Eve!" Fenmire yells.

The barn begins to crumble in on itself, the beams and board snapping and groaning like old bones breaking under the strain. I run back out of the paddock as the walls cave in and the roof slams down into the blaze. Fenmire grabs me and shuffles backward closer to the house, shielding me from the blast of embers and smoke with his wings. The ground shakes as the barn crashes to the ground, and I feel the heat of the fire even behind Fenmire's wings. When Fenmire parts his wings again, I cover my mouth with both hands at the sight of the flaming rubble where my family's barn used to be.

"Papa!" I scream, spinning around Fenmire and starting toward the house. "Papa, where are you?"

Please tell me he wasn't in there, I pray. *God, Seerraf, any and all divine powers who may be listening, please let my father be alright.*

Papa wouldn't have left a fire unattended.

"Papa!" I yell again, more urgently.

My father steps out onto the front porch.

"Thank the gods," I say in relief. "Papa, what…?"

Another man steps out of the house behind my father, and I freeze. Fenmire's hand grips my arm, tugging me protectively close as he growls under his breath. I pull his knife from my belt and hold it out in front of me.

Elias leers down at me from the porch. He's holding a gun, which is aimed at my father's back.

"I knew the smoke would draw you here," Elias says.

"Eve, run!" Papa orders. "He's lost his mind."

"I'm the only sane one here!" Elias cries. "I'm the only one willing to stand up to the devil. The rest are content to take the word of his minions and the witch who beds them." He glares at me. "I've seen it with my own eyes. Such disgusting, sinful behavior."

"I told you, Elias," Papa interjects, "it doesn't matter whom or what my child beds. Their words are truth, regardless."

"Your daughter fucks demons!" Elias shrieks, his gun bouncing as he shakes it in rage.

"And I love and trust them just the same as I did before I knew that."

Elias looks angry enough to chew nails. "Then you're no better than her. You're no better than any of them!"

"Elias," I spit angrily, "your quarrel is with me. If you hurt my father, I swear I'll—"

"You'll what?" Elias sneers. "What more could you do to me? Thanks to you and your demons' lies, I've been replaced as the head of our congregation. They took a vote last night. Not only am I no longer allowed to lead our village to righteousness, but I've been excommunicated from our church entirely. My father has disowned me. I've no family, no possessions, no money, nothing!"

Elias pokes my father in the back with the gun, and Papa starts down the steps with Elias on his heels. When they reach the bottom, Elias stops but gives my father a push, sending him across the yard toward me. I reach my hand out, eager for him to get as far away from Elias as possible.

"You've taken everything from me," Elias says, his hateful eyes boring into mine. "Allow me to show you how that feels."

Elias pulls the trigger, and I scream as Papa jolts, the bullet ripping clear through his chest. Just like in my dream, my hand gripping Fenmire's knife moves impossibly fast, and there's a loud clang of metal on metal and a flash of bright white light as the bullet strikes Fenmire's blade instead of my neck.

My father crumples to the ground.

Fenmire lets me go and, with a howl of pure rage, vaults through the air and lands on Elias, flattening him to the dirt and ripping the gun from his hands.

I run to my father, dropping to my knees in the dirt beside his lifeless body. I roll him into my lap and immediately place my hand over the hole in his chest. His eyes are closed.

"It's alright," I tell him softly as I will my powers to heal him. "You're going to be fine. I'll fix it. I'll…"

My palm heats as I focus on the wound, feeling its edges and willing them to close.

They don't respond.

I close my eyes and focus harder, seeing the bullet's path through my father's body in my head as I will it away.

Nothing.

"Fenmire!" I call. "Help me, please!"

Fenmire lifts his foot from Elias' chest. "Move, and I'll kill you," he snarls. He throws the gun to the ground and slams his foot down on it, crushing the weapon into useless bits before rushing to my side.

I hold my breath as Fenmire places his hand over mine, and I focus again on healing my father as Fenmire does the same. Nothing changes. Fenmire pulls away, his face falling as he looks into my eyes.

"I'm sorry," he says softly. "The bullet ripped through his heart."

"No," I mutter. "No, no, no. No!"

Again, I focus on my powers, but now that Fenmire has mentioned it, I can feel my father's heart, and it's been torn open. I detect no beat nor a drop of blood moving through his veins. Everything is still and quiet.

There's no life left to heal him with.

He's already gone.

My chest starts rising and falling painfully fast, my thoughts grow hectic, and my entire body feels like I've been thrown into the flames reducing the barn to ashes behind us. I finally take my hand away from my father's chest, and my palm is smeared with blood. My father's blood. A howl of pure agony escapes me as I gather him into my arms, hugging him to my chest.

It hurts.

I can't breathe.

This is one of Reilanna's nightmares. It has to be.

"Caliborne!" I cry. "Wake me up, please!" Wake up, damn it.

I don't wake up.

The pain doesn't stop.

This can't be happening.

I clutch my father and plant breathless kisses on his forehead. "I'm sorry," I whisper. "I'm so sorry. I love you. Please forgive me."

Fenmire silently holds me.

The sound of a boot shuffling across gravel makes me look up at Elias, who rises to his knees in the dirt nearby with a look of victory on his face at the sight of my pain.

I slide my father from my lap, gather Fenmire's knife from the ground, and stand. I only take one step toward Elias, however, before Fenmire grabs me by the arm.

"No," he says sternly.

"He killed my father!" I cry.

"I know, but this is what he wants."

I tear my eyes away from Elias to look up at Fenmire instead. "What?"

"He's got nothing left to live for; he said it himself. He expects you to end his miserable existence and make him a martyr. Don't give him the satisfaction."

I glare at Elias, weighing my desire for vengeance against Fenmire's words of wisdom.

Fenmire leans down near my ear. "I don't mean that he should go unpunished. There's always the offer I made you before. I'll gladly make his hands a gift. Just say the word."

I continue to stare at Elias as I consider the offer.

He glares back at me.

"Not his hands," I say. "His fingers. All of them." I hold out the knife.

Fenmire takes it with a nod.

We part ways, me going to kneel beside my father again and hold his hand while Fenmire stalks across the yard back toward Elias.

"Do it, you wretched creature!" Elias screams. "I'll be welcomed through heaven's gates with open… What are you doing? Stop! Let go! No, don't—"

Elias wails in fear and agony. I don't look. I tidy Papa's greying hair and count ten blood-curdling cries as Fenmire serves fair justice for the pain in my heart.

*****

I can't stay to help bury Papa. My mother and the village will want to do that, and Fenmire isn't convinced it's safe for me to stick around. Considering what happened here, I tend to agree. I have no desire to see my mother anyway. As much as I'd like to believe otherwise, I'm sure she voted not to excommunicate Elias. She's lost, and I won't sacrifice anymore of my heart for her to break. It breaks enough at the thought of leaving my father lying in the yard. We cover him with a blanket out of respect and leave a letter for my mother explaining everything.

We tie Elias to one of the porch beams for the village to do with as they see fit, though Fenmire is gracious enough to wrap Elias' mangled hands in bandages beforehand. I don't know where his fingers are, and I don't ask. Elias sits against the beam and sobs miserably, staring at his mangled hands and mumbling to himself.

I don't feel the least bit sorry for him.

The barn is still burning, and it will likely do so for many hours yet. Fenmire rips up the pieces of the paddock fence that the fire has already spread to and throws them into the heart of the blaze. We move anything else flammable a safe distance away then catch Papa's mare. I tie her to the side of the porch, but not before bringing her to Papa's body and letting her smell and nudge him.

She deserves to say goodbye too.

Once I've secured the mare, Fenmire touches my shoulder. "I think we're done here," he says softly.

I merely nod.

I should never have come here. Papa asked me to, but I knew it was selfish to agree. I put him in danger because I couldn't stand the thought of losing him, but I ended up losing him anyway.

I stare at the sheet-draped body as Fenmire picks me up and takes flight, and I look back over his shoulder until the farm is long out of sight.

The entire trip back to the castle is nothing but a blur. I blink, and I'm suddenly being set down on the stone steps of our home. I let myself inside and head immediately for the stairs in a daze so deep that when Fenmire calls my name, I jump, having forgotten he was there at all.

"Eve?"

I stop at the foot of the staircase and look back at him.

"I'm sorry," he says simply.

I have no words, and I don't try to find any. I turn back around and start climbing the stairs. I don't want his apologies. There's nothing for him to apologize for, and condolences born of obligation and pity don't bring back the dead.

I want to be alone, but a bigger part of me knows that's not what I need right now, so I seek out the one person I know will understand this darkness squeezing my heart.

I knock on Drixus' door, and when he answers, he takes one look at my face and draws me into his room and his arms.

"What's happened?" he asks, squeezing me tight.

"He's gone," I say quietly.

"Who?"

"My father."

A second of quiet surprise follows before he asks, "How?"

"Elias." I spit the name like a curse.

Drixus picks me up and carries me to his bed, lying down with me tucked close to his chest and his arms still wrapped around me. His thoughts are quiet, as always, and I realize that's what I came here for.

Silent solace.

Drixus doesn't offer me empty condolences. He knows more than most how useless they are. He simply holds me and exists in this space with me as I let myself feel things no words can banish.

Pure, hot grief swells in my chest, and I bury my face against Drixus' cool, leathery skin as I start to cry. Up until now, I was too numb for tears—my heart was in denial—but here, in the arms of the Gryxen who knows exactly how it feels to lose everything he loves, the numbness fades.

And gods does it hurt.

I cling to Drixus as if he might leave me, but he doesn't so much as move as I fall apart at the seams. I could never let go like this around the others. The pain of seeing me suffer this way would break their hearts, and I can't stand to bring them pain. Drixus knows pain. He knows it better than any of us. I can share some of mine with him, and he won't bat an eye, though I do feel guilty. I try to apologize through my tears, but he stops me with a thumb to my lips.

"No," he murmurs. "No 'sorry's, no 'forgive me's. Don't bottle an ounce of your pain up. Let it go, sweetheart. Let it all go."

So I do.

Drixus kisses the top of my head and holds me close as I sob harder than I ever have in my life. Just when I think the tears have dried up, they come again and again and again. Drixus starts to sing in that deep, rumbling voice of his, and I become mesmerized by the sound enough to calm my breathing. Eventually, the tears slow, though they don't stop entirely. I look up at Drixus, and his face holds nothing but love as he peers down at my tear-and-snot-smeared one.

"I failed him," I say weakly.

"You did no such thing. It's no one's fault but the one who pulled the trigger."

"I drove Elias to it."

"Only the foulest, most cowardly sort hurt others to heal their own pain. You are not responsible for his evil."

I rest my head on his collarbone. "I would have hurt Elias," I admit. "I would have killed him, but Fenmire stopped me."

"I'm sure he saw justice served, regardless."

"He did. Elias will never hurt another. Not by his own hands, anyway."

"Good."

More silence. More crying. The tears come in waves I don't bother to fight. Once the next one passes and I calm down again, I nuzzle my face into Drixus' cool neck.

"I can't see the others right now," I whisper.

"You don't have to. We can lay right here for as long as you need. Close your eyes and rest."

I appreciate that he doesn't say 'you'll feel better in the morning', because we both know that's not true. I am tired though, so tired, like I've worked all day in the fields with Papa. My eyes are so swollen and raw from crying that closing them brings some much-needed relief. I'm just conscious enough to hear Drixus start singing again before exhaustion sets in and yanks me into a deep, dreamless sleep.

Chapter 68

I spend the next week in Drixus' bed. The others deliver meals to his door, but Drixus is the only one to retrieve them. There's usually a quiet exchange as the dishes are passed over, concern for my well-being that's met with Drixus' assurances I am at least still breathing. I know the others are worried about me, but I don't have the strength to reassure them right now, and one look at me would likely only worry them further.

So, I stay in bed, eat, cry, and lie in Drixus' arms. And sleep. I sleep so much the days bleed together until I only realize how long it's been when I start to smell. When I bring it up to Drixus, he only shrugs.

"I've smelled worse," he says with a small smile.

I laugh.

Then I burst out crying again.

That night, long after everyone else has gone to bed, we sneak downstairs and bathe. It's a quick and quiet adventure as we simply scrub the smelly bits and head right back upstairs. I make a brief stop at my bedroom for clean clothes and my hairbrush, and I'm surprised to find a few additions to my bed, laid out neatly just below my pillows. There's a wooden box similar to the ones my mates' courting gifts were each delivered in, a few letters, a bundle of fur wrapped in ribbon, and several flowers in various stages of wilting.

They must be gifts from the others to let me know they love me and wish to heal some of my hurt.

I leave them untouched on the bed, gather my clothes and brush, and take my leave of the room with haste.

Drixus is waiting for me in the hall, and we walk silently back up to the third floor together. Back in his room, I change into fresh clothes then sit on the bed with my brush to try and work a week's worth of tangles from my hair. Drixus sits beside me and holds his hand out for my brush.

"May I?" he asks softly.

I'm touched by the offer, but I hesitate as I run my hand down my hair, feeling endless knots under my palm as I do. "It's pretty bad."

"Though the state you found me in before says otherwise, I know how to brush out the most stubborn knots. I just gave up caring for myself for a time. You helped me when I wasn't strong enough to help myself. I'd like to repay the favor."

I wordlessly set the brush in his hand and turn my back to him.

His touch is as gentle as my mother's used to be when I was a child and my hair would get tied up in horrible states from running around with Will all day. Drixus parts it in sections and works from the bottom, separating each knot with his fingers before softly brushing them out. When one section brushes cleanly from root to tip, he sweeps it over my shoulder to the front and moves on to the next. A week ago, I likely would have been embarrassed that I let myself get to this state, but now? Now, I'm surprised it's only been a week since I last brushed it. All I did today was bathe, and yet I'm exhausted and ready to crawl right back into bed.

"I'd like to show you something tomorrow," Drixus says. "Are you up for an excursion?"

"Where to?" I ask.

"It's a surprise."

The thought that Drixus has another secret he wishes to share with me piques my interest, sparking the slightest bubble of anticipation and excitement under all the grief and fatigue. "Is it very far?"

"It'll take several hours to walk there."

"I don't know if I'm up for that."

"Well, we could always fly."

I turn my head, pulling the section of hair he's in the middle of detangling from his hands as I regard him with raised brows. "You mean…?"

He smiles. "Would you like to meet Mara?"

"Is she friendly?"

"She's my best friend, and she's never attacked another unprovoked, not even Wexton."

"Oh, well, if she can put up with him…"

Drixus chuckles. "Exactly."

I turn back around, and Drixus goes back to brushing as I consider. I'm so tired right now that even the thought of walking across the hall to Mara's room feels daunting.

"I'll try," I say.

"It's only a suggestion," Drixus says as he runs the brush clear through the second section of my hair. "It doesn't have to be tomorrow. Whenever you're ready."

*****

It takes three days for me to build up the strength—or perhaps the courage—to join Drixus in crossing the hall to Mara's room. Her door was nailed shut long ago, so we have to pass through Drixus' old, smelly room and the hole in the wall to get inside.

The floor here is much cleaner than in Drixus' old space, and it's lit by natural light from the back wall that's torn completely open. The hole is easily ten feet across and stretches up through the roof of this room into some sort of attic space. The ceiling has been almost completely torn out to extend the height of the room. I can see the roof when I look up, and there are birds in what's left of the rafters as well as a few lengths of rope draped over the beams. A few of the birds take flight when we arrive.

Near the hole to the outside, curled up on a massive nest of sticks, leaves, bones, and feathers, sits a creature so large it nearly blocks the entire entrance. Drixus clicks his tongue, and the creature lifts its head to look at us. Its feathered face is flat with two large, black eyes and a short brown beak. Its neck is long and winding, like the one on the spitter that attacked Wexton and I. Four long legs are tucked up under the body, but I can see from here that they're covered in fur instead of feathers. Two wings are nestled close to its sides, and a long, scaly tail drapes out behind it, stretching clear to the back wall near the door. It has six sharp spikes at the end, each as long as my arm.

I swallow as the creature stretches its neck out toward Drixus and I and snorts in my direction.

Drixus puts his arm around me. "It's alright. Just reach your hand out."

I slowly lift my arm and reach out, palm up and fingers splayed.

That curving neck stretches impossibly far, and the beak reaches for my hand.

I force myself to remain still as it nudges one of my fingers, and a blast of warm air whips across my palm as it sniffs me. The creature starts clicking.

"Is that good or bad?" I ask nervously.

"Since she makes that same noise whenever Percival comes around and she hasn't tried to eat him yet, I'd say it's good," Drixus teases. "Evangeline, meet Mara. Mara, this is our new friend, Evangeline."

Mara blinks at me as if she understands Drixus' words and is studying me, committing me to memory. She inclines her head a few inches before drawing back and turning to stare out the open wall again.

"What do we do now?" I whisper.

"We get closer," Drixus says, and he takes a step forward, ushering me along at his side. When Mara doesn't react, he steps again, then again. She turns her head to look at us, but Drixus doesn't stop. He marches me right up to Mara's side, and she watches us closely the whole way. "Place your hand on her side, just above her wing."

I'm apprehensive, but I trust Drixus, so I reach out and gently place my hand on the feathered body in front of me. When I do, her side twitches under my hand like Papa's mare used to do when the flies would land on her in the summer months. I press harder and stroke one of the massive feathers. It's as wide as my hand is tall, and I pet it clear to the tip. I look over at Mara, and she tilts her head at me, turning her face nearly upside down as she continues to study me.

I giggle nervously.

She chitters at me as if trying to recreate the sound of my laugh.

"Hello," I say.

She snorts back at me.

Drixus sidesteps and takes her head between his hands. Mara straightens her long neck and faces him. He sets his forehead against hers, and she chitters again and closes her eyes as he scratches her neck.

"Good girl," he says softly. "Wanna stretch your wings a bit?"

Mara clicks her beak once.

"Evangeline is coming with us. They're important to me, so behave yourself."

She turns to look at me again then sighs loudly as if to say, 'If you insist.'

I laugh again, and again, Mara copies me.

Drixus lets her go and comes back to me. "Want to give it a try?"

The last thing I'm feeling right now is adventurous, but the glint of excitement in Drixus' eye is contagious, so I smile and nod.

I take a step back as Drixus leans over Mara's body, and with a hop and a quick swing of his leg, he's astride her. He beckons me over and easily lifts me up with one arm, settling me in front of him, close to his chest.

"Take hold of a few feathers," Drixus says, and he shows me how best to hold them so as not to cause Mara pain. "Keep your grip tight, but you want to move your body weight with her more than relying on your hands to keep you on. Squeeze with your thighs."

"I can't really. She's too big." I'm an experienced rider when it comes to horses, but Mara's body is so wide my legs are practically in a split.

"Here." Drixus reaches up and pulls down one of the ropes dangling from the rafters. He loops it around his waist, knots it, then loops it around mine and knots it again, tethering us together. "That should keep you from sliding around too much."

I nod, happy with this added safety feature.

"Lean forward so you're lying across her back," Drixus instructs. We both lean over so far that Drixus is practically lying on top of me. He clicks his tongue again. "Let's go, girl!"

Mara grunts as she gets to her feet, and my heart starts racing as she heads for the hole in the wall. She ducks her massive body so Drixus doesn't strike his back on the wood as she scoots through.

Then she leaps.

I scream as the wind rushes past us and my body tips forward. The rope around my middle is all that keeps me from tumbling clear over her head as Mara falls away from the castle wall into a short dive. A few seconds later, her wings shoot out, and the sudden force of the wind beneath them, pulling her up from the dive flattens me to her back even harder. Once everything evens out, I'm scared to sit up even after Drixus does so behind me.

He touches my shoulder. "Are you alright?"

I lift my head, and though I can't see anything but the sky, I can tell we're at least flying flat and straight now. I sit up on my elbows and see The Deadwood stretching as far as the eye can see. Drixus puts an arm across my chest to steady me further, and I'm finally brave enough to sit up straight. Mara's wings beat softly on either side, and I'm shocked at how long they are when fully extended.

"What do you think?" Drixus asks nervously.

This is much different than flying with Caliborne or Fenmire, but the feel of Mara's muscles shifting beneath me and the openness of the sky above and around me makes me feel so free. I don't think I'll ever be comfortable riding her alone or without the rope connecting me to Drixus, but…

"It's amazing," I say.

Drixus grabs both my wrists and tugs. "Let go."

I hesitate at first but slowly loosen my grip and release. He guides my arms out to my sides as if I'm the one with wings, then he lets go.

"Look up."

I look straight ahead and laugh.

I'm flying.

The wind hits my face so hard it brings tears to my eyes, and my hair whips out behind me as Mara glides over The Deadwood.

I get silly and tilt my arms one way then the other, pretending I'm a bird zigzagging through the air.

Drixus laughs and joins me.

We're both still giggling when the edge of The Deadwood comes into view.

"Alright, hold on," Drixus warns, and I manage to grab on to Mara's feathers again before he guides her into a wide turn. The sudden dip on the left side threatens to send me rolling, but I lean heavily to the right and balance myself on Drixus' arm.

We fly toward a spot far off on the castle's left side, the opposite direction of The Gate, and we're soon gliding over a section of The Deadwood I've never been to before. We fly for several minutes, at least twice as long as it takes to get to the arch. Drixus puts his arm around me again as he urges Mara down toward the ground, and though I still feel like I might tumble over her head, I'm far less nervous this time and simply lean back into Drixus' chest and grip his arms as we descend. There's a small clearing in the trees, and I duck my head as we fly through a few upper branches on our way down to it.

Mara lands with only the smallest jolt, tucking her wings in as soon as all four feet are on the ground. She slowly kneels, tucking said feet underneath her. Drixus slides off then reaches up to lower me to the ground beside him. Once we've dismounted, Mara stands again and shakes, ruffling her wings and swinging her tail from side to side across the ground.

"Take a quick lap if you like," Drixus tells her. "But come when I call."

Mara doesn't hesitate to spread her wings again. I shield my face from flying dust and leaves as she takes flight and soon disappears over the treetops.

"She understands you," I say in awe. "How intelligent is she?"

"When I first saved her from the others, she was vicious and driven by nothing but bloodlust and fear. But, after a while, Reilanna's hold on her weakened, and she started to trust me. It was years before I was able to ride her, but in that time, her true personality won out over Reilanna's poisonous influence. She's actually quite bright."

"What made you choose to save her? Of all the beasts that came through The Gate, why this one?"

Drixus picks up a stick and starts breaking it in pieces instead of looking at me. "When Caliborne shot her down, she crashed through The Deadwood near my location, so I was the first to find her. When I did, she was trying to take flight again, struggling through the pain of a broken wing to get back in the sky. Her eyes never left it, not even when I emerged from the brambles a few feet away. And her cries… they made me stop, and when I did, I saw a creature in pain, not just in body but in mind. Reilanna had taken her freedom of will, and we'd taken her wings. I knew how that felt. Instead of swinging my axe, I threw a rope and tethered her to the ground to stop her from damaging herself further.

"The others found me there moments later, and I forbade them from killing her. They didn't like that, but Wexton said, 'We can always kill it later if it becomes a problem'. I almost laughed because he could've easily been talking about me."

He starts throwing the pieces of the stick into the trees, one at a time. "We were a broken pair, Mara and I. We'd both suffered at Reilanna's hands and been ripped from the sky, grounded against our will. Only for Mara, it wasn't forever. She healed where I could not. I honestly think that's why she didn't kill me. She could have a few times, but I think she could sense that, for her, the grounding was temporary, but for me, something had been taken that I'd never get back. So she shared her flight with me instead, eventually, in exchange for saving her from Reilanna and the others."

"Perhaps you saved each other."

Drixus throws his last piece of wood and smiles shyly at me. "I like to think so."

Silence falls between us, so I turn and survey the little clearing we're now standing in. This portion of The Deadwood looks no different from any other.

"What is it you wanted to show me?" I ask.

"A secret. Come on." He takes my hand and begins leading me through the nearby trees.

Chapter 69

In his excitement to show me his big secret, Drixus takes great strides I have to run to match.

"Can we slow down a little?" I ask after a few minutes. I'm breathless from attempting to keep up.

"Sorry," he says sheepishly, and he slows to a much more manageable pace. After a few more minutes, he stops, peers around, turns a bit more to the right, and continues walking.

"Are we lost?" I ask, more out of curiosity than actual concern.

"Not lost, no. It's been many years since I've come here and the forest has changed since then. It's just up ahead."

This is the first time I've seen Drixus in bright, natural sunlight, and it makes the hundreds of scars across his body stand out even harsher on his dark blue skin. There are a few that were obviously earned sometime recently as they're a different color than the rest, but they're all in places where his armor should protect him from superficial injuries. The longer I look, the more I suspect…

"Drixus, do you wear armor on patrol?" I ask.

"No."

"Why not?"

"The truth?" he asks, but since my answer is obvious, he doesn't wait for a response. "For the past two thousand years, I didn't care what happened to me. I figured if one of Reilanna's beasts ended me, my suffering would be over and the others could continue on as they always have. They don't need me, and I barely cared if I lived or died most days, so…"

"Where is your armor now?"

"I lost it. Reilanna stripped it from me before she… you know."

"Can you make a new set? Heaven knows there should be enough gold about the castle to do so."

He peers down at me with a raised brow. "Gold? Our armor isn't made of gold."

"It's not? It looks just like gold."

"Gold is far too soft a metal for things like weapons and armor. Our equipment is made from a metal not found in your world. Its shade is similar to that of the metal you call by the color, but if you compare the two side by side, you'd see ours is actually a bit more reflective and a lighter shade."

"Does our gold exist in your world?"

"It does, though we have little use for it. It doesn't stand the test of time very well. It's usually used to make things for children, toys and furniture that are only meant to last a few thousand years at most."

I can't imagine a world where toys for children are made of pure gold.

We walk for a couple more minutes before a patch of thick brush comes into view through the trees. Upon closer inspection, it appears to be a mound of thick underbrush, a hill of woven vines and moss. We stop in front of it, and I look at Drixus, waiting for an explanation as to what I'm seeing.

Drixus walks over to the mound and starts ripping down vines and brushing away leaves, moss, and dirt as he slowly uncovers a flat piece of rock. It seems this patch of overgrowth has wound its way around a boulder, completely covering it from top to bottom. Drixus clears away the growth until his fingers grasp the edge of the stone, then he smiles at me over his shoulder before leaning to the side and, with a grunt of exertion, slides the stone away. Behind this initial flat piece at the front lies a larger piece of hollowed out rock that remains covered with vines and moss, hidden from sight.

Drixus slides the flat piece of stone clear over to the nearest tree and leans it against the trunk. It leaves a divot in the dirt where it was dragged, and when I look closer, I can see evidence that this is not the first time such a path has been gouged into the ground. This stone has been slid across the dirt and tree roots here many times in the past.

"What is this place?" I ask.

"It's something my brother found a long time ago. It was our little secret for many years, and after everything that happened, it didn't feel appropriate to finally show it to the others. But it feels alright, good even, to share it with you."

"You can share anything with me, Drixus. I promise never to harbor grudges or judgment."

He smiles at me. "I know. It's what I love most about you."

It's a common enough phrase I know I shouldn't read anything into it, and yet the thought that there may be other things, many things, he also loves about me makes my stomach fluttery. A blush heats my cheeks, but thankfully, he's too busy searching inside the cave entrance to notice. He gropes in the darkness and yanks something off the wall. It's a torch. He takes a small golden box from his pocket and clicks a button on the side, igniting a flame at the end that he uses to light the torch, only once it catches, the fire changes from orange to bright blue.

"Whoa," I utter. "How did you do that?"

"It's soaked in a special oil that takes days to burn out." He pockets the golden box and holds his hand out to me again.

"Actually… can I hold it?"

Drixus looks at the torch and passes it to me without hesitation. "Be careful not to get that oil on you. It's tough to get off, and I don't want you to get burned."

I know it's silly, but I can't help but give the torch a little wave to watch the flames dance and leave a blue streak in the air in front of me.

Drixus laughs. "I think your name might be too long to write, sweetheart."

For the second time, my stomach flutters, and I can't help but grin at him for the endearment. Our eyes meet, and his one grey one flicks back and forth between both of mine. His smile softens into something else, something heartfelt and kind like the look I saw on his face in the drawing in Wexton's room. In it, I see a glimpse of the Gryxen who captured Fenmire's heart.

And maybe mine as well.

Drixus ushers me ahead of him, and we walk at an incline through a dark tunnel. This passageway is made of the same stone as the castle with textured but no less perfectly straight and flat walls. The floor is broken into steps where the incline becomes too steep, though they look far too smooth to have been shaped with man-made tools.

"Horthos built this passage, didn't he?" I ask.

"He did. His powers allowed him to sense caverns and tunnels buried deep beneath the earth. It's what directed him to the molten rock that warms the bathing pool beneath the castle. He knew just where to dig and how deep to do so."

"What did he find down here?" There's a faint roaring sound in the distance that's growing louder with every step we take.

"This," Drixus says, and he takes the torch from me as we step out into a wide-open cavern. He lifts the flames high in the air, casting a blue glow all around the cave.

This place, unlike the tunnel we walked through to get here, is completely natural, and by that, I mean I can tell Horthos had no hand in its creation. There are stalactites dripping from the ceiling onto their stalagmite brothers below, and a few have connected in the middle to form pillars of stone. An underground pond dominates most of the space, its crystal-clear water lapping faintly at its stone shore a few feet away from us. Directly across the cavern from us, the pond is being fed by a large waterfall, which is the source of the roaring sound. A light mist of water continuously billows up all around the base of the falls. It catches the light from the torch and shimmers wildly.

Another shimmer, a brighter one, catches my eye, and I look up and gasp.

Hundreds of crystals of various sizes and shapes hang from the ceiling of this cave. Many of them are dripping, making it look like it's raining underground.

Drixus walks around the left side of the pond, stepping carefully along a narrow walkway at the edge of the water as he lights torches attached to the walls every six feet or so. He comes back and does the same on the right side. Soon, the entire cavern is lit brightly with blue light. The flames dance along the edges of the crystals like the grandest, most beautiful chandelier. Drixus slides our original torch into a crevice in the wall near the tunnel entrance and turns to me.

"What do you think?" he asks.

"It's beautiful," I say in awe. "Like a dream. Who would've thought something like this existed beneath our feet."

"Do you want to go in?"

"Can I?"

"As long as you don't mind the chill. There's no sun down here to warm the water, so it's quite cold. Don't drink any of it—there are way too many minerals in it for that—but it's safe to bathe in."

I start shuffling out of my clothes. "Are you coming in too?"

His eye peers across the pond toward the waterfall. "I haven't since…"

He doesn't have to explain.

I take both his gloved hands in mine. "Come make a happy memory with me?"

His face breaks into that soft, kind smile I saw before. "I feel like that applies to every minute I spend with you."

He steps out of his pants and drops them near my discarded clothes.

I tug him toward the water, and he follows as I step down into the shimmering blue pool. He's right, it's quite chilly, and I gasp and yelp a few times as I wade deeper and deeper, heading for the waterfall. When the floor drops out from under my feet, I let go of Drixus' hand and kick off to tread icy water up to my chin. Drixus seems unfazed by the temperature and dives right in, coming up on the other side of me. He takes my hand again, and we slowly make our way to the falls.

The mist speckles us as we get closer, beading on my face and in my hair then running in small streaks that tickle my nose. I'm getting used to the temperature, so it's less uncomfortable by the time we reach the falls. The water rushing from the rocks at the top of the cave is actually warmer than the pool, but I'm apprehensive about ducking under it, afraid it will suck me beneath the surface. Drixus must sense this, for he stands up—I hadn't noticed he could still touch the bottom here—and picks me up onto his shoulders. As I hold his hands and giggle in anticipation, he walks under the rushing water.

The feeling is like nothing I've ever experienced before. The water beats down on my head, shoulders, and back, warming me where my skin is burning from the cold of the pool below. I let go of Drixus' hands and reach up, splaying my fingers to feel the water rush between them and slap my palms. As it falls down over my ears, it muffles the sound of the falls crashing into the pool, and I close my eyes and just feel. I laugh and teeter on Drixus' shoulders, but he reaches up and steadies me with his hands on my waist. After another minute, he steps out of the falls and slides me off his shoulders back into the icy pool.

"That was amazing!" I cry, grabbing his arms and squeezing in my excitement. "Oh, I wish I could show this to Will. Can we bring him sometime? He'd absolutely love this."

"Whatever would make you happy, sweetheart," Drixus replies, his low, booming voice echoing back to me from around the cavern.

I look up into his face.

He stares back down into mine.

I tug on his arms.

He bends his knees and lowers himself so that we're face to face.

I put my arms around his neck and pull closer.

His arms slide behind my back and tug me closer still.

"Is this alright?" I ask.

Drixus smiles, bows his head, and kisses me. It's a long and slow kind of kiss, the kind that conveys far more feeling than words ever could, and when he pulls away, my eyes are burning with tears.

He nuzzles my cheek. "This is perfect."

As I tread water, my lips find his again, and as I kiss him back, I'm shocked when my body responds with a desire that's been dormant since I crawled into Drixus' bed over a week ago. I tilt my head and open my mouth, inviting Drixus in, but he doesn't take me up on the offer. I pull away.

"I'm sorry," I say bashfully. "I pushed too far."

"No, you didn't." He kisses me again, soothing my worries. "I was actually going to ask… would you… touch yourself? While I watch?"

I blink in surprise. "I thought you said you don't like doing those sorts of things."

"I have no desire to participate, but I love to be a spectator." He smiles at me with a hint of the same mischief in his eye that Wexton carries in his every minute of every day.

"Do you find satisfaction in that?"

"Not the kind you're thinking. It's less carnal and more delight in seeing the ones I care about bathed in pleasure."

"This is something you do frequently then?"

"It used to be."

I consider it. Do I feel up to this? Am I ready? My body certainly thinks I am. Drixus' kisses have stirred a desire deep in my belly. What he's asking for is something new but certainly no more erotic than anything I've already done.

"I think I need a few more kisses to help me make up my mind," I say.

Drixus chuckles and obliges.

A few more long and sensual presses of his lips to mine is all it takes to banish my qualms. I picture myself with my hand between my thighs while Drixus' icy grey eye watches my every move.

I moan.

"Is that a yes?" he asks.

"Yes," I utter against his lips.

He grabs me by the backside and lifts me up onto his hips as he starts making his way to the side of the pool. I wrap my legs around him and continue to kiss him as he carries me out of the water. The air is much warmer than the water, and so is the stone that rises to meet my back when Drixus sets me down. He lays beside me with his head propped up on one arm. Water runs from us both in rivers and streaks across the stone floor back into the pool as he stares at me, patiently waiting for me to begin.

I swallow down my nerves and spread my legs. I slide my hand down the icy, water-slicked skin of my stomach and one of my legs to my knee then back up my inner thigh into the curls of my pubic hair. I part myself with two fingers then slide a third into the soft heat of my sex, petting my entrance a few times before sliding up to circle my clit.

I close my eyes.

"Look at me," Drixus requests softly.

I look him in the eye instead, and I don't look away as I start to pleasure myself. Drixus' eye bores into mine with such intensity my face heats in another blush, and this time, he definitely notices. But he doesn't speak, and he doesn't move; he just watches.

I slip one finger inside me, pumping it in and out and spreading my own warm and slick arousal across my clit. I do this three times then rub my clit overwhelmingly hard a few times, making myself whimper and thrust my hips. I slow and go back to the soft circles I did before, extending my pleasure for a moment before repeating the whole process: fuck myself with my finger, spread the resulting moisture across my clit, overwhelm my nerves with so much sensation I cry out, then soften and ride the waves.

Drixus never looks away for a second.

My lips part, and I start to pant as my orgasm builds. After so long spent celibate lately, I want to have the most intense orgasm I can, so when I rub my clit this time, I don't stop, forcing my orgasm to rush to the forefront and slam into me. I force my eyes to remain open and locked onto Drixus' as I cry out and whimper and shake on the stone, continuing to pleasure myself to the point my legs quiver uncontrollably. When I can't take it anymore, I remove my hand and squeeze my thighs together, milking every sensation from each delicious wave of my orgasm until it fades away completely.

When I finally still, Drixus smiles. "Beautiful."

I smile shyly at him. "Did you like that?"

"*You* liked it, and that's what matters to me."

I slide closer across the wet stone. I'm beginning to shiver, but since Drixus' skin is so chilly, he can't warm me up like the others.

"May I suggest an addition to your cavern?" I ask.

"It's as much your cavern now as it is mine, so sure."

"Perhaps a fire?"

Drixus touches my arm with the back of his wrist where his skin isn't gloved. "You're cold?"

"A little."

He stands up and retrieves my clothes, and though I'm still pretty damp, I eagerly dress, grateful for their warmth.

"Should we go?" Drixus asks.

"Not yet." I tug him down to sit beside me on a dry section of stone then scoot into his lap. "I'm not done making my memory."

Drixus puts his arms around me, and we sit there for a while in our usual silence, stealing a kiss or two as we watch the blue flames flicker in the crystals and the mist.

Chapter 70

It's just after dusk when Drixus and I get back to the castle. The flight home is chillier than the one to the cave. Fall is starting to creep in, and I wonder if all of this—the castle, the forest, or even us—will be here to see The Deadwood's first natural snowfall in over two thousand years. As much as I love whatever is growing between Drixus and I, it also feels a little scary.

It feels like the beginning of the end.

Mara lands back in her room and kneels down in her nest to let us off. Before following Drixus back through the hole in the wall, I turn to her, and that long, twisting neck creaks around as she regards me.

"Thank you," I say. "For today, sure, but also for all the ones you've carried Drixus into battle. Thank you for giving back what Reilanna stole from him."

Mara is still for a moment before she stretches her long neck out toward me, stopping with her beak just inches from my face.

She blinks.

I blink.

She snorts, and the wind from it blows back my hair.

I laugh nervously.

Mara inclines her head, turns away, and lays down upon her sticks, feathers, and bones, staring once again out the hole at the sky.

Drixus and I leave her to return to his room, but when we step into the hall, we find a figure leaning against the stone wall beside Drixus' door. It's dark now, so it's hard to see who it is, but once my eyes adjust, I easily recognize him.

"Will," I say in surprise. "What are you doing up here?"

"I came to talk to you," Will says, pushing himself off the wall. "The others asked us all to give you space, but I couldn't wait."

"Did something happen?"

He smirks and runs his hand through his hair. "You could say that. I asked Jacob to marry me, and he said 'yes'."

I squeal with delight and cross the hall to my friend, wrapping him in a tight hug. "Of course he did. Why wouldn't he? Jacob knows how lucky he is to have you. If he doesn't, he's a fool."

We hug for a long moment, then Will lets me go and takes me by the shoulders to study my face. "Are you alright? I mean… obviously you're not happy, of course you're not, but are you…?"

"I'm managing." It's the best I can do. "I think I was in shock for a while, and then it all sort of crashed down on me, and it was a lot. I'm feeling better every day, but I was a wreck for a while. I couldn't let the others see me like that."

"I understand. Do you think you'll be joining us soon? I don't want to rush you, so please tell me to kick sand if you're not ready, but Jacob and I want to have a wedding before the season turns, and I won't do it without you."

"You better not or else Jacob will have no groom at all."

Will tilts his head.

"Oh, because I'd kill you, dearest."

Will nods with a chuckle. "Right. Got it."

"Perhaps this is a good thing. Maybe a little kick in the backside will help me pull myself together, at least enough to join society again… or whatever you want to call our merry bunch."

"I'm truly sorry, Evangeline. I know how much your father meant to you."

I shake my head, willing myself not to cry again. "I'm not ready to talk about it yet."

Will nods again. "Will you stand beside me as I marry the man I love?"

I beam at him. "I'd be honored. Why don't I come downstairs tomorrow morning, and we can look for the perfect place to hold a ceremony? I'm sure there are rooms in the castle with plenty of space for us all to gather and celebrate your union."

"Actually, Jacob was hoping for an outdoor ceremony, hence the worry about the season."

"In that case…" Drixus takes an uncertain step out of the shadows he's been standing quietly in during this whole conversation. "I may know a place."

"Really?" I ask.

"I haven't been there since the blizzard broke to know what it looks like now, but it used to be a beautiful place."

"We could take a look after breakfast. Can Mara carry the three of us?"

"Probably, but I wouldn't try it. It's easy to keep you on her back with me, but two of you is a risk I'd rather not take."

"I'd like Jacob to come too anyway," Will says. "Can we ask the others for a quick flight?"

"Would you mind the company?" I ask Drixus.

"Would you?" he asks.

I take a deep breath in and let it out slowly between pursed lips. "I think I'm ready. I miss them."

Drixus bows his head. "Company it is, then."

Will gives my shoulder a squeeze. "I'll see you in the morning?"

"In the morning," I say, and I put on my best smile for my friend as he wanders away down the hall, but it quickly fades again once he's out of sight.

Drixus silently lets us into his room, and once the door is shut and it's just the two of us again, he says, "You're *not* ready, are you?"

"I don't know," I say honestly. I sit heavily on the side of the bed. "I want to be, but I know that's not the same thing."

"It's not, but it's a good sign." He takes me by surprise by scooping me up and flopping down into the bed with a heavy sigh. "It's not all or nothing. If you decide tomorrow is too much too soon, you're always welcome to retire here with me until you're ready to try again."

I curl closer and slip the edge of a blanket free from the collection around us, yanking it over me. "I know," I say softly, shutting my eyes against the burn of fatigue. "I know I haven't said it out loud, but I hope you know how much I appreciate… well, you, I suppose. All of you. I don't know that I would've gotten through this without you."

Drixus sighs again and runs the tips of his gloved fingers up and down my arm, giving me goosebumps. "You would've faired just fine, sweetheart." He sounds sad but resolved, and I pry my tired eyes open again to look at him. "You're not the type to let anyone or anything knock you down for long. You've lost someone, and I know better than most how that feels, but you still have a lot left to live for. You would've found your way back to them without me."

"Maybe, but what condition would I have been in when I did? Kneeling there in the dirt, holding my father, realizing he was… something broke inside me. During the flight home in Fenmire's arms, there was only one person I wanted to see. Somehow, I knew I could trust you with my broken pieces and that you'd help me put them back together again. Or maybe not so much that you'd help put me back together but that you'd protect what was left of me while I put *myself* back together. Does that make sense?"

"It does. I know firsthand the pain of healing alone. I'm glad I could be there for you when you needed me. It's the least I could do after you were there for me in the same way."

"We may have started in a place of mutual healing, and perhaps I'm still too raw from mine to say this with certainty, but am I right to think there's more between us now? What happened in the cave today certainly felt like more than friendship."

"Yes, it did. And I don't regret it."

"Me neither."

He smiles. "I'd say there's more then. All things considered, perhaps we shouldn't give it too much thought yet. If it's meant to be, it will be. Don't you think?"

"I do. Let's focus on helping my best friend get married, and we'll see how things go from there. Deal?"

"Deal."

I touch Drixus' face, tracing the harsh line of his cheekbone as I sweep the hair from the scarred side of his face. "You're beautiful and broken. Like me. My beautiful, broken boy."

His arm tightens, dragging me closer as he leans down and kisses me softly on the lips. "You're not broken, sweetheart," he murmurs. "A little bruised maybe, but not broken." He palms my cheek, and I feel the icy cool of his powers through his leather gloves. "It'll take much more than this to break you. You may be small, but there's nothing but strength inside you. I can feel it."

I touch his hand, clutching it tighter to my face. "Will you come downstairs with me tomorrow?" I whisper.

Drixus visibly swallows, but after only a heartbeat's hesitation, he nods. "Now go to sleep. We have to deal with Wexton in the morning."

I laugh softly, get comfortable under my blanket, and sigh as my eyes close and refuse to open again this time.

*****

I'm anxious as I dress the next morning. I've finally broken from the Evangeline-only mood I've been in since losing my father, so I put on my favorite Evan outfit instead, the one I swiped from my room on my first visit to the farm. With each piece of clothing I put on, my nerves flare, but this outfit is one I longed for, for years, and its arrival was a dream come true for me. Seeing myself in it now helps me stand taller. Though my confidence leaves much to be desired, I'm resolved and as ready to face the day as I'll ever be.

Drixus steps up behind me in the mirror and studies us both. His hair is down across his marred face again, but he mirrors my stance, and we both cross our arms in unison.

Drixus nods. "Let's go."

We head downstairs together.

The halls are empty clear to the kitchen, and when I walk in, I'm met with a chorus of cheers and happy hellos.

"Look at you out and about," Levi says. "You're looking a little skinny though. I'll fix that in no time." He gives me a wink and sets about preparing me a tray. When he hands it over, he loses his smile. "I'm sorry to hear about your father."

My stomach drops as I take the tray with only a nod for a response.

"I'm sorry," he says again. "You must be sick to death of hearing that."

"It's alright," I say, though I don't deny it. "Thank you for all the meals lately."

"You're welcome. Now go." He shoos me toward the door. "Go work on putting some meat back on those bones." He drops his voice to a whisper. "And I'll start leaving you a midnight snack on your dresser. Something extra sweet."

"You spoil me… I love it."

I leave him laughing, and only when I turn around do I realize Drixus never followed me into the kitchen. I find him waiting with his back to the wall in the hall instead. To say he looks uncomfortable is an understatement.

"Is everything alright?" I ask.

"Sure," he says, though it comes out a bit choked. He motions me ahead of him down the hall toward the dining room, but when we approach the door and the sound of chatting and laughing voices reaches us, he stops again. He's visibly shaking.

I set my tray on the floor and go to him. "It's alright," I say with my hands on his chest. "It's just our friends."

"*Your* friends," he says miserably.

I search his face and find nothing but terror. His eye is fixed on the open doorway ahead of us, and at a particularly rowdy burst of laughter, he takes a step backward.

"Drixus?" I call softly.

He looks down at me.

"Go. It's alright."

"I wanted… I thought I'd…"

"You're not ready. I understand. Go. I'll come find you later."

He looks so sad and lost when he nods and turns away that I almost pick up my tray and go after him. Part of me would love nothing more than to go take my meal in his room again and let him surround me with his quiet affection and never-ending patience, but I have other friends and a few mates I've neglected too long already. So I pick up my tray and walk into the dining room instead.

The chatter I heard from the hallway dies to silence upon my arrival as all heads swivel to stare at me. I freeze and suddenly get an idea how Drixus must've felt just now as my heart starts to race. Thankfully, Will jumps into action. He's the first to turn away from me and spark the conversation anew.

"So Wexton," Will says. "I've got to ask, and feel free to tell me to go to hell if this question is too personal, but how'd you lose the arm? I've gotta know."

Wexton smiles wickedly from across the table. "That, my friend, is a long story."

There are no longer any eyes on me as they're all drawn into Wexton's tale, the one he told me in my sickbed months ago. I head for the empty seat between Will and Fenmire, and when I get close,

Fenmire tugs the stool out for me without even looking at me, silently welcoming me to the table without putting me on the spot. Once I'm seated, he leans down and softly kisses me on the top of the head. Wexton winks at me without pausing his story. Will slides his uneaten pie onto my tray. Jacob gives me the smallest wave before asking Wexton a question.

And just like that, I'm back amongst my family and friends with none of the fuss I'd been dreading. There are no 'I'm sorry's or 'how are you feeling's, no guilt for how long I've been hiding away upstairs.

There's only laughter and love and apple pie.

Chapter 71

Will and I explain our plans for the day to the others, and since Wexton is not ideal for helping us travel, he offers to relieve Caliborne of his patrol so he can fly us to Drixus' spot instead.

"Thank you," I tell Wexton with a parting kiss on the castle's front steps.

"You're welcome, darling," he replies, rubbing my arm. "I've missed you."

I hang my head.

He tilts it back up again by my chin. "Don't do that," he says softly.

"Do what?"

"Feel guilty. You mourn however and for as long as you need. I can't imagine what human grief must feel like. Your life is so short it must seem like you've barely accomplished anything at all before it's over, and you rarely get to accept death on your own terms. It's cruel."

I take his hand with a squeeze. "It makes each moment that much more precious. But you're right, it's not fair."

He strokes a finger down my cheek then picks up his sword. "I told Will and Jacob to meet Fenmire and Caliborne here so you can ride with Drixus."

I nod. "I love you."

He gives me a beaming smile, shakes out his wings, and takes off.

I head up to the third floor, but when I knock on Drixus' door, I get no answer. I look at the door to his old, filthy room and say a prayer. Please tell me he's not back in there. I knock on that door too and am met with the same silence, only this time, I open the door and peer in. The room is indeed empty, but I hear a low voice and some shuffling in the room next door and head for the hole in the wall. When I peek my head in, I find Drixus sitting at the edge of Mara's nest with his head against her neck, petting her and speaking in a low whisper.

"Drixus?" I say, softly so as not to startle him, but he jumps anyway. "Sorry."

He stands up and comes to the hole to take my hand as I step through. "Are the others ready?"

"They should be momentarily. What are you doing in here?"

"Visiting an old friend." He seems tired and sad.

"You don't have to come today," I say. "You can point me in the direction of your spot, and I'll fly with the others if—"

He shakes his head. "I want to come. It's just…" He looks away. "I'm ashamed. It's such a foolish thing. I've faced countless horrors with nary a qualm, but the thought of walking into a room scares me to my core. Pitiful."

"Oh, Drixus," I say. I hug him. "It's not foolish or pitiful. Please don't think that way. Think of it like… like a battle scar. There's nothing shameful about scars, right?"

"No. But this scar is of my own making."

"You were protecting yourself."

"I was being a coward."

I click my teeth irritably as I accept this battle is lost today. "Well, regardless of how or why it was born, it's here. And if it's something you wish to change, we'll work on it. Together."

He touches the back of my head, hugging me tighter to his chest. "No promises, remember?"

"No expectations," I say. I look up at him and smile. "Deal?"

He gives me a halfhearted grin and waves his arm toward Mara. "Shall we?"

*****

With Drixus and I back aboard Mara, we head for Drixus' spot, and the others take off from the castle steps when they see us pass overhead. Drixus leads us all in a direction I think I recognize.

"Isn't the cave this way?" I ask.

"The cave is there." He points to a place more to our right. "We're headed over here." He points off toward the left.

I don't see anything, and yet Mara starts to descend a moment later. We're headed straight for the trees with no clear landing space in sight.

"Hold on," Drixus advises.

I grip Mara's feathers more tightly as she angles even further down, and I hug close to her body as Drixus does the same behind me, all but flattening himself against me as we break through the trees. Thankfully, Mara glides down into the forest without much trouble, but as soon as her feet touch the ground, she's forced to stop rather suddenly to keep from running head-first into a tree. The rope attaching me to Drixus' waist is all that keeps me from sliding right out from under him.

Caliborne and Fenmire land soon after and set Will and Jacob on their feet.

Drixus unties my rope and lowers me to the ground. "It's just through those trees," he says quietly, pointing to a spot behind me. He doesn't get down from Mara's back.

"Aren't you coming too?" I ask.

His eye flicks toward the others and then immediately to the ground.

I touch his leg. "You can stay here if you like," I say quietly enough the others won't hear. "But I'd love for you to show me this place. If it's anything like the last secret you shared with me, I know it'll be wonderful."

Drixus looks at Fenmire, but the broody Gryxen in question isn't paying any attention to us, whether intentionally or by happenstance, I can't tell. After another moment's consideration, Drixus slides from his mount.

He turns to Mara and pets her long neck. "Stay," he orders her, and she nudges him with her head. "Good girl." He takes my hand, but the look on his face says it's more to bring himself comfort than anything else. He locks his eye forward and purposely avoids looking at the others as he heads off in the direction he pointed before. The others trail after us.

We don't have to walk far. Right on the other side of a grove, there's a break in the trees. It looks like a clearing, only it's not lit with bright sunshine like one would expect. We step out into an open space about half the size of the clearing that houses The Gate, and I look up to see the trees here have bowed inward, their branches intertwining to create a green ceiling. The ground is covered in a thick carpet of deep green moss, darted here and there with flowers of all different colors. Since the natural canopy blocks the sun, it's cooler here with a slight, pleasant breeze.

"Oh, wow..." Jacob says in awe. "It's a glade. Beautiful."

"It's like something from a fairytale," I say. I squeeze Drixus' hand. "Is this what it used to look like?"

"Yes," Drixus replies. "We never figured out what causes the trees here to grow like this, but—" He falls silent when Fenmire steps into the glade to our left. Drixus swallows and looks again at the ground.

"Walk with me?" I ask suddenly, tugging Drixus' hand as I step to the right, away from Fenmire.

Drixus and I walk along the outer edge of the glade, and once we're about a quarter of the way around, he says, "Thank you."

"Thank *you*, for this." I wave my arm at this magical place. "Will and Jacob have been through so much. They deserve the most fantastic wedding we can give them. This place is perfect."

When we're on the opposite side of the glade from the others, Drixus reaches down, plucks a small red flower from the moss, and presents it to me. I tuck it up into my braid then touch a large, flat section of moss near my feet. It's soft and squishy, so I plop down on it like a chair. Drixus sits beside me, though he's much heavier and sinks far deeper into the cushiony undergrowth.

The others are deep in talk, waving their arms and pointing about the space, no doubt working out the finer details of having a ceremony and celebration here while Drixus and I watch from afar. Eventually, Drixus relaxes and puts an arm around me.

I lean my head on his shoulder. "How did you find this place? Was it somewhere special for you?"

"Not really. Horthos and I used to explore the woods during our free time. This was one of many spots we stumbled across." He touches the ground between us. "Horthos liked to uncover all sorts of anomalies and wonders."

"Like the waterfall?"

"That's right. These woods are full of so many tunnels." He peers around at the surrounding trees. "I can only remember a few, but there are dozens."

"Can I ask you something?"

"Anything."

"Why do you think Horthos joined Reilanna?"

Drixus grunts and tugs me closer under his arm. "He loved her."

"Really? How? Why?"

"Horthos was the first one Reilanna came to in our dreams, only at that time, they weren't nightmares, not yet. He told me about them at first, but soon he stopped confiding even in me. It was the first time I suspected something was wrong.

"Our parents died when Horthos was only a couple hundred years old. He didn't even remember them. I was barely over three thousand myself when they died, but I asked to take him under my care rather than see him go to another family. I was all he had, and we never kept things from each other. When he started dodging my questions about his dreams, I was concerned but didn't tell the others.

"It turns out, Reilanna was whispering sweet things in his ears every night, promising him not only a place to call his own here in your world once she ruled it but a permanent place at her side as her lover, her king, so to speak. My brother was the lonely sort, and she promised him the one thing he'd wanted since he was a child: a family. She was cunning, and she chose him first because she thought he'd be the easiest to sway. And she was right.

"By the time he told me his plans, she had her claws so deep in him he was practically manic. He prattled on to me about the plans she had for them together, and no matter what I said, he would shake his head and tell me I didn't understand, that Reilanna wasn't evil, she didn't want to hurt the humans, she wanted to help them advance as a society, study them, and be their loving queen. And he would rule at her side as her true love. He said he was leaving to be with her, and he begged me to come too. I knew if I let him leave alone, I'd never get him back, so I went."

"Reilanna knew exactly what weaknesses to exploit to ensnare your brother," I say. "And she no doubt did the same to Jothrik and Breklen."

"She tried to ensnare me too. She promised me many things, and I usually nodded and thanked her, but I think she could tell my interest wasn't genuine. She kept me at a greater distance than the others. My mating bond with Fenmire no doubt made her leery. It's not an easy thing, betraying a mate, so she was suspicious from the start, but I never once showed any signs that fighting Fenmire and the others bothered me, so she let me stay. And while I stayed, I worked to fracture the hold she had on Horthos.

"I was subtle. I would ask him a question every once in a while that contradicted Reilanna's views, or sometimes I'd point out an inconsistency in her plans for after we took over your world. Sometimes, I'd stoke his jealousy by pointing out that, despite her claims to love him so dearly, she never treated him any differently from Jothrik or Breklen or even me. It was slow going, but day by day, I watched the veil lift in my brother's eyes. I was so close to convincing him to leave with me and return to the others. Another month or two and we'd have been far out of her reach, but she caught on to my plans, and everything fell apart."

"Evangeline."

Both Drixus and I jump when Fenmire calls my name, and Drixus stiffens beside me as Fenmire walks toward us across the glade.

I take Drixus' hand. "It's alright."

Fenmire stops several yards away. "We're ready to head back," he says. "We need to speak with Levi and Percival, but we plan to come back out here over the next couple of days to start setting things up."

"Alright," I say. "Why don't you all go on ahead. We'll catch up."

Fenmire nods then looks over at Drixus, who inhales sharply before he stops breathing altogether.

"This was a good idea," Fenmire says. "Well done."

"Th…thank you," Drixus replies.

Fenmire nods again then says, "I'll see you at home."

We watch him walk away until he rejoins the others, then I turn to Drixus excitedly. "Wow. That was almost pleasant."

Drixus has just the hint of a smile on his face. "That's the nicest he's been to me in over two thousand years."

I tug him down and kiss him on the cheek. "It's a start."

*****

Back at the castle, I don't go back to Drixus' room, at least not right away. I go to my own room to finally deal with the collection of gifts on my bed. The pile hasn't grown since the last time I was here, but someone has removed the flowers that were no doubt wilted and starting to rot. One remains that's still in seemingly perfect condition, but upon closer inspection, I discover it's actually made of paper. It's a perfectly-folded white lily with small dark speckles painted along the petals. There are even little stamens of tightly rolled paper in the center, which are painted green with red tips. One of the letters has a small white lily painted on its front, so I read that one first as I twirl the flower in my fingers.

It's from Jacob. The note is short and sweet but makes my chest hurt to read. I fold it back up and tuck it away in the drawer of my nightstand. The lily I place on the mantel above my fireplace. I'd put it in a vase, but it would only get broken the next time one of Reilanna's horrors comes through The Gate.

There are notes from Levi and Percival, which I read quickly and place in the drawer with Jacob's. I slide over the package wrapped in fur and pluck open the twine holding it all together. Inside are two folded stacks of cloth, one a deep royal blue, the other a light pastel pink. I unfold them to see how much there is and am shocked to find enough to make a few outfits in each color. A letter falls out from between the cloth. It's from Will.

Dearest Evangeline,

I tucked these fabrics amongst the offering from my father's store with plans to save them for your birthday, but since arriving in The Deadwood, I've realized how foolish it is to take any day for granted. If they make you smile, then they've done their job, birthday or not. I can't wait to see the beauty you'll no doubt create with them.

I'm so sorry, love, about your father. He was a good man, the kind our entire village should strive to be. Not Elias, that's for certain. I want to say I know your pain, having lost both my own parents over the years, but truth be told, I know that's a lie. The love and respect you and your father shared is something I never experienced with any of my blood, which means this loss you feel is no doubt much more intense than mine. I wish I could ease it, for I wish nothing but happiness for the best friend a man could ever ask for.

I know he is proud of you because I *am proud of you, and I like to think your father and I were of similar morals and values, or perhaps that's just me thinking too highly of myself. You'll no doubt tell me so if that's the case.*

I love you and am here for you should you need another shoulder to cry on, an ear to listen, or simply a distraction in the shape of an old friend who knows how to make you smile even on the darkest of days.

Love,
Will

I laugh and cry through the whole letter then hug it to my chest. I must remember to thank him when I can do so without sobbing. I put it, along with his other letters, on my mantel next to the lily.

The only thing left to open is the wooden box. It's pretty heavy when I pick it up, and something inside slides around when I jostle it. I open the lid and gasp.

Inside are two skeletal hands lying palms-down on red felt. The metacarpals and wrist bones are made of gold, or the Gryxen equivalent at least, but all eight of the fingers and both thumbs are bright white bone. I reach in and pick up one of the hands, and I'm shocked to discover all the joints move. The detail is astounding, though there are small nicks in the bones near where they attach to the golden ones.

So this is where Elias' fingers went.

Mesmerized, I put my hand against the skeletal one, palm to palm and fingers to fingers.

It's beautiful and disturbing.

I absolutely love it.

I put the hand back, and that's when I find the folded piece of paper in the bottom of the box. It's a small note, but it brings me just as much joy as Will's letter.

'The Touch of a True Monster'

A gift for a pet who deserves the world,
but since I can't give them that at present,
I'll give them justice instead.

I take the box to the mantel and place it beside my other gifts with the lid open and the note propped up in full view.

I take a step back and admire my collection. It's not nearly as large and impressive as Fenmire's, but it's a start.

And it's all me.

I go back to the bed and snatch up my new fabrics, holding them to my body as I imagine what I'd like to create with them first. I have a wedding to attend soon. I want to look my best for Will and Jacob's special day. And with that in mind, I pull out my sewing kit and get to work.

Chapter 72

The castle is bustling for the next few days as preparations are made for Will and Jacob's wedding. The kitchen is hard at work preparing food under Levi's direction, the Gryxen spend most of their time hauling materials to the glade, and the rest of the staff make decorations, which Percival helps organize. Most of the castle hasn't been to a wedding or any other kind of celebration in years, so everyone is happy to help, and they throw themselves into their tasks with full force.

As for me, I spend what free time I find between helping the others sewing my outfit, often staying up for hours after everyone else has gone to bed in order to get it done in time. Caliborne watches me work each night and makes me go to bed when I start nodding off over my stitching.

I admire your dedication, but you need rest too. It will be there in the morning.

I fly with Fenmire to The Gate to ask if we'll have any uninvited guests, but it reports Reilanna has been suspiciously still. It will be many more days before The Gate has the power to send through another quaheitan, if she does indeed plan to send anything at all. The Gate reports the city has been quiet since we defeated the last one.

She's waiting for something, preparing in silence for her strongest strike yet. I can see her, and she is in no hurry. Your human ceremony should be safe.

We don't have to ask what exactly she's planning for, but I'm no closer to breaking the spell now than I was weeks ago, due in part to the grief I've only just surfaced from and the hustle and bustle of preparing a wedding for my two closest friends. But there's also another reason why things have stalled when it comes to freeing us all from Reilanna's curse.

During the days it takes to prepare for Will and Jacob's ceremony, Drixus is nowhere to be found, and I don't mean he's simply holed up in his room away from all the chaos, for which I wouldn't blame him. The couple of times I go upstairs to see him, his room is empty, both of them are. I even check Mara's room only to find her alone in there as well. It's as if he's vanished entirely.

"Oh, don't worry about him," Wexton tells me when I express my concern over Drixus' disappearance. "I saw him this morning headed downstairs, probably to take a bath. He looked alright and waved when I called his name. He's probably just trying his best to avoid all the noise."

I don't have the time to go searching for him, so I let it go for the time being.

Finally, the day of the wedding arrives, and the mayhem intensifies, though I refuse to let Will or Jacob see it. I confine them to their room as Percival, Levi, and I shout orders, organize the staff, and cook food while the Gryxen take load after load of not only decorations and furniture but people to the glade.

Since the boys wish to exchange their vows in the evening, close to sunset, I find an hour or so in the afternoon to slip to my room and make the last couple of adjustments on my outfit, which is my most beautiful creation yet. I quite literally break the thread on the final stitch seconds before Wexton knocks on my door.

"Evangeline," he calls. "We're ready."

"Alright," I call back. "Just let me get dressed. Tell Caliborne I wish to go to the glade first to check everything is ready for the grooms before they arrive."

"Will do."

I quickly shuck my work clothes and get dressed in the outfit I only just finished in time. I pull on my new pants, which are made of various shades of blue fabric sewn together in a swirling pattern that starts out dark on the bottoms and slowly shifts to much lighter shades up the lengths of the legs and eventually to white at the waist.

The shirt that goes with them is sewn in the same fashion with white along the bottom that fades to pastel pink toward the top. Ruffles of pink, white, and blue line the shoulders and down the sleeves. The shirt buttons at the front and hangs loose and flowy about my torso, and I tuck it into the top of my pants to create a more billowed look at the waist.

I braid my hair forward over one shoulder like the day Caliborne compared me to one of the warrior priestesses, slide on my bronze bracelet, and step into my old, borrowed boots, which I pull the legs of my pants down over to hide as much as possible since they don't really fit the look. My mirror was smashed in the quake that knocked all the furniture around my room, so there's nowhere for me to check everything, but when I step into the hallway, I do so at the same time Caliborne steps out of *his* room dressed head to toe in gold, and his look of wide-eyed awe when he sees me tells me I must look as fabulous as I feel.

"Do you like it?" I ask, giving him a twirl.

His answering nod is so enthusiastic it's comical, and I laugh as I take his hand. "Why are you wearing your armor?"

We all are. The occasion is too special for nothing but leather pants.

"Aww, that's sweet. Thank you. Shall we go? Will you be coming back to help Fenmire collect Will and Jacob?"

Yes. Now stop fretting.

I grimace as we head for the foyer. "Have I been too overbearing?"

Overbearing? No. But I've watched you stress yourself far too much these past few days. You can breathe now and enjoy the day.

"I did throw myself rather hard into this, didn't I?"

A bit.

"I think I just wanted to keep myself busy. If I'm busy and exhausted, I don't have the time or the energy to be sad."

I don't think that's healthy, my stoferra.

"Probably not, but it's how I'm choosing to cope for now."

We leave the castle, and Caliborne picks me up, gingerly, so as not to ruin my clothes. One short flight later, we're landing in the woods in the same place we did the day Drixus first brought us here, only now there is a path carved through the thicket. I'm thankful I don't have to pick my way through brambles and branches this time as I head for the glade, and I laugh in delight when I step out of the trees into the open, mossy space.

The glade has been transformed, and it's a magical sight. There's a wooden arch in the center woven with vines and a few flowers for a splash of color. Moss has been strategically plucked and placed to create a perfect, green aisle that starts at the end of the path through the trees and ends at the arch. Along the sides of the aisle, logs are placed in equal intervals like church pews for seating. Bunches of flowers are planted at the ends of each log, and vines are draped between each bundle of blossoms to more definitively mark the edges of the aisle along with strategically placed, round cuts of wood each with a single candle sitting atop it. Behind the arch sits a ring of stones and several tables made of stumps.

"This is wonderful!" I say as I wander down the aisle.

"Thank you," says a voice to my left, and I turn to find Percival beaming as he joins me.

"Did you do all of this?"

"Everyone helped bring it to life, but I had the vision."

I kiss Percival on the cheek. "It's beautiful. Thank you."

He puts an arm around my shoulders. "It's been a long time since any of us had a reason to celebrate, and who knows if we'll get many more after this, so…"

I frown. "Do you think we're all going to…?"

"What? Of course not." He squeezes my shoulders. "You're going to send that bitch to hell and free us. We'll all go our separate ways, which is how it's supposed to be, but we've all become a family over the years. It'll be a bittersweet day. But that's not *this* day. Today is only a sweet day."

"Have we decided who will act as an officiant?"

"Levi has agreed to do the honors. He remembers more of the prayers than the rest of us and has spent the last day or two writing them down to recite for the ceremony."

"That's perfect. Is he here already?"

Percival points out the man in question, who's currently standing by the ring of stones on the other side of the glade with a few leafs of paper in his hands, which he's currently reading quietly to himself.

"All that's missing are the grooms," Percival says.

I turn to Caliborne. "Bring the boys," I say with a happy smile. "We're ready for them."

*****

"Will, wilt thou have this man to thy wedded husband, to live together after God's ordinance in the holy estate of matrimony? Wilt thou obey him, and serve him, love, honor, and keep him in sickness and in health, and, forsaking all others, keep thee only unto him, so long as ye both shall live?"

Will beams. "I will."

Will and Jacob stand facing each other in front of the arch, holding hands with such loving looks on their faces I can barely keep myself together for how happy I am for them both. The sun is setting, casting an orange glow across the glade that's slowly fading to a deep red. I'm standing behind Will with Jacob's ring in my pocket, opposite Percival who stands behind Jacob with a matching golden band in his possession. Levi stands below the arch with his papers open in his palms as he reads with a smile. He turns to Jacob.

"Jacob, wilt thou have this man to thy wedded husband, to live together after God's ordinance in the holy estate of matrimony? Wilt thou obey him, and serve him, love, honor, and keep him in sickness and in health, and, forsaking all others, keep thee only unto him, so long as ye both shall live?"

"I suppose," Jacob says.

Everyone chuckles.

"The rings," Levi says with a bow of his head, and Percival and I dutifully hand them over. Levi looks at Will. "Put the ring on Jacob's finger and repeat after me. 'I, Will, take thee, Jacob…'

Will slides the ring on Jacob's finger and holds his hand in both of his own. "I, Will, take thee, Jacob…"

"'…to have and to hold…'"

"…to have and to hold…"

Jacob's eyes well with tears as Will finishes his vows. Levi turns to Jacob next, who puts a ring on Will's finger and repeats the same lines with an unwavering voice despite the tears now trailing down his face.

"'…and thereto I give thee my troth.'"

"…and thereto I give thee my troth."

Levi smiles at both men. "Those whom God hath joined together let no man put asunder." He looks out amongst the many gathered faces behind the grooms. "Forasmuch as Will and Jacob have consented together in holy wedlock and have witnessed the same before God and this company, and thereto have given and pledged their troth, each to the other, and have declared the same by giving and receiving a ring, and by joining hands, I pronounce that they are man and husband. In the name of the Father, and of the Son, and of the Holy Ghost. Amen."

The humans in the crowd all murmur, "Amen."

Levi folds up his papers with a smile. "Would you like to kiss your—"

The grooms reach for each other in unison, and the witnesses laugh and cheer as the two men kiss and hug at length.

I'm a mess of tears I don't bother hiding as my best friend turns to me nearly the second he lets go of his beloved. Will grabs me up in a crushing hug.

"Thank you," he says simply.

"This is all your doing, dearest," I tell him. "I love you, and I'm so proud of you my heart may burst." I let him go so he can take Jacob's hand as rice begins to fly.

At the very back of the congregation where they won't block anyone's view, my mates stand together in a row, watching. Not watching the grooms, I realize—who are now taking the traditional walk back down the aisle—but watching me. Two loving smiles beam at me when I catch them staring. The third raises his hand, and a wave of love and admiration washes over me.

I smile, but as happy as I am for my best friend's good fortune today, I'm also a little sad. As hopeful as I've tried to be these past many weeks, knowing all I do about this spell and Reilanna's evil, twisted mind, I can't help but feel like this may be my last celebration.

*****

The ceremony is immediately followed by a more informal celebration. A few of the staff have instruments, all handmade, and they sit or stand at the edge of the flattest portion of the glade where several others gather to dance. The ring of stones I saw earlier turns out to be a firepit that's stacked high with wood and lit to light the glade after the sun finishes setting. The Gryxen move several of the logs from in front of the arch to the fire to provide seating between the tables, which are loaded with finger foods and drinks. There's even a cake, a double-layered one dripping with icing, which Levi unveils to cheers and applause. A large but slightly lopsided 'W' and 'L' are written across the top.

"That's the extent of my cake-decorating skills, I'm afraid," Levi says bashfully.

"It's perfect, Levi," Jacob says, and he hugs the older man with a clap on his back. "Thank you."

Levi is blushing at the praise when Jacob lets him go.

The cake is sweet and sticky and absolutely delicious. Even Wexton agrees as he sucks some runaway frosting from my fingers.

"Not bad," he says, then he leans down near my ear. "You're sweeter, though."

I swat at him. "Heathen."

He pretends to bite my neck until I laugh and push him away.

I glance around at our celebrating friends and spot a single frowning face amongst all the happy smiles. I wander over to a table where Percival sits alone, watching Will and Jacob dance together on the opposite side of the fire. I slide onto the log beside him with my back to the table, and he jumps before smiling at me.

"Having fun?" he asks.

"I am," I say, and it's only partly a lie. "But, I couldn't help but notice you don't look like you are. Is everything alright?"

"Oh, sure. It's just… missed opportunities and old memories, that's all."

"Do you want to talk about it?"

He looks again at Will and Jacob. "I've never told you why I was sent here, have I?"

"No, but I've guessed at it."

Percival sits up straighter and runs his hands up and down his pants. He smiles at me again, but this time it's sad. "I had my own Jacob, once upon a time, only his name was Roderick."

I blink in surprise when I recognize the name. "Old man Oren's son?"

Percival's smile brightens a bit. "That's the one. We were lovers for several years in secret. We were always so careful with our trysts, but the sneaking around and hiding our feelings took its toll on me. I made the mistake of confiding in my best friend, who promised to take my secret to the grave. I believed him.

"A few days later, Roderick and I were in the woods behind the church—our usual place—when Pastor Elias and some men from the village descended upon us. We heard them coming and fled into the trees. Roderick got away before the others got a look at him, but they caught me. It wouldn't have mattered if they hadn't because leading the group of torches and pitchforks that night was the man I told my secret to, my best friend, who had already condemned me by name."

"Who was the friend?"

He looks at me with bitterness and hate in his eyes. "Elias V."

I gasp. "That vile snake was your best friend?"

"He didn't used to be that way. He was once as caring as you, if you can imagine that. I honestly can't tell you what happened to change him into the beast he is today. It was as if he woke one day as a completely different person, one who had no qualms about ruining his best friend's entire life and casting him into exile."

"I'm so sorry, Percival. You didn't deserve that."

He nods. "I'm sorry too. I hear Elias was instrumental in your exile as well."

"He wanted me to marry him," I say in disgust. "To save my soul." I roll my eyes. "I wish they could all see how ridiculous they are."

"Me too." He looks again at the dancing grooms. "But, today, I wish most of all that Roderick had come with me to The Deadwood. I don't fault him for it, of course. He likely thought me killed just as we all assumed happened to the ones banished here. It would've been foolish for him to try. But still… missed opportunities."

"Roderick left the village. It was not but a couple of years ago. Perhaps, once we break Reilanna's spell, you can find each other again."

He gives me a more genuine smile. "The thought had occurred to me."

I hold out my hand. "In the meantime, care to dance with a friend? You don't deserve to sit here alone and lonely."

"Oh, I'm alright." He crosses one leg over the other and leans casually against the table. "I'm a hopeless dancer anyway." His eyes slide past me over my shoulder, and he raises a brow of surprise.

"Besides, I think there's someone else who might need that dance more than me."

"Who?" I turn, following his eyes across the glade, and I stifle a gasp behind my hand.

Drixus is walking across the glade, headed straight for me. He's dressed in golden armor that looks as shiny and new as the others' with his twin axes slung across his back. I can see the handles peeking over his shoulders. His hair is pulled back and no longer covering the scarred side of his face. He doesn't break his stride as he walks under the arch and into the light of the fire, through the clusters of dancing bodies, and past logs filled with those sipping drinks and nibbling on morsels. Everyone is staring, but Drixus looks only at me.

He walks up and kneels on one knee beside my log. "Care to dance with me," he asks, offering me his hand, which shakes quite intensely, though his voice is steady and strong.

I'm in shock, but I give myself a shake and set my hand in his. "I'd love to."

He curls his fingers around mine but doesn't pull me to my feet. Instead, he looks me in the eye and says softly, "I don't mean this as just a dance. What I'm offering you tonight is… me." He waves his free hand down himself. "Me. Us. Everything. I am not a jeweler or a skater or an artist. I have nothing to offer you, so when I considered what gift I could give you to show you what you mean to me and ask you to be my mate, I asked myself what grand feat I could possibly perform that would be enough. And, well…"

He tugs my hand to his neck and presses my palm to the side of his throat. His heart is thumping so hard and fast I'd swear he just finished fighting another quaheitan all on his own. Rebuilding his armor, walking past all these staring eyes, and kneeling in front of a crowd at my feet… I know how hard this is for him, how much strength it took for him to walk out of those trees. He's trembling. If Reilanna ever invaded his dreams to torture him, this is exactly the scene she would throw him into, and he walked into it willingly tonight. For me.

"Drixus…" I murmur.

"I'd walk through every horror in existence if I knew you'd be waiting for me on the other side," he says with an intensity that takes my breath away. "But I'd arrive with empty hands and pockets. It's just me, sweetheart. Am I enough?"

I touch his face. "Yes, Drixus, you're enough. I accept."

I get one of those breathtaking smiles I love so much in return.

Taking his hand, I stand and tug him through the tables and dancing bodies to an open spot. Drixus glances around and swallows at the number of staring eyes upon us.

I call his name softly, and when he looks at me again, I say, "Pretend we're the only ones here. This whole glade, the fire and music, it's all just for us. No one else."

He locks his eye on me and steps closer. "I know I asked you, but I don't know the first thing about human dancing."

"That's alright. Just follow my lead."

I wrap his arm around my back and take his hand, stepping into his space with a smile. I motion down to my feet, and he watches as I step, mirroring me slowly so as not to stomp on my toes. The staff takes notice of our slower dance and the song changes, growing softer and more sensual. It's a tune I recognize, and I alter our dance to fit. Once Drixus gets the steps down, he looks up at my face again, and his eye sweeps across it with such a look of loving awe my cheeks heat in response. Eventually, his eye settles on one of mine, and my heart turns to mush.

There's no doubt in my mind how this soft soul won Fenmire's heart, and while I've learned enough about Fenmire's past to understand the why, it breaks my heart to think he ever doubted Drixus' loyalty. Drixus is still shaking; I can feel his tremors the places his body touches mine. The mate he loves but can no longer have is no doubt watching our every move. Even I can feel Fenmire's eyes burning into us as we dance across slowly the mossy ground. And yet Drixus is here, locked onto my eyes as if they're tethered to his soul.

Or perhaps his heart.

"You look fantastic," I tell him. "I knew you would."

"I promised I'd take better care of myself," he says quietly, no doubt wishing this conversation to remain as private as the eye contact we've yet to break. "I figured this was the best way to show you I meant it."

I nod. "That's good, because I don't ever wish to lose a single one of my mates."

"Are you sure about this? About me? I don't want to give you the wrong idea by showing up here tonight. I'm not fixed. I don't think I'll ever be the same Gryxen I was before."

"I didn't know the Gryxen you were before, so it makes little difference to me. I know the Gryxen you are now, and I meant what I said: you're enough."

He pulls me closer and lets go of my hand so he can wrap both arms around me. We have to dance even more slowly this way, but I don't care. I hug him back and sway softly to the music long after the tunes change back to the livelier ones from before.

As usual, Drixus silently holds me for as long as I like.

Chapter 73

It's been a perfect day filled with love and excitement with nary a worry or foul word spoken throughout. Though I know not a soul here hasn't felt the increasing tension over the past few months as we get closer to breaking the spell, everyone seems determined to ignore it, if only for a day. A moment of calm before the inevitable storm, that's what it feels like. I refuse to let my brain wander to anything but laughing, eating, dancing, and eventually drinking as the men pull out bottles of their finest when evening turns to night. I don't partake too heavily, having learned long ago how easy it is to get carried away and regret it the next morning.

Jacob, on the other hand, drinks so much Caliborne has to carry him to the boys' room at the end of the night.

"He's never had such freedom before," Will explains with his arm over my shoulders, swaying slightly himself as we follow Caliborne down the hall. "I'll have to teach him to pace himself."

"What, like you?" I jeer.

"Pfft. I'm fine." I stop walking, and Will almost loses his balance, not realizing how heavily he's leaning on me until I duck out from under his arm. He staggers, stops, and rights himself, then he laughs. "Point taken."

I lead him into his room and make him sit on the bed while Caliborne lays Jacob down on the other side.

"Go to sleep, you glutton," I tease, and I kiss him on the cheek. "Congratulations again."

Will hugs me. "Thank you. For everything."

I pat him on the back. "You're welcome."

Both boys are snoring before Caliborne and I are even out the door.

Out in the hall, Caliborne touches my shoulder. *Where will you be spending the night?*

Between the excitement of today's celebration, the dancing, and Wexton's never-ending flirts throughout the evening after all the time I've spent cooped up in Drixus' room, I'm aching for something carnal. I've far too much pent-up sexual tension even for Caliborne's gentle hands to handle. I told Drixus goodnight before leaving the glade. As much as I adore his calm and loving nature, that's not what I need tonight either.

"I haven't decided yet," I say truthfully.

Well, my door is open, as always.

I tug him down for a kiss of appreciation before he goes to his room, leaving me alone in the hall, but not for long.

The front doors burst open, and two laughing Gryxen wander in. Having finished flying the others back from the glade, Wexton and Fenmire head for their rooms, joking and shoving each other like two old friends who've decided, like the rest, to put aside their worries over what's soon to come and enjoy a day of nothing but each other's company. When they spot me, however, their demeanor instantly changes. They both stand up straight and stalk down the hall, their eyes fixated on me and burning with intention.

I lick my lips, my gaze darting between them as my imagination runs wild with fantasies, each slightly varied depending on whose bed I end up in, but all equally delicious and as carnal as my desires tonight.

"Good evening, darling," Wexton purrs as he approaches. "Waiting for someone?"

I smirk. "Possibly."

Fenmire circles around me so that they're standing on either side of me, looming over me as they trap me between them. "What's the matter, pet? You look like prey caught in an impossible situation."

Wexton touches my chin, turning my face up toward his. "Can't you see it, Fen? Their eyes give it away."

Fenmire takes my chin next and looks me in the eyes too. "Hmm, yes. I guess they still don't understand."

"Understand what?" I ask breathlessly.

Fenmire keeps my chin captive as Wexton leans down near my ear. "We don't mind sharing… even at the same time."

I swallow as a rush of wicked desire sweeps over me, breaking my skin out in goosebumps. I squeeze my thighs together and peer up at them.

I can have them both?

Together?

Am I ready for that?

Truth be told, I made my choice the moment the option was presented to me. This is exactly what I want, what I need. I wish to experience the most libidinous pleasures a human can. Considering the Gryxen who stand before me now, the two of them combined can give me that and then some.

"Have you done that before?" I ask Fenmire.

"Many times."

Wexton wraps his arm around me, pulling my back against his front, and the bulge of his erections presses into me. "What do you say, darling?" he asks with a slight buck of his hips. "Care to let the beasts ravage you tonight?"

"Yes," I whisper.

Fenmire takes my face in his hand again, making me look up at him. "Again. Louder."

"Yes," I repeat, louder and more confidently. "Please."

"Such a sweet mouth." Fenmire squeezes the sides of my face until I open my mouth, and he slips one finger inside. "I'm going to fuck it."

I close my eyes on a groan as Wexton reaches down to stroke a finger between my legs over my pants. "There's a sweeter place I plan to taste while his cock is down your throat," he whispers.

Well, I wanted the most carnal things they can give me, and they certainly plan to deliver.

"Your bed or mine?" Fenmire asks Wexton while his finger slips lazily in and out of my mouth, mimicking the motion his cock will soon take.

"Yours, I think," Wexton replies. "It's bigger."

All of a sudden, Fenmire reaches down and grabs me, throwing me over his shoulder. I yelp and laugh as he stalks toward his room. Wexton follows.

In Fenmire's bedroom, he tosses me onto my backside on his bed as Wexton shuts the door, and suddenly, I'm nervous. I've been with them both, but at the prospect of pleasing them at the same time, I'm not sure I'll know what to do.

Whatever look I currently have on my face must tip Fenmire off to my anxiety because he says, "Don't worry, pet. We'll lead tonight."

Wexton wastes no time as he immediately shoves his pants to his ankles and steps out of them. He crawls up onto the bed on his knees and scoots around behind me, hugging me into the crook of his arm as he kisses my neck. *I've missed the taste of your sweet cunt on my tongue.*

I moan.

Fenmire starts unbuttoning my pants.

Wexton tugs my shirt up over my head.

I lift my hips so Fenmire can undress my lower half as Wexton kisses my shoulder over my mate mark there. He licks the spot as if it's still bleeding.

Once I'm naked, Fenmire strips his pants off, his eyes burning into me as he does. "Turn around," he orders as he strokes himself. "Lie on your back with your head hanging off the bed."

Wexton smiles at me as I turn to face him on the bed, and he steals a few tongue-thrusting kisses before I lay down as Fenmire instructed and stare at my upside-down mate, who's still stroking himself as he steps nearer. He looks at Wexton with a bob of his brow, and Wexton rearranges my legs before parting them. Wexton strokes his hand down my throat, my chest, my belly, then between my legs, where he parts me with his fingers before leaning down and swiping that wicked tongue of his across my clit.

I jump with a small gasp.

Fenmire touches my chin, tugging it up so my head lolls off the side of the bed. He smiles as he lays his palm across my throat. "I've wanted to fuck my cock here for a long time. Would you like that?"

"I don't know," I say. "I've never done it."

"If I have my way, you won't be able to breathe. If you ever want me to stop, snap your fingers and it's done. Do that for me now."

I snap my fingers once with each hand.

He strokes my cheek with one finger. "Good pet."

Wexton licks me again, only this time he doesn't stop as he bathes me with his tongue before slipping it inside me, fucking me with both his mouth and his fingers.

At the same time, Fenmire taps my lips. "Open up."

I swallow then do as I'm told.

The head of Fenmire's bottom cock slides into my mouth, and I bathe it with my tongue and suck on it as Wexton does the same to my clit. When I moan, Fenmire's cock pushes in deeper. Fenmire tilts my head down even further and places his hand on my throat again as he withdraws and pushes inside my mouth a few more times, coating himself in my saliva. When he enters my throat, I fight not to gag, but thankfully, he goes slow, giving me the smallest nudge before withdrawing and letting me swallow again. After a minute or two of this, I'm no longer compelled to gag, and he goes deeper.

Wexton is still making a meal of me between my thighs as Fenmire's cock cuts off my air. He fucks himself down my throat a few times then withdraws so I can suck in a few quick breaths of air before he thrusts again.

"I love feeling your throat bulge with my cock," Fenmire murmurs.

Wexton moans, and both the sound and the vibration from his mouth make all my muscles clench from the waist down. Despite the distraction of Fenmire's length sliding in and out of my throat, my orgasm is building, and whenever Fenmire lets me breathe, I do it moaning as my hips buck against Wexton's face.

"I'm going to hold my cock down your throat as you come," Fenmire says, rubbing the head across my lips, painting them with my spit. "I want to feel your body twitch and spasm around me as you choke for air. How does that sound?"

"Yes, please," I utter.

Fenmire strokes my throat with two fingers and looks me in the eyes. "You're safe with us, you know that right?"

I nod.

"Then take one last breath and open up."

I take a deep, cleansing breath, let it part way out, and open my mouth as my legs start to shake.

Fenmire fucks my throat with a vengeance, pumping his hips to the same rhythm Wexton flicks his tongue across my clit. I grab

Fenmire's leg as my whole body locks up. He buries himself to the hilt down my throat and stills there.

And I come.

I buck and writhe, completely silent since Fenmire's cock doesn't allow even the smallest sound to escape me.

My lungs begin to burn.

My nails dig into Fenmire's thighs, but even as my body begs for me to take a breath and my throat desperately tries to draw air, I don't snap my fingers. I choke, and for some reason, that just makes my orgasm even more intense coupled with Wexton's teasing fingers and tongue. My eyes are streaming with tears, and my nails rake across Fenmire's leather skin, but still, I don't snap, and he doesn't pull away.

My head starts to swim, and my hand drops from Fenmire's leg, but just before I lose consciousness, his cock slides out of my throat.

I cough and gasp and start to cry.

Fenmire lifts me up by the shoulders so I'm sitting on the bed. "You're alright, pet," he tells me softly. "Breathe now. Deep and slow." He wipes the tears from my cheeks and the spit from my chin. "You did so well."

"And you taste so fucking good," Wexton says, wiping his mouth and licking his fingers clean.

My throat hurts, but my skin is tingly and my head feels funny, like I drank way more than just a few sips of alcohol throughout the evening. My vision is swimming, the whole room tilting first one way then the other even though I'm sitting still on the bed in Fenmire's arms. I touch my temples.

"It's normal," Fenmire tells me as he plucks the tie from the end of my braid. "You're alright." He works my hair loose and pets it until it's flowing freely down my back, then he kisses me along my jawline. "You're more than alright. You're amazing."

"But you didn't…" I croak.

"We'll get there. Someday. Tonight, I want to fill your ass with my seed instead."

"Jesus Christ," I mutter.

"He can't save you tonight," Wexton says with a growl before capturing my mouth in a passionate kiss. He draws me toward the center of the bed and lies down, tugging me over top of him. I straddle his hips, and his cocks bounce against my lower belly as I lean over and continue to kiss him. He buries his fingers in my hair, but not to own or control me, he simply holds me as our tongues thrust and tease and taste. I bite his lower lip, hard, and he laughs.

A touch on my back makes me jump. I never heard Fenmire join us on the bed, but I sit up on my knees and am suddenly wrapped in his arms. Our bottle of oil sits on the mattress nearby.

"I want to watch you ride him," Fenmire murmurs in my ear. *While I sit back here and stretch your ass so I can fuck it.*

Wexton grins up at me and fists his lower cock, rubbing his thumb through the drop of liquid that weeps from the tip. *Fuck me.* "Pretty please?" he asks with a bob of his brow.

I giggle and lift my hips, inviting him underneath me.

He holds his cock beneath my opening, and I lower myself down onto him, groaning at the stretch.

Fenmire holds my throat and licks across my cheek to my mouth, which he captures in one of his hard, demanding kisses, his tongue fucking so deep in my mouth it practically goes down my throat too. He grabs me by the hair as he breaks away.

"Ride, pet," he orders, and he shoves me down so my hands are splayed on Wexton's chest.

I pump my hips, gliding my body up and down Wexton's hard length.

Wexton puts his arm under his head with a smirk. *I love when your breasts jiggle like that.*

I move harder and faster, spearing myself down onto his cock until it feels like it might split me in two.

Wexton reaches up and pinches one of my nipples.

"Fuck!" I exclaim.

Wexton laughs. "I think that's the first time I've heard you say that."

"It won't be the last," Fenmire says. He picks up the bottle of oil.

Focusing on Wexton, I reach down to hold his top cock against my clit as I continue to pump up and down his bottom one. The added friction makes my legs shake again, and I moan.

I slow down when Fenmire's fingers touch the other place he plans to use tonight.

"Don't stop," he says as one finger circles and presses against my hole. "But don't come until I tell you."

I go back to riding, though I let go of Wexton's top cock since it'll push me over the edge far too soon.

I want this to last.

"Yes," I croon when Fenmire's finger slips inside me. When a second digit joins in the fun, I arch my back and lean down over Wexton, giving Fenmire all the room he needs to open me up for his cock.

"Well, hello," Wexton says as our faces get closer. He leans up on his elbow and kisses me.

A third finger works its way into my ass.

I break away from Wexton's lips to pant. I've had both my holes filled before, but that doesn't make it any less overwhelming. Fenmire fucks his fingers inside me at the same pace I pump myself up and down Wexton's cock. He spreads his fingers, stretching me impossibly far until his hand disappears entirely.

I glance back at him over my shoulder in anticipation.

Fenmire straddles Wexton's legs and shoves me down again by the neck as he fists a palmful of oil around his lower cock. I've stopped moving, but that doesn't seem to bother either of them as Fenmire scoots closer. The head of his cock presses against my hole. My body accepts him, but I gasp at the stretch. His bottom cock is significantly larger than his top one, and I hold my breath without thinking as he inches it inside me.

"Breathe, pet," Fenmire reminds me, and I do, though it's shaky and hitched.

Fenmire goes slow, and Wexton waits patiently as my body adjusts. With small and gentle thrusts, Fenmire glides deeper, and my body feels so impossibly full, like it's going to burst.

You can take us, pet, Fenmire tells me. He leans down and bites his mating mark, not hard enough to break the skin again but hard enough to make me whimper. When his cock is about halfway inside me, he pulls out to the head and plunges back in, and I cry out. He grabs me by the throat and hauls me up to my knees so my back is pressed to his chest. He nods down at Wexton who starts pumping his cock inside me from below at the same time Fenmire fucks my ass. I'm mewling by the time he finally presses flush against my backside. He's fully inside me now, and he pumps himself in and out in short but rough thrusts that would send me sprawling across Wexton's chest if he weren't still holding me by the throat.

Wexton reaches up and plays with my breasts and nipples as Fenmire reaches down and holds Wexton's top cock against my clit.

I clutch Fenmire's arm and let myself be swept away by it all. The most animalistic sounds pour out of me, but I no longer care. My entire body begins to shake.

"Not yet, darling," Wexton says breathlessly. "We want to fill you with our seed first."

Fenmire lowers me back to my hands again and grabs my hair, holding it painfully tight as he deepens his strokes. Wexton leans up to kiss me, and he pinches my nipple again, making me cry out into his mouth. He breaks our kiss, pants against my lips, and growls as he thrusts hard up inside me and stills. A second later, his warm seed spills inside me.

Wexton collapses onto his back on the bed and Fenmire leans over us both, driving into me at a punishing pace as he growls, "My turn." He reaches down and rubs my clit.

"Please," I cry out over and over as he teases me. I'm so close to another mind-shattering orgasm, but I hold it back, waiting for him to release me.

"Now!" Fenmire cries, and he pinches my clit.

"Fuck!" I scream as I come and cry and quiver.

Fenmire thrusts a couple more times and stills deep inside me. His heat fills me just like Wexton's as he swears and twitches against my ass with his fingers still gripping my hair tight enough to make my scalp burn.

A few breathless moments go by as we all slowly come back to reality. I have two demons' cocks inside me with their seed running down my legs. My throat burns, my nipples ache, my clit is throbbing, and I can feel my heartbeat in my scalp.

I look from one of my mate's faces to the other… and burst out laughing.

Wexton is quick to follow.

Fenmire chuckles uncertainly a few times before he joins in as well.

I collapse across Wexton's chest, and Fenmire kisses me on the shoulder before flopping across the bottom of the bed in a sweaty, breathless heap.

There's a lot of kissing, cuddling, and cleaning up before I eventually drift off held between them, not willing to give either of them up tonight, not even in sleep.

Chapter 74

For the next several days, Drixus and I spend just about every waking minute together. He's giddy each morning when I bring breakfast to his room, and we eat it picnic-style on his bed. Though his message was clear the night he showed up at Will and Jacob's wedding, I don't want him to feel like he has to put himself in the company of others for me. I don't want him to change; I don't need him to. His quiet and reserved ways are what I love most about him, and seeing him grind his teeth and force a smile during the meals he chooses to spend with me in the dining room with the others makes my stomach cramp so badly it's hard to eat my food at all.

So instead, we eat in his room and spend the majority of our time either flying over The Deadwood on Mara's back or walking through the woods while he shows me the secrets he remembers from his years exploring this area with his brother. Sometimes we walk in silence broken only by our footfalls and the sounds of nature. So many of the animals come up to us, not the least bit afraid of us since they were raised by both humans and Gryxen. The staff at the castle still feeds most of them since they're not used to taking care of themselves, so I carry little treats in my pockets as well, which they happily accept before bounding away.

Other times, Drixus and I talk as we walk, about anything and everything. I tell him so many things, some deep and private things I've only ever told Will, and I don't feel the least bit apprehensive or guilty about any of it. Drixus listens and discusses it all with me with no judgment, and he usually follows each of my confessions with one of his own, like the fact that he misses his brother terribly and that, no matter Horthos' sins, he can't be angry at him. I don't tell him it's alright to feel that way. It would change nothing to tell him what he already knows, and the point of these talks, I soon realize, is not to reveal our burdens in hopes the other person will help lift them off.

The point is to bare the darkest portions of ourselves to someone who isn't afraid of the dark.

Sometimes, our talks follow us back to his room at dusk. Other times, silence falls with the sun, and we strip naked and hold each other in his bed while our fingers—my bare ones, his gloved ones—dance across each other's skin. Drixus never touches me intimately, so I don't touch him that way either, and we don't do what we did in the cave. We do kiss, though. We kiss a lot. It's relieving, in a way, that no more is expected. I love the others and the things we do in private, but I also love lying in Drixus' arms knowing it won't go any further than that. It's sensual and sweet.

"What do you feel when you touch me?" I ask as his fingers brush through a lock of my hair. "You say it's not sexual, so what is it?"

Drixus grunts as he considers. "It's admiration, affection, and wonder. I like touching you, holding you, and kissing you; it makes my heart happy. I hope it does yours as well."

I roll over to face him with a smile. "It does."

He brushes my hair over my shoulder and traces my ear with one finger, making me shiver.

After a few more moments of silence, I whisper, "Can I ask you something?"

"Anything."

"Why did Reilanna choose this Gate? Why my world to conquer?"

"Because your people rely heavily on their faith. She saw your kind as an easy path to godhood."

"She wants to be a god?"

"Yes. One that rules through fear. Since the human god isn't strong enough yet to show much of a presence amongst your people, humans accredit many things, both wonderful and terrible things, to a higher power, one that's supposed to be loving but is often malevolent toward the beings he claims to cherish so dearly. Reilanna would've stepped into that role perfectly, only she wouldn't have provided unexplained miracles. She would've used her magic, all the powers she stole from our world, to make the humans worship her instead as a god that doesn't just offer empty promises but takes action. No offense, but I believe she would've succeeded as humans are easily swayed by such things."

"Since magic doesn't exist in our world, they probably would've called her a witch first."

"She knew your kind's beliefs, like the fact that your people believe your god responsible for catastrophic events that lead to countless deaths, and they blame the humans every time. Reilanna would've worked within what humans believe godhood looks like, and she would've killed any who dared resist her, which follows your kind's false understanding of your god already. She knew exactly what she was doing when she chose your world, and she had many plans to make them worship her."

"Is she an older Gruxa?" In my head, I've been picturing an old, wrinkled witch, the villain from some child's fairytale, and her image in my dreams when I faced her only strengthened that assumption.

"Not at all," Drixus says. "She was quite young, barely an adult at just over three thousand years old, when she made her first attempt to pass through The Gate. It's one of the reasons we underestimated her so catastrophically. We didn't think of her as much of a threat, not at first. For someone so young to have such a black and ambitious heart… We didn't take enough precautions. That's how she was able to reach out and poison Horthos, Jothrik, and Breklen."

"Did she ever try influencing you and the others?"

"No. She wanted those three specifically because their powers were projected. She's no fighter, she knows that, so she wanted powers she could wield from a distance."

"She's clever."

Drixus grunts. "Too clever."

"What do you mean?"

He shakes his head. "I don't know. Sometimes I got the sense there was someone or something else pulling the strings, like she was a puppet for some higher power. It would explain how one so young knew so much and acted so malevolently."

"You said once she might've had help. Is that what you meant?"

"Yes. I could never prove it, though." He looks at me, and there's a flicker of fear but also resolve in his eye as he says, "We need to warn the others before we become mates so that they can be ready for whatever she plans to do afterward."

I nod. "Yes, we should." I look away shyly. "I… I just want you to know that I… Whenever you're ready, I'm…"

He smiles. "I have to admit, I've been stalling a bit. It's been so long since I've had someone to talk to, and I don't know what will happen after… I want to be your mate, Eve. I want to feel my soul join with one that cares for me back."

"Fenmire does care about you, Drixus," I say softly. "He just needs time."

"I know. But I'm afraid our time has run out."

"Do you think we're going to…?"

"Like I said, I don't know what will happen. Fenmire and I had our chance, and we both made mistakes to ruin what we had. But with you…" He scoots closer and sighs as he struggles to find the words. "With Fenmire, it felt like we belonged because we fit. He was a storm, and I was the calm, two pieces to complete a whole that complement each other, but we found each other by happenstance. With you, it feels like destiny. The moment I met you, your presence felt right in a way I've never felt before, as if our meeting was more than mere coincidence. And those days I closed my door to you and tried to slink back into my darkness, I was restless and unhappy. I'd known you only a few days, and something had already changed inside me, woken up.

"Correct me if I'm speaking in ignorance, but whatever is between us, it feels like something it would take far more than a few mistakes to break. I think my soul was yours the moment I opened my door to you. There's nothing left but to bond it to yours, where it belongs."

I touch his face. "I know what you mean. Ever since the day I stepped into The Deadwood, I've felt like I'm walking a path that was predestined for me long before I was born, perhaps even before Reilanna cast her spell. And now… we're nearing the end."

"Are you afraid?" he asks softly.

"Sometimes. I don't want to lose what I've found here."

"I don't think Seerraf will let that happen."

"If he could've intervened, wouldn't he have done so by now?"

"Probably. But we don't know what's holding him back or if breaking the spell will allow him to finally step in."

I shake my head, not willing to let myself hope.

"He helped you in your dreams," he reminds me.

"We don't know that. That could've just been my imagination."

He snorts. "That's Fenmire talking. He's always been one to apply the most logical explanation to any situation. Is that truly what you believe?"

"I don't know."

"If you believe your path is predestined, then—"

"Then I will follow it, as I'm meant to, to the end." I cuddle closer and curl up under Drixus' arm. "I don't see the point in worrying what that end will look like before I arrive at it. I'll face it like I've faced everything in my life: with the knowledge that, if given the choice, I wouldn't do anything different."

Drixus rests his chin on the top of my head. "I suppose there's no stalling anymore then, is there?"

"That's up to you, Drixus. I've followed your lead up to this point, and I don't plan to change that now."

He sighs. "One more day. One more day, then we'll step into the inevitable. Together."

I kiss his collarbone. "Deal."

*****

The next morning, on my way to the kitchen to grab Drixus and I's breakfast, I stop by Fenmire's room first. He's already up, of course—I'm convinced he never actually sleeps—and I let myself in his room at his call.

"Good morning," he greets.

I shut the door behind me. "Good morning." I'm nervous for this conversation, but I know that's foolish at this point.

Fenmire frowns. "What's the matter?"

"I came to warn you. Drixus and I… we plan to become mates. Tonight."

Fenmire nods slowly. "Alright."

"I think it's wise if we prepare for the worst."

"I agree. But is that why you look so pale right now?"

"No," I admit.

He opens his hand and bids me closer, and I step between his legs. "What is it, pet?" he asks, rubbing my arms.

"I don't want to disappoint you," I say quietly.

"And you think by mating with Drixus, you will be disappointing me?"

"Things are complicated between you. I don't know how you'll feel to see Drixus find what the two of you once had with someone else, someone you love just as much. I don't want to cause you pain."

"You forget that Drixus is still my mate. As complicated as it is between us, I still care about him, and that will never go away. If anything, seeing him happy again will bring me happiness, not pain."

"Are you sure?"

"Drixus and I both deserve to move on. If he does that with you like I have, then I'll be in your debt, not disappointed. Besides, you could never disappoint me, Eve. Never. Don't ever let that worry into your head."

"I lost your knife."

He blinks at me then looks down at my hip in disbelief only to find the weapon secured safely to my belt, as usual. He snorts. "Cheeky pet."

I put my arms around his neck. "Always."

He kisses me once, softly. "I'll start making preparations. Thank you for the warning."

I nod and step out of his arms. "I love you."

"And I love you. Always."

*****

I bring Drixus and I's breakfast to his room like I usually do, and just like he does every morning, he greets me with a smile. Neither of us bring up the fact that we plan to become mates today. We eat and talk and laugh and eventually leave the room to go flying with Mara as if it's just another day. We end up at the cave with the waterfall, which now has a new firepit built on the rocky bank by the water. There's wood cut and stacked neatly next to the wall, and Drixus arranges a few pieces in the pit and lights a fire. It allows me to swim much more comfortably since I can step out of the chilly water to warm up whenever my fingers and toes go numb. Drixus carries me on his shoulders under the falls so I can bask in the feel of the water cascading down on top of me. Then, after my skin has turned pruney and the fire has burned low, we lie naked on the stone together.

Just like the last time we were here, I touch myself while Drixus watches and kisses me, swallowing my moans as I bring myself pleasure for his enjoyment. I come with a cry that echoes throughout the cavern. Afterward, I drift off in Drixus' arms until he wakes me up in darkness broken only by the faintest blue glow from the torch by the entrance. Our fire has gone out, and I've started to shiver.

"We should go," he says regretfully.

We dress, and I stand at the edge of the pond and take in the cave one last time. I'm glad now that I never brought Will down here. This space is Drixus and I's little secret, and it gets to stay that way. That feels right in a way that makes me sad, but the feeling passes when Drixus takes my hand and leads me back outside to Mara. When we land back in Mara's room at the castle and slide off, I head for the hole in the wall, but Drixus hangs back.

"What's wrong?" I ask.

"You should go enjoy your dinner with the others," he says, then he takes Mara's face in his hands. "There's someone else I should spend some time with before…"

I nod in understanding and pat Mara affectionately on the side. "Do you want me to come to your room after dinner?"

"No. I'll meet you in yours."

"Alright." I give him a kiss then leave him and Mara to their farewells.

The dining room is every bit as lively as it always is. Not a single one of my friends seem worried or stressed for what will no doubt soon be the end of everything we know here in The Deadwood. It seems Fenmire hasn't told them yet what I plan to do tonight, and as the happy chatter around me helps soothe my nerves, I'm grateful he didn't. He winks at me, and I realize he did it on purpose. I can almost hear his reasoning in my head.

'Let them have one more night.'

I couldn't agree more.

I finish my meal and leave the dining room with the others, and after dropping off my dishes in the kitchen—with some cheerful small talk with Levi as I do—I head for my room with determination in my steps.

Drixus has lit a fire in the fireplace in my room, something I've been doing most evenings myself since the temperature in the castle has started dropping at night. Fall has arrived. The leaves in The Deadwood have begun to change colors as well, only further reminding me that nothing can stay the same forever.

I'm ready to step into the next season of my life.

Drixus is seated, cross-legged, on the floor in front of my fireplace. I smile at him as I shut my door behind me, and he reaches a hand out to me. I cross the room and take it. He tugs me into his lap with my back to his chest and wraps me in his arms as we stare into the fire.

"Are you nervous?" he asks.

"Not for you. Not for our bond."

He takes my hands in his gloved ones, interlacing our fingers as he says, "I am. I've never done this part myself before."

I look back at him. "Where is your other mating mark?"

He lifts my hand to his scarred shoulder. "The same place as yours." He runs my fingers along his burn scars in the same place Fenmire's fangs sank into my body. Under the taut, burnt skin, I can barely feel two small divots under my fingers. "Try as she might, Reilanna couldn't burn the scar away."

"Good. Fuck her."

Drixus barks in laughter. "I see Wexton's mouth has made an impression."

"Maybe a little."

He squeezes me tight. "You're right, though. Fuck her." He lets go of my hands and takes hold of the bottom of my shirt, giving it a tug. "May I?"

I lift my arms and let him strip the fabric off me. His cool skin rests against mine, giving me goosebumps. He kisses my shoulder, my unmarked one, and I wonder briefly if he'll choose to sink his fangs in there, opposite the place his other mate chose for our mating bond. His lips dance across the spot, though, and continue down my arm. He kisses the bend of my elbow, down my forearm, and around my wrist as he turns my hand. I turn in his lap as he kisses the tips of each of my fingers then my palm.

In a room lit only by faint firelight, his grey eye blazes as it looks into mine, and he holds my hand to his lips. I swallow, understanding his intention, and I nod. Without breaking eye contact, he pierces the palm of my hand with a single fang enough to draw a drop of blood.

It's enough.

A familiar heat sweeps over my body, and I gasp, but…

This is different.

This heat is so intense it hurts.

My eyes water, and my chest locks up momentarily as pure fire races through my veins, and judging by the low growl and grimace on Drixus' face, he's feeling the same pain as me. He pants as he licks the blood from my palm.

"Drixus?" I say with a small whimper.

"I know," he replies breathlessly. "I'm sorry."

I don't want his apologies. I want…

I want his hands on me.

His bare hands.

I grab one and start unfastening his glove.

"What are you doing?" he asks in a slight panic, but he doesn't pull away.

"Trust me." I tug the glove off and reach for his other hand. Once it's bare as well, I look him in the eye. "Touch me. Please."

Drixus hesitates but only for a heartbeat before he does as I ask and places both his hands on me, one on my chest and one on my back.

The burning immediately begins to fade under Drixus' chilly touch.

I sigh with relief as the usual wave of passion and love I feel with a new bond finally washes over me. Drixus is staring at me, wide-eyed and worried, but I don't feel any different. I feel fantastic. His hands glide across my chest and back up to my shoulders, my neck, then my face where he rests his palms on my cheeks.

I smile at him.

He laughs tearfully. "I haven't been able to touch someone, truly touch someone in so long… Oh, gods, Eve."

"Not even Fenmire?"

"No."

I take one of his hands and kiss his palm and every one of his fingers in the same way he kissed mine.

He tugs me into his arms and kisses me while his palms run over my bare back. His hands are still as cold as ever, but they don't bother me in the slightest anymore. "You're so soft and warm," he murmurs against my lips. "You're perfect."

I stand up from his lap and tug his hand so he stands beside me. We strip the rest of our clothes off then get into my bed. I pull him close and place his hand on my chest again.

"Touch me," I murmur. "Every inch of me."

He nods and gets to it, trailing his fingers and palms across every part of my body he can reach. I even roll onto my stomach so he can pet my shoulder blades, my back, my backside, and even the backs of my legs. He surprises me by rolling over and straddling me, and I groan as he starts massaging my neck and shoulders.

"I could get used to this," I mutter.

Drixus leans down near my ear. "You'd better. I have thousands of years' worth of touches to make up for." He kisses me on the side of my neck. "I love you, Eve."

"I love you," I murmur sleepily as my eyes drift shut at Drixus' pets.

He chuckles and goes on working knots from muscles I didn't even know I had as I fall asleep under his hands.

Chapter 75

The next morning, Drixus and I wake up in my bed and gaze at each other with matching, knowing looks. Neither of us are in a hurry to rise and face the day, which is why, by the time we head for the kitchen for our breakfast, we figure the dining room will be empty. We head there with our plates instead of back to bed. To our surprise, the dining room has one remaining occupant when we step in the door.

Fenmire sits across the table from us with his hands held together on the tabletop. It's clear he's been waiting for us. He looks at both of us in turns, studying us.

"It's done, then?" he asks.

"It's done," Drixus replies.

Fenmire nods. "Have a seat, both of you. Please."

We come to the table and sit.

Fenmire extends his arms with his hands still clasped in a way I've seen him do once before. He reaches out to Drixus, who opens his hands to accept whatever Fenmire means to pass him. I already know what it is, so I cup my hands under Drixus' just in case. Drixus jumps when the little mouse lands in his gloved palms, but he quickly contains the creature without dropping it.

"I don't understand," Drixus says.

"We should test the extent of whatever powers Evangeline received from you," Fenmire explains. "Their powers so far have manifested as the opposite of that of the mate who gave them, which means...?"

"Drixus takes life," I say. "So, I should be able to give it."

Fenmire nods. "Whether by simple reanimation or full resurrection, Evangeline should be able to raise the dead, but in order to test it, we need a body. A fresh one." He waves down at the mouse in Drixus' hands. "Care to do the honors?"

Drixus stares down at the mouse for a moment, watching it scurry over his hands, then he looks at me.

"Only if you're comfortable with it," I tell him softly. "If not, we'll find another way."

He passes me the mouse and removes his gloves. When I move to pass him back the creature, he says, "It won't take long, so be ready. We don't know how much time you have to act after."

I nod and set the mouse in his palm.

At the little rodent's size, it's almost instantaneous. It stands on Drixus' chilly palms for a second then gives one tiny squeak of distress before slumping over. Drixus immediately gives it back to me, and it's like holding an icicle in my palms. Again, I focus on the mouse's little body, but instead of searching it for illness or injury, I close my eyes and simply… ask for what I want.

Please give him life.

Just like last time, my palms heat until I fear I'm doing little more than roasting the poor creature between my hands, but then I feel a twitch, then another, and another until his little heart starts racing and blood starts pumping throughout his body again. He's already squeaking and wiggling when I open my hands and pass him back to Fenmire.

Fenmire searches for any sign of distress in the tiny body. Finding none, he gives Drixus a nod.

To my surprise, both Gryxen glance at me, and the looks on their faces are less than celebratory.

"Did I miss something?" I ask.

"This new power of yours," Fenmire says, "it's strictly monitored in our world."

"Bringing people back from the dead can be immoral depending on how it's done, when, and to whom," Drixus explains. "Powers that raise the dead must be recorded at the temple. The priestesses keep a close watch on them."

I draw my arms inward, recoiling.

"It's not forbidden magic, Evangeline," Fenmire says. "You've done nothing wrong. It just means that, when the day comes for you to visit our world, we'll need to make the temple aware of what you can do. They'll ask some questions and put your name in their records. They may check in on you occasionally. That's it."

"What if they decide I'm too dangerous?" I fret.

"Your abilities don't matter. It's how you choose to use them. And you're simply not capable of the sorts of things that would get you in trouble for your powers."

"What sorts of things?"

Again, the Gryxen exchange looks.

"Would the two of you stop doing that and spit it out?" I bark.

Drixus turns in his seat to face me. "Sometimes, people with your abilities see their powers as a way to ease or completely avoid the grief of losing loved ones," he says softly, and his eyes are full of sadness for me I don't understand until…

Grief. Loved ones.

Papa.

Instant tears well in my eyes, but I swallow them down. "Could I even do that?"

"It's not a matter of could," Fenmire says. "It's a matter of 'for how long'. With your powers, you could force a heart to beat no matter the condition the body was in, but it wouldn't last if the corpse was past the point of revivification. You'd only cause suffering, for both of you."

I hear what he doesn't say, what he would never say to me but knows to be true regardless.

If I'd had this power before, I could've saved him.

But I was too late.

"Not everyone wants to be brought back," Drixus says. "Even if it's only been a minute, some don't want their fate in life and death decided by any mortal."

I only nod.

"That's why these sorts of powers are monitored," Fenmire continues. "To be sure you're using them humanely, if at all. You'll have to have permission from the temple to use this power in our world. Here, though, there's no one and nothing stopping you but your own morals and judgment."

"How often does your kind have this sort of ability?" I ask, mostly just to change the subject.

"Not very often," Drixus says.

"It's not as rare as a reeshro, but it's close," Fenmire adds.

I nod again. "Alright."

Drixus puts his gloves back on. "How long do we have before Reilanna springs whatever trap she's strung for us?" he asks Fenmire.

I wipe my eyes behind Drixus' back.

Fenmire pretends not to notice. "Not long, I don't think. It's usually only a day or so after a new bond when she sends some fresh horror through The Gate. We need to be prepared. We're all dressing in our armor and keeping our weapons on us at all times. We're evacuating the castle as well. The structure seems stable for now, but it won't survive much more. It's safer if no one is inside when The Gate opens again. The staff is currently setting up a temporary camp at a safe distance in the woods. You two should get what you need from your rooms and join us there."

"What will you do with Mara?" I ask Drixus.

"I'll gather my things and fly her down into The Deadwood," he says. "Somewhere close enough she'll get to me quickly when I call her but far enough away she won't interfere with the human camp."

"I'll pack my things and go with you, if that's alright."

Drixus nods and stands with his plate. When I don't, he looks from me to Fenmire and back before taking the hint. "I'll meet you upstairs." He kisses me on the forehead and leaves.

Once we're alone, Fenmire and I look at each other.

"So…" I say, and I heave a great sigh. "This is it."

"It is," he says. "Have you changed your mind?"

"About our plans?"

He nods.

"No. You?"

He shakes his head.

"Not even after learning the truth about Drixus?"

He sits with that question for a moment then asks, "Remember when you promised you wouldn't break any more of me?"

"I remember."

"Losing you wouldn't break me, Evangeline. It would annihilate me. I would burn my world to the ground, and maybe yours as well, for allowing such a tragedy. Even Seerraf couldn't stop me. So no, I haven't changed my mind. We'll go together into the unknown and welcome whatever we find there, even if it's death."

"The others may try to stop us."

"I expect them to. Does that change things for you?"

"No, but… promise me something?"

"Anything."

"If any of them step between us and The Gate, don't hurt them. If the cost of victory is their blood, don't pay it."

He nods again. "I promise." He stands from his chair and releases the mouse to scurry around on the floor as he walks around the table and sits beside me instead. "There's one more story I want to tell you. The one of Seerraf's third acolyte, Poilam. I've saved him for last because… well, his story is relevant."

"Then tell me," I bid.

He reaches for me, and I slide off my stool into his arms. He lifts me up to sit on the table in front of him with his arms around me.

"Poilam was a Gryxen," Fenmire says. "The Gate he guarded was one of the most dangerous in our history. As soon as it opened, conflict ensued with the beings on the other side, the Onmirix. They're also a winged race, smaller than Gryxen but faster. Their lifespans are considerably shorter, shorter even than yours at an average of 40 years. What they lack in strength and longevity, they make up for in speed and numbers.

"Poilam led the team of Gryxen who held the Onmirix at bay, but teams of Onmirix began passing through The Gate nearly the day it arrived and never stopped coming. They were anything but friendly. It's because of the Onmirix that we take protecting our Gates much more seriously now. Our kind has never seen such conflict as the one we found ourselves in with this race. Each team that came through The Gate was larger and more brutal than the last. Poilam and his team didn't know why they kept coming. They defeated the Onmirix each time, but they had losses on the Gryxen side as well. Poilam feared the Onmirix were trying to gather information, probing the Gryxen's defenses, and perhaps planning a larger scale assault, so the priestesses in the nearby temple held a council with Poilam and his team to discuss a more permanent solution.

"The council proposed an assault of their own through The Gate to push back whatever settlement the Onmirix had around it and set up their own defense camp to help protect our world. Poilam was against the idea, very vocally so. He said pushing their own team through The Gate could be seen as an act of war, and he feared it would only worsen the situation. Instead, he proposed they send just one Gryxen through The Gate with the goal of conducting negotiations for peace. His argument was that they should try diplomacy before violence. When asked who they should send for such negotiations, Poilam volunteered for the job himself.

"The council agreed, hesitantly, to allow Poilam to try his method first with the understanding that, should he fail or at the news of his death, they would revert to their original plan. He agreed and went through The Gate alone. He was immediately apprehended by the Onmirix, which he expected, so he put up no fight. What he didn't expect, however, was to be imprisoned and tortured with seemingly no other goal than to see how much his body and mind could take.

"The Onmirix held Poilam captive for almost a century, putting him through the worst kind of physical and psychological horrors you can imagine. During it all, he never took a single life nor raised a hand in violence against them, which perhaps was why, for his entire imprisonment, the Onmirix stopped attacking through The Gate. Though Poilam had seemingly disappeared, the council honored their bargain with him and waited to send anyone else through until they received either word of his success in brokering peace or word of his death.

"During his imprisonment, Poilam learned the Onmirix language, customs, and some of their names. He even made friends, who grew to hate the suffering he endured at their hands day after day, year after year. Eventually, he earned enough trust among them to be given an audience with their leaders, first in the prison where he was held, then the settlement, the city, and on until he was finally able to discuss peace with ones in positions powerful enough to promise such things. It took time, but he was able to convince them our people could be trusted, and he was eventually returned to our world, peace treaty in hand.

"His return was considered a miracle straight from Seerraf, but his years of suffering took its toll on him. He had violent nightmares, hallucinations, and paranoia that made it impossible for him to trust even his closest family and friends. There were times he couldn't even remember his own name. His body pained him greatly as well since some of his injuries were so devastating even our finest healers couldn't bring him relief. He lived alone at the temple for another hundred and fifty years to be sure the peace he brokered held, then he asked to pass on, which he was permitted to do without delay.

"The peace Poilam brokered with the Onmirix still holds to this day. As ruthless as the race is, they are also very strict about their laws. The council didn't know this until Poilam came back, but if they had gone to war with the Onmirix, it would have been catastrophic. While Onmirix don't have the lifespan or hardiness of Gruxa or Gryxen, they would have overwhelmed us with their sheer numbers and ability to reproduce at a rapid rate. Poilam single-handedly saved our world from destruction, but it came at the highest cost: a hundred years' worth of painful suffering that stole his health and sanity and eventually his life."

Fenmire tightens his arms around me. "Poilam didn't know the cost before he went through The Gate, but to him, it didn't matter. He was willing to do or endure whatever he had to in order to save his people." He rests his forehead against mine. "I don't mean to scare you, which is why I left his story for last, but I need you to understand my mindset before we face whatever awaits us on the other side of The Gate: like Poilam, I don't care what price we must pay, I will pay it with you a hundred times over rather than let you face it alone." He tilts my chin up so our eyes meet. "But unlike Poilam, you have a mate who would do anything for you. Anything, Evangeline. If we jump through The Gate only to discover a fate worse than death, say the word and I will end it all."

"You mean…?"

He nods. "I won't let Reilanna enjoy a single moment of your suffering. You won't end up like Drixus; I won't allow it. You say the word, and it's done."

"But what about you?"

"I'll be quick to follow you, pet, don't you worry."

I've long thought of our trip through The Gate as a suicide mission, but not until Fenmire proposes the impossible choice of ending our lives ourselves does the full weight of our plans settle on my shoulders. I swallow and nod.

"Did I make a mistake in telling you all of this?" Fenmire asks softly.

I kiss him. "No. I've always appreciated your candor, and it's good to be prepared for the worst."

He kisses me back. "When the quake starts, look for me. I won't be far."

Just then, Wexton walks into the dining room dressed in his armor and carrying his sword. "There you are, Evangeline."

Fenmire pulls away.

I smile at Wexton, but it feels so forced on my own face I know it won't fool him. "Have you been looking for me?"

Wexton ignores my question as his eyes flick between me and Fenmire. "Is something wrong?"

Thankfully, Fenmire answers for me. "No." He lifts me from the table and sets me on my feet beside it. "Pack anything that means something to you," he advises me. "Then head for the lane. Percival will show you where to go. He's helping to organize the camp."

I pick up my dishes, which are full of food I have no desire to eat anymore. "Did you need something, Wexton?" I ask.

He walks to the table and sets his sword down on it. "No, darling," he says with a smile barely more believable than mine. "I was coming to tell you what Fenmire already has. I'll see you outside."

I leave, but I don't go far. I stop just on the other side of the doorway and lean against the wall beside it, listening. At first, the two Gryxen are silent, and I can picture them staring at each other, neither willing to begin what will no doubt be a tense conversation.

Wexton must grow impatient because he's the first to break the silence. "What are you planning, Fenmire?"

"I don't know what you're talking about."

Wexton scoffs. "Come now, friend, don't lie to me. It's an insult to our friendship to think I'd fall for it. What are you and Evangeline going to do?"

"It's better you not know."

"That means I'd disapprove."

"When have you ever approved of my plans?"

"This is different. This is our mate. *Ours*, Fenmire. It's not just *your* heart and soul on the line this time."

"I know that. But I also know Evangeline has the final say, not me, not you, not Caliborne or Drixus. Evangeline. That was what we agreed at the start, was it not?"

"Yes, but—"

"There are no buts. Trust that I follow their word and will to the end. Or don't, it makes little difference to me."

Wexton doesn't respond right away, but when he finally does, his voice is filled with the most anger I've ever heard from him before. "I swear on Seerraf and the five, if you get them killed, best friends or not, I'll kill you myself."

"Good," is Fenmire's only reply.

The silence that falls this time makes my skin crawl, so I step away from the door and go to my room.

*****

My courting gifts, Will's letters, Jacob's paper lily, my golden hands, the clothes that mean the most to me as well as a few spares, and my bath bag are all tucked neatly into two sacks when I leave my room and head upstairs for the last time. Drixus has very little by way of belongings, so it's not hard for him to secure everything onto Mara's back with us before we take flight and head down into The Deadwood. The staff have cleared some trees a few hundred yards down the lane from the castle and are setting up tents and shelters around a large firepit. Levi and the rest of the cooks already have a makeshift kitchen set up near the fire next to a large cart of food.

Drixus and I land Mara a short distance away, further into the forest, and Drixus orders her to stay put, on the ground, until she's called. She immediately lays down on the forest floor.

"Do you think she understands what's happening?" I ask as we make our way through the trees toward the camp.

"I do," Drixus says. He pulls off one of his gloves to take my hand as we walk. "Animals can sense these things naturally, but I explained it to her last night, that we'd soon have to face the witch that's responsible for all our pain. She knows. She's ready to see justice served at last for what Reilanna did to her, what she did to us both."

"Are *you* ready?"

He looks at me with determination on his face. "I am."

When we reach the camp, Caliborne waves us over and touches my arm. *There you are. I was worried with you in the castle so long.*

"Sorry. We were the last to hear the news." I wave a hand around at the camp full of bustling bodies. "This is impressive."

Fenmire and Percival organized most of it. Though it hasn't been decided where you should stay. You can share with one of the Gryxen, or I'll happily find the supplies to make you your own space.

"I'll bunk with one of you tonight. Save the supplies to make sure everyone has a place to sleep tonight."

Caliborne nods then sends some message I don't hear to Drixus with his palm.

Drixus pulls on his glove then shakes Caliborne's hand. "I don't know what it means to you, but you have my word."

I don't ask what agreement the two of them just made.

Caliborne waves for us both to follow him, and he leads us to the very outskirts of the camp where a stack of logs and a tarp sit at a distance from the other structures.

This is meant to be Drixus' space, if he wants it, Caliborne says with a hand on my shoulder.

When I relay this information to Drixus, he smiles and nods. "Thank you." He glances back toward the camp through the trees. "This is perfect."

I spend the rest of the day helping first Drixus then the others set up their shelters. Toward dusk, I help Levi stack and light the wood for our fire, then I busy myself further with helping him and the others make dinner. Levi pulls out all the stops for the meal, baking and roasting just about everything that could go bad out of the ice box.

"I didn't know when we'd get access to the storage rooms again," he explains as we finish stringing up another pork loin. "So I brought everything the cart could carry."

"We may as well eat it rather than let it get buried in rubble," I reply. "Besides, the Gryxen and I can always make a trip to the village if we run out."

Neither of us say it, but the look that passes between us is one of mutual understanding.

We won't be out here long enough to run out of food.

That night, with plans and worries running wild in my head, I can't stand the thought of hearing what the others are no doubt thinking in theirs, so I seek out the one Gryxen whose mind is as quiet as I wish mine was. I crawl into bed with Drixus, and we lie facing each other in the dark. I'm clothed, but Drixus' bare hand is under my shirt, softly stroking the skin of my belly as we stare at each other.

Eventually, he starts to sing, and the sound combined with his petting calms me enough my eyes finally drift shut, and I fall asleep in my mate's arms for what I suspect will be the last time.

…and Hell followed with him…

Chapter 76

The camp is silent when I step out of Drixus' shelter the next morning. The staff gather near the fire as breakfast is passed around, but no one is talking. Will and Jacob are sitting together on a log nearby, so I take the plate Levi offers me—without his usual warm greeting—and walk over to sit beside Will.

"Morning," he says quietly.

"How did you sleep?" I ask as I push my food around my plate.

"We didn't," Jacob says. He's holding one of his rats.

"And how are *they* doing?" I ask with a nod toward the creature.

"Fine," Jacob says as he hands a crumb from his untouched breakfast to his furry companion, who accepts it eagerly. "Percival helped me put together a temporary cage for them out here."

All three of us fall silent again, and my stomach cramps so badly I give up on breakfast entirely and set the plate on the ground. I turn to Will and open my mouth to tell him… I don't even know what exactly, but he holds up his hand before I can utter a word.

"Don't," he says sternly.

"Don't what?" I ask.

"Don't start saying goodbye. I won't accept that. We're going to get through this and go on living our lives free of the village *and* the spell. Wait and see."

I try to smile, but I just can't, so I only nod.

Will's hand slides across the log and settles on top of mine. He gives it a squeeze. *I believe in you.*

I stand up, afraid I'll start crying if I don't find something to occupy myself with. "You two stay out of harm's way today." I'm talking to them both, but I'm looking mainly at Will. "Don't try to be heroes. Leave the fighting to the demons with armor and weapons, alright?"

Jacob touches Will's knee. "Don't worry. I'll watch him."

I nod and walk away.

My mates are standing together near the edge of the trees, though one stands slightly apart from the others. They don't look quite as morose as the humans. The Gryxen look resolved and ready with their weapons either strapped on their bodies or resting nearby within arms' reach.

"Oh, good," Wexton says when I join them. "We were just discussing where best to place you when The Gate finally opens. Ideally, you should stay here with one of us to guard you while we fight what beasts Reilanna sends this time, but we know you'd never stand for that, so…"

As Wexton goes on talking about who might be best for me to fly with or where the safest place for me might be during what they predict will be as big of a battle as the one that ended The Great War, I glance at Fenmire, who gives away nothing. He's holding his shield, but his mace is on his belt, which I've never seen him do before. Eventually, the others settle on me staying close to Caliborne since his bow can help him keep our enemies at a distance more than the others' weapons and powers. I just nod, afraid anything I try to add to the discussion will only give away that I have plans of my own.

"Evangeline?" Fenmire calls when my attention wanders completely.

"Evan," I mutter since my bracelets are packed in my bags for safekeeping.

Fenmire looks me in the eyes. "It's going to be alright."

I know what he's actually saying.

I'm not alone.

We have a plan.

I know that, but choosing my fate doesn't make it any easier to face.

Out of the corner of my eye, I see Drixus tilt his head and try to get my attention. I don't look at him, knowing he'd read the truth on my face and confirm what he no doubt already suspects.

Thankfully, Caliborne steps between us to touch my shoulder. Whatever words of bravery or love he was about to impart are soon forgotten.

The ground shakes.

It's only a slight rumble at first, but then another hits, and another, and each one grows in intensity until the trees begin to creak and groan around us.

Wexton picks up his sword. "Finally…"

Caliborne sweeps me behind him as he pulls his bow off his shoulder. When he lets me go to yank an arrow from his quiver, I step back and away from him, out of his reach.

Fenmire and I lock eyes.

With a faint boom, the ground lurches and sends everyone sprawling. The humans scream and run for the trees. A chorus of cracking and snapping sounds makes my mates and I look toward the castle where it rises above the forest canopy. I get to my feet and conveniently stagger closer to Fenmire as great cracks form in the outer walls of our home. The castle begins to crumble, starting at the peaks of the giant stalagmite towers, which fall in on themselves, driving the rest of the stone toward the ground. The sound is deafening and heartbreaking as the structure collapses, and it sinks down past the tree line where we can no longer see it just as I take Fenmire's hand.

Now?

As if in answer to his question, a screech announces the first of Reilanna's beasts as it flies over the trees, its eyes scanning the forest for prey. It's quickly joined by a second, then a third, and a fourth, until the sky is full of circling black horrors just like in the dream I had what feels like a lifetime ago.

And just like in that dream, I'm ready to go to battle for all I hold dear.

"Now!" I cry, and Fenmire snatches me up in his arms and takes flight all in one motion.

"Fenmire!" Wexton screams in rage, and though I'm sure he takes flight as well, I know he won't catch us.

Fenmire is the fastest flier.

Fenmire's shield offers me cover as we break through the trees into a sky that's filled with Reilanna's monsters. We can't afford to even slow down as we soar right into the fray, and Fenmire is forced to dodge and weave between beasts that screech and reach for us at every turn. Fenmire's wings are faster even than theirs, and though a few slam into us and attempt to rip me from his arms, he easily outmaneuvers them and leaves them all behind as we make for The Gate. I hear the clang of Wexton's sword as one of our enemies draws him into battle, and I'm both grateful for anything that might slow him down and terrified for his safety at the same time.

Fenmire and I make our way over The Deadwood around the endless wave of Reilanna's beasts, and though we have a few close calls, between Fenmire's flying skills, the shield I'm ducked behind, and Fenmire's knife I have clutched in both hands so as not to drop it, not a single claw or tooth touches me. I can't say the same for Fenmire, though. He's bleeding from several cuts and bites, but he doesn't let them slow him down.

Peeking over Fenmire's shield, I can see the clearing where The Gate resides in the distance, but there is a never-ending swarm of black, winged vermin pouring up out of it. Up to this point, Fenmire has been thinking in his language, more a result of the heat of battle than an attempt to keep me out, I suspect. Just when I decide to ask him how he thinks we can get through the onslaught of Reilanna's army, the swarm suddenly comes to an end.

And somehow, I get the feeling that's worse.

"Fenmire?" I say in uncertainty.

"I see it." He doesn't slow down since, regardless of what Reilanna plans to throw at us next, our goal is The Gate, and there is nothing else for us to do but continue heading for it, to whatever end. "I'm going to loop around and come at it from the—"

A sudden and vicious wind whips up from below us. It's frigid and makes me hide my face against Fenmire's warm chest. I can't see through a sudden cloud of blowing white, but I hear Fenmire's blood-curdling scream.

We start to fall.

"Fenmire?" I scream.

"Hold on!"

He's struggling to keep us in the air, I can feel the momentum of his wings desperately trying to stay in flight. They're failing, though I don't know why. We drop into the trees, and Fenmire uses his shield to protect me from the worst of the branches. He hugs me tight to his chest with one arm as he grabs at the trees to slow our descent. It helps a little, but I still hit the ground so hard it knocks the wind out of me and sends me rolling across the forest floor.

Once I finally come to rest, I catch my breath for a moment and assess the damage. Other than a few throbbing places that will no doubt bruise magnificently later, I'm in one piece and nothing seems broken. I've dropped Fenmire's knife, so I sit up with a groan and immediately look around for it.

Fenmire is on his hands and knees a few yards away, panting and grimacing in pain.

I don't have to ask why.

His wings are full of holes, shredded by ice shards, a few of which are still stuck in his wings and back.

I get slowly to my feet and stagger over to him.

"I can fix it," I say, but at a closer glance, I don't know where to start. The leather spans between the bones of his wings are full of so many holes some of the pieces are barely hanging on by a thread. It would take forever to mend all of this.

Fenmire gets one leg underneath him and lurches up onto his feet with a groan of pain. He folds his wings in close to his back to protect them from further damage.

"We have to run," he says. "That was Breklen's magic. She's close."

"Are you alright?"

"Enough to finish this. You?"

I nod.

"Then run like I'm chasing you, pet."

We take off together toward the clearing again, weaving around trees, wading through streams, and jumping over fallen logs. Where I struggle to keep up, Fenmire carries me, but for the most part, we run together this time. I don't let myself look back to see if we're being followed. I lock my eyes straight ahead and run like there's a beast after me.

There is, and this time it truly is out for my blood.

When I see sunlight through the trees ahead, I point excitedly. "There!"

A scream, one I've heard before in my dreams, cuts through the woods from nearby, causing my entire body to shiver. She's close. Too close.

"Don't stop!" Fenmire yells, and he spins and raises his shield a split second before a spear whistles through the trees and clangs off its face as he knocks it out of the air.

I scream and duck and scramble through the last strip of woods between us and the clearing, and when I break the tree line, I practically fall on my face in the grass. Fenmire grabs me by my shirt and hauls me back to my feet. I can see the circle of stones ahead of us as well as the shimmering gateway between them that's open and waiting for me.

Reilanna screams again, and I hear the snapping and scraping of branches behind us. I finally look back in time to see her burst out of the trees, and she looks the same as she did in my dream: four arms, black wings, patchy orange hair… She spots me and smiles, showing me her black, rotting teeth. She has a quiver on her back that's full of her spears as well as one in each of her four hands. She throws one, but Fenmire easily knocks it away.

About halfway across the clearing, Fenmire slows and grabs his mace. "Keep running!" he yells, and though he's still following me, his attention is locked onto Reilanna.

Reilanna screams, and another burst of wind filled with ice shards streaks across the clearing. This time, it slams into Fenmire's shield, but it can't protect all of him. He growls in pain as ice shards stab into his legs and feet, and he's forced to slow down even further to keep a hold of the shield the wind threatens to snatch from him.

I don't slow down. The Gate is before me, and I put all of my strength into reaching it as fast as I can with Reilanna's ice on my heels. Reilanna's spears clang against Fenmire's weapons as I streak across the ground. When there's not but a couple of yards left for me to run, the ground shakes again, and I dig my heels into the dirt as another of Reilanna's beasts comes through The Gate. A small, bird-like creature comes streaking out of the gateway at full speed, headed straight for me.

"Evan!" Fenmire yells, but he's too far away to intervene.

I turn and run back toward him, but I don't make it more than a step or two before the creature's claws wrap around my upper arms and lift me off my feet into the air.

Reilanna laughs.

She knew. She knew this was our plan and made a plan of her own.

"Fenmire!" I scream in panic. The air rushes around me as the ground falls away, and I flail and kick and writhe, but the claws locked around my arms don't budge, and I can't reach them with my hands to use my powers. "Help!"

Fenmire is still locked in battle with Reilanna, but he turns and looks up at me briefly before pivoting to knock away another of her spears with his shield. In the same motion, he swivels on one heel and flings his shield into the air. The shield streaks up and slams into the legs of the creature that's holding me, severing one entirely. I'm dropped on one side so that I'm swinging from one arm, which feels like it's being ripped from its socket at my shoulder. But more importantly, I can now reach the creature's other leg. I wrap my fingers around the scaly limb just above the claw still holding me captive and focus on my powers.

Let. Me. Go!

The creature's talons slowly loosen and eventually release me.

It's not until I start plummeting toward the ground that I realize just how high in the sky I've been lifted. I'm far above the trees, and the ground is now rushing back up to meet me. I scream, knowing it's going to hurt when I land, if I survive at all. Fenmire sees the danger too and starts running, heading right for me. I pray he can reach me in time before—

Fenmire jerks and stumbles as not one but two spears slam into his back, their heads ripping through his chest on both sides. The last thing I see is him falling to his knees.

Then I hit the ground.

*****

I come to with a groan of utter agony. I'm alive, but part of me wishes I wasn't. My head feels as if one of Reilanna's beasts stomped on it, my left hand is on fire, and my chest aches so badly I can barely breathe through the pain. I taste blood in my mouth. I lift my head and immediately throw up. It's mostly blood. Where's Fenmire? I try to sit up, but all I manage is a slight shift of my body before I scream in agony and freeze.

I can't feel my legs, but I hear the bones in both of them grind together when I try to move.

My hand is skewered through the palm by a large splinter of wood.

I rip it out.

More vomiting.

"F…Fen…mire?"

The sunlight hurts my eyes, but I blink through the pain and search for him. There's a blue blob on the ground a short distance away, but I can't make my eyes focus on it. I close them and touch a shaking hand to my chest over the place that hurts so badly it's keeping me from breathing properly. A familiar laugh makes me look up at a black, winged form floating in the air to my left.

Reilanna has a spear in each hand again, and she stares down at me with a sick smile on her face as I try to heal the wounds in my torso enough I can at least stop puking blood.

"So, you're a mere mortal after all," she says. "You're nothing without Seerraf's tricks of the mind, are you?"

The ground beneath me moves, and something hard and sharp stabs me in the shoulder. I scream as a spear of stone pushes into my body, lifting me up in a semi-sitting position as it does. I keep my hand pressed against the pain in my middle and try not to move to keep the stone from impaling me any further as I heal myself. Reilanna slowly flies closer.

I hear a grunt of pain and turn my head to see Fenmire struggling up to his knees about ten feet away. The two spearheads are still sticking out of his chest, and he takes hold of them, one in each hand, and pulls. He screams as the spears slide through his body, but once there's about a foot of wood between the heads and his chest, he grabs one with both hands and snaps it off flush to his skin. He does the same with the other and points the bloodied end of one spear up at Reilanna.

"I'll see you dead by day's end," he hisses.

Reilanna rolls her eyes and tosses one spear up in the air, catching it above her shoulder in the perfect position to lob it down at us. "It would take a miracle for that to happen." She smiles at me. "And I'm—"

Reilanna screams, this time in pain. A spray of blood and a flash of gold erupts at the base of her left wing as it's cleaved off her back. One wing falls to the ground as Reilanna flounders in the air with her remaining one, spinning off to the side about fifteen feet before slamming into the dirt. Mara dives into the clearing with a terrifying screech, heading straight for Reilanna. Next to the lifeless wing, Drixus lands and stands up, one of his axes dripping black as he looks at Fenmire and I.

"Do what you've got to do," he says, then he turns to face Reilanna again as Mara descends upon her. "I'm owed one more wing." He starts running across the clearing toward our enemy.

Fenmire staggers to his feet.

My hand has healed the ache in my chest enough I can breathe now, but I'm still impaled on stone, and even the smallest attempt to move makes both my legs and hips pop and grind.

A ball of swirling black and red crashes to the ground a few yards away and rolls across the dirt. When it comes to rest, I see Wexton locked in a heated battle with one of Reilanna's winged beasts. He grunts and yells as he strikes the creature with the hilt of his sword, shoves it away from him, and skewers it through the middle. It twitches and snaps its teeth at him a few more times before it finally stills, and he kicks it off his blade. He turns to us, breathless and covered in gore.

"Don't you move," he says, pointing at me. "I'll get you in just a min—"

Another winged horror swoops down at him and tears his attention away from us, and he's drawn into battle once again.

Fenmire reaches me and takes my upper arms in his hands. "I'm sorry for this," he says, then he kicks the stone spear out from underneath me and rips it out of my body.

I scream in pain and cling to Fenmire's arms. "My bones… are broken," I utter miserably between gasps for air. "I can't… move."

He nods and reaches down to pick me up. I grab him around the neck as he slides his arm under my twisted, mangled limbs and hauls me up into his arms.

"I've got you," he says. He turns toward The Gate.

The ground shakes again.

We both freeze as another black, twisted creature streaks through The Gate and heads right for us. I scream and cower against Fenmire's chest, but just before the creature reaches us, a volley of arrows slams into its head and chest, knocking it out of the air entirely. It's dead before it hits the ground.

I look up at Caliborne, who's hovering in the air at the edge of the clearing. Our eyes meet for only half a heartbeat before he turns and shoots another of Reilanna's beasts, then another, and another. The number of beasts in the sky has increased dramatically, all of them drawn to the fighting and the gold-clad warriors picking off their brethren one by one.

Fenmire strengthens his grip on me and starts toward The Gate, one unsteady step at a time. We're almost halfway there when he stumbles and falls to one knee, nearly dropping me. The jostling makes me cry out in pain again.

"Evan!" Wexton yells. "Fenmire, don't you dare!"

Fenmire ignores him, gets back to his feet, and continues on.

We're no more than a dozen steps away when a gold-armored figure slams into the ground in front of us, sending up a shower of dirt and stones. Fenmire stops as Caliborne stands up tall between us and The Gate, blocking our way. He's covered in so much blood his armor is more black than gold, and he pants as he stands there staring at us through glaring, narrowed eyes.

"Move aside," Fenmire orders with a growl.

Caliborne shakes his head.

"It's the only way!"

Caliborne doesn't respond, but he draws another arrow from his quiver and nocks it with his eyes locked onto Fenmire.

"All of this will be for nothing if we don't finish what we started," Fenmire says. His voice sounds tired, and he's shaking as if he's fighting every muscle in his body to remain standing.

Again, Caliborne shakes his head. He draws his bow and aims at Fenmire with a look of determined sadness in his eyes.

"Caliborne!" I cry.

Hesitantly, his eyes slide away from Fenmire and lock onto me instead.

"Please," I beg. "This is what I'm meant to do. Let me do it."

He doesn't move or lower his weapon.

"Nothing against my will, remember?" I say tearfully. "This is what I want."

Caliborne's blazing white eyes burn into mine, and they fill with tears.

"Please," I say again, and I start to cry with him. "I love you. Please let me save you."

Caliborne looks from me to Fenmire, and a heartbeat later, he fires his bow. Fenmire and I both jump, but the arrow flies over us and slams into another of Reilanna's beasts that was descending on us from behind. Caliborne takes flight and flies over us, knocking another creature to the ground and firing three quick arrows into its chest before looking at me again.

He nods once and turns away, drawing the next closest creature's attention away from us and onto him instead.

Our path clear once more, Fenmire stumbles forward toward The Gate. The ring of grey stones is scattered now, but the doorway to the Gryxen homeworld is open and shimmering before us. Fenmire sinks to his knees at its edge. Blood from the wounds in his chest has soaked his front and me as well, and there's a trickle of it coming from his mouth. His breaths are ragged and raspy and cause the blood to bubble a bit on his lips. His eyes flutter when they look at me.

"Together," I whisper.

He wraps both arms around me, and I tighten my grip on his neck, trying my best not to let my fear show even though I'm shaking like a leaf.

"Together," he says, then he falls forward, sending us both plummeting through The Gate.

The journey from one world to the other is instantaneous, and we fall out of The Gate into the air above the Vorisca Desert. The first thing I notice is the heat. It's hotter here than the sunniest summer day in my village. I look up through The Gate over Fenmire's shoulder. Nothing looks different, and I'm still alive. The spell hasn't been broken yet.

That's when I realize The Gate was never meant to kill me. It was the fall. The genius of that on Reilanna's part could almost be commendable. In order for the spell to break, my mates would've had to willingly let me fall through The Gate and die upon the sands of their homeworld. Reilanna was smart to bet against such a thing, but she underestimated Fenmire.

She underestimated us all.

There's a scream of fury from above before Reilanna's face emerges, framed by the shimmering edges of The Gate. She has no more wings to fly after us with, and there's no point anyway since we're so far below her now she'd never reach us in time to stop the inevitable. Five hands grasp onto her from all sides as my mates yank her back, readying to finish the job once the spell is broken.

"Good riddance, witch," Fenmire mutters. The wind whipping by my ears is so loud I barely hear him.

There will be no intervention, not from The Gate, my mates, or Seerraf, but at least my death will be quick, like Vorilai's. I can hear her voice in my head, an echo from when she spoke to me in my dream. I look over my shoulder toward the ground and see blood red sand rising rapidly to meet us. Despite my resolve, I whimper a little at the sight.

"Don't look," Fenmire says. His voice is weak, and the grip of his arms around me is weakening.

I turn away from my doom and bury my face in his neck. "I love you."

Instead of saying it back, he kisses me softly on the cheek.

I close my eyes, hug my mate, and wait for the impact.

Chapter 77

I'm lying on hot sand. Its heat is burning into my back through my clothes. I dig my fingers into it.

Why aren't I dead?

I slowly lift my head. I'm lying on my back on the floor of the Vorisca Desert, but I don't recall hitting the ground. The last thing I remember is plummeting through the air, clinging to Fenmire's neck. I look up toward where The Gate was just seconds ago, but there's nothing but pale blue sky with no shimmering gateway in sight. I look all around me. There's no one and nothing but red sand as far as the eye can see.

"Fenmire?" I call as I climb to my feet. My legs are no longer broken, and all my pain is gone everywhere else. "Fenmire!" I scream loudly as I spin in a circle, searching.

"He's not here," says a deep and powerful voice from behind me.

I spin so fast I nearly lose my balance in the sand. Standing a few yards away is a Gryxen. At least, he's shaped like a Gryxen, but he's unlike any Gryxen or Gruxa I've ever seen before. He's very tall, taller even than Caliborne by several heads and twice as broad, and he has four arms instead of two. His hair and glowing eyes are as bright gold as his armor, which he's dressed in from head to toe. Even his skin has a slightly golden hue.

I've seen his likeness before, on the shelves in Fenmire's bedroom.

"You…" I utter in disbelief. "You're…"

He bows his head to me. "I am Seerraf, the Gryxen god, among other things. I have many shapes and names. I even have one in your world, though very few worship it, and fewer still worship it by my true teachings."

"Why are you here? Am I dead?"

"Strictly speaking, yes, though I stole your consciousness at the very moment of your end."

"Why?"

He smiles at me. "I came to congratulate you, Evan. I've waited for you to reach this moment for a very long time."

"Is that why you called me your champion in my dreams?"

"Yes."

I hug myself. Despite the warm desert air, I'm getting chilly. "When you say you've waited for me for a long time, do you mean you waited for *me* or for the human who would break Reilanna's spell."

"You, Evan. I waited for you."

"How long have you known I'd be the one standing before you now?"

"From the time Reilanna's spell was born, I knew. Or at least, I'd hoped."

"What does that mean?"

He laces two of his hands together as he regards me. "Reilanna was quite clever when she cast her spell. She knew I was watching very closely, so to stop me from intervening, she wove my people's fate with that of a human's. You see, believe it or not, we gods have our own rules, and the most important one is that we must never intervene in the fate of another god's people. Reilanna made a human the key to breaking her spell, so your human god was the only one who could intervene."

"But he didn't," I say bitterly. "Did he?"

"Not because he didn't want to. The others have explained to you how a god gains power, have they not?"

I nod.

"Your god was very young when Reilanna tried to take over your world. I went to him the moment Reilanna made her intentions known, but he lacked the strength to do more than make me a promise. He promised that as soon as he was able, he would set a certain soul on the path toward helping my people."

"A *certain* soul?"

He smiles again. "Yes, Evan. A certain soul. One I provided your god to be placed in his human world."

I blink at him. "My soul came from you?"

He bows his head in a nod.

"Does that mean I'm a Gryxen?"

"You were one, once upon a time. A soul is what it is. The vessel that contains it matters very little, though your previous lives no doubt influenced your actions in this one."

Lives. Plural.

My mind spins with endless questions at this news.

What sort of person was I in my previous lives? Does this mean I'm barred from heaven? Does heaven even exist, or do all souls get reborn in this way as something else, some completely different being?

Seerraf chuckles. "The sort I could trust to help me break this spell. No. Yes. And no, souls don't get passed from one god's beings to another. Yours was a special circumstance born of necessity. Neither I nor your human god even knew if it would work. You exceeded our highest expectations, and for that, we are both eternally grateful."

"So then, who is my true god, the one I'm meant to worship?"

"That is entirely up to you. Like I said, yours was a special circumstance. You could worship either of us, both of us, or neither one of us at all. You've earned the right to choose which of us is worthy of your soul's loyalty."

At mention of my soul, it prompts a question I've held in the back of my mind since childhood, and, knowing this is a once-in-a-lifetime opportunity to have it answered, I simply blurt it out, not caring a bit how foolish it might sound. "What does it look like?"

Seerraf tilts his head. "Your soul?"

I nod.

He smiles sweetly at me. "Would you like to see it?"

I nod again, and Seerraf reaches out his hand, palm pointed toward me much like Caliborne does. He closes his fist as if taking hold of something in midair, then he pulls his arm back toward himself, drawing a milky white orb from my chest. I don't feel a thing as it slips from my body and hovers between us, spinning slowly in the air. There are five tendrils floating around the outside, like whisps of milky smoke.

"What are those?" I ask.

"Your mating bonds."

"But there are five."

Seerraf nods. "Yes, you took one other mate, many lifetimes ago."

The fifth mating bond is different from the other four. It's longer and brighter, and where the others are like tentacles connected to the orb but moving in their own space beside it, the fifth is curled around the orb as if holding it close. I'm still wondering after this fifth mate of mine when a voice, like an echoing whisper, rises up from the orb. It speaks in the Gryxen's language, and yet I understand every word.

'I don't care what waits for me on the other side,' says a deep, masculine voice. *'If it means saving us from war, I'll gladly face it.'*

Another voice, this one neither strictly male nor female, says, *'They are* not *just mindless beasts! I'll prove it to you. I'll prove it to everyone!'*

Why does that sound familiar?

I frown, trying to think where I've heard those words before. "Are those…?"

"Moments from your previous lives, ones that left a permanent mark on your soul."

'The children!' cries a feminine voice. *'Quickly, save the children before the building collapses!'*

'I won't leave you here to rot in this prison,' says a masculine voice, though this one's not quite as deep as the first. *'I'll join the local guard and be here the day they set you free. I promise.'*

Lastly, another female voice speaks, this one full of determination. *'We've come too far to stop now. Yes, I know I'm fading. As long as my heart's still beating, we will continue the procedure. We have to.'*

"But… but those are…"

Seerraf bows his head to me again. "Yes, Evan. They are the stories of my acolytes. Or should I say, my acolyte. My champion."

My mouth falls open in a gasp. "They were… me? All of them?"

He nods.

"Those stories Fenmire told me, I did all of those things?" I ask tearfully.

"You did. You've done many remarkable things, even more than the legends mention. But throughout each of your lives, one thing remained constant: you never conformed to a specific gender. Born male or female never mattered to you, for your identity has always been as fluid as a rolling sea. Part of me thinks Reilanna chose the wording she did in her spell because she knew a soul like yours, like my acolyte's, was rare, and she never expected a human would be capable of hosting one. Little did she know, the very soul that inspired her choice in words would be the one to make her regret them."

I shake my head. There must be some mistake. "But I'm no one. I'm just… just me." I pat my chest as if to show what little there is of me.

He snorts. "Some things never change," he mutters, more to himself than to me. "You say that every time, or some version of it, anyway."

I wipe my eyes. "We've had this conversation before?"

"Many times."

"So I knew? About the previous acolytes?"

"At the end of each of your lives, yes, you knew."

I shake my head again. "Fenmire is never going to believe this."

Seerraf touches his chin. "You know, he nearly guessed it once. During his studies in his youth, he noted the timeline for each acolyte's life and death and wondered if there was a correlation. He'll no doubt be quite cross that he missed it."

I laugh. "He will indeed." I rub my arms as a sudden chill sweeps over me.

The orb flickers.

"You don't have much time left," Seerraf says, and he waves the orb back inside my chest. Again, I feel nothing. "Your soul will soon slip away. Where it goes will depend on the choices you make here."

"Is that why you've come? To let me choose my fate in death?"

"Not quite. My people have suffered greatly under Reilanna's ascendancy. The people of Michastiforo were slaughtered in numbers so grave I wept blood for years. They prayed endlessly for me to fix it, to end her cruelty and bring back peace, but I could do nothing. I, like your mates, had to wait for the right human to come along. I had to wait for you."

He opens his hand to me, his palm glittering gold in the sunlight. "And now, you've fulfilled my people's prayers where I could not. The moment your heart stops, Reilanna's spell will be broken. Even now, your mates lay waste to her beasts and overpower her. They will not let her slip through their fingers again. You've ended my people's suffering at last. And so, I've stretched a single heartbeat into these moments with you, to offer you something in return."

I shiver again. "What is it?"

"A wish. For all you've done for me and my people. The magic Reilanna used for her spell is very powerful, more powerful than any mortal has wielded before. The instant it's broken, you'll release a surge of energy so strong that—coupled with my own powers—could grant you anything you ask for. Anything at all. I feel it's only right that you get to use it. I've watched you throughout this life and known you in all your previous ones. You are pure of heart and soul and as clever as they come. I know you'll use this gift wisely.

"So, Evan, tell me. What is your wish?"

With such endless opportunities placed before me, how can I possibly choose? I could ask to live again. I could ask to live forever with my mates. I could give them back everything they've lost, including me.

But this was always much bigger than us.

While I worked hard to break Reilanna's spell over the past few months, that's just the last page of this story. The suffering, pain, and loss all started long before I was ever born. Drixus' loss of his brother and his torture at Reilanna's hands; Fenmire's loss of a mate he believed betrayed him and the two thousand years' worth of heartbreak that caused; Caliborne losing his sister, twice, who he loved more than life itself; Wexton's battle scars and the arm he still mourns, though he tries not to show it.

Every soul lost when Reilanna was sealed behind The Gate.

The leveled temple.

The golden city stained with black evil.

The unanswered prayers of thousands who died as Reilanna took her wrath out on those undeserving.

How can I possibly undo all of that?

By severing the common thread.

I look up at Seerraf, and through chattering teeth, I say, "I wish Reilanna never existed."

He tilts his head at me. "Do you realize what you're asking for? What it will mean for you? After all, erasing Reilanna would erase everything that came from her existence, including your mating bonds."

"Nothing can break a mating bond. Not even death."

Seerraf's smile spreads across his entire face, and he laughs. It's a deep, rich sound that brings some warmth back to my veins, if only temporarily.

"You never cease to amaze me," he says in awe, and his eyes glow even brighter. "I can do that, with a few *adjustments* of my own." Without seeing him move, he's suddenly right in front of me, so close I can feel the heat of him against my frigid skin. "Don't think I don't know what you're giving up," he says softly.

Seerraf touches my cheek, and I lean into his warmth, much like I did when I first met Caliborne. This touch is one I've felt before, standing in the clearing in my dream after defeating Reilanna. And just like that day, I'm filled with emotion and desperate for that touch never to leave me.

"We will meet again, my champion," he says. "When you're ready."

With nothing left to say, I close my eyes, suddenly too exhausted to keep them open anymore. And yet, I still see a golden light that burns brighter and brighter, overtaking the darkness closing in around me until the light is all that's left.

I'm no longer cold.

Evangeline

Charity suffereth long,
and is kind;
charity envieth not;
charity vaunteth not itself,
is not puffed up,
Doth not behave itself unseemly,
seeketh not her own,
is not easily provoked,
thinketh no evil;
Rejoiceth not in iniquity,
but rejoiceth in the truth;
Beareth all things,
believeth all things,
hopeth all things,
endureth all things.
Charity never faileth:
but whether there be prophecies,
they shall fail;
whether there be tongues,
they shall cease;
whether there be knowledge,
it shall vanish away.

-I Corinthians 13:4-8 KJV

Chapter 78

I walk the cobbled street toward the general store, waving to friends who greet me as I pass. A group of ladies walking the opposite way down the lane spot me, and they move over, their dresses whispering across the stone and their parasols bumping together as they group up and whisper excitedly.

"Morning ladies," I say, and I tip my hat as I pass.

"Good morning, Evan," they call back in unison, then they all fall into a fit of chittering giggles.

I count six steps before I look back. One of the ladies is still staring after me, and I give her a wink for good measure. Her smile is breathtaking, and yet it fails to stir even the tiniest hint of feeling in me. I sigh to myself as I continue up the street. Some days I fear I'll never find anyone, man or woman, who can make me feel… something, anything other than lonely and sad.

My woes ease a bit when I enter the general store and am greeted by the cheerful dinging of the bell as I walk in, followed immediately by a wide smile from my best friend.

"It's an Evan day, I see," Will says as I step up to the counter.

I'm dressed in my new riding boots and the shirt and vest set my mother just finished helping me make yesterday evening. My pants are an old pair of my father's I hemmed to fit my height, but I still have to wear a belt cinched tight around my waist to keep them up. I'm hoping to fix that soon, though. My long, dark brown hair is braided and pinned up under a black flat cap I bought two summers ago in the city when Will and I visited his aunt. All in all, I think I look pretty damn good.

"I came to pick up Mother's order," I say, then I lean over the counter. "Are they here yet?"

Will leans over his side of the counter as well. "Maybe."

"Don't tease me, Will. Did my packages arrive or not?"

"I counted no less than three parcels in the back with your name on them."

I clap with glee. "I was hoping they'd come before church this Sunday!"

"How do you know Sunday will be an Evan day?"

"I know. I'm so excited it can't be anything but."

Will retrieves both my mother's order and my parcels and stacks it all on the counter. "I'll help you carry these if you wait a few minutes until my father gets back."

"Give me a sweet for the trouble?"

Will rolls his eyes but dutifully takes down the glass jar full of my favorite peppermint candies, doling me out not one but three. "You're lucky my father likes you."

"*You're* lucky he likes me or else he'd make you pay for these when he catches you sneaking them to me." I smirk and pop one in my mouth.

The bell dings again, and Will and I both turn as Pastor Elias walks in.

"Good morning, Pastor," Will greets.

"Will," Pastor Elias says in surprise. "Don't tell me your father has you stuck in here all day."

"Just this morning while he runs a few errands."

"That's good. It's too fine a day for someone so young to be cooped up out of the sun."

Will and I roll our eyes in unison.

Pastor Elias looks over at me. "Oh, hello, Evan. I barely recognized you at first."

"It's the boots," I say with pride. "They make me taller."

The pastor surveys me for a moment. "No," he says thoughtfully. "I think it's that vest."

"Do you like it? I made it with Mother's help."

"It's quite dashing." He pats me on the shoulder. *I'll never understand youth these days.*

I resist the urge to snort.

Will is the only one who knows about my gifts, as we call them. Being able to read the thoughts of anyone who touches me is just one of them. We have no idea where they came from, and we've never told a soul. As understanding as our little village is about the odd or eccentric, even they have their limits on what they can tolerate.

And the things I can do fall far beyond odd.

Will helps Pastor Elias gather the things his wife sent him to fetch, and the pastor pays the bill before taking his basket.

"Good day, gentlemen," he bids, but then he gives me an extra little knowing smile before he heads for the door.

"What was that look about?" Will asks after the bell announces the pastor's exit.

"I have no idea," I reply.

I hear Will's father swap happy hellos with the pastor before he walks into the store a heartbeat later. I smile at the man who's been like a second father to me my whole life. Will and I have always been so close that his father no doubt thought, like many did, that I would one day become his daughter through marriage, but that's just not how things ended up. Not that I don't adore Will, but we'll never be anything more than friends, for several reasons.

Will's father gives me a beaming smile as he approaches the counter. "Evange—sorry, Evan. How are you this morning?"

"Fine, sir. Will snuck me three peppermint candies."

Will smacks my arm, and I laugh.

His father laughs too. "Be careful or I'll ask you to work a few hours behind my counter to pay me back for all the sweets you've made off with over the years."

"I'll gladly help, sir. Any time."

Will's father holds up his hand and turns away as he falls into a sudden coughing fit. It's a wet, horrible sound that fills me with great concern.

"Are you alright?" I ask.

"Oh sure," he wheezes out between coughs. "It's nothing. Just a lingering cold, is all."

He struggles to breathe as the fit continues, so I put a hand on his back, feigning a simple comforting pat and rub.

I can feel this sickness, deep down in his lungs, and I will it away, slowly, so it doesn't raise his suspicion. My palm heats against his shirt far more than one would expect from a simple touch, and I pray he doesn't notice. After a moment, the coughing eases and he stands upright.

"I'm alright," he says. His voice is stronger.

As he stands there catching his breath, I keep my hand on his back until I don't feel any hint of the sickness left, then I drop my arm and step away.

He blinks in surprise and takes a deep, clear breath. "There, you see," he says, "it's getting better. A day or two more and I'll be right as rain."

"I'm sure you're right," I say, then I give Will a wink.

"Are you done with your errands?" Will asks. "I told Evan I'd help them carry their parcels to their wagon across town."

Will's father narrows his eyes. "And then you plan to disappear to spend the afternoon with Jacob, no doubt."

Will rubs his neck. "He did mention maybe going swimming later."

His father grunts. "Your mother isn't expecting another mouth to feed at dinner tonight, so if Jacob will be joining us again, you'd better let her know or else she's liable to skin you this time."

"Yes, sir."

"Well, go on then."

We don't need to be told twice.

On our way back down main street, Will and I are stopped no less than three times by various groups of friends to chat. My arms are throbbing from carrying my mother's overflowing basket by the time we get back to my cart tied off to old man Oren's fence. Will takes the basket and lowers it into the cart, but his eyes are on something down the dirt lane behind me. I turn to see a young woman—the one who'd stared after me when I passed the group of them earlier—standing near the corner of the fence, talking to Oren. Every so often, her eyes flick up to me as Oren drones on about one of his various pieces of gossip.

"It seems you have an admirer," Will remarks.

"I guess so."

She's maybe a year or two younger than me, and as I watch her, her cheeks turn pink under my stare. She's beautiful, that wasn't just a trick of the light before, but again, there's no reaction from my body or my heart. I sigh again.

"Nothing?" Will asks.

"No."

"I don't get it, Evan. You don't like a single man *or* woman in this village. What is it you're looking for, exactly?"

"I wish I knew, Will. Trust me, I wish I could look at her and get all weak in the knees, make a fool of myself asking her name, maybe sit beside her at church on Sunday and feel… something. But I don't." It's deeper than that, but I've never successfully explained it to him before, and I won't waste my breath trying again.

There are no words to explain this ache in my chest day and night, like I've known some loss great enough it brings me to tears in bed when I'm alone with nothing left to distract me. All things considered, I have a great life full of people who love and accept me. I'm grateful, but at the same time, I long for something else, something more, though I have no idea what.

I shake my head and focus on other things like I always do when such thoughts threaten to overwhelm me. "How are things with you and Jacob?"

The little smile that crosses Will's face at my question tells me plenty, far more than the simple "Good" he gives me for an answer.

"When are you going to ask that boy to marry you?" I ask, taking no prisoners.

This time, Will chuckles and rubs his neck again. "I don't know."

"Perhaps sooner rather than later? Maybe I'll meet my special someone at your wedding."

My chest aches a little harder, and the thought that always seems to ruin every touching moment crashes into me once more.

There is no one and nothing for me here.

Chapter 79

Back home, I toss my parcels onto the kitchen table along with the basket.

"Mother!" I yell. "They came!"

"What are you hollering about, child?" she asks moodily as she comes into the kitchen a moment later. Her eyes fall on the packages on the table, and her scowl instantly smooths into a smile. "Is that your order?"

"I'm not expecting anything else."

She grabs sheers from a drawer and snips off the twine on each parcel, and I come along behind and rip open the paper. Out falls a pair of men's dress pants, a dress shirt, a cravat, dress shoes, three work shirts, and a pair of work pants, all brand new. My mother triple checked the measurements on the catalog form before we sent it to make sure every article of clothing was tailor made to fit my frame perfectly. No more cinched belts or wrapping my breasts to fit into my father's old clothes.

My mother picks up the dress pants and holds them against me. She clicks her tongue. "They still look about an inch too long, but I can fix that in an evening."

"Before Sunday?" I ask anxiously.

She huffs but says, "Yes, I can hem them up before Sunday." She picks up the dress shirt next, holding it against my chest and tucking it under my arms to check the fit. "It's hard to tell with your wrap on, but this looks right."

"Can I still wear my vest over it, do you think?"

"Not to church. It doesn't go with the pants or the cravat. We'll have to make you a jacket once the weather turns."

We're discussing fabrics and colors when there's a knock on the screen door.

The twinkle in my mother's eye says she knows who it is, but she doesn't say anything as she goes to answer the door. Her voice is one of feigned surprise as she says, "Good afternoon, Elias. What brings you out this way?"

"Afternoon, ma'am." Elias V, Pastor Elias' son, walks into the kitchen a few seconds later with his hat in his hands. He smiles at me. "Good afternoon, Evangeline."

"Good afternoon. It's Evan today," I correct him.

I always have to correct him.

He nods but doesn't apologize or correct himself. Instead, he asks, "Can I sit down with you and your parents for a moment?"

My mother answers for me. "Of course you can, Elias. Evan, offer your guest a drink while I round up your father."

She ushers us into the sitting room where my father is already hovering. He must've been told about this meeting in advance and ordered not to wander too far, which is likely pure torture for him since his mare is due to foal any minute. He's practically lived in the stables the past few days.

I narrow my eyes at him as I cross the room to my favorite chair. He could have warned me.

He merely shrugs back at me, looking sheepish.

Once we're all seated—except my father who chooses to stand next to my chair—my mother asks the question she no doubt already knows the answer to.

"What brings you by to see us today, Elias?"

Elias clears his throat and spins his hat in his hands. "Well, as you all know, I'm to take my father's place as the head of our little church in the years to come. In order to do that, it's important that I stand as a pillar of society and a prime example of the type of person we should all strive to be. For a man, that's a husband and a father to as many children as God will bless him with. My father and I have talked, and we've decided that, before I begin leading any sermons, I should take a wife."

Elias looks directly at me as he continues. "I'm young and healthy and have my own homestead next to my father's where I can build any house my wife would like with room to grow to fit the family I dream of having with her someday. All I need is the right woman to help me make that dream a reality. I've decided that woman is you, Evangeline."

"My name is Evan, and I am not a woman," I say testily.

My father's hand rests softly on my shoulder.

Dear Lord, grant my child the strength and patience to deal with this ignorant fool. This match could help make their every dream come true.

The fact that my father wants this so badly is all that keeps me from getting up from my chair, bidding Elias good day, and leaving the room.

"I understand you're... different," Elias says carefully. "That doesn't change my opinion that we'd be a good match." He looks up at my father. "I'm officially requesting your daughter's hand in marriage."

I look up at my father too, and he stares down at me, chewing his cheek as he considers.

"Evan has never spoken of a desire to wed you, Elias," my father says, slowly, choosing each word with care. "I am not altogether against the idea, but I won't force them to marry someone they don't want. If you want my child's hand, you'll have to earn their affection first."

I've never loved my father more than I do in this moment.

Elias looks at me. "Are you willing to spend some time with me—chaperoned, if you prefer—to see if we'd be a compatible match?"

"A chaperone won't be necessary," I say. "If you try anything unseemly in my company, no wife you ever take will give you children." When he blinks at me in confusion, I cross one leg over the other and lean back in my chair as I clarify. "I'll rid you of your manhood the instant you try to take anything I don't willingly give, including my hand in marriage."

"Evan," my mother hisses.

My father coughs to suppress a laugh.

To my surprise, Elias smiles. "This is why I think we'd be a good match. We're equally witty and independent people, you and I. We certainly won't be bored together."

"The question is whether or not we can stand each other."

"Care to find out?"

I consider it. Despite the fact that I have no desire for a husband or a wife, I've reached an age where I will soon become a burden to my parents. If I don't marry, the state of my family's land will be in constant question since I'm an only child with no male relatives. Marrying Elias would secure not only my own future but my parents' as well. And Elias is strong and handsome, if not a bit irritating at times. The question remains whether or not he can accept me for who I truly am, or if he's merely hoping for a good little housewife to latch onto his arm for appearances' sake.

"We can start now," I say, and I hop to my feet. "I need to do my chores. Feel free to join me, if you like."

"Oh, umm…" Elias looks at my mother and father, but when neither of them speaks a word to rescue him, he looks back at me. "I was thinking perhaps a picnic or a walk down the south road. The flowers at the woods' edge are beautiful. I saw them myself on the ride over."

"Like I said, I have chores to attend to. You can either join me, or I'll see you at church on Sunday."

Elias' mouth snaps shut, and he nods. "Alright. I'll join you."

I stop by the back door just long enough to grab the egg basket, then I stomp outside with Elias hot on my heels. We get about halfway across the yard before I stop and round on him.

"Now that we're alone,"—I cross my arms with the egg basket teetering on one finger—"Out with it. Why do you *really* want to marry me?"

He surprises me with a real answer. "You're a hard worker, you don't let anyone tell you what you want in life, but most of all, you didn't immediately start batting your eyes at me the moment you were of age."

I blink at him. "You like me because I *don't* like *you*?"

"It's more than that, but… yes? I want a partner in life who will love and respect me, sure, but mostly I want a partner who can stand on their own two feet, who can see me as their equal and not their prize to be won."

"That's a fair thing to want, I suppose." I uncross my arms. "But, Elias, you say you know I'm 'different', but do you really? Do you understand what it would mean for you if we got married?"

"Explain it to me."

"It would mean that some days you'd have a wife like you want, but there would also be days when you'd wake up with a husband instead. And there would be days when you'd have neither. Are you prepared for that?"

Elias' brow crinkles. "It's truly gone that far?"

"Not only has it gone that far, but I won't be going back. I'm not a woman. I've told you this many times. If we married, I'd expect you to respect my names, all of them, and never to call me 'she' ever again. You'd have no say over my wardrobe either. I'll wear whatever makes me happy in the moment. I'm a hopeless cook too. Just ask my mother. And I have no desire to learn. I'd rather be in the stables or fishing or"—I brandish the basket at him—"collecting eggs. I can sew a decent stitch, though, so I suppose we won't freeze while we starve to death."

Elias crosses his arms. "You're mocking it now."

"I'm not. I'm being honest. You say you like me because I never pursued you as a husband. That's because I have no desire to be a wife. If all you want is a partner to hook onto your arm in order to appease your father so you can take his place, I may be open to that arrangement, but it'll happen on my terms. And I don't know yet if I want children, so I can't even promise you that much."

He studies me, and I almost wish we were touching so I can hear what's going on in that mind. After a long silence, he lifts his chin and says, "If I hired a full-time cook and the best nanny I can find, would you consider children?"

So it's a negotiation now, is it? I consider my own terms. "As long as all my aforementioned conditions are met as well and my parents never want for anything as they age, I'd consider children."

He smiles at me. "Good."

"That's not me agreeing yet. We still don't even know if we can stand each other's company."

"If this conversation is any judge, I think we'll do just fine." When I open my mouth to argue, he holds up his hand. "But I understand. You want time. I'm a patient man—"

I snort. "There's no such thing."

He ignores my comment. "Just don't leave me waiting too long, alright?"

I nod.

He puts his hat back on, adjusting it just right before offering me his hand.

I shake it.

Father will be pleased.

"No promises," I remind him.

He bows his head at me. "I'll see you at church."

As he leaves, that ache in my chest intensifies, and I rub it. I want to cry, but I haven't done that in years. That overwhelming feeling of loss is back, and it has nothing to do with the man walking away from me, that much I'm sure of. I wish I knew how to banish it for good.

"Please tell me what I should do," I pray quietly. "Help me find what's missing, I beg you, because I can't take this anymore." I rub my chest and squeeze my eyes shut, willing the answers to come to me. I can feel them, like a tickle up the back of my neck, but all I get for my efforts is a headache.

I march off toward the chicken coop to collect the eggs.

Chapter 80

I'm flying. I don't have wings myself, but the being holding me tight in his arms does. I'm warm and comfortable and… happy. When I feel the dream slipping away, I want to cry.

Please don't leave me.

Evangeline.

The voice in my head is a low and powerful growl. It doesn't even sound human.

I realize the thought came from the being carrying me, and I look up, eager to see his face. I catch just a hint of glowing white before the dream is ripped away from me.

"No…"

"Evangeline!"

"Wh…what?" I blink awake. My father is standing by my bed, shaking my shoulder.

"The mare is foaling," he says in a rush. "Come quickly. I need you."

I sit up and throw my legs out of bed. "How is she?"

My father chucks my boots at me from the door. "Her water broke nearly an hour ago."

"An hour!" I've never gotten my boots and robe on so fast in my life.

We fly down the stairs, and it's a miracle neither of us breaks our neck.

"What's happening?" my mother calls sleepily from the top of the stairs.

"I need Evangeline's help in the stables," my father yells before we both sail out the door, slamming the screen in our wake.

The stables are warm, and I can smell blood before we even reach the foaling stall. The mare is on her side and breathing hard, clearly near exhaustion already from pushing and getting nowhere. When my father and I enter the stall, she has the energy for a twitch of her ears in our direction but not much else.

"I fear it's positioned badly and can't pass," Papa says, and he kneels next to the mare's back end. "I need to reach in and maneuver it. Can you try and keep her calm while I do?"

I kneel at the mare's head and start talking to her. She's tired enough now that she puts up no fight as Papa reaches inside her to check on her baby. I try to stay focused on her, but I keep peeking over at Papa, waiting anxiously for him to tell me what he feels. He grimaces, and my heart sinks.

"What is it?" I ask.

"It's backward."

"How many legs can you feel?"

He looks gravely up at me. "Only one."

"Can you reposition the other?"

"I'll try."

The wait is agony. My father grunts and groans as he works to free the foal's other hind leg without injuring the mother. She's so tired she's barely pushing anymore.

"Don't give up, mama," I tell her. "We'll give you a healthy baby yet. You just wait and see."

"I got it!"

I could cry with relief. "Can you grab them both?"

"I think so. Just give me a minute."

Several grunts and a few choice swear words later, my father has the foal's feet out, but the mare isn't pushing at all anymore.

"Come on, girl," he says. "Help an old man out, would you?"

To my surprise, she does. Whether because she understood him or because she can sense the end of this birth is near, she starts to push again, her stomach rippling as she puts the last of her strength into delivering her baby.

"Evangeline," my father hisses between puffing breaths. "I need you… to help… pull."

I leave the mare's head and come to my father's side. There isn't much room for both of us, but I take the leg Papa offers me, place my hands where he tells me, and pull.

Slowly but surely, the foal slides out of the mare. When its front feet are free, my father and I both whoop with joy, but it's a short celebration.

It's a beautiful jet-black colt.

He's not breathing.

"Come on, baby," my father says as he cleans the colt's mouth and nose. "The hard part's over. I just need you to breathe now. Come on."

I grab clean blankets from the top of the stall wall and start rubbing the colt down as my father pokes a long piece of straw into the baby's nose.

There's no response.

"Come on, pretty boy," my father coaxes. "Just one big breath."

When the colt still shows no signs of life, my father sniffs and wipes his face with his sleeve.

"Papa?" I call softly.

He looks up at me, and the tears in his eyes shatter my heart.

"Let me try."

I slide across the floor and take the baby into my lap. I don't care that he's filthy. With one hand, I rub him with the blanket as I speak to him the same way Papa did.

With my other hand, I touch my palm to his chest.

Please heal him. Please let him live. Please.

My palm heats up, and I pray and wish and hope with every ounce of my soul that this works.

At first, I think it's not going to.

But then…

It starts with a twitch of an ear, then one eye flutters, and after a moment, the nostrils flare as the colt takes one startled breath, then another. His long legs start kicking, and he lifts his head enough to look at my father.

"There you are," Papa utters, and he releases a shaky, emotional breath of relief. "Good job, Evangeline. I thought things had gone terribly wrong there for a moment."

"He's fine, Papa," I say, but I keep my hand on the colt's chest for as long as I can, flooding him with life through my palm until I'm sure he'll be alright when I let go. "Just fine."

*****

Both mother and baby make it through the night. As the sun rises, I stand outside the stall door, watching the colt wobble around after his mother, nursing and exploring this new world he came into so chaotically.

Papa names him Midnight. He's already absolutely smitten.

For a moment, I'm envious of my father. I wish I could love and enjoy something as fully as my father loves his animals. He's a farmer through and through. I wish I had that passion for it. I wish I had passion for anything. Everything feels so dull to me, like the world's been washed out, its colors faded like the paint on the barn we have to redo every couple of years.

I wish I could take a paintbrush to my soul.

After tending to a few chores, Papa joins me at the stall door and puts his arm over my shoulders.

"We did good, kid," he says.

I only nod.

He peers sideways at me. "What's wrong?"

I shrug. "I don't know."

"You've seemed unhappy since Elias' visit. If I'm honest, you've been unhappy for a long time before that, but it seems like that day made it worse."

I hug my filthy robes tighter around myself. "You're right on all accounts."

"You don't have to marry him, you know."

"I know, but I don't know what else to do. No one else has asked me, and I have no desire to ask anyone myself. I have no money and no other plans for my life. If Elias and I can at least tolerate each other, life with him wouldn't be so bad. I could do worse."

"You could leave and find better."

I bark with humorless laughter. "Where would I go?"

Papa shrugs. "You could go to the city. Perhaps Will's aunt would let you stay with her again while you figure out a plan for your life. Your own plan."

"I couldn't leave you and Mother like that," I scoff. "What would happen to you and the farm as you both age?"

"That's not your concern."

"Papa…"

"Evangeline… is it Evangeline today?"

"It's an Eve day, I think."

He turns to me, and I turn away from the stall to face him too.

"It's not your burden to bear that you were born an only child," he says. "I know you. This life isn't what you want. I've seen it in your eyes since you were a little thing. I confess that, when Elias first asked, I was happy for you and hoped the two of you could work it out, but now? Now, I think you're destined for something much, much bigger. Please don't marry Elias on your mother and I's account."

"I haven't decided anything yet."

"Well, whatever you decide, choose it because it will make *you* happy, first and foremost. Promise me."

I'm torn. On one hand, I'd love to prioritize my own happiness, but on the other, I don't know that I could live with myself if I simply walked away. At the thought of staying, though, my chest starts to hurt again. Perhaps this *is* the answer.

"Eve," Papa says sternly. "Promise me."

I haven't made Elias or anyone else any promises, so I refuse to feel guilty as I make this one to my father.

"I promise, Papa."

*****

Back in my room, I change out of my soiled nightgown and toss it and my robes into the hall for my mother to scrub. I wash up, but before I get dressed again, I study myself in the mirror next to my dresser, my eyes instantly going to the two small, round scars on my chest, just above my left breast. Birthmarks, I correct myself. Not scars. My mother swears they were there when I was born, but they don't look like any birthmark I've ever seen. I have the exact same marks on one of my shoulders as well as one high up on my inner thigh. There's also a small spot that could be another on the palm of my hand.

I reach up and touch the ones on my chest, feeling the divots at their centers. I know these aren't birthmarks, but I have no idea exactly what they are or where they came from. The ache in my chest intensifies, and I can't hold it together anymore. I sink to my knees in front of the mirror and burst into tears.

Something is horribly wrong.

I use my hand to search my body for any sign of illness.

I find none.

I ask, in my mind, for it to give me life.

Nothing happens.

"I don't understand," I say between sobs. I look up at my ceiling, though I'm not entirely sure why. I stopped praying to God years ago. "If you would just tell me where to go, I'll go. Tell me what to do, and I'll do it. Just please, make me whole."

As always, there is no answer, so I rise, dress, and climb into bed.

*****

I'm standing next to the halfway tree by the south road, staring down the footpath that leads into the forest. A slight breeze whips down the path and past my face, bringing with it the smell of ancient trees and moss. I take a single step, and suddenly, I'm so far down the path I can no longer see the road. I keep walking, letting the sounds and smells of this place wash over me.

I've always loved it here. The others fear these woods, but not me. They feel like home.

I step from the trees into a clearing. It's nothing special, just a clearing bathed in golden sunlight, but a peaceful haze washes over me nonetheless, as if that light is an old friend. A circle of grey stones sits in the center of this space, and the ground between them shimmers a bit as if flickering in and out of existence entirely.

The ground under my feet rumbles. I don't know what it means and yet I'm giddy with excitement. I walk over and kneel beside the circle. The ground is shaking so hard now the stones roll a bit, tapping against each other in a way that almost sounds like music. I reach out and touch one.

Hello again, *says a voice in my head that sounds like crumbling stone.* They're waiting for you.

I wake up with a start as my mother calls my name softly from the doorway, asking me if I'd like some lunch.

As I get up and dress, I think of that clearing and that voice in my head that sounded like gravel under wagon wheels, and I feel something I haven't felt in so long I'd forgotten such a thing existed until now.

Hope.

Chapter 81

Sunday is in fact an Evan day.

I wake up excited for the first time in a long while, and I avoid the mirror to keep from spoiling my mood as I button, tuck, and tie myself into my new outfit before pinning my hair up as tight as I possibly can. I won't be able to wear my hat to church, so this will have to do. Only once I'm dressed do I face my reflection, and the sound of giggling glee that escapes me makes me laugh twice.

I look handsome.

I practice my deep, masculine voice until my mother calls for me to hurry so we're not late. When I come down the stairs, she blinks up at me in happy surprise.

"That looks wonderful on you, dear," she says, though she fusses over my cravat and tells me to stand up straight.

When Papa rounds the corner from the sitting room, even he's stunned to silence momentarily before he nods with a smile of pride.

I beam back at him.

My mother utters my father's name like a curse. "You were in the stables in your Sunday clothes again, weren't you?" Before he can come up with some clever lie, she points down at the bottoms of his pants, which are flecked with little dots of mud.

"I was just checking on the baby before we left is all," he says, then he kisses her on the cheek. "Sorry, dear."

Her anger deflates under my father's loving stare. "I ought to make you change them, but we haven't the time. Let's go, both of you. I won't be late to service again because of your foolishness."

We take the south road to church, as always, and when we pass the halfway tree, I stare down the footpath beyond it, remembering the peaceful happiness I felt in that clearing in my dream and wishing more than anything I could find that feeling in the waking world. As our wagon drives by, I have to fight the temptation to jump out and run down the path in search of that clearing and its strange, talking circle of stones.

*****

Despite my mother's worries, we arrive at church in plenty of time. We pull our wagon in line with the others and swap greetings with neighbors and friends we rarely get time to see outside of Sunday service.

Percival and his husband park their wagon next to ours. "Good morning!" Percival bids cheerfully. "How's the new foal?"

Percival is married to old man Oren's son, Roderick. Together, they raise birds on a farm on the east side of the village. They raise everything from simple chickens to more exotic things like owls and peacocks. They even have a pet parrot. Will used to work there during the summer when we were younger, and I'd bring him lunch on occasion just to get a chance to see the animals. Percival and Roderick were always more than happy to give me a tour and show me all the new babies.

"He's doing just fine," Papa replies with pride.

"Oh, so it's a colt after all," says Levi as he and his wife walk by the back of our wagon.

I've been out to the feed mill with Papa on many occasions, so I've known Levi most of my life. There's never anything but kindness in his eyes, which is why, about two years ago, when he shot his neighbor's son early one morning while hunting, no one doubted for an instant it was anything more than a tragic accident. The boy almost died, but when I heard how bad it was, I convinced my mother to take a basket of preserves and fresh eggs over to the boy's mother, just to be neighborly. As the two women talked, no one paid me any mind as I touched the boy's shoulder and made sure, in my way, that he'd get better.

"It's a beautiful colt, Levi," I say. "He's black as the starless sky."

"How's his temperament so far?" Levi asks.

Papa reaches up to help my mother down from the wagon. "It's a bit early to tell for sure, but he seems like a curious, friendly, and independent little thing. His mother and I both have quite a time keeping him out of trouble, but he doesn't mind my fussing so far."

"Will you be gelding him?"

"I'm not sure yet. If his temperament continues to impress, he may make an excellent stud."

"Let me know. I have a mare I've considered breeding. She's a beauty herself and one of my sweetest. Oy, Percival! Roderick! Hold up a moment, please."

The two men pause on their way inside.

"Good morning, Levi," Percival greets.

"Good morning. I have a request to make of you, if you don't mind."

"What can we do for you?" Roderick asks.

"My granddaughter's got it in her head she wants to raise ducks. Can I bring her out to your place this week and let her see what it takes to raise them? I want to make sure she knows what she's getting into before her father and I build a second coop."

"If they already have a decent sized chicken coop, they can stay in there," says Percival. "No need to build a second one at all. But bring her on by anyway. If she's still set on it by the time you leave, I've got some babies she can take home with her."

A familiar wagon pulls up the church driveway, and I break away from the others to double back as Will and his family arrives.

"Good morning, Evan," Will's mother greets me warmly.

Will hops down out of the wagon before it even stops moving. He whistles as he looks me up and down. "Look at you! You look great."

"My mother had to hem the pants," I say. "But everything else fits me perfectly."

"Did you order these clothes from that catalog you were talking about?" Will's mother asks.

"Yes, ma'am."

She touches the sleeve of my shirt and looks down at my pants and shoes. "Very nice. I might have to order some things for Will and his father before the wedding."

"Wedding?" I ask. "Whose wedding?"

Will clears his throat. "Mine," he says sheepishly. "Jacob asked me last night."

The squeal of utter joy that comes out of me no doubt makes the whole church stare, but I don't care a bit as I throw my arms around my best friend and hug him so tight he grunts in my ear.

"I'm so happy for you," I say, then I kiss him on the cheek.

"Hey now," says a familiar voice from behind me, and I turn as Jacob walks up. "If I didn't know better, I'd think you were trying to steal him from me, Evan."

I haul Jacob into a far more dignified but no less happy hug. "Will just told me the news. Congratulations!"

"Thank you. I had a feeling he was going to ask himself eventually, but"—Jacob smirks—"he was taking too long."

I laugh. "I just told him that the other—"

"There you are, Evangeline," Elias says as he joins us. "I was looking for you."

"Evan," Will says, and his face loses all hint of a smile as he regards Elias. "It's clearly an Evan day today."

Elias studies me, pretending to notice how I'm dressed for the first time. "Ah… so it is." He smiles at me and manages not to make it look completely forced. "Would you join my mother and I for service this morning?"

"Oh, um…" I remember the promise I made to Papa, but I also did tell Elias I would spend time with him to see if we could possibly make this work. Sitting with him in church certainly isn't accepting his proposal. I can give him this much. "Alright."

Will wrinkles his brow but doesn't say anything. He doesn't have to. I know what he's thinking without having to touch him, and I give him an apologetic smile before we all head inside the church together.

It's stifling in here this morning. Elias motions me ahead of him down the aisle to the very front row where his mother is already perched. She looks up from her bible as Elias and I come to the end of the pew.

"Oh, good morning, dear," she says. She always calls me 'dear' or 'child' or 'sweetie'. Never my name. I know she does it to avoid having to call me by my preferred names, and though it annoys me, she's never been anything but kind to me, so I don't say anything. "Will you be joining us?"

"Yes, ma'am."

She scoots down the pew enough for Elias and I to sit beside her—Elias at the end with me sitting between them—and I immediately feel squashed and overheated. I peek over my shoulder at my parents to find my mother beaming at us. She gives me an excited little wave. My father is chewing his lip like he always does when he's bothered. I don't need my powers to know what he's thinking right now either.

The last of the village files in and sits down, and a hushed silence falls as Pastor Elias steps up to the pulpit with his bible. The book is so aged it looks ready to fall apart, but he gently sets it on the stand and lays it open with care so that none of the pages fall out of place. He clears his throat and smiles at his gathered flock, but before he starts service, his eyes fall on Elias and I, and he smiles in pleasant surprise.

As his father launches into his sermon, Elias sets his arm on the back of the pew behind me, and when he does, he drapes his hand across my shoulder.

That's right, father. Not only have I found a wife, but it's the woman no man ever thought they could convince to marry. You doubted me, but I'll show you. Once Evangeline and I have exchanged our vows, I'll do away with all this nonsense. Multiple names, men's clothing, chores not fit for a proper lady… I'll do away with it all and show you the strength of my faith as a man of God. Maybe then you'll be proud.

His hand squeezes my shoulder.

I launch out of the pew and onto my feet, stopping Pastor Elias mid-sentence as I round on his son.

"You wretched beast!" I snarl. "You lied to me!"

"Evangeline," Elias' mother says in shock. "Sit down this instant."

I ignore her and continue addressing her snake of a son. "You said you wanted to marry me because you respect me, but you only chose me to impress your father, didn't you?"

Elias narrows his eyes, no doubt confused how I know this. "I don't know what you're talking about."

"I don't care if you admit it or not, Elias. My answer is no. I wouldn't marry you if you were the last man on this Earth!"

I turn to walk back down the aisle.

Elias grabs my arm, painfully hard.

"Sit. Down," he says in a low voice between gritted teeth. "We'll talk about this later, but right now, you're causing a scene in the middle of service. Don't embarrass yourself any more than you already have."

I try to pull my arm free, but he refuses to let go. I reach down and take hold of his wrist.

Let. Me. Go.

Slowly, the strength in his whole arm slips away. His muscles twitch as he tries to regain control, and his eyes widen as his fingers slowly relax against his will. I pry them off of me.

"Don't ever touch me again," I hiss, then I march away down the aisle.

The pew creaks as he gets up to follow me, and I quicken my steps.

When I pass Will's pew, he stands and steps into the aisle, slamming his hand into Elias' shoulder and stopping him in his tracks.

"They said 'no'," Will says sternly.

I stand behind my best friend and glare at Elias over his shoulder.

"Stay out of this," Elias barks.

Jacob stands up from the seat next to Will's and steps into the aisle too. He stands next to his betrothed and crosses his arms.

Will's father stands up too. "I think you should go back to your seat, son," he says sternly.

Across the aisle, my father stands up next.

Two rows behind him, Percival and Roderick stand as well.

Then Levi in the back.

A handful of others follow suit, some I've barely exchanged more than a word or two with my entire life. They all lock hostile eyes on Elias, daring him to take one more step toward me.

I'm misty eyed with gratitude.

Elias looks livid.

"Elias," Pastor Elias calls, and when his son looks back at him, he shakes his head, his face one of deep disappointment.

Elias shoves Will's hand away and stalks back up the aisle. He plops into the seat next to his mother, lounges back, and crosses his legs like nothing happened at all. As everyone starts sitting back down, I turn and leave the church.

This service already taught me the lesson I needed.

Back outside in the fresh air, I stop on the steps and catch my breath. My heart is pounding painfully hard in my chest, and I can't stop my hands from shaking as I tuck a stray hair behind my ear. I'm angry, mostly at myself. I should never have given that weasel the benefit of the doubt. Above me, the sun is shining, bathing the church's front lawn in golden light. It reminds me of the clearing from my dream again, and I'm so absorbed in the hope and happiness the image brings me that I jump when the door opens behind me, but it's only Will.

"Are you alright?" he asks.

Am I? "I think so. I don't know, Will. Everything's just…"

"Why did you agree to sit with that bastard in the first place?"

I mentally prepare myself for the tongue lashing I know is coming as I say, "Elias asked me to marry him."

"I gathered that, but I don't understand why you didn't tell him no the moment he asked."

"I should have, I know that now, but… I thought that, at the very least, having a husband would protect my parents' farm when—"

"No one here would dare take your inheritance away from you," Will interjects with a stern look. "If anyone tried, the whole village would step in. You know we would. Or was that not proof enough for you." He gestures back toward the door of the church with his thumb.

He's right of course, and I know in my heart that was a weak excuse on my part to avoid confronting my true desires. "I'd hoped for a moment, a short and foolish one, that he might be the answer to this longing in my heart. Perhaps he wouldn't banish it completely, but I'd hoped a husband might fill it a little, enough that I could be happy."

"Elias is not the answer, Evan. He's a selfish bully. He hides it well, but we both know it's true. Just look how his friendship with Percival ended. That is not a man who can make you happy, and you know it."

I don't reply because there's nothing to say.

The door of the church opens again and Jacob steps outside. "Is everything alright?" he asks.

I manage a smile. "Yes. I think I'll just be going home."

"I'll go with you," Will says.

I nod and start down the steps as Will kisses Jacob goodbye.

"Don't be too long," Jacob says. "Your mother has brunch planned."

"I know. I'll meet you there."

We borrow two of Will's brothers' horses and head down the south road since it's the quickest way back to my family's farm.

As much as I hate to admit it, Elias was right about one thing: the south road is one of the most beautiful places to be this time of year. The wildflowers that grow in large blankets between the road and the edge of the woods have always been a haven for bees and butterflies as well as the occasional rabbit or even a fox or two, and since few travel this road from day to day, the creatures that venture out of the trees have little to fear. I once had a rabbit come take a carrot straight out of my hand. To me, this place feels like it belongs in a fairytale. And that's before you even enter the woods.

There's something about the trees here that feels otherworldly. They make most of the people in the village uncomfortable, though I don't understand why. These woods were like a second home to me growing up, but I never ventured too deep, mostly because that made it all the farther I had to walk back home. The forest calls to me today like it did when I explored here as a child, so much so that, when we reach the halfway tree, I rein my horse to a stop.

"What is it?" Will asks, swinging his horse back around to come up beside me in the road.

"I don't know," I say, my eyes finding the path beyond the halfway tree, the one I walked in my dream. Will and I used to adventure down it occasionally, though whenever we mention it in the village, no one else ever remembers such a path. I long to walk it again now. "I guess I just don't feel like going home yet."

Will follows my gaze. "What, you want to go in there instead?"

The ache in my chest intensifies at the question, so the answer comes out a tad bit breathless. "Yes."

Will shrugs. "I suppose I have time for a walk. A short one, mind you. I can't be gone too long because of—"

"Brunch," I say with a smirk. "I know."

"Pastor Elias is invited," he says. "We're to discuss dates and plans for the ceremony."

I turn my horse and head for the halfway tree. "It will no doubt be a beautiful day. Your mother will make sure of that."

Will follows me to the tree and slides off his horse, tying it to a post we installed out here years ago for just such a purpose. "Since Jacob's mother is no longer with us, I'm afraid mine is trying way too hard to make up the difference." He takes my horse's reins and ties them off too before I've even dismounted. "As soon as Jacob and I told her the news, she started making plans. Jacob says he's never seen her so… energetic."

I laugh as I slide out of the saddle. "I can only imagine. Mine would no doubt be the same. If she becomes too much, ask your father to gently reel her in."

Will snorts. "Like he could ever tell her no. She could say she wants to have the wedding on the moon, and he'd just smile and nod. 'Of course, dear. That would look lovely'." Will looks up at the bright white orb in question and frowns. "Speaking of which, it looks as if it's a full moon right now. Are you sure you want to go wandering in the woods?"

"Don't tell me you believe those old stories of beasts that transform by the light of a full moon," I say as I step toward the path.

"I believe that we can't possibly know everything there is to know about the world. Who's to say those stories aren't seeded in truth?"

I roll my eyes. "It's a good thing, then, that I've brought a strapping young man with me, isn't it?" I clap him on the shoulder.

He raises one brow at me. *If some werebeast* does *find us, I'm tripping you and leaving you behind.*

"That's alright. I'll be sure to haunt you and your new husband for all eternity. Try to outrun me then."

Will laughs heartily and throws his arm over my shoulders as we cross into the woods.

Chapter 82

The woods surround me like the hug of an old friend, and I find my mood lightening the further Will and I walk. Once we can no longer see the fields of flowers, the road, or our horses, I'm laughing and joking in a way I haven't since we were teens. I study the trees and try to figure out what it is about this place that makes others uncomfortable. They look no different than any others. The underbrush is green and inviting. There are birds chirping and rodents shuffling, so there's obviously life here. After about twenty minutes of walking, interrupted only by the sounds of nature and our footsteps, I think I've found my answer.

This place feels old.

No doubt such a thing could be said about many forests throughout the world, but this one…

Large sheets of moss hang between the trees, stretching from one trunk to the next and hanging clear to the forest floor like deep green blankets on some magical forest creature's clothesline. The trees are so tall I can't see the tops when I look up through the canopy, which is so dense the light here is muted to a dusky gold no matter the time of day. It's always warmer here, as if the closely packed trees are breathing, pumping the air with their hot breath to heat the space. It's so warm here in the winter that the snow rarely sticks.

And the smell.

There's nothing quite like it. The woods near the river by our farm don't smell anything like this, and again, I imagine the trees breathing like Will and I, exhaling their woodsy scents into the air hour after hour, day after day. It's so potent that, whenever I head home after spending any amount of time here, the smell clings to my clothes and hair for days afterward.

I breathe that scent deep into my lungs and run a hand across the bark of a tree that leans further into the path than the rest. The feel of it makes me giggle. Why don't I come here more often? Life, I suppose. There's always a hundred things to do and half as much time as I need to get it all done. I wish I knew what about this place brings me peace so I could find it out there.

Will and I continue our walk, but after another ten minutes, we come to a fork in the path.

"Do you remember there being a second path out here?" I ask.

"No," Will says, bewildered. He points down the right trail, the one that's a continuation of the path we're currently standing on. "This goes straight into the woods and stops at the base of that rocky ridge where you cut your knee that summer, remember?" He points down the left one. "But this one was never here before. It was always just the one trail."

I take Will's hand and tug him toward the left path. "Let's see where it goes."

"I was about to suggest we head back."

"Oh, come on. It hasn't been an hour. Service isn't even over yet."

"No, but an hour walk in is another hour walk out."

The thought of leaving makes that pain return to my chest. "Please?"

Will sighs, and after a moment's stern stare, he allows me to tug him along down the left path, deeper into the forest.

As we walk, the trees grow denser, the moss starts to dissipate, and the natural sounds of the woods die down as the birds and other creatures become scarce. It's as if we've stepped into the very heart of the woods, and as we keep walking, my own heart starts to race in excitement. I don't know why, but I feel drawn forward so hard I start walking faster until I'm almost running.

"Evan?" Will says as he struggles to keep up with me even with his much longer legs. "We should probably head back."

I stop, though it hurts my heart to do so, and turn around to face him. When I do, I blink in shock as I look past him back the way we came.

"What?" Will asks, his tone suddenly anxious at the look on my face. He spins around and swears, backing away so fast he almost trips over a stray root until I grab his arm to steady him.

The path is gone. We're clearly standing on it, but the trail we just came down is nowhere in sight. It ends a few feet behind us at a wall of trees and brush so dense we can't see through it much less find a path through.

"Witchcraft," Will mutters.

"It's alright," I say. I don't know where my sudden calm comes from, but somehow, in my heart, I know that whatever is responsible for this doesn't mean us any harm. "We just need to keep going."

"Are you crazy?" Will asks. His wide eyes stare down the path in front of us, which is still there, open and inviting us to continue deeper into the woods. "This is unnatural. Whatever lies at the other end, it can't be good."

"Do you trust me?"

Will's eyes bore into mine, and I can see the conflict in them. This place doesn't speak to him like it does to me. I take his hand.

I'm scared, he tells me.

"I'm not. I don't know how, but I feel like I know where I am. This place feels familiar."

He doesn't look convinced, but he stares again down the path before us and eventually nods. *I trust you.*

"Of course you do," I say with a smirk. "When am I ever wrong?"

When he opens his mouth, I put a finger over it.

"That was rhetorical."

He rolls his eyes at me, and I laugh as we start walking again.

We both try to resist the urge to look back, but we do so anyway every couple of minutes. Each time we do, we find the thick wall of trees right behind us. It's unnerving, even for me, but we continue trudging forward. An hour goes by then another with no end in sight.

"Jacob will be wondering where I am by now," Will comments.

"Don't worry, you can make it up to him later."

"If there is a later," he mutters.

I click my tongue at him but don't reply as we keep on walking.

Another twenty minutes later, I see sunlight ahead.

"Look, I think we're at the end!" I say, barely containing my excitement.

"Oh… great."

"Come on." I pick up speed, but Will grabs my arm.

"Slow down. We don't know what's up there."

But I do. I know because we're close enough now that I can see the clearing. The clearing from my dreams. Rather than slow down as Will requests, I want to run. My heart is racing as we enter the clearing at the exact place I did in my dream. The circle of grey stones is just ahead, and I strike out across the clearing toward it.

"What are you doing?" Will asks.

"I've been here before." I stop in front of the circle and kneel.

"Evan?"

I set my palm against the nearest stone.

Hello again.

A stifled sob of relief bursts out of me. "H…hello."

They're waiting for you.

"Who's waiting?"

"Who are you talking to?" Will asks.

Your stoferras.

"My what?"

"Evan, who—"

The ground begins to shake, and I fall over on my backside. Will hauls me up on my feet and pulls me back away from the circle as the ground inside it begins to shift and change. The air suddenly grows even warmer, and a circle of shimmering red appears between the stones. I see rolling hills of red sand for a split second before a large gold and dark blue figure bursts out from the circle and shoots straight up into the air. It's quickly followed by a second, then a third, and finally a fourth. Will and I clutch each other's arms as the figures land in front of us with hard slams that send bits of grass and dirt flying.

Once the dust settles, all four of them stand up straight.

They're massive creatures with great leathery wings, dark blue skin, fangs, and claws. Their eyes glow in colors that match their hair—white, red, black, and grey—and they're all locked onto me with an intensity that makes me shiver. They're dressed head to toe in bright golden armor. Three of them smile at me while one remains expressionless.

I want to cry, and I have no idea why.

"Holy Mary, Mother of God..." Will mutters.

"Who are you?" I ask.

The three smiling faces look at the emotionless one, the one with the bright white hair and eyes, who takes a step toward me.

Will takes two steps back, tugging on my arm to draw me away, but I don't let him.

"Stay back!" Will cries. "Evan, stay away from it!"

"It's alright," I say, and I tear my eyes away from the four giants in front of me to look at my best friend. "Trust me."

Will's face is full of panic as he looks from me to the beings in gold then back again. His fingers loosen, slowly, and I pull my arm free.

When I turn back to him, the one with the straight face kneels on one knee and holds out his hand. I don't hesitate to cross the distance between us and take it. It's so warm. He draws me closer and sets his palm on my chest, right over the mark above my left breast.

Seerraf and the five, please let this work, says this creature's deep and rumbly voice in my head.

"Who's—"

Another voice, an even deeper and more powerful one, speaks right next to my ear, so close I can feel the heat of his breath.

"I told you I'd see you again, my champion."

A warm palm touches my cheek, and my lips part on a startled gasp as an intense heat washes over me. There's a burst of bright gold light in my eyes, and then I... I...

I remember.

I remember the village and how different it was.

The Offering every full moon.

The night I was thrown into a world of blowing snow, twisted vines, and dead trees.

The Deadwood.

The castle of stone in the heart of that cursed forest.

The demons that lived there.

The Gryxen.

My Gryxen.

I remember their names, their scents, their voices, the feel of each of their fangs as they marked me as theirs... Every tender moment, every pleasure, every smile, laugh, and tear, it all comes back to me in a rush of white, red, black, and grey.

My stoferras.

My mates.

"Caliborne!" I cry as I throw my arms around his neck.

He hugs me so tight, kissing my cheek and nuzzling my hair.

Thank the gods. It's been so long…

The ache in my chest is gone. All this time, I missed them, the ones my heart longed for but couldn't remember. That hollow spot that hurt for so many years is full now, so full I burst into tears.

Caliborne pulls away and takes my face in his hands.

"I wished Reilanna never existed," I say between sobs.

We know. We remember everything.

"How?"

Seerraf. We've much to tell you, but we're here. We're all here and together again. He wipes the tears from my cheeks. *Don't cry, my stoferra. I hate to see you cry.*

"These are happy tears," I say with a shaky laugh.

I touch my forehead to Caliborne's before stepping out of his arms to face the red-haired Gryxen standing behind him who's smirking at me. I giggle and launch myself into his arms—both his arms, I note with glee—and he hauls me up onto his hips and spins us in a circle.

"Wexton!" I cry as I laugh.

"Did you miss me, darling?"

"More than you know."

"Was it me you missed or my mouth?"

I throw my head back on a laugh before said mouth captures mine in a heated kiss that makes me blush.

"All of you," I utter breathlessly against his lips. "Every last bit."

He smirks at me again, and a familiar, wicked little glint appears in his eyes before he peels my legs off his hips and throws me up into the air. I yelp as I fly, but I'm soon caught by another pair of strong Gryxen arms. I put my arm around the neck of a black-haired Gryxen whose smile is slight, but his eyes are full of far more feeling than he could ever put into words.

"Fenmire," I say softly.

"Oh great," Fenmire says with a roll of his eyes. "You again. I thought we'd gotten rid of you for good."

I bite my lip and shake my head. "You can't ever get rid of me. I thought you'd learned that by now."

Fenmire kisses me in that hard, demanding way of his, but when he breaks away, he's more breathless than I am. He closes his eyes and sets his cheek to mine.

"We did it," I whisper to him.

You *did it, pet. I only helped you a little along the way. Never leave me again. Please.*

"Never again. My heart could never take it."

Neither could mine.

He kisses me on the forehead before setting me down on my feet.

I turn to the last Gryxen, and for a moment, all I can do is stare.

He has both eyes, there are no scars, and his hair is long with a healthy shine, but the most startling difference is…

"Drixus," I utter in awe. "You have wings."

Drixus drops to both his knees in front of me, takes me in his arms, and holds me tight.

"My beautiful boy," I tell him as I stroke his silky hair. "You're not broken anymore."

"All thanks to you, sweetheart," he murmurs, and his deep, rumbling voice still gives me chills. "You gave me back everything the witch stole from me. You truly are a goddess sent straight from Seerraf." He peels off his gloves and touches my face with his chilly fingertips. "I missed you so much."

I put my arms around his neck and kiss him tenderly. "I know the feeling."

"I'm not all that's been fixed," he says quietly, and he looks over my shoulder at Fenmire with a smile.

I look at Fenmire too and gasp when he smiles lovingly back at Drixus.

My head whips back and forth between them. "You two… did you…?"

"We had a lot of time to work on things," Fenmire says. "All has been forgiven."

I squeal with delight for the second time today and hug Drixus again.

He kisses me on the shoulder. "Now I'm truly whole again."

"Me too."

I step back and take them all in.

"Evan?"

I jump and spin around. I'd nearly forgotten about Will.

"What just happened?" he asks.

"Um…" How am I going to explain this? I look at Caliborne. "Can you make him remember too?"

Caliborne shrugs.

"Can you try?"

He nods and offers Will his hand.

Will stares at that hand for a long time before looking at me again.

"It's alright," I say, and I beckon him over.

I've never seen Will move so slowly. He shuffles his feet across the dirt one half step at a time and pokes Caliborne's palm with two fingers before finally laying his whole hand in it. Will continues to stare blankly at Caliborne, his entire body stiff with one foot stuck out behind him as if he's prepared to take off running any second.

This time it's me who prays to Seerraf for this to work.

Will's eyes suddenly widen, and he swears. After about a minute, he blinks a few times and takes his hand back.

"Holy shit," he says as he relaxes. "We won!" He scoops me up in a bear hug.

"You remember!" I cry as I'm lifted off my feet.

He sets me back down. "The village… it's all so different now."

"Your village was allowed to flourish without The Deadwood or Reilanna's spell influencing it," Fenmire explains. "And, of course, it had Evan."

I suspect there was a much larger and more powerful force at play, but I keep my suspicions to myself. For now.

"Your powers," Will says. "My mother and father…" He hugs me again, tightly. "Thank you."

"I'd do it again in a heartbeat," I say. When he lets me go, I turn to my mates. "Michastiforo?"

"Perfectly fine," Wexton says.

"What about the others? Horthos, Breklen, and Jothrik?"

"They're alive," Fenmire replies. "But they were permanently removed from duty."

I turn to Drixus apologetically. "I'm sorry."

"Don't be," he says. "My brother is alive. He was ashamed at first, but he's worked hard to rebuild his reputation. He has a mate and three children now. He's happy. I couldn't ask for more."

"And your sister?" I ask Caliborne.

He takes my hand with a smile. *She is well. She can't wait to meet you.*

"Meet me? When? Where?"

They all exchange knowing glances.

"About that," Wexton says with one of his telltale smirks.

"What's going on?" I ask.

Caliborne kneels and offers me his palm, and I hold it to my face.

I'm standing on the dark red sands of the Vorisca Desert once again, looking out from Caliborne's eyes. In front of me stands Seerraf, and he looks exactly as I remember him from the day I made my wish.

"Caliborne," he says, "your mate has chosen to erase Reilanna from existence. I have to admit, I was impressed with their choice. With one stroke, Evan has wiped away all the hurt and death Reilanna has caused. They could have chosen a dozen different lives for themselves with the four of you, but they didn't. They looked beyond their own desires and granted the wishes and prayers of thousands. It's an act of sacrifice I haven't seen in a long time.

"Your mate is counting on the bond to bring you all together again, but I think we can do better than that."

Without seeing him move, Seerraf is suddenly standing right in front of me.

"I'll offer a bargain. And I'll offer the same bargain to all four of you, so don't worry, you won't be making this decision alone. I'm going to set back the clock to before Reilanna ever existed, thousands of years before Evan was ever born. The choice you have to make is this: I can erase the memories of everything you've lived through and set you back on the path you walked all those years ago. You'll remember none of the pain or the loneliness, but you won't remember your mate either, and whether or not you find them again will be entirely up to chance. No one will know the deeds Evan has done here for us all. It will truly be like Reilanna never existed, and life will go on naturally like it did before but without her in it.

"Or, I can allow the four of you to remember everything. You'll keep the memory of these past thousands of years while living them again. In this way, Reilanna will still have existed for you. You'll carry the pains of that

life with you into the next, but you'll also carry Evan's memory. You can tell their story and be sure our people know the fate they saved us all from, but you'll pine for them for thousands of years while you wait for them to be born again. In return, once you've relived those years, I will reunite you with Evan, when they're ready. It will be my gift to them and to you four for all you've done and all you've endured.

"I will make this offer to you, Wexton, Fenmire, and Drixus. All four of you must agree to remember or else you'll all forget. As we speak, the rest are choosing. So, tell me, what's your choice?"

Caliborne's response is immediate and resolute.

This is no choice at all. I want to remember. A few thousand years' worth of longing and painful memories is nothing compared to having my stoferra back. For Evan, I would wait a thousand lifetimes and suffer a thousand more. I will endure whatever I must to have them in my arms again.

Seerraf stands still for a moment before he smiles. "The decision has been made. All four are in agreement." Seerraf's eyes change. They bore into Caliborne's, but when he speaks again, it's clear he's not talking to him anymore. "Come to my temple, my champion. I have a gift for you, the highest blessing I can bestow."

A bright golden light surrounds me.

I'm in tears again when the memory fades away.

"You all chose to remember?" I ask, glancing between all four Gryxen. "You chose to remember all of that pain and heartache and spend thousands of years waiting for me?"

Caliborne nods.

"Of course we did," Wexton says.

"I'd do it all again in an instant," says Fenmire.

"As many times as I had to," Drixus adds.

"And Seerraf wants me to go to the temple?" I ask.

"After your wish," says Fenmire, "we were the only ones who remembered the past. Once we had the chance to talk, we chose to go to the temple and explain everything to the priestesses. Caliborne showed them all of his memories."

"Which took forever," Wexton mutters.

"Even with Caliborne's memories, they had a hard time believing us," Drixus says. "But they eventually prayed to Seerraf, and he confirmed the whole story. After that, the priestesses made a formal announcement and told the whole city our story, your story. Everyone's been waiting thousands of years to meet you."

Caliborne takes me by the chin so that our eyes meet. *The priestesses are waiting for you at the temple. We're to bring you back with us to Michastiforo where you'll be celebrated as the hero you are. But only if you want to, my stoferra.*

"What does Seerraf want to give me?" I ask.

"I have a few theories," Fenmire says.

"Of course you do," Wexton and I say in unison.

Fenmire rolls his eyes. "I don't want to say and get anyone's hopes up in case I'm wrong."

"But what if I choose not to go?" I ask.

"The Gate isn't going anywhere," Wexton says. "We have to be careful what we do while we're here so as not to cause mayhem in your world, but the door is always open for us to come and go."

"We could rebuild the castle," Drixus suggests. "Or perhaps something smaller. We could ask that much of Horthos. He'd be glad to do it."

"What do you say?" Fenmire asks me. "Do you want to come back with us to Michastiforo? If only temporarily."

I smile. "I'd love to. I want to see the temple and meet the priestesses. And your sister," I add with a glance at Caliborne. "Your brother too," I say to Drixus.

I get three beaming smiles and one bowing nod.

"Just so you know," Wexton says, "the entire city is anxious to see you. You're the hero who saved them all from Reilanna's horrors. They've waited for this day for a long time. We all have. But the priestesses have closed the temple to the public so they can be the first to welcome you."

Will clears his throat. "This all sounds fascinating, but I get the feeling I'm not exactly invited so—"

"You can come if you want to," Fenmire interjects.

"No, I can't. I have someone waiting for me."

"Will is engaged to Jacob," I explain. "Again."

He gets a round of congratulations, shoulder slaps, and handshakes.

"Thanks," Will says bashfully. "But I really need to get back to the horses. My mother is probably already fuming over my absence."

"I'll take you," Drixus offers.

Will nods but doesn't move. He looks at me. "So, I guess I won't be seeing you as much."

"It was inevitable," I say sadly. "You're getting married and moving on with your life. It's time I do the same."

"You'll come to the wedding, though, right?"

"I wouldn't miss that for the world. But can you do something for me?"

"Anything."

"My parents. They'll have questions and worries. Tell them I… I don't know… that I ran off with a man from the city I met when I was there with you visiting your aunt. Tell them I'm happy and that I'll come back and visit them soon."

"I can do that, no problem. Don't worry about them. Jacob and I will make sure they're taken care of."

I hug my best friend as tight as I can. "I know you will."

Will was always like a son to my father. I wouldn't be surprised if he leaves Will the farm. The next time I see my parents, I'll talk to them about it and make sure they know that's what I want as well.

This feels right. This feels perfect, like the bigger and better thing Papa says I'm meant for. I did promise him I'd seek my own happiness, after all. And this? This makes me so happy I'm about to start crying again, even if saying goodbye to Will is a bittersweet repercussion.

I'm whole again.

I'm home.

Chapter 83

After a final round of goodbyes, Drixus takes off with Will in his arms. Watching Drixus fly makes my heart soar just as high. Once he's gone, I turn to Fenmire.

"He looks good," I say.

"He was still pretty broken after everything that happened," Fenmire says. "But having Horthos back helped. We took some time apart at first. I did some traveling while he and Horthos rebuilt what broke between them. When I came back, everything felt different, in a good way, like we'd both had a chance to finally catch our breath. It took years, but we eventually forgave each other. The hurt took longer to mend, but we were determined to make things right again. I don't think we'll ever be the same as we were, but that's alright. *We're* not the same."

"I'm proud of you both."

Drixus returns a few short minutes later, and Wexton taps one of The Gate's stones with his foot. "Open up," he says.

"Be nice, Wexton," I chastise.

"Please," he adds with a roll of his eyes. When The Gate obeys, he walks over to me and holds out his arms. "Fly with me?"

I grin because I understand what this means to him. Of all my mates, he's the only one I haven't flown with yet since his missing arm made him worry he couldn't carry me safely. I step into his arms, and he hauls me up against his chest. His beaming smile of pride warms my heart before he launches into the air, spins, and shoots back down, headfirst, through The Gate.

"Wexton!" I scream and laugh and cling to him as we're instantly transported to his world. When Wexton finally stops his antics and flies straight, I turn to stare over the dark red sand toward the city I've only ever seen in Caliborne's memories. Michastiforo is as golden as ever with its shining, steepled roofs and the temple rising high above the rest of the city in its center. I can barely see the long golden walkway at the front.

My four mates and I soar over the Vorisca Desert with its rolling, sandy hills as far as the eye can see. The heat rolls off the sand in waves that makes the city in the distance shimmer and undulate like a mirage. When we finally reach the city, I peer down at the streets far below and see masses of people gathered in just about every open space. They're all watching and waving at us as we fly overhead.

"Told you the city was excited to see you," Wexton says.

"They're all gathered for me?" I ask in awe.

"Yes, but they'll have to wait to meet you. I can't speak for the others, but after these past many years without you, I won't be ready to share you for quite some time."

I lean my head against his shoulder. "I'm alright with that."

We approach the temple and land at the end of the golden walkway, the same place I've seen Caliborne land in his memories at least a dozen times. Behind us is a long staircase that leads down into the center of Michastiforo. It's usually bustling with foot traffic to and from the temple, but there's no one on it today. The walkway is long and lined with priestesses on either side. Some are dressed in golden robes, others golden armor, but they're all looking at us as Wexton sets me down on my feet.

One of the priestesses in golden robes, a female Gruxa with dark brown and curly hair, steps out of the line and approaches us.

"Welcome, Evangeline," she says to me. "We've been expecting you."

Am I supposed to bow or something? I look around at my mates, but they all remain upright, so I do as well.

"Hello," I say. "It's actually Evan today."

"Apologies," she says with a slight bow. "Evan. There's someone who wishes to speak to you right away. If you would please follow me."

I do, and my mates all follow closely behind me. The rest of the priestesses bow their heads and greet me as we pass, but about halfway down the walkway, a single Gruxa stands out to me from the rest of the figures in gold. She has familiar, bright white hair, and when she looks up, her eyes shine with the same light as her brother's.

"CeCe?" I say in awe, and when she smiles in acknowledgement, I break away from the others and go to her.

She's almost as tall as Caliborne, so she goes down on one knee when I approach. I instantly hug her. It should probably feel odd to hug a stranger as if she's some long-lost friend, but it doesn't. This Gruxa feels like anything but a stranger.

"I've heard so much about you," I say, but that doesn't come close to describing how it feels to finally meet a person I spent months getting to know through mere memories, a person I couldn't wait to meet, whose death by Reilanna's cruelty stole her away from me before I got the chance. But here she stands, perfectly happy and healthy before me at last. "You're a temple priestess?"

"I am," she says, and her voice stuns me. It's enchanting, like she's caught somewhere between talking and singing. She holds me by the shoulders and giggles, and her words break with emotion as she says, "You're so beautiful. Caliborne told me you were, of course, but I wouldn't let him show me what you looked like until I could see you with my own eyes. Welcome home, sister."

"Sister," I murmur. "I have a sister!"

CeCe laughs, mirroring my delight as we hug again.

Thank you so much for saving my brother, she tells me in her mind, and her voice inside my head sounds normal instead of the bewitching one she has when she speaks. *I can't imagine losing him, and I'm so grateful you replaced that life with the one I have now.*

"I'd do it all again if I had to," I whisper for her ears only. "This moment alone was worth it."

She gives me an extra tight squeeze and lets me go. "We'll talk more later."

CeCe stands, takes her place back in line, and gives me the same polite bow as the others as I walk past her and continue following the brown haired Gruxa down the long walkway.

From behind me, Caliborne places his hand on my shoulder. *My sister is still a wailer,* he explains. *That wasn't a product of Reilanna's shapeshifting but of CeCe's natural abilities.*

"Is that why her voice sounds like that?"

Yes. Wailers are very powerful and often feared for their abilities, so CeCe chose to join the temple where she would be safe and could use her powers for good. She is highly respected and loved throughout Michastiforo as a result. I am very proud of her.

I touch his hand. "Me too."

I'm starting to sweat rather profusely. The Gryxens' world is considerably hotter than mine, which will be a problem if I don't get out of this sun soon. Thankfully, when we step into the temple, the temperature drops considerably. It's still warm, but no more so than a sunny summer day in my world.

"This way," the priestess says as she motions us down a corridor to the left.

The temple is made of the same golden metal as the rest of the city. The walls and floors are made of bricks, and the windows are beautifully intricate mosaics that fill the halls with color. There are tapestries on the walls, sculptures set in deep alcoves, and, in a few places, the metal walls are ground smooth with scenes carved in them in striking detail. One such carving makes me pause, mostly because I recognize the creature in it. It's a large, four-legged beast with feathered wings, a long, curved neck, and a flat face with a short beak.

"Drixus," I say in surprise, pointing to the carving.

Drixus smiles and nods. "Fenmire carved it."

"Mara deserves to be celebrated as much as the rest of us," Fenmire says. "I made sure she'd never be forgotten." He looks at Drixus, who puts an arm around Fenmire's shoulders and taps his helmet against his mate's.

That's going to take some getting used to.

We continue down the hall until the priestess opens a set of double doors on the right and waves us in.

Fenmire grins like a fool as we enter.

"Why do you look so smug?" Wexton asks.

"No reason," Fenmire replies, but his smile only widens.

We're ushered into a large chamber with four golden pillars and massive golden tablets lining the walls. Each tablet is covered, top to bottom, in carvings that tell a story in a series of panels. I can see the carvings on the nearest one clear enough to recognize the tale. It's Poilam's, starting with the appearance of the first Gate and ending with his eternal rest at the temple. In between depicts the horrors he suffered to broker peace between his people and the beings from that other world.

The soft thump of the doors shutting makes me look back at my mates, but each of them are staring, awe-struck, at the back of the room. I step around the pillar currently blocking my view to see what's drawn their attention.

Sitting against the back wall of this chamber is a large golden chair, like a throne, only plain in its design. Upon that chair sits a familiar four-armed Gryxen dressed head to toe in golden armor and silently watching us with one leg crossed over the other, his hands folded in his lap, and a small smile on his face.

"Seerraf!" I say in happy surprise. There's a literal god sitting in front of me, and yet I'm not the least bit nervous or shy as I walk closer. "I came like you asked."

"My champion," Seerraf greets me warmly, and the joy that bubbles inside me at the sound of his voice makes me giggle. "Thank you for coming." He stands up, and he's even bigger than I remember. He reaches his hand out to me, and I happily give him mine. His fingers curl delicately around my hand, and his grip is warm and inviting. "Did you tell them?"

I shake my head.

"Do you want to?"

"Why don't you," I say, waving my arm toward my mates in welcome.

Seerraf nods and turns to the four Gryxen still standing near the door. "Come, my warriors, come." He motions them closer. "We have much to discuss."

At Seerraf's urging, they step across the room and gather in front of him.

With his hand on my shoulder, Seerraf clears his throat and looks at each of my mates in turns before speaking. "Before Evan made their wish, I shared a deep secret with them, one that I'll also share with you now. It's important this secret never leaves this room. Will you all swear to never speak a word of it to anyone? That includes writing it down, Fenmire," Seerraf says with a stern look at the Gryxen in question.

After a round of chuckles, all four of them nod. Three offer a verbal vow of silence. Caliborne offers a handshake instead, which Seerraf accepts.

"Very well then," says Seerraf. He waves an arm around at the carved walls. "What do you see here?"

"The stories of the acolytes," Fenmire answers.

"Right you are, *vauncidi*, but not completely." Seerraf squeezes my shoulder as he says, "My acolytes were in fact a single soul reborn into the lives you see carved around you. One soul. One acolyte. My champion."

Realization dawns first in Fenmire's eyes. He looks down at me with his mouth slightly agape.

"Champion…" Wexton mutters. "Isn't that what you call…?" He falls silent, and his face mirrors Fenmire's a second later. "Oh, shit."

I laugh.

Drixus laughs too when he finally understands. "I'd say I'm surprised, but honestly, it makes so much sense I'm not the slightest bit shocked."

Caliborne walks over to me and sinks to one knee at my feet. His eyes are full of tears as he takes one of my hands between both of his and bows his head over it. *I am not worthy to call you my stoferra. The lives you've saved, the deeds you've done… I am honored to know you, to love you, to be your mate. I fear I could never do enough to earn the privilege bestowed upon me, but I will spend the rest of my life trying.*

"Caliborne," I utter, wrapping my arms around his neck. "You owe me nothing. None of you do. I am the same person, the same *human* you know and love. That's all."

"Says the champion of a god," Wexton teases.

I stick my tongue out at him.

They all laugh, even Caliborne as he stands and wipes his eyes.

Seerraf clears his throat again. "I've called you all here for a very special purpose." He sweeps his arms about the room. "Each of Evan's previous stories are very different from the others, but they all end the same way: each time, they decided whether or not to add their story here, then they chose the fate of their soul in the afterlife."

"I get a choice?" I ask. "I thought all souls were reborn no matter what."

"We have a… special sort of arrangement, you and I. Your past deeds grant you a reprieve between lives, a time of peaceful rest, for as long as you wish. You choose when to move on."

"Where do I go during these times of reprieve?"

"With me," Seerraf says with a soft smile. "I've spent countless millennia in your company, my champion, until you tell me you're ready for your next adventure. All of this you usually learn at the end of each lifetime. But this time, your sacrifice, the wish you made, took a once-in-a-lifetime opportunity away from you, so I gave your mates the choice to alter your wish enough to bring you here. And now, I can give that opportunity back to you. This once, I will let you choose your future in life instead of in death. Simply make another wish."

"Anything I want?" I ask.

"Anything and everything."

"What would you ask in return?"

Seerraf shakes his head. "You are not my servant. You are a beacon of hope and virtue for my people, nothing more. Your more recent story would join the others'"—again, he waves an arm at the etchings around the room—"and be told throughout the ages, in both the hard times and the good, to show what true sacrifice looks like and to remind us that even just one person can make all the difference in the world. You've already paid the price, Evan. All that's left is your reward."

It seems too good to be true. How is it that I can have everything? That's not how it's supposed to work, I've been taught that all my life—both of them, actually. Happiness doesn't come without sacrifice.

'Don't think I don't know what you're giving up.' Seerraf's own words come back to me from the moment of my death.

I already sacrificed. We all did.

My mates sacrificed their families, friends, and entire lives to keep Reilanna at bay.

I sacrificed the life I found with them to free them all when I jumped through The Gate.

I sacrificed the wish I could have used for us to free everyone from Reilanna's poisonous influence.

Then my mates sacrificed again by agreeing to wait in longing for me for thousands of years. I know how painful and lonely my short twenty years have been. I can't imagine how it must have been for them.

We can be happy now. We've all earned it.

"Shall I add your most recent tale beside the others?" Seerraf asks.

"Yes, I think so."

Seerraf smiles and points his finger at a blank tablet to our left, and detailed scenes begin carving themselves into the metal. They tell our whole story, starting with my mates pushing Reilanna back through The Gate and ending with all five of us standing before Seerraf as we make our choices.

There is one last panel at the very bottom, the largest of them all, but it's blank.

Seerraf takes me gently by the shoulder and points to that blank panel. "What do you want your future to look like, Evan? What is it your heart desires above all else?"

It's not hard for me to imagine it since I've already seen it once as I fought Reilanna in my dreams. I'd still need to be able to go back to my world to visit those I still love there, and I admit it takes my mind a moment to work around that problem. Once I think I have everything I want, I picture it vividly, what my perfect future would look like if I could choose, and I look at Seerraf.

He grins and nods. "I can do that."

My eyes well with tears. "All of it?"

"Yes. As long as you're sure."

"I've never been more sure of anything in my life."

He offers me his hand, and when I take it, he pulls me close, drawing his wings in around us and cocooning me in gold. A bright, golden light envelopes me, making every inch of my body tingle as it seeps into my very skin.

"Close your eyes," Seerraf says. "Picture that life and will it into being."

Do I ever. I picture it and pray for it with all my heart and soul. I'm warm again, so warm and filled with so much excitement and happiness that I'm trembling. I look up at Seerraf to find him staring down at me with a look I've seen before on the faces of the Gryxen waiting for me across the room.

"I had a much happier life the second time around," I tell him.

"I'm glad," he replies softly.

"Why do I suspect you had something to do with that?"

He touches my cheek. "Because you know me too well."

My eyes flick back and forth between his. "My fifth mate," I whisper, "the one I took before… it's you, isn't it?"

Seerraf only smiles.

Will

To every thing there is a season, and a time to every purpose under the heaven:
A time to be born, and a time to die; a time to plant, and a time to pluck up that which is planted;
A time to kill, and a time to heal; a time to break down, and a time to build up;
A time to weep, and a time to laugh; a time to mourn, and a time to dance;
A time to cast away stones, and a time to gather stones together; a time to embrace, and a time to refrain from embracing;
A time to get, and a time to lose; a time to keep, and a time to cast away;
A time to rend, and a time to sew; a time to keep silent, and a time to speak;
A time to love, and a time to hate; a time of war, and a time of peace.

-Ecclesiastes 3:1-8 KJV

Epilogue

I start my long trek through the woods hours before dawn. Jacob thinks I've gone to the city to retrieve my best friend and travel back to the village with them, but where I'm going is far more magical and much closer to home. It's a good thing I have this path just about memorized by now since I have to walk it in the dark this time. Thankfully, there's a full moon tonight to help guide my way. Even so, I almost miss the fork and take the wrong path, but I eventually get myself straightened out and headed in the right direction.

I see the clearing at the end of the path up ahead as the sky begins to lighten in shades of red and gold. Dawn reminds me so much of the world where Evangeline spends most of their time now. I've been there myself a time or two, just for a visit. It's much too hot for me to linger there for more than a few hours. I always come back drenched in sweat and happy to be back on my side of The Gate where I know I belong.

For a few brief moments on mornings like this, it's like my best friend is peeking over the horizon at me, checking that all is well. Knowing Evangeline, that's probably a lot closer to the truth than I know. Their ability to know whenever I need them nowadays is uncanny, no doubt due in no small part to their new… job? Form? Powers? I don't know what to call it, and quite frankly, I don't care. All I know is that I've never seen my best friend so happy, and I didn't lose them, which is all that matters to me.

I finally break through the trees and step into the clearing. There's a circle of grey stones in its center that looks unremarkable, like something a child might create during some fanciful game. I walk over and knock on one of the stones with a single knuckle.

"Um… excuse me," I say awkwardly. "Can you tell them I'm here, please?"

The Gate never talks to me, but Evangeline swears it can hear. I feel foolish talking to rocks, regardless. The ground beneath my feet begins to rumble, and I take several steps back before a familiar golden figure streaks out through the rock circle and lands in front of me, far more gracefully than their mates do whenever they pass through The Gate. The figure plants their feet and stands up straight, and the face of my best friend beams at me from under their golden helmet.

Evangeline looks nothing like they did before. Their features are the same, but now there are wings sprouting from their back, large, feathered ones the same color as their armor, which covers them from head to toe. They carry a sword now too, a short and broad one made of smoking ice that never leaves their hip, as well as the same small knife they carried before, a gift from one of their Gryxen lovers, though I can't remember which one.

The wings, weapons, and armor disappear with a shrug of their shoulders, and the person standing before me looks exactly like they did before either of us ever entered The Deadwood, only now, there's a fiery confidence in their eyes that wasn't there before. They stand so tall and proud these days that even Elias, on the few occasions he sees them, falls silent in their presence. It's a beautiful thing that makes me smile every time.

"Good morning," I greet. I quickly assess their outfit: a crisp white dress shirt, black slacks, a matching vest, a cravat, dress shoes, and their golden bracelet. Their favorite Evan outfit. It will bring a deep scowl to Elias' face today.

Perfect.

"Good morning to you," Evan replies. "Are you nervous yet?"

I laugh. "Of course not. Whyever would I be? I've already done this once before, remember?"

"Of course I remember, but that was a very private ceremony. This time, you'll be wed in front of the entire village."

Despite my previous claims, a small knot of nerves twists painfully in the pit of my stomach.

Evan—who knows me well enough I swear they can detect my moods before I can most of the time—laughs and takes me by the arm. "Don't fret. I'll be right by your side just like last time. Today will be perfect, and you and Jacob will live long and happy lives together."

"Did your god tell you that?"

"He didn't have to. I just know."

We walk arm in arm through The Deadwood even though it's a long walk back to the village and Evan could easily fly us both there in minutes. This is our custom. The time we spend walking through these trees and talking is the only time we get alone anymore. Ever since they became Seerraf's newest acolyte and joined the Gryxen in protecting The Gate between our worlds, I don't see them nearly as often as I used to. I miss my friend, but we're both moving on with our lives, as one does. These walks are all I will ever get now, so I cherish every minute of them.

"How is Jacob doing?" Evan asks. "Does he remember anything at all?"

"Nothing," I say sadly.

"It's not too late, Will. I can make him remember too."

"*You* can do that now? I thought that was a temporary power your god gave Caliborne for you and he only made an exception for me."

"Technically, yes, that's true. But I can ask for another exception."

"Your god grants you whatever you want, does he?"

Evan gives me a mischievous smile. "Let's just say he likes to see me happy, and I don't ask him for much, so when I make a request, he usually grants it. He'd give Jacob back his memories if I asked, I have no doubts."

I consider the offer, but in the end, I shake my head. "Jacob is happy. To disrupt that with the memories of how badly he was treated before would be cruel. Plus, that means I get to make the good memories he's missing all over again, right?"

Evan smiles. "It does."

"Once we move into the new house, I plan to get him his first rat."

They laugh. "I thought you never cared for the creatures."

I shrug. "They grew on me, but it's more about how happy they made Jacob. I don't want him to miss out on a single thing in life."

"How is the house coming along?"

"It's going well. Your father stops by throughout the day whenever I'm not around to check the workers are following my instructions. He's going to be the best neighbor."

Since Evan has no plans to take over their family's farm, their father decided—no doubt with some extra encouragement from my best friend—that he wanted Jacob and I to inherit the place. An official contract has already been drawn up and signed that states we will become the new owners of the farm whenever Evan's father passes away. Until then, a smaller abode is being built in one of the northern pastures for me and Jacob until it's time for us to move into the main house.

I spend most of my days with Evan's father learning the finer skills of farming. Though I've never cared much for hard labor in the past, that was due mostly to the fact that, since I am the youngest of four sons, I knew our homestead would never be mine. Working for free on something I would never own didn't interest me, but now I'm proud of every drop of sweat I put into what will eventually be my home, Jacob and I's home.

Jacob, on the other hand, has considered taking over my father's store. Father made him the offer shortly after our engagement. Neither my brothers nor I have any interest in the store, and my father wants desperately to keep it in the family. I told Jacob it was his choice since he'd have to be the one to take care of the place most of the time. When last we talked, he was seriously considering it if only to have something to occupy his time so that he doesn't "go crazy alone in the house all day while you're out working in the fields," as he puts it.

In the end, I don't give a damn what he chooses to do as long as he's happy. With the memories of our old life in my head to remind me what could have been, I'll just be grateful for every day I wake up beside the man I love, and I'll do what I must to ensure he greets me with a smile with every sunrise.

*****

This wedding ceremony, though still tender and sweet, isn't quite the same as the one we held in the glade. I try not to compare, but with the eyes of the entire village—many belonging to people I've barely spoken to my entire life—locked onto us from all around the stifling church, I long for the breeze and the more intimate gathering we had the first time Jacob and I were wed. One thing remains the same, though.

My best friend stands at my back with Jacob's ring in their pocket, and when I turn to take it from them, they give me the biggest, most tearful smile that I can't help but swallow back tears of my own.

"I, Will, take thee, Jacob…" I slide Jacob's ring on his finger and repeat after Pastor Elias. We wanted him to be the one to marry us, not Elias V, who has already taken over leading our congregation in his father's stead. Pastor Elias was hesitant to do it, but Jacob and I both insisted, so he agreed under the condition that this would be his very last ceremony. I don't know what we would've done if he'd refused because there was no way I was going to let his beast of a son marry us.

I glance over at Elias V, who's sitting near the back with his new bride. She's young, only just turned eighteen, but she's pretty and acts and dresses like a proper lady and wife on Elias' arm.

Completely the opposite of the person Elias originally attempted to wed.

A very small part of me wishes Evan would've married Elias just so they could drive him mad for the rest of his life. They would've been miserable themself, though, so obviously I'm glad it turned out differently, but…

He deserves to suffer.

I banish the thought as soon as it's born. I can't hold the actions of a man from a previous life against the one in this one, even if that man has shown only the slightest improvements over the original version. That man is gone, and I can't say with certainty that this one would make the same mistakes.

I hope we never find out.

"…and thereto I give thee my troth," Jacob says as he finishes his vows.

Pastor Elias smiles at us both, and for as much as I doubt his son, I see genuine joy in his eyes for us. Perhaps there is hope for our little village yet.

"Those whom God hath joined together let no man put asunder," he says. He addresses our gathering and imparts the traditional blessing before closing his prayer book. "You may kiss."

I take Jacob in my arms and seal our marriage with a long kiss. He's shaking with nerves this time, only proving to me that our ceremony in the glade was still superior to this one. Jacob was barely even nervous that day. Still, we part with matching, happy smiles and face our friends, family, and acquaintances. Hand-in-hand, we walk back down the aisle and into our new life.

*****

I watch from the church's front steps as Evan hugs their father and laughs at something he says. It's selfish of me, but I'm happy I'll be living on their farm where I'll be around to see Evan more often. They'll always find the time to come back to see their father, and while he still lives, I won't have to give up my best friend.

Something tells me that won't be the case forever.

Jacob is talking with my father, deciding at last if he wishes to take over our store. I left myself out of that conversation. It's not my choice, and I don't want to influence Jacob in it.

Elias V and his wife head for their wagon, which is parked near Evan's parents'. When they pass Evan, Evan pats their father on the arm and follows Elias, calling to him. Evan draws Elias aside far enough their conversation won't be overheard by any of the guests now headed down the church driveway.

Evan starts talking, seemingly at ease and nothing but pleasant. Elias, on the other hand, looks uncomfortable and slightly confused, that is until Evan takes his hand. Nearly the moment they touch, a stream of emotions passes across Elias' face. What starts as a look of confusion and surprise turns to shock then pure horror as more than a minute passes. Finally, he wrenches his hand from Evan's and glances about, his eyes wide with fear. Evan speaks again, and Elias just listens, then, after the briefest of nods from the pastor, Evan walks away.

What the hell was that about?

I head across the yard and meet Evan halfway back to their parents' wagon.

"That looked like an interesting conversation," I say, and I let my eyes ask the obvious question.

"Oh, it was," Evan says with a twinkle of mischief in their eye. "I gave him a warning. I showed him what happened the last time he led the village astray and made it clear he'd know the same fate or worse should it happen again."

"You let him remember?"

"Not everything. Just enough to show him what I can and will do if he starts hurting others again. I told him he'd better treat both our village and his new wife with the respect they deserve because I'll be watching and will know if he doesn't. I told him my mates and I will happily come back and do much worse this time should he turn out the way he did before."

"The village might look the same as it did before, but the people are so different I doubt they'd let him get away with it anyway. Still, it was a lesson he likely needed. Only the good would suffer should he have to learn it twice."

"My thoughts exactly."

I touch Evan's shoulder. "How long can you stay?"

They smile. "You have me for the day, dearest. I plan to go back at sunset."

"Make it a couple of hours before. I plan to go with you and don't fancy walking back in the dark."

They frown. "Are you sure? It's your wedding day."

"I don't get to see you very often anymore. I can spare a few hours for you, regardless of the day."

"Will?" Jacob calls, and Evan and I turn to him as he joins us. "I told your father yes."

"You're taking over the store then?" Evan asks.

"Did Will tell you?"

I didn't, which is why I raise a curious brow at my best friend, who smiles at Jacob, giving nothing away.

"I think it's a wonderful idea," Evan says. "My mother always drove me mad while Papa was out tending to chores. She's often so bored and lonely. It's good to have your own interests. And this way, Will's father doesn't have to worry about the future of the store anymore."

Jacob nods. "A second source of income is always a good thing to have as well."

I put an arm around the shoulders of both my best friend and my husband. "Look at us." I give them both a little shake. "Let's go celebrate all of this day's good fortune, shall we?"

They smile at me with matching looks of love and affection as I usher them toward our waiting wagons.

*****

After hours of handshakes and thanks for all the well-wishes, I am beyond happy to walk in silence beside my best friend down the south road like we used to in our youth. I've taken off my stuffy vest and unbuttoned my shirt to let the fall breeze cool me off after sweating for most of the day. Jacob and I have a much more intimate gathering planned for this evening with our closest friends, and I'm looking forward to that more than I did the ceremony, when it's just me and him and the ones we care about most.

Minus one.

"Are you sure you can't stay?" I ask. "My brother promised to bring a couple of bottles of his homemade brew to our little gathering later."

Evan laughs. "I remember what happened the night of your first wedding. I have no desire to carry you to your bed again, dearest. You'll have to get Jacob to help you."

"I'm serious."

They sigh. "I know, but I can't stay." They don't elaborate, but the sad look on their face puts me on edge.

We arrive at the halfway tree, and I throw my vest over one of the lower branches. "You sure you want to fly us in? I don't mind walking."

"I thought you didn't want to walk home in the dark."

I shrug.

They shake their head at me. "Come here, you heathen."

I smirk as I join them near the edge of the forest. Evan glances around to be sure we don't have an audience, then they pick me up in their arms as if I weigh nothing at all. It's a bit unnerving and only serves to remind me they aren't the same person. Neither am I, not really, but it's sad to watch the ones you love change and grow and move on.

And leave you behind.

With a shrug, Evan summons their wings and takes off. We fly over the forest, and it only takes a couple of minutes to reach the clearing it took me hours to reach on foot early this morning. We land beside The Gate, and Evan sets me on my feet.

"When should I make the trek out here again?" I ask as I straighten my clothes and hair since the wind from our flight ruffled both. "Jacob and I will be in the city for two weeks, then I'm free after that."

"Actually…" That sad look is back on Evan's face, and my stomach twists uncomfortably. "I'm afraid you won't see me for a bit."

"Why? What's wrong?"

"Nothing's wrong. My mates and I are leaving to travel. There are several places in their world they want to show me. And there's something we need to look into as well. We suspect there might've been some higher power that influenced Reilanna to take over this world, so the temple is sending us to the other Gates to have a look and ask some questions. We're heading out tomorrow morning. We'll be gone a few months at least."

I blink in surprise and deflate a bit. "Oh."

They take both my hands in theirs. "Don't be sad. Not today."

I force a smile. "I'm not. Not really. I'm glad to see you finally living the life you deserve."

They smile. "You and Jacob are starting your new life together too. You'll be so busy loving each other, you won't have time to wander in here to see me twice a week like you do now. And that's alright." They squeeze my hands. "That's good."

"When will I see you then? And don't say never. I don't accept that."

"No, not never. I was thinking once a month might be good. At every full moon? After I get back from my travels, that is."

"How will I know when that is?"

"I'll leave you a message on the halfway tree. When you see it, you'll know to come at the next full moon."

"What kind of message?"

They wink. "One you won't miss, I promise."

I stare at my best friend, and though I am happy for us both and the lives we've found full of happiness and love, I'm disappointed and sad to see us drifting apart. Never in my life have I pictured a future without them. They've always been my rock, my constant, the one source of unconditional love I never doubted.

And now they're leaving me.

"Oh, Will," Evan says softly.

Oh, shit. We're touching.

I quickly take back my hands. "Sorry," I say with a snort of laughter that nearly breaks into a sob. "It's just that we've been through so much. I wouldn't be here without you. It feels wrong to say goodbye."

"Then we won't say it. I never could, not to you. I love you."

I hug them and kiss them on the forehead. "Be careful."

"You too."

They pull away, holding on to my hand until the last possible second before kneeling to touch one of The Gate's grey stones. "Send me home?" they request.

The Gate responds immediately, and the ground between the stones opens again to the deep red sands of the Vorisca Desert. Evan stands at the edge of the gateway and waves to me.

"I'll see you soon," they say.

I laugh tearfully. "See you soon."

They shrug out their wings, summon their armor and sword, and jump through The Gate.

The ground shimmers and solidifies once more, sealing my best friend behind millions of miles of space. I stand there for a long time, wiping my eyes as my heart accepts this change. I finally turn away and walk to the tree line, but before I start up the path that will take me home, I look back one last time at that circle of stones.

"Goodbye," I whisper.

Then I leave.

The End

If you liked this story, please consider leaving a review!

To stay up to date on new releases from this author, join their private Facebook reader group, Sir's Bibliophiles: https://www.facebook.com/groups/sirsbibliophiles

Other works by this author:

The Lady of the Mark – An adult historical fantasy romance

The Heart of Jesparia – An adult historical fantasy romance

Other works by this author under other names:

Show Me by Mx. Alex – A reverse age gap femdom romance

Rescue by Mx. Alex – An MM alien BDSM romance

Dollars to Collars by Mx. Alex – An MM contemporary BDSM novella

Just Call Me Sir by Mx. Alex – A collection of MM BDSM poetry

Made in United States
Troutdale, OR
09/09/2023

12769110R10445